TOPLINER REDSTARS

GENERAL EDITOR: AIDAN CHAMBERS

Wild and Penned

John Crompton has been fascinated by animals,
wild and tame, ever since he was a boy. Here
he brings together some of his favourite
stories by writers like Henry Williamson,
Gerald Durrell, Janet Orchard and Robert Bustard –
writers who have observed animals closely and
who know how to describe them vividly.
Wild and Penned is a book that will appeal to
everyone who enjoys entering into the rich
and varied life of nature.

Another TOPLINER by John Crompton

Up the Road and Back

TOPLINER REDSTARS

Wild and Penned

Nature stories compiled by
John Crompton

Macmillan

Selection © John Crompton 1978

First published 1978

Published in *Topliner Redstars* by
MACMILLAN EDUCATION LIMITED
Houndmills Basingstoke Hampshire RG21 2XS
and London
Associated companies in Delhi Dublin
Hong Kong Johannesburg Lagos Melbourne
New York Singapore and Tokyo

Printed in Hong Kong

British Library Cataloguing in Publication Data

Crompton, John
Wild and penned.
1. Animals – Juvenile literature
I. Title
591'.08   QL49
ISBN 0-333-24844-9

Contents

Acknowledgements

The author and publishers wish to thank the following who have kindly given permission for the use of copyright material:

William Collins Sons & Co. Limited for extract from *Kay's Turtles* by Robert Bustard;

The Countryman Limited for articles 'Collecting Foxes' by Gay A. Sagar, 'Seven Lame Badgers' by Janet Orchard, 'Battle Royal' by Anne Quekett and 'My Pine Martens' by H.G. Hurrell from *The Countryman Nature Book*;

Rupert Hart-Davis Limited/Granada Publishing Limited for extracts from 'Love and Marriage' and 'The Nightingale Touch' from *Menagerie Manor* by Gerald Durrell;

A.M. Heath & Co. Limited on behalf of The Estate of the late Henry Williamson for extracts from 'The Lone Swallows' and 'The Old Pond' from *The Lone Swallows* and 'Chakcheck's Raid on London' and 'No Eel for Nog' from *The Old Stag* by Henry Williamson;

Longman Group Limited for extract from 'A Hen and Some Eggs' from *The Stories of Frank Sargeson* by Frank Sargeson.

1 Love and Marriage
Gerald Durrell

Gerald Durrell always wanted as a boy to work with animals. He became a zoo keeper (at Whipsnade Zoo) as a youth, went collecting animals in Africa as a young man and now has his own zoo in the Channel Islands. This chapter from Menagerie Manor *describes the problems of breeding some kinds of animal, and Durrell uses his usual vividness and humour to help you imagine the creatures, and their young ones, at his zoo.*

You can tell if an animal is happy in captivity in a number of different ways. Principally, you can tell by its condition and appetite, for a creature which has glossy fur or feathering, and eats well to boot, is obviously not pining. The final test that proves beyond a shadow of doubt that the animal has accepted its cage as 'home' is when it breeds.

At one time, if an animal did not live very long in captivity, or did not breed, the zoos seemed to be under the impression that there was something wrong with it, and not something wrong with their methods of keeping it. So-and-so was 'impossible' to keep in captivity, they would say, and, even if it did manage to survive for a while, it was 'impossible' to breed. These sweeping statements were delivered in a wounded tone of voice, as if the wretched creature had entered into some awful conspiracy against you, refusing to live or mate. At one time there was a huge list of animals that, it was said, were impossible to keep or breed in confinement, and this list included such things as the great apes, elephants, rhinoceros, hippopotamus, and so on. Gradually, over the years, one or two more agile brains entered the zoo world, and to everyone's surprise and

chagrin it was discovered that the deaths and lack of babies were not due to stubbornness on the part of the creature, but due to lack of knowledge and experiment on the part of the people who kept them. I am convinced there are precious few species of animals which you cannot successfully maintain *and* breed, once you have found the knack. And by knack I mean once you have discovered the right type of caging, the best-liked food, and, above all, a suitable mate. On the face of it, this seems simple enough, but it may take several years of experiment before you acquire them all.

Marriages in zoos are, of course, arranged, as they used to be by the eighteenth-century mammas. But the eighteenth-century mamma had one advantage over the zoo: having married off her daughters, there was an end to it. In a zoo you are never quite sure, since any number of things may happen. Before you can even lead your creatures to the altar, so to speak, it is quite possible that either the male or the female may take an instant dislike to the mate selected, and so, if you are not careful, the bride or groom may turn into a corpse long before the honeymoon has started. A zoo matchmaker has a great number of matters to consider, and a great number of risks to take, before he can sit back with a sigh of relief and feel the marriage is an accomplished fact. Let us take the marriage of Charles as a fairly typical one.

Charles is – rather unzoologically – what is known as a Rock ape from Gibraltar. He is, of course, not an ape at all, but a macaque, one of a large group of monkeys found in the Far East. Their presence in North Africa is puzzling, but obviously they have been imported to the Rock of Gibraltar, and have thus gained the doubtful distinction of being the only European monkey. We were offered Charles when the troop on the Rock underwent its periodical thinning, and we were very pleased to have him. He was brought over from Gibraltar in style on one of Her Majesty's ships, and we duly took possession of him. He stood two feet six inches high, when squatting on his haunches, and was clad in an immensely long, thick, gingery brown coat. His walk was very dog-like, but with a distinct swagger to it, as befits a member of the famous Rock garrison. He had bright, intelligent brown eyes, and a curious pale pinkish face, thickly covered with freckles. He was undoubtedly ugly, but with an ugliness that was peculiarly appealing. Curiously enough, although he was a powerful monkey, he was excessively timid, and an attempt to keep him with a mixed group of other primates failed, for they bullied him unmercifully. So Charles was moved to a cage of his own, and a carefully worded letter was despatched to the Governor of Gibraltar, explaining in heart-rending terms, Charles's solitary confinement and hinting that he would be more than delighted if a female Rock ape should be forthcoming. In due course we received a signal to say that Charles's condition of celibacy had been reviewed and it had been decided that, as a special concession, a female Rock ape, named Sue, was going to be sent to us. Thus another of Her Majesty's ships was pressed into service, and Sue duly arrived.

By this time, of course, Charles had settled down well in his new cage, and had come to look upon it as his own territory, and so we had no idea how he would treat the introduction of a new Rock ape – even a female one – into his bachelor apartments. We carried Sue in her travelling crate and put it on the ground outside Charles's cage, so that they could see each other. Sue became very excited when she saw him, and chattered away loudly, whereas Charles, after the first astonished glance, sat down and stared at her with an expression of such loathing and contempt on his freckled face that our hearts sank. However, we had to take the plunge and Sue was let into the cage. She sprang out of her crate with great alacrity, and set off to explore the cage. Charles, who had been sitting up in the branches dissociating himself from the whole procedure up till then, decided the time had come to assert himself. He leapt down to the ground and sprang on Sue before she realised what was happening and could take evasive action. Within a second she had received a sharp nip on the shoulder, had her hair pulled and her ears boxed, and was sent tumbling into a corner of the cage. Charles was back on his branch, looking around with a self-satisfied air, uttering little grunts to himself.

We hastily went and fetched two big bowls of fruit and put them into the cage, whereupon Charles came down and started to pick them over with the air of a gourmet, while Sue sat, watching him hungrily. Eventually, the sight of the grape juice trickling down Charles's chin was too much for her, and she crept forward timidly, leant towards the bowl and took a grape, which she hastily crammed into her mouth, in case Charles went for her. He completely ignored her, however, after one quick glance from under his eyebrows, and, gaining courage, she again leant forward and grabbed a whole handful of grapes. Within a few minutes they were both feeding happily out of the same dish, and we sighed with relief. An hour later, when I passed by, there was Charles, lying on his back, eyes closed, a blissful expression on his face, while Sue, with a look of deep concentration, was searching his fur thoroughly. It seemed that his original attack on Sue was merely to tell her that it was *his* cage, and that, if she wanted to live there, she had to respect his authority.

Sometimes one acquires mates for animals in very curious ways. One of the most peculiar was the way in which we found a husband for Flower. Now, Flower was a very handsome North American skunk, and when she first came to us she was slim and sylph-like and very tame. Unfortunately, Flower decided that there were only two things in life worth doing: eating and sleeping. The result of this exhausting life, which she led, was that she became so grossly overweight that she was – quite literally – circular. We tried dieting her, but with no effect. We became somewhat alarmed, for overweight can kill an animal as easily as starvation. It was plain that what Flower needed was exercise, and equally plain that she had no intention of going out of her way to obtain it. We decided that what she needed was a mate, but, at that particular time, skunks were in short supply and none were obtainable, so Flower continued to eat and sleep undisturbed. Then, one day, Jacquie and I happened to be in London on business, and, being a bit early for our appointment, we walked to our destination. On rounding a corner, we saw approaching us a little man dressed in a green uniform with brass buttons, carrying in his arms – above all things – a baby chimpanzee. At first, with the incongruous combination of the uniform and the ape, we were rather taken aback, but as he came up to us I recovered my wits and stopped him.

'What on earth are you doing with a chimpanzee?' I asked him, though why he should not have a perfect right to walk through the streets with a chimpanzee I was not quite sure.

'I works for Viscount Churchill,' he explained, 'and he keeps a lot of queer pets. We've got a skunk, too, but we'll 'ave to get rid of that, 'cos the chimp don't like it.'

'A skunk?' I said eagerly. 'Are you sure it's a skunk?'

'Yes,' replied the little man, 'positive.'

'Well, you've met just the right person,' I said. 'Will you give my card to Viscount Churchill and tell him that I would be delighted to have his skunk, if he wants to part with it?'

'Sure,' replied the little man, 'I should think he'd be pleased to let you 'ave it.'

We returned to Jersey full of hope that we might have found a companion, if not a mate, for Flower. Within a few days I received a courteous letter from Viscount Churchill, saying that he would be very pleased to let his skunk come to us, and that, as soon as he had had a travelling cage constructed, he would send him. The next thing I received was a telegram. Its contents were simple and to the point, but I cannot help feeling that it must have puzzled the postal authorities. It read as follows:

GERALD DURRELL ZOOLOGICAL PARK LES AUGRES JERSEY CI: GLADSTONE LEAVING FLIGHT BE 112 AT 19 HOURS TODAY THURSDAY CAGE YOUR PROPERTY. CHURCHILL.

Gladstone, on being unpacked, proved to be a lovely young male, and it was with great excitement that we put him in with Flower and stood back to see what would happen. Flower was, as usual, lying in her bed of straw, looking like a black and white, fur-covered football. Gladstone peered at this apparition somewhat shortsightedly and then ambled over to have a closer look. At that moment Flower had one of her brief moments of consciousness. During the day she used to wake up periodically for about thirty seconds at a time, just long enough to have a quick glance round the cage to see if anyone had put a plate of food in while she slept. Gladstone, suddenly perceiving that the football had a head, stopped in astonishment and put up all his fur defensively. I am quite sure that for a moment he was not certain what Flower *was*, and I can hardly say I blame him, for when she was just awakened from a deep sleep like that she rarely looked her best. Gladstone stood staring at her, his tail erect like an exclamation mark; Flower peered at him blearily and, because he was standing so still and because she had a one-track mind, Flower obviously thought he was some new and exotic dish which had been put in for her edification. She hauled herself out of her bed and waddled across towards Gladstone.

Flower walking looked, if anything, more extraordinary than Flower reclining. You could not see her feet, and so you had the impression of a large ball of black and white fur propelling itself in your direction in some mysterious fashion. Gladstone took one look, and then his nerve broke and he ran and hid in the corner. Flower, having discovered that he was only a skunk, and therefore not something edible, retreated once more to her bed to catch up on her interrupted nap. Gladstone steered clear of her for the rest of the day, but towards evening he did pluck up sufficient courage to go and sniff her sleeping form and find out *what* she was, a discovery that seemed to interest him as little as it had done Flower. Gradually, over a period of days, they grew very fond of one another, and then came the great night when I passed their cage in bright moonlight and was struck dumb with astonishment, for there was Gladstone chasing Flower round and round the cage, and Flower (panting and gasping for breath) was actually enjoying it. When he at length caught her, they rolled over and over in mock battle, and, when they had finished, Flower was so out of breath she had to retire to bed for a short rest. But this was only the beginning, for after a few months of Gladstone's company Flower regained her girlish figure, and before long she could out-run and out-wrestle Gladstone himself.

So zoo marriages can be successful or unsuccessful, but if they are successful they should generally result in some progeny, and this again presents you with further problems. The most important thing to do, if you can, is to spot that a happy event is likely to take place as far in advance as possible, so that the mother-to-be can be given extra food, vitamins and so forth. The second most important thing is to make up your mind about the father-to-be: does he stay with the mother, or not? Fathers, in fact, are sometimes more of a problem than mothers. If you do not remove them from the cage, they might worry the female, so that she may give birth prematurely; on the other hand, if you do remove them, the female may pine and again give birth prematurely. If the father is left in the cage, he might well become jealous of the babies and eat them; on the other hand, he might give the female great assistance in looking after the young: cleaning them and keeping them amused. So, when you know that a female is pregnant, one of your major problems is what to do with Dad, and at times, if you do not act swiftly, a tragedy may occur.

We had a pair of slender loris of which we were inordinately proud. These creatures look rather like drug addicts that have seen better days. Clad in light grey fur they have enormously long and thin limbs and body; strange, almost human, hands; and large lustrous brown eyes, each surrounded by a circle of dark fur, so that the animal appears as though it is either recovering from some ghastly debauchery, or a very unsuccessful boxing tournament. They have a reputation for being extremely difficult and delicate to keep in captivity, which, by and large, seems to be true. This is why we were so proud of our pair, as we had kept them for four years, and this was a record. By careful experiment and observation, we had worked out a diet which seemed to suit them perfectly. It was a diet that would not have satisfied any other creature *but* a slender loris, consisting as it did of banana, mealworms and milk, but nevertheless on this monotonous fare they lived and thrived.

As I say, we were very proud that our pair did so well, so you can imagine our excitement when we realised that the female was pregnant: this was indeed going to be an event, the first time slender loris had been bred in captivity, to the best of my knowledge. But now we were faced with the father problem, as always; and, as always, we teetered. Should we remove him or not? At last, after much deliberation, we decided not to do so, for they were a very devoted couple. The great day came, and a fine, healthy youngster was born. We put up screens round the cage, so that the parents would not be disturbed by visitors to the Zoo, gave them extra titbits, and watched anxiously to make sure the father behaved himself. All went well for three days, during which time the parents kept close together as usual, and the baby clung to its mother's fur with the tenacity and determination of a drowning man clasping a straw. Then, on the fourth morning, all our hopes were shattered. The baby was lying dead at the bottom of the cage, and the mother had been blinded in one eye by a savage bite on the side of her face. To this day we do not know what happened, but I can only presume that the male wanted to mate with the female, and she, with the baby clinging to her, was not willing, and so the father turned on her. It was a bitter blow, but it taught us one thing: should we ever succeed in breeding slender loris again, the father will be removed from the cage as soon as the baby is born.

In the case of some animals, of course, removing the father would be the worst thing you could do. Take the marmosets, for instance. Here the male takes the babies over the moment they are born, cleans them, has them both clinging to his body and only hands them over to the mother at feeding time. I had wanted to observe this strange process for a long time, and thus, when one of our cotton-eared marmosets became pregnant, I was very pleased. My only fear was that she would give birth to the baby when I happened to be away, but luckily this did not happen. Instead, very early one morning, Jeremy burst into my bedroom with the news that he thought the marmoset was about to give birth, so, hastily flinging on some clothes, I rushed down to the Mammal House. There I found the parents-to-be both unperturbed, clinging to the wire of their cage and chittering hopefully at any human who passed. It was quite obvious from the female's condition that she would give birth fairly soon, but she seemed infinitely less worried by the imminence of this event than I. Getting myself a chair, I sat down to watch. I stared at the female marmoset, and she stared at me, while in the corner of the cage her husband – with typical male callousness – sat stuffing himself on grapes and mealworms, and took not the slightest notice of his wife.

Three hours later there was absolutely no change, except that the male marmoset had finished all the grapes and mealworms. By then my secretary had arrived and, as I had a lot of letters to answer, I made her bring a chair and sit down beside me in front of the marmoset cage while I dictated. I think that visitors to the Zoo that day must have thought slightly eccentric the sight of a man dictating letters, while keeping his eyes fixed hypnotically on a cageful of marmosets. Then, about midday, someone arrived whom I had to see. I was away from the cage for approximately ten minutes, and on my return the father marmoset was busy washing two tiny scraps of fur that were clinging to him vigorously. I could quite cheerfully have strangled the female marmoset: after all my patient waiting, she went and gave birth during the short period I happened to be away.

Still, I could watch the father looking after the babies, and I had to be content with that. He looked after the twins with great care and devotion, generally carrying them slung one on each hip, like a couple of panniers on a donkey. His fur was so thick and the babies so small that most of the time they were completely hidden; then, suddenly, from the depths of his fur, a tiny face, the size of a large hazelnut, would appear, and two bright eyes would regard you gravely. At feeding time the father would go and hang on the wire close alongside the mother, and the babies would pass from one to the other. Then, their thirst quenched, they would scramble back on to father again. The father was extremely proud of his babies, and was always working himself up into a state of panic over their welfare. As the twins grew older, they became more venturesome and would leave the safety of their father's fur to make excursions along the nearby branches, while their parents eyed them with pride, as well as a little anxiously. If you approached too near the cage when the twins were on one of their voyages of exploration, the father would get wildly agitated, convinced that you had evil designs on his precious offspring. His fur would stand on end, like an angry cat's, and he would chitter loud and shrill instructions to the twins, which were generally ignored as they grew older. This would reduce him to an even worse state of mind, and screaming with rage and fear, he would dive through the branches, grab the twins and sling them into place, one on each hip; then, muttering dark things to himself — presumably about the disobedience of the modern generation — he would potter off to have a light snack to restore his nerves, casting dark glances at you over his shoulder. Watching the marmoset family was an enchanting experience, more like watching a troupe of strange little fur-covered leprechauns than monkeys.

Naturally, the biggest thrill is when you succeed in breeding some creature which you know from the start is going to be extremely difficult. During my visit to West Africa I had managed to acquire some Fernand's skinks, probably one of the most beautiful of the lizard family, for their big, heavy bodies are covered with a mosaic work of highly polished scales in lemon yellow, black, white and vivid cherry-red. By the time the Zoo in Jersey was established I had only two of these magnificent creatures left, but they were fine, healthy specimens, and they settled down well in the Reptile House. Sexing most reptiles is well-nigh impossible, so I did not know if these skinks were a true pair or not, but I did know that, even if by some remote chance they were a true pair, the chances of breeding them were one in a million. The reason for this was that reptiles, by and large, lay the most difficult eggs to hatch in captivity. Tortoises, for example, lay hard-shelled eggs which they bury in earth or sand. But if you do not get the temperature and humidity just right in the cage, the eggs will either become mildewed or else the yolk will dry up. A lot of lizards, on the other hand, lay eggs which have a soft, parchment-like shell, which makes matters a bit more difficult, for they are even more sensitive to moisture and temperature.

Knowing all this, I viewed with mixed feelings the clutch of a dozen eggs which the female Fernand's skink laid one morning in the earth at the bottom of her cage. They were white, oval eggs, each about the size of a sugared almond, and the female (as happens among some of the skinks) stood guard over them and would attack your hand quite fearlessly should you put it near the eggs. With most lizards the female walks off, having laid her batch, and forgets all about it; in the case of some of the skinks, however, the female guards the nest and, lying on top of the soil in which the eggs are buried, urinates over the nest at intervals to maintain the right moisture content, in order to keep the delicate shells from shrivelling up in the heat. Our female skink appeared to know what she was doing, and so all we could do was to sit back and await developments, without any great hope that the eggs would hatch. As week after week passed, our hopes sank lower and lower, until, eventually, I dug down to the nest, expecting to find every egg shrivelled up. To my surprise, however, I found that only four eggs had done so; the rest were still plump and soft, though discoloured, of course. I removed the four shrivelled ones and carefully opened one with a scalpel. I found a dead but well-developed embryo. This was encouraging, for it proved at least that the eggs were fertile. So we sat back to wait again.

Then, one morning, I was down in the Reptile House about some matter, and as I passed the skink's cage, I happened to glance inside. As usual, the cage looked empty, as the parent skinks spent a lot of their time buried in the soil at the bottom of the cage. I was just about to turn away when a movement among the dry leaves and moss attracted my attention. I peered more closely to see what had caused it, and suddenly, from around the edge of a large leaf, I saw a minute pink and black head peering at me. I could hardly believe my eyes, and stood stock still and stared as this tiny replica of the parents slowly crept out from behind the leaf. It was about an inch and a half long, with all the rich colouring of the adult, but so slender, fragile and glossy that it resembled one of those ornamental brooches that women wear on the lapels of their coats. I decided that if one had hatched, there might be others, and I wanted to remove them as quickly as possible for, although the female had been an exemplary mother till now, it was quite possible that either she or the male might eat the youngsters.

We prepared a small aquarium and very carefully caught the baby skink and put him into it. Then we set to work and stripped the skinks' cage. This was a prolonged job, for each leaf, each piece of wood, each tuft of grass had to be checked and double checked, to make sure there was no baby skink curled up in it. When the last leaf had been examined, we had four baby Fernand's skinks running around in the aquarium. When you consider the chances of any of the eggs hatching at all, to have four out of twelve was, I thought, no mean feat. The only thing that marred our delight at this event was that the baby skinks had decided to hatch at the beginning of the winter, and as they could only feed off minute things the job of finding them enough food was going to be difficult. Tiny mealworms were, of course, our standby, but all our friends with gardens rallied round, and would come up to the Zoo once or twice a week, bearing biscuit tins full of woodlice, earwigs, tiny snails and other dainty morsels that gave the babies the so-necessary variety in diet. Thus the tiny reptiles thrived and grew. At the time of writing, they are about six inches long, and as handsome as their parents. I hope it will not be long before they start laying eggs, so that we can try to rear a second generation in captivity.

There are, of course, some animals which could only with the greatest difficulty be prevented from breeding in captivity, and among these are the coatimundis. These little South American animals are about the size of a small dog, with long, ringed tails which they generally carry pointing straight up in the air. They have short, rather bowed legs, which give them a bear-like, rolling gait; and long, rubbery, tip-tilted noses which are forever whiffling to and fro, investigating every nook and cranny in search of food. They come in two colours: a brindled greenish-brown, and a rich chestnut. Martha and Mathias, the pair I had brought back from Argentina, were of the brindled kind.

As soon as these two had settled down in their new cage in the Zoo they started to breed with great enthusiasm. We noticed some very interesting facts about this which are worth recording. Normally, Mathias was the dominant one. It was he who went round the cage periodically 'marking' with his scent gland so that everyone would know it was his territory. He led Martha rather a dog's life, pinching all the best bits of food until we were forced to feed them separately. This Victorian male attitude was only apparent when Martha was not pregnant. As soon as she had conceived, the tables were turned. She was now the dominant one, and made poor Mathias's life hell, attacking him without provocation, driving him away from the food, and generally behaving in a very shrewish fashion. It was only by watching to see which was the dominant one at the moment, that we could tell, in the early stages, whether Martha was expecting a litter or not.

Martha's first litter consisted of four babies, and she was very proud of them, and proved to be a very good mother indeed. We were not sure what Mathias's reactions to the youngsters was going to be, so we had constructed a special shut-off for him, from which he could see and smell the babies without being able to sink his teeth into them, should he be so inclined. It turned out later that Mathias was just as full of pride in them as Martha, but in the early stages we were not taking any risks.

Then the great day came when Martha considered the babies were old enough to be shown to the world, and so she led them out of her den and into the outside cage for a few hours a day. Baby coatimundis are, in many ways, the most enchanting of young animals. They appear to be all head and nose, high-domed, intellectual-looking foreheads, and noses that are, if anything, twice as rubbery and inquisitive as the adults'. Then they are natural clowns, forever tumbling about, or sitting on their bottoms in the most human fashion, their hands on their knees. All this, combined with their ridiculous rolling, flat-footed walk, made them quite irresistible. They would play follow-my-leader up the branches in their cage, and when the leader had reached the highest point he would suddenly go into reverse, barging into the one behind, who, in his turn, was forced to back into the one behind him, and so on, until they were all descending the branch backwards, trilling and twittering to each other musically. Then they would climb up into the branches and do daring trapeze acts, hanging by their hind paws, or one fore paw, swinging to and fro, trying their best to knock each other off. Although they often fell from quite considerable heights on to the cement floor, they seemed as resilient as india-rubber and never hurt themselves.

When they grew a little older and discovered they could squeeze through the wire mesh of the cage, they would escape and play about just inside the barrier rail. Martha would keep an anxious eye on them during these excursions, and should any real or imaginary danger threaten they would come scampering back at her alarm cry, and, panting excitedly, squeeze their fat bodies through the wire mesh and into the safety of the cage. As they grew bolder, they took to playing farther and farther afield. If there were only a few visitors about, they would go and have wrestling matches on the main drive that sloped down past their cage. In many ways this was a nuisance, for at least twenty times a day some kindly and well-intentioned visitor would come panting up to us with the news that some of our animals were out, and we would have to explain the whole coati-mundi set-up.

It was while the babies were playing on the back drive one day that they received a fright which had a salutary effect on them. They had gradually been going farther and farther away from the safety of their cage, and their mother had been growing increasingly anxious. The babies had just learnt how to somersault, and were in no mood to listen to their mother's warnings. It was when they had reached a point quite far from their cage that Jeremy drove down the back drive in the Zoo van. Martha uttered her warning cry, and the babies, stopping their game, suddenly saw they were about to be attacked by an enormous roaring monster that was between them and the safety of their home. Panic-stricken they turned and ran. They galloped flat-footedly down past the baboon cage, past the chimp's cage, past the bear cage, without finding anywhere to hide from the monster that pursued them. Suddenly, they saw a haven of safety, and the four of them dived for it. The fact that the ladies' lavatory happened to be empty at that moment was entirely fortuitous. Jeremy, cursing all coatimundis, crammed on his brakes and got out. He glanced round surreptitiously to make sure there were no female visitors around, and then dived into the Ladies' in pursuit of the babies. Inside, they were nowhere to be seen, and he was just beginning to wonder where on earth they had got to when muffled squeaks from inside one of the cubicles attracted him. He discovered that all four babies had squeezed under the door of one of these compartments. What annoyed Jeremy most of all, though, was that he had to put a penny in the door *to get them out*.

Still, whatever tribulations they might give you, the babies in the Zoo provide tremendous pleasure and satisfaction. The sight of the peccaries playing wild games of catch-as-catch-can with their tiny piglets; the baby coatimundis rolling and bouncing like a circus troupe; the baby skinks in their miniature world, carefully stalking an earwig almost as big as themselves; the baby marmosets dancing through the branches, like little gnomes, hotly pursued by their harassed father: all these things are awfully exciting. After all, there is no point in having a Zoo unless you breed the animals in it, for by breeding them you know that they have come to trust you, and that they are content.

2 The Old Pond

Henry Williamson

Henry Williamson is most widely known for his book Tarka
the Otter, *which is probably the best nature story ever written. But he wrote many other nature stories, long and short.
I like this one because it deals so well with creatures living
in the city. London, in fact; South-East London, to be more
exact.*

I remember trout lying in the sluice of the mill-wheel below
the culvert. Roach roamed along the weed-beds, grass-green
of back when the sun lit the water. Kingfishers, perching on
snags, looked at their own bright images, and very early in
the misty morning a grey heron stood on the rushes, sharp of
beak to spear the brown voles which burrowed in the banks.
The acre of water was fed by a brook, where wild duck
splashed in winter. Sometimes at night the miller heard the
whistles of a roaming dog-otter, and the moon jigged in
broken gold where its flat head set the ripples spreading.
The spirit of the water was joyous as it flowed through the
green Kent country, long ago.

Nowadays the waters of the pond are false-coloured with
tar and oil from the road. The trout are dead, and hundreds
of metal caps of beer bottles lie below the culvert, dirty-
white in the water, the saloon-bar Sunday trade of the red-
brick public house nearby. The fire-bellied efts and nine-
spined sticklebacks are dead, too. Beetles remain, and the red
wriggling larvae of the gnat. When the road was widened
for the tramcars of the London County Council, the corpora-
tion drained the pond, pulled down its daisied bank and
wooden posts and rails, filled in a third of its area, built
above its eastern edge a wall of bricks and concrete, and

planted an iron-spiked fence. Having ravished its spirit, the LCC stole the pond's birthright and severed the child from its lovely mother Kent, giving it to the County of London. A wild cherry tree used to lean out of an island in the middle of the pond when it was in Kent; but London cut down the tree, and erected a pole for the Union Jack. Perhaps, when there is no more war, the snowy blossoms of the wild cherry will drift over the water again. . . .

Tramcars stop by the pond, and return north again to the city, through the Old Kent Road. Motor-buses pass all day and most of the night. A pair of moorfowl live on the island of the pond, unafraid of traffic. The hen calls her mate by a cry of *teank!* and he replies with *teonk!* They are always calling one another, in voices croaking and watery, and they dive for beetles and red-thread gnat-worms. The pond is two feet deep, and the fowls swim by paddles on their long toes.

One March morning, while the birds were singing in sunlit County Kent, and a chill, choking yellow fog darkened the sky of County London, Teank rose with a tram ticket in her bill. She had been building a nest since the previous morning. Her skill in nest-building would not have turned a chaffinch, that perfect moss-moulder and feather-felter and cowhair-weaver, into a greenfinch with envy. She merely opened her bill and dropped the ticket on the meeting place of three thorn branches. She made many underwater journeys that day, and at nightfall the nest was finished. It was made of weed and tickets, a bootlace, a fragment of yellow cardboard with a print of *Every genuine cigarette bears the name W. D. & H. O.* upon it, and beakfuls of cat's hair. This was Teank's first nest to be made in a tree, and she had placed it there because of the rats which swarmed on the island.

The first egg was laid five days later. In size it was between that of a hen and a pigeon, the colour of dead oak leaves, freckled and spotted red-brown. Teank laid it before the wheels of the first early tramcar yarred and screaked on the rails in the wood-block road. She did not return to the nest during the day, but paddled about the pond and walked the grassy bank opposite the railings for snails and worms. The pond on this side was dammed by a bank higher than the flat allotments beyond, where cabbage leaves and old tins rotted. Willows and hawthorns and alders leaned over the bank.

The next morning, long before smoke began to rise from the chimney pots of the brick houses nearer London, Teank laid her second egg. As she jumped off the nest it fell to the ground and was smashed, and although she heard the noise of the breaking shell, she did not realise that it was her egg. The first egg remained in the centre of the platform, resting in a slight hollow. Then Teonk and Teank, their black-and-white tails flipping as they peered left and right, swam to the bank and walked down to the allotments through the thorn and willow trees. Many slugs and insects they found, but a dog disturbed them, and with heavy flight, for their wings were short, they returned and splashed into the pond.

The nest being as small as the palm of a man's hand, the third egg rolled off as soon as laid, and so did the fourth and the fifth and the sixth and the seventh eggs, but Teank did not miss them. The shattered yolks below gave a rat a small meal, and what he left the ants and flies removed. As soon as her seven were laid, Teank began to brood over the solitary egg. Previously she had roosted on a low bough of a box tree, near Teonk, but now she slept on the platform, with the egg between her legs. She was there during the daytime as well, except for hurried searches for food. While she brooded her blood was hotter, and she used to sink into a heavy state which was almost sleep.

In April a pair of swallows came back to the grass-grown chimney of the blacksmith's shop in the disused mill, where they had nested for five years. They twittered joyfully over the water, so happy to be back again, and took flying dips into the pond, making ripples which the sun turned to silver as of old. Two sedge-warblers from Africa had come with them, and at night the lights of motorbus and tramcar made the cock-bird sing his sweet chattering song among the flag irises. A cuckoo with a cracked voice could be heard calling far away in the very early morning, but the noises of traffic were often too loud during the day. Unemployed men and youths, including myself, loafed by the railings. I could see Teank as she sat on her egg.

One morning something began to tap-tip-tap inside this egg, and tip-tapped till the afternoon, when the shell opened and a head looked out. It had an appearance of old age, with tousled black down and weary time-worn eyes. *Weep-weep*, it said, opening its red bill. *Weep-weep*, as it kicked to be free of the shell; *weep-weep*, as it tried to stand on tiny legs. *Weep*, as it fell asleep. *Teank!* cried the mother, and *Teonk!* he answered. He did not go to her, but continued his task of trying to break up with his bill a floating crust he had been pursuing for over half an hour. Every time he pecked, the crust bobbed. The workless men were most interested in him.

The next day the mother carried her chick on her back to the water, and dived. It swam. The day was a Sunday, and at noon the railings held a line of human mothers and fathers and children, in best clothes, boots and hats. Hundreds of fragments of biscuit and bread were thrown into the pond of the broken-down mill. A pair of dingy swans had wandered there, and eaten their fill. They floated on the water, amidst specks of soot, with necks and heads laid between wings folded, but with open eyes. Sparrows fluttered and hovered over the sodden crusts, trying to peck a meal. Teonk was pushing another crust round the pond, ignorant of human encouragements and humour. Each time he knocked a bit off, he croaked in his watery voice. Banana skins and orange peel were flung in for him, but he did not want them.

Empty paper bags were blown out by small boys and girls, and cast away through the rails, their romantic voyagings watched by the owners. Three of them sank, two drifted into the island, one was wrecked upon a snag, another stayed by the body of a drowned cat floating with only part of its back visible, and one was taken by fair winds right across the ocean to America, or Africa, to the savages, where the jungle grew. The poor boy beside me had been reading Ballantyne, out of the Free Library. We talked. I wish I knew his name and where he lived, for I would send him a copy of Jeffries' *Bevis*, the best boy's book in the world. The blue eyes, widely spaced, the animation of the pale sensitive face, remain in my mind; he was trying for a scholarship – 'Mum wanted 'm to.' He was ten years old, and at a London County School at Greenwich – he found another crumb in his pocket, and ate it with delight. Mum gave him a penny a week for helping her Saturday mornings: he bought broken biscuits with this wage, and 'chewed 'm slow, to make 'm last, he did'.

A walking-stick was hurled over the railings, a strange-shaped hairy dog after it, amid the joyful shrieks and yells of the cockney kids thrusting arms and legs through the railings. Teank, in the lee of the island, called to Teonk. The wee black chick cried *weep*, and dived. It swam underwater until its lungs ached, and up it bobbed, a hundred kicks having taken it a few inches, and away from the island. It saw a great shaggy head, and bobbed again. It came up six inches further from the island. The dog barked as he neared the stick. *Weep-weep* the chick cried, alone in the world, having no more breath. It made for the island where Teank was calling. It was an immense and terrible journey, but at last it was among the thick growth, and safe with mother.

The fear of dog soon faded from the mind of mother and chick. Years ago there had been in the pond a terror to wild-fowl, when pike had lurked beside the weed-beds like dark logs sodden and sunken there. The last pike had been killed by the last roaming otter at the end of the nineteenth century, and in the belly of that pike at the time of its death, the miller told me, was a moorhen. The fear of pike was still in the mind of Teank, and whenever she saw the shadow of a tree move in the water, she would call the chick to her side.

In the third week of July the cuckoo with the cracked voice flew back to Africa, whence it had journeyed in the third week of April. During many springtimes its voice had been heard in the copses and spinneys which lay around a golf course, once a park owned by the Cator family. Other cuckoos' voices cracked in June, but this cuckoo's second, or dropped, note always split into keys like the voice of an adolescent schoolboy. I heard it first in May 1914, again in 1916; then in 1919 and the following year; and, yes, the same cuckoo in 1922, when Teank built her silly nest in the island hawthorn.

The chick had grown into a moorhen, and lived on the island with Teonk and Teank. She walked with them on the allotments in the early morning, and had no fear of the hissing, clanking traction engines and wasp-striped furniture vans that trundled along the broad main road. No longer did she say *weep-weep*, but *teunk*.

The cuckoo had been gone only a few days when Teank, the mother, began to build another nest. She made it not on the island, but among the sedges, treading a standing-place and putting weed and wet paper there. This nest was as large as a man's head, and was covered above by an arch of sedge. Teank laid five eggs on it, and then Teunk, her daughter, sat on them to hatch them. When Teunk was hungry she called Teank, who crept over the eggs and brooded them while Teunk swam away and fed herself.

Teonk, the father, slept as usual on the island, because the making of a nest and the hatching of eggs did not interest him. Teunk, the daughter, did not live to see her small brothers and sisters which her warmth had helped into life, because a ragged ex-soldier shot her with a gun with sawn barrels on the allotments early one morning, and took her home for his wife and children in Deptford.

Teank sat alone in the nest. There were but three eggs to sit upon after the eleventh day, because a pair of rats found them and stole two. One dropped into the water, but the other they got to their hole unbroken. A rat turned on his back, holding it in his paws, and his companion seized tail in teeth and dragged him as though he were a sled. They returned for more, but Teank and Teonk faced them furiously, stamping with their feet and pecking with their bills so hard that the rats ran away. Only two of the eggs hatched, for the third was addled; it had hardly grown cold after the departure of the chicks when a rook saw it, and took it on a branch to suck it. When he had opened it he cried 'Cor!' and, dropping it, flew away.

The two chicks were about a week old when the pond began to shrink. A channel had been cut in the bank above the allotments, for the weedy penstock by the mill was held by tons of mud. Boots, cans, sticks, an old sack or two with skull or bones near, dried on the shoals. Water receded from the island, until a narrow channel only was left, trickling through what looked like an estuary. The mud became pressed by the feet of birds and rats. It slowly dried, and cracks opened across it. Teonk and Teank took their chicks up the brook to the watercress beds above and there they lived happily on beetles and snails for many weeks.

A gang of men came with shovels and wheelbarrows, dug up the silt, wheeled their loads on plank-tracks to the allotments and dumped them there, burying cabbages and tins and mouldering scarecrows. One of the shovels struck something brittle, that knocked against the wooden side of a barrow as it was turned in − a human skull, with a narrow cleft in its top, as might be made by a light blow of an axe, or the cut of a sword, from behind. A small round skull, in the Celtic shape: struck down perhaps, by a Roman, for Caesar's legions passed by the pond on the way to Londinium. Perhaps a cottage murder − a weighted sack pushed in from the bank at night, to sink into mud, among the eels. . . . ' 'Ave a fag, mate,' said one of the men, wearing the watered-rainbow ribbon of the 1914 Star on his shabby waistcoat, taking the cigarette stump from his lips and sticking it between the bony jaws. No money reward for a skull and a few bones, so what use reporting it to the police? The dead could not help the living, or the living the dead. So it was wheeled away in the barrow, tipped out, and buried with the fag, among many other skulls and bones; and one of those lesser skulls may have rejoiced to be with it, for the bed of the pond was a dogs' golgotha.

A year passed, and another year, and I thought to myself, in the clear air of Devon, that never again would I go near the poor spoiled waters, where once a springtime snow of wild cherry blossom had floated above the grass-green roving roach. But one night, when I was stopping in London after a return from the Salient, I dreamed of the pond, and saw again the summer-quiet lilies, and the back fin of a carp glistening brown among the floating leaves. Clouds moved in sky and water, and the blue dragonflies were on the sedges. The ghosts fled when I awakened to hear the rain on my window, and all the morning I was restless, for the spirit of the pond was calling me. So we returned, my memory and I, and stood by the railings, while the cold wind of a late winter afternoon blew about the road. The mill-house was gone, and the hawthorn; and the little wooden shop where without shame we could ask the old woman for a ha'porth of mixed biscuits. She called every child 'Dear', and no one made a row in her shop, or cheeked her; she was so old and tiny.

New shops, a garage with plate-glass windows; the jolly inn by the pond, The Green Man, where carters took their quarts while on the night journey to Covent Garden Market, was pulled down. Well, it had been spoiled for some years, ever since the tramlines were laid; and they kept goldfinches in cages in the glittering lights of the saloon bar. The weekend crowds came and went, and it made a fortune; the new and larger brick building will make another.

Yes, I thought, the pond was dying, and London has quite killed it. The black County, with a millstone round its neck, had stolen more of the country, and the beautiful Seven Fields of Shrofften are to be part of a new suburb. I knew every nesting-hole in every tree in Shrofften . . . the Saxon

25

name is not good enough for a suburb; it will have a new name, easier for the suburban tongue. From the main road, by the bend where the great elms grow, the beautiful and green outline of the hills was the same as in boyhood; but what shall I see if I go there again?

And so I took my last look at the island, which during the cleaning of the pond had been cleared of its undergrowth of angelica and nettles. It was now tidy. The flagpole stood straight, not crooked like the cherry tree, which is gone. They had made the island circular, and bound its edge with wooden piles; the sedges were not there. A boathouse had been built on the allotments, and beside it many small cor- acles were stacked. A notice board said that this was the Children's Pool, and that all moneys from the hire of boats would be paid to a Children's Hospital in London. Then the pond had been cleaned so that tiny limbs should be set straight, and tiny faces made to unpucker, and lips to smile! I knew then why the spirit of the water, which might be of Bethesda, had come to me in a dream with a vision of its olden loveliness to be written not with sadness, but with joy. An omnibus with guardian lamps bore swiftly upon me, and as I turned to climb upon the step I heard from over the glimmering pond a watery cry of Teank! and an answer, Teonk!

3 My Pine Martens

H. G. Hurrell

Pine martens belong to the same family as ferrets, otters and mink, the latter being farmed for their beautiful coats. Weasels and stoats are the commoner relatives. It seems pine martens can act like ferrets.

It was in 1938 that I first acquired three pine martens which had been imported from Germany. I remember being impressed at once by their broad, rather flat heads and strong thick legs, with feet that leave tracks suggesting a larger animal.

I keep and breed the martens at my home on the southern fringe of Dartmoor in pens formerly used for silver foxes. They do not seem to be encumbered by their stout limbs, for they exercise themselves for hours and their movements are often very rapid. It is fascinating to watch the exciting chases of playful cubs rushing in wild pursuit from one end of their large pen to the other. Martens rarely walk; they normally progress by a succession of easy bounds with backs arched, thus showing their relationship to the weasel. They have a swinging rhythm, and I often picture them bounding through the forest like sprites. The names I give them – Zephyr, Ripple, Eddy, Swirl – suggest the movement which is their very essence.

A faulty door-catch allowed one of the two original males to escape. I hunted high and low but realised how hopeless it was to try to recapture an animal which could easily climb the guard fence that had prevented the escape of my silver foxes. Imagine my surprise and delight the following day to see him run along a wall, flip over the fence and go straight back to his pen, where a feed was waiting. This experience with a marten which was not even bred in this country encouraged me to let one out deliberately. I had fearful qualms about losing it, but within a day or so it returned; and this led me to try to control a marten while out, so as to get it back at will.

I have had a lot of experience in training hawks, especially goshawks, and wondered if martens could be trained by an adaptation of the method. Hawks must first be accustomed to human beings; then they are trained to feed on a lure. As soon as they are tame and know that the lure means food, the main problem is to ensure that they are keen before being flown. For my martens I have invented a special kind of lure, a pan on a long handle: I cannot help calling it a martinet, though it is not a spur but an enticement. Food can be placed in the pan and the animal encouraged to eat from it. Eventually he is taught to follow the pan for a reward and so can be allowed a short distance from the pen and lured back there. The training may take some time but, as with hawks, it becomes mainly a matter of keeping the creature tame and seeing that it has a good healthy appetite when at liberty. By tame I mean willing to feed close to a human being; my martens would strongly object to being handled.

The similarity of the response of hawk and marten is remarkable: if they are not keen they may go off on their own regardless of their owner and his lure. But there is one great difference. As a rule a hawk cannot be relied on to return home after it has been lost; eyases* will sometimes do so, but it is risky to depend on it. A marten is fortunately almost certain to come back, though it may keep one waiting many anxious hours. Scores of times I have had mine go off on their own, but only one has finally walked out on me in this way, though seven or eight others have got out accidentally and gone wild. One of these is known to have lived wild for two years and another for at least three.

One of the first climbing tricks I taught my martens was to go up a long pole which I had baited with food at the top. I now make it more interesting by using a fresh-cut thirty-foot larch, baiting the topmost twig which bends alarmingly when the animal approaches the food. Another stunt is to sweep the martinet over a line of fifteen-foot posts set about a yard apart, so that the martens will race along the tops of them after it. Various tightrope turns add variety to this performance.

A marten's hearing is acute, so I attached a hawk bell to the martinet to help them to locate the reward. When I felt I had reasonable control over them I began to take them to an adjoining wood. On a cord from my neck I hung a container with food, leaving both hands free to manipulate the martinet, the handle of which I had greatly lengthened with two joined bamboo poles. By raising this I encouraged the martens to climb and jump from tree to tree. Now the real fun began. There is something squirrel-like in the way they

* *Eyases*: young hawks from the nest, or incompletely trained.

clasp a tree trunk with side-stretched limbs and jerk their way up or down, but the bark of some trees – beech, for example – may be too smooth for them to climb the trunks: their claws cannot grip it. They are expert in assessing instantly whether a particular route from one tree to another is negotiable and in spotting an alternative, which may mean going back to the trunk and out on another branch. A troupe racing wildly through a wood, all eager for the reward in the martinet, is a remarkable sight. After this strenuous and exciting exercise the martens usually go back readily to their pens.

Some years ago I found an interesting way of hunting with a marten. Blondin, then my favourite and a talented tree climber, was exercised regularly in the wood and on one occasion discovered a rabbit in some bushes. He sprang on it and killed it. This encouraged me to take him out hunting. The method was to get him to enter likely bushes by throwing in a scrap of food. Sometimes he would scent or see a rabbit and try to capture it by a sudden rush. When one broke cover with Blondin in full pursuit I had a revelation. I had always thought that martens were built for endurance rather than speed, but the rabbit, racing away from cover with a five-yard start, was only a couple of yards ahead when it had travelled about twenty yards, though after that it began to pull away. I had grossly underestimated the marten's acceleration.

Blondin generally caught his rabbits before they had time to get going. Occasionally he got one after a chase of up to a hundred yards, usually when it took refuge in other bushes. I saw no evidence of the rabbits being inhibited by fear: they seemed to move as quickly as if chased by a dog, perhaps because the marten did not follow them underground and bolt them from the burrows. I did not encourage Blondin to go to ground because I should have been able to recover few, if any, of the rabbits he killed. In proportion to its size a full-grown rabbit is one of the strongest of prey, and I was astonished that a marten could hold on to one and kill it:

Blondin's total bag in the year before myxomatosis reached us was twenty-eight. He also killed a good-sized rat, a mole, a dormouse and, unfortunately, two or three birds in thick cover. In addition he caught field mice, which he hunted with stiff-legged jumps, as other animals do.

When I went hunting with Blondin I did not take the martinet but a walking-stick with a hawk bell attached to the handle. This helped him to find me in thick cover, though he would also come to my whistle. I think he chiefly relied on sight and scent to keep in touch with me. I used the stick also to pry into dense bushes and recover rabbits from thick brambles; Blondin always left them when they were dead. I am still puzzled by the way Blondin followed me close at heel. After dashing off in pursuit of a rabbit he would waste little time in returning if the quarry eluded him. We expect a dog to follow its master, but a marten is surely a lone hunter; why should it deliberately accompany a human being? I suspect that the reason is fundamentally the urge for food – the reason that prompts a falcon to wait on – whereas the dog's attachment to its master is largely the pack animal's craving for company.

I have had exceptional opportunities to observe what my martens will eat. I have known them catch frogs. Most ranch-bred martens will refuse slugs, but I had one which would drag them about under his front feet to de-slime them before eating them. All are fond of beetles and moths, and they will pick blackberries and rowan berries. So their diet can be very varied.

Not many generations ago martens were widespread in the British Isles. Now they have been banished from most of the country, surviving most successfully in the north of Scotland. They also exist as rarities in Wales, Ireland and the Lake District. The species cannot stand up to intensive persecution because its reproduction rate is low. Martens do not reach breeding age until they are two years old, and even then they produce only one litter, averaging three cubs, a year. They are not likely to become numerous because only a limited population is found even in virgin forests where they have never been hunted. If a few were present in our woodlands they would help to check the grey squirrel.

4   A Hen and Some Eggs

Frank Sargeson

Frank Sargeson was a well-known New Zealand writer of novels and short stories. He did not usually write about animals or birds, but I specially like this story (or memory) because of its clear description of a creature we have nearly all come across. And because it tells us something about the writer, too.

I think that one time when my mother set a hen on some eggs was about the most anxious time I've ever experienced in my life.

The hen was a big black Orpington, and Mother set her inside a coop in the warmest corner of our yard. My brother and I went out one night and held a candle, and mother put the hen in the coop and gave her thirteen eggs to hatch out. And the next morning we ran out and looked inside the coop, and it was wonderful to see the hen looking bigger than ever as she sat on the thirteen eggs.

But besides being wonderful to see the hen sitting on the eggs, it was a worry to see that she had one egg showing. And it was the same way each time we looked. It wouldn't have been so bad if we could have been sure that it was the same egg each time, because Mother had put the thirteenth egg in just to see if thirteen was an unlucky number, and if it hadn't hatched out it wouldn't have mattered much. But we couldn't be sure, and we'd go to school thinking that if our hen was silly enough to let each one of the thirteen eggs get cold in turn, then we wouldn't have any of the eggs hatch out at all.

Then an even worse worry was trying to get the hen to eat. We'd put her food just by the hole in the coop but she'd take no notice. And after we'd got tired of waiting to see her come out and eat and had gone away and left her, sometimes the food would disappear, but as often as not it wouldn't. And when it did disappear we could never be sure that it wasn't the sparrows that had taken it. So each time we looked inside the coop we thought our hen was getting thinner and thinner, and if there happened to be two eggs showing instead of one, we were sure that it was so, and we said that after all our trouble there probably wouldn't be one egg that'd hatch out after all. And we thought that our hen might be even silly enough to let herself starve to death.

Then one Saturday morning when it was nearly time for the eggs to hatch out, something terrible happened. My brother and I were chopping kindling wood in the yard and suddenly my brother said, Look! And there was the hen walking up and down inside the wire-netting part of the coop, something which we had never seen her doing before.

We thought she must be hungry, so as fast as we could we took her some wheat. But the hen didn't seem to be hungry, and instead of eating the wheat she started cackling, and if we stayed near her she'd run up and down inside the wire-netting instead of just walking. Well, we went and told Mother, and Mother told us to leave the hen alone and she'd go back to the eggs. So we stood in the yard and watched, and the hen went on walking up and down, so we went and told Mother again. And Mother looked at the clock and said, Give her five minutes from now and see what happens.

Well, the hen went on walking up and down, and we could hardly bear it. It was awful to think of the thirteen eggs getting colder and colder. Anyhow Mother made us wait another five minutes, then she came out and we tried to shoo the hen back into the coop. But it was no good, the hen went on like a mad thing, and Mother said we'd just have to leave her alone and trust to luck. We all went inside to look at the clock and we reckoned that the hen must have been off the nest for at least twenty minutes, and we said that the eggs couldn't help being stone cold by that time.

34

Then when we came outside again we saw the most astonishing thing happen. The hen suddenly left off cackling and walking up and down. She stood there without moving just as if she was trying to remember something, then she ran for the hole in the coop and disappeared inside.

Well, it was ourselves who went on like mad things then. But after a few minutes we started talking in whispers, and we chopped our kindling wood round the front of the house so as not to disturb the hen, and we'd keep coming back into the yard to creep towards the coop and look in from a distance, and it was more wonderful than ever to see the hen sitting there, even though she had the one egg showing as usual.

And a few days later twelve of the eggs hatched out, but the thirteenth egg was no good. To this day I've wondered whether it was the same one that was always showing, and whether that was the one that was no good. My brother said that the hen knew it was no good and didn't bother to keep it warm. He may have been right. Children are rather like hens. They know things that men and women don't know, but when they grow up they forget them.

5 The Lone Swallows

Henry Williamson

Henry Williamson died in 1977, aged over eighty. I had been meaning to write and tell him how much I loved his books for thirty years and never did. This is my favourite Williamson short story, because, I think, it is simply told and about a common, but beautiful summer-visiting bird, which nested in a shed near the house where I lived as a boy. The story helped me to see and value the birds.

Along the trackless and uncharted airlines from the southern sun they came, a lone pair of swallows, arriving with weakly and uncertain flight from over the wastes of the sea. They rested on a gorse bush, their blue backs beautiful against the store of golden blossom guarded by the jade spikes. The last day of March had just blown with the wind into eternity. Symbols of summer and of loveliness, they came with young April, while yet the celandines were unbleached, while the wild white strawberry and ragged robin were opening with the dog violet.

On the headland the flowers struggle for both life and livelihood, the sward is cropped close by rabbits and sheep, and the sea wind is damp and cold. Perhaps the swallows hoped to nest, as their ancestors had done centuries since, in the cave under the precipice at the headland's snout, or that love for its protection after the wearying journey was new-born in their hearts. One cannot say; but the pair remained there.

Days of yellow sunshine and skies blue as their wings greeted them. Over the wave crests and the foamed troughs they sped, singing and twittering as they flew. Kestrel hawks with earth-red pinions hung over the slopes of the cliffs, searching with keen eyes for mouse or finch, but the swallows heeded not. Wheatears passed all day among the rabbit burrows and the curled cast feathers of the gulls, chiffchaffs iterated their little joy in singing melody, shags squatted on the rocks below, preening metal-green plumage and ejecting fishbones.

The wanderer on the sheep track, passing every day, joyed in the effortless thrust of those dark wings, the chestnut stain on the throat, the delicate fork of the tail. Winter was ended, and the blackthorn blossoming – there would be no more snow or ice after the white flowers, fragile as vapour thralled by frost, had come upon their ebon wilderness of spines. The heart could now look forward, not backwards to other fled springtimes. The first swallows had come from distant lands, and three weeks before the winged hosts were due! One of the greatest of nature writers wrote, 'The beautiful swallows, be tender to them.' In fancy Richard Jefferies, too, was wandering on the headland, and watching the early vagrants, breathing the fragrance of the wild thyme that came like an old memory with the wind. Always dearly loved are the singing birds of passage, returning with hopeful wings to the land that means love and life to them, and love and life and beauty to us. Each one is dear; all the swallows returned are a sign and a token of loveliness being made manifest before our eyes.

The early April days passed, like the clouds in the sky, softly and in sunlight, merging into the nights when Venus lighted the western seas, and belted Orion plunged into the ocean. In the sheltered places the arums grew, some with hastate leaves purple-spotted, and showing the crimson *spadix* like the tip of a club. Brighter grew the gorselands, till from the far sands they looked like swarming bees gold-dusty from the pollen of the sun. The stonechat with white-ringed neck and dark cap fluttered into the azure, jerked his song in mid-air, then dived in rapture to his mate perched upon a withered bramble. In a tuft the titlark was building her nest, while the yellowhammer trilled upon a rusted plough-share in the oatfield.

Sometimes the swallows flew to a village a mile inland, and twittered about an ancient barn with grass-grown thatch, haunted by white owls, and hiding in dimness a cider press that had not creaked in turning for half a century. Once they were seen wheeling above the mill pond, and by the mossy waterwheel, hovering along its cool gushings and arch of sun-stealing drops thrown fanwise from the mouldered rim. Everywhere the villagers hailed them with delight, and we spoke in the inn at nights of their early adventuring. Such a thing had been unknown for many years; the oldest granfer had heard tell of it, but had never actually seen it before. The old man took a poet's delight in the news, and peered with rheumy and faded blue eyes, hoping to see them when tapping along the lane to his 'tetties'. It became a regular thing for the wanderer upon the headland to report their presence when he returned from the high solitude and the drone of the tide, and the yelping cries of gulls floating white in the sunshine above a sea of woad-blue.

Gulls selected nesting sites, and the sea-thrift raised pink buddings from its matted clumps. The ravens rolled in the wind uprushing from the rocks, and took sticks in black beaks to the ledge where they had nested throughout the years. The male bird watched upon a spur while his mate with throaty chucklings built anew the old mass of furze sticks where her eggs would be laid. Sometimes he fed her with carrion filched from a pearly gull by the flashing and sunpointed foam, and she gabbled with pleasure.

Ever and anon the fleeing specks of the swallows passed near, winding in and out, floating and diving, 'garrulous as in Caesar's time'. Like kittens in distress the buzzards wailed, spreading vast brown canvas that enabled them to sail high among those silver and phantom galleons, the clouds. Steamers passing to the Severn basin left smoke trails on the horizon; the life of the sea and land, wild and civilised, went on; but no other swallows arrived. Light of heart the wanderer watched, and waited. Any day, new born and blessed by Aurora, would see the arrival, any day now – two dark arrowheads fell with hissing swoop from heaven, arrowheads that did not miss their mark. There was a frail flutter of feathers in the sunshine, a red drop on the ancient sward, a scuttle of terrified rabbits, a faint scream trembling and dying in the blue. Then only the murmur of the sea far below and the humming of the single telegraph wire near the pathway. The peregrine falcons had taken the lone and beloved swallows.

6 Battle Royal

Anne Quekett

Conger eels can grow up to nine or ten feet long (three metres) and as thick as a man's thigh. Since they also have fearsome teeth and live on the sea bed they have always given me the shiver that a sea monster gives. Imagine those teeth sunk into your flesh and those coils round your neck. There is violence in nature all right.

As I sat on a rocky platform on the eastern side of Rathlin Island, some four miles off the north Antrim coast, I was startled to hear heavy breathing almost at my feet and saw that a big grey bull seal had come close inshore to inspect me. After some minutes he disappeared and I was looking for his partner, as seals are not often seen singly, when there was a sudden turmoil just off the rocks. The bull rose grunting and wheezing in his effort to maintain his grip on a giant conger-eel, which he held near the tail. The giant length of the eel's body arched high out of the water and then flattened along the surface. While the seal tried to take a surer grip near the head, the conger reared its gleaming coils up and above the seal's head, striking at the jaws and finally twisting in a stranglehold about the thick bull-neck. Time after time the pair submerged and rose struggling together, until the eel released its grip momentarily and was seized beneath the head and bitten deep in the belly, so that the water was crimson about them.

The seal now began to show signs of distress. He seemed to rest briefly, unable to do more than keep his hold on the eel, which was still fighting gamely, the slap of its tail sounding on the water and on its adversary's body. The end of the struggle was a breathtaking spectacle. The seal dipped his great head and, gripping the conger below the water with his flippers, raised himself slowly, drawing back his head; steadily he tore a long strip of living flesh from head to tail and devoured it. The sounds of tearing flesh and crunching jaws came sharply across to me on that still afternoon, until there remained only the tail and bared vertebrae, still lashing for release, though feebly now. Then these, too, were eaten to the last mouthful. Tired and replete, the seal heaved his great shining body on to the rock platform where, unconcerned at my presence, he lay basking in the last warmth of the sun. The whole struggle had occupied fully ten minutes.

7 Kay's Turtles

Robert Bustard

Kay is a seventeen-year-old South Sea Island girl. Through her great interest in the animals of her Pacific home she became a friend of an American marine biologist, Dr Robert Bustard. This is the opening chapter of his book about Kay's studies of turtles. The chapter is called 'First Meeting With Ruth', but I have used the title of the book here because it tells you better what both the chapter and the book are about – the girl and the animals.

As the day reluctantly gave way to night Kay left her home to walk around to the back of the island to look for nesting turtles. She carried a basket woven from pandanus leaves. Turtle eggs are a delicacy to Torres Strait Islanders and she hoped to find some nesting turtles and collect a clutch of eggs. In this way Kay had seen many hundreds of nesting turtles – mostly green turtles, but also a few hawksbill or tortoiseshell turtles – and had come to acquire a considerable fund of knowledge about turtles and their ways. While spearing fish on the reef flat she also often came in contact with turtles, and the relaxed tempo of island life meant that she could always stop what she was doing in order to watch and perhaps ponder. Life in the islands is kind in that there is always time to stand and stare.

The sun slipped behind the hill as Kay reached the beach, leaving a row of coconut palms silhouetted against the reddening sky. The rising tide lapped quietly against the sand and a few reef herons looking for fish rose languorously into the air at Kay's approach. The only other sign of life was a small, brilliantly-coloured kingfisher sitting on a pandanus branch. It was extremely alert and disappeared in a blur of iridescent blue well before Kay approached its look-out point.

High tide would occur shortly after dark, and, as Kay knew, the high tide would bring in the female green turtles which were ready to go through the arduous business of coming ashore, pulling their great weight up the soft sandy beach, and laying their eggs above the high-water mark in a specially constructed nest which would ensure the correct conditions for the developing young.

As darkness fell a few ghost crabs left their burrows, freshly constructed on the beach after each high tide destroyed them, and started to forage near the high-tide mark for food. These large ghost crabs are able to overpower baby green turtles, and later in the summer when the young turtles were hatching, life would be easy for the crabs. At present, however, things were far from easy, and the crabs had to hunt hard to find sufficient scraps to make a meal.

There were two species of ghost crab on the island, this large type which kept strictly to the beach, rarely venturing above the high-tide mark and taking refuge in shallow water when frightened, and another smaller, more colourful species, which dug its burrow inland from the beach and spent most of its time well above the high-tide mark.

It was early November and the green turtle nesting season had just begun. Only a few turtles were coming ashore to nest each night, sometimes only one. Later in the season several dozen each night would not be exceptional. Green turtles are strictly seasonal nesters in the Torres Strait where they lay from November to February inclusive. The tortoiseshell turtle, known simply as the 'shell turtle' to the Islanders, on the other hand nests throughout the year in the Torres Strait.

Kay had reached a sheltered crescent-moon-shaped bay at the back of the island, popular with nesting turtles, and sat down to await developments. There was no sound except the gentle lapping of the advancing tide on the sand and a faint rustle among the pandanus fronds caressed by a light onshore breeze. Kay was early this evening – no turtles had as yet come ashore – and she sat under a pandanus palm in an area much frequented by nesting turtles and wondered if any would in fact come ashore there that night. It was fruitless to speculate, so Kay stretched out on the sand and proceeded to tear strips off an old dead pandanus leaf and knot them together with her long slender fingers.

Her mother, like all the older generation, could make excellent mats and baskets from pandanus leaves but Kay had never been taught how to do this. Unfortunately the Islanders are rapidly losing their special skills handed down from generation to generation, and when the present older people die so much will have been lost for ever.

About an hour must have passed when she saw a dark shape emerging from the surf about fifty paces down the beach. The full moon provided excellent visibility and reflected off the wet shell of the green turtle, for that is what it was. As Kay watched, the turtle slowly hauled itself free from the gentle waves, stopping frequently to look about, and then started the slow process of ascending the beach. After some time the turtle disappeared into the vegetation zone, and shortly afterwards Kay heard the sound of sand spraying from pandanus leaves indicating that the turtle had selected a nesting spot and was digging in. Kay lay back to wait. After what probably amounted to a further forty-five minutes, she sauntered slowly along the beach towards the turtle.

There had been no sound for some time, indicating that the turtle had completed its preliminary construction and was now either digging the chamber which would hold the egg clutch or actually laying the eggs. Kay came up behind the turtle so as not to frighten it and bent down to see what stage of nesting it had reached. To her surprise it had scarcely dug any egg chamber. Then, as it started digging again after a rest period, she saw the reason. Its right rear flipper had been damaged, perhaps as the result of an attack by a shark, but instead of being bitten clean off as often happens, only part of the muscle had been cut. The flipper was no longer able to go through the normal, but incredible, motions in which it becomes virtually a hand-scoop to remove sand, so that all the digging activity had to be done by the left flipper. This is not an impossible task, although, naturally, it takes somewhat longer than when both flippers work alternately. However, the problem was much worse than this. When one digging flipper has been damaged, even when it has been reduced to a mere stump at the region of the upper thigh, that flipper still goes through the motions of digging in its turn. When the flipper has been damaged but not lost, it may actually impede the digging sequence and this was the case with the turtle Kay was watching.

The rear flippers alternately dig into the sand, loosen it, and then cup themselves to remove a flipperful which is deposited on the sand well clear of the developing egg chamber. When its turn came the right flipper made a very clumsy initial movement which caused sand to fall down into the hole, it was then inserted into the embryonic chamber where it twisted around but was unable to remove any sand. Hence progress was minimal, the digging effort of the left flipper being negated by the succeeding action of the right.

Kay watched for a while and then looked to see if any other turtles had come ashore. None had. She therefore decided to see if she could help the turtle dig its egg chamber for she knew that until it had dug an egg chamber no eggs would be laid. Kay lay down behind the turtle and removed sand with her hands working in the frequent rest periods which occurred between digging sequences by the turtle. At first the task looked hopeless as the damaged flipper continued to negate her efforts. She then saw that the trouble came from its action against the wall of the egg chamber and that if she enlarged the chamber on the right side the damaged flipper would have no effect as it would no longer strike any sand. This task completed, she continued to deepen the chamber and after a quarter of an hour it had reached the maximum depth that the undamaged left flipper could reach, which is the cue to the turtle, working by touch alone, that the chamber is ready to receive the eggs. The turtle made a few investigatory movements at the foot of the chamber with the left flipper and then, apparently satisfied, prepared to lay its eggs.

Egg-laying was preceded by several contractions of the tail region, and a quantity of clear fluid was exuded prior to the appearance of any eggs. Suddenly, following a more violent contraction, one egg was extruded and dropped to the foot of the egg chamber. It was soon followed by another and then another. Soon eggs started to appear two at a time and then sometimes three were laid one right after the other. Kay lay down flat on the sand and started to collect the eggs from the foot of the egg chamber taking care not to touch the female turtle's tail in the process. When she had scooped up all the eggs already deposited in the egg chamber, three at a time, and placed them in the basket she had made from pandanus leaves, she sat up and collected the eggs, each slightly larger than a ping-pong ball, that were now dropping from the turtle's cloaca. The turtle laid 154 eggs. These completely filled the large basket, and since each weighed more than one and a half ounces, making a total of 15 lb, they would constitute an excellent meal for the family. The eggs, rich in fat and protein, have a watery white which does not coagulate when cooked, and a fishy flavour. However, if the eggs are left in the sun for a day or so or soaked in salt water then the white coagulates as in hen's eggs. Kay went home with her basket of eggs, leaving the turtle to cover up the non-existent eggs and disguise the nest site before returning to the sea, unaware that its nest was now empty.

During the week that followed, Kay completely forgot about the turtle whose egg chamber she had helped to dig and did not again go egg hunting.

Just over a fortnight later she was again around at the back of the island one evening, when she again saw a turtle having difficulty in digging its egg chamber. Because of the large barnacle on the top of its head and the nature of the wound to the right rear flipper she knew at once that it was the same turtle. On examining it more closely she was able to confirm this by several other features: some of the scales on one side of the head were abnormal in number and of irregular shape and there were several large barnacles beneath the marginal shields at one side. The turtle was making extremely little progress as before and Kay decided to help it. This time she had no ulterior motive. There were numerous nesting turtles so eggs were plentiful, and besides, Kay had not brought a basket in which to place eggs. The sand was very dry as there had been no rain for several weeks and even with Kay's help digging was extremely difficult. The dry sand fell into the egg chamber as quickly as the turtle and Kay could remove it. After some strenuous digging efforts Kay realised it was useless and in moving, accidentally caused substantial sand slippage on to the undamaged left rear flipper. The turtle, which Kay had decided to name Ruth, after her mother, at once stopped digging and after a few minutes moved on to try again elsewhere.

The nest excavation commences with a large shallow depression, somewhat larger than the turtle, called the body pit. This generally allows the turtle to enter somewhat moist, more consolidated sand in which it can dig the egg chamber. Ruth was lucky in that in moving on she slid into the remains of a former body pit. The head-down inclination at once released the nesting urge and the turtle quickly completed the body pit and was ready to commence the egg chamber. Once again the sand was extremely dry and Ruth and Kay together could make little progress. When Kay realised this she purposefully dropped a stream of sand from her hands on to the left rear flipper. As before, the turtle stopped its attempts and rested. Purely by chance Kay had found the natural way in which a turtle is 'informed' when digging conditions are quite hopeless. One must remember that all the digging activity goes on behind the turtle, and, just as it cannot see someone lying behind it taking its eggs, it never sees the egg chamber, which is constructed purely by touch using the extremely sensitive rear flippers.

Ruth moved on several yards and started digging yet a third body pit. While the turtle was doing this it occurred to Kay that if she could only moisten the sand slightly it would be easy to dig an egg chamber. She looked round for something in which to carry water but was unable to find anything. She was wearing a red and white patterned towelling mini which would readily soak up water. She decided to use it so slipped it off and went down the beach to the sea. Kay returned with her dress soaked with sea water and waited impatiently for the turtle to complete the body pit and commence the egg chamber. As soon as it had started she carefully wrung out her dress on the precise spot where

48

digging was occurring and made several quick trips back to the sea for more water. She then returned to the turtle to help her to dig.

Progress was rapid once she had cleared sand well away from the region of the damaged flipper. She made a total of five more trips back to the sea then wrung her dress out as completely as possible and draped it over a nearby pandanus to dry in the faint breeze. The egg chamber was now two-thirds dug and had reached moister sand where digging was possible without additional water. Kay was lying flat on the ground in order to reach the foot of the egg chamber. Suddenly she felt something solid in the egg chamber and at its next dig Ruth's left flipper unearthed a tree root passing diagonally across the egg chamber. The root belonged to a nearby she-oak and was fully one inch in diameter. Neither Kay nor Ruth was able to break it. Attempts to dig the egg chamber round it failed to satisfy Ruth, so the third nesting attempt had proved a failure despite Kay's help and her idea of wetting the sand around the egg chamber. Kay and Ruth, simultaneously and independently, decided that they had done enough work for one night and that it was time to go home. Ruth slowly turned about and made for the beach accompanied by Kay. Kay was interested to see Ruth's response to her on the beach where the sudden appearance of a human usually sends returning turtles 'galloping' for the sea, and causes others that are emerging to lay to do a rapid about-turn and re-enter the water. However, she need not have worried. Ruth was completely undisturbed by Kay's presence and stopped frequently to rest between forward movements down the beach. Turtles are not responsive animals – they do not lick you like dogs – but are rather independently-minded creatures, a trait which will be immediately understood by cat lovers. In this connection it is interesting to note that Kay does not like dogs but is extremely fond of cats. What part this may have played in the friendship with Ruth is impossible to say but it may well have been significant. Kay, of course, had more sense than to walk down the beach standing up and towering over Ruth. Instead she moved alongside Ruth on all fours and during the longer rest periods sat down alongside. Sometimes she stroked Ruth's head.

The tide was now well out though it must have been nearly full when Ruth emerged to nest some four or five hours previously. Near the water's edge was an area of beachrock which was difficult for a turtle to climb from the landward side. Here began yet another co-operative activity between Kay and Ruth. On land, turtles are shortsighted and their heads are only a few inches above the ground, giving a very restricted range of vision. On reading the bedrock, Ruth turned left whereas Kay could see that only four or five yards to the right there was a break in the beachrock. She wondered how she could communicate this information to Ruth. While she pondered this, Ruth slowly and laboriously dragged her great weight for almost twenty yards along the beachrock before deciding to try in the other direction. As it was, she had only stopped several yards short of the end of the rock. Again Kay could not think how to tell her. Ruth now slowly retraced her steps, with frequent rest periods, and eventually reached and passed through the break that Kay had seen from the start. Soon she reached an area of muddy sand left by the receding tide and started to cross it. Kay remained with her until she was in water reaching halfway to Kay's knees, which was just deep enough to allow Ruth to swim. She then slowly swam out towards the edge of the reef and bed – which would be under a coral ledge with head facing inwards where she was comparatively safe from shark attack. Kay, clad in only a pair of bikini briefs as islanders seldom wear bras, was by now very cool. She ran up the beach, put on her dress, which was still slightly damp, and started out for home. On the way back Kay was quite excited and elated at the evening's happenings. However, she determined to say nothing as no one would believe that she had spent the evening making friends with a turtle.

The next night Kay returned to the same beach at the time of high tide. This evening she had brought a small red plastic bucket to wet the sand in the expectation that, having failed to lay her eggs the previous night, Ruth would return this evening to have another attempt. Kay detected three sets of tracks in the moonlight, one of which from its much smaller size she knew at once belonged to a shell turtle. The other two tracks, looking even larger than life in the moonlight – almost like those of a tractor – belonged to green turtles. Kay went up behind the first turtle which expired air with a hissing sound and drew in its head at her approach; clearly this nervous turtle was not Ruth. The other green turtle she knew at a glance was not Ruth because of its unusual coloration and exceptionally small head. The carapace was pale green with virtually no darker blotches or spots. The turtle had a well-dug chamber and, as Kay watched, it suddenly struck some obstruction, then brought up a flipperful of eggs, and then another and another. Some of the eggs were broken but others were intact.

Kay looked down the egg chamber and saw that the turtle had dug into the side of a previously laid nest. The carnage continued. As the nesting season had only recently begun, the embryos were still small and pink-coloured. Kay picked up one broken egg to look at it. The embryo had a huge head with enormous purple-black eyes, the shell was clearly visible, but completely soft to the touch, and pink, like the soft parts. As Kay turned the small embryo over, the heart was conspicuous and its pumping action could be clearly seen. Each time the embryo was touched it moved its tiny limbs. It would soon be dead and the intact eggs would be killed by the heat of the sun the next day in the unlikely event of seagulls not detecting them first. Kay decided to prevent this and collected fifteen intact eggs and sat down to dig an egg chamber for them. Having placed the eggs at the foot and covered them up in approved turtle fashion, Kay noticed two other turtles coming up the beach. As she watched in the overcast moonlight she fancied one was Ruth. She kept still and after a few minutes the turtle was abreast of her and she knew for sure that it was Ruth.

This evening Ruth had come ashore on part of the beach where there was a pronounced bank to climb and where some areas were too steep even for determined turtles. Kay moved slowly towards Ruth, on all fours, and Ruth, who had stopped to rest, showed no sign of fear. Ruth continued straight up the beach and it was clear to Kay that she was heading for an almost unscalable portion of the bank. Crawling up alongside her Kay accidentally placed her weight on her left fore flipper and Ruth made a slow deliberate turning movement to the right and then continued on up the beach at the new angle. However, the best approach to the bank lay slightly farther to the right so, noticing the previous response, Kay again placed her weight on the left front flipper. Ruth responded exactly as before moving even farther towards the right. Kay was delighted; she had found a way in which to guide her friend around obstacles and so save her considerable effort.

Turtles forsook the land to return to the sea at least seventy million years ago, and are therefore naturally adapted to life in the water. It is extremely difficult to obtain traction on soft sand but in the water support for the enormous weight is no problem. On land, shifting the weight across soft sand with limbs ill-adapted for terrestrial movement becomes a major task, hence the turtles' frequent rest periods. Furthermore, turtles, like whales, have problems in breathing when on land. Everyone has heard of the mass deaths of stranded whales. Most people know that whales are mammals like ourselves and also breathe by means of lungs but few people realise that stranded whales die ashore from slow asphyxiation. Due to their great weight, much of which is lying on top of the lungs, stranded whales are unable to inflate their lungs and so take in air. Turtles face a similar problem but can overcome it by elevating their head and pushing upwards slightly with their front flippers. Nevertheless this is a considerable effort and the whole nesting process is an arduous one, especially for the heavier turtles.

Green turtles have a further handicap not shared by most other species. When on land they do not walk by the alternate limb movements that characterise terrestrial animals and indeed most other turtles. Terrestrial animals move opposing limbs together so that the left front leg moves simultaneously with the right rear leg and vice versa. Green turtles, on the other hand, move by simultaneous movements of all four limbs. The front flippers are raised, moved forward, placed on the sand and used to drag the turtle forward. At the same time the rear flippers push forward. The overall action serves to slide the turtle across the sand without its being lifted clear off the ground. One has only to watch one of the other species of similar weight, such as a large loggerhead, walking across the beach to see just how inefficient is the green turtles' locomotory pattern.

With Kay's help – Kay acting as the brain and eyes and Ruth providing the motive power – Ruth had now reached an area of bank where ascent was possible and where there were no obstructions. Kay had often marvelled at the way in which turtles climb steep inclines to a height of twelve feet or more without apparent trouble. As soon as she had ascended the bank, using the rear flippers not only to push her forward but as props to stop her sliding backwards on her smooth lower shell, Ruth started a body pit and Kay lay down in front to watch her. Normally one has to stay behind a nesting turtle to avoid frightening it, at least until it has laid its eggs, but Kay now felt that Ruth was sufficiently accustomed to her presence not to worry about her, an assumption which proved correct. It is a great advantage to be able to sit in front of a nesting turtle as during the construction of the body pit sand is forcefully thrown backwards by powerful strokes of the front flippers and, as the turtle moves slightly from side to side, the sand spray covers almost one hundred and eighty degrees.

Kay watched Ruth's slow, purposeful, digging activity.

Her eyes remained open throughout the process, which seemed rather strange to Kay as clearly visual stimuli could not be necessary for digging the body pit when they were not needed for the construction of the infinitely more complex egg chamber. Kay noticed that streams of mucus ('tears') slowly oozed from Ruth's eyes and remembered that she had seen these previously on other nesting turtles. She wondered if these were produced to keep the eyes free of sand particles. (She did not know that these 'tears' are emitted even under water and are a method used by turtles to get rid of excess salt taken in with the food.)

As Kay watched, Ruth completed the body pit to her satisfaction and started on the egg chamber. As soon as Kay was quite certain of the exact spot which was to be excavated, she carefully sprinkled water over the area. She did this slowly, between flipper actions, and let it soak in before adding more so that the texture would not be too alien to Ruth. She then settled down as before to dig. This time the wet sand was extremely easy to remove – it was like digging into damp earth and in to time Ruth and Kay had the egg chamber half dug. Kay had been careful to make the hole wide on the right side so that the damaged flipper could not hit the rim and cause a cave-in. They were now digging into drier sand so Kay got up and went down to the sea to get more water.

As she entered the shallows several shovel-nosed rays scurried away from her feet. Smallish individuals up to about two feet have a marked penchant for lying in the shallowest water where they are constantly dragged back and forth by the waves. They are difficult to see as they lie half covered by sand beneath a water surface partly obscured by foam from the waves.

Kay walked back up the beach to Ruth with her bucket. She noticed several large ghost crabs foraging along the high-tide mark. They scuttled off sideways with a graceful, almost dancing action as she approached, and a large land hermit crab crawling slowly back up the beach left its characteristic track on the sand as if a miniature tank had passed that way. The hermit crab was brilliant red and protected its soft abdomen by living in a large whelk shell which the crab had obtained after the death of the original owner. It had been down to the sea to wet its gill chambers. Although living on land as an adult, it still needs to have wet gills in order to breathe. This necessitated a quick trip to the sea every third or fourth day. Kay had always been fascinated by the land hermit crabs. The smaller ones were a rather drab white colour and lived in white nerite shells. As they grew they changed gradually to orange, and finally red, and nerite shells became too small for them. Although there were plenty of suitable smaller shells, large shells were at a premium unless they were prepared to inhabit the delicate tun shells which offered little protection against a determined predator.

The shortage of large shells was so acute that the largest crabs often inhabited damaged shells, whereas the smaller hermits could afford to be very choosy. When frightened they retired within the shell closing the entrance with the tough keratinised limbs and one claw which was much larger than the other. Again the larger hermits were often unable to retreat fully into their shells because, due to the shortage of large shells, most of them inhabited shells which were on the small side, but Kay supposed these large individuals were better able to take care of themselves than the young crabs. The large red hermit had stopped and was eyeing Kay suspiciously as she stood several yards off looking down at it. However, it decided that she was not a threat and slowly continued on its way up the beach to its home in the debris below a scaevola bush.

In her absence Ruth had made considerable progress and all that was necessary to complete the egg chamber was about a third of the water in the bucket. Having helped her dig the chamber to its full depth, Kay sat back and allowed Ruth to put the finishing touches to widening the foot to receive the eggs.

Once practically no sand was being removed, Ruth stopped digging and took up a laying position. With Ruth, the left rear flipper was placed in the hole and curved slightly as it reached against the back of the chamber from left to right. The right flipper rested on the sand. This was a fairly common flipper position during egg laying.

With little prior warning an egg appeared from the cloaca and dropped into the chamber. The first five eggs were all laid singly, then two eggs were laid together and soon the normal pattern of eggs being expelled in two's and three's commenced. Ruth was a fast layer and it did not seem long before Kay had counted 166 eggs and Ruth had stopped laying and almost immediately started to cover the nest site.

Kay had decided carefully to mark the exact site of the nest as she hoped to be able to keep watch over it and with luck be present when the baby turtles hatched. After all, she had played a key role in providing their incubation conditions. Without her it seemed unlikely that an egg chamber could have been successfully dug and eggs laid. Furthermore, it was a way of continuing her association with Ruth. Strange though, she thought, that she would probably be there to watch Ruth's babies emerge but that Ruth would not be present. Nor would Ruth know anything about their future for there is no parental care in turtles, instinct equipping the babies for an independent life from the moment they emerge from the egg.

Knowing when to expect the young to hatch was not so difficult as it might seem. Kay knew that incubation took about six weeks, which would be about the time that Ruth was due to lay her fifth clutch of eggs. Kay would, of course, be present then to help Ruth and could easily keep watch over the other nest. A day or two before emergence takes place, a small depression usually develops at the surface and this would provide a cue for Kay that the next evening she should be beside the nest before sunset.

While she had been thinking about this, Ruth had completed covering the nest and was now flinging sand backwards as she filled in the body chamber and made some attempt to disguise the nest site. After what appeared to Kay to be a relatively short time, Ruth stopped this activity, climbed out of the shallow pit and headed seawards. She slid down the bank, crossed the beach and was in the sea all within ten minutes. Kay stood on the beach and watched her swim out to sea. She waited after she had disappeared from sight and, sure enough, in the bright moonlight saw her surface briefly to breathe, then she was gone.

8 Collecting Foxes

Gay Sagar

In the village I used to live in, near Nottingham, you sometimes met a tame fox out for a walk on a lead. So many wild animals can be kept as pets and people seem to love to keep all kinds of creatures. I always enjoy the stories which deal with the relationship between man and beast.

Nearly twenty years ago I was telling a farmer friend how much I would like to have a fox cub as a pet, and there and then he produced one – not out of a hat but from a sack. Ever since, fox cubs have been brought to me in sacks, boxes and other containers.

There was Barny, who had been found apparently abandoned at the age of about two months. I decided that he would have to accompany me wherever I went and so be accustomed to seeing a lot of people from the start. Every day he accompanied me to the office and curled up on a shelf by my desk, sleeping nearly all the time. Fortunately the factory was in the country, so I could take him for a lunch-time walk on his lead. If I went to see a film he had to come too. Cinema managers are not madly keen to have livestock on their premises; but how were they to know, when I walked in with a fox fur over my arm, that the bright eyes and quivering nose of Barny were tucked inside my coat? And if two people bought three tubs of ice-cream, in the dark no one could see a greedy fox cub licking his tub with relish. Barny seemed a success at first, but for one reason and another I had to leave him a good deal on his own and he became so timid with everyone else that it made me miserable. At last I let him go, and although I called him every evening for a time I did not see him again. If only, I sighed, one could have a cub that was free.

Not long afterwards I met a woman who was a whipper-in to a pack of foxhounds. She told me that she had had a very young cub and brought him up in her house with the hunt terriers. He went to live in the field next to the house when he was older, and stayed for about three years. I asked whether she had ever worried about the hounds hunting him. She told me how, when she was watching one side of a covert near home and listening to hounds working on the other, the fox Charlie bounded out very pleased to see her. Quietly she ordered him to go home, and he disappeared again into the undergrowth. Later a check on the time of his arrival at the kennels showed that he must have returned immediately after she had spoken to him.

This story stirred in me a longing to have a free fox and the following year, when the RSPCA inspector rang me up late one evening to say that he had another cub, this time injured, I agreed at once to have him. A poor weak creature, he had been rescued from a trap. How long he had been without food I have no idea, but for several days we had to feed him with milk from a spoon. At first we added a few drops of whisky, from which he got his name. Whisky was quite the most lovable cub I had ever had. Although, from the beginning, when I picked him up he would cough at me in the peculiar way of a fox – rather like a cat spitting – as soon as I began to bathe his injured leg he would lick my hand and sit quite still. There were times when I must have hurt him a great deal, but he never attempted to draw his leg away. I thought of the reactions of most dogs and cats to any kind of treatment and felt that the old story of removing the thorn from the lion's foot might well be true. I had Whisky for about three months. He gradually grew stronger and his leg healed, but he also was too old to tame; as he began to feel better he started to scratch at the wall to get out. Regretfully I released him one night, leaving his basket in a quiet spot with food beside it. I was overjoyed when he obviously returned at night to eat; but I did not see him again, and after the week the food remained untouched.

After this last disappointment I decided that I would never achive my ambition of having a fox cub as a pet and at the same time quite free. While I was ruminating about such things a large van stopped in the drive and a man got out. As he came up to me carrying a cardboard box, he began, 'I've got a—'

'Oh, no,' I interrupted, 'not a fox cub.'

He looked startled: 'Why yes, I found it on the road; its leg is a bit hurt.'

That is how I came to have Foxy, who had no other name because I was so sure she would not be with us long. She was a weedy-looking object the size of a large kitten – about seven weeks old, I guessed. As she was still too young to care for herself, we decided that we would have to keep her for a while. She soon became quite tame with the children and me, but like the others she remained very afraid of everyone she did not know. I took her about with me for a week or two, but it is difficult to carry a fox cub without being continually stopped by people who want to look at it; so I gave up trying to introduce her to the world at large.

I had not realised before how much foxes loved sweet things. Foxy would go crazy for bread and syrup or sweet milky coffee – in fact anything really sugary. She lived happily with us for a month or so, becoming very attached to our Alsatian bitch Belga, with whom she played every evening. Belga was thirteen and a great character; she was often likened to Nana in *Peter Pan*. One of her greatest virtues was her kindly acceptance of any animal we happened to adopt. At first Foxy was very hostile to her, but her unruffled calm, even when attacked by this wretched little cub, made Foxy realise that here was a friend.

In spite of all we did to make Foxy happy, she began to show all the signs of wanting to be free. After about six weeks I could bear it no longer, but this time I made some preparations before releasing her. I started to take her for walks on a collar and lead in the garden down to an old rabbit hole where a dachshund had once followed a rabbit and had to be dug out. It made an ideal earth, as it was well screened with bushes. After showing Foxy the way to it from all directions, one evening about a week later I set her free. She rushed round and round with the greatest joy but, to our amazement, did not run away. She played for a full two hours that evening, never still for a minute. When I retired to bed about midnight, I wondered if I would see her again.

In the morning I went to the entrance of her new home and called. At first there was no movement, but in a minute she popped out of the hole. As she stood and looked at me, gradually her ears went back and she began to wag her tail, very slowly at first. Then, as if she had suddenly decided that it really was me, she bounded forward and jumped up like a puppy, tail wagging furiously. We were very excited; at last a fox was staying with us of its own accord. For several nights I left open the door of the place where she had been sleeping, until I knew that she was perfectly content in her new home. Obviously she called in, for her new collar and lead vanished unaccountably. Other things, too, disappeared mysteriously, and if anything was missing we looked for it at the entrance of her earth; bathing trunks, towels, etc., have all been found there.

We did not see much of Foxy during the day, though she came out whenever she was called, so long as no strangers were about. Belga took to calling her, going to the hole, sticking her head down and whining until Foxy appeared. This odd pair were really fond of one another. In the evenings the cub was about the garden all the time and played with Belga as long as the dog would stay out with her, being especially fond of jumping on Belga's back and lying there until she was shaken off. When I saw how much energy Foxy used running round and wrestling with Belga, I realised how impossible it was to keep an animal so full of vitality contented in captivity. Belga unfortunately died in

September, and a few weeks later I bought an Alsatian puppy, which I introduced to Foxy. They soon made friends and began to romp about the garden; and they continued to play every evening when Foxy called.

One evening in June, when she had been with us for more than a year, Foxy came and took away a lot of food, returning several times for more. I was sure she had cubs not far away and was excited at the prospect of her bringing them with her when they were old enough. The following evening I sat in the garden until midnight and was puzzled that she did not appear. When I made inquiries next day I learnt that a vixen had been trapped not far away. The garden seemed empty in the evenings without the mischievous brown shadow that was Foxy. For days I searched the fields, calling her, but I never saw her again.

9 Chakchek's Raid on London

Henry Williamson

Peregrine falcons became very rare indeed in the 1960s. Now they are recovering from the effects of chemical farming treatments. And if the falconers who steal their young can be kept away from the nests it is possible this magnificent bird will return to London. Henry Williamson almost makes me feel I am, as I read, sweeping through the sky high over the city.

Again the dark sharp-winged bird cut a swift air-circle round the petrified figure standing on the column one hundred and forty-five feet above the earth. The figure was eighteen feet tall, and wore cocked hat, coat, knee-breeches, and shoes, all of stone. Sightlessly it stared, fixed and immobile, alone in the sky, the southern sun shining on its smoke-dark face. Thus had it been staring many years over the highway, on which proceeded perpetual lines of horse and motor traffic. Below the column were four bronze lions. Two fountains were playing. A dissonant hum of engines arose from the highway, up and down which thousands of men and women were hurrying.

Not one of the hurrying men and women looked up at the statue or saw the sharp speck flying in a circle above the monument to a dead admiral. The bronze lions were nothing to them, because they were not symbolic of the natural human spirit. These people were of a great town civilisation, whose human spirit was suppressed by a mind-layer of false thought. They believed newspapers, and hated others they had never seen. Many had forgotten the sky, and the green earth wearied them.

The gaze of the people was on the pavements and no

higher than omnibus driver or pedestrian immediately approximate. And at the moment most of them thought hatefully and scornfully of another nation, as that nation thought hatefully and scornfully of them. Among these people, determined in a conviction of their national righteousness, were many civil servants from the War and Admiralty Offices going to lunch in restaurants in the Strand, and old men wearing uniform, whose heels flashed.

The agitated streams of moving hats on the pavements, the dark dots passing through the traffic, the coloured motor-buses and cabs, were ignored by the bird above. The hum and shimmer and shuffle uprising in a hundred confused echoes smote continuously upon his senses of sight and sound, but he accepted them calmly as he had accepted the rivers and woods and towns over which he had passed since his escape from his master in Devon. He was Wizzle of the Chakcheks, a half-trained peregrine falcon. More than two centuries before, one of his ancestors had killed rooks which lived in the trees whose roots now rotted under the asphalt walks of Trafalgar Square, which was then called

Porridge Island in the village of Charing.

He flew with quick flutterings of pointed wings, followed by short level glides. His scaly yellow legs, with their four toes and black sickle-claws, were pressed into the brown plumage of his belly. His beak was blue and pointed. He had black patches on his cheeks. His eyes showed him to be noble; indeed, an English king had once conferred an earldom on one of his ancestors; his eyes were large and fierce and proud, of a beautiful brown, with liquid blue-black pupils. He was the last of the Chakchek family, peregrine falcons whose eyrie for centuries had been upon Bone Ledge, a hundred feet down a Devon sea precipice. He was Wizzle, son of the One-Eyed.

He flew seven hundred feet above Whitehall, seeing below him an immense wilderness of buildings, an immense spreading patch whose edges were lost in grey smoke rising in the windless air from a million chimneypots. He saw the river crossed by many bridges, its wide and silver flowing broken by tugs and barges, and its banks overcrowded with wharves and cranes, and tangled with spars and rigging. He climbed to a thousand feet, flying at sixty miles an hour, and turned suddenly by opening and depressing the stiff feathers of his tail, so that with a hissing of air he was flung up in a loop, at the top of which he rolled over, facing Trafalgar Square, and pointing at the figure on the top of the column. With wings half closed the tiercel* slanted down from the sky at a hundred miles an hour, breaking his point just before the statue by using wings and tail as brakes, thrusting out spread yellow feet, and alighting on the admiral's cocked hat with a tinkle of the silver bell tied to one leg. He preened the long flight-quills of his wings, drawing them through his beak and smoothing the ruffled filaments. When he had made these airworthy he preened his tail feathers in the same way, and cleaned his breast and toes. Afterwards he shook himself, stretched pinions and legs, and looked at the strange wilderness around and under him.

* *Tiercel*: the male of any hawk.

Immediately below the statue was a wide ledge, and on this were lying hundreds of skeletons and claws and scattered bones. And there were skulls, most of them about an inch and a half long, but there were smaller, blunter skulls as well. For this was a dying-place of London's birds. It was nearest the sky, and no bird likes to die on the ground. Here pigeons and sparrows who found their food in the Square flew with last wingbeats when they felt the world they knew passing away from them. There was the body of a humble-bee lying on its side by a sparrow skull, with frayed vanes folded tranquilly over its black and gold body. It had died that morning, having come to London in a Kentish flower wagon, wearily clinging in the starlit frosty night to an aster flower. The beams of the sun had given it enough strength to fly up, but its spirit had gone back to the happy meadows as its body dropped on the ledge.

Suddenly the perching bird stiffened. A flock of pigeons had flown up from somewhere behind the Admiralty Arch. He was not hungry, having gorged himself on a chicken taken from a garden in Woking half an hour previously. In the arrogancy of his young life he stared at them. They floated to the Square, with wings held at a high angle. He watched with fierce eyes all their movements. They fluttered round a woman who held a paper bag, from which she took handfuls of maize to scatter for them. The pigeons walked quickly on the asphalt, picking up the grains and having no fear of the idlers. She held out a palmful and two birds perched on her wrist. Then something little, which had been standing like a tree stump rooted in the pavement, with a paper-bill stuck to it, became alive, and slouched big-booted to her. It wore a dinted bowler hat with a a brass band shining with the letters STAR round the crown. It had fed many generations of pigeons with corn on the brim of that official hat. The woman dropped a trickle of maize over it. Three birds fluttered round it. One perched on the crown. The tree stump became human. It smiled. It held newspapers under one arm, and cried *Brisharmgravictryspeshl.*

The tiercel fixed the pigeon on the hat with the stereoscopic sight of his eyes, leaned forward, and slipped off his perch. He fell almost perpendicularly, with wings arched back, sharply, like the barbs of an iron arrowhead. He fell thus half the height of the Nelson Column, and then he opened and beat his wings, swooping low and fast just above the heads of the two uniformed Eastern Telegraph boys. A sparrow sipping water on the stone edge of the fountain basin saw him, and fell into the water with fright. The newspaper seller, faithful purveyor of racing selections during thousands of lunch hours, patron of pigeons and worthy citizens, was offering his double newssheet which told of the *British Army's Great Victory – Special –* to a pale-faced shipping clerk, when the bird on his hat was knocked three yards in a horizontal direction towards Cockspur Street, and half a hundred pigeons and a dozen sparrows on the ground scattered like spoke-splinters and felloes of a grey limber-wheel struck by a noiseless shell.

No one with human intelligence knew what had happened. The pigeon was picked up in one place, and its head several paces beyond, where it had rolled. Its crop was ripped open, and maize-berries fell out. The shipping clerk asked if it were dead.

'Dead?' replied one of the cheeky Telegraph boys. 'What yer fink 'e is? Springcleaning 'isself?'

A tall policeman strolled over with noiseless tread, controlled and immaculate. The newspaper man held out the decapitated pigeon, an appealing look on his barky face. A dozen voices tried to tell the policeman what had happened. Somone suggested it must have been shot. Someone else said a stone must have been thrown at it. An office boy munching a beef sandwich tried to assume a knowing expression, as though to direct upon himself the prominence of suspicion. He was an opportunist with imagination, as yet undeveloped, and he was being wasted as an envelope flap-licker and stamp-thumper. Another individual suggested that a German spy was concealed among the chimneypots, sniping with an airgun the military staff of the War Office. Hearing this, a territorial rifleman with blistered feet, recruit of three days training (it was the September of Nineteen Fourteen), looked alarmed, and the policeman produced his notebook. A crowd of several hundreds had been formed. The policeman ordered people to move on, and they shuffled a few feet. The crowd blocked the road, and immediately the fluid traffic lines began to coagulate. The word *Germans* made a sibilance on the tongues of the people.

Soon the people wandered away, the traffic pulsed again up and down Whitehall, Cockspur Street, and the Strand; back went the notebook into the policeman's breast pocket. The paper 'boy' rolled the body of the pigeon in one of the news-bills of the lunch edition of the *Star*, and put it in his pocket, muttering 'Lor, won't it be loverly in a poie for Sunday's dinner! Lor, won't it taste loverly!' Sparrows and pigeons came back to the Square, and the fountains splashed in the great stone basins, casting sun-dogs out of the rising waterspray which the passersby did not see.

That afternoon Wizzle stooped at three pigeons from the gilt cross on the dome of St Paul's Cathedral, losing the first bird, striking the second above an omnibus but missing a clutch, so that it hit the wooden surface of the street with such force that it bounced a yard. The third he missed in his first plunge but recovering immediately he circled under it and drove it up to an altitude about thrice the height of the cathedral. Then his relentless round-and-round tactics changed; the steady beating of his wings became agitated; with a burst of speed he dashed at the tail of the dingy pigeon, who towered and escaped, to fall towards a retreat below the lead dome where scores of its brethren were crouching. Wizzle fell upon it before it had dropped two hundred feet, and the people watching below saw the two birds meet and become one which faded into the dome, leaving only feathers in the air where they had apparently joined.

Wizzle stood on the small pigeon, descendant of a stock

68

dove, and plucked, skinned, and ate it. He tore the flesh from the frame, often pausing to peer from the ledge as though fearing disturbance. What he left ten minutes later weighed about an ounce – tail and pinion feathers, part of the breastbone, mandibles and part of the skullbone, legbones, feet, and gizzard.

For two days he harried the pigeons of St Paul's Cathedral, and then he left, making a temporary roost in one of the elms of Hyde Park. He killed a green woodpecker as it was pushing itself up a trunk with its pointed tail feathers, to the excitement of a falcon-eyed, white-bearded man who had been watching it through glasses; for the old gentleman had been observing birds in Hyde Park for many years, and he knew that the peregrine falcon was a rare visitor. In this pleasaunce a grey American squirrel ceased to live, after a chase among yellowing leaf-patches and a bounding run among the grasses that ended in sharp death for one of the invading tribe which had helped decimate the brown English squirrel.

Other strange things happened. The sexton of a church at Hampstead was surprised one morning to find the remains of a bantam cock lying on one of his tombs; but he was not more surprised than the gunner subaltern at the RA mess, Woolwich, whose horse shied and threw him during a canter round Blackheath when a rook sprawled through the air, broken-backed, and fell just before its nose. The striking-down of the rook from eleven hundred feet took place less than a quarter of an hour after Wizzle had flown up from the cockerel, and as Hampstead is some miles to the north-west of Piccadilly, and Blackheath is some miles to the south-east, one may estimate his roving pace.

He had no fixed eyrie or base; he was not yet mated; three months ago he had been a helpless and weak eyas upon Bone Ledge, watched over and fed by Mousing Keekee, the childless kestrel hawk who had adopted him. For a few weeks he hunted in Greater London, and many adventures he had, including a terrible minute when near Eltham he stooped at

69

the decoy bird of a netter, tied to a post in a wasteland to attract passing finches. For the netter concealed behind a bush jerked the cord to release the clap net, which held him captive. Wizzle's hind claw missed the decoy bird, a bullfinch, but so great was the terror of the little bird that it fell into a swoon, and hung by one frail leg from its foul perch. The netter, an unshaven and insignificant individual who worked for a 'birdfancier' in Whitechapel, ran forward to see what strange thing was struggling in his net. It was a bird with eyes fiercer than any he had seen before, with yellow legs trousered with feathers, gripping the meshes by sharp black claws. The sight of the silver bell made him imagine that it was a rare kind of parrot escaped from a cage, and he thought of a reward.

He was afraid to take it in his hands, and went back to his hiding place behind a willow stole to fetch the sacking with which he covered the cages when he travelled — for magistrates had been known to fine trappers the sum of half a crown and more for breaking the law that protected the nation's wild songsters from ravagement by mercenary wretches. He had two cages, of wood and iron wire, nine inches long, five inches wide, and eight inches high. He had twelve linnets and two goldfinches in one, and nine chaffinches in the other, all struggling to escape, clawing one another, beating wings and pushing blooded beaks through the bars to find a way to the wandering air and the thistle-heads.

He knelt by the net through which Wizzle was trying to thrust himself with foot and pinion. He smothered him with the sacking, and lifted the cane hoop of the net. The talons of one foot pierced the sacking and the skin of the thumb of the dirty hand pressing upon it, but the netter, thinking of his luck and determined not to lose the 'parrot', held on. The thorn-prick tightened, and was as the piercing of steel fish-hooks. He threw the other piece of sacking over the head, grasped it firmly, released the hold of his other hand, and sought to draw Wizzle from the net.

But Wizzle was held to the net by his clutch on the sacking through the meshes. He threshed so powerfully with his wings that the netter became afraid and tried to smother him in the covering by which he held his head. To do this he had to shift his hold, and immediately he did so Wizzle bit him in the index finger, breaking the nail. In pain the man snatched away his hand, bringing the beak near his face. Wizzle struck with a taloned foot at his ear, and clenched; at the same time he nicked with his beak and ripped the flesh under the cheekbone. The man shut his eyes, threw away the bird, and hid his face in his arms; then blundering to his feet he ran to his hiding place, his boots snapping and tearing the meshes of his net. He kicked over one of the cages, and the door opened, releasing linnets and goldfinches which fluttered away with sweet twitters of joy. The chaffinches remained, however, and eventually they were taken to an East End slum, where some were blinded with red-hot needles to make their song brighter, where their feather colours faded, and where those that did not die of a broken heart (being older birds) lived in tiny cages and ate seed and sang and sang and sang to blackened heaven. . . .

For a week more Wizzle remained near London, and during that time he hunted a stretch of the Thames some miles above Richmond, where among the reeds of the eyots* thousands of swallows were gathered for the autumnal migration. There was another bird preying upon the pilgrims, a bird swift as Wizzle, and very much like him in shape, but smaller. He weighed nine ounces. The stranger was about twelve inches long, with white neck and chin and black cheeks; he had a yellowish-white breast streaked broadly with brown, and his back was the colour of dark slate. He had the magnificent eyes of the noble falcons, the bluish curved beak with the notch, and yellow skin, or cere, round its base. He used to dash into the twittering clouds of swallows and seize one. Sometimes the chosen bird dodged him, but the little pirate, who was one of the rare hobby falcons,

* *Eyots*: small islands in a river.

71

would follow its every twist and turn and tumble until with a sudden stroke he caught it. Wizzle's way was not the hobby's way, for when he missed his swallow in the first swoop he used to leave it, and pursue another.

One afternoon as he was flying over Richmond Bridge he saw a long formation of birds in the air about a mile from him. The formation was constantly changing. As the birds wheeled in unison their broad wings made the flight like an eyebrow above the horizon; but after the turning movement it became as a string of dust. They were peewits, or green plover, which had come from the snows of Scandinavia to the English autumn ploughlands so rich with worm and grub. The leaders dived soughing over a field, and the birds sank down together. Their plumage was a harmony of tarnished green, black, white, and brown and each bird had a plume on its poll. They ran to their feeding, all running one way, and suddenly the thousand birds ceased movement, for Wizzle was above them.

He stooped, and they took to the air. He cut in among them, and missed his bird, for it tumbled out of the air-path of his swoop. He looped and cut at it again, and it fled before him, twisting and tumbling, the spread tips of its flight quills making a gruff noise. Four times Wizzle slid down in his half-point at the plover, and then he gave up the chase and followed another bird. This was one of the season's youngsters, and it was not so quick at twisting as an old bird. It was struck underneath by the tiercel who had turned on his back, and two hind talons ripped half the feathers from its breast; its wings became workless, and as it dropped limp it was clutched and borne to the middle of the field, and eaten.

For several days the swallows gathered in the river eyots, made their false starts in migration, and every hour new wanderers from the north joined the excited throng. The red sun going down in the west made them strangely agitated, and one morning when the life-giver came up beyond the sea at the Thames mouth they were gone. The hobby was gone too, and all the long and weary journey down the west coasts of France and Spain, and so to Africa, over the deserts and the mountains, it followed with other hobbies, harrying the blue birds who bring happiness to our countryside in spring.

Wizzle had set out on a journey before them, and he did not return to the Devon precipice of his birth until he had girdled the earth in flight.

10   The Nightingale Touch
Gerald Durrell

The zoo keeper is not only the marriage maker and midwife,
but the doctor for his animals. We seem to like programmes
and stories about hospitals, doctors, nurses and operations –
judging by the number of them. If one likes animal stories as
well, this one is perfect, having the medical details as well as
the animal interest. The story is also from Gerald Durrell's
Menagerie Manor, *my favourite Durrell book.*

Whether you run a pig farm, a poultry farm, a mink farm or
a zoo, it is inevitable that occasionally your animals will
damage themselves, become diseased, and eventually that
they will die. In the case of death, however, the pig, mink or
poultry farmer is in a very different position from the
person who owns a zoo. Someone who visits a pig farm and
inquires where the white pig with the black ears has gone, is
told that it has been sent to market. The inquirer accepts this
explanation without demur, as a sort of porcine kismet. This
same person will go to a zoo, become attracted to some
creature, visit it off and on for some time, and then, one
day, will come and find it missing. On being told that it has
died, they are immediately filled with the gravest suspicion.
Was it being looked after properly? Was it having enough to
eat? Was the vet called in? And so on. They continue in this
vein, rather like a Scotland Yard official questioning a murder suspect. The more attractive the animal, of course, the
more searching do their inquiries become. They seemed to
be under the impression that, while pigs, poultry or mink
die or are killed as a matter of course, wild creatures should
be endowed with a sort of perpetual life, and only
some gross inefficiency on your part has removed

them to a happier hunting ground. This makes life very difficult, for every zoo, no matter how well fed and cared for are its animals, has its dismal list of casualties.

In dealing with the diseases of wild animals you are venturing into a realm about which few people know anything, even qualified veterinary surgeons, so a lot of the time one is working, if not in the dark, in the twilight. Sometimes the creature contracts the disease in the zoo, and at other times it arrives with the disease already well established, and it may well be a particularly unpleasant tropical complaint. The case of Louie, our gibbon, was a typical one.

Louie was a large black gibbon with white hands, and she had been sent to us by a friend in Singapore. She had been the star attraction in a small RAF zoo where – to judge by her dislike of humans, and men in particular – she had received some pretty rough handling. We put her in a spacious cage in the Mammal House, and hoped that, by kind treatment, we would eventually gain her confidence. For a month all went well. Louie ate prodigiously, actually allowing us to stroke her hand through the wire, and would wake us every morning with her joyous war cries, a series of ringing 'Whoops' rising to a rapid crescendo and then tailing off into what sounded like a maniacal giggle. One morning Jeremy came to me and said that Louie was not well. We went down to have a look at her, and found her hunched up in the corner of her cage, looking thoroughly miserable, her long arms wrapped protectively round her body. She gazed at me with the most woebegone expression, while I racked my brains to try to discover what was wrong with her. There seemed to be no signs of a cold, and her motions were normal, though I noticed her urine was very strong and had an unpleasant pungent smell. This indicated some internal disorder, and I decided to give her an antibiotic. We always use Tetramycin, for this is made up in a thick, sweet, bright red mixture, which we have found by experience that very few animals can resist. Some monkeys would, if allowed, drink it by the gallon. At first, Louie was clearly so poorly that she would not even come to try the medicine. At last, after considerable effort, we managed to attract her to the wire, and I tipped a teaspoonful of the mixture over one of her hands. Hands, of course, are of tremendous importance to such an agile, arboreal creature as a gibbon, and Louie was always very particular about keeping her hands clean. So to have a sticky pink substance poured over her fur was more than she could endure, and she set to work and licked it off, pausing after each lick to savour the taste. After she had cleaned up her hand to her satisfaction, I pushed another teaspoonful of Tetramycin through the wire, and to my delight she drank it greedily. I continued this treatment for three days, but it appeared to be having no effect whatsoever, for Louie would not eat and grew progressively weaker. On the fourth day I caught a glimpse of the inside of her mouth, and saw that it was bright yellow. It seemed obvious that she had jaundice, and I was most surprised, for I did not know that apes or monkeys could contract this disease. On the fifth day Louie died quite quietly, and I sent her pathetic corpse away to have a post-mortem done, to make sure my diagnosis was correct. The result of the post-mortem was most interesting. Louie had indeed died of jaundice, but this had been caused by the fact that her liver was terribly diseased by an infestation of filaria, a very unpleasant tropical sickness that can cause, among other things, blindness and elephantiasis. We realised, therefore, that, whatever we had tried to do, Louie had been doomed from the moment she arrived. It was typical that Louie, on arrival, had displayed no symptoms of disease, and had, indeed, appeared to be in quite good condition.

This is one of the great drawbacks of trying to doctor wild animals. A great many creatures cuddle their illnesses to themselves, as it were, and show no signs of anything being wrong until it is too late – or almost too late – to do anything effective. I have seen a small bird eat heavily just after dawn, sing lustily throughout the morning, and at three o'clock in the afternoon be dead, without having given the slightest sign that anything was amiss. Some animals, even when suffering from the most frightful internal complaints, look perfectly healthy, eat well, and display high spirits that delude you into believing they are flourishing. Then, one morning, it looks off-colour for the first time, and, before you can do anything sensible, it is dead. And, of course, even when a creature is showing obvious symptoms of illness, you have to make up your mind as to the cause. A glance at any veterinary dictionary will show a choice of several hundred diseases, all of which have to be treated in a different manner. It is all extremely frustrating.

Generally, you have to experiment to find a cure. Sometimes these experiments pay off in a spectacular way. Take the case of the creeping paralysis, a terrible complaint that attacks principally the New World monkeys. At one time there was no remedy for this, and the disease was a scourge that could wipe out your entire monkey collection. The first symptoms are very slight: the animal appears to have a certain stiffness in its hips. Within a few days, however, the creature shows a marked disinclination to climb about, and sits in one spot. At this stage both hind limbs have become paralysed, but still retain a certain feeling. Gradually the paralysis spreads until the whole of the body is affected. At one time, when the disease reached this stage, the only thing to do was to destroy the animal.

We had had several cases of this paralysis, and lost some beautiful and valuable monkeys as a result. I had tried everything I could think of to effect a cure. We massaged them, we changed the diet, we gave them vitamin injections, but all to no purpose. It worried me that I could not find a cure for this unpleasant disease, since watching a monkey slowly becoming more paralysed each day is not a pretty sight.

I happened to mention this to a veterinary surgeon friend, and said that I was convinced the cause of the disease was dietary, but that I had tried everything I could think of without result. After giving the matter some thought, my friend

77

suggested that the monkeys might be suffering from a phosphorus deficiency in their diet, or rather that, although the phosphorus was present, their bodies were unable, for some reason, to assimilate it. Injections of D3 were the answer to this if it was the trouble. So the next monkey that displayed the first signs of the paralysis was hauled unceremoniously out of its cage (protesting loudly at the indignity) and given an injection of D3. Then I watched it carefully for a week, and, to my delight, it showed distinct evidence of improvement. At the end of the week it was given another injection, and within a fortnight it was completely cured. I then turned my attention to a beautiful red West African patas monkey, who had had the paralysis for some considerable time. This poor creature had become completely immobile, so that we had to lift up her head when she fed. I decided that if D3 worked with her, it would prove beyond all doubt that this was the cure. I doubled the normal dose and injected the patas; three days later I gave her another massive dose. Within a week she could lift her head to eat, and within a month was completely cured. This was a really spectacular cure, and convinced me that D3 was the answer to the paralysis. When a monkey now starts to shuffle, we no longer have that sinking feeling, knowing that it is the first step towards death; we simply inject him, and within a short time he is fit and well again.

Another injection that we use a lot with conspicuous success is Vitamin B12. This acts as a general pick-me-up and, more valuable still, as a stimulant to the appetite. If any animal looks a bit off-colour, or starts to lack interest in its food, a shot of B12 soon pulls it round. I had only used this product on mammals and birds, but never on reptiles. Reptiles are so differently constructed from birds and mammals that you have to be a bit circumspect in the remedies you employ for them, as what may suit a squirrel or a monkey might well kill a snake or a tortoise. However, there was in the Reptile House a young boa constrictor which we had obtained from a dealer some six months previously. From the day the boa arrived he had shown remarkable tameness, but what worried me was that he steadfastly declined to eat. So, once a week, we had to haul the boa out of its cage, force open his mouth and push dead rats or mice down his throat, a process which he did not care for, but which he accepted with his usual meekness.

Force-feeding a snake like this is always a risky business, for, however carefully you do it, there is always the chance that you might damage the delicate membranes in the mouth, and thus set up an infection which quickly turn to mouth canker, a disease to which snakes are very prone, and which is very difficult to cure. So, with a certain amount of trepidation, I decided to give the boa a shot of B_{12} and see what happened. I injected halfway down his body, in the thick, muscular layer that covers the backbone. He did not appear even to notice it, lying quite quietly coiled round my hand. I put him back into his cage and left him. Later on that day he did not seem to be any worse for his experience, and I suggested to John that he put some food in the cage that night. John placed two rats inside, and in the morning reported to me delightedly that not only had the boa eaten the rats, but had actually struck at his hand when he had opened the cage. From that moment on, the boa never looked back. As it had obviously only done good to the snake, I experimented with B_{12} on other reptiles. Lizards and tortoises I found benefited greatly from periodical shots, especially in the colder weather, and on several occasions the reptiles concerned would certainly have died but for the injections.

Wild animals, of course, make the worst possible patients in the world. Any nurse who thinks her lot is a hard one, handling human beings, should try her hand at a bit of wild animal nursing. They are rarely grateful for your ministrations, but you do not expect that. What you do hope for (and never, or hardly ever, receive) is a little co-operation in the matter of taking medicines, keeping on bandages, and so forth. After the first few hundred bitter experiences you reconcile yourself to the fact that every administration of a

79

medicine is a sort of all-in wrestling match, in which you are more likely to apply more of the healing balm to your own external anatomy than to the interior of your patient. You soon give up all hope of keeping a wound covered, for nothing short of encasing your patient entirely in plaster of Paris is going to prevent it from removing the dressings within thirty seconds of their application.

Monkeys are, of course, some of the worst patients. To begin with, they have, as it were, four hands with which to fight you off, or remove bandages. They are very intelligent and highly-strung, on the whole, and look upon any medical treatment as a form of refined torture, even when you know it is completely painless. Being highly-strung means that they are apt to behave rather like hypochondriacs, and quite a simple and curable disease may kill them because they just work themselves into a state of acute melancholy and fade away. You have to develop a gay, hearty bedside manner (rather reminiscent of a Harley Street specialist) when dealing with a mournful monkey who thinks he is no longer for this world.

Among the apes, with their far superior intelligence, you are on less shaky ground, and can even expect some sort of co-operation occasionally. During the first two years of the Zoo's existence we had both the chimps, Chumley and Lulu, down with sickness. Both cases were different, and both were interesting.

One morning I was informed that Lulu's ear was sticking out at a peculiar angle, but that, apart from this, she looked all right. Now Lulu's ears stuck out at the best of times, so I felt it must be something out of the ordinary for it to be so noticeable. I went and had a look at her and found her squatting on the floor of the cage, munching an apple with every sign of appetite, while she gazed at the world, her sad, wrinkled face screwed up in intense concentration. She was carefully chewing the flesh of the apple, sucking at it noisily, and then, when it was quite devoid of juice, spitting it into her hand daintily, placing it on her knee and gazing at it with the air of an ancient scientist who has, when he is too old to appreciate it, discovered the elixir of life. I called to her and she came over to the wire, uttering little breathless grunts of greeting. Sure enough, her ear looked most peculiar, sticking out at right angles to her head. I tried to coax her to turn round so that I could see the back of the ear, but she was too intent in putting her fingers through the wire and trying to pull the buttons off my coat.

There was nothing for it but to get her out, and this was a complicated procedure, for Chumley became most jealous if Lulu went out of the cage without him. However, I did not feel like having Chumley as my partner during a medical examination. So, after much bribery, I managed to lure him into their bedroom and lock him in, much to his vocal indignation. Then I went into the outer cage, where Lulu immediately came and sat on my lap and put her arms round me. She was an immensely affectionate ape, and had the most endearing character. I gave her a lump of sugar to keep her happy, and examined the ear. To my horror, I found that, behind the ear on the mastoid bone, there was an immense swelling, the size of an orange, and the skin was discoloured a deep purplish black. The reason this had not been noticed in the early stages was that Lulu had thick hair on her head, and particularly behind her ears, so that – until the swelling became so large that it pushed the ear out of position – nothing was noticeable. Also Lulu had displayed no signs of distress, which was amazing when one considered the size of the lump. She allowed me to explore the exact extent of the swelling gently, without doing anything more than carefully and politely removing my fingers if their pressure became too painful. I decided, after investigation, that I would have to lance it, as it was obviously full of matter, so I picked Lulu up in my arms and carried her into the house, where I put her down on the sofa and gave her a banana to keep her occupied until I had everything ready.

Up till now, the chimps had only been allowed in the house on very special occasions, and Lulu was, therefore, charmed with the idea that she was getting an extra treat without Chumley's knowledge. She sat on the sofa, her mouth full of banana, giving a regal handshake and a muffled hoot of greeting to whoever came into the room, rather as though she owned the place and you were attending one of her 'At Homes'. Presently, when everything was ready, I sat down beside her on the sofa and gently cut away the long hairs behind the ear that was affected. When it was fully exposed, the swelling looked even worse than before, a rich plum colour, and the skin had a leathery appearance. I carefully swabbed the whole area with disinfected warm water, searching to see if I could find a head or an opening to the swelling, for I was now convinced that it was a boil or ulcer that had become infected, but I could find no opening at all. Meanwhile, Lulu, having carefully and thoroughly scrutinised all the medical paraphernalia, had devoted her time to consuming another banana. I took a hypodermic needle and gently pricked the discoloured skin all over the swelling without causing her to deviate from the paths of gluttony, so it was obvious that the whole of the discoloured area was dead skin.

I was faced with something of a problem. Although I was fairly sure that I could make an incision across the dead skin, and thus let out the pus, without Lulu suffering any pain, I was not absolutely certain about it. She was, as I have remarked, of a lovable and charming disposition, but she was also a large, well-built ape, with a fine set of teeth, and I had no desire to enter into a trial of strength with her. The thing to do was to keep her mind occupied elsewhere while I tackled the job, for, like most chimps, Lulu was incapable of thinking of more than one thing at a time. I enlisted the aid of my mother and Jacquie, to whom I handed a large tin of chocolate biscuits, with instructions that they were to be fed to Lulu at intervals throughout the ensuing operation. I had no fears for my aides' safety, as I knew that if Lulu was provoked into biting anyone it would be me. Uttering up a brief prayer, I sterilised a scalpel, prepared cotton wool swabs, disinfected my hands and went to work. I drew the scalpel blade across the swelling, but, to my dismay, I found that the skin was as tough as shoeleather, and the blade merely skidded off. I tried a second time, using greater pressure, but with the same result. Mother and Jacquie kept up a nervous barrage of chocolate biscuits, each of which was greeted with delighted and slightly sticky grunts from Lulu.

'Can't you hurry up?' inquired Jacquie. 'These biscuits won't last for ever.'

'I'm doing the best I can,' I said irascibly, 'and a nurse doesn't tell a doctor to hurry up in the middle of an operation.'

'I think I've got some chocolates in my room, dear,' said my mother helpfully. 'Shall I fetch them?'

'Yes, I should, just in case.'

While Mother went off to fetch the chocolates, I decided that the only way to break into the swelling was to jab the point of the scalpel in and then drag it downwards, and this I did. It was successful: a stream of thick putrid matter gushed out from the incision, covering both me and the sofa. The smell from it was ghastly, and Jacquie and Mother retreated across the room hastily. Lulu sat there, quite unperturbed, eating chocolate biscuits. Endeavouring not to breathe more often than was necessary, I put pressure on the swelling, and eventually, when it was empty, I must have relieved it of about half a cupful of putrefying blood and pus. With a pair of scissors I carefully clipped away the dead skin and disinfected the raw area that was left. It was useless trying to put a dressing on for I knew that Lulu would remove it as soon as she was put back in her cage. When I had cleaned it up to my satisfaction, I picked Lulu up in my arms and carried her back to her cage. Here she greeted Chumley with true wifely devotion, but Chumley was deeply suspicious. He examined her ear carefully, but decided that it was of no interest. Then, during one of Lulu's hoots of pleasure, he leant forward and smelt her breath. Obviously, she had been eating chocolate, so Lulu, instead of receiving a husbandly embrace, received a swift clout over the back of the head. In the end, I had to go and fetch the rest of the chocolate biscuits to placate Chumley. Lulu's ear healed up perfectly, and within six months you had to look very closely to see the scar.

About a year later Chumley decided that it was his turn to fall ill, and of course he did it – as he did all things – in the grand manner. Chumley, I was told, had toothache. This rather surprised me, as, not long before, he had lost his baby teeth and acquired his adult ones, and I thought it was a bit too soon for any of them to have decayed. Still, there he was, squatting forlornly in the cage, clasping his jaw and ear with his hand and looking thoroughly miserable. He was obviously in pain, but I was not sure whether it was his ear on his jaw that was the cause of it. The pain must have been considerable for he would not let me take his hand away to examine the side of his face, and when I persisted in trying he became so upset that it was clear I was doing more harm than good, so I had to give up. I stood for a long time by the cage, trying to deduce from his actions what was the matter with him. He kept lying down, with the bad side of his head cuddled by his hand, and whimpering gently to himself; once, when he had climbed up the wire to relieve himself, he lowered himself to the ground again rather awkwardly, and as his feet thumped on to the floor of the cage he screamed, as though the jar had caused him considerable pain. He refused all food and, what was worse, he refused all liquids as well, so I could not give him any antibiotics. We had to remove Lulu, as, instead of showing wifely concern, she bounded round the cage, occasionally bumping into Chumley, or leaping on to him and making him cry out with pain.

I became so worried about his condition by the afternoon that I called into consultation Mr Blampier, a local veterinary surgeon, and our local doctor. The latter, I think, was somewhat surprised that he should be asked to take a chimpanzee on to his panel, but agreed nevertheless. It was plain that Chumley's jaw and ear would have to be examined carefully, and I knew that, in his present state, he would not allow that, so it was agreed that we would have to anaesthetise him. This is what had to be done, but how to do it was another matter. Eventually, it was decided that I should try to give Chumley an injection of a tranquilliser which would, we hoped, have him in an agreeable frame of mind by the evening to accept an anaesthetic.

The problem was whether or not Chumley was going to let me give him the injection. He was lying huddled up in his bed of straw, his back towards me, and I could see he was in great pain, for he never even looked round to see who had opened the door of his cage. I talked to him, in my best bedside manner, for a quarter of an hour or so, and at the end of that time he was allowing me to stroke his back and legs. This was a great advance, for up till now he had not let me come within stroking distance. Then, plucking up my courage, and still talking feverishly, I picked up the hypodermic and swiftly slipped the needle into the flesh of his thigh. To my relief, he gave no sign of having noticed it. As gently and as slowly as I could, I pressed the plunger and injected the tranquilliser. He must have felt this, for he gave a tiny, rather plaintive hoot, but he was too apathetic to worry about it. Still talking cheerful nonsense, I closed the door of his bedroom and left the drug to take effect.

That evening Dr Taylor and Mr Blampier arrived, and I reported that the tranquilliser had taken effect: Chumley was in a semi-doped condition, but, even so, he still would not let me examine his ear. So we repaired to his boudoir, outside of which I had rigged up some strong lights and a trestle table on which to lay our patient. Doctor Taylor poured ether on to a mask, and I opened Chumley's bedroom door, leant in and placed the mask gently over his face. He made one or two half-hearted attempts to push it away with his hand, but the ether combined with the tranquilliser was too much for him, and he slipped into unconsciousness quite rapidly. As soon as he was completely under, we hauled him out of the cage and laid him on the trestle table, still keeping the mask over his face.

Then the experts went to work. First, his ear was examined, and found to be perfectly healthy; just for good measure, we examined his other ear as well, and that, too, was all right. We then opened his mouth and carefully checked his teeth: they were an array of perfect, glistening white dentures without a speck of decay on any of them. We examined his cheeks, his jaw and the whole of his head, and could not find a single thing wrong. We looked at his neck and shoulders, with the same result. As far as we could ascertain, there was nothing the matter with Chumley whatsoever, and yet *something* had been causing him considerable pain. Dr Taylor and Mr Blampier departed, much mystified, and I carried Chumley into the house, wrapped in a blanket, and put him on a camp-bed in front of the drawing-room fire. Then Jacquie brought more blankets, which we piled on top of him, and we sat down to wait for the anaesthetic to wear off.

Lying there, his eyes closed, breathing out ether fumes stertorously, he looked like a slightly satanic cherub who, tired out after a days's mischief-making, was taking a well-earned rest. The amount of ether he was expelling from his lungs made the whole room reek, so that we were forced to open a window. It was about half an hour before he began to sigh deeply and twitch, as a preliminary to regaining consciousness, and I went over and sat by the bedside with a cup of water ready, since I knew from experience the dreadful thirst that assails you when you come out from under an anaesthetic. In a few minutes he opened his eyes, and as soon as he saw me he gave a feeble hoot of greeting and held out his hand, in spite of the fact that he was still half asleep. I held up his head and put the cup to his lips and he sucked at the water greedily before the ether overcame him again and he sank back into sleep. I decided that an ordinary cup was too unwieldly to give him drinks, as a considerable quantity of liquid was spilt. I managed, by ringing up my friends, to procure an invalid's cup, one of those articles that resemble a deformed teapot, and the next time Chumley woke up this proved a great success, as he could suck water out of the spout without having to sit up.

Although he recognised us, he was still in a very drugged and stupid state, and so I decided that I would spend the night sleeping on the sofa near him, in case he awakened and wanted anything. Having given him another drink, I made up my bed on the sofa, turned out the light and dozed off. About two o'clock in the morning I was awakened by a crash in the far corner of the room. I hastily put on the light to find that Chumley was awake and wandering round the room, like a drunken man, barging into all the furniture. As soon as the light came on and he saw me, he uttered a scream of joy, staggered across the room and insisted on embracing and kissing me before gulping down a vast drink of water. I then helped him back on to his bed and covered him with his blankets, and he slept peacefully until daylight.

He spent the day lying quietly on his bed, staring up at the ceiling. He ate a few grapes and drank great quantities of glucose and water, which was encouraging. The most encouraging thing, however, was that he no longer held the side of his face and did not appear to be suffering any pain. In some extraordinary way we seemed to have cured him without doing anything. When Dr Taylor telephoned later that day to find out how Chumley was faring I explained this to him, and he was as puzzled as I. Then, later on, he rang up to say that he had thought of a possible explanation: Chumley might have been suffering from a slipped disc. This could have caused intense pain in the nerves of jaw and ear, without there being anything externally to show what caused it. When we had Chumley limp and relaxed under the anaesthetic we pulled his head around quite a lot during our examination, and probably pushed the disc back into place, without realising it. Mr Blampier agreed with this diagnosis. We had no proof, of course, but certainly Chumley was completely cured, and there was no recurrence of the pain. He had naturally lost a lot of weight during his illness, and so for two or three weeks he was kept in a specially heated cage and fed up on every delicacy. Within a very short time he had put on weight and was his old self, so that whenever anyone went near his cage they were showered with handfuls of sawdust. This, I presume, was Chumley's way of thanking one.

Sometimes animals injure themselves in the most ridiculous way imaginable. Hawks and pheasants, for example, are the most hysterical of birds. If anything unusual happens they get into a terrible state, fly straight up, like rockets, and crash into the roof of their cage, either breaking their necks or neatly scalping themselves. But there are other birds equally stupid. Take the case of Samuel.

Samuel is a South American seriama. They are not unlike the African secretary bird. About the size of a half-grown turkey, they have long, strong legs, and a ridiculous little tuft of feathers perched on top of their beaks. In the wild state seriamas do not fly a great deal, spending most of their time striding about the grasslands in search of snakes, mice, frogs and other delicacies. I had purchased Samuel from an Indian in Northern Argentina, and as he had been hand-reared he was of course, perfectly (and sometimes embarrassingly) tame. When I finally shipped him back to Jersey with the rest of the animals, we took him out of his small travelling crate and released him in a nice, spacious aviary. Samuel was delighted, and to show us his gratitude the first thing he did was to fly up on to the perch, fall off it and break his left leg. There are times when animals do such idiotic things that you are left bereft of words.

Fortunately for Samuel, it was a nice clean break, half-way down what would be the shin in a human being. We made a good job of splinting it, covered the splint with plaster of Paris bandage, and, when it was dry, put him in a small cage so that he could not move around too much. The following day his foot was slightly swollen, so I gave him a penicillin injection – which he took great exception to – and his foot returned to normal size as a result. When we eventually took off the splint, we found the bones had knitted perfectly, and today, as he strides importantly around his aviary, you have to look very closely to see which leg it was that he broke. Knowing Samuel for the imbecile he is, it would not surprise me in the least if he did not repeat the performance at some time in the future ... probably on a day when I am up to my eyes in other work.

During the course of your Florence Nightingale work you become quite used to being bitten, scratched, kicked and bruised by your patients, and on many occasions, having performed first aid on them, you have to perform it on yourself. Nor is it always the bigger creatures that are the most dangerous to deal with. A squirrel or a pouched rat can inflict almost as much damage as a flock of Bengal tigers when they put their minds to it. While anointing a fluffy, gooey-eyed bushbaby once for a slight skin infection on the tail, I was bitten so severely in the thumb that it went septic, and I had to have it bandaged for ten days. The bushbaby was cured in forty-eight hours.

Human doctors are covered by the Hippocratic Oath. The wild animal doctor employs a variety of oaths, all rich and colourful, but which would, I feel, be frowned upon by the British Medical Council.

11 Seven Lame Badgers

Janet Orchard

I once found a hideout of mountain hares in a snow-hole in Scotland. One by one I dragged them out, chopped them, karate-style, across the neck and dumped them on the snow behind me. Thirteen I pulled out. But when I looked round for my pile of dinners there were thirteen hares staggering down the hillside, fast recovering from my deathblows. This story reminds me of that and of the many puzzles of animal behaviour.

Once when my brother and I were badger-watching in late August we saw six good-sized cubs leave the set, followed by a curious little creature not much bigger than a hedgehog. This was the dilling of the litter – small and stunted but very pert. After playing round the set on a heap of sand the cubs filed down a narrow path quite close to us, Dilly in the rear. They disappeared over a small ditch and up a bank on the far side into a thick clump of rhododendrons. There we heard much rustling of leaves and occasional growls and snufflings. When the troop reappeared about twenty minutes later, it was almost too dark to see. They filed past within a few feet of us, and to our amazement all seemed to be lame. We were mystified by this and determined to discover the cause.

Every evening for nearly a week we went to the same place, and exactly the same thing happened: the cubs all went out sound and and came home lame. At last we were able to watch the return journey by the light of a good moon and saw each cub hobbling home on three legs; with the fourth it clasped to its chest a pawful of leaves, evidently stripped from the rhododendrons on the far bank.

Dilly came last again and missed his footing as he crossed the ditch, dropping his leaves in midstream. His look of dismay as he set to work retrieving them was a wonderful sight. As soon as he picked up one he dropped another, but after exactly ten minutes of determined effort (timed by my brother's wristwatch) Dilly limped home triumphantly clasping his small bunch of leaves.

Meanwhile the mother, with much snuffling and grunting, had raked the bedding clear of the set and sorted out all the dirt, which she carefully buried in the sand. She took the cleaned bedding and the fresh leaves brought by the cubs into the set and finally disappeared backwards, raking in Dilly's load as she went. After listening to the thuds and grunts of the underground bedmaking, we decided to go home too, having solved a great mystery, though we still do not know if what we saw is common practice among badgers or peculiar to this one family.

12   No Eel for Nog
Henry Williamson

Henry Williamson again. No apologies for working in four stories from my favourite (and, I believe, the greatest) writer of animal stories. This one shows perfectly, I think, Williamson's ability to give you a clear picture of the everyday life of a creature and yet make it exciting and dramatic.

On a certain afternoon in the early spring a solitary heron was standing on an islet in the estuary, near the overturned hulk of a gravel barge. The islet was formed of sand lodging against a tree uprooted in winter floods and partly reburied by the lapse and flow of a hundred salt-water tides. He had flown there from the heronry in the oakwood four miles away, and a strong east wind had swept him forward with hardly a thrust of his broad vanes. He was Old Nog, and for a living he speared fish with a long sharp beak. The old bird was working very hard just now. Gone were the easy days when with a full crop the grey fisher used to walk on his lanky legs to the middle of the sandbank, draw up one foot, lay his head in the middle of his back, and sleep, motionless as grey, dry seaweed on two sticks. No naps for Nog nowadays. He'd got two growing young 'uns, old enough, thought Nog, to leave the treetop nest and learn to fish for themselves. As, however, they wouldn't leave, Old Nog had to work thrice as hard, for unknown to him his mate had been struck down and killed by peregrine falcons a week ago as she was spearing her seven-hundredth yearling in a trout farm. He missed her very much, and since the moon had grown bright he had fished all night, being so hungry.

The tide on this afternoon was nearly slack, and he peered keenly at the water in which he was wading to his knee

joints. The little light-coloured eyes saw a disturbance of sand grains, the narrow head peered forward, while the wind stirred black plumes on the long neck that was scarcely thicker than his spindle-shanks. Many times he had been angered to see a wriggling and doleful specimen of a heron looking at himself out of the water. It had blue-grey plumage, streaked with black, and white in parts. Old Nog threatened it many times a day for coming where he was. It threatened him, too, holding out its ragged wings, dancing on tottery legs, and opening its beak. Fancy not knowing himself! A dull old bird, a silly old bird, so thought the carrion crows of the higher reaches of the estuary. They knew why his mate had not returned. But Old Nog was not so dull or silly as they thought, for on this particular afternoon . . . but as yet no bird of the estuary had seen the specks of death waiting on in the sky, waiting on. . . .

Old Nog continued to peer. The movement of sand was made by a dab, or small flatfish, rising off the bed of the estuary where it had been lying invisible owing to a back speckled and dotted like sand. Old Nog darted at the movement, transfixing the dab with the two tips of his beak just opened. Lifting it, he threw it on his tongue, and swallowed with a shake of his head that scattered the water out of his eyes. Another movement, in water deeper by two inches. He waded on legs like stilts, and green as rushes, peered low, struck with hardly a splash, and swallowed a shrimp. Thus he fished for several minutes, taking many dabs and shrimps, until five herring gulls which had been patrolling the tideline, looking for carrion or fish, alighted on the water near the heron and paddled around the tree. None dared to swim near that spear of a beak.

Old Nog had many fishing places in the muddy creeks and dykes of the low marshland country of the Two Rivers' estuary. He visited them one after another, beginning at dawn, and going on all night, from drain to mill-leat, from mill-leat to brook, from brook to creek, and, at low tide, to the estuary islet. This afternoon he had just flown from the duck ponds a mile away, after taking a rainbow trout, a frog, a rat, a beetle, and a duckling. The keeper had tried to stalk him, but the old heron had been standing where he could see the approach of man beyond gunshot range.

The gulls paddled around the islet, ignored by Old Nog. At the tideline of the muddy shore four yards away a curlew was walking, thrusting a curved delicate bill into craters small as pennies, drawing out worms that lay beneath, and swallowing them without a jerk, with head still lowered. Neither gull nor heron, with their proportionately shorter beaks, could suck up the food like this. The gulls watched both feeding birds. Every time the heron struck and withdrew with a headshake the gulls screamed, lest the beak lose its grip and fling its prey aside. Every time the curlew bowed, keen and pale eyes watched for sight of wriggling worm. A blackpoll gull was near her when this happened, and ran to steal it; the curlew lifted her brown freckled wings and ran, uttering a trill of notes ascending in scale. From the beak of the gull a raucous scream came, and he ran after the curlew, but when he reached her the worm was swallowed. His ferocious attitude fell from him, and both birds went on with the intent search for food.

A small bird piped a shrill *peet-peet* as it flew across the river to the islet. It was the size of a sparrow, but sturdier, with white throat, black beak, rich auburn breast, wings and back a greenish-blue, the head and neck being barred with brilliant azure. To the tree it flew with quick flutters, perching with pink feet on a weed-hung twig. It gazed at the water, being a kingfisher, and it fished the higher reaches of the estuary every day, as regularly as the heron, flying zigzag from bank to bank, from one perching rock or twig to another. It saw nothing, and restlessly piping *peet-peet* it flew away, and had gone less than fifty yards when it saw a little fish and splashed into the water, returning to the tree to kill and swallow its catch.

Another bird was fishing near, like a large scarecrow of a duck turned pirate, black as coal with a greenish sheen on its oily feathers. His beak was as long as the beak of Old Nog, only black, and hooked at the tip. He was Oylegrin the shag, one of the pelican family, but, unlike his large relative, his beak had not the capacity of his belly. He paddled with black webbed feet in deeper water, and every minute he bobbed his head, tipped up and swam to the river bed. Looking up, with his green eyes he could see any fish swimming over him as a shape shown up by the quicksilvery surface. In one of his underwater swims, as he thrust along with strong pushes, his neck stretched out, he espied an eel, and opened his beak. The eel was near the islet, and as Oylegrin snapped at its tail, Old Nog, who had suddenly waded into deeper water, darted his neck forward and speared. So swift the judgement, so precise the angle of striking, that the points pierced the slimy skin of the eel and drew it curling and lashing from the water.

Observing the eel the five herring gulls screamed, and beat their wings to arise and fly about the heron. Out of the water bobbed the head of the shag, and the eel's tail was seized in the hook-tip. The kingfisher flew up estuary, the curlew walked away, for she was a gentle bird, a lover of water-murmurous solitude, and disliked the wrangling of gulls. From the speartip of heron's beak the eel was pulled by Oylegrin, and it dropped into six inches of water, to be gripped by the sharp edge of the shag's mandibles before it had time to writhe in one curl. Spray was beaten by the big black wings immediately, for Nog speared the eel again. Shag tried to swallow it, his green eye fierce, and the crest of feathers on his head risen with fury. He threatened with a greasy mutter in his throat, while two beachcombing crows flew over the water to see what might be doing for themselves. They perched on the hulk and waited; eel, wounded heron, maimed shag – and what might be in their crops – anything and everything, dead or alive, was food for crows.

Old Nog got the eel again, but before he could throw it up and gulp it into a crop already laden, Oylegrin the shag had gripped the tail end. The spearing and buffeting and nipping soon killed the eel, although its nerves continued to twitch and flick in death.

While the birds were struggling, neither managing to swallow the eel, something was seen by the gulls and crows. The effect was immediate. *Krok-krok-krok* said one of the crows, and they were gone from the hulk, beating wings faster than usual as they fled silently over the water to the oak trees on the bank. With a gabbling cry one of the herring gulls made off, followed by four others and the smaller blackpoll. Oylegrin the shag, at the verge of the scratched and spurred sand of the islet, wary for the stroke of the heron's spear-tip, suddenly turned away and vanished under a bulking water ring. From this ring ripples spread out and disappeared in the frothy tops of wavelets. Oylegrin bobbed up fifty yards away, breathed, took a glance skywards, bobbed under. Beside a stone crouched the curlew, head to wind, immobile and coloured as the stone. Only the heron had not seen what the others had seen.

Squark! cried Old Nog, very satisfied, as he picked up the eel. After many tosses and jerks it joined the duckling, the beetle, the rainbow trout, the frog, and the rat. Then leisurely spreading his grey vanes he jumped into the wind, tucked a scraggy neck between shoulders, stretched out his long thin legs behind him, and beat towards the heronry, four miles away. Half a mile above him, steady on pitches in the wind, three birds, sharp in outline like specks of slate, were watching him, and – in an ancient term of falconry – were waiting on.

They were peregrine falcons of the ancient and noble house of Chakchek. A Chakchek was famous among falconers throughout Europe during the reign of Queen Elizabeth. A Chakchek founded the northern eyrie upon Lundy Island, whose cream-breasted peregrines are still considered the finest in the world. A Chakchek surveyed the battle of Trafalgar. Another slew the Frenchman's message pigeons before Sedan. One was in Ypres during the first bombardment. A Chakchek was hunting the airways of the Two Rivers' estuary as the ships went over the bar to join Drake's fleet; centuries before, when Phoenicians first came to trade; long, long before, when moose roamed in the forest which is now gone under the sand, drowned by the sea.

They were Chakcheks, father and mother and son – tiercel and falcon, and a young male bird of immature plumage, an eyas hatched and reared less than a year before, in the month of May. There had been two daughters. One hunted in Scotland with a mate; the other had been shot off the coasts of Florida. Chakcheks have wandered from Spitzbergen to Samoa; they are free of the winds of the world. They attack eagles. No man knows where the old birds go to die; for there are no old Chakcheks. They die young, beloved of their god. Noble they are, of lineage as ancient as the first gods of man, and their god is older, being Altair in the constellation of Aquila, a night sun with gold-flickering wings.

The wind of early spring blew cold at a thousand feet, but the peregrines, one above and beyond the other, felt neither heat nor cold. Their feathers were tight against bodies. The parent birds were slatey-blue of back and creamy of breast, which was thinly barred in black. The eyas had a dark brown back and dingy white breast, draggled down. He was the heir to the eyrie of Bone Ledge. Their beaks were short and curved, with yellow skin round the base, and their eyes were full, liquid, and dark, steadfast with an untameable hauteur, eyes which saw many times as keenly as man.

The wind did not rock them. They were as though fixed in the sky. They waited on. They saw the gulls, the shag, the crows. These slunk away, and the lank grey bird launched himself. He had gone two hundred vane-flaps when the tiercel cried *Chak-chek-chek!*, turned on his side and slipped from his pitch. With beak to earth he beat his wings ten times, then closed them. The falcon followed, and the eyas. The triple-cut air whined as though in complaint.

Old Nog saw the tiercel falling upon him, and shifted with violent flaps, and Chakchek dropped below him. Two seconds later the falcon swished past him, and the eyas followed so quickly that he was struck at an elbow joint, and feathers were struck away. He cried *Krark!* and as the three made their points – shooting up perpendicularly with the impetus – the heron climbed, swinging round with the wind and making ring after ring. In long spiral curves he mounted towards the clouds, but ring after ring the peregrines made also, rushing downwind for half a mile and tearing round in a great banking circle that shot them up hundreds of feet. Chakchek mounted to his pitch above, at such a height that a man watching below could not see him. Again the grand stoop, again Chakchek fell past the heron four hundred feet before he could make another point. Old Nog tried desperately to climb. He was too weary. He opened his beak and the eel fell out.

Down came the falcon – than whom the tiercel was smaller by a tierce, or third – driving at him with yellow feet spread for black sickle-claws open to rip up his back. Old Nog rocked, and nearly overturned. He could see the leafless oak trees of the heronry, and young birds standing in the topmost branches, beyond the winding of the river and its sandy wastes. The clouds were high above him, but reach them he must. He cried out in his fear as the eyas fell upon him. The dabs, the rat, and the rainbow trout followed the eel. The tiercel was ringing again, climbing three yards to the heron's one, level but distant half a mile upwind at one moment, two hundred yards over and passing downwind at a hundred miles an hour a few seconds afterwards, and three minutes later almost out of sight. *Krark! Krark!!* cried Old Nog dolefully, and breathing fast with his efforts. Tiercel poised in his pitch for a grand stoop, his eyes fixed on the labouring expanse of wings, every nerve and sinew tightened for the downward drive at two hundred miles an hour. He waited, his pinions crooking back with nervous false starts many times in the ten seconds during which he was poised. *Chak-chek-chek!* He saw the line, tipped up sideways, beat a dozen swift strokes, closed pinions, and pressed

99

every feather into a taut and quivering body, and stooped. The rush of air against his eyes was so keen and hard that he blinked the third eyelids over the dark orbs, so that he saw but dimly. Larger and larger grew the heron, and Chakchek's eyes became clear and brown; he held his breath for the impact and spread his talons – *whish!* he had passed Old Nog. The heron escaped by a falling spin, losing in ten seconds the height he had gained by two minutes' ringing. Down fell duckling, frog, and beetle. He recovered his balance in time to avoid the falcon's stoop, but the eyas, pressing hard behind his mother, hit him between the shoulders. Old Nog tumbled, and abandoned hope of climbing above his enemies. He was flustered and shaken. He began to flap wildly in the direction of the heronry. No other birds were visible in the air. He cried out in his helplessness, and the third *Krark!* ended abruptly, for Chakchek had made his point above him and stooped so surely that he struck him and bound to the grey back with his claws. Down came falcon and eyas, giving him two more tremendous jolts, and Old Nog sank down under the weight, crying for help.

All four fell on a mudbank, near the eel, and the blow knocked the heron feeble. Immediately falcon and tiercel began to rip with their beaks, and the eyas flew arrogantly at the head. Old Nog lifted a muddy spear and stabbed so swift and true that he shattered an eye of the young peregrine. Chattering with pain he flew up, as Old Nog feeling stronger jumped up on tottery legs and faced the pair with vanes held around him like shields. The feathers of his throat and breast were muddy, and a froth of blood was on his beak. In the ragged tent of his wings he stood grey and anxious and lank, holding up a crimsoning spear. The tiercel uttered the ringing cry of his race, *Chak-chek-chak!*, and dashed at him, to swerve as the spear flashed at his throat. Upwind flew the falcon, and cut at Nog, followed by the wounded eyas, whose hind claws nearly ripped open the narrow skull. Swoop after swoop Old Nog met with a stab; and then they flew away.

But the heron did not move, crouched in the mud, his head trembling between narrow shoulders, gazing fixedly at the sky. He watched the three birds cutting circles higher and higher, farther and farther away, where the wind had torn wiisps of mist from the cloud-laden wains of sky. The heron watched the specks slipping downwind, swinging round, and the specks gave out a minute flickering as the peregrines climbed up against the wind. Minute after minute Old Nog stood in his tent, taking counsel with himself, his spear upright. The specks vanished in a cloud.

Old Nog flapped his vanes, and cried *Squark!* He preened his flight-quills by drawing them through his beak, and looked about him. He took several steps forward, then sideways, then round. Again he shook himself, and flapped his vanes. *Squark!* a cry of satisfaction. A scrutiny of the sky revealed nothing of his enemies, so he looked around him, to see the eel lying not far off. Gravely he walked over to it, leaving the spurs of his three big toes on the mud along worm castings and empty mussel shells. Picking it up in his beak he tossed it until the head was on his tongue, and with shake and gulp it disappeared into his crop. Forthwith he looked around for the duckling. He found it. And the rat. *Squark!* said Old Nog, stalking on stilty legs after the rainbow trout. Afterwards he stood on one leg and tried to scratch mud off his plume. Thence an amble to a water-filled creek, where he watched for dab and shrimp. They had ceased feeding, and were invisible. He climbed out of the creek, and launched himself homeward.

He had flown, stiffly and laboriously, about half the way to the heronry when the three Chakcheks, who from pitches two miles away had watched him picking up the eel, half closed their pinions, and shot down an incline at nearly twice flying speed. Their wings made the shape of an anchor head with shortened shank and crooked flukes. The pain of a shattered eye went from the eyas in jubilation of feeling his tail thrumming, his pinions hissing. He opened the toes of his feet pressed into his feathers, and the air whined as the claws scratched eight unseen lines in the sky. Behind his noble parents he stooped, and when the heron saw them he cried aloud in distress. A hundred pairs of pale yellow eyes were watching them from the heronry. They saw Old Nog shift as the falcon stooped, but he was tired, and his broad vanes too clumsy for so light a body. He tried to stab her, she crashed into the long, black flight-quills, passed behind him, turned in a short swishing curve and passed under his breast, on her back, bursting away hundreds of feathers. Seven seconds later she was bound to his back, sinking with him. The tiercel joined her. They bore the old bird down, and Old Nog ceased to struggle, and closed his vanes. But seeing below him the river, which was tidal for three miles beyond the heronry, he gave a cry and opened them in order to beat into a position for diving. With two of his enemies on his back, and a third chattering around him, Old Nog plunged headfirst into the river.

Not long afterwards nearly a hundred young herons dozing on flat piles of sticks in the treetops, while waiting for food, poked up their heads again.

The arrival of Old Nog, bedraggled, with skinny breast unfeathered, frayed vanes, and red beak, was welcomed by a hubbub of gutteral squawks. Slowly and heavily he sailed nearer to the uproar of flapping wings, stretching necks, and opening beaks. Was this a demonstration of victory, of greeting the conquering hero? Oh no, for the fight was already forgotten and Old Nog was merely a parent bird coming with food, a parent claimed by every youngster, frenziedly implored to alight at every nest and to give up what he had got. Old Nog flapped over the heronry, sailed to a branch near his nest, closed his tattered vanes, and perched swaying six feet away from his noisy sons. He hunched up his shoulders and sank his head between them, desiring only to rest after the contest, and digest his meal. Far away over Exmoor a young peregrine was soaring alone – his parents drowned. Chakchek is dead – long live Chakchek the One-Eyed!

Seeing him huddled on the tree, the sons of Nog, who had learned during the past few days to walk on branches, went foot by foot to where he was perched, and yelled *Pa! Pa!* so loudly that Old Nog opened his eyes. Seeing he was awake they flapped their vanes and pulled down his head. Old Nog pulled it up again; but one or the other got hold of it, and pulled it down again. *Krark!* said Old Nog, but the two grawbeys would not be quiet. Old Nog yawned, and bending down, yielded trout and rat to one, and duckling and eel to the other. Such robbery had happened to Old Nog for over twenty years – every spring he fished and toiled all day and half the night, and whenever he flew home for rest and quiet, the nestlings not only pestered him with their noisiness, but took away his food. With a melancholy *Krark!* Old Nog flapped away from the heronry, and after filling himself with dabs, walked wearily and stiffly to the middle of a sandbank, secure from man and nestlings, and slept until the tide wetted him four hours afterwards. Then, fishing for half an hour, he filled his crop, and went back to the heronry to see how the young 'uns were getting on.

More TOPLINERS for your enjoyment

Escapers
Compiled by Aidan Chambers
True accounts of men who attempted to escape from captivity during the Second World War. Stories of men digging tunnels, hijacking an aeroplane, disguising themselves, joining resistance fighters: using every ounce of their ingenuity, determination and courage.

Ghosts 4
Malcolm Blacklin
Here are terrifying spectres, fearsome manifestations, weird spectres and malicious beings that stalk the night. These are the ghosts that walked the earth in the days when the houses were lit by candlelight. ...

I Want to Stay Here!
Christine Dickenson
When Sue's family decide to emigrate, she refuses to leave home. She wants to be a vet and has a job she likes in the local animal surgery. This is the story of how she gets her way and begins life alone for the first time at 17.

Vicky Takes a Chance
Jenny Hewitt
Fifteen-year-old Vicky starts shoplifting apparently for fun. But of course she gets caught. Her family and boyfriend are upset and she faces up to the chance that comes her way in approved school.

TOPLINERS from Macmillan

More TOPLINER REDSTARS for your enjoyment

The Siege of Babylon
Farrukh Dhondy
Three West Indians rob an office, but the plan goes wrong and they find themselves holding hostages in a siege above a London street. As the long siege goes on, we discover who these three men are . . . what it is they want from life, themselves and the society in which they live.

Maybe I'm Amazed
Chris Hawes
Six stories about people leaving school. They range from the clever boy who rejects academic standards for success, to The Mob, the 'failures' who wreck the place and cause trouble. What brings them together is their surprise at discovering the truth about themselves and what school has meant to them, and their determination to be themselves whatever the consequences.

What It's All About
Vadim Frolov
Translated by Joseph Barnes
Present-day Leningrad is where Sasha has always lived with his father and actress mother. But this summer his mother hasn't returned from her summer touring season. Sasha begins to realise that everyone but he knows why, and that something has gone wrong. When a spiteful schoolmate blurts out the crude truth, Sasha beats him up in rage. And that begins a rebellious, unhappy time for Sasha, his relatives and friends. Until Sasha sets about finding out for himself what it's all about. . . .
It's a quest he begins as a boy and ends as a man.

The editor of Topliners and Topliner Redstars is always pleased to hear what readers think of the books and to receive ideas for new titles. If you want to write to him please address your letter to: The Editor, Topliner Redstars, Macmillan. Houndmills, Basingstoke, Hampshire RG21 2XS.

TOPLINER REDSTARS published by Macmillan

D0671539

LANGENSCHEIDT'S
UNIVERSAL POLISH
DICTIONARY

POLISH-ENGLISH
ENGLISH-POLISH

First edition

LANGENSCHEIDT
NEW YORK · BERLIN · MUNICH
VIENNA · ZURICH

Compiled by
Michał Jankowski, Tadeusz W. Lange, Grzegorz Skommer

Contents – Spis treści

Neither the presence nor the absence of a des-
ignation that any entered word constitutes a
trademark should be regarded as affecting the
legal status of any trademark.

Zgodnie z praktyką przyjętą w publikacjach encyklopedycz-
no-słownikowych nazwy handlowe wyrobów i produktów podaje
się w niniejszym słowniku bez informacji dotyczącej możliwych
ważnych patentów, zastrzeżonych wzorów użytkowych lub zna-
ków towarowych. Brak odnośnych wskazówek nie uzasadnia
więc przypuszczenia, że dana nazwa handlowa nie podlega
ochronie.

© 1999 Langenscheidt KG, Berlin and Munich
Printed in Germany by
Druckhaus Langenscheidt, Berlin-Schöneberg

Zasady posługiwania się słownikiem
Notes on the Use of the Dictionary

Tylda (~) używana jest jako znak zamiany – dla oszczędności miejsca wyrazy o podobnej formie są często grupowane razem; używa się wówczas tyldy, która zastępuje w takich wypadkach cały wyraz hasłowy, lub tylko tę jego część, która występuje przed pionową kreską (|):

atten|tion uwaga *f*; **~ive** (= **attentive**) uważny

Jeżeli zmienia się pisownia pierwszej litery wyrazu, z dużej na małą i na odwrót, tylda (~) występuje z kółeczkiem (⊙):

Ang|ielka *f* Englishwoman; **⊙ielski** English

Odmienne kroje czcionek pełnią różną funkcję:

wytłuszczenie używane jest dla wyrazów hasłowych w hasłach głównych oraz dla cyfr arabskich, które dzielą hasło na części odpowiadające częściom mowy, a także gramatycznym formom wyrazu:

flow ... **1.** ⟨po⟩płynąć; **2.** strumień *m*, potok *m*

The swung dash or tilde (~) serves as a replacement mark. For reasons of space, related words are often combined in groups with the help of the swung dash, which in these cases replaces either the entire entry word or that part of it which precedes the vertical bar (|):

atten|tion uwaga *f*; **~ive** (= **attentive**) uważny

If there is a switch from a small first letter to a capital or vice-versa, the standard swung dash (~) appears with a circle (⊙):

Ang|ielka *f* Englishwomen; **⊙ielski** English

The various typefaces fulfil different functions:

bold type is used for main entries and for the Arabic numerals which structure the entry into the various parts of speech and the different grammatical forms of a word:

flow ... **1.** ⟨po⟩płynąć; **2.** strumień *m*, potok *m*

kursywa używana jest dla skrótów nazw kwalifikatorów gramatycznych (*adj, pf* itp.), nazw rodzajów gramatycznych (*m, f, n*), kwalifikatorów zakresowych (*ecol., med.* itp.) oraz dla wszelkich dodatkowych uwag odnoszących się do wyrazu hasłowego lub jego tłumaczenia:

lakier *m* ...; *do paznokci a.*: enamel; *samochodowy*: paint

Przykłady zdaniowe, ilustrujące użycie wyrazu hasłowego, jego formy fleksyjne – włącznie z nieregularnymi formami fleksyjnymi – oraz używane z nim przyimki, wydrukowane są przy użyciu **wytłuszczonej kursywy**:

drive ... (*drove, driven*)
easy ...; *take it* ∼! spokojnie!, nie przejmuj się!
nalegać insist (*na* on)
wbić → **wbijać**

Wszystkie zaś tłumaczenia wydrukowano czcionką zwykłą.

Przy zapisie wymowy angielskich wyrazów hasłowych i ich form fleksyjnych użyte zostały znaki Międzynarodowego Stowarzyszenia Fonetycznego (IPA) (patrz str 8). W zapisie wymowy, w celu uniknięcia powtórzeń, także używa się tyldy; za-

italics are used for grammatical abbreviations (*adj., pf* etc.), the gender abbreviations (*m, f, n*), subject labels (*econ., med.* etc.) and for all additional explanatory notes on an entry or a translation:

lakier *m* ...; *do paznokci a.*: enamel; *samochodowy*: paint

The example sentences illustrating the use of an entry, the prepositions, and inflected as well as irregular forms and cross references all appear in *boldface italics*:

drive ... (*drove, driven*) ...,
easy ...; *take it* ∼! spokojnie!, nie przejmuj się!
nalegać insist (*na* on)
wbić → **wbijać**

Finally, all translations are given in normal type.

The symbols of the International Phonetic Association (IPA) are used to indicate the pronunciation of the English headwords (cf. p. 8). The swung dash (∼) is also used here to avoid repetition and replaces the symbols already given. The correct intonation

stępuje ona ciąg znaków podanych już wcześniej. Właściwy przycisk wyrazowy – akcent – oznaczany jest symbolem ('), który występuje przed akcentowaną sylabą:

four ... [fɔː] ...; **~teen** [~'tiːn] ...

Nie podaje się wymowy wyrażeń złożonych, jeżeli poszczególne części składowe wyrażenia pojawiają się osobno jako wyrazy hasłowe w Słowniku:

im'partial bezstronny

W obu częściach słownika podaje się zawsze rodzaj gramatyczny polskich rzeczowników, także we frazach, jeżeli właściwy rzeczownik nie występuje jako wyraz hasłowy:

godzina *f* hour
ry|nek ...; **~kowy** *adj*: *gospodarka f ~kowa* market economy
leisure ... wolny czas *m*

Polskie czasowniki dokonane umieszczone zostały albo we właściwym miejscu alfabetycznym w Słowniku wraz z odsyłaczem do formy niedokonanej czasownika, albo też mogą być podane w nawiasach trójkątnych bezpośrednio po formie niedokonanej czasownika:

dać *pf* → **dawać**
czytać ⟨**prze-**⟩ read
namydl|ać ⟨**-ić**⟩ soap

---

is indicated by the symbol ', which appears before the stressed syllable:

four ... [fɔː] ...; **~teen** [~'tiːn] ...

No details of pronunciation are given for compound entries if the individual parts of the compound appear as full headwords in the Dictionary:

im'partial bezstronny

The gender of the Polish nouns is always given in both parts of the Dictionary. This also applies to compounds if the noun is not the headword:

godzina *f* hour
ry|nek ...; **~kowy** *adj*: *gospodarka f ~kowa* market economy
leisure ... wolny czas *m*

Perfective Polish verbs appear either at the appropriate alphabetical position in the Dictionary with a cross-reference to the imperfective verb or, alternatively, in angle brackets ⟨ ⟩ immediately after the imperfective verb:

dać *pf* → **dawać**
czytać ⟨**prze-**⟩ read
namydl|ać ⟨**-ić**⟩ soap

7

Ta część bezokolicznika, która zmienia formę czasownika na niedokonaną, podawana jest w okrągłych nawiasach w obu częściach Słownika:

select ... wyb(ie)rać

Różnice między pisownią brytyjską a amerykańską ukazywane są albo w formie odsyłacza:

archeology *Am.* → **archaeology**

albo przez jawne wskazanie pisowni amerykańskiej w samym wyrazie hasłowym:

flavo(u)r ... (*Am.* = flavor)
centre, *Am.* **-ter** ...

Nieregularne wyrazy angielskie zostały oznaczone gwiazdką, zaś w Dodatku umieszczono spis najważniejszych nieregularnych czasowników.

Gdy wyraz hasłowy ma diametralnie różne znaczenia, opisywany jest on w dwóch hasłach, lub większej ich ilości, wyróżnionych kolejnymi cyframi w indeksie górnym:

fly¹ ... mucha *f*
fly² ... rozporek *m*
fly³ (*flew, flown*) ⟨po⟩lecieć

Znaczenia, które wykształciły się z podstawowego znaczenia danego wyrazu, nie są rozróżniane w ten sposób.

The part of the infinitive ending that makes the verb imperfective is given in round brackets in both parts of the Dictionary:

select ... wyb(ie)rać

Differences between British and American spelling are indicated either by a cross reference:

archeology *Am.* → **archaeology**

or by an explicit reference to the American form in the headword:

flavo(u)r ... (*Am.* = flavor)
centre, *Am.* **-ter** ...

English verbs marked with an asterisk are irregular. A list of the most important irregular verbs can be found in the Appendix. Where a word has fundamentally different meanings, it appears as two or more separate entries distinguished by exponents, or raised figures:

fly¹ ... mucha *f*
fly² ... rozporek *m*
fly³ (*flew, flown*) ⟨po⟩lecieć

This does not apply to senses which have evolved directly from the primary meaning of the word.

Transkrypcja fonetyczna

ʌ	punk [pʌŋk]		a *krótkie jak w* bank
ɑː	after [ˈɑːftə]		a *długie jak w* Saara, Saab
æ	flat [flæt]		*pośrednie między* a i e
ə	arrival [əˈraivl]		*brzmi pośrednio między* a i y
e	men [men]		e *krótkie jak w* Ren, deszcz
ɜː	first [fɜːst]		*pośrednie między* e i u
ɪ	city [ˈsɪtɪ]		i *krótkie, pośrednie między* y i i
iː	see [siː], weak [wiːk]		i *długie, podobnie jak w* i inni
ɒ	shop [ʃɒp]		o *krótkie jak w* lot, stop
ɔː	course [kɔːs]		o *długie, podobnie jak w* zoo
ʊ	good [gʊd]		u *krótkie, jak w* ruch
uː	too [tuː]		u *długie, podobnie jak w* tu u nas
aɪ	punk [naɪt]		aj *jak w* rajd
aʊ	now [naʊ]		au *jak w* auto
əʊ	go [həʊm]		*zbliżone do* eu *w* neurologia
eə	air [eə]		*wymawia się jak* e^a
eɪ	eight [eɪt]		ej, *podobnie jak w* hej
ɪə	near [nɪə]		*zbliżone do jednosylabowej wymowy* ie^a
ɔɪ	join [dʒɔɪn]		oj, *podobnie jak w* bojkot
ʊə	tour [tʊə]		*zbliżone do jednosylabowej wymowy* ue^a
j	yes [jes], tube [tjuːb]		j *jak w* Jan
w	way [weɪ], one [wʌn]		*jak* ł *w* tłum (u *niezgłoskotwórcze*)
ŋ	thing [θɪŋ]		n *tylnojęzykowe, podobnie jak w* bank
r	room [ruːm]		r *jak w* rura, ruch
s	service [sɜːvɪs]		s *jak w* serwis
z	is [ɪz], zero [ˈzɪərəʊ]		z *jak w* zero
ʃ	shop [ʃɒp]		sz *jak w* szopa
tʃ	cheap [tʃiːp]		cz *jak w* czub
ʒ	television [ˈtelɪvɪʒən]		ż *jak w* żona
dʒ	just [dʒʌst]		dż *jak w* dżuma

θ	thanks [θæŋks]	*spółgłoska bezdźwięczna jak seplenione s (wymawia się kładąc czubek języka między zęby)*
δ	that [δæt]	*dźwięczny odpowiednik* θ *(jak seplenione z)*
v	very ['verı]	*w jak w* woda
x	loch [lɒx]	*ch jak w* loch
:		*poprzedzająca ten znak samogłaska jest długa*

Spis przyrostków

-ability [-ə'bılətı]
-able [-əbl]
-age [-ıdʒ]
-al [-(ə)l]
-ally [-əlı]
-an [-ən]
-ance [-əns]
-ancy [-ənsı]
-ant [-ənt]
-ar [-ə]
-ary [-ərı]
-ation [-eıʃn]
-cious [-ʃəs]
-cy [-sı]
-dom [-dəm]
-ed [-d; -t; -ıd]
-edness [-dnıs; -tnıs; -ıdnıs]
-ee [-i:]
-en [-n]
-ence [-əns]
-ency [-ənsı]
-ent [-ənt]
-er [-ə]
-ery [-ərı]

-ess [-ıs]
-est [-ıst; -əst]
-fold [-fəʊld]
-ful [-fʊl]
-hood [-hʊd]
-ial [-əl]
-ian [-ən]
-ibility [-əbılətı]
-ible [-əbl]
-ic(s) [-ık(s)]
-ical [-ıkl]
-ie [-ı]
-ily [-ılı; -əlı]
-iness [-ınıs]
-ing [-ıŋ]
-ish [-ıʃ]
-ism [-ızəm]
-ist [-ıst]
-istic [-ıstık]
-ite [-aıt]
-ity [-ətı; -ıtı]
-ive [-ıv]
-ization [-ə'zeıʃən];
  Brt. [-aı'zeıʃn]

10

-ize [-aɪz]
-izing [-aɪzɪŋ]
-less [-lɪs]
-ly [-lɪ]
-ment(s) [-mənt(s)]
-ness [-nɪs]
-oid [-ɔɪd]
-or [-ə]
-o(u)r [-ə]
-ous [-əs]
-ry [-rɪ]
-ship [-ʃɪp]

-(s)sion [-ʃn]
-sive [-sɪv]
-some [-səm]
-ties [-tɪz]
-tion [-ʃn]
-tional [-ʃənl]
-tious [-ʃəs]
-trous [-trəs]
-try [-trɪ]
-ward [-wə(r)d]
-y [-ɪ]

Skróty
Abbreviations

a.	*also* też, również	*comb.*	*combination* połączenie
abbr.	*abbreviation* skrót	*comp*	*comparative* stopień wyższy
adj	*adjective* przymiotnik		
aer.	*aeronautics, aviation* lotnictwo	*constr.*	*construction* składanie
agr.	*agriculture* rolnictwo	*contp.*	*contemptuously* pogardliwy
Am.	*American English* amerykański	*eccl.*	*ecclesiastical* kościelny
anat.	*anatomy* anatomia		
appr.	*approximately* w przybliżeniu	*econ.*	*economics* ekonomia
arch.	*architecture* architektura	*electr.*	*electrical engineering* elektrotechnika
attr	*attributive* przydawkowo	*esp.*	*especially* szczególnie
		etc.	*and so on* i tak dalej
biol.	*biology* biologia	F	*familiar, colloquial* wyraz potoczny, poufały
bot.	*botany* botanika		
Brt.	*British English* brytyjski	*f*	*feminine* żeński (rodzaj)
chem.	*chemistry* chemia		
cj	*conjunction* spójnik	*fig.*	*figuratively* w znaczeniu przenośnym

form.	*formal* formalny
gastr.	*gastronomy* kucharstwo
GB	*Great Britain* Wielka Brytania
geogr., *geogr.*	*geography* geografia
gr.	*grammar* gramatyka
hist.	*history* historia
hunt.	*hunting* gwara myśliwska
inf	*infinitive* bezokolicznik
instr.	*instrumental* (*case*) narzędnik
int	*interjection* wykrzyknik
itd.	*i tak dalej* and so on
itp.	*i tym podobne* and the like
jur.	*legal term* prawo, prawniczy
ling.	*linguistics* językoznawstwo
m	*masculine* męski (rodzaj)
mar.	*nautical term* okrętownictwo, żegluga
math.	*mathematics* matematyka
med.	*medicine* medycyna
meteor.	*meteorology* meteorologia
mil.	*military term* wojskowość
mot.	*motoring* motoryzacja
mst	*mostly* w większości wypadków
mus.	*musical term* muzyka
n	*neuter* nijaki (rodzaj)

np.	*na przykład* eg., for example
num	*numeral* liczebnik
o.s.	*oneself* się, siebie, sobie
opt.	*optics* optyka
parl.	*parliamentary term* parlamentaryzm
pf	*perfective aspect* czasownik dokonany
phls.	*philosophy* filozofia
phot.	*photography* fotografia
phys.	*physics* fizyka
physiol.	*physiology* fizjologia
pl	*plural* liczba mnoga
poet.	*poetical* poetycki
pol.	*politics* polityka
post.	*post and telecommunications* poczta i telekomunikacja
pp	*past participle* imiesłów czasu przeszłego
pred.	*predicative* orzecznikowy
pres	*present* czas teraźniejszy
pres p	*present participle* imiesłów czasu teraźniejszego
print.	*printing* drukarstwo
pron	*pronoun* zaimek
prp	*preposition* przyimek
psych.	*psychology* psychologia
rail.	*railroad, railway* kolejnictwo
rel pron	*relative pronoun* zaimek względny

12

s	*substantive, noun* rzeczownik
s.o., s.o.	*someone* ktoś
s.th., s.th.	*something* coś
sg	*singular* liczba pojedyncza
sl.	*slang* wyrażenie slangowe
sp.	*sport, sports* sport
sup	*superlative* stopień najwyższy
tech.	*technology* technika
teleph.	*telephony* telekomunikacja
thea.	*theater, Brt. theatre* teatr
tj.	*to jest* i.e.
TM	*trademark* chroniona nazwa towaru
TV	*television* telewizja
typ.	*typography* typografia
univers., uni.	*university* uniwersytecki
usu.	*usually* zwykle
v	*verb* czasownik
v/aux	*auxiliary verb* czasownik posiłkowy
v/i	*intransitive verb* czasownik nieprzechodni
v/t	*transitive verb* czasownik przechodni
zo.	*zoology* zoologia
→	*see, refer to* patrz

* nieregularne czasowniki angielskie zostały oznaczone gwiazdką

A

a *cj* and; (*ale*) but; ~ **jednak** and yet

abażur *m* lamp shade

abecadło *n* the ABC

abon|ament *m* subscription; **~ent** *m* subscriber

absolutny *adj* absolute

absorbować ⟨**za-**⟩ *fig. używane biernie*: absorb, engross

absurd *m* absurdity; **to** ~ that's absurd

aby *cj* (in order) to

aczkolwiek *cj* although, albeit

administr|acja *f* administration; **~ator** *m* administrator; **~ować** administer

admirał *m* admiral

adnotacja *f* note

adres *m* address; **~at** *m* addressee; **~ować** ⟨**za-**⟩ address (**do to**)

adwokat *m* lawyer, solicitor

afisz *m* poster

Afryka *f* Africa; **~nka** *f* (**~ńczyk** *m*) African; **2ński** *adj* African

agen|cja *f* agency; **~t** *m* (secret) agent; *econ.* agent

agrafka *f* safety pin

agresja *f* aggression

agrest *m* gooseberry

akacja *f* acacia

akademi|a *f* academy; **~cki** *adj* academic; **~k** *m* F (*dom studencki*) hall of residence *Brt.*, dormitory *Am.*, dorm F *Am.*

akcent *m* accent; *ling.* stress

akcesoria *pl* accessories *pl*

akcj|a *f* action; *econ.* share; **~onariusz** *m* shareholder

akompani|ament *m* *mus.* accompaniment; **~ować** accompany

akord *m* *mus.* chord; **praca** *f* **na** ~ piece-work

aksamit *m* velvet

akt *m* act; *obraz itp.*: nude; *dokument*: certificate; ~ **oskarżenia** indictment; **~a** *pl* file, records *pl*

aktor *m* actor; **~ka** *f* actress; **~stwo** *n* acting

aktówka *f* briefcase

aktualny *adj* current

aktyw *m* activists *pl*; **~a** *pl* *econ.* assets *pl*; **~ność** *f* activity; **~ny** *adj* active

akumulator *m* battery

akwarela *f* watercolour

akwarium *n* aquarium

alarmować ⟨**za-**⟩ alert

albo *cj* or; ~ **...** ~ either ... or

album *m* album

ale cj but

aleja f alley

alergiczny adj allergic

alimenty pl alimony

alkohol m alcohol; **~owy** adj alcoholic

alpejski adj alpine

altan(k)a f arbour, bower

aluzja f allusion (**do** to), hint (**do** at)

amator m amateur; lover; **~ski** adj amateur ...

ambasad|a f embassy; **~or** m ambassador

ambi|cja f ambition; **~tny** adj ambitious

ambona f pulpit

ambulatoryjn|y adj: **leczenie ~e** out-patient's treatment

Ameryka f America; **~nin** m (**~nka** f) American; **2ński** American

amnestia f amnesty

amortyz|acja f tech. shock absorption; econ. amortisation; **~ator** m shock absorber; **~ować** tech. absorb, cushion; **~ować się** econ. amortise, pay off

amputować amputate

amunicja f ammunition, ammo F

analiz|a f analysis, **~ować** analyse

ananas m pineapple

anarchia f anarchy

anatomia f anatomy

anegdota f anecdote

aneks m appendix

anemiczny adj anaemic

Angielka f Englishwoman; **2ielski** English; **po 2ielsku** (in) English; **ziele n 2ielskie** pimento; **~lia** f England; **~lik** m Englishman

ani not a; **~ ... ~** neither ... nor

anioł m angel; **~ stróż** guardian angel

ankiet|a f (opinion) poll; (formularz) questionnaire; **~ować** poll

anonimowy adj anonymous

anons m advertisement, ad F

antybiotyk m antibiotic

antyczny adj antique; (klasyczny) ancient

antyk m (starożytność) antiquity; (mebel itp.: antique

antykoncepcyjny adj: **środek ~** med. contraceptive

antykwariat m second-hand bookshop

antypat|ia f antipathy; **~yczny** adj disagreeable

aparat m apparatus; **radiowy, telewizyjny:** set; **~ fotograficzny** camera

apartament m **hotelowy:** suite

apatyczny adj apathetic

apel m appeal; **obozowy:** roll-call

apelacja f appeal

apety|czny adj appetising; **~t** m appetite

aprob|ata f approval; **~ować** ⟨**za-**⟩ approve (**coś** of s.th.)

aptek|a f **domowa:** medicine chest; **podręczna:** first-aid kit; **~ka** f pharmacy, chemist's *Brt.*, drugstore *Am.*

Arab(**ka** f) m Arab; **⚥ski** adj Arab ...; *język, cyfra*: Arabic; *Półwysep*: Arabian

arbuz m watermelon

archipelag m archipelago

architekt m architect; **~ura** f architecture

arcybiskup m archbishop

arcydzieło n masterpiece

areszt m *pomieszczenie*: gaol *Brt.*, jail *Am.*; *jur.* short confinement; **~ować ⟨za-⟩** v/t arrest; **~owanie** n arrest

arkusz m sheet

armator m shipowner

armia f army; **⚥ Zbawienia** Salvation Army

arogancki adj arrogant

arteria f (a. ~ **komunikacyjna**) artery

artretyzm m arthritis

artykuł m article; **~y** pl *spożywcze/żywnościowe* groceries pl

artyleria f artillery

artyst|**a** m (**~ka** f) artist; **~yczny** adj artistic

arytmetyka f arithmetic

asfaltowy adj asphalt ...

astronomiczny adj astronomical

atak m assault; attack (a. *fig.*); **~ować ⟨za-⟩** assault; attack (a. *fig.*)

atlas m atlas

atłas m satin

atlanty|**cki** adj Atlantic; *Ocean* **⚥cki** the Atlantic (Ocean); **⚥k** *F* m the Atlantic

atmosfera f atmosphere

atom m atom; **~owy** adj atomic

atrament m ink

atut m asset; *w kartach*: trump card

audycja f broadcast

Australi|**a** f Australia; **~jczyk** m (**~jka** f) Australian, Aussie F; **⚥jski** adj Australian

Austria f Austria; **⚥cki** adj Austrian; **~czka** f (**~k** m) Austrian

autentyczny adj genuine, authentic

auto F n car; **~bus** m bus; **~kar** m coach *Brt.*, bus *Am.*

automat m (automatic) machine; F (*broń*) sub-machine gun; **~ telefoniczny** pay phone; **~yczny** adj automatic

autor(**ka** f) m author

autostrada f motorway

autostop F m hitch-hiking; *jechać* **~em** hitch-hike; hitch F; **~owicz** F m hitch-hiker

awans m promotion; **~ować** v/i get* a promotion; v/t promote

awantur|**a** f row; **~nik** m (*osoba terroryzująca otoczenie*) bully F; **~ować się** bicker, brawl

awaria f failure; *samochodu*: break-down

Azja f Asia; **~ta** m (**~tka** f) Asian; **⚥tycki** adj Asian, Asiatic

azot *m* nitrogen

azyl *m* asylum

aż *cj* (a. ~ **do**) until

ażeby *cj* in order to, so as to; ~ **nie** in order not to, so as not to

B

bab|a *f* (old) woman; *wiejska:* (old) countrywoman; ~**cia** *f* granny; ~**ka** *f* grandmother; *gastr. kind of Easter cake;* F *(dziewczyna)* bird F *Brt.,* chick *Am.*

bachor *m* brat

baczn|ość *f* attention; ~**y** *adj* attentive, watchful

bać się fear, be* afraid of

bada|cz *m* researcher; ~**ć** ⟨**z-**⟩ examine; *naukowo* a. research; ~**nie** *n* examination; ~**nia** *pl* research; ~**wczy** *adj* research ...

bagaż *m* luggage, baggage; ~**nik** *m samochodowy:* boot *Brt.,* trunk *Am.; na dachu:* (roof) rack; *rowerowy:* carrier; *~owy* **1.** *m* porter; **2.** *adj* luggage ...

bagn|isty *adj* boggy, marshy, swampy; ~**o** *n* bog, marsh, swamp, mire

baj|eczny *adj* fabulous; ~**ka** *f gat. literacki:* fable; *dla dzieci:* fairy tale; *fig.* fable, fabrication, invention

bajer F *m* gimmick

bak *m* petrol tank *Brt.,* gas(oline) tank *Am.*

bakier: na ~ *adv* cocked, tilted

bakteriobójczy *adj* germicidal

bal *m* ball

balanga F *f (pijaństwo)* drinking spree, booze-up F *Brt.,* piss-up V *Brt.*

baleron *m* (kind of) smoked ham

balet *m* ballet; ~**nica** *f* ballet dancer

balkon *m* balcony; *thea. 1* piętro dress circle

balon *m* balloon; ~**ik** *m* (toy) balloon; F *test alkoholowy:* Breathalyser *TM*

balowy *adj* ball(room) ...

bałagan *m* mess

Bałka|ny *pl* the Balkans *pl;* 2**ński** *adj* Balkan

bałty|cki *adj* Baltic; *państwa ~ckie* the Baltic States *pl; Morze* 2**ckie** the Baltic Sea; 2**k** *m* the Baltic (Sea)

bałwan *m* snowman; *fig.* blockhead

banda *f* gang, band

bandaż *m* bandage; ~**ować** ⟨**za-**⟩ bandage, dress

bandy|cki *adj: napad m ~cki* criminal assault; ~**ta** *m* bandit, thug

bank *m* bank

bankiet *m* banquet

banknot m (bank) note; bill Am.

bankru|ctwo n bankruptcy; **~tować** ⟨z-⟩ go* bankrupt

bańka f bubble; F *pojemnik*: can, (metal) container; **~my-dlana** soap bubble

bar m snack-bar, diner Am.; *hotelowy itp.*: bar

barak m hut; (*prowizoryczny dom*) makeshift house

baran m ram; **~ek** m lamb; **~ina** f (meat), mutton

barbarzyń|ca m barbarian, savage; **~stwo** n barbarity, savagery

barczysty adj broad-shouldered, square-built

bardzo adv very; **~iej** more; **tym ~iej że** the more (so) because

barki pl shoulders pl

barman m barman, bartender Am.; **~ka** f barmaid

barszcz m borsch

barw|a f hue, colour(ing); **~ić** ⟨za-⟩ colour, dye; **~nik** m dye, tint; **~ny** adj colourful; *fig.* vivid

barykada f barricade

bas m bass

basen m basin; **~ pływacki** swimming pool

baśń f fairy tale

bat m whip; **~y** pl beating, lashing; (*lanie*) licking F

bateria f battery

bawełn|a f cotton; **~iany** adj cotton ...

bawić (*śmieszyć*) amuse; *gości*: entertain; **~ się** play (**w kogoś** s.o.); toy (**czymś** with s.th.)

baza f (*danych* data) base

bazar m bazaar

bazgra|ć ⟨na-⟩ scribble; **~ni-na** f scribble

bażant m pheasant

bąbel m na ciele: blister; *powietrza*: bubble

bądź v. **~ ... ~** either ... or; **co ~** (just) anything; **kto ~** (just) anyone/anybody

bąk m (*owad*) gadfly; (*zabawka*) top; **~ać** ⟨~nąć⟩ mutter, mumble

beczeć *owce*: bleat; F (*płakać*) blubber F

beczka f barrel, cask

befsztyk m (beef)steak

bejc|a f stain; **~ować** ⟨za-⟩ stain

bek m owiec itp.: bleat; F (*płacz*) blubbering F

bekon m bacon

bela f materiału: bale; **pijany jak ~** drunk as a lord

Belg m Belgian; **~ia** f Belgium; **~ijka** f Belgian; **£ijski** adj Belgian

belka f arch. beam; stalowa: girder; drewniana: log

bełkot m blithering, gibberish; **~ać** ⟨wy-⟩ gibber

benzyn|a f petrol Brt., gasoline Am., gas F Am.; **~owy** adj petrol – Brt., gasoline – Am.; zapalniczka: benzine ...; **stacja ~owa** f filling station *Brt.*, gas(oline) station *Am.*

berbeć F *m* toddler, tot

beret *m* beret

bestia *f* ⟨*zwierzę*⟩ beast; ⟨*człowiek*⟩ brute; **~lski** *adj* bestial, atrocious

besztać ⟨z-⟩ scold, rebuke

beton *m* concrete; **~owy** *adj* concrete ...

bez¹ *m bot.* lilac

bez² *prp* without; **~ mała** almost; **~ ustanku** continually

bezalkoholowy *adj* non-alcoholic

bezbarwny *adj* colourless

bezbłędny *adj* faultless

bezbolesny *adj* painless

bezbożny *adj* godless, impious

bezbronny *adj* defenseless

bezbrzeżny *adj* boundless

bezcelowy *adj* aimless, purposeless; pointless

bezcen: za ~ *adv* dirt cheap, for a song

bezcenny *adj* priceless

bezchmurny *adj* cloudless

bezczelny *adj* insolent, impudent, cheeky F

bezczynny *adj* idle

bezdomny *adj* homeless

bezduszny *adj* soulless; *człowiek*: insensitive, unfeeling

bezdzietny *adj* childless

bezgotówkowy *adj* by *cheque or money transfer*

bezgraniczny *adj* boundless, limitless

bezimienny *adj* nameless, unnamed

bezinteresowny *adj* disinterested

bezkarny *adj* unpunished

bezkompromisowy *adj* uncompromising

bezkonkurencyjny *adj* unrivalled, matchless

bezkrytyczny *adj* uncritical

bezkształtny *adj* shapeless

bezlitosny *adj* pitiless, merciless

bezludn|y *adj* ⟨*wyludniony*⟩ deserted; **~a wyspa** desert island

bezład *m* disorder

bezmyślny *adj* thoughtless

beznadziejny *adj* hopeless

bezokolicznik *m* infinitive

bezosobowy *adj* impersonal

bezowocny *adj* fruitless, futile

bezpański *adj* ownerless; derelict; *pies a.:* stray

bezpardonowy *adj* pitiless, merciless, ruthless

bezpartyjny *adj* non-partisan

bezpiecze|ństwo *n* ⟨*brak zagrożenia*⟩ safety; ⟨*zabezpieczenie*⟩ security; **~nik** *m* elect. fuse; *mil.* safety (catch); **~ny** *adj* ⟨*nie zagrożony/zagrażający*⟩ safe; ⟨*zabezpieczony*⟩ secure

bezpłatny *adj* free (of charge)

bezpłodny *adj* sterile, barren

bezpodstawny *adj* unfounded, groundless, baseless

bezpośredni *adj* direct;

człowiek a.: straightforward

bezprawny *adj* unlawful, illegal

bezpretensjonalny *adj* unpretentious; *człowiek*: unassuming

bezprzewodowy *adj* cordless

bezradny *adj* helpless

bezrobo|cie *n* unemployment; **~tny** *adj* unemployed, out of work

bezsenność *f* sleeplessness, insomnia

bezsensowny *adj* (*nonsensowny*) nonsensical; (*nie wart zachodu*) pointless

bezsilny *adj* helpless, powerless

bezskuteczny *adj* ineffective, futile

bez|sporny, ~sprzeczny *adj* unquestionable, undisputed; *fakt, argument*: irrefutable

bezstronny *adj* impartial, unprejudiced, unbiased

beztroski *adj* careless; *człowiek a.*: carefree

bezustanny *adj* continual

bezwartościowy *adj* worthless

bezwarunkowy *adj* unconditional

bezwiedny *adj* (*nieświadomy*) unconscious; (*nie zamierzony*) unintentional, involuntary

bezwład *m* inertia; **~ny** *adj* inert

bezwstydny *adj* shameless

bezwzględny *adj człowiek*:

ruthless; *phys., math.* absolute

bezzębny *adj* toothless

bezzwłoczny *adj* immediate

bezzwrotny *adj* not repayable

beżowy *adj* beige

bęben *m* drum; **~ek** *m anat.* eardrum

bębnić drum; *deszcz*: pelt

biadać lament (**nad czymś** s.th.)

biał|aczka *f* leukemia; **~ko** *n* protein; **~y** *adj* white

Biblia *f* the Bible

bibliote|czka *f mebel*: bookcase; **~ka** *f* library; **~karka** *f* (**~karz** *m*) librarian

bibuła *f* blotting paper; **~ka** *f* tissue (paper); *papierosowa*: cigarette paper

bicie *n* beating; **~ serca** heartbeat; **~ zegara** striking (of the clock)

bić beat*, thrash; *zegar*: strike*; *monety*: mint; *dzwon*: peal, toll; *serce*: beat*; **~ się** fight*

biec run*; ⟨**po-**⟩ *a.* dash, rush

bied|a *f* poverty, distress; **~ak** *m* poor/needy person; **~aku!** poor you!; **~ny** *adj* poor, needy; **~ować** live in poverty, suffer want

bieg *m* run; *sp.* race; *mot.* gear; **~ zjazdowy** downhill race; **z ~iem czasu** in the course of time; **~acz** *m* runner; **~ać** run*; *dla zdrowia*: jog;

~le *adv* efficiently; *mówić:* fluently; **~ły 1.** *adj* expert, efficient; **2.** *m* expert; **~nąć →** *biec*

biegun *m* pole

biegunka *f* diarrhoea

biel *f* white(ness); **~eć ⟨z-⟩** whiten, turn white; **~ić ⟨po-⟩** whitewash; **⟨wy-⟩** bleach, whiten; **~izna** *f* washing, laundry; *osobista:* underwear; *damska a.:* lingerie; **~iźniarka** *f* chest of drawers

bierny *adj* passive (*a.* gr.), listless

bierzmowanie *n* Confirmation

bieżąc|y *adj* current; **~a woda** running water

bieżni|a *f* racetrack; **~k** *m* mot. (tyre) tread

bigos *m* sauerkraut stewed with sausage, pork, mushrooms etc.

bijatyka *f* brawl

bilans *m* balance

bilard *m* billiards, pool; F *a.* snooker

bilet *m* ticket; **~ powrotny** return ticket; **~ wstępu** ticket, admission card; **~er(ka** *f)* *m* ticket collector

bilon *m* (small) change

bimber F *m* hoo(t)ch *Am.,* moonshine *Am.*

biodro *n* hip

biskup *m* bishop

biszkopt *m* sponge cake

bitka *f* gastr. cutlet; F *w kartach:* trick

bitwa *f* battle (**pod** of)

biuletyn *m* bulletin; *drukowany a.:* newsletter

biur|ko *n* desk; **~o** *n* office; **~o podróży** travel bureau/agency; **~owiec** *m* office building

biust *m* bust; **~onosz** *m* brassière, bra

biżuteria *f* jewellery

blacha *f* sheet metal; *na kuchni:* top plate (of kitchen range); *do pieczenia:* baking pan/tin; **~rz** *m* mot. panel beater

blady *adj* pale

blaknąć ⟨wy-⟩ fade

blankiet *m* form

blask *m* brightness, brilliance; *fig.* glamour

blaszan|ka *f* (tin) can; **~y** *adj* tin ...

blat *m* (desk/table) top

blednąć ⟨z-, po-⟩ grow*/turn pale; *kolor:* fade; *fig.* pale

blisk|i *adj* close, near, nearby; **z ~a** at close quarters; **~o** *adv* close, near, nearby; **~oznaczny** *adj* synonymous

blizna *f* scar

bliźni *m* neighbour; **~aczka** *f* twin (sister); **~aczy** *adj* twin ...; **~ak** *m* twin (brother); **~ęta** *pl* twins *pl*

bliż|ej *adv* closer, nearer; **~szy** *adj* closer, nearer

blok *m* block; (*budynek*) block (of flats); *papierowy:* pad; **~ować ⟨za-⟩** block, obstruct

blond adj blond

blondynka f blonde

bluszcz m ivy

bluzka f blouse

bluźnierstwo n blasphemy

błaga|ć beseech*, implore, beg F (**o** for); **~lny** adj beseeching, imploring

błah|ostka f trifle; **~y** adj trifling, trivial

błazen m jester; fig. fool, buffoon, clown; **~enada** f tomfoolery, buffoonery; **~eński** adj clownish

błąd m mistake, error; (gafa) blunder

błądzić err; (błąkać się) wander about

błędny adj incorrect, erroneous

błękit m azure; **~ny** adj azure

błogi adj blissful, sweet

błogosławi|ć ⟨po-⟩ bless; **~eństwo** n blessing; eccl. benediction; **~ony** adj blessed

błona f anat. membrane, dziewicza: hymen; zo. web; phot. film; **~ śluzowa** mucous membrane

błotn|ik m rowerowy: mudguard; samochodowy: wing; **~isty** adj muddy; **~o** n mud

błysk m flash, sparkle; **~ać** v/t flash; v/i flash, sparkle, glitter; **~awica** f (flash/stroke of) lightning; **~awiczny** adj rapid, swift; **~** a. **zamek**; **~otliwy** adj brilliant; (dowcipny) witty; **człowiek** a.:

quick-witted; **~owy** → **lampa**

błysnąć flash

błyszcz|eć ⟨za-⟩ glitter, glimmer; **~ący** adj brilliant, shiny

bo F cj because, for

boazeria f wainscot, panelling

bobkowy adj: **liść** m **~** bay leaf

bochen(ek) m loaf (of bread)

bocian m stork

boczek m bacon

boczyć się sulk

bodziec m stimulus, incentive

boga|cić ⟨wz-⟩ **się** become*/get* rich; **~ctwo** n wealth; riches pl; **~ctwa** pl **naturalne** natural resources pl; **~ty** adj rich, wealthy, affluent

bohater m hero; **~ka** f heroine; **~ski** adj heroic; **~stwo** n heroism

boisko n szkolne: playground, playing field; sp. pitch

bojaź|liwy adj timid, fearful; **~ń** f fear, fright

bojow|nik m (**~niczka** f) fighter; **~y** adj combat ..., battle ...

bok m side

boks|er m boxer; **~ować (się)** box

bol|ączka f ailment; **~eć*** hurt*, ache; **~i mnie ...** my ... hurts; **~esny** adj sore, painful, aching; *cios itp.* painful; *wiadomość itp.* sad, sorrowful; **~eść** *f* anguish; (*smutek*) sorrow, grief

bomb|**a** *f* bomb; **~ardowanie** *n* bombing; **~ka** F *f* coloured glass ball for Christmas tree; **~owiec** *m* bomber (plane)

bon *m* coupon, ticket

bonifikata *f* discount

borowik *m* species of edible fungus; *zo.* cep

borówka *f* bilberry; **~ bruśnica** cranberry

borsuk *m* badger

bosaka: *na* **~** barefoot(ed)

bosk|**i** *adj* divine; **Matka £a** *f* Our Lady, Mother of God

bos|**o** *adv.*, **~y** *adj* barefoot(ed)

Bośnia *f* Bosnia; **£cki** *adj* Bosnian; **~czka** *f* (**~k** *m*) Bosnian

bowiem *cj* as, because, since

boż|**ek** *m* idol; **~y** *adj* God's; **£e Ciało** *n* Corpus Christi; **£e Narodzenie** *n* Christmas

bób *m* broad bean

bóbr *m* beaver

Bóg *m* God; *Pan m* **~** *zapłać!* may Heaven reward you!

bój *m* combat, battle; **~ka** *f* brawl, fight

ból *m* pain, ache; **~ gardła** sore throat

bóstwo *n* divinity, deity; (*bożek*) idol

brać take*****; **~ się** set***** about (*do robienia czegoś* doing s.th.)

brak *m* lack, want; *od-*

czu(wa)ć **~** lack; **~ować** be***** missing

bram|**a** *f* gate; gateway; **~ka** *f* *sp.* goal; **~karz** *m* *sp.* goalkeeper, goalie F; F (*wykidajło*) bouncer, chucker-out

bransolet(k)a *f* bracelet

branża *f* line of trade/business

brat *m* brother; **~ cioteczny** **stryjeczny** first cousin; **~anek** *m* nephew; **~anica** *f* niece

bratek *m* pansy

brat|**erski** *adj* brotherly; **~erstwo** *n* brotherhood; **~owa** *f* sister-in-law

brąz *m kolor*: brown; *metal*: bronze; **~owy** *adj kolor*: brown; (*z brązu*) bronze ...

bre|**dnie** *pl* nonsense, rubbish, drivel; **~dzić** talk nonsense/rubbish, drivel on

brew *f* eyebrow

brezent *m* tarpaulin, canvas

brnąć flounder, to work one's way

broczyć: **~ krwią** bleed*****, shed***** blood

broda *f* beard; *anat.* chin; **~ty** *adj* bearded

brodawka *f* wart; *piersi*: nipple

brodzić wade

broić ⟨z-⟩ do***** mischief

bro|**nić** defend; **~ń Boże!** God forbid!

broń *f* weapon(s *pl*), arms *pl*; **~ jądrowa** nuclear weapons *pl*

broszka *f* brooch

broszur(k)a *f* pamphlet

browar *m* brewery

bród *m* ford; **w ~** galore

bru|d *m* dirt, filth, grime; **~dny** *adj* dirty, filthy, grimy; **~dzić** ⟨za-⟩ soil, smear, dirty

bruk *m* cobbles *pl*, cobblestones *pl*; pavement *Am.*

brukow|ać ⟨wy-⟩ cobble, pave; **~any** *adj* cobbled, paved; **~iec** *m* cobblestone, paving stone; *gazeta*: tabloid; **~y** *adj prasa*: tabloid

brukselka *f* Brussels sprouts *pl*

brulion *m* rough draft; (*zeszyt*) notebook

brun|atny *adj* brown; **~et** *m* dark-haired man; **~etka** *f* brunette

brutalny *adj* rough, brutal

bru|zda *f* furrow; **~ździć**: **~ździć** ⟨na-⟩ *komuś* F put* a spoke in s.o.'s wheel

brwi *pl* eyebrows *pl*

bryk|ać ⟨nąć⟩ *koń*: buck; *dziecko*: romp

brylant *m* diamond

bryła *f* block, lump; *ziemi*: clump; *lodu*: block; *math.* solid

Bryt|ania *f geog.* Britain; *fig.* Britannia; **Wielka ~ania** Great Britain; **~yjczyk** *m* (**~yjka** *f*) Briton, Britisher, Brit F; **2yjski** *adj* British

bryzol *m* (thin) steak

brzeg *m* edge; *filiżanki itp.* rim; *morza*: shore; *rzeki*: bank

brzemię *n* burden

brzęcze|ć ⟨za-, brzęknąć⟩ *metal*: rattle, clank, clink; *szkło*: chink, clink; **~nie** *n metalu*: rattling, clanking, clinking; *szkła, monet*: chinking, clinking

brzęk *m metalu*: rattle, clank, clink; *szkła, monet*: chink, clink; **~nąć** → **brzęczeć**

brzmie|ć ⟨za-⟩ sound; be* heard; *tekst*: read*; **~nie** *n* sound; *głosu*: ring

brzoskwinia *f* peach

brzoza *f* birch (tree)

brzu|ch *m* stomach, belly F; *anat.* abdomen; **~chacz** *m* big-bellied person; **~chaty** *adj* pot-bellied; **~szek** *m dziecięcy*: tummy; **~szny** *adj anat., med.* abdominal

brzyd|ki *adj* ugly, unsightly, unlovely; *pogoda*: bad, foul, nasty; **~nąć** ⟨z-⟩ become*/ grow* ugly; lose* one's looks; **~ota** *f* ugliness, unsightliness

brzydzić się abhor

bubel F *m* unsaleable product, trash F

buch|ać ⟨nąć⟩ burst*; *ogień*: flare up, flame out; *krew itp.*: gush

buczeć hoot

bud|a *f* shed; *dla psa*: kennel; F (*szkoła*) school; **~ka** *f* booth

budow|a *f* construction; building; *plac*: construction site; **~ać** ⟨z-⟩ build*; construct;

~la f building, edifice; **~lany** adj construction ..., building ...; **~nictwo** n construction, building; **~nictwo mieszkaniowe** housing

budu|jący adj edifying; inspiring; **~lec** m building material; *drewno*: timber

budynek m building

budyń m (*sweet creamy*) pudding

budzi|ć ⟨z-⟩ wake* (up); waken; *uczucia itp.* evoke; **~ć się** wake* (up), awaken; **~k** m alarm clock

budżet m budget; **~owy** adj budget ..., fiscal; **sfera z ~owa** state employees pl

bufet m cafeteria, snack bar; **zimny** ~ buffet; **kolejowy** itp.: buffet; **~owa** f barmaid

buja|ć rock; F (*kłamać*) kid; **~ się** rock

bujny adj lush, luxuriant, rank; *włosy*: luxuriant, thick

buk m beech (tree)

bukiet m bouquet; *kwiatów a.*: bunch

bulgotać bubble

buł|eczka, **~ka** f roll; *słodka*: bun

Bułgar m Bulgarian; **~ia** f Bulgaria; **~ka** f Bulgarian; **2ski** adj Bulgarian

bunt m mutiny, rebellion; **~ować** ⟨z-⟩ incite; **~ować się** mutiny, revolt, rebel; **~ownik** m mutineer, rebel

bura F f dressing-down, talking-to

burak m beet, beetroot Brt; ~ **cukrowy** sugar beet; **zaczerwienić się jak** ~ go* beetroot Brt F

bur|czeć *żołądek*: rumble; *a.* ⟨~knąć⟩ growl

burda F f brawl

burmistrz m mayor

bursztyn m amber; **~owy** adj amber ...; **barwy bursztynu:** amber-coloured

burta f side; **lewa** ~ port (side); **prawa** ~ starboard (side)

bury adj dull brown/grey

burz|a f storm; *zaczyna się* stormy; **~yć** ⟨z-⟩ pull down, demolish; **~yć się** seethe; → *a.* **buntować się**

but m shoe; *wysoki*: boot

buta f arrogance, haughtiness

but|elka f bottle; **~la** f (big) bottle, demijohn, carboy; *tech.* stalowa: steel) cylinder

butwieć ⟨z-⟩ moulder, rot

buzia f (girl's/child's) face; **~k** F m kiss

by cj (in order to)

być be*; ~ **może** maybe, perhaps

bydl|ę n beast, animal; *fig.* V bastard, skunk; **~ęcy** adj cattle ...; **~o** n cattle

byk m bull; F (*błąd*) mistake; **strzelić ~a** put* one's foot in it, make* a blunder

byle¹ adv (no)(-); ~ **co** anything, any old thing F; ~ **gdzie** any place, anywhere; ~ **kto** anyone

byle² *cj* in order to, so as to;
on condition that, provided
that; as/so long as

były *adj* former, ex-

bynajmniej *adv* by no means;
w odpowiedzi: not at all

bystry *adj* sharp, keen, bright;
wzrok: keen; *nurt*: rapid

byt *m phls.* existence, being;
zapewnić ~ provide for;
~ność *f* stay

bywa|ć frequent (*w czymś*

s.th.); be* often (*w* in; *u* at
...'s); go* often (*w* to; *u* to
...'s); **~lec** *m* habitué

bzdur|a *f* nonsense, rubbish,
humbug; **~ny** *adj* silly, ridiculous, preposterous

bzik F *m* craze, fad; **mieć ~a**
be* potty, be* off one's
rocker; **mieć ~a na punkcie**
... be* crazy about ..., be* a
... buff

bzyk|ać ⟨**~nąć**⟩ buzz

C

cackać się (*z czymś*) handle
(s.th.) delicately/gently

cacko *n* a beauty

cal *m* inch; **~ówka** *f* folding
ruler

całkowi|cie *adv* entirely,
wholly; **~ty** *adj* entire

cało *adv* **wyjść ~** escape un-
hurt/unharmed

cało|dzienny *adj* daylong,
all-day; **~kształt** *m* the whole; **~ść** *f* the whole; entirety
całować ⟨**po-**⟩ kiss; **~ować
się** kiss (each other); **~nasto-
latki**: neck F; **~us** *m* kiss;
posłać komuś ~usa blow
s.o. a kiss

cały *adj* whole; entire; all; **~ i
zdrowy** safe and sound; **~mi
dniami** for days on end

campingowy → **kempingowy**

cebul|a *f* onion; **~ka** *f bot.*
bulb; **~owy** *adj* onion ...

cech *m* guild

cech|a *f* feature, characteris-
tic; **~ować ⟨s czymś⟩** be*
characterised by s.th.

cedz|ak *m* colander; **~ić**
⟨**prze-, od-**⟩ strain

ceg|ielnia *f* brickyard; **~lany**
adj brick ...; **~lasty** *adj*
brick-red, orange-red; **~ła** *f*
brick

cel *m* (*zamiar docelowy*) aim,
objective, purpose (*czegoś*
of s.th.); *mil.* target

cela *f* cell

celem *adv* in order to

celnik *m* customs officer

celn|y¹ *adj dotyczący cła*: cu-
stoms ...; **odprawa** *f* **~a** customs clearance

celny² *adj* (*trafny*) well-aim-
ed, accurate

celow|ać ⟨**wy-**⟩ aim, take*
aim (*do* at); **~nik** *m mil.*
sight(s *pl*)

celow|o adv deliberately, on purpose; **~ość** f advisability; **~y** adj deliberate, purposeful

cementownia f cement works

cen|a f price; **~ić** appreciate; **~nik** m price list; **~ny** adj valuable, precious

centr|ala f head office; teleph. exchange; **~um** n centre

cera[1] f (skóra twarzy) complexion

cera[2] f na ubraniu: mend

ceramicz|ny adj ceramic; **~ka** f ceramics; pottery

cerata f oilcloth

ceregiel|e pl: bez **~i** unceremoniously

cerować ⟨za-⟩ darn, mend

certować się make* a pretence of declining

cesarz m emperor; **~owa** f empress

cęgi pl pliers pl

cętkowany adj spotted

chaber m cornflower

chałup|a f (old, rambling) house; (wiejska chata) cottage; **~nictwo** n cottage work; **~nik** m cottage worker

cham m boor; **~ski** adj boorish; **po ~sku** boorishly

charakter m character; nature; **~ pisma** handwriting; **~ystyczny** adj characteristic (dla of); typical (dla of)

charczeć wheeze

chata f (country) cottage

chcieć want; wish; **~ałbym** I'd like

chciwość f greed; **~y** adj greedy, mean with money

chełpić się brag; boast; **~liwy** adj boastful

chemi|a f chemistry; **~czny** adj chemical; **~k** m chemist

cherlak M m weakling

chę|ć f wish, desire; dobre **~ci** pl good intentions pl; mieć **~ć na coś** fancy s.th., feel like s.th.; **~tka** F f sudden desire, whim; **~tny** adj willing

chichotać giggle

Chi|nka f Chinese; **~ny** pl China; **~ńczyk** m Chinese; **2ński** adj Chinese;

chlapa|ć ⟨~nąć⟩ splash, spatter, splutter

chleb m bread

chlipać sob

chlor m chlorine

chlub|a f pride (czegoś/kogoś of s.th./s.o.); credit (czegoś/kogoś to s.th./s.o.); **~ić się** pride oneself (czymś on s.th.), take* pride in s.th.); **~ny** adj glorious; creditable

chlup(ot)ać lap

chlus|tać ⟨~nąć⟩ v/t splash; v/i spurt (out), spout (out), gush

chłeptać lap (up)

chło|dnia f cold store; samochód **~dnia** refrigerated lorry; **~dnica** f mot. radiator; **~dnik** m cold borsch; owocowy: cold fruit soup; **~dny** adj cool; dzień, wiatr: chilly;

~dziarka → **lodówka**; **~dzić** ⟨**o-**⟩ cool (down), chill

chłonąć ⟨**w-**⟩ absorb; *fig. a.* drink* in

chłop *m* peasant; F (*mężczyzna*) man; **~ak** *m* boy; F *sympatia*: boyfriend; **~czyk** *m* (little) boy; **~iec** *m* boy; **~ięcy** *adj* boy's; boyish, puerile; **~ka** *f* peasant woman; **~ski** *adj* peasant ...

chłód *m* cold, chill

chmiel *m bot.* hop

chmu|ra *f* cloud; **~rzyć** ⟨**za-**⟩ become* overcast

chociaż, choć *cj* although, though

cho|dnik *m* pavement *Brt.*, sidewalk *Am.*; *tech.* gallery; *rodzaj dywanu*: carpet, runner; **~dzić** walk, go* (**na coś** *(uczęszczać)* **na coś** s.th.); **~dzić do szkoły** go* to school; **~dzić z kimś** go* out with s.o.; **jeśli ~dzi o ...** as far as ... is concerned

choinka *f sosna*: pine-tree; *świerk*: spruce; *świąteczna*: Christmas tree

cholera *f med.* cholera; **~jasna!** V damn it! V

chomik *m* hamster

chorągiew *f* flag, banner, standard

choro|ba *f* illness, sickness; *med.* disease; **~bliwy** *adj* morbid; **~bowe** F *n* sick leave; **~bliwy** be* ill, suffer (**na** from), be* down (**na** with) F; **~wity** *adj* sickly

Chorwa|cja *f* Croatia; 2**cki** *adj* Croat(ian); **~t(ka** *f) m* Croat(ian)

chory *adj* ill; **być ~m** suffer (**na** from), be* down (**na** with)

chować ⟨**s-**⟩ hide*, conceal; **~ się** hide*; → *a.* **wychowywać się**

chód *m* gait

chór *m* choir

chrap|ać snore; **~anie** *n* snoring; **~liwy** *adj* hoarse, husky

chroniczny *adj* chronic

chronić ⟨**o-, u-**⟩ protect; shield (**od/przed** from/ against); **~** ⟨**s-**⟩ **się** seek* shelter

chrop|awy, ~owaty *adj* rough, coarse

chrup|ać crunch; **~iący** *adj* crunchy, crispy

chryja *f* row, scandal

chryp|(k)a *f* hoarseness; **mieć ~ę** be* hoarse, have* a frog in one's throat V

chrzan *m* horseradish

chrzą|kać ⟨**~nąć**⟩ clear one's throat; *świnia*: grunt

chrząstka *f* w *mięsie*: gristle; *anat.* cartilage

chrząszcz *m* beetle

chrz|cić ⟨**o-**⟩ baptise, christen; **~ciny** *pl*, **~est** *m* baptism, christening; **~estny** *adj*; **~estna matka** *f* godmother; **~estny ojciec** *m* godfather

chrześcija|nin *m* (**~nka** *f*) Christian; **~ński** *adj* Christian

chrześnia|czka f goddaughter; **~k** m godson

chrzę|st m clank, clatter, clang; **~ścić** clank, clatter, clang

chuch|ać ⟨**~nąć**⟩ breathe

chud|nąć ⟨**s-**⟩ become* thinner; lose* weight; **~ość** f thinness; **~y** adj thin; lanky

chuligan m tough, rowdy, hooligan; **~ić** brawl

chust(ecz)ka f na głowę: kerchief; **~ do nosa** handkerchief, hanky F

chwa|lebny adj commendable, praiseworthy; **~lić** ⟨**po-**⟩ praise, commend; **~lić się** brag, boast (**czymś** about/of s.th.); **~ła** f glory; **~ła Bogu!** thank God!

chwast m weed

chwi|ać ⟨**za-**⟩ shake*, rock; **~ać się** shake*, rock; na nogach: stagger, totter; **~ejny** adj stół itp.: unsteady; fig. a. shaky; człowiek: irresolute, vacillating

chwil|a f moment, while; **~eczke!** just a moment!; **~owo** adv momentarily; (czasowo) temporarily; **~owy** adj momentary; (czasowy) temporary

chwyt m grasp, grip, hold; **~ać** ⟨**chwycić**⟩ grasp, grip; gwałtownie: grab

chyba F surely; **~ że** unless

chybi|a(ć) miss; **~ony** adj ineffective, unsuccessful; uwaga: pointless

chylić bend*; głowę: bow; **~ ⟨po-⟩ się** bend* (down); do przodu: lean forward

chytry adj sly, clever

ci¹ F pron (tobie) you

ci² pron pl these

ciało n body; **~ a. boży**

ciarki pl shudder, the shudders pl, the creeps F pl

ciasn|ota f lack of room/ space; **~y** adj pokój itp.: (too) small; (wąski) narrow, poky F; ubiór: tight, close-fitting

ciast|ko n cake; **~o** n masa: dough, batter; produkt: cake

ciąć ⟨**po-**⟩ cut*

ciąg m sequence; **~ dalszy** (nastąpi) (to be) continued; **dalszy ~** continuation; filmu: sequel; **jednym ~em** at a stretch; **w ~u** during, in the course of; **~le** adv continually, constantly, all the time; **~ły** adj continuous; continual

ciągn|ąć ⟨**po-**⟩ pull; **~ienie** n loteryjne: draw; **~ik** m tractor

ciąż|a f pregnancy; **być w** ⟨**drugim miesiącu**⟩ **~y** be* (two months) pregnant; **~yć** weigh/lie* heavy (komuś on s.o.)

cich|aczem adv on the sly, stealthily; **~nąć** ⟨**u-**⟩ człowiek: grow* silent, quiet down Am.; wiatr itp.: die down; subside; **~y** adj człowiek: quiet; głos itp. low

ciec → cieknąć

ciecz f liquid

ciekaw|ość f curiosity; **~y** adj człowiek: curious; film itp.: exciting, interesting

ciek|ły adj liquid; **~nąć** ⟨-⟩ trickle; rura itp.: leak

ciel|ak m, **~ę** n calf; **~cina** f veal; **~ęcy** adj calf ...; kotlet itp.: veal ...

ciemię n the crown of the head; fig. **nie w ~ bity** F no fool

ciemn|ia f darkroom; **~ieć** ⟨**po-, ś-**⟩ grow* dark; **~o** adv dark; było **~o** it was dark; **~ość** f dark, darkness; **~y** adj dark

cienki adj thin; fine

cień m człowieka itp.: shadow; osłonić to miejsce: shade

ciep|larnia f hothouse, greenhouse; **efekt** m **~larniany** greenhouse effect; **~lny** adj thermal; **~ło 1.** n warmth; phys. heat; **2.** adv warm; witać: warmly; **tu jest ~ło** it's warm here; **~łota** f: **~łota ciała** (body) temperature; **~łownia** f heating plant; **~ły** adj warm

cierpi|eć suffer (**na** from); **nie ~ę** ... I cannot stand/bear ...; **~enie** n suffering, torment

cierpki adj bittersweet

cierpliw|ość f patience; **~y** adj patient

cierpnąć ⟨**ś-**⟩ grow* numb; skóra: creep*

cieszyć ⟨**u-**⟩ please; **~ się** be* pleased/glad/happy

cieśnina f straits pl

cięcie n cut

ciężar m (obciążenie) load; fig. a. burden; (waga) weight (a. phys.) (**czegoś** of s.th.); **~ny** adj pregnant; **~ówka** f lorry Brt., truck Am.

ciężki adj heavy; praca itp.: hard

ciocia f auntie

cios m blow

ciot|eczny adj: **~eczny brat** m, **~eczna siostra** f (first) cousin; **~ka** f aunt

cis|kać ⟨**~nąć**⟩ hurl

cisnąć¹ pf → **ciskać**

cisnąć² ⟨**na-**⟩ press; but: be* tight; **~ się** press, crowd

cisza f silence; quiet

ciśnienie n a. phys. pressure

ciuch F m piece of clothing

ciułać ⟨**u-**⟩ v/t scrape up/together

ckliwy adj mawkish; człowiek: maudlin

clić ⟨**o-**⟩ collect duty (**coś** on s.th.)

cło n (customs) duty

cmentarz m graveyard, cemetery; **przykościelny**: churchyard

cnot|a f (zaleta) virtue; (dziewictwo) virginity; **stracić ~ę** lose one's virginity; **~liwy** adj chaste

co pron what; rel. which; **~ do** ... concerning/regarding ...; **~ godzinę** every hour; **~ za** ...

what ...; **w razie czego** if anything should happen, if the worst comes to the worst; **po czym** after which, whereupon

codzienny adj everyday; daily

cof|ać ⟨-nąć⟩ pojazd itp.: back; słowo itp. take* back, withdraw*; **~ać się** step back; pojazd: back up; wojsko: withdraw*

cokolwiek pron anything, whatever

coraz adv: **~ lepiej** better and better; **~ więcej** more and more

coroczny adj yearly, annual

coś pron something

cór|eczka f (little) daughter; **~ka** f daughter

cóż pron: **~ dopiero** let alone; **no ~** well

cuchnąć reek (**czymś** of s.th.)

cucić revive; ⟨o-⟩ bring* to/round

cud m wonder, miracle; **~aczny** adj weird, bizarre; **~ny** adj lovely; **~owny** adj wonderful; zjawisko: miraculous

cudzoziem|iec m (**~ka** f) foreigner, alien; **~ski** adj foreign; **Legia** f **2ska** Foreign Legion

cudzy adj somebody else's; **~słów** m quotation marks pl, inverted commas pl

cuk|ier m sugar; **~ierek** m bonbon; candy Am.; **~iernia** f confectioner's; **~ierniczka**

f sugar bowl; **~rownia** f sugar factory; **~rzyca** f diabetes

cumować ⟨przy-, za-⟩ moor

cwał m gallop

cwan|iak m crafty fellow; **~y** adj crafty, sly

cyfr|a f figure; tech. digit; **~owy** adj digital

Cygan m (**~ka** f) gypsy

cygaro n cigar

cylinder m (kapelusz) top hat, topper F; tech. cylinder

cyna f tin

cynamon m cinnamon

cynkować ⟨o-⟩ zinc, coat with zinc

cypel m promontory

Cypr m Cyprus; **~yjczyk** m (**~yjka** f) Cypriot, Cypriote; **2yjski** adj Cyprian, Cypriote

cyrk m circus

cysterna f (pojemnik) tank; (samochód) tanker

cyt|at m quotation, quote; **~ować** ⟨za-⟩ quote

cytryna f lemon

cywil m civilian; **~ny** adj civilian

czad m chem. carbon monoxide; **da(wa)ć ~u** F play (music) very loud

czaić się lurk

czajnik m kettle

czapka f hat; miękka: (cloth) cap

czar m (urok) charm; rzucony: spell

czarn|orynkowy   adj black-market; **~y** adj black

czaro|dziej *m* (**~ka** *f*) magician; **~dziejski** *adj* magic; **~wać** *v/i* use/do*/work magic; *v/t* (**o-**) charm, enchant; **~wnica** *f* witch

czar|ujący *adj* charming; **~y** *pl* magic

czas *m* time; **w/na ~** in time; **po pewnym ~ie** after a while, some time later; **~ami**, **~em** *adv* sometimes, at times; **~opismo** *n* magazine; **~owo** *adv* temporarily; **~owy** *adj* temporary

czaszka *f* skull

czatować lie* in wait (**na** for); **~ pl** czaić się

cząsteczka *f* molecule

cześć worship; **święto** itp. worship; **święto** celebrate, observe

czcionka *f* type

czczo: na ~ *adv* on an empty stomach

Czech *m* Czech; **~y** *pl* Czech Republic; *hist.* Bohemia; **£osłowacki** *adj* Czechoslovak

czego F *pron:* **~?** What do you want?

czek *m* cheque *Brt.*, check *Am.*

czekać (**za-**, **po-**) wait (**na** for)

czekolad|a *f* (bar of) chocolate; **~ka** *f* (small) chocolate

czele: na ~ *adv* at the head

czemu F why, how come

czepi(a)ć się F find* fault (**kogoś** with s.o.); pick (**na kogoś** on s.o.)

czereśnia *f* cherry

czer|nić (**po-**) blacken; **~nieć** loom black; (**s-**) turn black; **~ń** *f* blackness, black

czerpać scoop, ladle; *fig.* draw* (**z** from, on)

czerstwy *adj* chleb: stale; *staruszek:* hale; still going strong F

czerwiec *m* June

czerw|ienić (**za-**) **się** *człowiek:* blush, redden; **~ień** *f* redness, red; **~onka** *f* dysyntery; **~ony** *adj* red

czesać (**u-**) comb; **~ się** comb one's hair

czeski *adj* Czech; *hist.* Bohemian

Czeszka *f* Czech

cześć *f* worship, (religious) veneration, (*respekt*) reverence; *fig.* worship; **oddawać ~ → czcić;** **~!** hullo!; (*pożegnanie*) bye!, see you!

często *adv* often, frequently; **~kroć** oftentimes, many a time; **~tliwość** *f* frequency

częstować (**po-**) offer (**kogoś s.o.** s.th.); treat (**kogoś czymś** s.o. to s.th.)

częsty *adj* frequent

częściow|o *adv* partly, in part; **~y** *adj* partial

część *f* part; (*udział*) share

czkawka *f* hiccups *pl*

człon *m* segment, section; **~ek** *m* member; *anat. a.* penis; (*ręka, noga*) limb; **~ek rodziny** family member; **~kostwo** *n* membership

człowiek *m* man, human being

cmych|ać ⟨~nąć⟩ flee*, bolt

czołg *m* tank; **~ać się** crawl, creep*

czoł|o *n* brow; **~ówka** *f sp.* lead; *filmu:* opening credits

czosnek *m* garlic

czół|enka *pl* pumps *pl*; **~no** *n* canoe

czter|dzieści *num* forty; **~naście** *num* fourteen; **~osuwowy** *adj* four-stroke; **~y** *num* four; **~ysta** *num* four hundred

czub *m* tuft; **mieć w ~ie** F be* tipsy; **~ek** *m* tip; F *(wariat)* loony F; **~ić się** bicker

czucie *n* feeling

czuć ⟨po-⟩ feel*

czujny *adj* alert, watchful; *sen:* light

czuł|ość *f* tenderness; *phot.* speed; **~y** *adj (kochający)* tender, affectionate; *(wyczulony)* sensitive (**na** to); *phot.* fast

czupryna *f* mop/crop of hair

czupurny *adj* defiant

czuwać be* vigilant, be* on the alert; **w nocy:** keep*/hold* a vigil

czwart|ek *m* Thursday; **~y** *num* fourth

czwor|aczki *pl* quadruplets, quads F *pl*; **~o** *num* four *(children, people of different sexes)*

czwórka *f cyfra:* (a) four; *ludzi:* foursome; *ocena:* good mark; *(powóz)* four-in-hand

czy *pron w pytaniach:* **~ jesteś zdrowy?** are you well?; *rel pron* if, whether; **nie wiem, ~ ...** I don't know if/whether ...

czyhać lurk; lie* in wait *(na* for*)*

czyj (**~a, ~e**) *pron* whose; **~kolwiek** *pron* anybody's

czyli *cj* or, that is to say, in other words

czyn *m* act, deed; **~ić** ⟨u-⟩ make*; **~ić postępy** make* progress; **~ić trudności** make* difficulties; **~ić cuda** work miracles; **~nik** *m* factor; **~ność** *f* activity; *organu, mechanizmu:* function, action; **~ny** *adj* active; *sklep itp.:* open

czynsz *m* rent; **~owy** *adj:* **kamienica ~owa** tenement house

czyrak *m med.* boil

czy|stość *f* cleanness; *osobista:* cleanliness; *tech., fig.* purity; *dźwięku:* clearness; **~sty** *adj* clean; *tech., fig.* pure; **~szczenie** *n* cleaning, cleansing; **~szczenie chemiczne** dry-cleaning; **~ścić** ⟨wy-⟩ clean; cleanse; **~ściec** *m* purgatory

czyt|ać ⟨prze-⟩ read*; **~elnia** *f* library; *sala:* reading-room; **~elnik** *m* reader; **~elny** *adj* legible

ćma *f* moth

ćwiartka f quarter; F *a quarter-litre bottle of vodka*

ćwicz|enie n practice; *fizyczne, pisane:* exercise; **~enia** pl univ. seminar, class; **~yć**

practise; *fizycznie:* exercise; ⟨**wy-**⟩ master; **~yć się** practise (**w czymś** s.th.)

ćwikła f beetroot and horseradish puree

D

dach m roof; **~ówka** f (roof)tile

da|ć pf → **dawać;** **~j mi spokój!** leave me alone!

dal f distance; → a. **skok**

dale|j adv o odległości: farther/further away/off; *fig.* further; *w czasie:* next; later; **i tak ~j** and so on; (**no**) **~j(że)!** come on!; **~ki** adj far-off, remote, distant; **~ko** adv far (away); **z ~ka** from far away; *poet.* from afar

dalekobieżny adj: **pociąg** m ~ long-distance train

dalekowzroczność f med. hyperopia; *fig.* foresight

dalszy adj further

dama f lady; *w kartach:* queen

damski adj ladies', lady's

dancing m dance; **iść na ~** go* to a dance

dane pl data

Dania f Denmark

danie n dish; (*część posiłku*) course; **drugie ~** main course

dar m gift

daremny adj vain, futile

darmo, za ~ adv free (of charge)

darow(yw)ać present (**ko-**

muś coś s.o. with s.th.); *jur.* donate; **winę** itp. forgive*; **życie** spare

daszek m czapki: visor, peak

dat|a f date; **~ować** date; **~ownik** m date-marker

daw|ać give*; **~ca** m donor; **~ka** f dose; **~kować** dose; **~kowanie** n dosage

dawn|iej adv formerly, in the past; **~o** adv long ago; **~o, ~o temu** once upon a time; **od ~a** for a long time; **~y** adj ancient; (*były*) ex-, former

dąb m oak (tree)

dąć ⟨**za-**⟩ blow*

dąsać się sulk

dąż|enie n, **~ność** f striving; **~yć** strive* (**do** for)

dba|ć take* care (**o** of); look after (**o kogoś** s.o.); **nie ~m o** to I don't care; **~łość** f care; **~ły** adj careful

debil F m moron F

decy|dować ⟨**z-**⟩ decide; **~dować się** make* up one's mind; **~zja** f decision

dedykować ⟨**za-**⟩ dedicate

defekt m fault, flaw, damage; *mot.* break-down; *silnika:* engine trouble

defraudacja f embezzlement

deko F n 10 grams (*1/45 of a pound*)

dekolt m décolletage

dekoracja f decoration

dekret m decree

delegat m delegate

delikatesy pl (*smakołyki*) delicacies pl; (*sklep*) delicatessen

delikatny adj delicate, gentle

demaskować ⟨z-⟩ *coś*: unmask; *kogoś*: find* out

demokratyczny adj democratic

demolować ⟨z-⟩ smash up

denat m the deceased

denerwować ⟨z-⟩ irritate, vex; ~ **się** be* angry (*na kogoś* with s.o.); *na egzaminie itp.*: be* nervous/uneasy

dentyst|a m dentist; ~**yczny** adj dentist's; dental

deponować ⟨z-⟩ deposit

deptać ⟨z-⟩ trample, tread*

deseń m pattern

deser m dessert, pudding Brt.

deska f board

deszcz m rain; ~ **pada** it's raining; ~**owy** adj rain ...; *dzień*: rainy

detaliczny adj retail

dębowy adj oak ..., oaken

dętka f mot. inner tube

diabe|lny adj devilish; ~**lski** adj devil's, diabolic(al); ~**ł** m devil, fiend

diament m diamond

diet|a f diet; ~**y** pl travelling allowance

dla prp for; ~**czego** pron why; ~**tego** adv that's why; therefore; ~**tego że** because

dławić choke, smother; *fig.* stifle, smother

dłoń f hand, palm (of the hand)

dłuba|ć F tinker (**przy** at); ~**nina** F f tiresome detailed work

dług m debt

dług|i adj long; ~**o** adv long; **na** ~**o** for a long time

długofalowy adj long-term

długoletni adj of many years

długonogi adj long-legged

długopis m ball-point pen, Biro Brt.

długość f length

długoterminowy adj long-term

długotrwały adj prolonged; long-lasting

długowłosy adj long-haired

dłużej adv longer

dłużn|ik m debtor; ~**y** adj indebted; **być komuś** ~**ym** owe s.o.

dłużyć się drag on

dmucha|ć ⟨~**nąć**⟩ blow*

dnie|ć: ~**je** the day is dawning

dniówka f day's work; (*zapłata*) day's wages pl

dno n bottom; F (*osoba, sytuacja*) the pits F pl

do prp for; *wewnątrz*: into; ~ **domu** home

doba f twenty-four hours, day and night

dobierać select; pick

dobi|(ja)ć give* the coup de grace, finish off F; **~tka:** *na* **~tkę** F to make matters worse, on top of it all F

dob|orowy *adj* choice; *mil.* elite ...; **~ór** *m* selection; **~rać** *pf* → **dobierać**

dobranoc! good night!

dobro *n* prosperity; **~byt** *m* prosperity; **~czynność** *f* charity; **~czynny** *adj* charitable; **~ć** *f* kindness, goodness; **~duszny** *adj* good-natured, kindly; **~tliwy** *adj* good-humoured, kind-hearted

dobrowolny *adj* voluntary

dob|ry *adj* good; **~rze** *adv* well

dobytek *m* belongings *pl*

doby(wa)ć take* out, pull out; *i pokazać:* produce

docelowy *adj* target ...

doceni(a)ć appreciate

dochodowy *adj* profitable; **podatek** *m* **~** income tax

docho|dzenie *n jur.* investigation; **~dzić** reach (*dokądś* a place); **~dzić do czegoś** *fig.* be* successful

dochód *m* income; *z czegoś:* profit

dociąć *pf* → **docinać**

docier|ać ⟨**dotrzeć**⟩ *v/i* reach (*dokądś* s.th.); arrive (*do* at, in); *v/t mot.* run* in

docin|ać tease (*komuś* s.o.); pick (*komuś* on s.o.); **~ek** *m* jibe

docis|kać ⟨**~nąć**⟩ press home; (*dokręcać*) tighten

doczekać się live to see

doczepi(a)ć attach

doda|ć *pf* → **dodawać**; **~tek** *m* addition; *gazetowy:* supplement; *finansowy:* allowance; *na* **~tek** in addition, on top of it all F; **~tkowo** *adv* in addition, additionally; **~tkowy** *adj* extra, additional; **~tni** *adj* positive; *fig.* favourable, beneficial; **~dawać** *adj:* measure add; **~wanie** *n* addition

dogad|ać się *pf* → **dogadywać się**; **~ywać** ⟨**~ać**⟩ *v/i* **docinać**; **~ywać się** come* to an agreement, make* a deal F

dogadzać please; *dziecku:* pamper

doganiać catch* up with

doglądać supervise; *pacjenta itp.* look after

dogodny *adj* convenient; opportune

dogodzić *pf* → **dogadzać**

dogonić *pf* → **doganiać**

dogorywać *człowiek:* be* dying, be* on one's deathbed; *ogień:* be* dying out

dogryzać → **docinać**

doić ⟨**wy-**⟩ milk

doj|azd *m* access, approach; **~azdowy** *adj* access ...; **~echać** *pf* reach (*do czegoś* s.th.); **~eżdżać** *v/i* commute; → *a.* **dojechać**

dojrza|ły *adj* of maturity; **~y** *adj* mature; *owoc, a. fig.:* ripe

dojrze|ć *v/t* (*zauważyć*) notice, spot

dojrze|ć² *v/i pf* → **~wać** mature; *owoc, a. fig.*: ripen

dojść *pf* → **dochodzić**

dokazywać romp (about), frolic (about)

dokąd *pron* where (to)

dokładać add

dokładn|ość *f* accuracy, precision, exactitude; **~y** *adj* exact, precise, accurate

dokoła *prp* round; → *a. dookoła*

dokon(yw)ać perform, carry out, execute; *przestępstwa* commit

dokończ|enie *n* end, conclusion; **~yć** complete, finish (off)

dokręc|ać **⟨~ić⟩** tighten

dokształc|ać **⟨~ić⟩** give* additional training

doktor *m* doctor; **~at** *m* doctorate, doctor's degree, Ph.D. F; *(praca doktorska)* Ph.D. dissertation

dokucz|ać tease; **~liwy** *adj* *człowiek*: trying; *rzecz a.*: persistent; **~yć** *pf* → **dokuczać**

dokument *m* document; **~y** F *pl tożsamości*: identification, I.D. F

dolać *pf* → **dolewać**

doleg|ać trouble, hurt*; ache; **~liwość** *f* complaint

dolewać pour (in) more; *drinka*: top up

dolicz|ać **⟨~yć⟩** add; *do ceny*: charge extra

dolina *f* valley

dolny *adj* lower, bottom ...; ⛿

geogr. Lower

dołącz|ać **⟨~yć⟩** *v/t* attach, connect; **~ać** *(się) v/i* join *(do kogoś* s.o.)

dołożyć *pf* → **dokładać**

dom *m (budowla)* house; *rodzinny*: home

domagać się demand *(czegoś* s.th., *żeby* ... that ...); insist *(czegoś* on s.th., *żeby* ... that ...)

domek *m* cottage

domiar *m podatkowy*: surtax; **na ~ złego** to make matters worse

domiesz|ać add; **~ka** *f* addition; *gastr.* dash

domniemany *adj* alleged

domo|stwo *n* (farm)house; **~wnik** *m* member of the household; **~wy** *adj* house ...; home ...; domestic; → *wojna*

domy|sł *m* guesswork; **~ślać ⟨~ślić⟩ się** guess, suspect, surmise; **~ślny** *adj* *osoba*: smart, bright

doniczka *f* flowerpot

donie|sienia *pl* news *sg*; report(s *pl*); **~ść** *pf* → **donosić**

doniosł|ość *f* importance, significance; **~y** *adj* important, significant

donosi|ciel *m* informer; **~ć ⟨donieść⟩** inform *(na* on, against); *gazeta*: report

donośny *adj* sonorous, loud

dookoła *adv* around; → *a. dokoła*

dopadać hunt down, get*;

(*chwytać*) grab, seize
dopasow(yw)ać fit; adjust
dopaść *pf* → **dopadać**
dopełni|(a)ć complete; **~acz** *m* gr. genitive
dopędz|ać ⟨**~ić**⟩ catch* up with
dopiąć button up; *fig.* ~ **swego** have* one's way
dopie|c *pf* → **~kać** give* a hard time; → *a.* **docinać**
dopiero *adv* barely, scarcely, only; ~ **co** only just
dopilnować see* (*czegoś* to s.th.)
dopis|(yw)ać add; **~ek** **~(yw)ać** fail; **~ek** *m* postscript
dopła|cać ⟨**~cić**⟩ pay* an extra charge; **~ta** *f* extra charge, surcharge
dopom|agać ⟨**~óc**⟩ help
dopom|inać ⟨**~nieć**⟩ się demand; claim (*o coś* s.th.)
dopóki *adv* as long as
dopomóc *pf* → **dopomagać**
doprawdy *adv* really, indeed
doprawi(a)ć *gastr.* season
doprowadz|ać ⟨**~ić**⟩ lead* (*do* to); result (*do* in)
dopu|szczać allow (*do czegoś* s.th.); **~szczać się** commit, perpetrate; **~ścić** *pf* → **dopuszczać**
dopyt(yw)ać się inquire (*o* about)
dorabiać ⟨**~robić**⟩ *v/t* make* (a missing part *etc.*); *v/i* earn extra money; ~ **na boku** F moonlight F

dora|dca *m* adviser (*-or*); **~dzać** ⟨**~dzić**⟩ counsel, advise
dorastać ⟨**~rosnąć**⟩ grow* up
doraźny *adj* immediate; summary; emergency ...
dorę|czać hand in; deliver; **~enie** *n* delivery; **~yciel** *m* postman; **~yć** *pf* → **doręczać**
dorob|ek *m* achievements *pl*; *literacki*: output; **~ić** *pf* → **dorabiać**; **~kiewicz** *m* upstart
doroczny *adj* annual, yearly
dorodny *adj* healthy
doros|ły *adj* adult, grown-up; **~nąć** *pf* → **dorastać**
dorożka *f* cab
dorówn(yw)ać equal
dorsz *m* cod
dorywcz|y *adj*: **praca** *f* **~a** odd job
dorzuc|ać ⟨**~ić**⟩ add, throw* in F
dosięg|ać ⟨**~nąć**⟩ reach
doskonal|e perfect; **~ić** się strive* for perfection (*w* in); **~łość** *f* perfection; **~ły** *adj* perfect
doskwierać trouble
dosłowny *adj* literal
dosłyszeć: **nie** ~ (*mieć słaby słuch*) be* hard of hearing
dostać *pf* → **dostawać**
dostarcz|ać ⟨**~yć**⟩ supply, provide (*coś komuś* s.o. with s.th.); **przesyłkę** *itp.* deliver

dostateczny *adj* sufficient; *ocena*: fair

dostat|ek *m* affluence; **~ni** *adj* affluent

dostawa *f* delivery

dostawać get*, obtain

dostaw|ca *m* supplier; *form.* purveyor; **~i(a)ć** supply; *przesyłkę* deliver

dostęp *m* access; **~ny** *adj miejsce*: accessible; *towar*: available

dostojn|ik *m* dignitary, high official, V.I.P.; **~y** *adj* dignified

dostosow(yw)ać adapt, adjust; **~ się** adapt, conform (*do czegoś* to s.th.)

dostrze|c *pf* **~gać** notice; **~galny** *adj* perceptible, noticeable

dosyć *adv* (*całkiem*) pretty, fairly, rather; (*wystarczająco*) sufficient; *po przymiotniku*: enough; **~ tego!** enough is enough!

dosyp(yw)ać add

doszczętnie *adv* totally, utterly

dosztukow(yw)ać attach

dościg|ać (**~nąć**) catch* up with

dość → **dosyć**

doświadcz|alny *adj* experimental; **~enie** *n phys.*, *chem.* experiment; *życiowe itp.*: experience; **~ony** *adj* experienced; *podróżnik*: seasoned

dotąd *adv o czasie*: till now, until now, to date; *o miejscu*:

up to here; *jak* **~** so far, as yet

dotk|liwy *adj* severe, intense, keen; **~nąć** *pf* → **dotykać**; **~nięcie** *n* touch

dotrzeć *pf* → **docierać**

dotrzym(yw)ać keep*

dotychczas *adv* so far; as yet; **~owy** *adj* ... so far, ... till now

dotycz|ący *adj* relating (*czegoś* to s.th.); concerning (*czegoś* s.th.); **~yć** concern

dotyk *m* touch; **~ać** touch

dowcip *m* joke, witticism; **~ny** *adj* witty

dowi|adywać się inquire (*o* about); *then* (**~edzieć się**) learn*, find* out

dowierzać: nie **~** distrust

dowieść *pf* → **dowodzić²**

dowieźć *pf* → **dowozić**

dowodowy *adj*: **materiał ~** the evidence

dowodzić¹ *armią itp.*: command

dowodzić² *prawdy itp.*: prove

dowolny *adj* (*jakikolwiek*) any; (*przypadkowy*) random

dowozić bring*/supply by car

dowód *m* proof; *form.* evidence; **~ osobisty** identity card, I.D.

dowód|ca *m* commander; **~ztwo** *n* command

dowóz *m* delivery

doza *f fig.* degree

dozgonny *m* lifelong, undying

dozna(wa)ć feel*; experience

dozor|ca *m* caretaker; janitor

Am.; **~ować** supervise

dozować → **dawkować**

dozór *m* supervision; *bez ~oru* unattended

dozwolony *adj* allowed; permitted; *~ od lat 18* X-rated

dożylny *adj* intravenous

dożynki *pl* harvest home (festival)

doży|(wa)ć live (*do* till; to be); **~wocie** F *n jur.* life F; **~wotni** *adj* life(long)

dół *m* (*dziura*) hole (in the ground); (*dolna część*) bottom; (*parter*) downstairs; *w ~* down(wards)

drabina *f* ladder

dramat *m* drama; *fig.* tragedy

drań *m* scoundrel, cad F

drapać ⟨**po-**⟩ scratch; *~ się* scratch oneself; F ⟨**w-**⟩ (*wspinać*) climb

drapieżni|k *m* predator, beast of prey; **~y** *adj* predatory

dra|snąć ⟨**za-**⟩ graze; **~śnięcie** *n* cut, graze

draż|liwy *adj* sensitive; **~nić** ⟨**po-**⟩ irritate, annoy

drąg *m* pole, rod

drążyć ⟨**wy-**⟩ hollow (out)

dres *m* tracksuit

dreszcz *m* shiver, shudder, quiver; **~e** *pl* chill; *mieć ~e* shiver, shudder

drewn|iany *adj* wooden; **~o** *n* wood; (*budulec*) timber

dręczyć torment

drętwieć ⟨**z-**⟩ grow* numb

drg|ać tremble; *usta itp.*: twitch; *tech.* vibrate; **~awki**

pl convulsions *pl*; **~nąć** *pf* → **drgać**

drob|iazg *m* trifle; (*przedmiot*) knick-knack; **~iazgowy** *adj* detailed; meticulous; (*zmiana*) **~ne** *pl* change; **~nostka** *f* trifle; **~ny** *adj* tiny, small; *osoba*: petite

droga *f* road, way

drogeria *f* chemist's *Brt.*, drugstore *Am.*

drogi *adj* expensive; dear; (*kochany*) dear

drogocenny *adj* precious

drogow|skaz *m* (road) sign; **~y** *adj* road ...; traffic ...; *wypadek m ~y* road accident

drożdż|e *pl* yeast; **~owy** *adj* leavened

droż|eć ⟨**po-**⟩ go* up in price; rise* in price; **~yzna** *f* high cost of living

drób *m* poultry

drug|i *num* second; *z dwóch*: the other; *~a godzina* two o'clock; *po ~ie* secondly; **~orzędny** *adj* secondary; (*lichy*) second-rate

druk *m* print; **~arka** *f* printer; **~arnia** *f* printing shop; **~arski** *adj* printing ...; **~arz** *m* printer; **~ować** ⟨**wy-**⟩ print

drut *m* wire

druzgotać ⟨**z-**⟩ shatter, smash; crush

drużyn|a *f* sp. team; *mil.* squad; *harcerska:* troop; **~owy 1.** *adj* team ...; **2.** *m* scoutmaster

drwa *pl* (fire)wood; **~l** *m* lumberjack

drwić

drwi|ć ⟨za-⟩ ridicule (**z kogoś** s.o.), scoff, sneer, jeer (**z** at); **~na** *mst* **~ny** *pl* ridicule, jibe, sneer; jeers *pl*

drzazga *f* splinter

drzeć ⟨po-⟩ tear*

drzem|ać doze, nap; **~ka** *f* doze, nap

drzewo *n* tree; (**drewno**) wood

drzwi *pl* door

drżeć ⟨za-⟩ tremble, shiver (**z** with)

duch *m* ghost; spirit

duchow|ieństwo *n* clergy; **~ny 1.** *m* clergyman; priest; **2.** *adj* ecclesiastic; **~y** *adj* spiritual

dud|ek *m*: **wystrychnąć kogoś na ~ka** *fig.* make* a fool of s.o.

dudnić ⟨za-⟩ rumble; thunder

duma *f* pride; **~ny** *adj* proud

Du|nka *f* (**~ńczyk** *m*) Dane; **2ński** *adj* Danish

dur *m* *mus.* major; *med.* typhoid

dur|eń *F m* fool, nitwit F; **~ny** *F adj* stupid, foolish

durzyć się *F* have* a crush (**w** on)

dusić ⟨u-⟩ choke, stifle; (**by zabić**) strangle; throttle; ⟨z-⟩ **papierosa** put* out; (fig.) suppress, stifle; **~ się** choke, suffocate

dusza *f* soul

duszkiem *adv* in one gulp/ draught

duszny *adj* *pogoda*: sultry; *pokój*: stuffy; *zapach*: sickly

duszony *adj* *gastr.* stewed

dużo *adv wody, miłości itp.*: a lot, much; **za ~o wody** too much water; *książek, ludzi itp.*: a lot, many; **za ~o ludzi** too many people; **~y** *adj* big, large

dwa *num* two; **~dzieścia** *num* twenty; **~naście** *num* twelve

dwieście *num* two hundred

dwo|ić się : **~ić się i troić** bustle about; **~isty** *adj* dual, twofold; **~jaczki** *pl* twins *pl*; **~jaki** *adj* twofold; **~je** *num* two (*children, people of different sexes*)

dworcowy *adj* station ...

dworek *m* (small) manor-house

dworzec *m* (**kolejowy/autobusowy**) railway/coach) station

dwójka *f* (**cyfra**) (a) two; *ludzi*: twosome, couple; *w kartach*: deuce; (*ocena*) fail, bad mark

dwór *m* manor (house)

dwubarwny *adj* two-coloured

dwucyfrowy *adj* two-digit

dwudniowy *adj* two-day

dwudziestoletni *adj* twenty-year-old

dwudziesty *num* twentieth

dwukołowy *adj* two-wheeled

dwukropek *m* colon

dwukrotnie *adv* twice

dwukrotny *adj* repeated

dwulicowy *adj* double-faced, double-dealing

dwunasty *num* twelfth

dwuosobowy *adj* for two persons; *mot.* **samochód** *m* ~ two-seater

dwupiętrowy *adj* two-storey

dwupokojowy *adj* two-room

dwustronny *adj* two-sided; *polit.* bilateral

dwutygodnik *m* biweekly

dwuznaczny *adj* ambiguous

dygnitarz *m* dignitary, V.I.P. F

dygotać shiver, tremble

dykta → **sklejka**

dykt|ando *f* resignation; **~ator** *m* dictator; **~atura** *f* dictatorship; **~ować** ⟨**po-**⟩ dictate

dym *m* smoke; **~ić (się)** smoke

dymisj|a *f* resignation; **podać się do ~i** hand in one's resignation

dyndać dangle

dynia *f* pumpkin

dyplom *m* certificate

dyploma|cja *f* diplomacy; **~ta** *m* diplomat; **~tyczny** *adj* diplomatic

dyrek|cja *f* management, board of directors; **~tor** *m* director

dyryg|ent *m* conductor; **~ować** conduct

dysk *m* disc Brt., disk Am.; *sp.* discus; **komputerowy:** disk; **twardy** ~ hard disk; **~ietka** floppy (disk)

dyskretny *adj* discreet

dyskrymin|acja *f* discrimination; **~ować** discriminate (**kogoś** against s.o.)

dysku|sja *f* debate; **~tować** debate

dyskwalifik|acja *f* disqualification; **~ować** ⟨**z-**⟩ disqualify

dystans *m* distance

dystyngowany *adj* dignified

dysza *f* jet

dyszeć pant

dywan *m* carpet

dyżur *m* duty; **nocny** ~ night duty; **~ny** *m* mil. orderly; **szkolny:** prefect Brt.

dzban(ek) *m* jug Brt., pitcher Am.

dziać się occur, happen; **co się dzieje?** what's going on?, what's up?

dziadek *m* grandfather

dział *m* section, department

działa|cz *m* activist; **~ć** be* active; **maszyna:** work; **~lność** *f* work; **~nie** *n* activities *pl*

działka *f* plot (of land)

działo *n* gun, mil. artillery piece

dziarski *adj* brisk, lively

dziczyzna *f* game

dzieci|ak *m*, **~ę** *n* child; **~ęcy** *adj* child ..., children's; **~nny** *adj* infantile; **~ństwo** *n* childhood; **~ko** *n* child

dziedzi|ctwo *n* heritage; **~czny** *adj* hereditary; **~czyć** ⟨**o-**⟩ inherit

dziedzina *f* field

dziedziniec *m* courtyard

dzieje *pl* history; **~owy** *adj* historical

dziel|enie n distribution; *math.* division; **~ić ⟨po-⟩** distribute; *math.* divide; **~ić się** share (**z** with); *math.* divide; **być** divisible; **~nica** f quarter, district; neighbourhood F

dzieln|ość f gallantry; **~y** adj gallant

dzieło n work; **~ sztuki** work of art

dzie|nnie adv daily; **~ś** a day's; **~nnik** m daily; **~nnikarz** m journalist; **~nny** adj day; **~ń** m day; **co ~ń** daily, every day; **~ń powszedni** weekday; **~ń dobry!** good morning!; **po południu** : good afternoon!

dzierżaw|a f lease; **~ca** m leaseholder; **~ić** hold* on lease; **⟨wy-⟩** lease

dziesiąt|ka f (a) ten; **~aty** num tenth; **~eciobój** m decathlon; **~eciolecie** n decade; **~eć** num ten; **~etny** adj decimal

dziewcz|ęcy adj girlish; **~yna** f girl; (*sympatia*) girlfriend; **~ynka** f little girl

dziewiąt|ka f (a) nine; **~y** num ninth

dziewi|ca f virgin; **~czy** adj virgin ...

dziewięć num nine; **~dziesiąt** num ninety; **~set** num nine hundred; **~tnaście** num nineteen

dziew|ka, ~ucha f wench

dzięcioł m woodpecker

dzięk|czynny adj thanksgiving; **~i 1.** pl thanks pl; **2.** prp thanks, owing (**czemuś** to s.th.); **~i Bogu!** thank God!; **~ować ⟨po-⟩** thank (**za** for)

dzik m (wild) boar

dziki adj wild

dzioba|ć ⟨~nąć⟩ peck; **~ty** F adj pock-marked

dzi|obowy adj fore(...); **~ób** m zo. beak; bill; mar. bow(s pl)

dzisiejszy adj today's; fig. present-day; **~siaj**, **~ś** adv today

dziur|a f hole; **~awić ⟨po-⟩** make* a hole, make* holes; **~awy** adj with holes in it; (*cieknący*) leaky; **~ka** f little hole; **~kować** punch, perforate

dziw|actwo n eccentricity; **~aczny** adj eccentric; **~ak** m eccentric, crank F, oddball F; **~ić ⟨z-⟩ się** be* surprised (**czymś** at s.th.)

dziwka V f contp. slut F, tramp F; (*prostytutka*) whore

dziw|ny adj strange; odd; funny; **~oląg** m freak

dzwon m bell; **~y** pl spodnie: bell-bottoms pl; **~ek** m do drzwi: doorbell; **~ić ⟨za-⟩** ring* (**czymś** s.th.); (*telefonować*) ring* up; call Am. (**do kogoś** s.o.); **~nica** f belfry

dźwię|czeć ⟨za-⟩ ring*; **~czny** adj głos: sonorous; głoska: voiced; **~k** m sound, noise; **~kowy** adj sound ...

dźwig m crane; → a. **winda**; **∼ać** ⟨**∼nąć**⟩ lift; **∼nia** f lever
dżdżownica f earthworm
dżdżysty adj rainy

dżem m jam
dżins m (*materiał*) denim; **∼y** pl jeans pl
dżungla f jungle

E

echo n echo
edy|cja f edition; **komputerowe ∼cje tekstu** word processing; **∼tor** m **tekstu** word-processing program
efek|ciarski adj flashy; **∼ciarz** m show-off; **∼t** m effect; **∼towny** adj strój itp.: showy; *uroda*: striking, impressive; (*widowiskowy*) spectacular
egoistyczny adj egoistic, selfish
egzamin m exam(ination)
egzekucja f execution
egzemplarz m copy; (*okaz*) specimen
ekipa f team
ekonomi|a f economy; **∼sta** m economist
ekran m screen
ekspe|dient(ka f) m shop assistant; **∼dycja** f (*dział*) dispatch office, shipping department; (*wyprawa*) expedition
ekspert m expert
eksploatacja f operation; (*utrzymanie*) maintenance
eksplo|dować explode; **∼zja** f explosion
eksponat m exhibit

ekspres m (*pociąg*) express (train); (*list*) express letter *Brt.*, express delivery letter *Am.*
ekwipunek m equipment, gear
elastyczny adj elastic; *fig.* flexible
elegancj|a f elegance; **∼ki** adj elegant, smart *Brt.*
elektrociepłownia f heat- and power-generating plant
elektroni|czny adj electronic; **∼ka** f electronics sg
elektrownia f power plant
elektrowóz m electric locomotive
elektryczn|ość f electricity; **∼y** adj electric(al)
element m element; **∼arny** adj elementary, fundamental; **∼arz** m ABC-book
eliminacje pl sp. preliminaries pl
emaliowany adj enamelled
emblemat m emblem
emeryt|(ka f) m old-age pensioner, OAP *Brt.*; **∼ura** f retirement; (*świadczenie*) old age pension *Brt.*; **przejść na ∼urę** retire, be* pensioned off

emigra|cja f emigration; **~nt** m emigrant; *polityczny*: émigré

energi|a f energy; **~czny** adj vigorous, energetic

entuzjazm m enthusiasm; **~ować się** be* enthusiastic

epilepsja f epilepsy

epizod m (unimportant) event

epok|a f epoch; **~owy** adj epoch-making

erekcja f erection

erotyczny adj erotic

erozja f erosion

esencja f essence

eskort|a f escort; **pod ~ą** under escort; **~ować** escort, follow

estetyczny adj pleasing to the eye; *phls.* (a)esthetic

Esto|nia f Estonia; **~nka** f (**~nczyk** m) Estonian; **2ński** adj Estonian

etap m stage

etat adj post, position; **~owy** adj full-time

ete|r m fig.: **na falach ~ru, w ~rze** on the air

etykiet(k)a f (*nalepka*) label

Europej|czyk m (**~ka** f) European; **2ski** adj European

ewakua|cja f evacuation; **~ować (się)** evacuate

ewangeli|cki adj Protestant; Lutheran; **~k** m Protestant; Lutheran

ewentualny adj possible

ewidencja f records pl, files pl

F

fabry|czny adj factory ...; **znak** m **~czny** trademark; **~ka** f factory, plant; **~kować** ⟨**s-**⟩ fabricate

fabularny adj: **film** m **~** feature film

fabuła f plot, story F

facet F m bloke F *Brt.*, guy F *Am.*

fachow|iec m professional, expert; **~y** adj professional

fajka f pipe

fajny F adj terrific, great, neat *Am.*

fakt m fact; **~yczny** adj actual; real

fal|a f a. phys. wave; **~isty** adj wavy; **~ochron** m breakwater; **~ować** wave

fałda f fold; *na materiale*: crease

fałsz m insincerity, falsity; **~erstwo** n forgery, falsification; **~erz** m forger; **~ować** ⟨**s-**⟩ forge, counterfeit; *zawartość dokumentu itp.* falsify; *mus.* sing*/play out of tune; **~ywy** adj fake, counterfeit; *człowiek*: false; *mus.* out of tune

fantazja f (*wyobraźnia*) imagination; (*wymysł*) fiction;

(*kaprys*) whim

farb|a *f* paint; **~ować** ⟨**po-**⟩ dye

fartuch *m* apron

fasola *f* bean(s *pl*)

fason *m ubioru*: cut; *fig.* dash, style; **z ~em** with a dash, in style

faszy|zm *m* fascism; **~stow-ski** *adj* fascist

fatalny *adj* wretched

fatyg|a *f* trouble; **~ować** trouble; **~** ⟨**po-**⟩ **się** bother to go* (and get*)

faul *m* foul; **~ować** foul

faza *f* phase

federa|cja *f* federation; **~lny** *adj* federal

feralny *adj* ill-fated

fermentować ⟨**s-**⟩ ferment

festyn *m* festival, carnival, fair

fig|a *f* fig (tree); **~ę z makiem!** F nothing doing! F

figiel *m* joke, trick, prank, lark *Brt.*

figura *f* figure; *fig.* V.I.P. F

filc *m* felt; **~owy** *adj* felt ...

filharmonia *f* philharmonic

filia *f* branch (office *etc.*); *przedsiębiorstwa*: subsidiary (company)

filiżanka *f* cup

film *m* film; **~ować** ⟨**s-**⟩ film; **~owy** *adj* film ...; *form.* cinematic

filozof *m* philosopher; **~ia** *f* philosophy

filtr *m* filter

Fin *m* Finn

finał *m* final

finans|e *pl* finances *pl*; **~ować** ⟨**s-**⟩ finance; sponsor

finisz *m* the finish; the final spurt; **~ować** make* the final spurt in a race

Fin|ka *f* Finn; **~landia** *f* Finland

fiński *adj* Finnish

fioletowy *adj* purple, violet

fiołek *m* violet

firanka *f* net curtain

firm|a *f* company, firm; **~owy** *adj* company ...; **danie** *n* **~owe** chef's special; **znak** *m* **~owy** trademark

fizy|czny *adj* physical; **pra-cownik** *m* **~czny** blue-collar worker; **~ka** *f* physics *sg*

flaga *f* flag

flaki F *pl* guts *pl*; *gastr.* tripe

flakon *m* flower vase

fladra *f zo.* flounder

flegmatyczny *adj* phlegmatic; F sluggish

flesz *m* flashlight, flash F; (*sprzęt*) flashgun

flet *m* flute

flirtować flirt

flota *f* fleet

foka *f* seal

folia *f* wrapping film; *aluminiowa*: foil

folklor *m* folk traditions *pl*; folklore

form|a *f* form; **~alność** *f* formality; **~ować** ⟨**u-**⟩ form; **~uł(k)a** *f* formula

forsa F *f* dough F, bread F

forsow|ać advocate; ⟨prze-⟩ *mięsień itp.* strain; ⟨s-⟩ *drzwi itp.* force; **~ny** adj strenuous

fortepian m (grand) piano

fortuna f fortune

fotel m armchair; easy chair

fotograf m photographer; **~ia** f (odbitka) photo(graph), print F; *sztuka, rzemiosło:* photography; **~iczny** adj photographic; **~ik** m photographer; **~ować** ⟨s-⟩ photograph

fotokopia f photocopy

fracht m carriage, freight; (towar a.) consignment, shipment; **~owiec** m freighter

frak m tails pl

Franc|ja f France; **2uski** adj French; **~uz** m Frenchman; **~uzka** f Frenchwoman

frędzl|a f tassel; **~e** pl fringe

front m mil. front line; **~**

~owy adj front-line

fryz|jer(ka f) m hairdresser; **~jer męski** a. barber; **~ura** f hairstyle, hairdo F

fund|acja f foundation; **~ować** ⟨u-⟩ sponsor; ⟨za-⟩ F buy* (coś komuś s.o. s.th.); treat (coś komuś s.o. to s.th.); **~usz** m fund

funkcj|a f function; **~onariusz** m operative; **~onować** function

funt m pound

furgonetka f (delivery) van

furia f fury

furt(k)a f gate

fusy pl grounds pl

fuszer|ka f botch(-up); **~ować** ⟨s-⟩ botch (up), bungle

futerał m case

futro n fur; (płaszcz a.) fur coat

futryna f door frame; okienna: window frame

futrzany adj fur ...

G

gabinet m office; (prywatny pokój do pracy) study; **~ lekarski** surgery Brt., doctor's office Am.

gablot(k)a f showcase, glass case

gad m reptile

gada|ć F chatter; **~anie** m chatter; **~anina** F f idle talk; **~atliwy** adj talkative; **~uła** f chatterbox

gafa f blunder, bloomer

gaj m grove; **~owy** m game warden

galanteria f accessories pl

galaret(k)a f jelly

galeria f gallery

galon m (miara) gallon

galop m gallop; skrócony **~** canter; **~ować** ⟨po-⟩ gallop; krótki: canter

galowy adj: strój m **~** full dress

gałąź f branch

gałka f ball, knob; ~ **oczna** eyeball

gama f muz. scale; fig. range, gamut, array

ganek m porch

ganić ⟨z-⟩ rebuke, blame

gap|a f sleepyhead; **na ~ę** adv without paying the fare; **pasażer m na ~ę** a passenger without a ticket; mar. stowaway; ~**ić się** stare, gape; ~**iowaty** F adj thick, slow (on the uptake)

garaż m garage

garb m hump

garb|aty adj with a hump; ~**ić się** ⟨z-⟩ stoop, hunch

garbus m contp. humpback, hunchback

gardło n throat; fig. **wąskie ~** bottleneck

gardzić → **pogardzać**

garmażeryjn|y: **wyroby** pl ~**e** ready-to-cook/-serve foods

garnek m pot

garnitur m suit

garsonka f twin-set

gar|stka, ~ść f handful

gasić ⟨z-⟩ papierosa, ogień put* out, extinguish; światło, silnik switch/turn off; ~**nąć** ⟨z-⟩ go out, die down

gaśnica f fire extinguisher

gatun|ek m (jakość) quality; (rodzaj, typ) brand; zo., bot. species; ~**kowy** adj high-quality

gawę|da f tale; ~**dzić** ⟨po-⟩ chat

gaworzyć babble

gaz m (łzawiący/ziemny tear/natural) gas

gaza f gauze

gazet|a f (news)paper; ~**owy** adj newspaper ...

gazo|ciąg m gas main; ~**mierz** m gas meter; ~**wnia** f gasworks sg; ~**wy** adj gas ...

gaźnik m carburettor

gąbka f sponge

gąsienica f zo. caterpillar; tech. caterpillar track

gąszcz m thicket

gbur m boor; ~**owaty** adj boorish

gderać grumble; nag

gdy cj when; as; ~**by** cj if; ~**ż** cj because

gdzie pron where; ~ **indziej** pron somewhere else, elsewhere; ~**kolwiek** pron anywhere

generał m general

geniusz m genius

geografi|a f geography; ~**czny** adj geographic(al)

geologi|a f geology; ~**czny** adj geological

geometr|ia f geometry; ~**yczny** adj geometrical

gęba F f mug F

gęst|nieć ⟨z-⟩ thicken; ~**y** adj płyn: thick; mgła, tłum a.: dense

gęś f goose

giąć ⟨z-⟩ bend*

giełda f stock exchange

giętk|i adj elastic; człowiek a.: flexible; ~**ość** f elasticity; flexibility

gimnasty|czny adj gymnastic; **~ka** f gymnastics sg

ginąć ⟨z-⟩ (tracić życie) perish, die; (przepadać) be* gone, disappear; rzecz a.: be* lost

ginekolog m gyn(a)ecologist

gips m plaster; **~ować** ⟨za-⟩ plaster

gitara f guitar

glazura f glaze; (płytki) tiles

gleba f soil

glin|a f clay; **~iany** adj clay ...; **~iasty** adj clay-like

glista f worm

glon m alga, mst algae pl

gła|dki adj smooth; **~dzić** ⟨wy-⟩ smooth

głaskać ⟨po-⟩ stroke, pet

głaz m boulder, (big) stone

głębi|a f depth; fig. profoundness; **~ia ostrości** depth of field; **w ~i** in the background; **~ina** f the deep; **~oki** adj deep; **~okość** f depth

głod|ny adj hungry; **~ować** starve; **~owy** adj hunger ..., starvation ...; **~ówka** f hunger strike

głos m voice; polit. vote; **na ~** adv aloud; **prosić o ~** ask leave to speak; **~ić** preach; **~ka** f speech sound; **~ować** vote; **~owanie** n vote, voting

głoś|nik m loudspeaker; **~no** adv aloud; loudly; **~ny** adj loud

głow|a f head; **~ica** f tech. head

głód m hunger; (klęska głodu) famine

głów|nie adv mostly, chiefly, mainly, for the most part; **~y** adj chief, main, principal

głuch|awy adj hard of hearing; **~nąć** ⟨o-⟩ grow*/become* deaf; **~oniemy 1.** adj deaf and dumb, deaf mute; **2.** m deaf-and-dumb person; deaf-mute; **~ota** f deafness; **~y** adj człowiek: deaf; dźwięk: dull, hollow

głup|i adj stupid; **~iec** m fool; **~ota** f stupidity, foolishness; **~stwo** n blunder; palnąć **~stwo** put one's foot in; (drobiazg) trifle; **to ~stwo!** don't mention it!

gmach m edifice

gmatwać ⟨po-, za-⟩ confuse, muddle up

gmin|a f commune; F (urząd gminny) local administration; **~ny** adj community ...

gnębić harass, pester; hist. oppress

gniazd|ko n tech. socket; fig. love nest; **~o** n nest

gnić ⟨z-⟩ decay, rot

gnieść ⟨z-⟩ crush, press, squash

gniew m anger; wrath; **~ać** ⟨roz-⟩ anger; **~ać się** be* angry (na with; at); **~ny** adj angry

gnieździć się fig. w ciasnym pokoju: be* cooped up

gno|ić ⟨z-⟩ F humiliate; **~jówka** f liquid manure

gnój m manure

godn|ość f dignity; **~y** adj worthy (**czegoś** of s.th.); ...worthy; **~y pochwały** praiseworthy; **~y podziwu** admirable; **~y pogardy** contemptible, despicable; **~y poża-łowania** regrettable, lamentable

godzić ⟨po-⟩ się : **~ z kimś** be* reconciled with s.o.; **~ z czymś** reconcile o.s. with s.th.

godzina f hour; **która ~ ?** what's the time?; **pierwsza ~** one o'clock

godziwy adj fair

goić ⟨wy-⟩ heal; **~ się ⟨za-⟩** heal

gol m goal

golas F m naked person; **na ~a** F adv in the nude, naked

golenie n shaving; **maszyn-ka** f **do ~a** shaver

goleń f shinbone

golić ⟨o-⟩ (się) shave

golonka f pickled knuckle of pork

gołąb m pigeon, dove; **~ek** m gastr. stuffed cabbage

gołoledź f black ice

gołosłowny adj unfounded

goły adj naked

goni|ć chase, pursuit; sp. race **~ec** m office boy; szachy: bishop; **~twa** f chase, pursuit; sp. race

gont m shingle

gończy adj: **list ~** warrant; plakat: wanted poster

gorąc|o 1. n heat; **2.** adv hotly, hot; **jest ~o** it's hot; **jest**

mi ~o I'm hot; **~y** adj hot

gorączk|a f fever; **~ować** have* a fever, be* feverish; **~ować się** F be* all worked up

gorliw|ość f zeal, ardour, eagerness; **~y** adj zealous, ardent, eager, keen

gorsz|ący adj scandalous; disgraceful; **~y** adj worse; inferior; **~yć ⟨z-⟩** shock; (demoralizować) **~yć ⟨z-⟩ się** be* scandalized/ shocked

gorycz f bitterness

goryl m zo. gorilla; F (ochroniarz) bodyguard

gorzał|ka f F booze F

gorzej adv comp. worse

gorzk|i adj bitter; **~nieć ⟨z-⟩** grow*/become* bitter

gospod|arczy adj economic; **~arka** f economy; **~arny** adj thrifty; **~arować** keep house; run (a farm); **~arstwo** n: **~arstwo domowe** household; **~arstwo rolne** farm; **~arz** m host; na wsi: farmer; **~yni** f hostess; na wsi: farmer's wife

gość|ić v/t a. **⟨u-⟩** receive, have*, entertain; v/i be* a guest, be* received/entertained; **~cina** f visit; **być u ko-goś w ~cinie** be* s.o.'s guest; **~cinny** adj hospitable; **pokój ~cinny** guest room; **~ć** m guest; → **↓ facet**

gotowa|ć ⟨u-⟩ cook; **~ny** adj boiled

got|owość f readiness; **~owy**,
~ów adj ready; **~ówka** f cash

goździk m bot. carnation; **~i**
pl gastr. cloves pl

góra f (górna część) top;
geogr. mountain; (górne
piętro) upper floor; **w ~rę**
up(wards); **~ral(ka** f) m
highlander; **~rka** f mound,
hillock; **~rnictwo** n mining;
~rniczy adj mining ...; **~rnik**
m miner; **~rny** adj upper;
~rować dominate, dwarf
(nad czymś s.th.); człowiek :
outshine* (nad kimś s.o.);
~rski adj mountain ...; **~ry** pl
mountains pl; **~rzysty** adj
mountainous

gra f game

grabić¹ ⟨o-⟩ (łupić) plunder,
pillage, loot

grabić² ⟨z-⟩ grabiami: rake
(up); **~e** pl rake

grabieć ⟨z-⟩ grow* numb
(with cold)

grabież f plunder, pillage

gracz m player

grać ⟨za-⟩ play; **~ w karty**
play cards; **~ na fortepianie**
play the piano

grad m hail; (kulka) hailstone

grafi|czny adj graphic; **~k** m
graphic artist; **~ka** f graphics
pl; (obrazek) etching, engra-
ving, print F

gramatyka f grammar

gramofon m gramophone,
record player

granat¹ mil. grenade; bot.
pomegranate

granat² m (kolor) navy blue;
~owy adj navy blue

granda F f scandal

grani|ca f border, frontier;
fig. limit; **~ce** pl bounds pl,
confines pl, frontiers pl;
(być) za **~cą** (be*) abroad;
jechać za **~cę** go* abroad;
~czyć border (z on)

grat F m (samochód) bone-
shaker, banger Brt.; **~y** pl
(stare meble itp.) lumber,
junk

gratis(owy) adj free (of charge)

gratulacje pl congratulations
pl

grdyka f Adam's apple

Gre|cja f Greece; **2cki** adj
Greek; **~k** m (**~czynka** f)
Greek

grobow|iec m tomb; **~y** adj
fig. dismal, gloomy

groch m pea(s pl); **~ówka** f
pea soup

grodzić ⟨o-⟩ fence

groma|da f herd, bunch F;
~dzić ⟨na-, z-⟩ accumulate,
gather; **~dzić się** gather

grono n cluster, bunch; **~ zna-
jomych** acquaintances; **~wy**
adj grape ...

grosz m penny

grosz|ek m gastr. green pea(s
pl); bot. sweet pea; **w ~ki**
polka-dotted

groza f terror; **~zić** threaten;
~źba f threat, menace; **~źny**
adj threatening, menacing,
sinister; choroba: grave; wy-

padek: serious, ugly F, nasty F

grób *m* grave

grubas F *m* fatty F, fatso F

grubia|nin *m* boor; **~ński** *adj* rude, coarse, boorish

grubość *f* thickness

gruboziarnisty *adj* coarse-grained

gruby *adj* thick; *człowiek*: fat

gruchać coo

gruczoł *m* gland

grudzień *m* December

grunt *m* (*ziemia*) land; **~owny** *adj* thorough; *wiedza a.*: profound

grup|a *f* group; **~owy** *adj* group ...; (*wspólny*) common

grusz|a *f* pear (tree); **~ka** *f* pear; → *a.* **grusza**

gruz *m* rubble; **~y** *pl* débris, rubble; *fig.* ruins

gruźlica *f* tuberculosis, TB F

grypa *f* influenza, flu F

gryzący *adj* pungent, acrid

gryzmolić ⟨na-⟩ scrawl, scribble

gryzoń *m* rodent

gryźć ⟨u-⟩ bite*

grzać ⟨o-⟩ heat, warm (up)

grzałka *f* heater; *tech.* heating element

grzanka *f* toast

grząski *adj* miry, sticky

grzbiet *m* back; *anat. a.* spine; *górski*: ridge

grzebać *v/i* fumble; ⟨po-⟩ *v/t* bury

grzebień *m* comb

grzech *m* sin

grzechot|ać rattle; **~ka** *f* rattle

grzeczn|ość *f* politeness, courteousness; (*przysługa*) favour; **~y** *adj* polite, courteous; *dziecko*: good

grzejnik *m* heater; (*kaloryfer*) radiator

grzeszyć ⟨z-⟩ sin

grzęznąć ⟨u-⟩ get* stuck

grzmieć ⟨za-⟩ roar; *piorun*: thunder; *głos itp.*: boom; **~ot** *m* thunder(bolt)

grzyb *m* mushroom; *med., bot.* fungus

grzyw|a *f* mane; **~ka** *f* fringe

grzywna *f* fine

gubić ⟨z-⟩ lose*

gum|a *f* rubber; *w odzieży*: elastic; **~a do żucia** chewing gum; **~ka** *f* eraser *Am.*, rubber *Brt.*; *do włosów itp.* rubber/elastic band; **~owy** *adj* rubber ...

gust *m* taste; **~owny** *adj* tasteful, in good taste

guz *m* bump; *med.* tumour

guzdrać się F dawdle, dally

guzik *m* button

gwałcić ⟨z-⟩ rape; *fig.* violate; **~t** *m* rape; **~towny** *adj* violent

gwaran|cja *f* guarantee; **~tować** ⟨za-⟩ guarantee

gwiazd|a *f* star (*a. fig*); **~ka** *f* star; (*aktorka*) starlet; **Ջka** *f* Christmas; **~kowy** *adj* Christmas ...; **~ozbiór** *m* constellation

gwiezdny *adj* star ...; *form.* astral

gwint m thread

gwizd m whistle; *syreny itp.*: hoot, toot; **~ać** v/i whistle; *syrena itp.*: hoot, toot;

~ek m whistle; **~nąć** F v/t pf pinch F, rip off F; → a. **gwizdać**

gwóźdź m nail

H

haczyk m hook; **~owaty** adj hooked

haft m embroidery; **~ka** f hook and eye; **~ować** ⟨wy-⟩ embroider

hak m hook

hala f wystawowa itp.: hall; *górska*: mountain pasture; *fabryczna*: shop

halka f slip

hała|s m noise; din; **~sować** ⟨na-⟩ make* a noise; **~śliwy** adj noisy

hamak m hammock

ham|ować ⟨za-⟩ brake; **~ulec** m brake; **~ulec bez-pieczeństwa** emergency cord Am., communication cord Brt.

hand|el m business, commerce; *(detaliczny/wewnętrz-ny/zagraniczny* retail/do-mestic/foreign) trade; **~larz** m trader, tradesman; **~lo-wać** trade, deal (**czymś** in s.th.); **~lowiec** m salesman; **~lowy** adj trade ..., commercial

haniebny adj shameful, dis-graceful

hań|ba f disgrace, shame, dis-honour; **~ić** ⟨z-⟩ disgrace

harce|rstwo n scouting; **~rka** f scout Am., girl guide Brt.; **~rz** m (boy) scout

hardy adj haughty

harmoni|a f harmony; F (*in-strument*) accordion; **~jka** → **organki**

harować toil

hart m fortitude; **~ować** ⟨za-⟩ tech. temper, anneal; *fig.* toughen

hasło n slogan; *słownikowe*: entry

hazard m gambling

hełm m helmet

herb m (coat of) arms; (*tarcza herbowa*) escutcheon

herbat|a f tea; **~nik** m biscuit

herezja f heresy

hetman m szachy: queen

higien|a f hygiene; **~iczny** adj hygienic

hierarchia f hierarchy

hipno|tyczny adj hypnotic; **~za** f hypnosis

hipopotam m hippopotamus, hippo F

hipoteka f mortgage

hister|ia f hysteria; **~yczny** adj hysterical

histor|ia f history; (*opowieść*) story; **~yczny** adj historical;

~yk m historian
Hiszpa|nia f Spain; **~n(ka** f) m Spaniard; **2ński** adj Spanish
hodowl|ać ⟨**wy-**⟩ raise; zwierzęta a. breed, rear; rośliny a. grow; **~ca** m zwierząt: breeder; roślin: grower; **~la** f zwierząt: breeding, farming; roślin: growing; (zakład) farm; (dziedzina) animal husbandry
hojn|ość f generosity; **~y** adj generous
hokej m: **~ na lodzie** ice hockey; **~ na trawie** hockey Brt., field hockey Am.
hol m (przedpokój) hall; mar., mot. tow line; **na ~u** on tow
Holl|andia f the Netherlands pl, Holland; **~ender** m Dutchman; **~enderka** f Dutchwoman; **2enderski** adj Dutch
holow|ać ⟨**od-**⟩ tow; **~nik** m tug (boat)
hołdować zasadom: profess; modzie: follow indiscriminately
hołota f rabble, riffraff
honor m honour; **słowo ~u!** take my word for it!, honour bright! F Brt.; **~arium** n fee;

~owy adj człowiek, wyjście: honourable; (tytularny) honorary
horyzont m horison
hotel m hotel
hrabi|a m count, earl Brt.; **~na** f countess
hucz|eć ⟨**za-**⟩ roar, boom; **~ny** adj (okazały) ostentatious; (hałaśliwy) riotous
huk m bang, boom, roar; **~nąć** bang; (krzyknąć) bellow, roar
hula|ć carouse; **~noga** f scooter
humor m humour; (nastrój) mood
huragan m hurricane
hurt m wholesale trade; **~em** adv wholesale; **~ownia** f wholesale outlet
huśta|ć (się) rock, swing; **~wka** f swing; pozioma: seesaw
hut|a f: **~a szkła** glassworks; **~a żelaza** ironworks; **~nictwo** n metallurgy; **~niczy** adj metallurgic; **piec ~ niczy** blast furnace; **~nik** m ironworker
hydraulik m plumber
hymn m państwowy: anthem

I

i cj and
ich pron their(s)
idea f idea, notion; **~lny** adj ideal, perfect

idiota m idiot, moron F
igła f needle
igra|ć play; **~szka** f play
igrzyska pl: **2 olimpijskie**

Olympic Games

ile *pron* wody, miłości how much; książek, ludzi how many; **~kroć** *adv* every time, whenever

ilo|czyn *m* product, ratio; **~raz** *m* quotient; **~ść** *f* quantity, amount

iluzjonista *m* conjurer, (stage) magician

im: ~ ... tym ... the ... the ...; ~ **wcześniej tym lepiej** the sooner the better

imadło *n* vice

imbryk *m* teapot

imi|eniny *pl* nameday; **~ennik** *m* namesake; **~ę** *n* Christian name *Brt.*, first name *Am.*

imponować impress (**komuś** s.o.); **~ujący** *adj* impressive

import *m* import; **~owany** *adj* imported

impreza *f* artystyczna: show; F (przyjęcie) party

inaczej *adv* differently; (w przeciwnym razie) otherwise

incydent *m* incident, (unimportant) event

indy|czka *f* turkey hen; **~k** *m* turkey (cock)

inform|acja *f* (piece of) information, dope F; **~ować** inform; **~ować się** inquire

inny *adj* (some) other; (różny) different (**niż** from)

inspekcja *f* (tour of) inspection

instalator *m* fitter; (hydraulik) plumber

instrukcja *f* instruction; ~ **obsługi** instruction book/ manual

instrument *m* instrument

instytucja *f* institution

inteligen|cja *f* (grupa) intelligentsia; *psych.* intelligence; **~tny** *adj* intelligent, bright F

intencja *f* intention

interes *m* interest; *econ.* business; **~ant** *m* member of the public who has business in an office; (osoba pytająca) inquirer; (klient) customer; (klient) customer; ~**ować się** be* interested (**czymś** in s.th.); **~ujący** *adj* interesting; exciting

interpretacja *f* interpretation

intratny *adj* lucrative, profitable

intruz *m* intruder

inwalida *m* disabled person, invalid

inwentaryzacja *f* cataloguing; (remanent) stocktaking

inżynier *m* engineer; graduate of a school of engineering

Irlan|dczyk *m* Irishman; **~dia** *f* Ireland; **~dka** *f* Irishwoman; **~dzki** *adj* Irish

irytacja *f* irritation, vexation

isk|ra *f* spark; **~rzyć** spark; **~rzyć się** sparkle

Islan|dczyk *m* (**~dka** *f*) Icelander; **~dia** *f* Iceland; **~dzki** *adj* Icelandic

istn|ieć exist; **~ota** *f* (stworzenie) creature, being; (rzeczy) essence, gist; **~otny** *adj* es-

sential, fundamental, crucial
iść → chodzić
izol|acja f isolation; tech. in-

sulation; **~ować** a. ⟨**wy-**⟩
isolate; tech., a. ⟨**za-**⟩ insulate

J

ja pron I
jabł|ecznik m (placek) apple
pie; (wino) cider; **~ko** n
apple; **~oń** f apple tree
jad m venom
jadaln|ia f dining room; **~y**
adj edible
jadło|dajnia f (cheap) restau-
rant; **~spis** m menu
jadowity adj venomous
jagnię n lamb
jagoda f berry; czarna: blue-
berry
jaj|(k)o n egg; **~ecznica** f
scrambled eggs pl; **~nik** m
ovary
jak 1. pron how; **2.** cj as; **~
najszybciej** as soon as possible; **~i** pron what (... like); **~a
ona jest?** what is she like?;
~iś pron some; **~ tako** not too bad; **~oś** pron
somehow; one way or an-
other
jakość|ć f quality; **~ciowy** adj
qualitative
jałowy adj barren; fig. futile
jama f (nora) cave(rn), den, hollow;
anat. cavity
Japo|nia f Japan; **~nka** f
(**~ńczyk** m) Japanese; **2ński**
adj Japanese
jarmark m (country) fair

jarski adj vegetarian
jarzeniówka f glow lamp; neon light
jarzyna f vegetable
jaskinia f cave
jaskółka f swallow
jaskrawy adj bright; loud
jasn|o- light ...; **~ość** f bright-
ness; **~owidz** m clairvoyant;
~y adj light; (zrozumiały)
clear
jastrząb m hawk
jaszczurka f lizard
jaśnieć shine*; gleam
jaw: wyjść na ~ come* to
light, transpire; **~ny** adj
open, public, overt
jazda f ride, riding; **~ konna**
horseback riding; → a.
prawo
jądro n biol., fiz. nucleus;
owocu, tech., fig. core; orze-
cha: kernel; anat. testicle;
~wy adj nuclear
jąkać się stammer
jątrzyć provoke, irritate; **~
się** rana: fester
jechać ⟨**po-**⟩ go*; (prowadząc
pojazd) drive*; **~ konno** ride
jed|en num one; **wszystko
~no** it makes no difference
jedena|sty num eleventh;
~ście num eleven

jednak adv however; still; yet

jednakowy adj identical

jednoczesny adj simultaneous

jednoczyć ⟨z-⟩ (się) unite

jednodniowy adj one-day

jednogłośny adj unanimous

jednokierunkowy adj one-way

jednolity adj uniform, homogenous

jednomyślny adj unanimous

jednoosobowy adj one-man; pokój: single

jednorodzinny adj: dom m ~ detached house

jednorzędowy adj garnitur: single-breasted

jednostajny adj unvarying, monotonous, steady

jednostka f ludzka: individual; fiz., mil. unit

jednostronny adj one-sided; polit. unilateral

jedność f unity

jednoznaczny adj unequivocal

jedwab m silk; **~ny** adj silk ...

jedyn|ie adv merely; only; **~ka** f (a) one; **~y** adj (the) only; (the) sole

jedzenie n food

jego pron his

jej pron her(s)

jeleń m hart, stag, deer

jelit|o n intestine; **~a** pl a. entrails pl

jeniec m captive; ~ **wojenny** prisoner of war, p.o.w.

jesien|ny adj autumn ...; **~eń** f autumn Brt., fall Am.; **~onka** f (type of) overcoat

jeszcze adv (nadal) still; (dodatkowo) ... more; ~ **nie** (...) not (...) yet

jeść ⟨z-⟩ eat*; ~ **śniadanie** itp. have* breakfast etc.

jeśli cj if

jezdnia f roadway; street

jezioro n lake

jeździ|ć travel; pojazdem, konno: ride; **~ć konno** ride a horse; **~ć na rowerze** ride a bicycle; **~ć na nartach** ski; **~ec** m rider

jeż m hedgehog

jeżeli cj if

jeżyna f blackberry; (krzak a.) bramble

jęczeć moan, groan

jęczmień m barley; med. stye

jęk m groan, moan; **~nąć** pf → jęczeć

język m anat. tongue; ling. language; ~ **ojczysty** mother tongue; **~oznawstwo** n linguistics sg

jodła f fir (tree)

jogurt m yoghurt

jubiler m jeweller

jubileusz m jubilee

Jugosł|awia f Yugoslavia; **~owianin** m (**~owianka** f) Yugoslav; **Łowiański** adj Yugoslav(ian)

jur|or m member of the jury; **~y** n jury

jut|ro, adv tomorrow; ~ **rzejszy** adj tomorrow's; **~ rzenka** f dawn; poet. aurora

już adv already; w pytaniach: yet

K

kabanos *m* type of thin, smoked and dried pork sausage

kabina *f* cabin; *kierowcy:* cab; *pilota:* cockpit; **~ telefoniczna** (tele)phone booth/box, call box

kacz|ka *f* duck; **~or** *m* drake

kadłub *m samolotu:* fuselage; *statku:* hull

kadra *f* staff, personnel

kafel(ek) *m* tile

kaftan *m* jacket; *hist.* doublet; **~ bezpieczeństwa** straitjacket

kajak *m* kayak

kajdan|ki *pl* handcuffs *pl;* **~y** *pl* shackles *pl*

kajuta *f* cabin

kalafior *m* cauliflower

kale|ctwo *n* (physical) handicap; disability; **~czyć ⟨s-⟩ (się)** hurt/injure (oneself); **⟨o-⟩** cripple; **~ka** *m, f* disabled person, cripple F

kalendarz *m* calendar; **~yk** *m terminowy:* diary

kalesony *pl* long johns *pl*

kalka *f maszynowa:* carbon paper; *techniczna:* tracing paper

kalkulator *m* calculator

kaloryfer *m* radiator

kalosz *m* rubber boot

kał *m* excrement; *med.* faeces *pl*

kałuża *f* puddle, pool

kamera *f* camera; **~ filmowa** cine camera

kamienica *f* tenement house

kamie|niołom *m* quarry; **~nisty** *adj* stony; **~nny** *adj* stone...; **~ń** *m* stone

kamizelka *f* waistcoat *Brt.,* vest *Am.*

kampania *f* **(wyborcza** election) campaign

kamy(cze)k *m* small stone, pebble

kana|lizacja *f* plumbing; **~ł** *m a. tech.* channel; *sztuczny:* canal

kanap|a *f* sofa; **~ka** *f* sandwich; *(tartinka)* canapé

kanciasty *adj* angular

kantor *m hist.* merchant's office; **~ wymiany** bureau de change

kantować ⟨o-⟩ F cheat, swindle, trick

kapać drip

kapelusz *m* hat

kapitał *m* capital

kapitan *m* captain

kaplica *f* chapel

kapłan *m* priest

kapral *m* corporal

kapry|s *m* caprice, whim; **~sić** be* capricious; *(grymasić)* be* fussy, fuss; **~śny** *adj* capricious; moody

kaptur *m* hood

kapu|sta *f* cabbage; **~sta**

biała white cabbage; **~sta czerwona** red cabbage; **~sta kiszona** sauerkraut; **~sta włoska** savoy; **~śniak** *m* cabbage soup

kara *f* punishment; *jur.* penalty; **~ć** ⟨**u-**⟩ punish (**za** for)

karabin *m* rifle; **~ maszynowy** machine gun

karaluch *m* cockroach, roach F

karb *m fig.*: **złożyć na ~ czegoś** put down to s.th.

karcić ⟨**s-**⟩ rebuke, scold

karczować ⟨**wy-**⟩ clear, grub up, root up

karetka *f*: **~ pogotowia** ambulance

kark *m* nape (of the neck); **~ołomny** *adj* hazardous, risky; *tempo*: breakneck

karłowaty *adj* dwarf ..., midget ...

karmić ⟨**na-**⟩ feed*

karnawałowy *adj* carnival ...

karo *n* diamonds *pl*; **trójka** *f* **~** three of diamonds

karp *m* carp

kart|a *f* card; **~ka** *f* sheet of paper; *w książce*: leaf; *pocztowa*: postcard

kartof|el *m* potato; **~lanka** F *f* potato soup

karuzela *f* merry-go-round, roundabout *Brt.*, carousel *Am.*

karygodny *adj* (*skandaliczny*) unpardonable; *błąd*: gross

karzeł(ek) *m* midget, dwarf

kasa *f* dworcowa: booking of-

fice *Brt.*, ticket office *Am.*; *sklepowa*: cash desk; *tech.* cash register; *teatralna, kinowa*: box office, booking office *Brt.*

kaset|a *f* magnetofonowa, *video*: cassette; **~ka** *f* casket, jewel box

kasjer(ka *f*) *m* cashier

kasować ⟨**s-**⟩ *taśmę* erase; *komputer a.* delete

kasza *f* grits *pl*; (*potrawa*) gruel; **~nka** *f* black/blood pudding, blood sausage *Am.*

kasz|el *m* cough; **~leć** cough

kasztan *m* chestnut

kat *m* hangman, executioner

katar *m* catarrh, runny nose F

katedra *f* cathedral; *uniwersytecka*: chair

katoli|cki *adj* Catholic; **~czka** *f* (**~k** *m*) Catholic

kaucja *f jur.* bail; *za butelkę itp.*: deposit

kawa *f* coffee

kawale|r *m* bachelor; **~rka** *f* bedsitter; **~ria** *f* cavalry; **~rzysta** *m* cavalryman

kawał *m* (*część*) (large) piece, chunk; (*dowcip*) joke; **~e(cze)k** *m* bit, (small) piece

kawiarnia *f* café, coffee bar; **~owy** *adj* coffee-coloured; **bar** *m* **~owy** coffee shop

kazać order, tell*

kazanie *n* sermon

każd|orazowo *adv* each time; **~y** *adj* every, each

kąpać ⟨**wy-**⟩ bath *Brt.*, bathe *Am.*; **~ać się** bathe;

take* a bath; **~iel** f bath; **~ielisko** n bathing place; **~ielowy** adj bathing ..., bath...; **strój** m **~ielowy** bathing costume/suit, swimsuit; **~ielówki** pl swimming trunks pl

kąs|ać bite*; **~ek** m bite, morsel

kąt m corner; math. angle

kelner m waiter; **~ka** f waitress

kemping m camping site, campsite, campground Am.; **~owy** adj: **domek** m **~owy** (holiday) cabin

kędzierzawy adj curly

kęs m bite

kibic m piłkarski: (football) fan

kich|ać ⟨**~nąć**⟩ sneeze

kiedy pron when; **~ś** adv o przeszłości: once; at one time; o przyszłości: one day

kieliszek m (small) glass

kiełbasa f sausage

kiepski adj poor, lousy F

kier m hearts pl; **walet** m **~** jack of hearts

kierow|ać ⟨**po-**⟩ run*, manage; ⟨**s-**⟩ direct (**do** to); samochodem: drive*; **~ca** m driver; **~nica** f steering wheel; **~nictwo** n management; **~nik** m (**~niczka** f) manager

kierun|ek m direction; **~kowskaz** m mot. indicator

kiesze|ń f pocket; **~onkowiec** m pickpocket; **~onkowy** adj pocket ...

kij m stick

kilka a few, some, several; **~krotnie** adv several times, repeatedly, more than once; **~naście** a dozen or so

kilo|bajt m kilobyte; **~gram** m kilogram; **~metr** m kilometre

kim: **z** ~ with whom; **o** ~ about whom

kiosk m kiosk

kipieć ⟨**za-**⟩ boil over; fig. seethe

kisić ⟨**za-**⟩ pickle

kisiel m kind of fruit-flavoured jelly

kiszony → kapusta

kit m putty

kiw|ać ⟨**~nąć**⟩ ręką: wave; beckon (**na** to); głową: nod; **~ać się** sway, rock

klakson m horn

klamka f doorknob

klamra f tech. clamp, brace; pasa: buckle

klapa f flap, cover; włazu itp.: trapdoor; thea. itp. flop

klasa f class; **w szkole** a.: form, grade Am.

klaskać clap (one's hands), applaud

klas|owy adj class ...; **~ówka** f class test

klasyczny adj classic (starożytny) classical

klasztor m żeński: convent; męski: monastery

klatka f cage

klawi|atura f keyboard; **~sz** m key

kląć ⟨za-⟩ swear*

klecić ⟨s-⟩ cobble together

kle|ić ⟨s-⟩ glue, stick*; paste; **~ik** m pap; **~isty** adj gluey, sticky; **~j** m glue

klejnot m jewel; *herbowy*: crest

klekotać ⟨za-⟩ clatter

klepać clap, slap

kler m the clergy

kleszcze pl (pair of) tongs pl; *med.* forceps pl

klę|czeć kneel*; **~kać** ⟨~nąć⟩ kneel* down

klęska f defeat, failure

klient m customer; *form.*, *adwokata*: client

klimat m climate; **~yzacja** f air-conditioning; (*urządzenie*) air conditioner; **~yzowany** adj air-conditioned

klinika f teaching hospital

kloc m log; block of wood; **~ek** m (building) block

klomb m flowerbed

klon m maple (tree)

klops(ik) m meatball

klosz m lampy: lampshade

klucz m key

kluski pl noodles pl

kłam|ać ⟨s-⟩ lie; **~ca** m liar; **~stwo** n lie

kłaniać się bow

kłaść put*; *starannie*: lay*; **~ się** lie* down; (*iść spać*) go* to bed/sleep

kłębek m ball, bundle

kłoda f log

kłopot m problem; *poważny*: trouble; **~liwy** adj inconve-

nient, troublesome

kłos m ear (of corn)

kłócić ⟨po-⟩ **się** quarrel, squabble

kłódka f padlock

któt|liwy adj quarrelsome; **~nia** f quarrel; squabble

kłuć ⟨po-, u-⟩ prick

kłus m trot; **~ować** koń: trot; (*polować nielegalnie*) poach; **~ownik** m poacher

kminek m caraway

knajpa F f pub Brt., saloon Am.; joint F

kobie|cy adj (*typowy dla kobiet*) feminine, womanly; *o-dzieś itp.*: women's; **~ta** f woman, female

koc m blanket

kocha|ć love; **~ć się wzajemnie**: love each other; (*odbywać stosunek*) make* love, have* sex; **~nek** m lover; **~nka** f lover, mistress; **~ny** adj darling

kod m code

kodeks m code; **~ drogowy** traffic rules pl, Highway Code Brt.; **~ karny** penal code

kogo pron who(m)

kogut m cock, rooster Am.

koić ⟨u-⟩ soothe

kojarzyć ⟨s-⟩ associate; (*łączyć*) match

kokarda f bow

koktajl m cocktail; (*przyjęcie*) cocktail party; **~ mleczny** milk shake

kolacj|a f supper; *gorąca*:

dinner; **jeść ~ę** have* supper/dinner, sup, dine
kolano n knee
kola|rstwo n cycling; **~rz** m cyclist, rider F
kolba f mil. butt (of a rifle/pistol); chem. flask; (kukurydzy) cob
kolczasty adj prickly; **drut m ~** barbed wire
kolczyk m earring
kolebka f cradle
kolec m spike; bot. thorn
kolega m mate; form. colleague
kolej f railway; railroad Am.; (kolejność) turn; **~ podziemna** the underground Brt., subway Am.; **~arz** m railwayman Brt., railroad worker Am.; **~ka** f **~ kolej**; (ogonek) queue Brt., line Am.; **stać w ~ce** queue (up) Brt., line Am.; **~no** adv in turn, one after the other; **~ny** adj subsequent; **~owy** adj railway ...
kolekcj|a f collection; **~ono-wać** collect
koleżeński adj sporting
kolęda f Christmas carol
kolizja f conflict; mot. collision
kolor m colour; **~owy** adj colour ..., colourful; **~owy telewizor** m colour TV
kolumna f column
kołatać bang, knock
kołdra f quilt
kołek m peg

kołnierz m collar
koło¹ prp ground
koło² n mot. itp. wheel; (figura) circle
kołys|ać (się) rock, swing*; **~ka** f cradle
komar m gnat, mosquito
kombinerki pl combination pliers pl
kombinezon m overalls pl, boiler suit Brt.
komedia f comedy
komenderować command; fig. boss (kimś s.o. around/about); lord it (kimś over s.o.)
komiczny adj comical
komin m chimney; **~ek** m fireplace; **~iarz** m chimney sweep
komis m (sklep) second-hand shop
komisariat m police station
komisja f committee, commission
komitet m committee
komor|a f chamber; **~ne** n rent; **~nik** m bailiff
komórka f biol. cell
komplet m set; **~ny** adj complete
kompot m stewed fruit
kompres m compress
kompromit|ować f blunder; **~ować ⟨s-⟩** compromise
komputer m computer
komu pron (to) whom
komunik|acja f (public) transport; ... service; **~at** m announcement; **~ować ⟨za-⟩** announce

komuni|styczny adj Communist; **~zm** m Communism

koncert m concert; (*utwór*) concerto

koncesja f licence

kondolencje pl condolences pl

konduktor m conductor

kondycja f (physical) shape, form

kondygnacja f floor, storey; level

konfitury pl candied fruit

koniczyna f clover

koniec m; **w końcu** in the end, finally, eventually

konieczn|ie adv necessarily; F absolutely; **~y** adj necessary

konik m fig. hobby-horse

konkretny adj definite, concrete

konkurencja f competition; sp. event

konkurs m contest, competition

konno → **jechać**, **jeździć**

konsekwentny adj consistent

konserwować ⟨za-⟩ preserve

konspiracja f clandestine resistance movement

konstytucja f constitution

konsumpcja f consumption

kontakt m contact; F electr. switch; **~ować się** ⟨s-⟩ contact (**z kimś** s.o.), make* contact, get* in touch (**z kimś** with s.o.)

kontener m (shipping) container

kontrakt m contract

kontrol|a f inspection; **~er** m inspector; **~ować** ⟨s-⟩ inspect

kontuzja f injury

kontynu|acja f continuation; **~ować** continue, carry on

konw|ojent m guard, escort; **~ojować** escort; **~ój** m convoy

koń m horse; **~ mechaniczny** horsepower, HP

koń|cowy adj final, end ...; **~ckówka** f final part; **~czyć** ⟨s-⟩ finish; ⟨za-⟩ a. complete; ⟨za-⟩ a. end; **~czyć się** end, finish

kooperacja f cooperation

kopa|ć ⟨~nąć⟩ nogą: kick

kopa|ć² ⟨u-⟩ w ziemi: dig*; **~lnia** f mine; **~rka** f excavator

koper m dill

koperta f envelope

kopia f duplicate; w sztuce: replica

kopi|arka f copier; **~ować** ⟨s-⟩ copy

kopul|acja f copulation; **~ować** copulate

kopuła f dome

kopyto n hoof

kora f bot. bark

korale pl bead necklace; z koralu: coral necklace

korek m cork; drogowy: traffic jam

korekta f proof-reading

korepetycj|e pl private lessons pl; **udzielać komuś ~i** coach s.o.

korespondencja *f* correspondence; **~t** *m* correspondent

korko|ciąg *m* corkscrew; **~wać** ⟨za-⟩ cork (up)

korona *f* crown; **~ka** *f* (*tkanina*) lace

kort *m* (tennis) court

korytarz *m* corridor, passage(way)

korze|nić ⟨za-⟩ **się** take* root; **~ń** *m* root

korzy|stać ⟨s-⟩ benefit (z from); (*używać*) use; **~stny** *adj* favourable; *econ.* profitable; **~ść** *f* benefit

kos *m* blackbird

kosa *f* scythe; **~iarka** *f* mower; **~ić** ⟨s-⟩ mow*

kosmety|czka *f* beautician; (*torebka*) vanity bag; **~k** *m* cosmetic

kosm|iczny *adj* space ...; *form.* cosmic; **~os** *m* outer space; (*wszechświat*) the universe/cosmos

kosmyk *m* wisp (of hair)

kostium *m* costume; *damski*: suit; **~ kąpielowy** bathing suit/costume *Brt.*, swimsuit

kost|ka *f lodu itp.*: cube; *anat.* ankle; → *a.* **kość**; **~nieć** ⟨s-⟩ (*drętwieć*) grow* numb; **~ny** *adj* bone ...

kosz → **koszyk**

koszary *pl* barracks *pl*

koszt *m* cost; **~orys** *m* estimate; **~ować** *v/i* cost*; *ile to ~uje?* how much is it?; *v/t* ⟨s-⟩ taste; **~owny** *adj* costly,

precious

koszula *f* shirt

koszyk *m* basket; **~ówka** *f* basketball

kości|elny *adj* church ...; *instytucja*: ecclesiastical; **~ół** *m* church

kościsty *adj* bony; **~ć** *f* bone

koślawy *adj* crooked

kot *m* cat

kotara *f* curtain

kotlet *m* chop; *siekany*: hamburger

kotlina *f* dell, valley

kotłować ⟨za-⟩ **się** swirl, whirl

kotłownia *f* boiler room/house

kotwica *f* anchor

koza *f zo.* (nanny) goat; **~ica** *f* chamois; **~ioł** *m* (*samiec kozy*) (billy) goat

kożuch *m* sheepskin coat

kółko *n tech.* wheel; (*figura*) circle

kpi|ć ⟨za-⟩ (**sobie**) mock (z *kogoś* at s.o.); **~na** *f* (**~ny** *pl*) mockery

kra *f* cake of ice; *w morzu*: ice floe

kraciasty *adj* check(er)ed

kradzie|ż *f* theft; **~ony** *adj* stolen

kraj *m* country

kraj|ać ⟨po-⟩ cut* (up); *w plasterki*: slice (up)

krajobraz *m* landscape

krakowski *adj* Cracovian, of Cracow

kran → **kurek**

krasnoludek m dwarf

kraść ⟨u-⟩ steal*

krat|(k)a f (wzór) check; w oknie itp.: grating, grill(e), bars pl; w ~ę, ~kowany adj check ..., check(er)ed

krawat m (neck)tie

krawcowa f seamstress, dressmaker

krawę|dź f edge; ~żnik m kerb Brt., curb Am.

krawiec m tailor

krąg m circle

krążek m disc

krążenie n circulation; ~yć circle, hover

kreda f chalk

kredens m cupboard

kredka f crayon; ~ do ust lipstick

kredyt m credit

krem m cream; ~owy adj creamy

kresk|a f line; ~owany adj lined

kreślić draw*

krew f blood; ~ki adj hot-blooded; ~niak, ~ny m relative, relation

kręc|ić ⟨po-, za-⟩ turn (round); spin; ~ić się revolve, rotate; włosy: curl; dziecko itp.: fidget; ~ony adj włosy: curly; schody: winding

kręgle pl skittles pl, ninepins pl Am.; (gra a.) bowling

kręgosłup m spine, backbone

krępować ⟨s-⟩ (wiązać) tie (up); (żenować) embarrass; ~

się feel* embarrassed

krępy adj stocky, squat, thickset

kręt|acz m wriggler, dishonest person; ~y adj winding

kroczyć pace

kroić ⟨u-⟩ cut* (off); ⟨po-, s-⟩ cut* (up)

krok m step

kromka f slice (of bread)

kronika f chronicle; (film) newsreel

kropić ⟨po-⟩ sprinkle; deszcz: drizzle; ~ka f dot; ~la f drop; ~lówka f drip

krosta f pimple

krowa f cow

krój m cut

król m king; ~estwo n kingdom; ~ewski adj royal

królik m rabbit

król|owa f queen; ~ować reign

krótki adj short; (krótkotrwały) a. brief

krótkometrażowy adj: film m ~ short

krótkoterminowy adj short-term

krótkotrwały adj brief; short-lived

krótkowzroczny adj (a. fig.) short-sighted

kruchy adj fragile, brittle

kruk m raven

krupnik m gastr. barley soup

kruszyć ⟨po-, s-⟩ crumble, crush

krwaw|ić bleed*; ~ienie n bleeding; ~y adj bloody

krw|iobieg m blood circulation; **~iodawca** m blood donor; **~ionośny** adj: **naczynie** n **~ionośne** blood vessel; **~iożerczy** adj: blood-thirsty; **~otok** m h(a)emorrhage

kry|ć ⟨s-, u-⟩ hide*, conceal; **~ć się** hide*; **~jówka** f hiding place; ludzka a.: hideout

krymina|lny adj criminal; **~ł** F m (więzienie) prison; (powieść) detective story

kryształ m crystal

kryty adj sp. itp. indoor

krytyczny adj critical; **~ka** f criticism; **~kować** ⟨s-⟩ criticize

kryzys m crisis

krzak m bush

krzątać się busy oneself (przy czymś with s.th.), bustle about/around

krzep|ić ⟨po-⟩ invigorate; **~ić się** fortify oneself; **~ki** adj vigorous; **~nąć** ⟨s-⟩ coagulate

krzesło n chair

krzew m shrub; **~ić** teach*, promulgate, promote

krzy|czeć cry, shout; **~k** m cry, shout; **~kliwy** adj loud, noisy

krzywa f curve

krzyw|da f wrong, harm; **~dzić** ⟨s-⟩ harm, wrong

krzywi|ć ⟨s-⟩ bend*; **~ć się** frown (na at); **~zna** f curvature; **~y** adj crooked

krzyż m cross; **~ować** ⟨s-⟩ cross; **~ówka** f crossword

(puzzle); biol. cross

kserokopia f Xerox TM copy

ksiądz m priest

książeczka f booklet; **~ oszczędnościowa** savings-bank book

książę m prince; duke

książka f book

księg|arnia f bookshop Brt., bookstore Am.; **~owość** f accountancy, bookkeeping; **~owy** adj accountant, bookkeeper

księ|stwo n duchy; **~żna** f duchess; **~żniczka** f princess

księżyc m moon

kształ|cić ⟨wy-⟩ educate; **~cić się** study, train; **~t** m shape, form; **~tny** adj shapely; **~tować** ⟨u-⟩ shape, form, fashion; **~tować się** take* shape/form

kto pron who; **~kolwiek** pron anybody, anyone; whoever; **~ś** pron somebody, someone

któr|ędy pron which way; **~y** pron which; rel a. that; rel o ludziach: who, that; **~ykolwiek** pron any, whichever

ku pron towards

kube|k m mug; **~ł** m bucket; na śmieci: bin

kuch|arka f cook; **~arski** adj cooking ...; **książka** f **~arska** cookery book, cookbook; **~arz** m cook; **~enka** f cooker; **~enny** adj kitchen ...; **~mistrz** m chef, head cook; **~nia** f (pomieszczenie) kitchen; fig. cuisine, cooking

kuć

kuć *żelazo* forge; ⟨o-⟩ *konia* shoe; ⟨u-⟩ *słowo* coin

kudłaty *adj* hairy, shaggy

kufel *m* beer mug

kukułka *f* cuckoo

kukurydza *f* maize *Brt.*, corn *Am.*

kula *f* ball; *geom.* sphere; *mil.* bullet

kul|a² *f inwalidzka*: crutch; **~awy** *adj* lame; **~eć** *v/i* limp

kulisty *adj* spherical, ball-shaped

kulk|a *f* small ball; **~owy** *adj*: *łożysko* *n* **~owe** ball bearing

kultura *f* culture; **~lny** *adj* *człowiek*: cultivated, well-mannered

kundel F *m* mongrel

kunsztowny *adj* ingenious

kupa *f* heap

kup|ić *pf* → **kupować**; **~iec** *m* merchant; **~no** *n* purchase; **~ować** buy*

kura *f* hen

kuracj|a *f* treatment, cure; **~usz** *m* patient (*esp.* in a spa)

kurcz *m* cramp

kurcz|ak *m*, **~ę** *n* chicken

kurcz|owy *adj* convulsive; **~yć** ⟨s-⟩ **się** shrink*; contract; *liczba*: dwindle

kurek *m tech.* tap

kuropatwa *f* partridge

kurs *m* course; **~ować** run*

kurtka *f* jacket

kurtyna *f* curtain

kurz *m* dust; **~yć** raise dust; **~**

66

się (*zbierać kurz*) gather dust

kusić ⟨s-⟩ tempt

kuszetka *f* couchette

kuśnierz *m* furrier

kuzyn *m* (male) cousin; **~ka** *f* (female) cousin

kwadrans *m* quarter (of an hour)

kwadrat *m* square

kwalifik|acje *pl* qualifications *pl*; **~ować się** ⟨za-⟩ qualify

kwarta|lnik *m* quarterly; **~lny** *adj* quarterly; **~ł** *m* quarter (of a year)

kwa|s *m* acid; **~sić** ⟨za-⟩ → **kisić**; **~skowaty** *adj* sourish; **~śny** *adj* sour

kwatera *f* quarters *pl*; *mil. a.* billet

kwesti|a *f* question; **~onariusz** *m* questionnaire; **~onować** ⟨za-⟩ (call into) question

kwia|ciarnia *f* florist's; **~t** *m* flower

kwiczeć ⟨za-⟩ squeal

kwiecień *m* April

kwiecisty *adj* flowery

kwit *m* receipt; **~** *bagażowy* luggage receipt, luggage token

kwitnąć ⟨za-⟩ bloom, blossom; *drzewo a.*: be* in bloom/blossom

kwitować ⟨po-⟩ sign (*coś* for s.th.)

kwota *f* amount, sum

L

lać v/t *płyn* pour; *krew, łzy* shed*; F (*tłuc*) lick F; v/i pour (with rain); ~ **się** flow, run*, pour (forth)

lada f counter

laik m layman

lakier m varnish; *do paznokci a.*: enamel; *samochodowy*: paint; **~ki** pl patent-leather shoes pl; **~ować** (**po-**) varnish; *samochód* paint

lakować (**za-**) seal

lalka f doll; *thea.* puppet

lamentować wail; lament (**nad czymś** s.th.)

lampa f lamp; ~ **błyskowa** flashlight

lampart m leopard

lampka f small lamp; ~ **wina** glass of wine

lanie F n licking F

laryngolog m ENT specialist

las m wood, (*iglasty/liściasty* coniferous/leafy) forest

laska f walking stick

latać fly*; (*biegać*) run* around/about

latar|ka f torch *Brt.*, flashlight *Am.*; **~nia** f lantern; **~nia morska** lighthouse

lato n summer; **~em, w lecie** in (the) summer

laur m laurel; **~eat** m prize winner; *form.* laureate

ląd m land; **~ować** (**wy-**) land; **~owanie** n landing

lecieć (**po-**) pf → **latać**; **muszę** ~ I must dash

lecz cj but, however

lecz|enie n treatment, cure; **~nica** f hospital, infirmary; **~nictwo** n medical care, health service; **~niczy** adj curative; *ćwiczenia itp.*: remedial; **~yć** treat; (**wy-**) cure; **~yć się** undergo* treatment

ledw|ie, ~o adv barely, hardly, scarcely

legitymacja f identification, ID (card) F; *członkowska*: membership card

lejek m funnel

lek m remedy, medicine; **~arka** f (woman) doctor; **~arski** adj doctor's ...; **~arstwo** n medicine (**na** for); **~arz** m (medical) doctor, physician

lekceważ|ący adj supercilious, disrespectful; (**z-**) (*okazywać lekceważenie*) disdain; *niebezpieczeństwo itp.* ignore

lekcj|a f lesson, class; **na ~i** in class

lekki adj light

lekkoatletyka f athletics, track-and-field *Am.*

lekko|myślny adj reckless; **~ść** f lightness

lemoniada f lemonade

len m flax

lenić się laze about; **~wy** *adj* lazy; idle

leń *m* lazybones, idler

lepić mould; **~ się** be* sticky

lepiej *adv* better

lepki *adj* sticky

lepszy *adj* better; *form.* superior

leszczyna *f* hazel

leśn|ictwo *n* forestry; (*okręg*) forest district; **~iczówka** *f* forester's lodge; **~iczy** *m* forester; forest ranger *Am.*; **~y** *adj* forest ...

letni *adj* summer ...; *płyn itp.*: tepid, lukewarm; **~k** *m* holidaymaker *Brt.*, vacationer *Am.*

lew *m* lion

lewarek *m mot.* jack

lew|ica *f pol.* the left; **~icowy** *adj* left-wing; **~ostronny** *adj* left-sided; *ruch*: on the left-hand side of the road; **~y** *adj* left; **na ~o** on the left(-hand side); **w ~o** left, to the left

leż|ak *m* deckchair; **~anka** *f* couch; **~eć** lie*

lęk *m* fear; **~ać się** fear, be* afraid

libacja F *f* drunken orgy

liceum *n* secondary school

lichy *adj* poor-quality, shoddy

licytacja *f* auction; *w kartach*: bidding

licz|ba *f* number; **~nik** *m* meter; **~ny** *adj* numerous; **~yć** ⟨**po-, z-**⟩ count

lider *m* leader

likier *m* liqueur

lil|a, ~iowy *adj* lilac, purple

lin|a *f* rope; **~ia** *f* line; **~iowy** *adj* linear

lipa *f* lime/linden (tree)

lipiec *m* July

lis *m* fox

list *m* letter

lista *f* list

listonosz *m* postman, mailman *Am.*

listopad *m* November

listwa *f* batten

liść *m* leaf

litera *f* letter; **~cki** *adj* literary; **~tura** *f* literature

litewski *adj* Lithuanian

lito|ść *f* mercy; **~ściwy** *adj* merciful; **~wać się** feel* pity (*nad* for); *a.* ⟨**u-**⟩ take* pity (*nad* on)

litr *m* litre (*1.76 pints*)

Litw|a *f* Lithuania; **~in(ka** *f*) *m* Lithuanian

liz|ać ⟨**~nąć**⟩ lick

lo|dowaty *adj* ice-cold; **~dowisko** *n* ice rink; **~dowy** *adj* ice ...; **~dówka** *f* refrigerator, fridge F; **~dy** *pl* ice cream; **~dziarz** *m* ice-cream man

lokator *m* lodger

lokomo|cja *f*: *środek m ~cji* means of transport; **~tywa** *f* railway engine, locomotive

lokować ⟨**u-**⟩ place; *econ.* invest

lornetka *f* binoculars *pl*, field-glasses *pl*

los *m* (*przeznaczenie*) fate, destiny; *(dola)* lot; *loteryjny*: (lottery) ticket; **ciągnąć ~y** draw* lots; **~ować ⟨wy-⟩** draw* lots

lot *m* flight; **~nictwo** *n* aviation; **~nik** *m* flyer, pilot; **~nisko** *n* airport; *mil.* airfield; **~niskowiec** *m* aircraft carrier

loża *f thea.* box; *masońska*: lodge

lód *m* ice; *gastr.* ice-cream

lub *cj* or

lubić like, be* fond of

lud *m* people; **~ność** *f* population; **~owy** adj people's

ludz|ie *pl* people; **~ki** adj human

luka *f* gap

luksusowy adj luxury ..., luxurious

lust|erko *n* kieszonkowe: vanity mirror; **~erko wsteczne** rear-view mirror; **~ro** *n* mirror, looking-glass

luty *m* February

lu|z *m* w linie itp.: play; F w zachowaniu: ease; *mot.* neutral gear, the neutral; **~zować ⟨z-⟩** relieve; **~źny** adj loose

lżej adv, **~szy** adj easier

Ł

łabędź *m* swan

łachman *m* rag

łaciaty adj spotted

łaci|na *f* Latin; **~ński** adj Latin

ład *m* orderliness, order

ładny adj pretty, nice, cute *Am.*

ładow|ać ⟨za-⟩ load; **~nia** *f* hold

ładunek *m* load, freight; *mar.* cargo

łago|dny adj mild; *człowiek*: gentle; **~dzić ⟨z-⟩** soothe

łajdak *m* scoundrel, rascal

łakomy adj greedy

łam|ać ⟨po-, z-⟩ break*; **~liwy** adj brittle

łańcu|ch, ~szek *m* chain

łap|a *f* paw; **~ać ⟨z-⟩** catch*; *ręką*: grab; **~czywość** *f* greediness; **~ownictwo** *n*

bribery; **~ówka** *f* bribe

łaska *f* grace; **~wy** adj kind, gracious

łaskotać tickle

łat|a *f* patch; **~ać ⟨za-⟩** patch (up)

łatwo|palny adj (in)flammable; **~ść** *f* easiness; **~owierny** adj credulous; **~y** adj easy

ław|(k)a *f* bench; **~a os-karżonych** the dock; **~nik** *m* member of the jury

łazienka *f* bathroom

łaźnia *f* bathhouse

łącz|nie adv inclusive (**z** of), together/along (**z** with); (**w** sumie) altogether; **~nik** *m mil.* liaison officer; **~ność** *f* communications *pl*; **~ny** adj total, global; **~yć ⟨po-, z-⟩** connect, join; *fig.*

combine; **~yć się** ⟨z-⟩ unite; ⟨po-⟩ teleph. get* a connection
łąka f meadow
łeb F m zwierzęcia: head
łkać sob
łobuz m rascal
łodyga f stem; liścia: stalk
łokieć m elbow
łom m crowbar
łono n lap; matki: womb
łopata f spade; **~ka** f ogrodowa: trowel; anat. shoulder blade
łoskot m rumble, thud
łosoś m salmon
łotewski adj Latvian
łotr m knave, scoundrel
Łot|wa f Latvia; **~ysz(ka** f) m Latvian
łowi|ć ⟨z-⟩ catch*; **~ecki** adj hunting ...; **~ectwo** n hunting
łożysko n tech. bearing

łó|dka, ~dź f boat; **~dź podwodna** submarine
łóżko n bed
łuk m arch; (broń) bow
łup m booty; **~ać** orzechy crack; szczapy split
łupież m dandruff
łupina f peel; (skorupka) shell
łuska f scale; mil. cartridge case; **~ć** shell, scale
łuszczyć się flake (off)
łydka f calf
łyk m gulp; **~ać** ⟨~nąć⟩ swallow, gulp down
łykowaty adj tough
łys|ina f bald spot; **~y** adj bald
łyż|eczka f teaspoon; czegoś: teaspoonful; **~ka** f spoon; czegoś: spoonful
łyżw|a f skate; **~iarstwo** n skating

łza f tear; **~wić** water

M

macać ⟨po-⟩ feel*
mach|ać ⟨~nąć⟩ swing*; ręką, chusteczką itp.: wave
macierzyństwo n maternity
macocha f stepmother
maczać dip
magazyn m store, warehouse; (pomieszczenie) storeroom; (czasopismo) magazine; **~ier** m storekeeper; **~ować** ⟨z-⟩ store
magiel m mangle; **~lować** ⟨z-⟩ mangle
magnes m magnet; **~tofon** m

tape recorder; **~towid** m video cassette recorder, VCR
maj m May
maj|ątek m fortune; ziemski: estate; econ., jur. assets pl
majonez m mayonnaise
majsterkować tinker
majtki pl damskie: panties, knickers pl; dziecięce: pantiesy pl; męskie: underpants pl
mak m poppy; (ziarno) poppy seed
makaron m noodles pl, macaroni

makijaż m make-up

makowiec m poppy-seed cake

mala|rstwo n painting; **~rz** m painter

malina f raspberry (bush)

malow|ać ⟨na-⟩ paint; **~idło** n painting; **~niczy** adj picturesque

mało adv little; **~letni 1.** adj under age; **2.** m minor; **~mówny** adj taciturn; **~obrazkowy** adj 35-millimetre; **~stkowy** adj petty; człowiek: narrow-minded

małpa f zo. monkey; duża: ape

mały adj small, little

małż|eński adj marital; **~eństwo** n marriage; **~onka** f husband; spouse; **~onka** f wife; spouse; **~onkowie** pl husband and wife, married couple

mamrotać ⟨wy-⟩ mumble

mandarynka f tangerine, mandarin

mandat m polit. mandate; (kara) fine, ticket F

manewr m man(o)euvre

mankiet m cuff; u spodni: turn-up

mańkut m left-hander

mapa f map

marchew(ka) f carrot

margaryna f margarine, marge F

margines m margin

marka f towaru: brand; samochodu: make; (waluta) mark

markotny adj sullen

marmolada f jam

marmur m marble

marn|ieć ⟨z-⟩ deteriorate; człowiek : waste away; **~otrawstwo** n waste; **~ować ⟨z-⟩** waste

marny adj poor

marsz m march

marszałek m marshall

marszczyć ⟨z-⟩ crease; **~ się** crease; człowiek : frown

martwić ⟨z-⟩ worry; **~ się** worry, be* anxious (o about)

martwy adj dead

marudzić F grumble; (guzdrać się) dally

marynarka¹ f jacket

marynar|ka² f wojenna: navy; handlowa: merchant marine; **~rz** m seaman

marynować ⟨za-⟩ marinate, pickle

marzec m March

marzenie n dream

marznąć freeze*

marzyć dream(*) (o about)

masa f mass

masaż m massage

mask|a f mask; mot. bonnet Brt., hood Am.; **~ować ⟨za-⟩** camouflage

masło n butter

masować massage

mas|owy adj mass ...; **~ówka** F f mass production

maszt m mast

maszyn|a f machine; **~a do pisania** typewriter; **~a do szycia** sewing machine; **~ista** m engine driver; **~istka** f typist

maszynka f kuchenna: cooker; **~ do golenia** safety razor; *elektryczna*: (electric) shaver

maść f ointment

matematy|czny adj mathematical; **~ka** f mathematics sg, math(s) F

materac m mattress

materia f matter

materiał m material; (*tkanina*) a. cloth, fabric

matka f mother

matowy adj dull; *farba*: matt

matura f secondary school finals

matrymonialn|y adj: *biuro* ~**e** marriage bureau

mazać ⟨za-, po-⟩ smear

mącić ⟨z-⟩ cloud

mądr|ość f wisdom; **~y** adj wise

mąka f flour

mąż → **małżonek**

mdleć ⟨o-, ze-⟩ faint

mdł|ości pl nausea; **~y** adj insipid

mebel m piece of furniture; **~lować** ⟨u-⟩ furnish; **~lować się** furnish one's flat

mech m moss

mechanik m mechanic

mecz m match

medal m medal

medy|cyna f medicine; **~czny** adj medical; **~k** m medic F

meldować ⟨za-⟩ report; ~ **się** report (*gdzieś* to somewhere); *w hotelu*: check in in

melon m melon

menstruacja f menstruation

meta f sp. goal, winning post

metal m metal; **~owy** adj metal ...

meteorologiczny adj: **komunikat** m ~ weather report

metr m metre

metro n underground Brt., subway Am.

metryka f birth certificate

mewa f seagull

męcz|ący adj strenuous, tiring; **~yć** ⟨z-⟩ tire; ⟨za-⟩ (*gnębić*) nag, pester, torment; **~yć się** suffer

męka f torment

męski adj men's, male; *gr.*, *mężczyzna*: masculine

mętny adj cloudy; (*niejasny*) vague, obscure

męż|atka f married woman; **~czyzna** m man; **~ny** adj gallant, brave

mglisty adj misty, foggy; *fig.* vague; **~ła** f fog, mist

mgnienie n: **w ~u oka** in a flash

mianować appoint

mianowicie adv namely

miara f measure

miasto n town; *duże*: city

miażdży|ca f med. sclerosis; **~ć** ⟨z⟩ crush

miąć ⟨z-⟩ crumple; ~ **się** crease

miecz m sword

mieć have*

miednica f (wash) basin; *anat.* pelvis

mie|dziany adj copper ...; **~dź** f copper

miejsc|e n place; (*przestrzeń*) room, space; **~owość** f locality, town/village; **~owy** adj local; **~ówka** f (seat) reservation ticket

miejski adj city ...; *form.* municipal

mielić grind*

mieli|zna f shallows pl; sandbank; **na ~źnie** aground, on the rocks

mielon|y 1. adj ground; 2. F m kotlet: hamburger; **~e** n mięso: minced meat

mienie n possessions pl; property

mierny adj mediocre

mierzyć ⟨z-⟩ measure, gauge

miesi|ąc m month; **~ączka** f menstruation; **~ęczny** adj monthly

miesza|ć ⟨z-⟩ mix, blend; np. herbatę stir; **~nina, ~nka** f mixture, blend

mieszczański adj middle-class

mieszka|ć live; czasowo: stay; **~nie** n flat Brt., apartment Am.; **~niec** m inhabitant; **~niowy** adj housing

mieścić contain; **~ się** be* situated

miewać się: *Jak się miewa ...?* How is ...?

między 1. prp between; 2. prefix: inter-; **~miastowy** adj teleph. trunk ...; long-distance ... Am.; **~narodowy** adj international

mięk|ki adj soft; **~nąć** ⟨z-⟩ soften

mięsień m muscle

mięs|ny adj meaty, meat ...; **~o** n flesh; w handlu: meat

mięta f mint; **~owy** adj mint ..., mint-flavoured

mig: **w ~** adv in no time, in a flash; **~acz** m indicator; **~ać** flash; **~awka** f news flash; *phot.* shutter

migdał m almond; *anat.* (a. **~ek**) tonsil

migotać ⟨za-⟩ flicker, glimmer

mija|ć v/t a. ⟨wy-⟩ pass (by); go* past; v/i pass; **~nie** n → **światło**

mikro|bus m minibus; **~fon** m microphone, mike F

mikser m kuchenny: blender

mila f mile

milcze|ć be*/keep* silent; **~nie** n silence

mile, miło adv pleasantly, agreeably

miłosierny adj merciful

miło|sny adj love ...; **~ść** f love; **~śnik** m lover

miły adj pleasant, agreeable, nice

mimo prp in spite of; **~ to** nevertheless, nonetheless; **~ woli** unwittingly; **~wolny** adj unwitting, involuntary

min|a¹ f facial expression; **robić ~y** make* faces

mina² f mil. mine

min|ąć pf → **mijać**; **~iony** adj past

minister *m* minister; **~stwo** *n* ministry; **2stwo Spraw Wewnętrznych** Ministry of the Interior, Home Office *Brt.*; **2stwo Spraw Zagranicznych** Ministry of Foreign Affairs, Foreign Office *Brt.*, State Department *Am.*

minuta *f* minute

miotła *f* broom

miód *m* honey; **~ pitny** mead

mis(k)a *f* bowl

misja *f* mission

mistrz *m* master; *sp.* champion; **~ostwo** *n* mastery; *sp.* championship; **~owski** *adj* masterly; **~yni** *f sp.* (woman) champion

miś *m* bear; (*zabawka*) teddy bear

mit *m* myth

mizern|ieć ⟨**z-**⟩ grow* wan/ haggard; **~y** *adj* wan, haggard

mlecz|arnia *f* dairy; **~arski** *adj* dairy ...; **~ny** *adj* milk ...

mleć → **mielić**

mleko *n* milk

młod|ociany 1. *adj* juvenile; **2.** *m* juvenile, minor; **~ość** *f* youth; **~szy** *adj* younger; *form.* junior; **~y** *adj* young

młodzie|niec *m* young man, youth; **~ńczy** *adj* youthful; **~ż** *f* youth

młot(ek) *m* hammer

młyn *m* mill; **~ek** *m*: **~ek do kawy** coffee grinder

mnich *m* monk

mnie *pron* me; **u ~** at my place

mniej *adv* less; **~ więcej** more or less; **~szość** *f* minority; **~szy** *adj* smaller; *form.* lesser, minor

mniema|ć presume, suppose, believe, be* of opinion; **~nie** *n* conviction, opinion

mnoż|enie *n* multiplication; **~yć** ⟨**po-**⟩ multiply

mnóstwo *n* plenty (**czegoś** of s.th.), multitude (**czegoś** of s.th.), loads (**czegoś** of s.th.) F

moc *f* power; **na ~y**, **~ą** by virtue of; **~arstwo** *n* world power; **~ny** *adj* powerful; **człowiek**: strong; **~ować się** wrestle

moczyć ⟨**za-**⟩ drench, wet, soak

moda *f* fashion, vogue

model *m* model

modli|ć ⟨**po-**⟩ **się** pray; **~twa** *f* prayer

modny *adj* fashionable, in fashion

mok|nąć ⟨**z-**⟩ get*/become* wet, soak; **~ry** *adj* wet

molo *n* jetty, pier

moneta *f* coin

monitować send* reminders

montaż *m* assembly, assembling; **~er** *m* fitter

moralność *f* morals *pl*; morality

mord|erca *m* murderer; **~erstwo** *n* murder; **~ować** ⟨**za-**⟩ murder; *form.* assassinate

morela *f* apricot (tree)

morski *adj* sea ...; *form.* maritime

morze *n* sea

mosi|ądz *m* brass; **~ężny** *adj* brass ...

most *m* bridge; **~ek** *m* (small) bridge; *anat.* breastbone, sternum

motłoch *m* mob, rabble

moto|cykl *m* motorcycle, motorbike; **~r** *m* → **silnik**; F (*motocykl*) bike F; **~rniczy** *m* tram driver; **~rower** *m* moped; **~rówka** *f* motorboat

motyl *m* butterfly

motyw *m* motive; *artystyczny*: motif; **~ować** ⟨**u-**⟩ justify

mowa *f* speech; **~ ojczysta** mother tongue

mozolny *adj* arduous

moździerz *m* mortar

może perhaps, maybe; **~liwość** *f* possibility; (*sposobność*) opportunity; **~liwy** *adj* possible; feasible; **~na** *pred* ... one can ...; → *wolno*; **czy ~na?** may I?

móc can*; be* able to

mój *pron* my, mine

mól *m* (clothes) moth

mów|ca *m* speaker; **~ić** speak*; talk

mózg *m* brain

móżdżek *m gastr.* brains *pl*

mroczny *adj* dark, gloomy

mrok *m* darkness, the dark

mrowisko *n* ant hill

mro|zić ⟨**za-**⟩ freeze*; **~źny** *adj* frosty; **~żonki** *pl* frozen foods *pl*

mrówka *f* ant

mróz *m* frost

mruczeć murmur; *kot:* purr

mrug|ać ⟨**~nąć**⟩ blink; *porozumiewawczo*: wink; → *a. migać*

mrzonka *f* fantasy, daydream

msza *f* Mass

mścić ⟨**po-**⟩ avenge

much|a *f* fly; **~omor** *m* toadstool

muł¹ *m zo.* mule

muł² *m* (*błoto*) ooze, mud

mundur *m* uniform

mur *m* wall; **~arz** *m* bricklayer; **~ować** ⟨**wy-**⟩ build* (in brick)

Murzyn(ka *f*) *m* Negro; *w USA:* black person

musieć must*; have* to

muskularny *adj* muscular

muszka *f* (*krawat*) bow tie; *zo.* midge

muszla *f* shell; *klozetowa:* bowl

musztarda *f* mustard

Muzułma|nin *m* (**~nka** *f*) Muslim; **2ński** *adj* Muslim

muzyk *m* musician; **~a** *f* music; **~alny** *adj* musical

my *pron* we

myć ⟨**u-**⟩ (**się**) wash

mydl|ić ⟨**na-**⟩ soap; **~ło** *n* soap

myjnia *f samochodowa:* car wash

mylić ⟨**po-**⟩ confuse (**z** with); mistake* (**z** for); **~ić** ⟨**o-**⟩ **się** err; be* wrong/mistaken; **~ny** *adj* wrong; erroneous

mysz *f* mouse

myśl *f* thought; **~eć** ⟨po-⟩ think*; **~enie** *n* thinking;

~iciel *m* thinker

myśli|stwo *n* hunting, shooting *Brt.*; **~wy** *m* hunter

mżawka *f* drizzle; **~yć** drizzle

N

na *prp stole itp.*: on; *konferencji/weselu/zebraniu*: at; **~ bok** aside; to the side; **~ końcu** at the end

nabawić się contract, develop

nabiał *m* dairy produce

nabić *pf* → **nabijać**

nabierać fill (*czegoś do czegoś* s.th. with s.th.); scoop; (*oszukiwać*) put* on, kid F

nabija|ć *broń* load; **~ty** *adj* (*załoczony*) crammed; *broń*: loaded

nabożeństwo *n* service

nabój *m* cartridge

nabrać *pf* → **nabierać**

nabrzeże *n* wharf; embankment

nabrzmie(wa)ć swell*

naby|cie *n*: *do ~cia* available; **~ć** *pf* → **nabywać**; **~tek** *m* purchase, buy F; **~wać** (*kupować*) purchase; (*przyswoić sobie*) acquire; **~wca** *m* buyer

nachyl|ać ⟨**~ić**⟩ **się** bend*, lean* forward

naciąć *pf* → **nacinać**; **~ się** be* tricked

naciąga|ć ⟨**~nąć**⟩ *v/t* (*na-*

prężać) tighten; (*oszukać*) take* in; trick (*kogoś, żeby coś zrobił* s.o. into doing s.th.); *v/i herbata*: draw*

nacierać *v/t* (*smarować*) rub; *v/i* (*atakować*) attack

nacinać incise

nacis|k *m* pressure; **~kać** ⟨**~nąć**⟩ (de)press

naczeln|ik *m* head; **~y** *adj* leading; chief, main

naczynie *n* vessel; *kuchenne*: dish

nad *prp* over; **~ rzeką** on the river

nada|ć *pf* → **nadawać**; **~jnik** *m* transmitter

nadal *adv* still, as before

nadaremny *adj* vain

nadaw|ać *post.* post; *tel.* transmit; (*udzielać*) grant; **~ca** *m* sender

nadąż|ać ⟨**~yć**⟩ keep* up (*za* with)

nadchodzić approach

nadciśnienie *n* hypertension

nadczynność *f* excessive functional activity

naddźwiękowy *adj* supersonic

nadejś|cie *n* arrival; approach; **~ć** pf → **nadchodzić**

nadepnąć step, tread* (**na** on)

nader adv most, extremely, exceedingly

nadgodziny pl overtime (hours)

nadje|chać pf **~żdżać** arrive, come*

nadliczbow|y adj supernumerary; **godziny ~e** → **nadgodziny**

nadludzki adj superhuman

nadmiar m excess

nadmieni(a)ć mention

nadmierny adj excessive

nadmuch(iw)ać inflate, blow* up

nadprogramowy adj additional, supplementary

nadprzyrodzony adj supernatural

nadr|abiać **~obić** make* up (**coś** for s.th.)

nadruk m imprint

nadrzędny adj superior, primary

nadspodziewany adj ... beyond expectation

nadużyci|e n abuse; **~a** pl jur. embezzlement

nadwag|a f: **mieć ~ę** be* overweight

nadwerężać **~yć** strain

nadwozie n (car) body

nadwyżka f surplus

nadziej|a f hope; **mieć ~ę** hope

nadz|orca m supervisor; **~orować** supervise; **~ór** m supervision

nadzwyczaj adv exceedingly, exceptionally; **~ny** adj extraordinary

naft|a f petroleum, oil; **do lamp itp.**: paraffin, kerosene Am.; **~owy** adj petroleum ..., oil ...

nagabywać trouble

nagana f reprimand

nagi adj nude, naked

nagl|ący adj urgent; **~e** adv suddenly

nagły adj sudden

nago adv naked; in the nude; **~ść** f nakedness, nudity

nagr|adzać **~odzić** reward

nagrobek m tombstone

nagroda f reward; **oficjalna**: award, prize

naiwny adj naive

najazd m invasion

nająć pf → **wynajmować**

najmować → **wynajmować**

najem|ca m tenant; **~nik** m mil. mercenary; **~ny** adj hired

najeźdźca m invader

najgorszy adj the worst

najlepszy adj the best

najpierw adv first (of all)

najwięcej adv the most

nakaz m jur. warrant; **~(yw)ać** order, command

nakle|jać **~ić** paste, stick, glue; **~jka** f sticker; (**etykieta**) label

nakład m gazety itp.: circulation; książki: print-run; ~**y** pl expenditure; ~**ać** put* on

nakł|aniać ⟨~**onić**⟩ persuade (*kogoś do zrobienia czegoś* s.o. to do s.th.)

nakręc|ać ⟨~**cić**⟩ wind*; ~**tka** f na śrubę: nut; na tubke: cap

nakry|cie n stołu: tableware; ~**(wa)ć** cover; ~**wać do stołu** lay* the table

nalać pf → **nalewać**

nalega|ć insist (*na* on); urge (*żeby ktoś coś zrobił* s.o. to do s.th.)

nalep|i(a)ć paste; ~**ka** f → **naklejka**

naleśnik m pancake

nal(ew)ać pour (out)

należ|eć belong (*do* to; *być* among; ~**ność** f amount due, charge; ~**ny** adj due, owed

nalot m air raid; F policji: bust F

naładować broń load; akumulator itp. charge

nałogowiec m addict

nałożyć pf → **nakładać**

nałóg m bad habit, addiction

namacalny adj tangible

namawiać incite (*do* to); persuade (*kogoś do zrobienia czegoś* s.o. to do s.th.); talk (*kogoś do zrobienia czegoś* s.o. into doing s.th.)

namiastka f substitute, ersatz

namiętność f passion

namiot m tent

namoczyć soak

nam|owa f incitement; instigation; ~**ówić** pf → **namawiać**

namydl|ać ⟨~**ić**⟩ soap

namyśl|ać ⟨~**ić**⟩ **się** make* up one's mind

naoczny → **świadek**

naokoło prp around

napad m assault; ~**ać** assail; fizycznie: assault (*na kogoś* s.o.)

napast|liwy adj aggressive; ~**nik** m assailant

napaść 1. pf → **napadać**; **2.** f → **napad**

napchać pf → **napychać**

napełni(a)ć fill (up)

napę|d m drive; ~**dzać** ⟨~**dzić**⟩ drive*

napiąć pf → **napinać**

napić się have* a drink

napięcie n tension; electr. voltage

napinać string*

napis m inscription

napiwek m tip

napły|nąć pf → **napływać**; ~**w** m influx; ~**wać** pour in

napominać admonish

napomk|nąć pf → **napomykać**

napomnieć pf → **napominać**

napomykać mention

napot(y)kać come* across

napój m drink

napraw|a f repair(s); ~**i(a)ć** repair, fix F

naprawdę adv really, truly; indeed

naprzeciw(ko) adv, prp opposite

naprzód prp forward; ahead

naprzykrz|ać ⟨~yć⟩ się make* a nuisance of oneself

napychać stuff

narada f council; conference

naradz|ać ⟨~ić⟩ się confer

naraz adv at the same time; (nagle) suddenly, all of a sudden

nara|zić pf ~żać expose (na to)

narcia|rski adj skiing ...; ~rstwo n skiing; ~rz m skier

nareszcie adv at last, finally

narko|man m drug addict; ~tyk m drug; ~tyzować się take* drugs; be* on drugs; be* a drug addict

narodow|ość f nationality; ~y adj national

Narodzenie n: Boże Narodzenie Christmas

narośl f growth

naroż|nik m corner; ~y adj corner ...

naród m nation; (lud) people sg

narta f ski

narusz|ać infringe; ~enie n infringement; ~yć pf → naruszać

narząd m organ

narzecz|eni pl engaged couple; ~ona f fiancée; ~ony m fiancé

narzekać complain

narzędzie n tool

narzu|cać ⟨~cić⟩ impose; ~t

m econ. surcharge

nas pron us; u ~ at our place

nasada f base

nasenny adj: środek m ~ sleeping pill/tablet

nasienie n bot. seed; ludzkie: semen

nasilenie n increase, escalation

naskórek m epidermis

nasmarować tech. grease, lubricate

nasta(wa)ć v/i follow; come* (about)

nastawi(a)ć set*; ~ się prepare (na for)

nast|ąpić pf → następować; ~ępca m successor; ~ępnie adv next; subsequently; ~ępny adj next; ~ępować follow (po czymś s.th.); ~ępstwo n sequence; ~ępująco adv as follows; ~ępujący adj following

nastraszyć frighten

nastręcz|ać ⟨~yć⟩ trudności itp.: present, offer

nastr|ojowy adj romantic; ~ój m mood; atmosphere

nasu|nąć pf ~wać się occur (komuś to s.o.)

nasyc|ać ⟨~ić⟩ saturate; głód itp. satisfy

nasyp m embankment; ~(yw)ać pour (out)

nasz pron our's

naszy|ć pf → naszywać

naszyjnik m necklace

naszywać sew* on

naśladować imitate, copy

naśmiewać się poke fun, laugh (**z** at)

naświetlać ⟨**~ić**⟩ *phot.* expose

natar|cie *n* advance; **~czywy** *adj* importunate; insistent

natężenie *n* intensity

natłu|szczać ⟨**~ścić**⟩ grease

natomiast *adv* however

natrafi|ać come* across/upon (**na kogoś, coś** s.o., s.th.)

natrętny *adj* importunate, insistent

natrysk *m* shower

natrząsać się to make* a laughing stock (**z kogoś** of s.o.)

natrzeć *pf* → **nacierać**

natura *f* nature; **~lny** *adj* natural

natychmiast *adv* immediately; **~owy** *adj* immediate

naucz|ać ⟨**~yć**⟩ teach*; **~yć się** learn*; **~yciel(ka** *f*) *m* teacher

nauk|a *f* science; (*uczenie się*) study, studying; **~owiec** *m* scientist; (*humanista*) scholar; (*nauki*) **~owy** *adj* scientific; **w humanistyce**: scholarly

naumyśln|ie *adv* deliberately, on purpose; **~y** *adj* deliberate, purposeful

nawałnica *f* (rain)storm

nawet even

nawias *m* parenthesis; **~em mówiąc** by the way, incidentally

nawierzchnia *f* (road) sur-

face

nawieźć *pf* → **nawozić**

nawij|ać ⟨**~nąć**⟩ wind*, coil

nawle|kać ⟨**~c**⟩ thread

nawoływać exhort (**to** to)

naw|ozić fertilize; **~óz** *m* fertilizer; **naturalny**: manure

nawr|acać; **~ót** *m* sp. round; *med.* relapse

nawyk|ać ⟨**~nąć**⟩ become* accustomed, get* used (**do** to)

nawzajem *adv* (*wzajemnie*) mutually; **~!** the same to you!; **się/sobie ~** one another, each other

nazbyt *adv* too

naz|wa *f* name; **~wać** *pf* → **nazywać**; **nazwisko** *n* surname *Brt.*, last name *Am.*; **~ywać** call; **~ywać się** be* called*; **~ywam się ...** my name is ...

neg|atyw *m* negative; **~atywny** *adj* negative; **~ować** ⟨**za-**⟩ negate

neonowy *adj* neon ...

nerka *f* kidney

nerw *m* nerve; **~ica** *f* neurosis; **~owy** *adj* nervous; **człowiek**: excitable, jumpy, irritable

nędz|a *f* poverty; **~ny** *adj* wretched; (*kiepski*) trashy, lousy F

nękać harass

niby (*jakby*) as if/though; (*podobny do*) like; (*udawany, pozorowany*) sham, make-believe ..., mock ...

nic *pron* nothing; ~ **a** ~ nothing at all

niczyj *adj* nobody's

nić *f* thread

nie zaprzeczenie: no; *z czasownikiem*: not

niebezpiecz|eństwo *n* danger, peril; **~ny** *adj* dangerous

niebieski¹ *adj kolor*: blue; *na niebie*: sky ...

niebieski² *adj* (*niebiański*) heavenly, divine

niebo¹ *n* sky

niebo² *n eccl.* Heaven

nieboszcz|ka *f*, **~yk** *m* the deceased

niebywały *adj* unheard-of

niecały *adj* less than

niech: ~ **pan(i)** ... will you please ...; ~ **żyje** ...! long live ...!

niech|cący *adj* unintentionally; **~eć** *f* dislike (**do** for); bias (**do** against); **~ętny** *adj* reluctant, unwilling

niecierpliw|ić się *be** impatient/restless; **~y** *adj* impatient

nieco *adv* somewhat

nieczuły *adj* callous, insensitive

nieczynny *adj sklep*: closed; *urządzenie*: out of order

nieczytelny *adj* illegible

niedalek|i *adj* close, nearby; **~o** *adv* close, near, nearby

niedawno *adv* recently, not long ago

niedba|lstwo *n* carelessness, negligence; **~ły** *adj* careless, sloppy F

niedobór *m* deficiency, shortage

niedobry *adj* (*niewłaściwy*) wrong; (*niegrzeczny*) naughty

niedogodny *adj* inconvenient

niedojrzały *adj* immature; *owoc*: not ripe

niedokładny *adj* inaccurate, inexact

niedokończony *adj* unfinished

niedomagać *be** ailing

niedopałek *m* cigarette end, fag end F

niedopuszczalny *adj* unacceptable, inadmissible

niedorzeczny *adj* absurd, preposterous

niedoskonały *adj* imperfect

niedostate|k *m* scarcity, shortage; (*bieda*) want; **~czny** *adj* insufficient; *ocena*: unsatisfactory

niedostępny *adj* inaccessible

niedoświadczony *adj* inexperienced

niedowidzieć *be** short-sighted

niedozwolony *adj* prohibited

niedożywiony *adj* underfed, undernourished

niedrogi *adj* inexpensive

nieduży *adj* not large

niedziel|a *f* Sunday; **w ~ę** on Sunday; **~ny** *adj* Sunday ...

niedźwiedź *m* bear

niefachowy *adj* inexpert

niegdyś *adv* once, in the past

niegościnny adj inhospitable

niegrzeczny adj naughty

nieistotny adj immaterial, inessential

niejadalny adj inedible

niejaki adj: ~ **pan X** a Mr. X

niejasny adj obscure, vague

niejednokrotnie adv repeatedly, many a time

niekiedy adv sometimes, now and then

niekorzystny adj unfavourable; econ. unprofitable

niektórzy adj some (people)

nielegalny adj illegal, unlawful

nieletni 1. adj juvenile, under age; **2.** m minor, juvenile

nieliczn|i pl few (people); **~y** adj small (in number)

nieład m disorder, disarray, mess

nieładny adj not nice; (nieurodziwy) plain, unattractive

nie ma z l. pojedynczą: there isn't any; z l. mnogą: there aren't any; ~ **za co** not at all

niemały adj considerable, pretty big F

Niem|cy pl Germany; **~iec** m German; **2iecki** adj German; **~ka** f German

niemodny adj out of fashion

niemowlę n baby, infant

niemożliwy adj impossible

niemy adj dumb, mute

nienaganny adj impeccable, faultless

nienaruszalny adj inviolable

nienawi|dzić hate, loathe;

~ść f hatred, hate

nieobecny adj absent

nieobliczalny adj unpredictable

nieoczekiwany adj unexpected

nieodłączny adj inseparable

nieodpowiedni adj unsuitable

nieodpowiedzialny adj irresponsible

nieodwołalny adj irrevocable

nieograniczony adj unlimited

nieokreślony adj undefined, nondescript

nieomylny adj infallible, unerring

nieopanowany adj uncontrollable

nieopisany adj indescribable

nieostrożny adj careless, uncautious

nieostry adj obraz: blurred

niepalący m non-smoker

nieparzysty adj odd

niepełny adj incomplete

niepewny adj uncertain

niepijący m teetotaller

niepoczytalny adj insane

niepodległość f independence; **~y** adj independent

niepodobny adj unlike (do czegoś, kogoś s.th., s.o.), dissimilar (do to)

niepogoda f bad weather

niepok|oić ⟨za-⟩ trouble; bother; worry; **~oić się** worry, be* anxious; **~ój** m anxiety

niepokonany *adj* unconquerable, invincible

niepomyślny *adj (niekorzystny)* unfavourable; *wróżba*: ill-boding

niepoprawny *adj człowiek*: incorrigible; *gr.* incorrect

nieporozumienie *n* misunderstanding

nieporządek *m* disorder

nieposłuszny *adj* disobedient

niepospolity *adj* uncommon

niepotrzebny *adj* unnecessary; *(do wyrzucenia)* useless

niepowodzenie *n* failure

niepozorny *adj* inconspicuous, nondescript

niepożądany *adj* undesirable

nieprawd|a *f* untruth, lie; **~a?** isn't that so?; **~opodobny** *adj* improbable, unlikely

nieprawdziwy *adj* untrue; *(udający)* fake, not genuine

nieprawidłowy *adj* incorrect

nieproszony *adj* unwelcome

nieprzeciętny *adj* uncommon, extraordinary

nieprzekupny *adj* incorruptible

nieprzemakalny *adj* waterproof, water-resistant

nieprzepuszczalny *adj* impenetrable

nieprzerwany *adj* uninterrupted

nieprzetłumaczalny *adj* untranslatable

nieprzewidziany *adj* unforeseen

nieprzezroczysty *adj* opaque

nieprzychylny *adj* unfriendly

nieprzydatny *adj* useless

nieprzyja|ciel *m* enemy; **~zny** *adj* hostile

nieprzyjemn|ości *pl* trouble; **~y** *adj* unpleasant

nieprzystępny *adj* unapproachable

nieprzytomny *adj* unconscious

nieprzyzwoity *adj* indecent

niepunktualny *adj* unpunctual

nieraz *adv* many a time, repeatedly

nierdzewny *adj* stainless

nieregularny *adj* irregular

nierentowny *adj* unprofitable

nierozłączny *adj* inseparable

nierozpuszczalny *adj* insoluble

nierozsądny *adj* unwise

nierozważny *adj* imprudent, rash

nierów|ność *f powierzchni*: unevenness; **~ny** *adj powierzchnia*: uneven

nieruchomy *adj* motionless, immobile

nierząd *m* prostitution

nieskazitelny *adj* unblemished

nieskończony *adj* endless

niesłowny *adj* unreliable

niesłuszny *adj* unjust; *(bezpodstawny)* groundless

niesłychany *adj* unheard-of, incredible

niesmaczny adj unseemly

niespodzi|anka f surprise; **~any, ~ewany** adj unexpected

niespokojny adj restless; (zaniepokojony) anxious

niesprawiedliwy adj unjust, unfair

niestety adv unfortunately, alas

niestosowny adj improper

niestrawny adj indigestible

niesumienny adj unconscientious

nieszczery adj insincere

nieszczęś|cie n (tragedia) misfortune, disaster; **~liwy** adj unhappy

nieszkodliwy adj harmless

nieścisły adj inexact

nieść carry

nieślubny adj illegitimate

nieśmiały adj shy, timid

nieśmiertelny adj immortal

nieświadomy adj unaware/ unconscious (**czegoś** of s.th.)

nieświeży adj not fresh; chleb: stale; mięso, oddech: bad

nietakt m tactlessness; **~owny** adj tactless

nietoperz m bat

nietrzeźwy adj intoxicated, tipsy F

nietypowy adj sposób: unconventional

nieuczciwy adj dishonest

nieudany adj unsuccessful, failed

nieufność f distrust; **wotum**

n **~ci** a vote of no confidence

nieuleczalny adj incurable

nieunikniony adj inevitable, unavoidable

nieumiejętny adj unskilful

nieumyślny adj unintentional

nieunikniony adj inevitable, unavoidable

nieurodzaj m bad harvest

nieustanny adj continual, unceasing

nieustraszony adj fearless

nieuważny adj careless

nieuzasadniony adj unjustified

nieuzbrojony adj unarmed

nieważny adj szczegół: unimportant; dokument: invalid, null and void

niewątpliwy adj undoubted, unmistakable

niewdzięczny adj dziecko: ungrateful; praca: thankless, unrewarding

niewesoły adj sytuacja: unpleasant; mina: sad

niewiadoma f math. unknown quantity

niewiara f lack of confidence (**w coś** in s.th.)

niewidomy adj blind

niewidzialny adj invisible

niewiel|e światła, wody itp.: little, not much; **~e, ~u** few, not many; **~ki** adj little, small

niewier|ność f małżeńska: infidelity; **~y 1.** adj mąż: unfaithful; **2.** m infidel

niewierzący m atheist, unbeliever

niewinny *adj* innocent; *jur.* not guilty

niewłaściwy *adj* improper; *odpowiedź*: incorrect, wrong; *człowiek*: wrong

niewol|a *adj* captivity; **~nica** *f* (**~nik** *m*) slave

niewrażliwy *adj* insensitive (**na** to)

niewskazany *adj* inadvisable

niewybaczalny *adj* unforgivable

niewygodny *adj fotel*: uncomfortable; *fakt*: unfortunate; (*niedogodny*) inconvenient

niewykształcony *adj* uneducated

niewypłacalny *adj jur.* insolvent

niewyraźny *adj obraz*: fuzzy, blurred; *głos*: indistinct

niewyspany *adj* sleepy

niewytłumaczalny *adj* inexplicable

niezadowol|enie *n* dissatisfaction (**z czegoś** with s.th.), discontent (**z czegoś** with s.th.); **~ony** *adj* dissatisfied (**z czegoś** with s.th.)

niezależny *adj* independent (**od** of)

niezamężny *adj kobieta*: unmarried, single

niezapominajka *f bot.* forget-me-not

niezapomniany *adj* unforgettable

niezasłużony *adj* undeserved

niezawodny *adj* dependable, reliable

niezbędny *adj* indispensable, necessary

niezdatny *adj* unfit (**do** for)

niezdecydowany *adj* undecided; *człowiek*: hesitant

niezdrowy *adj* unwell, unhealthy

niezgrabny *adj* (*niezdarny*) clumsy, awkward

niezliczony *adj* countless, innumerable

niezły *adj* not bad, quite good

niezmienny *adj* unchangeable, invariable

nieznaczny *adj* inconsiderable, slight; *zwycięstwo*: narrow

nieznajom|a *f* stranger; **~y 1.** *m* stranger; **2.** *adj* strange, unknown

nieznany *adj* unknown

nieznośny *adj* intolerable, unbearable

niezręczny *adj* clumsy

niezrozumiały *adj* incomprehensible

niezupełnie *adv* not exactly, not quite

niezwłocznie *adv* at once, immediately

nieźle *adv* quite well

nieżonaty *adj mężczyzna*: unmarried, single

nieżyczliwy *adj* unfriendly

nieżywy *adj* dead; *noworodek*: still-born

ni|gdy *adv* never; **~gdzie** nowhere; *Gdzie byłeś? - 2gdzie*. Where have you

been? - Nowhere.; **~gdzie
nie pójdę** I'm not going anywhere
nijaki *adj* indistinct; *gr.* neuter
niknąć <z-> *v/i* disappear,
vanish
ni|kogo, **~komu** *pron* → **~kt**
pron nobody, no one; *Kto tu
był?* - **~kt.** Who was here? -
Nobody.; **~kogo nie ma**
there's nobody here; **nie
ufam ~komu** I don't trust
anybody
nim 1. *cj* before; → **zanim**;
pomyśl (za)~ coś powiesz
think before you say anything; **2.** *pron o ~* about him;
z ~ with him
nisk|i *adj* low; **człowiek:**
short; **głos:** low (**basowy**)
deep; **~o** *adv* low
niszcz|eć <z-> *v/i* deteriorate; **~yciel** *m* mil. destroyer;
~yć <z-> *v/t* destroy, devastate; **zdrowie ruin**; **~yć się
płaszcz itp.:** wear* out;
wzajemnie: destroy one another
nit *m* rivet
nitka *f* thread
nizina *f* lowlands *pl*
niż[1] *cj* than
niż[2] *m meteor.* depression; **~ej**
adv comp. of **nisko** lower; **~ej
podpisany** the undersigned;
~szy *adj comp. of* **niski** lower; **człowiek:** shorter
no *int* well; F yes, yeah F; **~ ~!**
F podziw: wow! F; **~ cóż** oh

well; **~ dalej!** *(pospiesz się!)*
come on!; **~ to co?** so what?
noc *f* night; **w ~y, ~ą** at night;
całą ~ all night (long); **~leg**
m: **dawać komuś ~leg** put
s.o. up (for the night); **~nik**
m (chamber) pot, potty; **~ny**
adj night ...; **~ować** <prze->
v/i spend* the night (**u kogoś**
with s.o.)
noga *f* leg; **do góry ~mi** upside down; **~wka** *f* (trouser)
leg
nominacja *f* nomination (**na**
for); appointment
nora *f* burrow; *(mieszkanie)*
pigsty F, dump F
norma *f* społeczna itp.: norm;
przemysłowa itp.: standard;
pracy: quota
Norwe|g *m* Norwegian; **~gia**
f Norway; **2ski** *adj* Norwegian; *mówić po 2sku* speak*
Norwegian; **~żka** *f* Norwegian
nos *m* nose
nosi|ciel *m* wirusa itp.: carrier; **~ć** carry; **ubranie** wear*
nosorożec *m* rhinoceros, rhino F
nosze *pl* stretcher
nośnik *m* magnetyczny itp.:
medium
notariusz *m* notary
not|atka *f* note; **~atnik** *m*, **~es**
m notebook; **~ować** <za->
write* down, make* a note
of
nowoczesny *adj* modern,
up-to-date

noworodek *m* newborn baby
nowość *f* novelty
now|**y** *adj* new; **~o** *adv* newly;
na ~o, od ~a all over again
noży|**ce, ~czki** *pl* scissors *pl*
nóż *m* knife
nud|**a** *f* boredom; *pl* **~ności** *pl*
nausea; **~ny** *adj* boring, dull
nudysta *m* nudist
nudzi|**arz** *m* bore; **~ć** bore
(**czymś** with s.th.); **~ć się** be

bored
numer *m* number; (*egzem-plarz*) issue; **~ować ⟨po-⟩**
number
nur|**ek** *m* diver; **~kować**
⟨za-⟩ dive
nurt *m* current
nuta *f mus.* note
nuż|**ący** *adj* tiresome; **~yć**
⟨z-⟩ *kogoś* make* (s.o.) tired

O

o *prp* mówić, martwić się: a-
bout; *opierać się*: against,
on; *prosić, walczyć*: for; *os-karżyć*: of
ob|**a, ~aj** both
obal|**ać ⟨~ić⟩** *rząd, ustrój*
overthrow; *teorię* disprove
obaw|**a** *f* fear; **~iać się** fear;
~iam się, że nie masz racji I
am afraid you are wrong
obcas *m* heel; *buty pl* **na wy-sokich ~ach** high-heeled
shoes *pl*
ob|**cęgi, ~cęgi** *pl* pincers *pl*
obchodzić *miejsce* walk
round; *święto* celebrate; **to**
mnie nie~ I don't care about
that; **~ć się** handle (**z czymś**
s.th.); *bez czegoś*: do* without (s.th.)
obchód *m w szpitalu*: round
obciąć *pf* → **obcinać**
obciąż|**ać ⟨~yć⟩** *weight,
kosztami*: charge
obcinać cut* (off)

obcisły *adj* tight, close-fitting
obcokrajowiec *m* foreigner
obcować be in contact (**z**
with)
ob|**cy 1.** *adj człowiek, miejsce*:
strange, unknown; *ciało*:
foreign; **2.** *m* stranger;
~czyzna *f*: **na ~czyźnie** in
exile
obdarz|**ać ⟨~yć⟩** present
(**czymś kogoś** s.th. to s.o.,
s.o. with s.th.); **~ać kogoś
zaufaniem** put* one's trust
in s.o.; **~ony** endowed
(**czymś** with s.th.)
obecn|**ie** now, at present;
~ość *f* presence; **~y** *adj* present
obej|**mować ⟨objąć⟩** *ramio-
nami*: embrace; (*dotyczyć*)
include, comprise; **~mować
urząd** take* office
obejrzeć *pf* → **oglądać**
obejść *pf* → **obchodzić**
obel|**ga** *f* insult; **~żywy** *adj*

insulting, offensive
oberwać pf → **obrywać**
obfity adj abundant
obgry|zać ⟨**~źć**⟩ kość gnaw; paznokcie bite*
obiad m wieczorem: dinner; po południu: lunch
obi|cie n upholstery; **~ć** pf → **obijać**
obie → **oba**
obiec pf → **obiegać**
obiec(yw)ać promise
obieg m circulation; **~ać** run* round
obiekt m object; sportowy, przemysłowy: complex
obie|rać ziemniaki, owoce peel; **~rzyny** pl peelings pl
obietnica f promise
obijać meble upholster
objaśni|(a)ć explain; **~enie** n explanation
objaw m symptom; **~ienie** n revelation
objazd m detour; **~owy** adj teatr: travelling
objąć pf → **obejmować**
obje|żdżać ⟨**~chać**⟩ tour
objętość f volume
obl(ew)ać wodą itp.: pour (water etc.) on; F egzamin flunk F; **~ się** wodą itp.: spill* (water) on oneself
oblężenie n siege
oblicz|ać calculate; **~enie** n calculation; **~yć** pf → **obliczać**
obligacja państwowa: bond
obliz(yw)ać lick
oblodzony icy

obława f manhunt
obł|ąkany adj mad; **~ęd** m madness; **~ędny** F adj fabulous
obłud|a f hypocrisy; **~nik** m (-nica f) hypocrite; **~ny** adj hypocritical
obmac(yw)ać feel* (with one's fingers)
obm|awiać ⟨**~ówić**⟩ slander
obmyśl|ać ⟨**~ić**⟩ devise
obnażony adj naked
obniż|ać ⟨**~yć**⟩ lower; **~ać się** temperatura: drop; **~ka** f reduction, drop; cen: (price) cut; **~ony** adj cena: reduced
obojczyk m collarbone
oboje → **oba**
obojętn|ość f indifference; **~y** adj indifferent (na to); chem.: neutral
obok prp by, next to; mieszkać: next door
obora f cowshed
obowiąz|ek m duty; **~kowy** adj przedmiot: obligatory, compulsory; uczeń: conscientious; **~ywać** be obligatory
obozow|ać camp out; **~isko** n encampment
obój m mus. oboe
obóz m camp
obrabia|ć metal shape; **~rka** f machine tool
obrabować rob; na ulicy: mug
obracać turn; **~ na drugą stronę** turn over; **~ się** turn round

obrać *pf* → **obierać**

obrad|ować deliberate; **~y** *pl* deliberations *pl*; *rządu:* debate

obraz *m* picture; *malowany:* painting; *w wyobraźni:* image, (mental) picture; *TV* picture; *phys., phot.* image

obraza *f* insult

obrazek *m* picture

obrazić *pf* → **obrażać**

obrazowy *adj* picturesque

obraźliwy *adj* offensive, insulting

obrażać insult, offend; **~ się** take* offence (**o** at)

obrażenia *pl* injuries *pl*

obrączka *f (ślubna* wedding) ring

obręb *m*: **w ~ie** within; *poza* **~em** beyond

obrobić *pf* → **obrabiać**

obro|na *f* defence (**przed** against); **~ńca** *m* defender; *moralności:* guardian; *jur.* counsel for the defence, advocate

obrotowy *adj* revolving

obroża *f* (dog) collar

obró|cić *pf* → **obracać**; **~t** *m* *koła:* revolution; *ciała:* turn

obrus *m* tablecloth

obrywać *guzik, liść* tear* off

obrząd|ek *m* → **~ed** *m* ceremony

obrzęk *m med.* swelling

obrzuc|ać ⟨**~ić**⟩ pelt (**czymś** with s.th.)

obrzy|dliwy *adj* disgusting; **~dzenie** *n* disgust

obsa|da *f film., thea.* cast; **~dzać** ⟨**~dzić**⟩ cast*

obserw|acja *f* observation; *policyjna:* surveillance; **~ator** *m* observer; **~atorium** *n* observatory; **~ować** observe; *(śledzić)* watch

obsłu|ga *f* service; *(pracownicy)* personnel, staff; **stacja** *f* **~gi** service station; **instrukcja** *f* **~gi** instructions (booklet); **~giwać** ⟨**~żyć**⟩ serve; *w restauracji:* wait on; *maszynę* operate, work

obstawa *f* bodyguard

obstrzał *m* gunfire; **pod ~em** under fire

obsyp|(yw)ać *kwiatami, prezentami:* shower (**kogoś czymś** s.o. with s.th.); *pochwałami:* heap (**kogoś czymś** s.th. on s.o.)

obszar *m* area; *lądu, wody:* stretch

obszarpany *adj* ragged

obszerny *adj* large; *sprawozdanie:* extensive, exhaustive

obu → **oba**

obudowa *f* cover

obudzić *pf* → **budzić**

oburz|ać ⟨**~yć⟩ się** become* indignant (**na** at); **~enie** *n* indignation; **~ony** *adj* indignant (**na** at)

obustronny *adj rozmowy:* bilateral; *zaufanie, korzyść:* mutual

obuwie *n* footwear

obwąch(iw)ać sniff (**coś** at s.th.)

obwiąz(yw)ać *ranę* bandage (up); *paczkę* tie up

obwieszczenie *n* announcement

obwini(a)ć blame (*kogoś o coś* s.o. for s.th.)

obwodnica *f* bypass

obwód *m* *math.* circumference; *electr.* circuit; **~ w pasie** waist measurement

obyczaj *m* custom; **~owy** *adj* customary

obyć się *pf* → **obywać się**

obydwa, ~oje → **oba**

obywać się manage (*bez* without)

obywatel∥(ka *f*) *m* citizen; **~stwo** *n* citizenship

ocal∥ać ⟨**~ić**⟩ rescue; *komuś życie* save s.o.'s life; **~eć** *pf* survive; **~enie** *n* rescue

ocen∥a *f* evaluation; *szkolna:* grade, mark; **~i(a)ć** evaluate; *prace uczniów* mark

ocet *m* vinegar

ochlap(yw)ać splash (*kogoś czymś* s.o. with s.th.)

ochładzać, ochłodzić → **chłodzić**

ochot∥a *f* willingness, desire; *mieć ~ę na coś* feel* like (doing) s.th.; **~niczy** *adj* voluntary; **~nik** *m* volunteer

ochrania∥cz *m* *sp.* pad; **~ć** → **chronić**

ochron∥a *f* protection; *osobista:* bodyguard; **~iarz** F *m* bodyguard; **~ny** *adj* protective

ociemniały → **niewidomy**

ocieplać ⟨**-lić**⟩ *dom itp.* insulate; **~ się** get* warmer

oclenie *n:* *coś do ~a* something to declare

oczarować enchant; **~ny** *adj* enchanted

oczekiwa∥ć await (*kogoś, czegoś* s.o., s.th.), wait (*kogoś, czegoś* for s.o., s.th.); **~nie** *n* expectation

ocz∥ko *n igły:* eye; *w pończosze:* ladder *Brt.*, run *Am.*; (*gra*) blackjack; **~ny** *adj* *nerw:* optic; **gałka** *f* **~na** eyeball; **~y** *pl* → **oko**

oczy∥szczać ⟨**~ścić**⟩ *skórę, ranę* cleanse; *teren* clear; **~szczalnia ścieków** sewage farm; **~szczanie** *n* purification; **~szczony** purified; *cukier:* refined

oczytany *adj* well-read

oczywi∥sty *adj* obvious; **~ście** obviously; (*na pewno*) certainly

od *prp miejsca:* from; *roku, godziny:* for; *w porównaniach:* than; *starszy ~ ciebie* older than you; *młodszy ode mnie* younger than me; **~ samego początku** from the very beginning

odbi∥ć *pf* → **odbijać**; **~cie** *n w lustrze:* reflection; *piłki o ziemię:* bounce; *piłki do przeciwnika:* return; *phys. fali:* deflection

odbiegać ⟨**~c**⟩ *run* away (*od* from); *od tematu:* deviate (from)

odbierać take* away (*komuś* from s.o.); *bagaż itp.* collect (**z** from); *telefon itp.* answer; *wiadomość* receive

odbijać *światło* reflect; *piłkę o ziemię* bounce; *piłkę do przeciwnika* return; F (*kopiować*) photocopy, run* off; **~ się** *światło*: reflect; *piłka*: bounce (**o** off); deflect

odbiorca *m* recipient; **~ornik** *m* receiver (*a. radio*) TV, radio: set; **~ór** *m* TV, radio: reception; *listu itp.*: receipt

odbitka *f* phot. print; (*ksero*) Xerox TM (*copy*)

odbudow|a *f* reconstruction; **~(yw)ać** reconstruct

odby *pf* → **odbywa**

odbyt *m* anat. anus

odbywać *karę* serve; *szkolenie* take*, undergo*; *rozmowę* hold*; **~ się** take* place, be* held, happen

odchody *pl* faeces *pl*; **~dzić** walk away (*od* from); *pociąg*: leave*; (*opuszczać*) leave* (**od kogoś** s.o.)

odchudz|ać ⟨**~ić**⟩ **się** slim

odciąć *pf* → **odcinać**

odciąg|ać ⟨**~nąć**⟩ pull away (*od* from)

odcień *m* shade

odci|ęty *adj* cut off (*od* from); **~nać** cut* off (*od* from); **~nek** *m* section; *drogi*: stretch; *serialu*: episode; *biletu*: stub; *math.* line segment

odcisk *m* imprint; *na stopie*: corn; **~ palca** fingerprint

odczyt *m* (*wykład*) lecture; *pomiaru*: reading

oddać *pf* → **oddawać**

odda|lać ⟨**~ić**⟩ **się** (*odchodzić*) walk away; **~ony**: **~ony o 10 kilometrów od czegoś** situated 10 kilometres away from s.th.

odda|ny *adj* devoted (*komuś, czemuś* to s.o., s.th.); **~wać** *pieniądze, książkę* return, give* back (*komuś* to s.o.); *głos w wyborach* cast* (**na kogoś** on s.o.); *myśl* express, render; **~wać mocz** urinate, pass water; **~wać się** (*zajmować się*) devote oneself (*czemuś* to s.th.); **~wać się w ręce władz** give* oneself up to the authorities

od|dech *m* breath; **~dychać** breathe; **~dychanie** *n* respiration

oddział *wojska*: troop; *w szpitalu*: ward; (*filia*) branch; **~ intensywnej opieki medycznej** intensive-care unit

oddziaływać affect (**na kogoś** s.o.), have* an effect (**na kogoś** on s.o.); *wzajemnie*: interact (**na siebie** with one another)

oddziel|ać ⟨**~ić**⟩ separate (*od* from); **~nie** *adv* separately; **~ny** *adj* separate

oddzierać tear* off

oddźwięk *m* repercussions *pl*

ode → **od**

odebrać pf → **odbierać**
odedrzeć pf → **oddzierać**
odegnać pf → **odganiać**
odegrać pf → **odgrywać**
odejmować math. subtract
odejście n departure; od tematu: deviation
odejść pf → **odchodzić**
odepchnąć pf → **odpychać**
oderwać pf → **odrywać**
odesłać pf → **odsyłać**
odetchnąć take* a deep breath
odezwać się pf → **odzywać się**
odgad|ywać ⟨~nąć⟩ guess
odgłos m noise
odgrywać play (back)
odgryzć bite* off
odgrz(ew)ać warm up
odjazd m departure
odjąć pf → **odejmować**
odjeżdżać ⟨-jechać⟩ depart, leave* (do for)
odkąd prp since
odklejać unstick*; ~ **się** unstick*, come* unstuck
odkładać na miejsce: put* away; pieniądze save; spotkanie: postpone, put* off; słuchawkę replace, put* down
odkop(yw)ać dig* out
odkorkow(yw)ać uncork
odkręcać ⟨-ić⟩ unscrew
odkry|cie n discovery; ~ty adj stadion: uncovered, outdoor; ~(wa)ć uncover; nieznany kontynent discover; ~wca discoverer

odkurz|acz m vacuum cleaner; ~ać ⟨~yć⟩ półkę dust; dywan vacuum
odlać pf → **odlewać**
odl|atywać ⟨~ecieć⟩ fly* away; samolot z lotniska: depart
odległ|ość f distance; **w** ~**ości 10 mil** 10 miles away; ~**y** distant
odlew|ać wodę pour off; (robić odlew) cast*; ~**nia** f foundry
odlot m departure; czas m ~**u** departure time
odłam|ek m fragment; mil. piece of shrapnel; ~(yw)ać break* off
odłącz|ać ⟨~yć⟩ część od całości: detach (**od** from); ~**ać się** break* away (**od** from)
odłożyć pf → **odkładać**
odmawiać refuse, deny; ~ **modlitwę** say* a prayer
odmi|ana f change; (urozmaicenie) variety; gr. declension; bot. variety; **dla** ~**any** for a change; ~**eni(a)ć (się)** gr. inflect; ~**enny** pogląd, płeć: opposite; gr. inflected
odmierz|ać ⟨~yć⟩ measure, gauge
odmł|adzać ⟨~odzić⟩ kogoś make* (s.o.) look younger; zespół inject new blood into
odmow|a f refusal; ~**ny** odpowiedź: negative
odmówić pf → **odmawiać**
odmr|ażać ⟨-ozić⟩ lodówkę

defrost; **~ozić** *sobie stopę* get* one's foot frostbitten; **~ożenie** *n* frostbite

odna|jdywać ⟨**~leźć**⟩ find*, discover; **~jdywać się** be discovered, turn up F

odnawiać *dom* redecorate, renovate; *znajomość* renew

odn|iesienie *n*: *punkt m* **~iesienia** point of reference; **~osić** ⟨**~ieść**⟩ *na miejsce*: take* back, carry back; **~osić się** refer (*do* to); **~oszący się do czegoś** relating to s.th.

odnowić *pf* → **odnawiać**

odosobnienie *n* in isolation

odpa|dać *z konkursu*: drop out (*of*); **~dki** *pl* rubbish *Brt.*, garbage *Am.*; **~dy** *pl* **przemysłowe** industrial waste; **~ść** *pf* → **odpadać**

odpędzać ⟨**~ić**⟩ chase off

odpiąć *pf* → **odpinać**

odpiłow(yw)ać saw* off

odpinać unfasten

odpis(yw)ać *na list*: reply; (*ściągać*) cheat, copy (*od* from), crib F

odpły|w *m* ebb; (*otwór, rura*) outlet; **~wać** ⟨**~nąć**⟩ *pływak*: swim* away; *jacht*: sail away

odpocz|ąć *pf* → **odpoczywać**; **~ynek** *m* rest; **~ywać** rest

odporn|ość *f* resistance; *med.* immunity (*na* to, against); **~y** *adj* immune (*na* to, against)

odpowi|adać¹ ⟨**~edzieć**⟩ answer, respond (*na coś* to s.th., *czymś* with s.th.); (*być odpowiedzialnym*) be* responsible (*za* for); *na list*: answer, reply (to); **~adać na pytanie** answer a question

odpowi|adać² suit; *opisowi*: answer (to); **~edni** *adj* suitable (*do* for); (*odnośny*) relevant; **~ednik** *m* counterpart; *w innym języku*: equivalent

odpowiedzialn|ość *f* responsibility (*za* for); **~y** *adj* responsible (*za* for); (*solidny*) reliable

odpowiedź *f* answer (*na* to), response (*na* to); *na list*: reply (*na* to)

odpraw|a *f* (*zebranie*) briefing; **~a celna** customs clearance; **~a pasażerów** check-in; **~i(a)ć** *towary* dispatch; **~iać Mszę** celebrate Mass

odpręż|ać ⟨**~yć**⟩ **się** relax; **~enie** *n* *pol.* détente

odprowadz|ać ⟨**~ić**⟩ see* off; **~ać kogoś do samochodu** see* s.o. to the car; **~ać kogoś do domu** see* s.o. home

odpychać push away (*od siebie* from one)

odrabiać *zaległości* catch* up on; **~ lekcje** do* one's homework

odra|dzać ⟨**~dzić**⟩ advise (*komuś coś* s.o. against s.th.)

odr|astać ⟨**-osnąć**⟩ *włosy itp.* grow* back

odra|za *f* disgust, abhorrence; **~żający** *adj* disgusting, repulsive

odrębny *adj* separate, distinct

odręczny *adj list*: hand-written; *rysunek*: free-hand

odrętwienie *n* numbness

odrobić *pf* → **odrabiać**

odrobina *f (trochę)* a little bit *(czegoś* of s.th.)

odro|czenie *n* postponent; *jur.* reprive; **~czyć** *pf* → **odraczać**

odro|dzenie *n* revival; *hist.* Renaissance; **~dzić się** *pf* → **odradzać się**

odróżni|a(ć) differentiate, tell* *(jedną rzecz od drugiej)* one thing from another); **~ się** stand* out

odruch *m* reflex

odrywać *guzik* tear* off; *nie mogę od nich oderwać oczu* I can't wrench my eyes away from them; **~ się** break* off

odrzu|cać ⟨**-cić**⟩ *piłkę* throw* back *(do kogoś* to s.o.); *propozycję* reject; **~cenie** rejection; **~t** *m towar*: reject; *broni palnej*: recoil; **~towiec** *m* jet plane

odsetki *pl econ.* interest

odsk|akiwać ⟨**-oczyć**⟩ jump back; **~akiwać na bok** jump aside

odsł|aniać ⟨**-onić**⟩ *coś zakrytego* uncover, expose;

pomnik unveil; **~aniać okno** draw* the curtain; **~ona** *f thea.* scene; **~onięcie** *n pomnika*: unveiling

odstawa(ć) *(wyróżniać się)* stand* out *(od* from)

odstawi|a(ć) *na miejsce*: put* away, put* back

odstąpić *pf* → **odstępować**

odstęp *m* distance; *między wyrazami*: space; *między wierszami tekstu*: line spacing

odstrasz|ać ⟨**-yć**⟩ scare away, *form.* deter; **środek** *m* **~ający** deterrent

odsu|wać ⟨**-nąć**⟩ push away *(od* from); **~wać na bok** push aside; **~wać do tyłu** push back; **~wać się** draw* back

odsyła|cz *m w tekście*: reference; **~ć** send* back; *do literatury*: refer (back) (to)

odszkodowanie *n (pieniądze)* damages *pl (za* for)

odszukać *pf* find*; **~ się** *wzajemnie*: find* one another

odśwież|ać ⟨**-yć**⟩ *meble itp.* restore; *powietrze* freshen; *po podróży*: refresh (**się** oneself); **~ać komuś coś w pamięci** refresh one's memory about s.th.

odświętny *adj nastrój*: festive; **~ strój** *m* (one's) Sunday best

odtąd *prp (od teraz)* since; *(od teraz)* from now on

odtłuszczon|y *adj* low-fat; **~e**

mleko n skim(med) milk

odtwarzać ⟨~orzyć⟩ recreate

oducz|ać ⟨~yć⟩: **~ać kogoś robić coś** train s.o. not to do s.th.; **~ać się** (*odzwyczajać się*) break the habit (**robić coś** of doing s.th.); (*przestawać umieć*) unlearn (**czegoś** s.th.)

odurzający adj hallucinogenic

odwaga f courage

odważnik m weight

odważny adj brave, courageous; **~yć się** have* the courage (**zrobić coś** to do s.th.)

odwdzięcz|ać ⟨~yć⟩ **się** return the favour

odwet m retaliation

odwiąz|yw|ać untie

odwie|dzać ⟨~dzić⟩ **kogoś** visit (s.o.), call (on s.o); **~dziny** pl visit

odwieźć pf → **odwozić**

odwijać unwrap

odwilż f thaw

odwinąć pf → **odwijać**

odwoł|anie n ze stanowiska: dismissal, removal; od decyzji: appeal; **do ~ania** until further notice; **~yw|ać ze stanowiska**: dismiss; spotkanie call off, cancel; **~ywać się** appeal (od to s.th.)

odwozić take*/drive* back; **~ kogoś do domu** drive* s.o. home

odwr|acać turn; uwagę divert; **~acać się** turn round;

~otnie adv the other way round; **~otny** adj reverse; **~ócić** pf → **odwracać**; **~ót** m retreat; **na ~ocie** overleaf

odwzajemni(a)ć uczucia return

odziedzicz|ać ⟨~yć⟩ inherit

odzież f clothing, clothes pl; **~przemysł** m ~owy textile industry

odzna|czać się stand* out; **~czenie** n decoration, medal; **~ka** f badge

odzwierciedl|ać ⟨~ić⟩ reflect

odzwycza|jać ⟨~ić⟩ **się** break* the habit (od robienia czegoś of doing s.th.)

odzysk|iw|ać recover; niepodległość regain

odzywać się speak*

odży|wa|ć come* back to life

odży|wi|a|ć nourish; **~wiać się zwierzę**: feed* (czymś on s.th.); **~wka** f do włosów: conditioner, tonic; dla dzieci: baby food, formula Am.

ofensywa f offensive

ofer|ować ⟨za-⟩ offer; **~ta** f offer

ofiar|a f victim; wypadku: casualty; (poświęcenie) sacrifice; **~ność** f dedication; **~ny** adj dedicated; **~ow|yw|ać** donate

oficer m officer; **~jalny** adj official; zaproszenie: formal; osoba: stand-offish

ogień m fire; **sztuczny ~** sparkler

ogier *m* stallion

oglądać look at, view; *film, telewizję* watch; **~ się do tyłu** look back; **~ się dookokoła** look round

oględziny *pl* inspection

ogłaszać ⟨**~osić**⟩ announce; *zwycięstwo* proclaim; **~oszenie** *n* announcement; **~oszenia** *pl drobne* small ads *pl Brt.*, classified ads *pl Am.*

ogłuchnąć go* deaf

ogłuszać ⟨**~yć**⟩ deafen

ognio|trwały *adj* fireproof; **~sko** *n* (bon)fire; *optyczne:* focus

ogniwo *n łańcucha:* link

ogon *m* tail; **~ek** *m liścia, owocu:* stalk

ogólnie *adv* generally; **~ie mówiąc** broadly/generally speaking; **~okrajowy** *adj* nationwide; **~oświatowy** *adj* worldwide; **~y** *adj* general

ogół *m* (*wszyscy ludzie*) society, the public; **~em** *adv* in general, all in all; **na ~** generally; **w ogóle** on the whole; (*wcale*) at all

ogórek *m* cucumber

ogranicz|ać ⟨**~yć**⟩ limit, restrict; **~enie** *n handlu itp.:* restriction; **~enie prędkości** speed limit; **~ony** *adj* limited, restricted; *człowiek :* narrow-minded

ogrodni|ctwo *n* gardening; (*nauka*) horticulture; **~k** *m* gardener

ogrodzenie *n* fence

ogromn|ie *adv* extremely; **~y** *adj* huge; *obszar:* vast

ogród *m* garden

ogrz|(ew)ać *dłonie* warm; *dom, wodę* heat; **~ewać się** warm oneself; (*centralne*) **~ewanie** (central) heating

ogumienie *n* tyres *pl*

ojciec *m* father; **~ciec chrzestny** godfather; **~ costwo** *n* fatherhood; **~czym** *m* stepfather

ojczy|sty *adj* native; **→ mowa**; **~zna** *f* homeland, native country

okalecz|ać ⟨**~yć**⟩ maim; **→ kaleczyć**

okaz *m* specimen; *zdrowia itp.:* picture; **~ać** *pf →* **okazywać**

okazja *f* opportunity, chance; *specjalna:* occasion; (*korzystny zakup*) bargain; *sp.* chance

okazywać show*; *uczucie* demonstrate

okiennica *f* shutter

oklaski *pl* applause; **~wać** applaud

okład *m med.* compress; **~ka** *f książki:* cover; *płyty:* sleeve

okłam|(yw)ać lie* (*kogoś* to s.o.); **~samego siebie** deceive oneself

okno *n* window

ok|o *n* eye; *widzieć coś gołym ~iem* with the naked eye; *na czyichś oczach* in front of/before/

under one's eyes; **na pierwszy rzut** ~**a** at first glance; **w mgnieniu** ~**a** in the twinkling of an eye; **tracić** ⟨**s-**⟩ **coś z oczu** lose* sight of s.th.

okolica f area

okoliczności pl circumstances pl; ~ **łagodzące** extenuating circumstances

około about, approximately; ~ **czwartej** at about four o'clock

okoń m zo. perch, bass

okop m trench

okra|dać ⟨**~ść**⟩ rob (**kogoś z czegoś** s.o. of s.th.)

okrąg m circle; ~**gły** adj round; ~**żać** ⟨**~żyć**⟩ surround; (omijać) walk/drive/ sail round; ~**żenie** n sp. lap

okres m period; polowań: season; u władzy: term; ~**owy** adj periodical; (tymczasowy) temporary

określ|ać ⟨**~ić**⟩ przyczynę itp. determine; ~**ony** adj definite

okręg m wyborczy: constituency; rolniczy itp.: region; administracyjny: province, district; ~**owy** regional

okręt m ship; ~ **podwodny** submarine; ~ **wojenny** battleship

okrężn|y adj; **droga** f ~**a** detour

okropny adj awful

okruch m crumb (a. fig.)

okru|cieństwo n cruelty; ~**tny** adj cruel

okry(wa)ć cover

okrzyk m shout, cry

okul|ary pl glasses pl; ~**ista** m optician

okup m ransom

okupacja f occupation

olbrzym m giant; ~**i** adj enormous, colossal

olej m oil; F (obraz) oil (painting); ~ **napędowy** diesel (oil); ~**ek** m (do opalania sun tan) oil); ~**ny obraz** m oil painting

olimpi|ada f the Olympics pl; ~**jski** adj Olympic; **igrzyska** pl ~**jskie** the Olympic Games pl

oliw|a f oil; ~**ka** f bot. olive; ~**kowy** adj olive (green)

ołów m lead

ołówek m pencil

ołtarz m altar

omal (nie) nearly; **omal nie upadł** he nearly fell

omawiać discuss

omdle|nie n faint; ~**wać** → **mdleć**

omijać ⟨**~nąć**⟩ miasto itp. bypass

omlet m omelette

omówić pf → **omawiać**

omy|lić pf się → **mylić**; ~**łka** f mistake

on pron he; ~**a** pron she; ~**e**, ~**i** pron they

onieśmielony adj abashed

ono pron it

opad m deszczu: rainfall; śniegu: snowfall; ~**ać** fall*; poziom: drop; ~**y** pl precipitation

opakow|anie n towaru: packaging, wrapping; jedno: packet; **~(yw)ać** wrap up

opal|ać się sunbathe; **~ić się** pf tan, get* a suntan; **~enizna** f (sun)tan; **~ony** adj (sun-)tanned, sunburnt Brt.

opał m fuel

opanow|anie n self-control; umiejętności: command (**czegoś** of s.th.); **~any** adj człowiek: composed; **~(yw)ać** take* control of; strach itp. fight* back, hold* back; umiejętność: master; **~ywać się** control oneself

oparcie n krzesła: back; dla głowy: (head)rest; w kimś: support

oparzenie n burn; parą, wrzątkiem: scald; słoneczne: sunburn

opaska f band

opasły adj fat, obese

opaść pf → **opadać**

opat|runek m med. dressing; **~runek gipsowy** med. (plaster) cast; **~rywać** (**~rzyć**) ranę dress

opera f opera; (budynek) opera house

operac|ja f operation, surgery; **~yjny** adj: **system ~yjny** komputer: operating system

operator m operator

operetka f operetta

operować operate (**kogoś** on s.o.)

opiec pf → **opiekać**

opieczętować seal

opieka f medyczna itp.: care; (odpowiedzialność) charge (**nad** of)

opiek|ać się take* care (**czymś** of s.th.), look after; **~un** m prawny: guardian; (przełożony) supervisor; **~un(ka f) do dziecka** babysitter

opierać głowę rest (**na** on); film base (**na** on); rower itp. lean (**o** against); **~ się** lean (**na** on, **o** against)

opini|a f reputation; (pogląd) opinion, view (**na** on); **~a publiczna** public opinion; **~ować** ⟨**za-**⟩ review

opis m description; **~(yw)ać** describe

opłac|ać ⟨**~ić**⟩ pay* for; **~ać się** pay* off; **~alny** adj profitable; **~ony** adj paid for

opłakiwać mourn (**coś** for/over s.th.)

opłata f fee; za przejazd: fare; za usługi: charge

opły|wać ⟨**~nąć**⟩ dookoła: swim* round; jachtem: sail round

opodatkow|anie n taxation; **~(yw)ać** tax

opona f tyre Brt., tire Am.

oporn|ik m resistor; **~y** adj stubborn

opowi|adać ⟨**~edzieć**⟩ tell*; **~adanie** n story; **~eść** f tale

opór m a. phys., electr. resistance; **bierny** ~ passive resistance; **stawi(a)ć** ~ **komuś/czemuś** resist s.o./s.th.; **ruch** *m* **oporu** the resistance movement

opóźni|**(a)ć** delay; ~**(a)ć się** be delayed; ~**enie** *n* delay; ~**ony** *adj* late, delayed; *w rozwoju*: retarded

opracow(yw)ać *plan itp.* devise, work out; *muzycznie*: arrange

oprawa *f* setting; *książki*: binding; *obrazu*: frame; *okularów*: frames *pl*; **~i(a)ć** *obraz* frame; *książkę* bind*; **~ka** *f okularów*: frames *pl*; *żarówki*: socket

oprocentowanie *n bankowe*: interest

oprogramowanie *n* software

oprowa|**dzać** ⟨**~dzić**⟩ **kogoś** (**po czymś**) show* s.o. around (s.th.)

oprócz *prp* besides, apart from; **~ tego** (*poza tym*) besides, apart from that

opróżni|**(a)ć** empty

oprysk|**iwacz** *m ogrodowy*: sprinkler; **~(iw)ać** splash (**czymś** with s.th.)

oprzeć *pf* → **opierać**

optyk *m* optician

optymalny *adj* optimum

optymi|**sta** *m* optimist; **~styczny** *adj* optimistic; **~zm** *m* optimism

opuch|**ły**, **~nięty** *adj* swollen

opustoszały *adv* deserted

opuszcz|**ać** ⟨**~ścić**⟩ *dom*, *rodzinę* leave*; *lekcję*, *dzień pracy* miss, skip; *statek* abandon; (*pomijać*) leave* out, omit; (*obniżać*) lower; **~ony** *adj* abandoned; (*pominięty*) omitted, left out

orać ⟨**za-**⟩ plough

oranżada *f* lemonade

oraz *cj* and

orbita *f* orbit

orchidea *f bot.* orchid

order *m* medal

ordynarny *adj* vulgar; *człowiek*: crude

organ *m* organ; *władzy*: authority, body; **~iczny** *adj* organic; **~izacja** *f* organization; **O~izacja Narodów Zjednoczonych** the United Nations (Organization); **~izator** *m* organizer; **~izm** *m* organism; *ludzki*: system; **~izować** ⟨**z-**⟩ organize

organki *pl harmonica*; **~y** *pl mus.* organ

orgazm *m* orgasm

orient|**acja** *f* orientation; (*znajomość*) acumen, sense; *politycznа*: tendencies *pl*; **~acyjny** *adj pomiar*, *cena*: approximate; **~ować się** know* one's way about/ around; **~ować się, że ...** be aware that ...; **nie ~uję się** I don't know

orkiestra *f* orchestra

ortografia *f* spelling

orygina|**lny** *adj* original; **~ł** *m* original

orzech *m* nut; **~owy** *adj* nutty; *kolor*: nut-brown

orzeczenie *n sądu*: ruling; *gr.* predicate

orzeł *m zo.* eagle

orzeźwiając|y *adj* refreshing

osa *f zo.* wasp

osa|d *m* sediment; *na zębach*: plaque; *na języku, garnku*: fur; *chem.* precipitate; **~da** *f* settlement; **~dnik** *m* (*osada*) settler; **~dzać się** *kurz itp.*: settle; *chem.* precipitate

osądz|ać ⟨**~ić**⟩ judge

oset *m bot.* thistle

osiad|ać → **osiadłać się**; **~ać na mieliźnie** run*/go* aground; **~ły** *adj* settled

osiąg|ać ⟨**~nąć**⟩ achieve; *porozumienie* reach; *popularność* gain, win*; **~nięcie** *n* achievement

osiąść *pf* → **osiadać**

osiedl|ać ⟨**~ić**⟩ **się** settle (down); **~e** *n* (*osada*) settlement; **~e mieszkaniowe** housing development, housing estate *Brt.*

osiem *num* eight; **~dziesiąt** *num* eighty; **~naście** *num* eighteen; **~set** *num* eight hundred

osioł *m* donkey; F *fig.* nitwit F

oskarż|ać accuse (**o** of); *jur.* charge (**o** with); **~enie** *n* accusation; *jur.* charge, indictment; **~ony 1.** *m jur.* defendant; **2.** *adj* accused; **~yciel** *m jur.* prosecutor; **~yć** *pf* → **oskarżać**

osłabi|(a)ć weaken; *wiarę*

shake*; *władzę* diminish, blunt; **~enie** *n* weakening

osł|aniać ⟨**~onić**⟩ protect; **~ona** *f* cover; *maszyny*: guard, hood; *części ciała*: guard, shield; *przed deszczem, wiatrem*: shelter; **pod ~oną nocy** under cover of the night

osłupienie *n* amazement

osob|a *f* person, individual; *gr.* person; **we własnej ~ie** in the flesh; **~istość** *f* personality, celebrity; **~isty** *adj* personal; **~iście** *adv* personally; **~liwość** *f* (*osobliwa rzecz*) curiosity; (*niezwykłość*) idiosyncrasy, peculiarity; **~liwy** *adj* idiosyncratic, peculiar; **~no** → **oddzielnie**; **~ny** → **oddzielny**; **~owy** *adj* personal; *pociąg*: local

ostat|eczność *adv* (*w końcu*) finally, **~eczność: w ~eczności** in the last resort; **~eczny** *adj* final; **~ni** *adj* last; **~nio** *adv* late, recently

ostro *adv krytykować*: sharply; **~ść** *f* sharpness

ostrożn|ość *f* caution; **~y** *adj* careful, cautious

ostry *adj* sharp; *med.* acute; *potrawa*: hot; *kolor*: vivid; **kąt m ~** *math.* acute angle

ostryga *f* oyster

ostrze *n* blade

ostrze|gać ⟨**~c**⟩ warn (**przed** against)

ostrzel(iw)ać shoot* at; *artylerią*: shell

ostrzeżenie n warning
ostrzyć ⟨na-, za-⟩ sharpen; *na osełce*: hone
ostudzić pf → **studzić**
oswajać ⟨∼oić⟩ tame; **∼ajać się** get* accustomed (**z** to)
oswob|adzać ⟨∼odzić⟩ liberate
ozaleca go* mad
oszczep m spear; sp.: javelin; **∼nik** m sp. javelin thrower
oszczerstwo n slander; jur. libel
oszczę|dnie adv economically, frugally; *używać*: sparingly; **∼dności** pl savings pl; **∼dność** f economy; *przezadna*: thrift; (*zysk*) saving (*czegoś* in s.th.); **∼dny** adj economical; *człowiek, tryb życia*: frugal; sparing (**w używaniu czegoś** with s.th.); *przesadnie*: thrifty; **∼dzać** ⟨∼dzić⟩ save; economize (**na** on); *kogoś, komuś zmartwień itp.*: spare
oszklony adj drzwi itp.: glazed
oszpec|ać ⟨∼ić⟩ disfigure (a. fig.)
oszu|k(iw)ać v/t deceive; **∼kiwać** v/i cheat (**w** at); **∼kiwać się** deceive oneself; **∼kiwanie** n deceit; **∼st(ka** f) m cheat, fraud; **∼stwo** n cheat, deception
oś f axis; mechanizmu: pivot, shaft; wozu, samochodu: axle
ość f fishbone
oślep|i(a)ć światłem: blind, dazzle; **∼iający** adj dazzling;

∼nąć go* blind
ośmiel|ać ⟨∼ić⟩ encourage; **∼ać się** dare (**zrobić coś** (to) do s.th.)
ośmiornica f zo. octopus
ośrodek m centre; **∼ zdrowia** health centre
oświadcz|ać ⟨∼yć⟩ state, declare; **∼ać się** propose (**komuś** to s.o.); **∼enie** n statement; **∼yny** pl proposal (of marriage)
oświata f (system of) education; **∼towy** adj educational; **∼ecenie** n hist. the Enlightenment
oświetl|ać ⟨∼ić⟩ light* (up), illuminate; **∼enie** n lighting, illumination; **∼ony** adj illuminated, lighted/lit (up)
otacza|ć surround; (*stawać dookoła*) encircle, surround; (*osaczać*) close in (*kogoś* on s.o.)
oto here ... is/are etc.; **∼ jestem** here I am
otocz|enie n environment, surroundings pl; **∼ony** adj surrounded; **∼yć** pf → **otaczać**
otóż → **oto**; **∼ to** that's it
otruć pf poison (**się** oneself)
otrząsa|ć ⟨∼nąć⟩ **się** recover (**z** czegoś from s.th.)
otrzym(yw)ać get*, receive
otwar|cie 1. adv bluntly; **2. ∼** opening; **godziny** pl **∼cia** opening hours; **∼ty** adj open; wrogość: overt; rana: gaping

otw|ieracz m opener; **~ieracz do konserw** tin opener Brt., can opener Am.; **~ierać** ⟨**~orzyć**⟩ open; **zamek kluczem** unlock; **pochód, listę** head; **~ór** m opening; **na monete**: slot; **wiercony**: hole

otyły adj obese

owad m insect

ow|ca f sheep; **~czarek** m sheepdog

owies m oats pl

owi|jać ⟨**~nąć**⟩ wrap (up) (**w** in); wind (**coś czymś** s.th. round s.th.)

owłosiony adj hairy

owoc m fruit; **~owy** fruit ...; **smak, zapach**: fruity

owszem yes

ozd|abiać decorate; **~oba** f decoration; **~obić** pf → **ozdabiać**; **~obny** adj decorative

ozięb|i(a)ć (się) chill; **~ły** adj cool; **kobieta**: frigid

oznacz|ać¹ ⟨**~yć**⟩ mark

oznaczać² mean*; **skrót**: stand* for

oznaka f **czegoś**: sign

oży|(wa)ć come* back to life; **~wi(a)ć** bring* back to life

Ó

ós|emka f (an) eight; **~my** num eighth; **~ma godzina** eight o'clock

ów that; **~czesny** adj contemporary; **premier, dyrektor itp.**: the then

ówdzie: **tu i ~** here and there

P

pach|a f armpit; **pod ~ą** under one's arm

pachnieć ⟨**za-**⟩ smell*

pacierz m prayer

paciorki pl (string of) beads

pacjent(ka f) m patient

pacz|ka f parcel, package; (**opakowanie**) packet; (**grupa**) pack; **~uszka** f packet

padać fall*; → **deszcz, śnieg, ~lina** f carrion

pagórek m hill

pająk m spider; **~ęczyna** f

(**cob**)web

pak|iet m **listów itp.**: bundle; **econ. papierów wartościowych**: portfolio; **transakcyjny akcji**: lot; **~ować** ⟨**za-**⟩ pack (up), wrap (up)

pakt m pact

pal m stake, pale

pal|acz m **papierosów**: smoker; **~arnia** f smoking area; **~ący** m smoker; **przedział** m **dla** (**nie**)**~ących** (non-) smoking compartment

papierek

palec *m u ręki:* finger; *u nogi:* toe

palenie *n* smoking; **~ wzbronione** no smoking

paletka *f* bat

pal|ić ⟨s-⟩ *v/t* burn*; *tytoń* smoke; *kawę* roast; **~ić się** burn*; *v/i* **⟨na-⟩** *w domu:* heat (house *etc.*); **~iwo** *n* fuel

palma *f* palm tree

palnik *m* burner

palto *n* coat

pałac *m* palace

pał|eczka *f dyrygenta, w sztafecie:* baton; *perkusisty:* drumstick; *do chińskich dań:* chopstick; **~ka** *f* club; *policyjna:* baton, truncheon

pamiątka *f* souvenir; **~owy** *adj znaczek, medal:* commemorative

pamię|ć *f a. komputer:* memory; **na ~ć** by heart; **~tać** remember (**o** about); **~tnik** *m* diary; **pisać ~tnik** keep* a diary; **~tniki** *pl* memoirs *pl*; **~tny** *adj* memorable

pan *m* gentleman; *przed nazwiskiem:* Mr; **to ~ Smith** this is Mr Smith; *w bezpośrednich zwrotach:* sir, you; **dzień dobry ~u** good morning, sir; **jedzie ~ do domu?** are you going home?; *w listach:* Sir; **Szanowny ~ie** Dear Sir; *dla psa, niewolnika, służby:* master; **~ młody** (bride)groom

pance|rny *adj wóz itp.:* armoured; **~rz** *m* armour

pan|i *f* lady; *przed nazwiskiem:* Mrs, Ms, Ms; **to ~i Smith** this is Mrs Smith; *w bezpośrednich zwrotach:* madam, miss, you; **dzień dobry ~i** good morning, madam; **jedzie ~i do domu?** are you going home?; *w listach:* Madam; **Szanowna ~i** Dear Madam; *dla psa, niewolnika, służby:* mistress; **~ieński** *adj* **nazwisko ~ieńskie** maiden name; **~na** *f* unmarried woman, girl; *przed nazwiskiem:* Miss; **to ~na Smith** this is Miss Smith; **~na młoda** bride; **stara ~na** old maid

pan|ować *król:* rule, reign; *tradycja, styl itp.:* prevail; **~ować nad kimś** control s.o.; **~owanie** *n* rule, reign; **~ujący** *adj władca:* ruling; *pogląd:* prevalent

pańsk|i *adj w bezpośrednich zwrotach:* your(s); **czy to ~ki płaszcz?** is this your coat?; **~two** *n* state; *przed nazwiskiem:* Mr and Mrs; **~two Smith poszli do domu** Mr and Mrs Smith have gone home; *w bezpośrednich zwrotach:* you; **czy ~two tu mieszkają?** do you live here?; **~twowy** *adj zakład:* state-owned; *wizyta:* state ...; *flaga:* national

papier *m* paper; **~ listowy** notepaper; **~ ścierny** sandpaper; **~ toaletowy** toilet paper; **~ek** *m od cukier-**

papierniczy

ka: wrapper; *na ziemi*: paper; ~**niczy** *adj*: **sklep** *m* ~-**niczy** stationer('s); **artykuły** *pl* ~*nicze* stationery; ~**os** *m* cigarette; ~**owy** *adj* paper ...

papież *m* (the) Pope

paproć *f bot.* fern

papryka *f* pepper; *w proszku*: paprika

papu|ga *f* parrot; ~**żka** *f* **fali-sta** budgerigar

para¹ *f* (*ława*) pair

para² *f wodna itp.*: steam

parada *f* parade

paradox *m* paradoks

parafia *f* parish; ~**nin** *m* parishioner

paraliż *m* paralysis; ~**ować** ⟨**s-**⟩ paralyse

parametr *m* parameter

parasol *m* umbrella; *prze-ciwsłoneczny*: parasol, sunshade

parę a couple (of); ~ **dni temu** a couple of days ago

park *m* park

parkan *m* fence

parkiet *m* parquet

park|ing *m* car park *Brt.*, parking lot *Am.*; ~**ować** park; ~**owanie** *n* parking; **zakaz** *m* ~**owania** no parking

parlament *m* parliament; ~**arny** *adj* parliamentary

parow|ać ⟨**wy-**⟩ *v/i woda*: evaporate; *v/t (gotować na parze)* steam; ~**iec** *m* steamer; ~**óz** *m* steam locomotive; ~**y** *adj* steam ...

parówka *f* frankfurter, sausage

parter *m* ground floor *Brt.*, first floor *Am.*; ~**owy** *adj* **bu-dynek**: one-storey *Brt.*, one--story *Am.*

partia *f polityczna*: party; *to-waru*: batch, consignment

partner *m* partner; *w inter-esach a.*: associate

partyzant *m* guerilla

parzyć¹ ⟨**s-**⟩ **kawę, herbatę** make*

parzyć² ⟨**o-**⟩ burn* (**się** oneself); *wrzątkiem*: scald (**się** oneself)

parzysty *adj math.* even

pas¹ *m jezdni*: lane; (*wąski ob-szar*) strip; (*część ciała*) waist; ~ **bezpieczeństwa** safety belt; ~ **startowy** runway

pas² *m w kartach*: pass

pasażer *m* passenger; ~**ski** *adj* passenger

pas|ek *m do spodni itp.*: belt; *przy spódnicy, spodniach*: waistband; (*wzór*) stripe; *pa-pieru*: strip; *do walizki*: strap; ~ **do zegarka** watchband

pasierb *m* stepson, stepchild; ~**ica** *f* stepdaughter

pasja *f* passion

pasjans *m* patience

paskudny F *adj* lousy F; *rana*: bad, nasty

pasmo *n zwycięstw itp.*: run; *włosów*: strand; *tech. radio-we*: band

pasować fit; *ubranie*: suit (*komuś s.o.*); *do siebie wza-jemnie*: match

pasożyt *m* parasite

pewny

pasta f spożywcza: paste; *do chleba a.*: spread; **~ do butów** shoe polish; **~ do zębów** toothpaste

pasterz m shepherd

pastor m minister

pastować ⟨wy-⟩ *buty* polish; *podłogę* wax

pastylka f tablet, pill

pasza f feed; *krów, koni*: fodder

paszport m passport

pasztet m âté

paść v/t *zwierzęta* graze; v/i pf fall*; **~ się** *animals*: graze

patelnia f frying pan

patent m patent

patriot|a m patriot; **~yzm** m patriotism

patrol m patrol

patrzeć look (**na** at)

paw m zo. peacock

pawian m zo. baboon

paznokieć m (finger)nail

pazur m claw

październik m October

pączek m (*ciastko*) doughnut; *na drzewie*: bud

pchać push; *mocno, gwałtownie*: shove; *nożem itp.*: stab

pchła f flea

pchn|ąć pf → **pchać**; **~ięcie** n push; **~ kulą** *sp.* shot put

pechowy adj unlucky

pedagog m educationalist

pedał m pedal; F (*homoseksualista*) gay F, queer F

pediatra m p(a)ediatrician

pejzaż m landscape

pełn|ia f (**~ księżyca**) full moon; **w ~i** fully; **~o** F adv (*dużo*) lots (of); **~oletni** adj adult; **~omocnik** m plenipotentiary; **~y** adj full (**czegoś** of s.th.), filled (**czegoś** with s.th.)

pensja f salary; *tygodniowa*: wages pl

pensjonat m boarding house

perfumy pl perfume, scent

periodyk m periodical

perkusja f percussion

perła f pearl

peron m platform

person|alny adj personal; **dział m ~alny** personnel (department); **~el** m personnel, staff

perspektywa f prospect; *optyczna*: perspective

peruka f wig

peryferie f outskirts pl, suburbs pl

pestka f *jabłka, pomarańczy*: pip; *wiśni, śliwki*: stone

pesymi|sta m pessimist; **~styczny** adj pessimistic; **~zm** m pessimism

pew|ien adj (*jakiś*) some; *form.* certain; **~nego dnia** one day; **jestem ~ien** I am sure; **~no** adv: **na ~no** definitely; **~nie** adv (*mocno*) firmly; (*chyba*) probably; **no ~nie!** certainly; **~ność** f certainty; (*pewność siebie*) assurance, self-confidence; **z ~nością** surely; **~ny** adj sure, certain (**czegoś/kogoś** of s.th./s.o.); *osoba, źródło*: reliable; *dowód, informacja*: firm; **~ny siebie** self-assured, self-confident

pęcherz *m* bladder; *na skórze*: (water) blister; **~yk** *m powietrza*: bubble

pęczek *m rzodkiewek*: bunch

pęd *m* rush; *bot.* bud

pędzel *m* (paint)brush

pęk *m* bunch

pęk|ać ⟨**~nąć**⟩ crack; *balonik, serce*: burst*; **~nięcie** *n* crack; **~nięty** cracked

pępek *m* navel

pętla *f* loop; *na szyi*: noose

piać ⟨**za-**⟩ *kogut*: crow

piana *f* foam; *z mydła*: lather; *na wodzie*: froth; *na piwie*: head

pianino *n* upright piano; **~sta** *m* pianist

piasek *m* sand; **~kowiec** *m* sandstone; **~kownica** *f* sandpit *Brt.*, sandbox *Am.*

piasta *f* hub

piaszczysty *adj* sandy

piąt|ek *m* Friday; **~ka** *f* (*cyfra*) (a) five; (*ocena*) very good; **~y** *num* fifth

pi|cie *n* drinking; F drink(s); **woda** *f* **do ~cia** drinking water; **~ć** ⟨**wy-**⟩ *v/i* drink*; *v/t* drink*, have*

piec¹ *m* stove; *przemysłowy*: furnace

piec² ⟨**u-**⟩ *ciasto* bake; *mięso* roast

piec³ *oczy, rana*: sting*

piechota *f mil.* infantry; **~ą, na ~ę** on foot

pieczar|a *f* cavern; **~ka** *f* champignon, mushroom F

pieczątka *f* (rubber) stamp

pieczeń *f* roast

pieczęć *f* seal; *gumowa*: rubber stamp; **~tować** ⟨**za-**⟩ seal

pieczony *adj chleb*: baked; *kurczak*: roast; **~ywo** *n* bread

pieg *m* freckle; **~owaty** *adj* freckled

piekarnia *f* bakery; (*sklep*) the baker('s), bakery; **~arz** *m* baker

piekło *n* hell

pielęgn|iarka *f* nurse; **~ować** care for, nurse

pielgrzym *m* pilgrim; **~ka** *f* pilgrimage

pieluszka *f* nappy *Brt.*, diaper *Am.*

pieniądz *m* (*moneta*) coin; *econ.* currency; **~e** *pl* money

pienić się foam

pień *m* trunk

pieprz *m* pepper; **~ny** peppery; *dowcip*: dirty; **~yć** ⟨**po-**⟩ *v/t* pepper; F *v/i* talk nonsense

piernik *m* gingerbread

pierś *f* breast; (*górna część tułowia*) chest

pierścionek *m* ring

pierwiastek *m chem.* element; *math.* root

pierwotny *adj* primeval; *człowiek*: primitive; (*pierwszy*) original

pierwsz|eństwo *n* priority; **~eństwo przejazdu** right of way; **~orzędny** *adj* first-class, first-rate; **~y** *adj* first

pierz|e *n* down; **~yna** duvet *Brt.*

pies *m* dog

pieszczot|a *f* caress; **~liwy** *adj* tender

piesz|o *adv* on foot; **~y** *m* pedestrian

pieścić caress

pieśń *f* song

pietruszka *f* parsley; (*korzeń*) parsnip

pięcio|bój *m* pentathlon; **~raczki** *pl* quintuplets *pl*, quins *pl* F

pięć *num* five; **~dziesiąt** *num* fifty; **~set** *num* five hundred

piękn|o *n* beauty; **~y** *adj* beautiful

pięść *f* fist

pięta *f anat.* heel

piętnaście *num* fifteen

pięt|ro *n* floor; (*kondygnacja*) storey *Brt.*, story *Am*; **na drugim ~rze** on the second (third *Am.*) floor *Brt.*

pigułka *f* pill

pija|cki *adj śmiech, zabawa*: drunken; **~k** *m* drunk, drunkard; **~ny** *adj* drunk, drunken; **jestem ~ny** I'm drunk; **~ny kierowca** *m* drunken driver

pik *m* spades; **dama** *f* **~** queen of spades

pikantny *adj* piquant

pilnik *m* file

pilność *f* diligence

pilnować *więźniów, drzwi*: guard; *dzieci*: look after,

watch over

pilny *adj* diligent; *uczeń*: studious; *wiadomość*: urgent

pilot *m* pilot; F *do telewizora itp.*: remote control (unit)

pilśniowy *adj*: **płyta** *f* **~a** hardboard

piła *f* saw; **~ mechaniczna** power saw

piłka *f* ball; **~ nożna** soccer, football *Brt.*; **~rz** *m* footballer

piłować saw*

pinezka *f* drawing pin *Brt.*, thumbtack *Am.*

pingwin *m zo.* penguin

pion *m* the vertical; *szachovy itp.*: pawn; **~ek** *m* counter; *szachowy*: pawn; **~owy** *adj* vertical

piorun *m* thunder

piosenka *f song*; **~rka** *f* (**~rz** *m*) singer

pióro *f* pen; *ptaka*: feather

pirat *m* pirate

pisać 〈**na-**〉 write*; **~ak** *m* felt-tip (pen); *gruby*: marker; **~arka** *f* (**~arz** *m*) writer; **~emny** *adj test itp.*: written

pisk *m* squeak, squeal, screech; *opon*: screech; **~lę** *n* chick, fledgling

pis|mo *n* writing; *odręczne*: handwriting; (*list*) memorandum, note; **2mo Święte** the Scripture; **~ownia** *n* spelling

pistolet *m* pistol, gun F

piszczeć squeak, squeal, screech; *opony*: screech

piśmienn|ictwo n literature; **~y** adj literate

piw|iarnia f pub; **~nica** f cellar; mieszkalna, użytkowa: basement; **~o** n beer

piżama f pyjamas pl

plac m square; **~ zabaw** playground

placek m cake, pie

plakat m poster

plam|a f stain; **~ić ⟨po-, s-⟩** stain

plan m plan; **~ lekcji** timetable, class schedule; **~ miasta** city map; **pierwszy ~** foreground; **~ować ⟨za-⟩** plan; **~owanie** n planning; **~owy** adj planned

planeta f planet

plaster m plaster; miodu: honeycomb; **~ek** m sera: slice

plastyczka f (graphic) artist

plast|ik m plastic; **~ikowy** adj plastic; **~yk¹** → **plastik**

plastyk² m (graphic) artist

platyna f platinum

plaża f beach

plebania f rzymsko-katolicka: presbytery; anglikańska: vicarage

plec|ak m rucksack; **~y** pl back

plemię n tribe

plemnik m sperm

plene|r m filmowy: location; **w ~rze** in the open air; film: on location

pleść ⟨za-⟩ włosy plait Brt., braid Am.; **~ bzdury** F talk nonsense/rubbish

pleś|nieć ⟨s-⟩ gather mould; **~ń** f mould

plik m papierów: pile; listów: bundle; banknotów: wad; komputer: file

plomba f seal; med. filling

plon m crop, harvest

plotk|a f rumour, (a piece of) gossip; **~ować** gossip

pluć spit*

plus m plus; (zaleta) advantage, asset; **~ minus** more or less, give or take

plusk|wa f bedbug; **~iewka** f → **pinezka**

pluton m żołnierzy: platoon; chem. plutonium; **~ egzekucyjny** firing squad

płac|a f pay; **~ić ⟨za-⟩** pay*; **~ić gotówką** pay* (in) cash; **~ić czekiem** pay* by cheque (check Am.)

płacz m crying; **~kać** cry

płask|i adj flat; **~orzeźba** f relief; **~owyż** m plateau

płaszcz m coat; **~ kąpielowy** bathrobe

płaszczyzna f surface; math. plane

płat|ek m śniegu: flake; kwiatu: petal; **~ki owsiane** oatmeal; **~ki kukurydziane** cornflakes pl

płat|nik m payer; **~ość** f payment; **~ny** adj paid; rachunek: payable; **~e przy odbiorze** cash on delivery, COD

płaz m zo. amphibian

płciowy adj sexual; **stosunek** m **~** sexual intercourse

płeć f sex

płetwa f fin; *nurka:* flipper

płomie/ń m flame; **stanąć w ~niach** burst* into flames

płon/ąc adj flaming; **~ąć** burn*, blaze

płoszyć ⟨s-⟩ scare away

płot m fence; **~ek** m sp. hurdle

płód m f(o)etus; **~ody** pl *rolne* produce

płótno n cloth, fabric; *obrazu:* canvas; *(obraz)* canvas

płuco n lung

pług m plough

płukać ⟨wy-⟩ rinse; **~ gardło** gargle

płyn m liquid; *tech.* fluid; **~ do mycia naczyń** washing-up liquid *Brt.*, dishwashing liquid *Am.*; **~ po goleniu** aftershave; **~ąć** *statek:* sail; *człowiek:* swim*; *płyn, elektryczność:* flow; **~nie** *adv mówić:* fluently; **mówić ~nie po polsku** speak* fluent Polish, be* fluent in Polish; **~ny** adj liquid; *mowa:* fluent; *ruch, granica:* fluid

płyt/a f *z kamienia, drewniana, betonowa:* slab; *metalowa:* sheet; *(metalowa pokrywa)* plate; *gramofonowa:* record; **~a kompaktowa** compact disc, CD; **~ka** f tile

płytki adj shallow

pływ/ać sail; *człowiek:* swim*; **~ający** adj *tech.* buoyant; **~ak** m swimmer; **~ać** float; **~alnia** f swimming pool

po *prp powierzchni, terenie:* on, over, around; **~ podłodze** on the floor; *pióro sunęło ~ papierze* the pen flowed over the paper; *biegła ~ trawie* she ran over the grass; **~ mieście/kraju** around the city/country; *czasie:* after; **~ śniadaniu** after breakfast; **~ drugiej** after two o'clock; *na zegarku:* past; **~ piąć ~ szóstej** five past six; **~ co?** what for?; **~ schodach** up/down the stairs; **~ cichu** quietly; **~ ciemku** in the dark; **~ pierwsze** first(ly); **~ polsku** mówić ~ polsku speak* Polish; **powiedzieć coś ~ polsku** say* s.th. in Polish; **przyjść ~ pomoc** come* for help

pobić beat* up; *(pokonać)* beat*

pob(ie)rać collect; *z banku:* withdraw*; **~ się** get* married

pobliż/e: w ~u in the vicinity *(czegoś* of s.th.)

pobłażliwy adj lenient

pobocze n roadside *Brt.*, shoulder *Am.*

pobory pl salary

pobożny adj pious

pobór m conscription, draft *Am.*

pobrudzić soil, dirty

pobu/dka f *mil.* reveille; *(bodziec)* motive; **~dzać ⟨~dzić⟩** stimulate; *emocjonalnie:* rouse; **~dzający**

stimulating; *emocjonalnie*: rousing; (*odświeżający*) invigorating; **środek** *m* ~*dzający* stimulant

pobyt *m* stay, visit

pocał|ować kiss, give* a kiss; ~**unek** *m* kiss

pochleb|ny *adj* flattering; ~**stwo** *n* flattery

pochł|aniać ⟨~**onąć**⟩ absorb; *książki* devour; *jedzenie* gobble (up) F

pochmurny *adj* cloudy

pochodnia *f* torch

pochodz|enie *n* origin; *Amerykanie polskiego* ~*enia* Americans of Polish descent; *Rosjanin z* ~*enia* a Russian by birth; *~ić* come* (**z** from); *zabytek itp.*: date (**z** from, back to)

pochód *m* march

pochwa *f* anat. vagina; *na pistolet*: holster; *na nóż*: sheath; *na miecz*: scabbard

pochwała *f* praise

pochyl|ać ⟨~**ić**⟩ bend*; ~**ać się** stoop (down), bend* (down); ~**ony** *adj* bent (**nad** over)

pochyły *adj* inclined

pociąć cut* (up)

pociąg *m* train; (*pragnienie*) drive* (*do robienia czegoś* to do s.th.); ~ **ekspresowy** express train; ~ **towarowy** goods train *Brt.*, freight train *Am.*; *~ać* → **ciągnąć**; ~**ać za** *ze szklanki*: sip; *nosem*: sniff; *fizycznie*: attract; ~**ać za**

sobą (*powodować*) cause; ~**nąć** *pf* → **pociągać**; ~**nięcie** *n ze szklanki*: sip; *nosem*: sniff; *pędzlem*: stroke; *za linę*: tug (at sth.)

pocić ⟨**s-**⟩ **się** perspire, sweat*

pociecha *f* consolation

pocierać → **trzeć**

pociesz|ać ⟨~**yć**⟩ comfort, console; ~**ający** *adj* comforting; ~**enie** *n* consolation; → **nagroda**

pocisk *m karabinowy*: bullet; *artyleryjski*: shell; *rakietowy*: missile

począ|ć *pf* → **poczynać**; ~**tek** *m* beginning, start; **na** ~**tku** in the beginning; **zacząć od** ~**tku** start from scratch; ~**tkowo** *adv* in the beginning, initially; ~**tkowy** *adj* initial; ~**tkujący** *m* beginner

poczekać *pf* → **czekać**; ~**lnia** *f* waiting room

poczt|a *f* post, mail; (*urząd*) post office; ~**a lotnicza** airmail; ~**owy** *adj* postal; ~**ówka** *f* postcard

poczucie *n* sense (*czegoś* of s.th.)

poczynać conceive

pod *prp* under; ~ **ścianą** at the wall; ~ **kątem** at an angle; ~ **wiatr** against the wind; ~ **wieczór** towards evening; ~ **warunkiem że ...** on condition that

poda|ć *pf* → **podawać**; ~**nie** *n* (*pismo*) application; *sp. piłki*: pass

podar|ować present (*komuś coś* s.o. with s.th.); **~unek** *m* gift

podat|ek *m* tax; **~nik** *m* tax payer

podawać *do ręki:* hand, give*; *do stołu:* serve; *przy stole:* tapes; *informacje* give*; *piłkę* pass; **~ się** pose (*za* as)

podaż *econ.* supply

podbiegać run* up (*do* to)

podbi|(ja)ć *kraj* conquer; *serca* win*; **~ój** *m* conquest

podburz|ać ⟨**~yć**⟩ incite (*przeciw* against)

podchodzić walk up (*do* to); *do problemu, osoby:* approach

podchwytliwy *adj pytanie itp.:* tricky

podczas *prp* during; **~ gdy** while

podda|ć *pf* → **poddawać**; **~ny** *m* subject

poddasze *n* attic

poddawać *miasto* surrender (*komuś* to s.o.); *krytyce, próbie:* subject (*czemuś* to s.th.); *pomysł* suggest; **~ się** surrender, give* in

podejmować *kwiaty* receive

podejrz|any 1. *m* suspect; **2.** *adj* suspicious; **~enie** *n* suspicion; **~ewać** suspect (*kogoś o coś* s.o. of s.th.); **~liwość** *f* mistrust; **~liwy** *adj* mistrustful

podejś|cie *n* approach; (*próba*) attempt; **~ć** *pf* →

podchodzić

podeprzeć *pf* → **podpierać**

podeptać *pf* trample

poderwać *pf* F (*zapoznać*) pick up F

podeszwa *f* sole

podglądać → **podpatrywać**

podgłówek *m na łóżku:* bolster; *w samochodzie:* headrest

podgrz(ew)ać warm up, heat up

podjazd *m przed domem:* driveway

podjąć *pf* → **podejmować**; **~ się** undertake (*zrobić coś* to do s.th.)

podje|żdżać ⟨**~chać**⟩ *samochodem:* drive* up (*do* to); *samochód:* pull in

podkład *m muzyczny:* backing; *pod farbę:* primer; *rail.* sleeper *Brt.*, tie *Am.;* **~ka** *f tech.* washer

podkoszulek *m* vest *Brt.*, undershirt *Am.*

podkowa *f* horseshoe

podkreśl|ać ⟨**~ić**⟩ underline, underscore; (*akcentować*) stress, emphasize, underscore

podlać *pf* → **podlewać**

podległy *adj* subordinate

podl(ew)ać *kwiaty:* water

podlicz|ać ⟨**~yć**⟩ sum up

podłoga *f* floor

podłoże *n* foundation

podłużny *adj kształt:* elongated; *przekrój:* longitudinal

podły *adj* mean

podmiejski *adj* suburban

podmiot *m gr.* subject

podmorski *adj* undersea

podmuch *m wiatru*: gust; *powietrza*: blast

podmy(wa)ć undermine

podnie|**cać** ⟨**~cić**⟩ excite; *seksualnie*: turn on F; ~**cać się** get* excited; *seksualnie*: get* aroused; ~**cenie** *n* excitement; ~**ta** *f* incentive

pod|**nosić** ⟨**~nieść**⟩ raise, lift; *z ziemi*: pick up; ~**nosić się** (*wstawać*) stand* up, rise*; *z ziemi*: pick oneself up; ~**noszenie** *n* **ciężarów** *sp.* weightlifting; ~**nośnik** *m mechaniczny*: hoist; *ręczny*: jack

podnóże *n góry*: foot; ~**k** *m* footstool

podobać się appeal (*komuś* to s.o.); ~**asz mi się** I like you; ~**ał ci się film?** did you like the film?; ~**ieństwo** *n* similarity (*pomiędzy* between, *do* to); *fizyczne*: resemblance (*pomiędzy* between, *do* to); ~**nie** *adv* similarly, in a similar way; ~**ny** *adj* similar (*do* to)

podpal|**ać** ⟨**~lić**⟩ *coś* set* fire to (s.th.), set* (s.th.) on fire

podpatrywać peep (*kogoś* at s.o.)

podpierać (**się**) support (oneself)

podpinka *f kurtki itp.*: detachable lining

podpis *m* signature; ~**(yw)ać** sign; *pisarz*: autograph

podpły|**wać** ⟨**~nąć**⟩ *statek*: sail up (*do* to); *człowiek*: swim* up (*do* to)

podpora *f* support

podporządkow(yw)ać subordinate (*coś czemuś* s.th. to s.th.); ~ **się** toe the line, conform (*czemuś* to s.th.)

podpowi|**adać** ⟨**~edzieć**⟩ prompt

podrabiać forge, counterfeit

podrapać *pf* → **drapać**

podraźni|(**a**)**ć** irritate; ~**ony** *adj* irritated

podręczn|**ik** *m* textbook; ~**y** *adj*: **bagaż** *m* ~**y** hand luggage

podrobi|**ć** *pf* → **podrabiać**; ~**ony** *adj* forged, counterfeit

podrożeć *pf* → **drożeć**

podróż *f ogólnie*: travel; *krótka*: trip; *dłuższa*: journey; *morska, kosmiczna*: voyage; *promem itp.*: crossing; ~**nik**, ~**ny** *m* traveller; ~**ować** travel (*po czymś* around s.th.)

podrzędny *adj* secondary

podrzu|**cać** ⟨**~cić**⟩ *przedmiot do góry* throw* (s.th.) up (in the air), toss*; F → **podwozić**

podsk|**akiwać** *na jednej nodze*: hop; *na drugą stronę*: skip; ~**oczyć** *w górę*: jump up, spring*, leap*; ~**ok** *m* hop, skip

podsłuch *m telefoniczny*: wire-tapping; ~**(iw)ać** *telefon* wire-tap, listen in (*coś* to s.th.); *ludzie*: eavesdrop (*coś* on s.th.)

podstaw|a f basis; (dolna część) base; **na ~ie czegoś** on the basis of s.th., based on s.th.; **~ka → spodek**; **~owy** adj basic, elementary, essential; **~y** pl essentials f
podstęp m trick
podsumow|anie n summary; **~(yw)ać** sum up
podszewka f lining
podświadom|ość f the subconscious; **~y** adj subconscious
poduszk|a f do spania: pillow; do siedzenia: cushion; **~owiec** m hovercraft
podwajać double
podważać lever, prise; argument challenge
podwieczorek m (afternoon) tea Brt.
podwieźć pf → **podwozić**
podwijać ⟨~nąć⟩ rękawy roll up
podwładny m subordinate
podwodny adj underwater; → **łódź**
podwoić pf → **podwajać**
pod|wozić osobę samochodem give* (s.o.) a lift (**do** to); **~wozie** n samochodu: chassis; samolotu: undercarriage
podwójny adj double
podwó|rko n, **~rze** n yard
podwyż|ka f płacy: rise Brt., raise Am.; **~ka cen** price increase; **~szać** ⟨~szyć⟩ raise
podział m division (**na** into); (konflikt) split

podziel|ać poglądy share; **~ić** pf → **dzielić**; **~ny** adj divisible; **~ony** adj divided; (skłócony) split
podziem|ie n underground; przestępce: underworld; **~ny** adj underground
podziękowanie n gratitude
podziwiać admire
podzwrotnikowy adj subtropical
poe|mat m (longer epic or lyric) poem; **~ta** m ⟨~tka⟩ f poet; **~zja** f poetry
pogada|ć F chat; **~nka** f talk
poganiać kogoś hustle (s.o.)
poganin m pagan
pogar|da f contempt; **~dzać** despise; **~dzić** refuse
pogarszać coś make* (s.th.) worse; **~ się** deteriorate
pogląd m view
pogłębi(a)ć (się) deepen
pogłoska f rumour
pogod|a f weather; **jutro będzie ~a** it will be fine tomorrow; **~ny** adj dzień: nice, fine; człowiek: cheerful
pogodzić się → godzić; (akceptować) resign oneself (**z czymś** to s.th.)
pogoń f pursuit, chase
pogorsz|enie n worsening; **~yć** pf → **pogarszać**
pogotowie n (gotowość) readiness; mil. itp. alert; **~ ratunkowe** (część szpitala) casualty (ward) Brt., emergency ward Am.; (stacja) emergency clinic; (karetka) ambulance

pogranicze n frontier; *fig.* borderland

pogrzeb m funeral

pogrzebacz m poker

pohamow(yw)ać się control oneself

pojawi(a)ć się show* up, turn up

pojazd m vehicle

pojąć pf → **pojmować**

pojechać pf → **jechać**

pojedyn|czy adj singular; **~ek** m duel

pojemn|ik m container; **~ik na śmieci** (litter) bin, garbage can Am.; **~ość** f capacity

poję|cie n idea (**o czymś** of s.th.); *logiczne itp.*: notion; **nie mam ~cia** I have no idea

pojutrze adv the day after tommorow

pokarm m feed

pokaz m *mody itp.*: show; *ogni itp.*: display; *umiejętności*: exhibition; **na ~** for show; **~(yw)ać** show*; *publicznie*: display

pokaźny adj fair, considerable

poklask m *fig.* approval

pokła|d m *na statku*: deck; *węgla*: seam; **na ~d** aboard; **na ~dzie** on board; **na ~dzie statku** aboard the ship

pokłon m bow

pokochać *kogoś* fall* in love with (s.o.)

pokoj|owy adj *traktat*: peace ...; *rozwiązanie*: peaceful; *temperatura*: room ...; **~ów-**

ka f chambermaid

pokolenie n generation

pokon(yw)ać *trudności* overcome*; *odległość* cover; *przeciwnika* defeat, beat*

pokor|a f humility; **~ny** adj humble

pokój¹ m *(pomieszczenie)* room

pokój² m (*nie wojna*) peace

pokrajać pf cut* up; *chleb, ciasto* slice

pokrew|ieństwo n kinship; **~ny** adj related

pokroić pf → **pokrajać**

pokropić pf → **kropić**

pokrótce adv briefly, in short

pokry|cie n *(materiał)* covering; *czeku*: cover, coverage; **~ć** pf → **pokrywać**

po kryjomu adv in secret, by stealth

pokry|wać cover; **~ty** adj covered; **~wa** f cover; **~wka** f *na garnek*: lid

pokusa f temptation

pokuta f atonement

pokwitowanie n receipt

polać pf → **polewać**

Polak m Pole

polana f clearing

pole n field; *math.* area

poleca|ć ⟨**~ić**⟩ recommend; *do wykonania*: → **zlecać**; **~enie** n recommendation; *wykonania*: instruction; **~ony** adj: *list* **m ~ony** registered letter

polegać depend (**na** on); (*obejmować*) consist (**na** in)

polewa *f* glaze; *czekoladowa*: icing; ~**ć** *czymś kogoś*: pour (s.th. on s.o.); *wodą*: water (s.o.)

polędwica *f* sirloin

policja *f* police; ~**nt** *m* policeman; ~**ntka** *f* policewoman

policzek *m* cheek; *(cios)* slap in the face

poliklinika *f* out-patient clinic

politechnika *f* polytechnic

polisa *f* *ubezpieczeniowa*: policy

polity|czny *adj* political; ~**k** *f* politician; ~**ka** *f* politics

Polka *f* Pole, Polish woman

polny *adj* field ...

polow|ać hunt *(na coś* s.th.); ~**anie** *n* hunt *(na coś* for s.th.)

Polsk|a *f* Poland; 2**i** *adj* Polish

polubić *kogoś* get* to like (s.o.), take* a liking to (s.o.)

połączenie *n* link *(między* between); *electr.* contact; *kolejowe*: connection; *uzyskiwać ~ teleph.* get* through *(z kimś* to s.o.)

połknąć *pf →* **połykać**

połow|a *f* half; *w ~wie maja* in the middle of May; *do ~wy, w ~wie* halfway

położe|nie *n* position; ~**na** *f* midwife; ~**yć** *pf →* **kłaść**

południ|e *n geogr.* south; *czas*: noon; *przed ~em* in the morning; *po ~u* in the afternoon; *w ~e* at noon; ~**owy**

adj south(ern); *wiatr, kierunek*: southerly

połykać swallow

połysk *m* shine

pomagać help, aid

pomału *adv* slowly

pomarańcza *f* orange

pomiar *m* measurement

pomidor *m* tomato

pomieszczenie *n* room

pomiędzy → *między*

pomi|jać ⟨~nąć⟩ ignore

pomimo → *mimo*

pomnażać → *mnożyć*

pomniejszać *pf →* **zmniejszać**

pomnik *m* monument

pomoc *f* help; *przy pracy, rada, pieniądze*: assistance; *medyczna, żywnościowa*: aid; *(ratunek)* rescue; **przyjść** *(komuś)* **z ~** come* to the/ one's rescue; *za ~ą czegoś* with the aid of s.th., by means of s.th.; *pierwsza ~* first aid; ~**niczy** *adj sprzęt itp.*: auxiliary; ~**nik** *m* helper; ~**ny** *adj* helpful

pomost *m na jeziorze*: pier

pomóc *pf →* **pomagać**

pomp|a *f* pump; *fig.* pomp; ~**ować ⟨na-⟩** pump

pomy|lić się be*/go* wrong, make* a mistake; *z czymś*: get* (s.th.) wrong; ~**łka** *f* mistake, error; *teleph.* wrong number

pomysł *m* idea; ~**owy** *adj* clever, ingenious

pomyśln|ość *f* prosperity; ~**y**

adj skutek: positive; zbieg okoliczności: happy; wiatr: favourable

ponad adv above; obszarem: over; w złożeniach: super-, ultra-; **~to** besides, moreover

ponętny adj tempting

poniedziałek m Monday

poniekąd adv in a way, as it were

ponieść pf → **ponosić**

ponieważ cj because

poniż|ać ⟨**~yć**⟩ humiliate

poniżej adv below

ponosić skutki, koszty itp. bear*

ponown|ie adv again; **~y** adj renewed

pończocha f stocking

poparcie n support

popatrzeć pf look (na at)

popchnąć pf → **popychać**

popełni(a)ć błąd make*; zbrodnię, grzech commit

popęd m (żądza) urge; psych. drive; (żądza) impulsive

popękany adj talerz itp.: cracked

popiel|aty adj grey, gray Am.; **~niczka** f ashtray

popierać support; wniosek a. second

popiersie n bust

popiół m ash(es pl)

popis m show

popołudni|e n afternoon; **~owy** adj afternoon; → **południe**

popraw|a f improvement; econ. recovery; **~i(a)ć** im-

prove; prace uczniów, błędy correct; **~i(a)ć się** improve; jur. a-mendment (do to); egzaminu: makeup examination Am.; **~ność** f correctness; **~ny** adj correct

poprzecz|ka f sp. bar; **~ny** adj element: transverse; **przekrój m ~ny** cross-section

poprzeć pf → **popierać**

poprze|dni adj previous; **~dnik** m predecessor; **~dnio** adv previously, formerly; **~dzać** ⟨**~dzić**⟩ precede

poprzek: w ~ across

poprzez → **przez**

popsuty adj telewizor itp.: broken, out of order

popularn|ość f popularity; **~y** adj popular

popychać push, shove

popyt m econ. demand

po|ra f time; **~ra roku** season; **do tej ~ry** so far, up till now; **od (tam)tej ~ry** from then on; **od teraz) ~ry** from now on; **o tej ~rze** at this time; **w samą ~rę** just in time; **pora da** f (a piece) of advice; **~dnia** f medyczna: clinic; **~dnik** m guide(book); **~dzić** pf → **radzić**

poran|ek m morning; **~ny** adj morning

porażenie n med. stroke

porażka f defeat
porcelana f china
porcja f portion
poręcz f banister, rail; **~e** pl sp. parallel bars pl
poręczny adj handy
pornografia f pornography
poronienie n miscarriage
porosnąć pf → **porastać**
porozumie|nie n agreement; **~(wa)ć się** communicate
poród m delivery
porówn|anie n comparison; **~awczy** adj comparative; **~(yw)ać** compare (**coś do czegoś** s.th. to s.th.)
port m (basen wodny) harbour; (miasto, teren) port; **~ lotniczy** airport
portfel m wallet
portret m (obraz) portrait; (opis) portrayal
porucznik m lieutenant
porusz|ać ⟨**~yć**⟩ move; **~ temat** touch (up)on; **~ać się** move; **~enie** n commotion; **~ony** adj agitated
por|wanie n kidnapping; samolotu: hijacking; **~ywacz** m kidnapper; samolotu: hijacker; **~ywać** ⟨**~wać**⟩ wiatr, prąd rzeki itp.: catch*; dla okupu: kidnap; samolot hijack
porząd|ek m order; **w ~ku** (zgoda) fine, all right; **ona jest w ~ku** she's all right; **coś jest nie w ~ku** something's wrong; **~ki** pl (wiosenne) (spring) cleaning; **~kować**

⟨**u-**⟩ pokój itp. tidy; **~ny** adj (czysty) neat; (uczciwy) honest, decent
porzuc|ać ⟨**~ić**⟩ abandon
posa|da f post, position; **~dzić** pf → **sadzać, sadzić**
posag m dowry
posądz|ać ⟨**~ić**⟩ kogoś accuse (s.o.) **o coś** of s.th.
posąg m statue
poseł m member (of parliament), MP Brt.; (przedstawiciel) envoy
posiad|acz m owner; dokumentu: bearer, holder; **~ać** own; **~łość** f estate
posiedzenie n (zebranie) session
posiłek m meal
posła|ć send*; **~niec** m messenger; **~nka** f member (of parliament), MP Brt.
posłu|szeństwo n obedience; **~szny** adj obedient
pospiech → **pośpiech**
pospolity adj common
post m fast
postać f (forma) form, shape; literacka: character; sławna: celebrity; (sylwetka) figure
postan|awiać ⟨**~owić**⟩ decide (**coś zrobić** to do s.th.)
postarać się pf arrange (**o coś dla kogoś** s.th. for s.o.)
postaw|a f posture; fig. stand (**wobec** on), attitude (**wobec** to/towards); **~ić** pf stand*
postąpić pf → **postępować**
postęp m progress; **~ować** (zachowywać się) act, behave

(*w stosunku do* towards), deal* (with); **~owanie** *n* behaviour; **~owy** *adj* progressive

postój *m* stop; **~ taksówek** taxi rank *Brt.*, taxi stand *Am.*

postrzelić shoot*

posu|nięcie *n* move; **~wać ⟨~nąć⟩ (się)** move; *do przodu*: advance

posyłać → (po)słać

posyp(yw)ać sprinkle (*czymś* with s.th.)

poszerz|ać ⟨~yć⟩ widen

poszukiwa|ć search (*czegoś* for s.th.); **~nie** search (*czegoś* for s.th.); **w ~niu czegoś** in search of s.th.

pościć fast

pościel *f* bed linen

pościg *m* pursuit (*za czymś/ kimś* of s.th./s.o.)

pośliz|g *m* skid; **wpaść w ~g** go* into a skid; **~nąć się** slip

pośmiertny *adj* posthumous

pośpie|ch *m* haste, hurry; **w ~chu** in haste, in a hurry; **~szny** *adj* hasty

pośredni *adj* indirect; **~ctwo** *n* mediation; **za ~ctwem czegoś** with the aid of s.th.; **~czyć** mediate; **~k** *m* mediator

pośród *prp* among

poświadcz|ać ⟨~yć⟩ certify; **~enie** *n* certificate

poświęc|ać ⟨~ić⟩ devote (*coś/się czemuś* s.th./oneself to s.th.); *w ofierze*: sacri-

fice; **~enie** *n* devotion (*czemuś* to s.th.); (*ofiara*) sacrifice; **~enie się** dedication

pot *m* sweat

potajemny *adj* secret

potem *adv* after that, afterwards; **na ~** for later; **→ wkrótce**

potęga *f* power

potępi(a)ć condemn

potężny *adj* powerful, mighty F

potknąć się *pf* **→ potykać się**

potoczny *adj* colloquial

potok *m* stream; *fig.* torrent, deluge

potom|ek *m* descendant; **~stwo** *n* offspring

potop *m* deluge

potrafić can*, be* able to, be* capable of; **nie ~** cannot, be* unable to, be* incapable of

potrawa *f* dish

potrąc|ać ⟨~ić⟩ *samochodem*: hit*, knock down, knock over

potrójny *adj* triple

potrzeb|a 1. *f* need (*czegoś* for s.th., *zrobienia czegoś* to do s.th.); **2.** *pred* it is necessary; **a nam cierpliwości** what we need is patience; **~ny** *adj* necessary; **~ować** need

potwierdz|ać ⟨~ić⟩ confirm; **~enie** *n* confirmation

potwór *m* monster

potyka|ć się stumble (*o* on), trip (*o* over)

poucz|ać ⟨~yć⟩ instruct

poufny *adj* confidential
powabny *adj* seductive
powaga *f sytuacji*: gravity
powalić *pf* → **obalać, przewracać**
poważ|ać respect; **~anie** *n*: *z ~aniem w liście*: yours sincerely; **~nie** *adv* seriously; *uszkodzić*: badly, **~ny** *adj* serious; *sytuacja*: grave
powiać *pf* → **wiać, powiewać**
powiad|amiać ⟨**~omić**⟩ *f* inform
powiązanie *n* connection
powiedzieć say*; *komuś*: say* (to s.o.), tell* (s.o.); **~ prawdę** tell* the truth
powieka *f* eyelid
powielać duplicate
powierzchnia *f* surface
powiesić *pf* → **wieszać**
powieś|ciopisarka *f* ⟨**~ciopisarz** *m*⟩ novelist; **~ć** *f* novel
powietrz|e *n* air; *na ~u* outdoors; **~ny** *adj* air ...; *fotografia*: aerial
powiew *m* gust; **~ać** *flaga itp.*: flutter
powiększ|ać ⟨**~yć**⟩ enlarge; *optycznie*: magnify; **~enie** *n phot.* enlargement, blow-up; *mikroskopu itp.*: magnification
powin|ien, ~na, ~no he, she, it should; **~ien być ostrożniejszy** he should be more careful; **nie ~ien tyle pracować** he should not work so much; **~ien był to**

zrobić he should have done it
powitanie *n* welcome
pow|lekać ⟨**~lec**⟩ *warstwą*: coat; **~łoka** *f* layer; *farby*: coat
powodować ⟨**s-**⟩ cause; **~ się czymś** be* prompted/ motivated by s.th.
powo|dzenie *n przedsięwzięcia*: success; *materialne*: prosperity; **~dzenia!** good luck!; **~dzić się** *jak się panu ~dzi?* how are you getting on?; **~dzi im się dobrze** they are doing fine/ well
powojenny *adj* post-war
powol|i *adv* slowly; **~ny** *adj* slow; *człowiek*: languid
powoł|anie *n* calling, vocation; *do wojska*: call-up *Brt.*, draft *Am.*; **~(yw)ać** *na stanowisko*: appoint; **~** *do wojska*: call up, draft *Am.*; **~ywać się** refer (*na coś* to s.th.)
powl|ód *m* reason; *z ~odu* because of, due to
powódź *f* flood
powr|otny *adj*: *bilet m ~otny* return (ticket) *Brt.*, round-trip ticket *Am.*; **~ót** *m* return; *z ~otem iść, jechać*: back
powsta|ć *pf* → **(po)wstawać**; **~nie** *n zbrojne*: uprising; (*początek*) establishment; **~wać** come* into being
powsze|chny *adj* universal; *opinia itp.*: public; *wybory*:

general; **~dni** adj common;
dzień m ~dni workday

powtarzać repeat; *przed eg-
zaminem*: revise; **~ się** repeat
oneself/itself

powtór|ka F f revision; **~rnie**
adv again; **~rnie użyty**
re-used; **~rny** adj done
again; **~rne wybory** pl
re-election; **~rzyć** pf → **powtarzać**

powyżej adv above

poza¹ f pose

poza² prp *krajem itp.*: out of;
granicami: beyond; *kimś*:
apart from; **~ tym** besides

pozbawi(a)ć deprive (*kogoś
czegoś* s.o. of s.th.)

pozby(wa)ć się *czegoś*: get*
rid of (s.th.)

pozdr|awiać ⟨**~owić**⟩ *kogoś*
say* hallo to (s.o.); **~ów go
ode mnie** say hallo to him
for me; **~owienie** n greeting;
~owienia z Londynu greet-
ings from London

poziom m level; *math.* the
horizontal; **~y** adj horizontal

pozłacany adj gold-plated

pozna|ć pf → **poznawać**;
~nie n: **zmienić się nie do
~nia** change beyond recogni-
tion; **~wać** ⟨**poznać**⟩ get* to
know (s.o.); **~wać się** get* to
know each other; (*rozpoz-
nać*) recognize; **miło mi cię
pani ~ć** I'm pleased to meet
you, Madam

pozosta|ć pf → **pozostawać**;
~łość f remainder; **~ły** adj

remaining; **~wać** stay; *bez
zmian*: remain; **~wać z tyłu**
stay/lag behind; **~wi(a)ć**
leave*

poz|ory pl, **~ór** m pretence,
appearances pl; **na ~ór** to/by
all appearances; **pod żadnym ~orem** on no account

pozwa|ć pf → **pozywać**

pozwalać let* (**komuś coś
zrobić** s.o. to s.th.), allow
(**komuś coś** s.o. s.th., **komuś coś zrobić** s.o. to do
s.th.); **~ sobie na coś** allow
oneself s.th., afford s.th.; **~
sobie na zrobienie czegoś**
allow oneself to do s.th., afford to do s.th.

pozwany m defendant

pozwol|enie n permission;
~enie na pracę work permit; **~ić** pf → **pozwalać**

pozycja f position; *społeczna*: status; *listy*:

pozywać *do sądu*: sue, take*
to court

pożar m fire; **~ny** adj → **straż**

pożądan|y adj desirable; **~ie**
n desire

pożegna|ć się say* goodbye
(**z kimś** to s.o.); **~lny** adj
farewell ...; **~nie** n farewell

pożycz|ać ⟨**~yć**⟩ lend* (**coś
komuś** s.th. to s.o.); borrow
(**coś od kogoś** s.th. from
s.o.); *zwłaszcza pieniądze*:
loan (**komuś** to s.o.); **~ka** f
loan

pożyte|czny adj useful; **~k m**
benefit

pożyw|ienie *n* food; **~ny** *adj* nutritious

pójść *pf* go*; → **iść, chodzić**

póki *cj* while; **~pamiętam** before I forget

pół half; **na ~ ugotowany** half-cooked; **przeciąć coś na ~ cut*** s.th. in half; **dzielić coś ~ na ~** split* s.th. fifty-fifty; **~ do piątej** half past four

półfinał *m* semi-final

półgłówek *m* half-wit

półka *f* shelf

półkole *n* semicircle

półksiężyc *m* crescent

półkula *f geogr.* hemisphere

półmisek *m* dish

północ *f geogr.* north; *czas:* midnight; **o ~y** at midnight; **~ny** *adj* north(ern); *wiatr, kierunek:* northerly

półtora one and a half

półwysep *m* peninsula

póź|niej *adv* later; **~niejszy** *adj* later; **~y** *adj* late

pra|- great ...; **~babka** *f* great grandmother

prac|a *f* work; *fizyczna:* labour; (*posada*) job; **~a naukowa** research; **~ochłonny** *adj* laborious; **~ować** work; **~owity** *adj człowiek:* hard-working; *dzień:* busy; **~ownia** *f naukowa:* lab(oratory); *artystyczna:* studio; **~ownica** *f* (**~ownik** *m*) worker; **~ fizyczny, umysłowy**

prać wash; **~ chemicznie** dry-clean

pradziadek *m* great grandfather

pragn|ąć desire, hanker (**czegoś** after/for s.th.); **~ę** *form.* I'd like; **~ienie** *n* desire, wish; *silne:* hankering; *wody itp.:* thirst

prakty|czny *adj* practical; **~ka** *f* (*nauka*) on-the-job training; (*doświadczenie*) on-the-job experience

pra|lka *f* washing machine; **~lnia** *f* laundry; **~lnia chemiczna** dry-cleaner('s); **~nie** *n* (*rzeczy*) laundry, wash, washing; (*czynność*) wash; **w ~niu** in the wash

pras|a[1] *f tech.* press; **~ować** ⟨**wy-**⟩ iron, press

prasa[2] *f* (*gazety, dzienniki-rze*) the press; **~owy** *adj rzecznik, konferencja:* press ...

prawd|a *f* truth; **~ę mówiąc** to be honest; **~a?** right?

prawdopodob|ieństwo *n* probability; **~nie** *adv* probably; **~ny** *adj* probable

prawdziwy *adj* real; (*typowy*) real, true; *historia:* true

prawic|a *f pol.* the right; **~owy** *adj* right-wing

prawidłowy *adj odpowiedź:* right, correct

prawie *adv* almost

praw|niczy *adj* legal; **~nik** *m* lawyer; **~ny** *adj* legal; **~o[1]** *n* law; *człowieka, obywatela:* right; **~o jazdy** driving licence *Brt.*, driver's license *Am.*;

~o natury the law of nature

prawo² adv: **na ~** on the right(-hand side); **w ~** right, to the right

prawosławny rel. orthodox

praw|ostronny adj right-sided; *ruch*: on the right-hand side of the road; **~y** adj right; *człowiek*: honourable; *burta statku*: starboard ...

prąd m current; **~ stały** direct current, DC; **~ zmienny** alternating current, AC; **~nica** f generator

premedytacj|a f: *morderstwo n z ~ą* premeditated murder

premier m prime minister; **~a** f premiere, first night

prenumer|ata f subscription; **~ować ⟨za-⟩** subscribe (*coś* to s.th.)

preria f prairie

prestiż m prestige

pretekst m pretext

pretensj|a f (*żal*) grudge; **~onalny** adj pretentious

prezent m present, gift; **~ować** present

prezerwatywa f condom

prezes m president, chairman (of the board)

prezydent m president

prę|dko adv quickly; fast; **~dko czy później** sooner or later; *im ~dzej tym lepiej* the sooner the better; **~dkość** f speed; *tech.* velocity

prędzej → **prędko**

pręga f streak

pręt m rod

prima aprilis m April Fools' Day

problem m problem

proboszcz m katolicki: parish priest; protestancki: rector

probówka f test tube

procent m per cent; (*część*) percentage

proces m process; *jur.* trial

proch m gunpowder; **~y** pl sl. drugs pl

prochowiec m trench coat

produ|cent m manufacturer, producer; **~kcja** f production; **~kować ⟨wy-⟩** produce; *w fabryce*: manufacture; **~kt** m product

prognoza f (*pogody* weather) forecast

program m programme, program Am.; *komputerowy*: program; **~ nauczania** curriculum; **~ista** m programmer; **~ować ⟨za-⟩** program

projekt m (*plan budowy*) design; **~ant** m designer; **~or** m projector

prokurat|or m prosecutor; **~ura** f prosecutor's office

prom m ferry; **~ kosmiczny** space shuttle

promie|niotwórczy adj radioactive; **~niować** radiate; **~niowanie** n radiation; **~ń** m świata, nadziei: ray; słońca, latarki: beam; math. radius

promocja *m* promotion; *(za-kończenie szkoły)* graduation

propo|nować ⟨za-⟩ suggest, propose; **~zycja** *f* suggestion

pro|sić ⟨po-⟩ ask (**kogoś o zrobienie czegoś** s.o. to do s.th., **kogoś o coś** s.o. for s.th.); **~szę** please; *podając coś*: here you are; *(co) ~szę bardzo (nie ma za co)* it's all right *Brt.*; you're welcome *Am.*; **(co) ~szę?** (I beg your) pardon?, sorry? *Brt.*, excuse me? *Am.*; **~ pana** Sir; **~ panią** Madam

prost|a *f math., sp.* straight; **~acki** *adj* coarse; **~o** *adv* straight; **~okąt** *m* rectangle; **~opadły** *adj* perpendicular; **~ota** *f* simplicity; **~ować ⟨wy-⟩ (się)** straighten; **~y** *adj* simple; *(nie krzywy, pionowy)* straight; **kąt ~y** right angle

prostytutka *f* prostitute

prosz|ek *m* powder; **~ek do prania** washing powder *Brt.*, laundry detergent *Am.*

pro|szę → prosić; ~śba *f* request (**o coś** for s.th.)

protest *m* protest; **~ować ⟨za-⟩** protest

proteza *f* prosthesis; *dentystyczna*: denture

protokół *m z zebrania*: minutes *pl*

prowadz|enie *n* running *w sklepie*: running; *lekcji*: conducting; *pojazdu*: driving; *sp.* lead; **~ić**

v/t **⟨po-⟩** *kogoś* lead*; *sklep* run*; *lekcje* conduct; *pojazd* drive*; *v/i* *w wyścigu, droga*: lead*

prowincja *f* the provinces, *negatywnie*: backwater; *(okręg)* province

prób|a *f* attempt; *thea.* rehearsal; *laboratoryjna*: test, trial; **~ka** *f* sample; **~ny** *adj* test ...; **~ować ⟨s-⟩** attempt, try (**coś zrobić** to do s.th.); *potrawę* taste; **⟨wy-⟩** *nowy sposób itp.* test

próch|nica *f med.* caries; **~nieć ⟨s-⟩** *zęby itp.*: decay

prócz → oprócz

próg *m* threshold; *domu*: doorstep

próżni|a *f* vacuum; **~ak** F *m* slacker

próżn|o *adv (a. na ~o)* in vain; **~ować** loaf (about/around)

próżny *adj człowiek*: vain; *zbiornik*: empty

prys|kać ⟨~nąć⟩ splash

pryszcz *m* pimple, spot

przebacz|ać ⟨~yć⟩ forgive*; **~enie** *n* forgiveness

przebić *pf* → **przebijać**

przebie|c *pf* → **przebiegać**; **~g** *m wydarzeń*: course; **~gać** *przez las, tłum*: run* through; *przez ulicę, most*: run* across/over; *przez pokój*: run* across; **~gły** *adj* shrewd, sly

przebierać *nie ~ w słowach* not to mince words; **~ się** change

przebijać pierce; (*być widocznym*) show through (*przez coś* s.th.)

przebój hit

przebywać stay

przeceni(a)ć overestimate, overrate; *towary* reduce the price of

przech|adzka *f* stroll; **~odzić** *v/i* pass (**obok** by), walk; *przez las, tłum*: walk through; *przez ulicę, most*: walk across/over; *przez pokój*: walk across; *na następnej sprawy*: go* on (to), proceed (to); *v/t operację* undergo; *chorobę itp*. cover; **~odzień** *m* passer-by

przechow|alnia bagażu *f* left luggage office *Brt.*, baggage room *Am.*; **~(yw)ać** store; **~ywanie** *n* storage

przechy|lać ⟨**~lić**⟩ tip, tilt; **~lać się** tilt; *teren*: slope; → *a.* chylić

przeciąć *pf* → przecinać

przeciąg *m* draught, draft *Am.*; **~ać** ⟨**~nąć**⟩ (*przedłużać*) drag out; **~ać się** *człowiek*: stretch

przeciąż|ać ⟨**~yć**⟩ overload (*czymś* with s.th.); **~enie** *n* overload; **~ony** *adj* overloaded (*czymś* with s.th.); *pracą*: overworked

przeciek *m* leak (*a. fig.*)

przecie(k)ać *pf* → przeciąć

przecier *m jabłkowy itp*.: purée

przecież *adv* after all

przeciętn|a *f* the average; **~ie** *adv* on average; **~y** *adj* average

przecin|ać cut*; **~ać się** cross; **~ek** *m* comma

przecisk|ać ⟨**~nąć**⟩ (*się*) push through

przeciw *prp* against; *sp., jur.* versus

przeciwdziałać oppose, counteract

przeciwko → przeciw

przeciwległy *adj* opposite

przeciwn|ie *adv* contrary (*do* to); (*wprost*) **~ie** on the contrary; **~iczka** *f* (**~nik** *m*) opponent, adversary; *czegoś*: opponent, enemy; (*konkurent*) rival; **~y** *adj* kierunek: opposite; *człowiek*: opposed (*czemuś* to s.th.); **w ~ym razie** otherwise

przeciwpożarow|y *adj* firefighting; *przepisy* **~e** fire regulations *pl*

przeciwstawi(a)ć contrast (*coś czemuś* s.th. to s.th.); **~ się komuś** stand* up (to s.o.); *władzy itp.* defy (*czemuś* s.th.)

przeczenie *n gr.* negation

przeczyszczający *adj* (*a. środek m ~*) laxative

przeczytać *pf* read* (from cover to cover); *coś krótkiego* read* through

przed *prp punktem w czasie*: before; *okresem*: ago; *domem*: in front of; (*wcześniej niż*) before, ahead of;

przyszła ~ *drugą* she arrived before two o'clock; *przyszła* ~ *dwiema minutami* she arrived two minutes ago

przed|dzień m: *w* ~*dzień, w* ~*edniu* the day before, *form.* on the eve of

przede → **przed**

przedimek m *gr.* article

przedłuż|acz m extension lead *Brt.*, extension cord *Am.*; ~*ać* ⟨~*yć*⟩ prolong, extend

przedmieście n suburb

przedmiot m object; *szkolny:* subject

przedmowa f preface

przedni *adj* front ...

przedostatni *adj* penultimate, next-to-last

przedosta|(wa)ć się get* (through) (*do* to); *do prasy:* be* leaked

przedpokój m hall(way)

przedpołudnie n morning; → *południe*

przedramię n forearm

przedsię|biorca m businessman; ~*biorstwo* n business, firm, company; ~*wzięcie* n undertaking; *ryzykowne:* venture, enterprise

przedstawi|ać introduce (*kogoś komuś* s.o. to s.o.); *argument, propozycję* put* forward (*komuś* to s.o.); *obraz, fotografia:* show, represent; ~*ciel(ka* f) m representative; ~*cielstwo* n agency;

~*enie* n *thea.* performance

przedszkole n kindergarten

przedtem *adv* before

przedwcze|sny *adj* premature; ~*śnie* *adv* prematurely

przedwczoraj *adv* the day before yesterday

przedwojenny *adj* pre-war

przedzia|ł m *rail.* compartment; ~*elać* ⟨~*lić*⟩ separate

prze|dzierać ⟨~*drzeć*⟩ tear*; *przez* tear* one's way (*do/przez* into/through)

przedziwny bizarre, weird

przegapi(a)ć F overlook; *autobus itp.* miss

przegląd m review; *wiadomości:* roundup, newsflash; *twórczości:* retrospective; ~ *techniczny samochodu:* MOT test; ~*ać* look over, look through; *książkę* thumb through

przegra|ć *pf* → *przegrywać*; ~*na* f defeat

przegrywać *mecz, bitwę* lose*

przegry|zać ⟨~*źć*⟩ *coś* bite* through (s.th.)

przegub m wrist

przejaśni(a)ć się *pogoda:* clear up

przejaw m manifestation

przejazd m passage; ~ *kolejowy* crossing

przejażdżka f ride

przeją|ć *pf* → *przejmować*

prze|jeżdżać ⟨~*chać*⟩ *v/i przez las:* drive* through;

przez most: drive* across/
over; *przez plac*: drive*
across; *przez past*: drive*
past (s.th.); *v/t człowieka*
run* over

przej|ęcie *władzy*: takeover,
seizure; *przedsiębiorstwa*:
takeover; **~ęty** *adj* (*zaniepokojony*) worried; (*podnie-
cony*) excited; **~mować**
władze seize, take* over;
przedsiębiorstwo, stanowisko
take* over; **~mować się**
czymś: take* (s.th.) to heart,
take* (s.th.) seriously; (*niepokoić się*) worry about
(s.th.); **nie ~muj się** don't
worry

przejrz|eć *pf* → **przeglądać**;
~ysty *adj* transparent

przejście *n* passage; *między
rzędami, regałami*: aisle; *z
jednego stanu w drugi*: tran-
sition; **~cie dla pieszych** pedestrian crossing; **~cie podziemne** underpass; **~ciowy**
adj (*tymczasowy*) temporary; *okres, stan*: transitional;
~ść *pf* → **przechodzić**

przekaz *m*: **~ pocztowy** money order; **~(yw)ać** *dokument* hand over; *tradycje*
hand down; *sygnały* trans-
mit; *wiadomości* communicate; *na konto*: transfer

przekaźnik *m tech.* relay

przekąska *f* snack

przekl|eństwo *n* curse;
(*słowo*) swearword; **~inać**
curse

przekład *m* translation; **~ać**
(*tłumaczyć*) translate; *w inne
miejsce*: move; **~nia** *f* gear

przekłu(wa)ć pierce

przekon|anie *n* conviction;
~any *adj* convinced;
~(yw)ać convince (*kogoś o
czymś* s.o. of/about s.th.);
persuade (*kogoś by coś zrobił* s.o. to do s.th.); **~ujący**
adj convincing

przekracz|ać *próg, rów* step
over; *rzekę, granicę* cross;
poziom, budżet exceed; *prze-
pisy* break*; **~ać dozwoloną
prędkość** exceed the speed
limit, speed F

przekrawać cut* (*na połowę*
in two)

przekreśl|ać ⟨**~ić**⟩ *słowo*
cross out

przekręc|ać ⟨**~ić**⟩ *gałkę*
turn; *słowa* distort

przekrocz|enie *n przepisów*:
breach; **~enie dozwolonej
prędkości** speeding; **~yć** *pf*
→ **przekraczać**

przekr|oić *pf* → **przekrawać**;
~ój *m tech., fig.* cross-section

przekształc|ać ⟨**~ić**⟩ (**się**)
transform; **~enie** *n* transfor-
mation

przekup|stwo *n* bribery;
~ywać ⟨**~ić**⟩ bribe

przelać *pf* → **przelewać**

przel|atywać ⟨**~ecieć**⟩ *nad
czymś*: fly* (over s.th.);
wiatr, samochody: sweep*

przelew *na konto*: transfer;
~ać *płyny*: pour (*z czegoś*

do czegoś from s.th. to s.th.); *krew, łzy* shed*; *na konto*: transfer; **~ać się** overflow

przelicz|ać ⟨~yć⟩ *pieniądze* count (out); **~yć się** miscalculate

przelot *m* flight (*nad czymś* over s.th.)

przeludnienie *n* overpopulation

przełam(yw)ać break* (*na połowę* in two)

przełącz|ać ⟨~yć⟩ *TV na inny kanał*: switch over (to); **~nik** *m* switch

przełęcz *f* pass

przełom *m* breakthrough

przełoż|ony *m* superior; **~yć** *pf* → **przekładać**

przełyk *m* gullet; **~ać** swallow; (*szybko albo dużo*) gulp

przemar|zać ⟨-znąć⟩ freeze*

przemęczenie *n* exhaustion

przemi|ana *f* change; **~eni(a)ć (się)** change (*w coś* into s.th.)

przemie|szczać ⟨~ścić⟩ **(się)** move

przemi|jać ⟨~nąć⟩ pass, go* by

przemoc *f* violence

przemoczyć *pf* soak

przemówienie *n* speech; *form.* address

przemy|cać ⟨~cić⟩ smuggle (*do/z* into/out of, *przez granicę* across the border)

przemyć *pf* → **przemywać**

przemysł *m* industry; **~owy** *adj* industrial

przemyśleć *pf coś* think* (s.th.) over; *jeszcze raz*: reconsider

przemyt *m* smuggling; *towary*: contraband; **~nik** *m* smuggler

przemywać wash

przenie|sienie *n* transfer; **~ść** *pf* → **przenosić**

przeno|sić carry; *pracownika* transfer; **~śny** *adj* magnetofon *itp.*: portable; *zwrot, znaczenie*: figurative

przeobra|żać ⟨~zić⟩ **(się)** transform

przeocz|ać ⟨~yć⟩ overlook; **~enie** *n* oversight

przepa|dać **~dać za czymś/kimś** be crazy about s.th./s.o.

przepalać ⟨~lić⟩ **się** *bezpiecznik*: blow*

przepaść *f* abyss

przepełniony *adj* crowded

przepędz|ać ⟨~ić⟩ drive* away

przepis *m* regulation; *gastr.*: recipe; **~(yw)ać** copy (out); *lekarstwo* prescribe

przepłuk|(iw)ać *naczynie*: rinse out

przepły|wać *v/i rzeka*: flow through; *v/t* ⟨~nąć⟩ *rzekę* swim* across; *statkiem*: sail across

przepona *f anat.* diaphragm

przepow|iadać ⟨~iedzieć⟩ predict

przepracowany adj overworked

przepr|aszać ⟨**~osić**⟩ apologize (**kogoś** to s.o.); **~aszam!** excuse me!; wyrażając żal: I'm sorry

przeprowadz|ać ⟨**~ić**⟩ badania conduct, carry out; kogoś np. przez ulicę help (s.o. across the street); **~ać się** move (**z - do** from - to); do kogoś: move in (**do** with); **~ka** f move

przepuklina f hernia

przepu|stka f pass; **~szczać** ⟨**~ścić**⟩ kogoś (robić komuś miejsce) let* (s.o.) through; zdającego egzamin pass

przepych m splendour; **~ać się** push (one's way) (**przez coś** through s.th.)

przerabiać dom, pokój remodel; odzież alter; temat cover

przera|żać ⟨**~zić**⟩ horrify; **~żający** adj horrific, terrifying; **~żenie** n horror; **~żony** adj terrified

przer|obić pf → **przerabiać**; **~óbka** f odzieży: alteration

przer|wa f break; w rozmowie: pause; w obradach: recess; w podróży: stopover; w filmie, koncercie: intermission; **~wać** pf → **~ywać** komuś: interrupt (s.o.), cut* (s.o.) off; pracę, budowę stop; bójkę, przyjęcie, spotkanie break* up; znajomość break* (off); łączność break*

przesa|da f exaggeration; **~dny** adj exaggerated; **~dzać** ⟨**~dzić**⟩ v/i exaggerate, overdo (**z czymś** s.th.); v/t drzewo itp. transplant

przesąd m superstition; **~ny** adj superstitious

przesia|dać ⟨**~ąść**⟩ się podczas podróży: change (**z czegoś na coś** from s.th. to s.th.), change trains, buses etc.

przesk|akiwać ⟨**~oczyć**⟩ coś jump over (s.th.)

przesłać pf → **przesyłać**

przesłuch|(iw)ać podejrzanego interrogate; **~anie** n podejrzanego: interrogation; przed sądem: hearing; kandydatów: interview; aktorów itp.: audition

przesta(wa)ć stop (**robić coś** doing s.th.); (uprawiać nałóg) give* up (**robić coś** doing s.th.)

przestawi(a)ć move; **~ się** switch (**z czegoś na coś** from s.th. to s.th.)

przestęp|ca m criminal; **~czość** f crime; **~czy** adj criminal; **~stwo** n offence; poważne: crime

przestra|ch m fright; **~szyć** pf frighten, scare; **~szyć się** get* scared; take* fright (**czegoś** of s.th.)

przestrze|gać zwyczaju, prawa: observe; **~c** kogoś warn, caution

przestrzeń f space; **~ kos-**

miczna outer space, cosmos; **~ powietrzna** airspace

przesu|wać ⟨~nąć⟩ (się) move

przesył|ać *pocztą:* send*, mail *Am.* (*komuś* to s.o.); *towary* ship; **~ka** *f* delivery

przeszczep *m* transplant

przeszk|adzać ⟨~odzić⟩ *v/i* disturb, interfere; (*stać na drodze*) be in the way; *v/t* prevent (*komuś w zrobieniu czegoś* s.o. from doing s.th.); **~oda** *f* obstacle, hindrance

przeszł|o *adv* over; **~ość** *f* (the) past; **~y** *adj* past

przeszuk|iwać *dom* search (*w celu odnalezienia czegoś* for s.th.)

prześcieradło *n* sheet

prześladow|ać oppress; *myśl:* haunt, nag; **~ca** *m* oppressor

prześliczny *adj* lovely

przeświadczenie *n* conviction

prześwietl|ać ⟨~ić⟩ X-ray; **~enie** *n* X-ray

przetarg *m* auction

przetrwać survive

przetw|arzać ⟨~orzyć⟩ process; **~arzanie** *n* processing

przewaga *f* advantage (*nad* over); *liczebna:* predominance; *przemysłowa, militarna:* supremacy

przewi|dywać ⟨~dzieć⟩ forecast*

przewie|trzać ⟨~trzyć⟩ po-

kój itp. air; **~w** *m* draught *Brt.*, draft *Am.*; **~wny** *adj* airy

przewieźć *pf* → **przewozić**

przewij|ać ⟨~nąć⟩ *taśmę* rewind*, wind* back; *do przodu:* wind* forward

przewodni *adj* leading; **~ cząca** *f* chairperson, chair; (*mężczyzna*) chairman; (*kobieta*) chairwoman; **~k** *m* guide; (*książka*) guide-(book); *electr.* conductor

przewodzić *strajkowi itp.* lead*; *prąd itp.* conduct

przewozić transport; *samolotem:* fly*; *samochodem:* drive*

przewód *m electr.* cable, lead; *zasilający:* flex *Brt.*, cord *Am.*; *med.* duct, tube, tract; **~ pokarmowy** digestive tract; **~ kominowy** flue

przewóz *m* transport

przewr|acać ⟨~ócić⟩ *osobę* knock down, knock over; *przedmiot* knock over, upset*, overturn; **~acać coś do góry nogami** turn s.th. upside down; **~acać ⟨~ócić⟩ się** fall* (over/down), overturn; **~ót** *m* revolution; *wojskowy:* takeover; coup; *społeczny:* upheaval

przez *prp czas:* for; *cały okres:* through(out); *most:* across; over; *rzekę, pole, pokój:* across; *las, tłum, okno, miasto, ścianę:* through; *telefon:* on; *dzielić,* *zrobione itp.*: by; *miasto na trasie*: via

przeziębi(a)|ć się catch* cold; **~enie** *n* cold; **~ony** *adj*: **jestem ~ony** I've got a cold

przeznacz|ać ⟨**~yć**⟩ allocate; *fundusze a.* appropriate; **~enie** *n* destiny; **~ony** *adj* intended (**na coś** for s.th., **dla kogoś** for s.o.)

przezorny *adj* cautious

przezrocz|e *n* slide; **~ysty** *adj* transparent

przeżegnać się cross oneself

przeży|cie *n* experience; **~(wa)ć** experience; *katastrofę* survive

przod|ek *m* ancestor; **~ujący** *adj* leading

prz|ód *m* front; **w ~ód, do ~odu** forward; **~odem, na ~edzie, z ~odu** in front; **z ~odu czegoś** in the front of s.th.

przy *stole, oknie, drzwiach*: at; *pracy*: at; *kimś*: beside; *ulicy*: on; *sobie*: on; *brzegu*: off

przybierać *v/i rzeka*: rise*; *v/t* (*zdobić*) decorate (**czymś** with s.th.); **~ na wadze** put* on weight

przybi|jać ⟨**~ć**⟩ nail (**coś do czegoś** s.th. to s.th.)

przybliż|ać ⟨**~yć**⟩ **się** approach (**do czegoś** s.th.); **~ony** *adj* approximate

przybory *pl* accessories *pl*; *wędkarskie*: tackle *sg*; **~ do golenia** shaving things *pl*

przybra|ć *pf* → **przybierać**; **~ny** *adj* ojciec, *syn*: foster; **pod ~nym nazwiskiem** under an assumed name

przybrzeżny *adj* coastal

przyby|cie *n* arrival; **~(wa)ć** arrive

przych|odnia *f* clinic, health centre *Brt.*; **przy szpitalu**: outpatient clinic; **~odzić** come*; **~odzić komuś do głowy** occur* to s.o.; **~odzić z pomocą** come* to the rescue; **~odzić do kogoś z wizytą** pay* s.o. a visit; **~odzić do siebie** come* to; **~ód** *m* proceeds *pl*

przychyl|ać ⟨**~ić**⟩ **się** (*zgodzić się*) accede (**do czegoś** to s.th.); **~ny** *adj* sympathetic; *opinia itp.*: favourable

przyciąć *pf* → **przycinać**

przyciąg|ać ⟨**~nąć**⟩ attract; **~ać czyjąś uwagę** attract s.o.'s attention

przycinać trim

przycis|kać ⟨**~nąć**⟩ press (**coś do czegoś** s.th. to s.th.)

przyczep|a *f mot.* trailer; **~a kempingowa** caravan *Brt.*, trailer *Am.*; **~i(a)ć** attach (**coś do czegoś** s.th. to s.th.)

przyczyn|a *f* reason; **~i(a)ć się** contribute (**do czegoś** to s.th.)

przyda|tny *adj* useful; **~(wa)ć się** be* of use (**do czegoś, na coś** for s.th., **jako coś** as s.th.)

przydział m allocation; _żywności_: ration

przydziel|ać ⟨~**ić**⟩ allocate; _do pracy_: assign

przyglądać się look (_czemuś_ at s.th.); (_sprawdzać_) inspect (_czemuś_ s.th.)

przygnębienie n depression

przygod|a f adventure; _miłosna_: affair, fling F; **~ny** adj znajomy: casual

przygotow|anie n preparation; **~ania** pl arrangements pl; ⟨~**(yw)ać** ⟨**się**⟩⟩ prepare (oneself) (_na coś, do czegoś_ for s.th., to do s.th.)

przyimek m gr. preposition

przyjaci|el m friend; **~elski** adj friendly; **~ółka** f friend

przyjazd m arrival

przyja|zny adj friendly; ⟨~**źnić się**⟩ be* friends (_z kimś_ with s.o.); **~źń** f friendship

przyjąć pf → **przyjmować**

przyjechać pf → **przyjeżdżać**

przyjemn|ość f pleasure; _z ~ością_ with pleasure; **~y** adj pleasant

przyjeżdżać arrive, come*

przyj|ęcie n party, reception; _pomocy, nowego członka_: acceptance; (_nie_) _do ~ęcia_ (un)acceptable; **~mować** accept; _gości_ receive; _pacjentów_ admit; _nie ~mować_ refuse; **~mować się** _poglądy, nowa moda_: catch* on

przyjrzeć się pf → **przyglądać się**

przyjś|cie n arrival; **~ć** pf → **przychodzić**

przykazanie n commandment

przyklej|ać ⟨~**ić**⟩ stick* (_coś do czegoś_ s.th. to s.th.)

przykład m example; _na ~_ for example

przykład|ać put* (_coś do czegoś_ s.th. to s.th.); **~ się** apply oneself (_do czegoś_ to s.th.)

przykręc|ać ⟨~**cić**⟩ _śrubę_: screw (_coś do czegoś_ s.th. to s.th.)

przykr|o adv: _~o mi_ I'm sorry; **~ość** f: _robić komuś ~ość_ hurt s.o.; _z ~ością zawiadamiam, że..._ I am sorry to inform you that...; _z ~ością muszę przyznać, że..._ I regret to admit that...; **~y** adj unpleasant

przykry(wa)ć cover (up)

przylądek m cape

przylegać adhere (_do czegoś_ to s.th.)

przylepi(a)ć ⟨się⟩ stick*

przylot m arrival (by plane)

przyłącz|ać ⟨~**yć**⟩ attach; _electr._ connect; **~ać się** join (_do czegoś_ s.th.)

przyłożyć pf → **przykładać**

przymi|arka f u _krawca_: fitting; **~erzyć** try on

przymiotnik m adjective

przymocow(yw)ać fasten (_coś do czegoś_ s.th. to s.th.)

przymus m compulsion; **~owy** adj _praca, lądowanie_: forced

przynajmniej adv at least

przynależność f do organizacji: membership

przynęta f bait (a. fig.)

przy|nosić ⟨~nieść⟩ bring*; (iść i wracać z czymś) fetch

przypad|ek m chance, accident; gr., med. case; ~kiem| przez ~ek by accident, by chance; w ~ku czegoś in the event of s.th., in case of s.th.; ~kowo adv accidentally, by chance; ~kowy adj accidental

przypal|ać ⟨~ić⟩ żelazkiem: scorch, singe; ogniem: singe; ~ać (się) jedzenie: burn*

przypilnować pf → **pilnować**

przypi|nać ⟨~nać⟩ pin (up)

przypis m (foot)note; ~(yw)ać attribute (coś komuś s.th. to s.o.)

przypływ m (incoming) tide; uczucia: rush, surge

przypom|inać ⟨~nieć⟩ remind (komuś o czymś/kimś s.o. of s.th./s.o.); (być podobnym) remind (komuś coś/ kogoś s.o. of s.th./s.o.), resemble (coś/kogoś s.th./s.o.), ~inać komuś by coś zrobił remind s.o. to do s.th.; ~inać sobie remember, recall

przypra|wa f condiment, seasoning; korzenna: spice; ziołowa: herb; ~wy pl seasoning(s pl); ~wi(a)ć season

przyprowadz|ać ⟨~ić⟩ bring* (along)

przyroda f nature

przyrodni adj: ~ brat m step-brother; ~a siostra f step-sister

przyrodni|czy adj natural; ~k m naturalist

przyrost m growth, increase; ~ naturalny birth rate; ~ek gr. suffix

przyrząd m instrument; ~dzać ⟨~dzić⟩ potrawę make*

przyrze|czenie n promise; ~kać ⟨~c⟩ promise (coś komuś s.th. to s.o.)

przysiąg|a f oath; ~ać ⟨~nąć⟩ swear*; ~ły m jur.: ~ława f ~łych jury

przysłać pf → **przysyłać**

przysłowie n proverb

przysłówek m adverb

przysługa f favour

przysmak m delicacy, titbit

przyspiesz|ać ⟨~yć⟩ accelerate, speed up; ~ać kroku quicken one's pace; ~enie n acceleration, pickup F

przysta|nąć pf → **przystawać**; ~nek m stop; ~ń f harbour; fig. a. haven; ~wać stop, halt

przystawka f gastr. starter, hors d'oeuvre

przyst|ąpić pf → **przystępować**; ~ępny adj clear; cena: moderate, reasonable; ~ępować: ~ępować do p-

rozmów: enter into (e.g. talks)

przystojny *adj* good-looking, handsome

przystosow(yw)ać (się) adapt (*do czegoś* to s.th.)

przysu|wać ⟨∼nąć⟩ *krzesło* pull up; **∼wać się** come*/move closer (*do kogoś* to s.o.)

przysyłać send* (*coś do kogoś* s.th. to s.o.)

przyszł|ość *f* future; **∼y** *adj* future; *tydzień, miesiąc*: next

przyszy(wa)ć *guzik* sew* (*do czegoś* onto s.th.)

przyśrubow(yw)ać screw (*coś do czegoś* s.th. to s.th.)

przytom|ność *f* consciousness; **∼ność umysłu** presence of mind, wits; **∼ny** *adv* conscious

przytrzym(yw)ać hold* down

przytul|ać ⟨∼ić⟩ cuddle; **∼ić się** cuddle up F (*do kogoś* to s.o.); **∼ny** *adj* cosy

przywiąz|anie *n* fig. attachment; **∼any** *adj* attached (*do czegoś* to s.th.); **∼(yw)ać** fix (*coś do czegoś* s.th. to s.th.); **∼ywać się** fig. become* attached (*do kogoś* to s.o.)

przywieźć *pf* → **przywozić**

przywilej *m* privilege

przywitać welcome

przywozić *samochodem, pociągiem*: bring*

przywódca *m* leader

przywyk|ać ⟨∼nąć⟩ get* used/accustomed (*do czegoś* to s.th.)

przyzna|nie *n*: **∼nie się do winy** admission of guilt

przyzna|(wa)ć admit; *nagrodę, tytuł* award; *fundusze* appropriate; **∼wać komuś rację** admit that s.o. is right; **∼wać się do czegoś** admit s.th., confess to s.th.

przyzwoit|ość *f* decency; **∼y** *adj* decent, respectable

przyzwycza|jać ⟨∼ić⟩ accustom (*do czegoś* to s.th.); **∼jać się** get* accustomed/used (*do czegoś* to s.th.); **∼jenie** *n* habit; **∼jony** *adj* accustomed

pseudonim *m* pseudonim; *literacki*: nom de plume

psi *adj* canine; **∼akrew!** *int* damn it!

psota *f* prank, mischief

pstrąg *m zo.* trout

psuć ⟨po-, ze-⟩ *zabawę, widok, dziecko* spoil*; *maszynę* break*, damage; *reputację* harm, damage; **∼ się** *maszyna*: break* (down); *jedzenie*: go* bad; *ząb*: rot

psych|iatra *m* psychiatrist; **∼iatryczny** *adj* psychiatric; **∼iczny** *adj* psychic(al); *choroba f ∼iczna* mental disease; **∼ika** *f* psyche; **∼olog** *m* psychologist; **∼ologia** *f* psychology; **∼ologiczny** *adj* psychological; **∼opata** *m* psychopath

pszczoła f bee

pszen|ica f wheat; **~ny** adj wheat ...

pta|ctwo m fowl; **~ctwo domowe** poultry; **~k** m bird

płyś m (ciastko) puff

publi|czność f audience; **~czny** adj public; **~kacja** f publication; **~kować ⟨o-⟩** publish

puch m down

puchar m cup

puchnąć ⟨s-⟩ swell*

pucz m wojskowy: (military) coup

pudel m poodle

pudełko n box; **~ zapałek** box of matches

puder m (face-)powder; **~niczka** f (powder) compact

pudło n (big) box; F (niecelny strzał) miss

pukać ⟨za-⟩ knock (do drzwi at/on the door)

pula f pool

pulchny adj plump

puls m pulse; **~ować** throb

pułapka f trap

pułk m regiment; **~ownik** m colonel

puma f puma

punkt m point; na liście: item; w tekście: section; programu: event; **~ kontrolny** checkpoint; **~ kulminacyjny** climax, culmination; **~ obserwacyjny** viewpoint, vantage point; **~ orientacyjny** landmark; **~ oparcia** purchase; **~**

sporny point at issue; **~ widzenia** point of view, viewpoint, standpoint; **~ zapalny** pol. hot spot; **~ zwrotny** turning point, watershed; **martwy ~** standstill, deadlock; **mocny ~** asset

punktualn|ie adv on time; **~y** adj punctual

pupa F f bottom

pustelni|a f hermitage; **~k** m hermit

pust|ka f emptiness, vacuum; **mam ~kę w głowie** my mind's a blank; **~kowie** n wastes pl; **~oszeć ⟨o-⟩** o sala itp.: empty; **~oszyć ⟨s-⟩** devastate; **~y** adj empty; **w środku:** hollow

pustyn|ia f desert; **~ny** adj desert ...

puszcza f forest

puszczać z ręki: let* go (coś of s.th.); na ziemię: drop; na wolność: let* (s.o.) go; wodę run*; taśmę play; **~ coś w obieg** pass s.th. round; **~ się** czegoś: let* go (of s.th.); F kobieta: sleep* around F

puszka f tin Brt., can Am.

puścić pf → puszczać

puzon m mus. trombone

pył m dust; **~ek kwiatowy** pollen

pysk m mouth; psa: snout, muzzle

pyszny adj delicious

pyta|ć ⟨s-, za-⟩ ask (kogoś o coś s.o. about s.th.); **~nie** n question

R

rabarbar *m* rhubarb
rabat *m* discount
rab|ować ⟨**ob-**⟩ rob (*kogoś z czegoś* s.o. of s.th.); ⟨**z-**⟩ steal* (*coś komuś* s.th. from s.o.); **~unek** *m* robbery
rachu|ba *f*: *tracić* **~bę** *czasu* lose* track of time; **~nek** *m w restauracji*: bill, check *Am.*; *w banku*: account; **~nkowość** *f econ.* accounting, book-keeping
racja¹ *f* ration
racja² *f*: *mieć* **~ę** be* right (*co do czegoś* about s.th.); *przyznać komuś* **~ę** admit that s.o. is right
raczej *adv* rather
rad|a *f* (*a piece of*) advice; (*grupa*) council; *dawać sobie* **~ę** cope (*z czymś* with s.th.), manage (*z czymś* s.th.); **~ca** *m* counsellor
radi|o *n* radio; *przez* **~o** by radio; *w* **~u** on the radio; **~oodbiornik** *m* radio receiver; **~ostacja** *f* radio (station); **~owóz** *m* patrol car; **~owy** *adj* radio
radny *m* councillor
rado|sny *adj* joyful, cheerful; **~ść** *f* joy
radykalny *adj* radical
radzić ⟨**do-, po-**⟩ advise (*komuś* s.o.); ~ ⟨**po-**⟩ *sobie*

cope (*z czymś* with s.th.); ~ ⟨**po-**⟩ *się* consult (*kogoś*
rafa *f* reef
rafineria *f* refinery
raj *m* paradise
rajd *m* rally; *pieszy*: hike
rak *m* crayfish; *choroba*) cancer
rakieta¹ *f kosmiczna*: rocket
rakieta² *f sp.* racquet, racket
rama *f* frame
rami|ączko *n* shoulder-strap; (*wieszak*) hanger; **~ę** *n* arm; (*bark*) shoulder
rana *f* wound
randka *f* date
ranek *m* morning
ran|ić ⟨**z-**⟩ (**się**) injure (oneself), hurt* (oneself); **~ni** the wounded *pl*; **~ny¹** *adj* wounded, injured
ran|ny² *adj* morning ...; **~o 1.** *n* morning; **2.** *adv* in the morning
raport *m* report
ras|a *f* race; *konia, psa*: breed; **~owy** *adj* racial; *kot, pies*: pedigree ...
rat|a *f* instalment; *na* **~y** in instalments; **~alny** *adj*: *sprzedaż* *f* **~alna** hire purchase *Brt.*, installment plan *Am.*
ratow|ać ⟨**u-**⟩ save (*kogoś przed czymś/od czegoś* s.o.

from s.th.); *z pożaru*: rescue; **~niczy** *adj sprzęt itp.*: ..., emergency ...; **~nik** *m* rescuer; *na plaży*: lifeguard

ratun|ek *m* rescue; **~ku!** help!; **~kowy** *adj* akcja, samolot: rescue ..., emergency ...

ratusz *m* town hall

ratyfikować ratify

raz 1. *adv* once; **2.** *m* time; *(jeden)* **~** once; *dwa* **~y** twice; *trzy* **~y** three times; *choć* **~** for once; *jeszcze* **~** one more time; *następnym* **~em** next time; *innym* **~em** some other time; *tym* **~em** this time; *za* **~em** for the time being; F *pożegnanie*: see you; *od* **~u** at once; *na* **~ie** at present, for the time being; *w ~ie potrzeby* if need be; *w żadnym* **~ie** by no means

razem *adv* together; **~ z** along with

razić *światło*: glare

razowy *adj*: *chleb* **~** wholemeal bread

rażący *adj* glaring

rąbać ⟨po-⟩ chop (up)

rączka *f torby*: handle

rdza *f* rust; **~wy** *adj kolor*: rusty

rdzewieć ⟨za-⟩ rust

rea|gować ⟨za-⟩ react *(na coś* to s.th., *przeciw czemuś* against s.th.); **~kcja** *f* reaction; **~ktor** *m* reactor

real|istyczny *adj* realistic; **~izować** realize, fulfil; *czek* cash

recenzja *f* review

recepc|ja *f* reception; **~onista** *m* (**-tka** *f*) receptionist

recepta *f fig.* recipe; *med.* prescription

redak|cja *f tekstu*: editing; *(redaktorzy)* editorial staff; *(biuro)* editorial office; **~cyjny** *adj* editorial; **~tor** *m* editor

refleksja *f* reflection

reflektor *m* searchlight; floodlight; *thea.* spotlight; *mot.* headlight

reforma *f* reform

regał *m*: **~** (*na książki*) bookcase

region *m* region; **~alny** *adj* regional

regula|cja *f* adjustment; *prawna*: regulation; *cen itp.*: controls *pl*; **~min** *m* regulations *pl*, code (of practice)

regu|larny *adj* regular; **~lować** ⟨wy-⟩ adjust; *ceny* control; *spór* *f* rule

rejestr *m* record, register; **~acja** *f* registration; **~ować** (się) register

rejon *m* region

rejs *m* voyage

rekin *m* shark

reklam|a *f* advertising; *(promocja)* publicity, promotion; *w gazecie*: ad(vertisement); *w telewizji*: commercial; *na planszy*: hoarding *Brt.*, billboard *Am.*; **~acja** *f* complaint; **~ować** *(promować)* advertise; *(składać reklamację)* complain, make* a complaint (*coś* about s.th.)

rekord *m* record; **~owy** *adj*
record ...

rektor *m* vice-chancellor *Brt.*,
president *Am.*

relacja *f* relation; (*sprawozdanie*) account

religia *f* religion; **~ijny** *adj*
religious

remis *m* sp. draw, tie

remont *m* renovation, overhaul; **~ować ⟨wy-⟩** renovate, overhaul

ren|cista *m* (**~cistka** *f*) pen-
sioner; **~ta** *f* pension

rentgen F *m* X-ray

reorganiz|acja *f* reorganiza-
tion; **~ować ⟨z-⟩** reorganize

reperować ⟨z-⟩ repair

repertuar *m* repertoire

reporter *m* reporter, correspondent

represja *f* repression

reprezent|acja *f* representa-
tion; **~ant** *m* representative;
~ować represent

reprodukcja *f* reproduction

republika *f* republic

resor *m* mot. spring

restauracja *f* restaurant

reszt|a *f* rest; *w sklepie*:
change; **~ki** *pl* remains *pl*;
jedzenia: leftovers *pl*, scraps
pl

reumatyzm *m* med. rheumatism

rewanż *m* sp. return match;
~ować ⟨z-⟩ się reciprocate,
repay (**komuś za coś** s.o. for
s.th.)

rewelac|ja *f* revelation; **~yj-**

ny *adj* sensational

rewia *f* variety, revue

rewi|dować ⟨z-⟩ search (**ko-
goś w poszukiwaniu czegoś**
s.o. for s.th.); **~zja** *f* search

rewoluc|ja *f* revolution; **~yj-
ny** *adj* revolutionary

rewolwer *m* revolver

rezerw|a *f* reserve; **w ~ie** in
reserve; **~acja** *f* reservation,
booking; **~ować ⟨za-⟩** reserve, book

rezultat *m* result, conse-
quence

rezygnować ⟨z-⟩ z czegoś:
give* (s.th.) up; *z rezerwacji*:
cancel (**z czegoś** s.th.); *ze
stanowiska*: resign (**z czegoś**
from s.th.)

reżyser *m* director; **~ia** *f* direction; **~ować ⟨wy-⟩** direct

rę|cznik *m* towel; **~czny** *adj*
manual; **~czyć ⟨po-, za-⟩**
vouch (**za kogoś** for s.o.);
~ka *f* (*dłoń*) hand; (*ramię*)
arm; **~ce do góry!** hands
up!; *pod ~ką* (close) at hand;
trzymać coś pod ~ką keep*
s.th. handy; **~kaw** *m* sleeve;
~kawiczka *f* glove; **~kojeść**
f handle; **~kopis** *m* manuscript

robak *m* worm; F (*insekt*) bug
F

robić ⟨z-⟩ do*; *błąd, obiad,
wyjątek, postępy* make*

robo|czy *adj* strój *itp.*: work-
ing; **~t** *m* robot; *kuchenny*:
food processor; **~tnica** *f*
(**~tnik** *m*) worker

roczn|ica f anniversary; **~ik** m (*czasopismo*) yearbook; *ludzi*: age group; *wina*: vintage; **~y** m annual, yearly

rod|ak m compatriot; **~owity** adj native; **~ówód** m origin; *psa*: pedigree

rodz|aj m kind, sort, type; *gr.* gender; **~ajnik** m gr. article; **~eństwo** n siblings pl; **~ice** pl parents pl; **~ić ⟨u-⟩** *dziecko* have*, give* birth to; *uczucia* give* rise to; **~ić się** be* born; **gdzie się urodziłeś?** where were you born?; **~ina** f family; **~inny** adj family ...

rodzynek m (a. **rodzynka** f) raisin

rogalik m croissant

rogi pl → **róg**

rok m (pl **lata**) year; **~ temu** a year ago; **w zeszłym/ przyszłym ~u** last/next year; **za ~** in a year; **ile masz lat?** how old are you?; **mam 25 lat** I am 25 years old; **lata osiemdziesiąte** the (nineteen) eighties, the 80s

rola f role; *filmowa*: part

rolka f roll

rolni|ctwo n agriculture; **~k** m farmer

roman|s m romance; (*przygoda miłosna*) affair, fling F; **~tyczny** adj romantic

rondo n roundabout Brt.; traffic circle Am.; *kapelusza*: brim

ropa f *naftowa*: oil; *med.* pus

ropucha f toad

rosa f dew

Rosja f Russia; **~nin** m (**~nka** f) Russian

rosnąć ⟨u-⟩ grow*

rosół m broth

rosyjski adj Russian

roślin|a f plant; **~ność** f vegetation; **~ny** adj plant ...; *olej itp.*: vegetable ...

rowek m groove

rower m bicycle, bike F; **~zysta** m cyclist

rozbawi(a)ć amuse

rozbier|ać *kogoś* undress (s.o.); *coś* take* (s.th.) a-part; **~ się** undress

rozbi(ja)ć break* (up); *namiot* put* up

rozbiór m partition; **~ka** f demolition

rozbr|ajać ⟨~oić⟩ disarm; **~ojenie** n disarmament

rozbudow|a f development; **~(yw)ać** develop

rozchodzić się *thm.*: disperse; *małżeństwo*: break* up; *plotki*: get* round/about; *ciepło*: radiate

rozchorować się pf fall* ill

rozcią|ć pf → **rozcinać**

rozciąg|ać ⟨~nąć⟩ (się) stretch

rozcieńcz|ać ⟨~yć⟩ dilute

rozcinać cut* (*na pół* in half)

rozczarowa|nie n disappointment; **~ć** disappoint, let* down; **~ć się** be* disappointed; **~ny** adj disappointed, discontented

rozda(wa)ć (*podawać, wręczać*) give* out, hand out; *majątek* give* away; *karty* deal*

rozdrażnі|enie *n* irritation; **~ony** *adj* irritated

rozdwojenie *n*: **~ jaźni** split personality

rozdzі|ał *m* chapter; **~elać** ⟨**~elić**⟩ (**się**) separate (**na grupy** into groups, **coś od czegoś** s.th. from s.th.)

rozdzierać tear*; *na kawałki*: tear* apart; **~ się** tear*

rozebrać *pf* → **rozbierać**

rozedrzeć *pf* → **rozdzierać**

rozegrać *pf* → **rozgrywać**

rozejm *m* truce

rozejrzeć się *pf* → **rozglądać się**

rozejść się *pf* → **rozchodzić się**

rozerwać *pf* → **rozrywać**

rozesłać *pf* → **rozsyłać**

roześmiać się *pf* burst* out laughing

rozglądać się look around

rozgnі|atać ⟨**~ieść**⟩ crush

rozgniewać *pf kogoś* make* (s.o.) angry; **~ć się** *pf* get* angry; → **gniewać (się)**; **~ny** *adj* angry

rozgotowa(ny)wać się get* overcooked

rozgrywka *f sp.* game

rozgrzesz ać ⟨**~yć**⟩ absolve (**kogoś z czegoś** s.o. of s.th.); **~enie** *n* absolution

rozgrz|(ew)ać *ciało* warm

(up); **~(ew)ać się** warm oneself; *sp.*, *fig.* warm up; **~ewka** *f* warm-up (*a. sp.*)

rozkaz *m* order, command; **~(yw)ać** *komuś* order, command (**komuś zrobienie czegoś** s.o. to do s.th.)

rozkład *m biol.*, *chem.* decay, decomposition; (*rozmieszczenie*) distribution; *jazdy lotów/zajęć* timetable, schedule; **~ać** *ramiona, mapę, gazety* spread* (out); *na części*: take* apart; *składane meble* set* up; *biol.*, *chem.* decompose, break* down; **~ać się** *chem.* decompose; *ciało*: putrify

rozkosz *f* delight; **~e** *pl* pleasures *pl*; **~ny** *adj* delightful; **~ować się** bask (**czymś** in s.th.); delight (**czymś** in s.th.)

rozkwit *m* boom; **~ać** ⟨**~nąć**⟩ blossom, flourish

rozlać *pf* → **rozlewać**

rozl|atywać ⟨**~ecieć**⟩ **się** F fall* apart

rozległy *adj* extensive

rozlewać spill*

rozluźnі|ać (**się**) relax; **~enie** *n* relaxation (**czegoś** of s.th.)

rozład|ow(yw)ać unload; *sytuację* defuse; **~unek** *m* unloading

rozłą|czać ⟨**~czyć**⟩ disconnect; *ludzi* separate; **~czać się** get* disconnected; **~ka** *f* separation

rozłożyć pf → **rozkładać**
rozmaity adj various
rozmawiać talk (z kimś, o czymś to s.o., about s.th.)
rozmiar m odzieży: size; zniszczeń: extent
rozmieni(a)ć pieniądze change
rozmie|szczać ⟨~ścić⟩ arrange, place; wojsko, rakiety deploy; **~szczenie** n arrangement
rozmn|ażać ⟨~ożyć⟩ (się) reproduce; **~ażanie** n reproduction
rozmow|a f conversation, talk; **~ny** adj talkative
rozmów|ca m interlocutor; **~ić się** have* a word (z kimś with s.o.); **~ki** pl phrase book
rozmraż|ać ⟨~ozić⟩ defrost
rozmyśl|ać meditate (nad czymś on/upon s.th.); **~ić się** pf change one's mind; **~ny** adj deliberate
rozn|osić ⟨~ieść⟩ listy deliver
rozpacz f despair; **~ać** despair (nad czymś at s.th.); **~liwy** adj desperate
rozpad m break-up, dissolution; **~ać się** rodzina itp.: break* up; **~ać się na kawałki** break* into pieces
rozpakow(yw)ać (się) unpack
rozpal|ać ⟨~ić⟩ kindle
rozpaść się pf → **rozpadać się**

rozpat|rywać ⟨~rzyć⟩ sprawę, podanie consider
rozpę|d m momentum; **~dzać** ⟨~dzić⟩ demonstrację break* up; **~dzać się** pick up speed
rozpiąć pf → **rozpinać**
rozpie|szczać ⟨~ścić⟩ spoil; **~szczony** adj spoilt
rozpinać undo*, unbutton
rozplą|t(yw)ać untangle
rozpłakać się burst* out crying, burst* into tears
rozpocz|ęcie n beginning; **~ynać** ⟨~ąć⟩ (się) begin*, start
rozporek m fly
rozpowszechni|(a)ć informacje disseminate; **~anie** n dissemination; **~ony** adj widespread
rozpozna|(wa)ć recognize; **~nie** n recognition
rozpraw|a f sądowa: trial; doktorska: thesis, dissertation; **~ić się** crack down (z kimś on s.o.)
rozprowa|dzać ⟨~dzić⟩ distribute
rozprzestrzeni(a)ć się proliferate
rozpusta f debauchery
rozpu|szczać ⟨~ścić⟩ (się) dissolve; **~szczalnik** m solvent; **~szczalny** adj soluble; **kawa ~szczalna** instant coffee
rozpyl|acz m atomizer; **~ać** ⟨~ić⟩ atomize
rozróżni(a)ć tell* apart

rozru|chy pl riots pl; **~sznik** m mot. starter

rozryw|ać tear* apart; **kopertę** tear* open; **~ka** f entertainment; **~kowy** adj entertainment ...

rozrzu|cać ⟨**~cić**⟩ scatter; **~tność** f extravagance; **~tny** adj extravagant

rozsąd|ek m sense; **zdrowy ~ek** common sense; **~ny** adj sensible

rozst|anie (się) n parting; **~(aw)ać się** part (**z kimś** with s.o.)

rozstrzel|anie n death by firing squad; **~(iw)ać** execute

rozstrzyg|ać ⟨**~nąć**⟩ decide; **~ający** adj decisive; **~nięcie** n solution

rozsyp(yw)ać spill*

rozszerz|ać ⟨**~yć**⟩ broaden, widen; **~ać się** broaden, widen; **metal:** expand; **~enie** n broadening

rozśmieszyć kogoś make* (s.o.) laugh

roztl|apiać ⟨**~opić**⟩ → **topić**

roztargniony adj absent-minded

roztropny adj cautious

roztrzask(iw)ać smash

roztwór m solution

rozum m reason; **~ieć** ⟨**z-**⟩ understand*; **~ieć się** understand* each other; **~ny** adj reasoning; **~owanie** n reasoning

rozwaga f prudence

rozwal|ać ⟨**~ić**⟩ smash

rozważ|ać ⟨**~yć**⟩ consider; **~ny** adj prudent

rozwiąz|anie n solution (**czegoś** to s.th.); **~(yw)ać:** **węzeł** untie; **organizację** dissolve; **problem** solve

rozwie|dziony adj divorced; **~ść się** pf → **rozwodzić**

rozwij|ać ⟨**~nąć**⟩ develop; **bandaż** itp. unwind; **~jać się** develop, evolve

rozwo|dnik F m divorcee; **~dowy** adj divorce ...; **~dzić się** divorce (**z kimś** with s.o.); dwell (**nad czymś** on s.th.)

rozwolnienie n diarrhoea

rozwód m divorce; **~ka** f divorcée

rozwój m development, evolution

rozwścieczony adj furious

rozżalony adj bitter

rozżarzony adj glowing

rożen m spit; **ogrodowy:** barbecue

róg m byka: horn; jelenia: antler; ulicy itp.: corner; **na rogu** on the corner

rów m ditch

równ|ać się equal (**czemuś** s.th.); **~anie** n equation; **~ie** adv equally

również adv also

równik m equator

równina f plain

równo adv equally; **~czesny** adj simultaneous; **~legły** adj parallel (**do czegoś** to s.th.); **~leżnik** m parallel; **~mierny**

adj steady; **~rzędny** *adj* equivalent

równość *f* equality

równowa|ga *f* balance; **~żny** *adj* equivalent

równy *adj* equal (*czemuś* to s.th.); *powierzchnia*: even, level; (*stały*) steady

róża *f* rose; **~niec** *m* rosary

różdżka *f* divining rod; **~ cza-rodziejska** magic wand; **~rstwo** *n* dowsing; **~rz** *m* dowser

róźni|ca *f* difference; **~ć się** differ (*od czegoś* from s.th.)

różnorodn|ość *f* variety, diversity; **~y** *adj* varied

różny *adj* (*nie ten sam*) different; → **różnorodny**

różowy *adj* pink

ruch *m* motion, movement; (*posunięcie*) move; **~ uliczny** traffic; **w ~u** in motion; **~li-wy** *adj* mobile; *ulica*: busy; **~omy** *adj* mobile, moving; **~omy czas ~ pracy** flexitime

ruda *f* ore; F *kobieta*: redhead

rud|owłosy, ~y *adj* red-haired

ru|ina *f* ruin; **~jnować** ⟨z-⟩ ruin

rum *m* rum

rumieni|ć ⟨za-⟩ **się** blush; **~ec** *m* blush

rumsztyk *m* rumpsteak

Rumun *m* Romanian; **~ia** *f* Romania; **~ka** *f* Romanian; 2**ński** *adj* Romanian

runda *f* round

rur|a *f* tube, pipe; **~a wyde-**

chowa exhaust pipe; **~ka** *f* tube; *do picia*: straw; **~ociąg** *m* pipeline

rusz|ać ⟨~yć⟩ move; (*dotykać*) touch; *samochodem*: pull away; **~ać się** move

ruszt *m* grill; **~owanie** *n* scaffolding

rwać ⟨wy-⟩ *ząb* pull (out); ⟨ze-⟩ *owoc, kwiat* pluck

ryb|a *f* fish; **~acki** *adj* fishing ...; **~ak** *m* fisherman; *przy* *adj*: *zupa* **~na** fish soup; **~ołówstwo** *n* fishing

rycerz *m* knight

ryczeć roar, bellow (*ze śmie-chu* with laughter); *lew*: roar; *krowa*: moo, low; *byk*: bellow; *osioł*: bray; F (*płakać*) blubber

ryk *m* roar; **~nąć** *pf* → **ryczeć**

rym *m* rhyme; **~ować się** rhyme

ryn|ek *m* market; **~kowy** *adj*: **gospodarka** *f* **~kowa** market economy

rynna *f* gutter

rys *m* sketch; **~y** features *pl*

rys|a *f* scratch; **~ik** *m* lead; **~opis** *m* description; **~ować** ⟨na-⟩ draw*; **~ownica** *f* drawing board; **~unek** *m* drawing

ryś *m zo.* lynx

rytm *m* rhythm; **~iczny** *adj* rhythmic

rywal *m* rival

ryzykow|ać ⟨za-⟩ risk, take* a chance; **~ny** *adj* risky

ryż *m* rice

rzadk|i adj rare, uncommon; (nie często) infrequent; dym, płyn, las: thin; **~o** adv rarely, seldom; **~ość** f rarity

rząd m row; biol., math. order; pol. government, administration Am.; (ministrowie) cabinet; **~owy** adj government ...

rządzić rule; państwem: govern

rzecz f thing; **~y** F pl clothes pl

rzecznik m spokesman

rzeczownik m noun

rzeczoznawca m expert

Rzeczpospolita f (Polska Polish) Republic

rzeczywi|stość f reality; **~sty** adj actual, real; **~ście** adv really

rzeka f river

rzemie|ślnik m craftsman; **~osło** n craft

rzepa f bot. turnip

rzetelny adj reliable

rzeźb|a f sculpture; **~iarz** m

sculptor; **~iarstwo** n sculpture; **~ić ⟨wy-⟩** sculpture

rzeźni|a f slaughterhouse; **~k** m butcher; (sklep) the butcher's

rzeżączka f med. gonorrhea

rzęsa f eyelash

rzodkiewka f radish

rzu|cać ⟨~cić⟩ throw*; mocno: hurl, fling*; w gniewie: dash; mocno, celując: pitch (w coś at s.th.); (upuszczać) drop; palenie, pracę give* up, quit* F; przekleństwa: hurl; światło, cień, spojrzenie cast*; wszystko drop; **~cać monetą** toss (a coin); **~cać komuś wezwanie** challenge s.o.; **~cać się** throw* oneself, fling* oneself; podczas snu: toss; za czymś: dive* (for s.th.); **~t** m throw; **~t oka** glimpse, look; **~t dyskiem** sp. discus; **~t karny** sp. penalty kick; **~t rożny** sp. corner kick

rzymski adj Roman

S

sad m orchard

sadza f soot

sadzać kogoś sit* (s.o.) (down)

sadzić ⟨za-⟩ plant; **~onka** f seedling

sadzony adj: jajka pl **~e** fried eggs pl

sakrament m sacrament

saksofon m saxophone

sal|a f room; lekcyjna: classroom; **~a gimnastyczna** gymnasium, gym F; **~a koncertowa** concert hall; **~a operacyjna** operating theatre Brt.; **~on** m lounge; mody, fryzjerski, artystyczny: salon

sałat|a f lettuce; **~ka** f (vege-
table) salad

sam¹ adv alone, on one's
own; **byłem ~** I was alone;
osobiście: -self; **~ reżyser
tam był** the director himself
was there; **→ ten**

sam² F m self-service shop,
supermarket

sami|ca f female, she-; **~ca
żaby** female frog; **~ca słonia**
she-elephant; **~ec** m male,
he-; **~ec żaby** male frog; **~ec
słonia** he-elephant

samo- self-

samobój|ca m (**~czyni** f) sui-
cide; **~stwo** n suicide

samochód m car; **~ ciężarowy** lorry Brt., truck Am.

samodzielny adj independent

samogłoska f gr. vowel

samokrytyka f self-criticism

samolot m aeroplane Brt.,
airplane Am., plane F

samo|obrona f self-defence;
~obsługa f self-service;
~obsługowy adj self-service
...; **~poczucie** n mood, state
of mind; **~rząd** m self-gov-
ernment

samotn|ość f (stan) solitude;
(uczucie) loneliness; **~y** adj
spacer, dom: solitary;
człowiek: lonely

samouk m self-taught person

sandał m sandal

sanie pl sleigh

sanitar|iusz m orderly; **~ny**
adj sanitary

sankcja f sanction

sanki pl sledge Brt., sled Am.

sardynka f sardine

sarna f (female) deer

satelit|a m satellite; **~rny** adv
satellite ...

satyr|a f satire; **~yczny** adj
satirical

są → być

sąd m court; (opinia) view,
claim; **~ apelacyjny** court of
appeal; **~ dla nieletnich** juvenile court; **~ wojenny**
court-martial; **przed ~em**
on trial; **~owy: medycyna ~
~owa** forensic medicine

sądzić v/i (uważać) feel*,
think*, believe; v/t w sądzie:
try (kogoś za coś s.o. for
s.th.)

sąsiad|(ka) m f neighbour;
~adować pokój: adjoin (z
czymś s.th.); **~edni** adj
neighbouring; pokój: adjoining; **~edztwo** n neighbour-
hood

scen|a f scene; w teatrze:
stage; **~ariusz** m screenplay;
~iczny adj stage...

sceptyczny adj sceptical

schabow|y adj: **kotlet ~** m
pork chop

schemat m diagram

schnąć <wy-> dry (up)

scho|dy pl stairway; wew-
nętrzne: staircase; **~dy ruchome** escalator; **~dzić** descend, go* down, come*
down, get* down; **~dzić się**
get* together, gather

schow|ać (się) hide*; **~ek** *m* hiding place; *na dworcu, w szatni*: locker; *mot.* glove compartment

schron *m* shelter; **~ienie** *n* shelter, refuge; **~isko** *n* hostel; **~isko górskie** mountain refuge; **~isko młodzieżowe** youth hostel

schwycić *pf* → **chwytać**

schylać *pf* → **chylić**

scyzoryk *m* pocket knife, penknife

seans *m filmowy*: show

sedno *n* crux, essence

sejf *m* safe

Sejm *m* Polish parliament

sekcja *f* section, division; **~ zwłok** autopsy, post mortem

sekret *m* secret; **~ariat** *m* secretary's office, secretariat; **~arka** *f* (**~arz** *m*) secretary

seks *m* sex; **~owny** *adj* sexy; **~ualny** *adj* sexual

sektor *m* sector

sekunda *f* second

seler *m bot.* celery

semafor *m rail.* semaphore

seminarium *n* seminar

sen *m* sleep; (*wizja, marzenie*) dream

senat *m* senate; **~or** *m* senator

senny *adj* sleepy

sen|s *m* sense; **to nie ma ~su** it doesn't make sense; **nie ma ~su czekać** it's no use waiting, there's no point in waiting; **w pewnym ~sie** in a way

sensacj|a *f* sensation; **~yjny** *adj* sensational

sensowny *adj* reasonable, sensible

seplenić lisp

ser *m* cheese

serc|e *n* heart; **z całego ~a** with all one's heart; **~deczne życzenia** *pl* best wishes *pl*

seria *f* series, sequence; *wydarzeń*: rash, string; *modeli*: line

serio *adv* (*a.* **na ~**) seriously

sernik *m* cheesecake

serw|eta *f* tablecloth; **~etka** *f* napkin; **~is** *m* service; *telewizyjny*: coverage; *sp.* serve; **~ować** serve

seryjny *adj* serial

sesja *f* session

set *m sp.* set

setka *f* (a) hundred; F *sp.* 100-metre dash; F *a 100-millilitre shot of vodka*

sezon *m* season; **poza ~em** out of season; **w ~ie** in season

sędzi|a *m* judge; *sp.* umpire; *piłka nożna, boks, zapasy*: referee; **~a liniowy** linesman; **~a śledczy** magistrate; **~ować** umpire; *w piłce nożnej, boksie, zapasach*: referee

sęp *m zo.* vulture

sfera *f* sphere

siać ⟨za-⟩ sow*

siadać sit* (down)

siano *n* hay

siarka *f* sulphur

siatk|a *f* net; **~ówka** *f anat.*
retina; *sp.* volleyball

siąść *pf →* **siadać**

siebie *pron* oneself (myself,
yourself *etc.*); *wzajemnie:*
each other, one another;
zrobiłem to dla ~ I did it for
myself; **zaadresowała list
do ~** she addressed the letter
to herself; *nie patrzymy na ~*
we aren't looking at each
other; *oni piszą do ~* they
write to each other; *→ sobą,
sobie*

sieć *f* network; *rybacka:* net

siedem *num* seven; **~dziesiąt**
num seventy; **~naście** *num*
seventeen; **~set** *num* seven
hundred

siedz|ący *adj* sitting; **~enie** *n*
seat; **~iba** *f organizacji:* seat;
~ieć sit* (down); **~ieć w
więzieniu** F be* in prison

siekiera *f* axe

sierota *f* orphan

sierpień *m* August

sierść *f* fur

się *pron* oneself (myself,
yourself *etc.*); *wzajemnie:*
each other, one another; *bez-
osobowo:* one, you, *etc.*; *za-
ciąłem ~ przy goleniu* I cut
myself shaving; *odwiedza-
liśmy ~ co tydzień* we visited
each other every week; *gazety dostarcza ~ samolo-
tem* newspapers are delivered by air; *szybko ~ o tym
zapomina* one quickly forgets about that

sięg|ać ⟨**~nąć**⟩ reach ((**po**)
coś (for) s.th.)

silnik *m* engine; *elektryczny:*
motor

silny *adj* strong; *uderzenie:*
powerful, hefty; *światło, ból:*
intense; *zapach:* powerful;
chwyt: firm; *opozycja:* stout;
osoba: powerful, sturdy,
lusty; *wiatr:* up; *akcent:*
broad

sił|a *f* *fizyczna:* strength;
*(zdolność oddziaływania na
otoczenie)* power; *phys.*
force; **z całej ~y** with all
one's strength; **~a ciężkości**
gravity; **~a robocza** man-
power, labour; **~a woli** willpower; **~y zbrojne** the (ser-
vices *pl*) armed forces *pl*, the ser-
vices *pl*

sin|iec *m* bruise; **~y** *adj* blue

siodło *n* saddle

siostr|a *f* sister; **~rzenica** *f*
niece; **~rzeniec** *m* nephew

siód|emka *f* (a) seven; **~my**
num seventh

sit|o *n* sieve; **~ko** *n do herbaty:*
strainer

siwy *adj* grey; *człowiek:*
grey-haired

skafander *m* (*kurtka*) an-
orak; **~ kosmiczny** spacesuit

skakać jump, leap*; *na jednej
nodze, ptak:* hop; *do wody:*
dive; *ceny:* rocket, zoom

skala *f* scale

skaleczenie *n* cut

ska|listy *adj* rocky; **~ła** *f* rock

skamieniały *adj* petrified

skandal *m* scandal; **~iczny** *adj* scandalous

skarb *m* treasure; **~ państwa** treasury; **~iec** *m* vault; **~nik** *m* treasurer; **~onka** *f* moneybox; *(świnka)* piggy bank

skarga *f* complaint

skarpet(k)a *f* sock

skarżyć ⟨**za-**⟩ *do sądu*: sue *(kogoś za coś* s.o. for s.th.); ⟨**na-**⟩ sneak *(na kogoś* on s.o.); ⟨**po-**⟩ **się** complain *(komuś na coś* to s.o. about s.th.)

skaz(yw)ać condemn *(na coś* to s.th.); *(wydawać wyrok)* convict, sentence *(na* to)

skąd *adv* where from; **~ jesteś?** where are you from?

skąpy *adj* stingy, tight-fisted *F*; *(skromny)* meagre

skierow(yw)ać *pf* → **kierować**

skinąć beckon *(na kogoś* to s.o.); **~ głową** nod (one's head)

sklejać ⟨**~ić**⟩ *coś* glue (s.th.) together; **~ka** *f* plywood

sklep *m* store *Am.*

sklepienie *n arch.* vault

skład *m (magazyn)* store, warehouse; *chemiczny*: composition; *drużyny*: line-up; **~ać na pół**: fold; *namiot, koszulę, gazetę, stolik itp.* fold (up); *z części*: put* together; *jajko* lay*; *zamówienie, plac: pieniądze* deposit; **~ać przysięgę** take* an oath; **~ać coś w ofierze** sac-rifice s.th.; **~ać skargę** complain; **~ać się** consist *(z czegoś* of s.th.), be composed *(z czegoś* of s.th.); *(stanowić)* constitute *(na coś* s.th.); *stolik, scyzoryk*: fold (up); **~ak** *F m* folding bicycle; **~any** *adj* folding; **~ka** *f* członkowska: (membership) fee; *F (zbiórka)* collection; **~nia** *f gr.* syntax; **~nica** *f* store; **~nik** *m* constituent, component; *potrawy*: ingredient; **~ować** store; **~owy** *adj* constituent

skł|aniać ⟨**~onić**⟩ *kogoś* induce (s.o.) *(do zrobienia czegoś* to do s.th.); **~onność** *f* tendency, inclination; **~onny** *adj* inclined *(do zrobienia czegoś* to do s.th.)

skocz|ek *m* jumper; *wzwyż*: highjumper; *spadochronowy*: parachutist, skydiver; *szachowy*: knight; **~nia** *f*: *narciarska* ski jump; **~yć** *pf* → **skakać**

skojarzenie *n* association

skok *m* jump, leap; *na jednej nodze, ptaka*: hop; *do wody*: dive; *cen itp.*: increase, hike *F*; **~o tyczce** *sp.* pole vault; **~ w dal** *sp.* long jump; **~ wzwyż** *sp.* high jump

skomplikowany *adj* complicated

skończony *adj* finished, through *F*

skoro *cj* since

skoroszyt *m* folder

skorowidz m index

skorpion f scorpion

skorup|a f crust; *orzecha, żółwia, ślimaka*: shell; **~ka** f *jajka*: eggshell

skos m slant; **na ~** at a slant

skośny adj oblique

skowronek m lark

skó|ra f *człowieka*: skin; *zwierzęca*: skin, pelt, hide; (*surowiec*) leather; **~rka** f *jabłka, ziemniaka, banana*: skin; *chleba*: crust; *szynki, sera, cytryny*: rind; **~rzany** adj leather...

skracać shorten

skradać się sneak up (**za kimś** behind s.o.)

skradziony adj stolen

skrajn|ość f extremity; **~y** adj extreme

skrapiać sprinkle (**coś czymś** s.th. with s.th.)

skreśl|ać ⟨**~ić**⟩ cross out

skręc|ać ⟨**~ić**⟩ v/i turn (**w lewo/prawo** left/right); *nagle*: swerve; v/t *nogę* sprain, turn, twist, wrench; *papierosa* roll; **~ać się** squirm (**z czegoś** with s.th.)

skrępowany adj uneasy

skromn|ość f modesty; **~y** adj modest; (*zwykły, prosty*) humble

skroń f temple

skropić pf → **skrapiać**

skró|cić pf → **skracać**; **~t** m (*krótsza droga*) short cut

skrupulatny adj meticulous

skrupuły pl scruples pl,

qualms pl

skry|ć pf → **kryć, skrywać**; **~tka** f hiding place; *w samochodzie*: glove compartment; **~tka bankowa** safe-deposit box; **~tka pocztowa** post-box; **~wać (się)** hide*

skrzydło n wing

skrzyn|ia f box, chest; **~ia biegów** gearbox; **~ka** f box; *do towarów*: crate; **~ka pocztowa** post-box, mailbox Am.

skrzyp|aczka f violinist; **~ce** pl violin; **~ek** m violinist; **~ieć** ⟨**~nąć**⟩ creak

skrzywi(a)ć → **krzywić**

skrzyżowanie n cross (**czegoś z czymś** between s.th. and s.th.); *dróg*: crossroads

skupi|(a)ć concentrate; *uwagę* focus; *wzrok* focus one's eyes; **~ać się** concentrate; **~enie** n concentration

skurcz m spasm

skut|eczny adj effective; **~ek** m effect, result; **~ek uboczny** side-effect

skuter m scooter

skutkować ⟨**po-**⟩ work, be effective

slajd F m slide

sleeping m sleeping car, sleeper F

slogan m slogan, catch-phrase

słab|nąć ⟨**o-**⟩ weaken; *deszcz, chwyt*: slacken; *ból, wiatr, głos*: subside; *wiara*: waver; **~ość** f weakness; **~y**

adj weak; (*niezadowalający*) poor

słać¹ ⟨po-, wy-⟩ *list* send*

słać² ⟨po-⟩ *łóżko* make*

sław|a *f* fame; **~ny** *adj* famous

słod|ki *adj* sweet; **~kowodny** *adj* fresh-water; **~ycze** *pl* sweets *pl*, candy *Am.*

słodzić ⟨o-, po-⟩ sweeten; *herbatę* sugar

słoik *m* jar

słom|a *f* straw; **~iany** *adj* straw ...; **~ka** *f* straw

słoneczn|ik *m* sunflower; **~y** *adj* sunny; *układ m* **~y** solar system

słonina *f* pork fat

słoniowy → **kość**

słony *adj* salty

słoń *m* elephant

słońce *n* sun

Słowa|cja *f* Slovakia; **⟨cki** *adj* Slovak; **~czka** *f* ⟨**k** *m*⟩ Slovak

Słowenia *f* Slovenia

Słowia|nin *m* ⟨**nka** *f*⟩ Slav; **⟨ński** *adj* Slavonic, Slavic

słowik *m zo.* nightingale

słow|nie *adv* verbally; **~nik** *m* dictionary; **~ny** *adj* verbal; **~o** *n* word; **~em** in a word; **~o w ~o** word for word; **w kilku ~ach** in a nutshell, briefly

słój *m* jar

słuch *m* hearing; **~acz** *m* listener; **~ać** ⟨po-⟩ listen (*czegoś/kogoś* to s.th./s.o.); **~am?** pardon? *Brt.*, excuse

me? *Am.*; **~awka** *f* earphone; *telefonu:* receiver

słup *m* pillar; *metalowy, drewniany:* pole; *latarni:* lamp-post; *electr.* pylon; **~ek** *m* post; *mot.* bollard; *sp.* goalpost

słuszn|ość *f:* **masz ~ość** you are right; **~y** *adj* right; *wyrok:* just, fair

służąca *f* maid; **~ący** *m* servant; **~ba** *f* service; *domowa:* servants *pl*; **~ba wojskowa** military service; **~bowy** *adj* *podróż:* business ...; **~yć** serve

słychać: *nic nie* **~** I can't hear anything; *co* **~?** how are you?

słynny *adj* famous

słysz|alny *adj* audible; **~eć** ⟨u-⟩ hear* (*coś* s.th., *o czymś* of s.th.)

smacz|ny *adj* tasty; **~nego!** said before a meal

smak *m* taste; **~ować** taste; *to mi* **~uje** I like it, it tastes good; **~owity** *adj* tasty

smalec *m* lard

smar *m* grease; **~ować** ⟨po-⟩ *mechanizm* grease, lubricate; **~ować chleb masłem** spread* butter on bread, butter bread; **~ować twarz kremem** put* cream on the face

smaż|ony *adj* fried; **~yć** ⟨u-⟩ (*się*) fry

smoczek *m do zabawy:* dummy *Brt.*, pacifier *Am.*; *do* *karmienia*: teat *Brt.*, nipple *Am.*

smok *m* dragon

smoła *f* tar

smród *m* stink, stench

smucić ⟨za-⟩ sadden; ~ **się** feel* sad

smutek *m* sadness, sorrow; **~ny** *adj* sad

smycz *f* leash

smyczek *m* bow; **~ki** *pl* the strings *pl*; **~kowy** *adj*: **kwartet** *m* **~kowy** string quartet

snuć *nić*, *pajęczynę itp.* spin*; ~ **opowieść** tell* a story; ~ **się** *bezczynnie*: moon about/around

sobą, **~ie** *pron* self (myself, yourself *etc.*); *(wzajemnie)* each other, one another; **bądź ~ą** be yourself; **przyglądał się ~ie w lustrze** he was looking at himself in the mirror; **nie rozmawiają ze ~ą** they are not talking to each other; **powiedzieli ~ie prawdę** they told each other the truth; **był ~ie ...** there once was ...

sobota *f* Saturday

sobowtór *m* double

socj|alistyczny *adj* socialist; **~alizm** *m* socialism; **~olog** *m* sociologist; **~ologia** *f* sociology

soczewka *f* lens

soczysty *adj* juicy

sod|a *f* soda; **~owy** *adj*: **woda** *f* **~owa** soda water

soj|a *m* soy (bean); **~owy** *adj* soy

sojusz *m* alliance; **~nik** *m* ally

sok *m* juice

sokół *m* falcon

solić ⟨po-⟩ salt

solidarność *f* solidarity

solist|a *m* (**~ka** *f*) soloist

sol|niczka *f* salt cellar, salt shaker *Am.*; **~ony** *adj* salted

solo *n* solo; **~wy** *adj* solo

sonda *f* probe; **~ż** *m*: **~ż opinii publicznej** public opinion poll

sortować ⟨po-⟩ sort

sos *m* sauce; *do mięsa*: gravy

sosna *f* pine

sowa *f* owl

sól *f* salt

spacer *m* walk; **~ować** ⟨po-⟩ walk; **~ówka** *f* pushchair *Brt.*, stroller *Am.*

spać sleep*; **iść ~ go*** to sleep; **chce mi się ~** I'm sleepy

spadać fall*; *liczby, ceny*: plunge, plummet; **~ek** *m* decrease; *temperatury*: drop; *wydajności*: fall; *cen*: plunge; *jur.* inheritance

spadkobierca *m* inheritor, beneficiary

spadochron *m* parachute; **~iarz** *m* parachutist; *sp.* skydiver; *mil.* paratrooper

spadzisty *adj dach*: slanting

spalać ⟨~ić⟩ **(się)** burn* (down); **~anie** *n phys.* combustion; **~inowy** *adj*: **silnik** *m* **~inowy** internal combustion engine; **~iny** *pl* exhaust (fumes *pl*); **~ony** *adj* burned; *dom*: burned down; **na ~onym** *sp.* offside

spaść *pf* → **spadać**

spawać weld

specjal|ista *m* specialist, expert; **~istyczny** *adj* specialist; **~izacja** *f* specialization; **~izować się** specialize (**w czymś** in s.th.); **~nie** *adv* specially; (*celowo*) deliberately, on purpose; **~ność** *f* speciality *Brt.*, specialty *Am.*; **~ny** *adj* special

spełni|a(ć) funkcję, cel, obietnicę, wymagania, życzenie, groźbę fulfil; *obowiązek*, *rozkaz* carry out; *oczekiwania* live up to, meet*; *potrzeby*, warunki meet*; **~(a)ć się** nadzieja, sen: come* true; **~enie** *n* obietnicy, marzeń: fulfilment (**czegoś** of s.th.)

sperma *f* semen

spędza|ć ⟨**~ić**⟩ czas, wakacje spend*

spiąć *pf* → **spinać**

spierać się argue (**z kimś o coś** with s.o. about s.th.)

spieszyć ⟨**po-**⟩ *się* hurry (up), be* in a hurry; *zegarek*: be* fast

spięcie *n* short-circuit

spiker(ka *f*) *m TV* announcer

spin|acz *m* paper clip; **~ać** ⟨**~ać**⟩ kartki clip together; **~ka** *f do włosów*: hair-grip, hairpin; *do mankietów*: cufflink;

do krawata: tie-pin

spirala *m* spiral; *grzejna*: element

spis *m* list; **~ treści** table of contents; **~ ludności** census

spisek *m* plot, conspiracy

spis(yw)ać copy down; **~ na straty** write* off

spiżarnia *f* larder, pantry

spłaca|ć ⟨**~ić**⟩ pay* off

spłonąć burn* down

spłuk(iw)ać rinse; *toaletę*: flush

spły|wać ⟨**~nąć**⟩ łzy itp.: flow (**po czymś** down s.th.)

spocony *adj* sweaty

spocz|ynek *m* rest; **~ywać** rest (**na czymś** on s.th.); ⟨**~ąć**⟩ *odpowiedzialność*: rest (**na kimś** with s.o.)

spod *prp* from under

spod|ek *m* saucer; **~enki** *pl* shorts *pl*; **~nie** *pl* trousers *pl*, pants *pl Am.*

spodziewać się expect (**czegoś** s.th., **że ktoś coś zrobi** s.o. to do s.th.)

spo|glądać ⟨**~jrzeć**⟩ look (**na kogoś** at s.o.); **~jrzenie** *n* look; *krótkie*: glance; *gniewne*: glare; *długie*: gaze

spok|ojny *adj* calm; *miejsce*, *ludzie*: peaceful, restful; *las*, *łąka*: still, tranquil; *dzień*, *podróż*: uneventful; *lot*: smooth; *kolor*: quiet, soft; *głos*: steady; **~ój** *m* peace; (*cisza*) calm

spokrewniony *adj* related

społecz|eństwo *n* society;

~ność f community; **~ny** adj social

spomiędzy prp from among

sponsor m sponsor; **~ować** sponsor

spontaniczny adj spontaneous

sporo adv a great deal (**czegoś** of s.th.)

sport m sport; **dzień** m **~u** sports day; **~owiec** m athlete, sportsman, sportswoman; **~owy** adj sporting; **zachowanie**: sportsmanlike, sporting; **~owy samochód** m sportscar; **~owa odzież** f

sporządz|ać ⟨**~ić**⟩ listę draw* up, make* (up)

sposobność f opportunity

sposób m way, manner; **w ten ~** like this, this way; thus; **w pewien ~** in a way; **~ postępowania** procedure

spostrze|gać ⟨**~c**⟩ notice; **~żenie** n observation

spośród prp out of, from (among)

spot|kanie n meeting, encounter form., get-together F; **umówione**: appointment, date F; **~(y)kać (się)** meet* (**z kimś** s.o., with s.o. Am.)

spowi|adać ⟨~wy~⟩ się confess (**z czegoś** s.th.); **~edź** f confession

spożywczy adj: **sklep** m **~** grocer's Brt., grocery store Am.

spód m beczki, łodzi: bottom;

samochodu: underneath; **~nica** f skirt

spójnik m gr. conjunction

spółdziel|czy adj cooperative; **~nia** f cooperative, coop F; **~nia mieszkaniowa** housing cooperative

spółgłoska f gr. consonant

spółka f company

spór m dispute

spóźni|(a)ć się be* late; na pociąg: miss; zegarek: be* slow; **~enie** n delay

spragniony adj thirsty

spraw|a f matter; pol. affair; jur. case; **zdawać sobie ~ę** be* aware (**z czegoś** of s.th.); **to nie twoja ~a** that's none of your business; **~ca** m perpetrator, culprit; **~dzać** ⟨**~dzić**⟩ check; prawdziwość: verify; słowo w słowniku look up; **~dzić się** prognoza: come* true; **~dzian** m test; **~i(a)ć** kłopot cause

sprawiedliw|ość f justice; **~y** adj just, fair

spraw|ność f efficiency; fizyczna: fitness; **~ny** adj efficient; fizycznie: fit; **~ować** funkcję, kontrolę perform; **~ować się** behave; **~owanie** n behaviour; **~ozdanie** n report; (relacja) account; sp. commentary; **~ozdawca** m reporter; sp. commentator

spręż|ać ⟨**~yć**⟩ compress; **~arka** f compressor

spręży|na f spring; **~sty** adj resilient

sprostać *pf trudnościom, obowiązkom*: cope (**czemuś** with s.th.)

sprowadz|ać ⟨**~ić**⟩ bring*, fetch; **~ać się do czegoś** boil down to s.th.

spryskiwacz *m* sprinkler

spryt *m* artfulness; **~ny** *adj* artful

sprzączka *f* buckle

sprzątaczka *f* cleaning lady; **~ać** ⟨**~nąć**⟩ clean (up)

sprzeciw *m* opposition; *słowny*: objection; **~i(a)ć się** oppose (**czemuś** s.th.); *słownie*: object (**czemuś** to s.th.)

sprzecz|ać się quarrel, argue; **~ka** *f* argument; **~ność** *f* contradiction; **~ny** *adj* contradictory

sprzeda|(wa)ć sell*; **~wca** *m* (**~wczyni** *f*) shop assistant *Brt.*, salesclerk *Am.*; **~ż** *f* sale

sprzęgło *n mot.* clutch

sprzęt *m* equipment; *komputer*: hardware; **~ kuchenny** kitchen utensils *pl*; **~ gospodarstwa domowego** (home) appliances *pl*

sprzyjać favour (**czemuś** s.th.)

sprzymierz|eniec *m* ally; **~ony** *adj* allied

sprzysięg|ać ⟨**~ąc**⟩ się conspire (**przeciwko komuś** against s.o.); **~ężenie** *n* conspiracy

spust *m pistolecie*: trigger; *phot.* shutter (release)

spu|szczać ⟨**~ścić**⟩ na zie-

mię: drop; (*obniżać*) lower; *psy* release; **~ścizna** *f* legacy

sputnik *m* satellite

spychacz *m* bulldozer

srebr|ny *adj* silver; **~o** *n* silver

sroka *f* magpie

ssa|ć suck; **~k** *m* mammal

stac|ja *f* station; → **benzynowy, obsługa**; **~yjka** F ignition

staczać roll (**z czegoś** down s.th.); *bitwę* fight*; **~ się** roll (**z czegoś** down s.th.)

stać¹ stand*; *maszyna, fabryka*: be* idle; **~ się** *pf* happen, take* place

stać²: (*nie*) **~ mnie na nowy samochód** I can(not) afford a new car

stadion *m* stadium

stadium *n* stage

stad|nina *f* stud (farm), stable(s); **~o** *n* herd; *wilków, psów*: pack; *owiec, kóz*: flock; *ptaków*: flight, flock

stajnia *f* stable

stal *f* steel

stał|ość *f* constancy; **~y** *adj* (*niezmienny*) permanent, constant; *wzrost, praca*: steady; *klient, praca*: regular; *adres*: permanent

stan *m* condition, shape; *zdrowia, finansowy*: state; **2y** *pl* **Zjednoczone** (**Ameryki**) the United States (of America); **2y** F the States F; **~ąć** *pf* → **stawać**

stanik *m* bra

stanowczy *adj osoba*: wilful, determined; *decyzja*: firm

stanowić constitute; **~sko** *n* (*pogląd*) position, opinion; (*posada*) position, post; (*miejsce*) post

stara|ć się try one's best; (*zabiegać*) try ⟨**o coś** for s.th./to get s.th.); **~nia** *pl* efforts *pl*; **~nny** *adj* careful, accurate

starcie *n demonstrantów z policją*: clash; *fig.* clash, skirmish, brush

starcz|eć ~yć⟩ suffice

staro *adv* old; **~dawny** *adj* old-fashioned; **~ść** *f* old age; **~świecki** F *adj* old-fashioned; **~żytny** *adj* ancient

start *m* start; *samolotu*: take-off; **~ować** start; *samolot*: take* off

star|uszek → **starzec**; **~uszka** *f* old woman; **~y** *adj* old; *chleb*: stale

starz|ec *m* old man; **~eć** ⟨**ze-**⟩ **się** age

statek *m* ship; **~ kosmiczny** spaceship

statut *m* charter

statyst|a *m* (**~ka** *f*) *film*: extra

statysty|czny *adj* statistical; **~ka** *f* statistics *sg*

statyw *m* tripod

staw *m* pond; *anat.* joint

staw|ać (*zatrzymywać się*) stop; (*podnosić się*) stand* (up); *maszyna*: break* down; *zegar*: stop; **~ać na baczność** stand* at attention; **~ać się** become*; **~iać**

⟨**postawić**⟩ stand*, put*, set*; *namiot, ścianę* put* up; **~iać coś komuś** stand* s.o. s.th., treat s.o. to s.th.; **~ka** *f godzinowa itp.*: rate; *w grach*: stake

staż *m* training (period); **~ysta** *m* trainee

stek *m gastr.* steak

stempel *m* (rubber) stamp; **~lować** ⟨**o-**⟩ stamp

ster *m* rudder

sterczeć stick* out

stereo: **zestaw ~** stereo (equipment); **~foniczny** *adj* stereo

sternik *m* helmsman

sterta *f* heap

stęk|ać ~nąć⟩ groan

stęż|enie *n* concentration; **~ony** *adj* concentrated

sto *num* hundred

stocznia *f* shipyard

stoczyć *pf* → **staczać**

stodoła *f* barn

stoisko *n* stand*

stok *m* slope

stokrotka *f bot.* daisy

stolarz *m meblowy*: cabinet--maker; *budowlany*: joiner

stolec *m med.* stool

stolica *f* capital

stolik *m* coffee table; **~ nocny** bedside table

stołek *m* stool; **~owy** *adj* table ...; **~ówka** *f* cafeteria

stop *m metali*: alloy

stopa *f* foot; **~ procentowa** interest rate; **~ życiowa** standard of living

stop|ień m degree; *schodów*: step; (*ocena szkolna*) mark, grade; *wojskowy*: rank; **~niowy** adj gradual

stos m stack, pile

stosow|ać ⟨**za-**⟩ use; **~ać się** (*dotyczyć*) apply (**do czegoś/kogoś** to s.th./s.o.); *do przepisów itp.*: follow (s.th.); **~ny** adj appropriate

stosun|ek m attitude; (*zależność*) relation(ship); *math.* ratio; **~ek płciowy** sexual intercourse; **~kowo** adv relatively

stowarzyszenie n association

stożek m cone

stół m table

strach m fear (**przed czymś** of s.th.); **mieć ~a** F be afraid; **~ na wróble** scarecrow

stragan m stall, stand, booth

strajk m strike; **~ować** ⟨**za-**⟩ strike*, go* on strike

strasz|liwy adj horrible; **~nie** adv: **~nie mi przykro** I'm awfully sorry; **~nie za tobą tęsknię** I miss you terribly; **~ny** adj horrible; **~yć** ⟨**prze-, wy-**⟩ frighten, scare

strata f loss; *czasu, pieniędzy*: waste

straż f guard; **~ pożarna** fire brigade *Brt.*, fire department *Am.*; **~acki** adj: **wóz ~acki** fire engine *Brt.*, fire truck *Am.*; **~ak** m fireman; **~nik** m guard

strąc|ać ⟨**~ić**⟩ knock off (**z czegoś** s.th.)

strefa f zone

stres m stress

streszczenie n summary; *artykułu, referatu*: abstract

stroić ⟨**na-**⟩ tune; **~ się** org *orkiestra*: tune up; ⟨**wy-**⟩ **się** dress (oneself) up

stromy adj steep

stron|a f side; *książki*: page; *gr.* voice; **w tę ~ę** this way; **w ~ę czegoś** towards s.th.; **z drugiej ~y** *fig.* on the other hand

stronnictwo n *pol.* party

strop m ceiling

strój m dress, *form.* attire; *specjalny, sportowy*: outfit

stróż m watchman

struga f *cieczy*: stream

struktura f structure

strumień m stream

struna f *mus.* string; **~ głosowa** vocal cord

strup m scab

struś m ostrich

strych m attic, loft

strzał m shot; **~a** f arrow; **~ka** f arrow

strzec guard; **~ się** beware (**czegoś** of s.th.)

strzel|ać ⟨**~ić**⟩ shoot*; *ogień, silnik*: sputter; **~anina** f shoot-out; **~ba** f shotgun; **~ec** m shot; **~ec wyborowy** marksman; **~nica** f rifle range

strzemię n stirrup

strzępić ⟨**po-, wy-**⟩ **się** fray

strzyc ⟨o-⟩ *coś* cut*/trim (s.th.); *trawnik* mow*; *kogoś* cut*/trim (s.o.'s) hair

strzykawka *f* syringe

stud|encki *adj*: **dom** ~**encki** hall of residence *Brt.*, dormitory *Am.*; ~**ent(ka** *f*) *m* student; ~**ia** *pl* studies *pl*; ~**io-wać** study

studnia *f* well

studzić ⟨o-⟩ cool (down)

stuk|ać ⟨~**nąć**⟩ clatter; ~**ać do drzwi** knock at/on the door

stulecie *n* century; *(rocznica)* centenary

stwarzać create

stwierdz|ać ⟨~**ić**⟩ state; ~**enie** *n* statement

stworz|enie *n* creation; *(istota żywa)* creature; ~**yć** *pf* → **stwarzać**

Stwórca *m* the Creator

styczeń *m* January

stygnąć ⟨o-⟩ cool (down)

styk *m* contact; ~**ać się** come* into contact (**z czymś/kimś** with s.th./s.o.); *ze sprawą*: encounter (**z czymś** s.th.), come* across (**z czymś** s.th.)

styl *m* style; *pływacki*: stroke

stypend|ium *n* scholarship; ~**ysta** *m* scholar

subiektywny *adj* subjective

sublokator *m* lodger

substancja *f* substance

subtelny *adj* subtle

suchy *adj* dry

su(cz)ka *f* bitch, she-dog

sufit *m* ceiling

sugerować suggest (*coś komuś* s.th. to s.o.)

sukces *m* success; *odnosić* ~ succeed

suk|ienka *f* dress; ~**nia** *f* (*esp. formal*) dress

suma *f* sum

sumi|enie *n* conscience; ~**enny** *adj* diligent

supeł *m* knot

surow|iec *m* raw material; ~**y** *adj* (*nie ugotowany*) raw; (*bez litości*) harsh, hard, strict, stern; *klimat*, *warunki*: harsh, hard

surówka *f* (raw vegetable) salad

susz|a *f* drought; ~**arka** *f* dryer; *do włosów*: (hair)dryer; ~**yć** ⟨**wy-**⟩ (**się**) dry

sutek *m* nipple

suw|ać slide*; ~**ak** *m tech.* slider; (*zamek błyskawiczny*) zip (fastener) *Brt.*, zipper *Am.*

suwerenny *adj* sovereign

sweter *m* sweater

swędzi(e)ć itch

swobod|a *f* freedom; ~**ny** *adj* free; *strój*: casual

swój *pron* one's (my, your *etc.*); **mam** ~ **własny pokój** I have my own room

syczeć hiss

sygnał *m* signal; *teleph.* tone

syk *m* hiss; ~**nąć** *pf* → **syczeć**

sylaba *f gr.* syllable

Sylwester *m* New Year's Eve

szczepić

sylwetka f silhouette

symbol m symbol; **~iczny** adj symbolic

symfonia f symphony

sympat|ia f liking (**do kogoś** for s.o.); (*dziewczyna*) girl-friend; (*chłopak*) boyfriend; **~yczny** adj likeable

symulować simulate

syn m son; **~owa** f daughter-in-law

synte|tyczny adj synthetic; **~za** f synthesis

sypać ⟨**się**⟩ pour

sypia|ć sleep*; **~lnia** f bedroom

syrena f morska: mermaid; alarmowa: siren

syrop m syrup

system m system; **~atyczny** adj systematic

sytuacja f situation

szabla f sabre, sword F

szablon m template

szach|ista m chess player; **~ownica** f chessboard; **~y** pl chess

szacować ⟨**o-**⟩ estimate

szacun|ek m respect (**dla kogoś** for s.o.); **~kowy** adj approximate

szafa f na rzeczy: wardrobe

szafka f cabinet

szajka f gang

szal m shawl

szale|ć człowiek: be* crazy (**za kimś** about s.o.); burza: rage; **~nie** adv madly; **~niec** m madman, lunatic F; **~ńczy** adj mad; **~ństwo** n madness, insanity

szalik m scarf

szalony → **szaleńczy**

szalupa f ratunkowa: lifeboat

szał m frenzy; **wpaść w ~** go* berserk; **doprowadzać kogoś do ~u** drive* s.o. crazy

szałas m shed

szampan m champagne

szampon m shampoo

szanow|ać kogoś respect (s.o.); **~ać się** (*dbać o siebie*) take* care of oneself; **~ny:** **Żny Panie** Dear Sir

szansa f chance

szantaż m blackmail; **~ować** blackmail; **~ysta** m blackmailer

szarfa f sash

szarlotka f apple pie

szarp|ać ⟨**~nąć**⟩ ⟨**się**⟩ jerk

szary adj grey

szata f robe; graficzna: layout

szatan m Satan

szatnia f cloakroom; (*przebieralnia*) locker room

szczątki pl remains pl, fragments pl; samolotu, budynku: debris, wreckage

szczebel m rung

szczególny adj particular

szczegół m detail; **~owo** adv in detail; **~owy** adj detailed

szczekać ⟨**za-**⟩ bark

szczel|ina f crack, chink; w skale: fissure, crevice; **~ny** adj tight

szczen|iak m, **~ię** n puppy

szczep m Indian: tribe; **~ić**

⟨za-⟩ vaccinate; **~ienie** n vaccination; **~ionka** f vaccine

szczer|ość f sincerity; **~y** adj sincere, frank

szczęka f jaw; **sztuczna ~** denture

szczęś|cie n happiness; (*nie pech*) (good) luck; **mieć ~cie** be* lucky; **na ~cie** luckily; **~liwy** adj happy

szczodr|ość f generosity; **~y** adj generous

szczot|eczka f: **~eczka do zębów** toothbrush; **~ka** f brush; **~kować** ⟨wy-⟩ brush

szczudło n stilt

szczupak m zo. pike

szczupl|eć ⟨ze-⟩ lose* weight; **~y** adj slender, slim

szczur m rat

szczyp|ać pinch; **~ce** pl pincers pl

szczypiorek m bot., gastr. chives

szczyt m top, peak, summit; pol. summit (meeting); dachu: gable; **~owy** adj top

szef m boss; ~ **kuchni** chef

szele|st m rustle; **~ścić** ⟨za-⟩ rustle

szelki pl braces pl Brt., suspenders pl Am.

szep|t m whisper; **~tać** ⟨~nąć⟩ whisper

szereg m row; (*pewna liczba*) several, some; **~ować** ⟨u-⟩ sort; **~owiec** m mil. private

szermie|rka f fencing; **~rz** m fencer

szerok|i adj broad, wide; uśmiech: broad; **~o** adv wide; **~o otwarty** wide open; **~ość** f width, breadth; **~ość geograficzna** latitude

szesnaście num sixteen

sześcian m cube; **~cienny** adj cubic; **~ć** num six; **~ćdziesiąt** num sixty; **~ćset** num six hundred

szew m seam

szewc m shoemaker

szkatuł(k)a f casket

szkic m sketch; **~ownik** m sketchbook, sketchpad

szkielet m skeleton

szk|lanka f glass; **~lany** adj glass ...; **~larz** m glazier; **~lić** ⟨o-⟩ glaze; **~liwo** n na porcelanie: glaze; na zębach: enamel; **~ło** n glass; **~ła** pl **kontaktowe** contact lenses pl

Szkoc|ja f Scotland; **2ki** adj Scottish, Scots; whisky: Scotch; **2ki angielski** (*język*) Scots

szkod|a f damage; **~!** pity!, that's too bad; **~liwy** adj harmful; **~nik** m pest

szkodzi|ć ⟨za-⟩ harm (*komuś* s.o.); *jedzenie*: disagree (*komuś* with s.o.); **nic nie ~** that's all right, no harm done F

szkol|enie n training; **~ić** train; **~nictwo** n the school system; (*nauczanie*) education; **~ny** adj school ...

szkoła f school; ~ **podstawo-**

wa primary (elementary *Am.*) school (6-14); ~ **średnia** secondary (high *Am.*) school (15-18); ~ **zawodowa** vocational school (15-18)

Szkot *m* Scot, Scotsman; **~ka** *f* Scotswoman

szlach|cic *m* nobleman; **~ectwo** *n* nobility; **~etny** *adj* noble; **~ta** *f* the nobility

szlafrok *m* dressing gown

szlak *m* route; *turystyczny*: trail

szlif|ierka *f* sander, **~ować** ⟨o-⟩ sand

szmat|a *f* rag, **~ka** *f* cloth

szmer *m* (rustling) noise

szminka *f* lipstick

sznur *m* rope; *tech* string; **~ować** ⟨za-⟩ *buty itp.* do up, lace (up); **~owadło** *n* (shoe)lace

szofer → **kierowca**

szok *m* shock; **~ować** ⟨za-⟩ shock

szopa *f* shed

szor|ować scrub; **~stki** *adj* rough

szorty *pl* shorts *pl*

szosa *f* main road, highway *Am.*

szósty *num* sixth

szpada *f* sword

szpara *f* crack, chink

szparag *m bot.* asparagus

szpic *m* point

szpieg *m* spy; **~ostwo** *n* spying; **~ować** spy (*kogoś* on s.o.)

szpik *m* (bone) marrow

szpilka *f* pin

szpinak *m* spinach

szpital *m* hospital; **~ny** *adj*: *leczenie n* **~ne** hospital treatment

szpon *m* claw

szprycha *f* spoke

szpul(k)a *f* spool, reel

szron *m* frost

sztab *m* staff

sztaba *f* bar

sztandar *m* flag, banner

sztorm *m na morzu*: storm

sztruks *m* cord(uroy)

sztucz|ka *f* trick; **~ny** *adj* artificial; *zęby, wąsy itp.*: false

sztućce *pl* cutlery

sztuka *f* art; *teatralna*: play

szturch|ać ⟨~nąć⟩ poke; *łokciem*: nudge

szturmować storm

sztylet *m* dagger

sztywn|ieć ⟨ze-⟩ stiffen; **~y** *adj* stiff; *przepis*: rigid

szubienica *f* gallows *sg, pl*

szuf|elka *f* dustpan; **~la** *f* (*łopata*) shovel

szuflada *f* drawer

szukać search, look (*czegoś* for s.th.)

szum *m* hum; **~ieć** hum

szwagier *m* brother-in-law; **~ka** *f* sister-in-law

Szwajcar *m* Swiss; **~ia** *f* Switzerland; **~ka** *f* Swiss; **~ski** *adj* Swiss

Szwe|cja *f* Sweden; **~d(ka** *f*) *m* Swede; **~dzki** *adj* Swedish

szyb *m* shaft; **~ naftowy** oil well

szyba *f* (glass) pane; **~ przed-**

nia ~ mot. windscreen Brt., windshield Am.

szybk|i adj fast, quick; **~ościomierz** m speedometer; **~ość** f speed

szybowiec m glider

szyć ⟨u-⟩ sew*

szydełko n crochet needle; **~wać** crochet

szyfr m code, cipher; do sejfu:

combination

szyj|a, ~ka f neck

szyk m chic

szykować ⟨na-, przy-⟩ ⟨się⟩ prepare

szyld m signboard

szympans m zo. chimpanzee

szyn|a f rail; med. splint

~ka f ham

szyszka f cone

Ś

ściana f wall

ściąć pf → **ścinać**

ściąg|ać ⟨~nąć⟩ w dół: take* down; odzież take* off; (naciągać) tighten; F (odpisywać) crib (od kogoś off/from s.o.)

ściec pf → **ściekać**

ściek m sewer; **~i** pl sewage; **~ać** flow down, trickle down

ścielić pf → **słać²**

ściemni(a)ć dim; ~ się get* dark

ścienny adj wall ...

ścier|ać wipe off; do kurzu: duster; do wycierania naczyń: tea-towel Brt., dish towel Am.

ścieżka f path; na taśmie: track

ścięgno n anat. sinew, tendon

ścigać chase; ~ się race (z kimś against) s.o.

ścinać cut* down; kogoś behead

ścisk m squeeze; **~ać** squeeze; w dłoni: clutch; w ramio-

nach: hug

ścisł|ość f: jeśli chodzi o **~ość** to be exact; **~y** adj związek: close; dyscyplina: strict; nauki pl **~e** exact sciences

ścisnąć pf → **ściskać**

ślad m stopy: (foot)print; obecności: trace; (wskazówka) clue; (trop) trail; bez **~u** without trace; **~y** tracks pl

śle|dczy m (oficer) investigator; **~dzić** follow, shadow F

śledziona f anat. spleen

śledztwo n investigation

śledź m herring

śle|piec m blind man; **~pnąć** ⟨o-⟩ go* blind; **~pota** f blindness; **~py** adj blind

śliczny adj lovely

ślimak m snail

ślin|a f saliva; **~a(cze)k** m bib

śliski adj slippery

śliwka f plum; ~ suszona prune

ślizga|cz m speedboat; **~ć**

(się) slide*; **~wka** f slide
ślub m wedding; **~ny** adj wedding ...; **suknia** f **~na** wedding dress; **~ować** vow; **~owanie** f vow
ślusarz m locksmith
śluz m mucus
śluza f sluice
śmiać się laugh
śmiał|ość f courage; **~y** adj courageous, bold, brave
śmiech m laughter, laughing
śmieci|arka F f dustcart Brt., garbage truck Am.; **~arz** F m dustman Brt., garbage collector Am.; **~ć** ⟨na-⟩ litter; **~(e)** pl rubbish, garbage Am.
śmieć dare; **jak ~sz!** how dare you!
śmiercionośny adj deadly, lethal
śmierć f death
śmier|dzący adj smelly; **~dzieć** stink* (**czymś** of s.th.)
śmierteln|ość f mortality; (liczba) death rate; **~y** adj mortal; wypadek: fatal
śmiesz|ny adj funny; **~yć** ⟨roz-⟩ amuse (**kogoś** s.o.)
śmietan|a f (bita whipped) cream; **~ka** f cream
śmietni|czka f dustpan; **~k** m rubbish dump Brt., trash-heap Am.; (pojemnik) dustbin Brt., garbage can Am.; fig. mess; **~sko** n rubbish tip Brt., garbage dump Am.
śmigło n propeller
śniadanie n breakfast
śnić dream* (**o czymś** of s.th.)

śnieg m snow; **pada ~** it is snowing
śnież|ka f snowball; **~yca** f blizzard
śpiący adj sleepy, drowsy
śpieszyć → spieszyć
śpiew m singing; **~aczka** f singer; **~ać** sing*; **~ak** m singer; **~nik** m songbook; **~ny** adj melodious
średni adj (przeciętny) average; temperatura: mean; wielkość: middle; **~ca** f diameter; **~k** m semicolon; **~o** adv on average; **~owiecze** n the Middle Ages
środ|a f (popielcowa Ash) Wednesday; **~ek** m middle, centre; (zapobiegawczy preventive) measure; **~ki pieniężne** means pl, funds pl; **~kowy** adj middle, central; **~owisko** n biol. environment; (otoczenie) surroundings pl
śród|mieście n city centre; **~ziemnomorski** Mediterranean
śrub|a f screw; okrętowa: propeller; **~okręt** m screwdriver
śrut m shot
świad|czenia pl services pl; **~czyć** bear* witness (**o** to), testify (**o** to); **~ectwo** n certificate; **~ek** m (naoczny eye-) witness; **~omość** f consciousness, awareness; **~omy** conscious (**czegoś** of s.th.), aware (**czegoś** of s.th.)
świat m world

świat|ło n light; **~a** pl drogo-welmijania main/dipped beam; **~okopia** f photocopy; **~omierz** m exposure meter

świato|pogląd m outlook on life; **~wy** adj world, worldwide

świąt|eczny adj holiday ..., festive; **~ynia** f temple

świd|er m drill; **~rować** drill

świe|ca f candle; **~ca zapłonowa** mot. spark plug; **~cić** shine*

świecki adj lay, secular

świecznik m candlestick

świerk m spruce

świerszcz m zo. cricket

świetlica f dayroom, common room

świetl|ny adj light ...; **~ówka** f fluorescent lamp

świetn|ość f magnificence, splendour; **~y** adj splendid, great, terrific

śwież|ość f freshness; **~y** chleb, powietrze: fresh; farba: wet; **na ~ym powietrzu** in the open air

świę|cić ⟨po-⟩ rocznicę celebrate; dzień keep*; **~to** n holiday, feast; **~tokradztwo** n sacrilege; **~tość** f (cecha) holiness, sacredness; narodowa itp.: sanctity; **~ty** adj holy, sacred; **Wszystkich Świętych** All Saints' Day

świ|nia f pig; contp. człowiek: swine; **~nka morska** guinea pig; **~ński** adj piggish, piggy; fig. dirty; **~ństwo** n dirty trick

świs|nąć pf → świstać; F (ukraść) nick F, pinch F; **~t** m whistle; kuli: zip; bata: swish; **~tać ⟨za-⟩** whistle

świt m dawn, daybreak; **~ać** dawn

T

ta pron → **ten**

tabaka f snuff

tabela f table

tabletka f pill, tablet

tabli|ca f (black)board; **~ca rejestracyjna** numberplate Brt., license plate Am.; **~ca rozdzielcza** switchboard, panel board; **~czka** f (small) board; pamiątkowa itp.: plaque; na drzwiach: plate; **~czka czekolady** bar of chocolate; **~czka mnożenia** multiplication table

taboret m stool

tac(k)a f tray

taczka f (wheel)barrow

tafla f slab; lodu itp.: sheet

taić ⟨za-⟩ conceal, hide*

tajać ⟨roz-⟩ thaw, melt

tajemni|ca f mystery; (sekret) secret; **~czy** adj mysterious

tajny adj secret

tak yes; so; **i ~ dalej** and so on/forth

taki pron such; so; **~ sam**

identical; ~ **sobie** so-so

taks|a f rate; **~ować** ⟨o-⟩ assess; **~ówka** f taxi, cab; **~ówkarz** m taxi driver

takt m tact; **~owny** adj tactful

taktyczny adj tactical

także also, too; w przeczeniu: either; ~ **nie** nor, neither

talent m talent, gift (**do** for)

talerz m plate

talia f waist; kart: pack, deck

talk m talc, talcum powder

tam (over) there; ~ **i z powrotem** to and fro

tam|a f dam, dike; **~ować** ⟨za-⟩ stem, stop; ruch clog; krew staunch

tam|ten that; **~tędy** that way, the other way

tance|rka f ⟨**~rz** m⟩ dancer

tandeta f trash, rubbish; **~ny** adj shoddy, trashy

tani adj cheap

taniec m dance

tanieć ⟨po-⟩ cheapen

tankowiec m tanker

tańczyć ⟨po-, za-⟩ dance

tapczan m couch

tapicer m upholsterer

tarapat|y F pl straits pl; **być w ~ach** be* in trouble

taras m terrace

tarcie n friction

tarcz|a f shield; (cel) target; zegara: face, dial; **~yca** f anat. thyroid (gland)

targ m market(place); **~i** pl econ. fair

targ|ać ⟨**~nąć**⟩ drag, pull; F ⟨dźwigać⟩ lug

tarka f grater

tartak m sawmill

taryfa f tariff

tarzać się roll, wallow

tasiemka f ribbon, band

taśma f tape; **~ klejąca** adhesive tape, Sellotape TM Brt., Scotch tape TM Am.

tata m dad(dy)

tatuaż m tattoo

tchawica f anat. windpipe, trachea

tchórz m coward, chicken F; **~liwy** adj cowardly; **~ostwo** n cowardice

te pron → **ten**

teatr m theatre; **~alny** adj theatrical

techni|czny adj technical; **~k** m technician, engineer; **~ka** f technology; (metoda) technique; **~kum** n technical college

teczka f briefcase

tekst m text

tektura f cardboard

telefon m (tele)phone; **~ować** ⟨za-⟩ phone, call (**do kogoś** s.o.)

tele|graf m telegraph; **~grafować** ⟨za-⟩ telegraph, cable; **~gram** m telegram, wire; **~komunikacja** pl; **~turniej** m TV quiz show; **~wizja** f TV, television; **~wizor** m TV, television (set)

temat m pracy: subject; rozmowy a.: topic; utworu a.: theme; gr. stem

temperatura f temperature
temper|ować ⟨za-⟩ sharpen; **∼ówka** f (pencil) sharpener
ten pron m, **ta** f, **to** n ⟨**ci, te** pl⟩ this (these); ∼ **sam, ta sama, to samo** the same
tendencyjny adj biased; osoba a.: partial
tenis m (**stołowy** table) tennis; **∼ista** m tennis player
teoretyczny adj theoretical
teraz now; **∼źniejszość** f the present; **∼źniejszy** present; (bieżący) current
teren m (obszar) area; (budowy itp.): site; ground; **∼owy** local, regional
termin m deadline; (nazwa) term; **∼owy** adj prompt
termo|metr m thermometer; **∼s** m Thermos TM flask, flask F
terrorystyczny adj terrorist ...
teściowa f mother-in-law; **∼ć** m father-in-law
też also, too
tęcza f rainbow
tędy adv this way
tęgi adj stout
tęsknić miss (za kimś/czymś s.o./sth.); **∼ota** f longing
tętn|ica f artery; **∼ić** pulsate, throb; **∼o** n pulse
tka|ć ⟨u-⟩ weave; **∼nina** f fabric; **∼nka** f biol. tissue
tkliwy adj tender, loving

tknąć pf touch
tlen m oxygen; **∼ek** m chem. oxide
tlić się smoulder
tło n background
tłocz|yć ⟨-⟩ olej itp. press; wodę itp. pump; ∼ **się** crowd
tłok¹ m crush, squeeze
tłok² m tech. piston
tłu|c ⟨po-, s-⟩ break; (miażdżyć) crush; **∼czek** m pestle
tłum m crowd
tłumacz|(ka f) m translator; ustny: interpreter; **∼enie** n translation; **∼yć¹** ⟨prze-⟩ translate; ustnie: interpret; **∼yć²** ⟨wy-⟩ explain; **∼yć się** explain oneself
tłumić ⟨s-⟩ bunt suppress; ogień extinguish, put* out; śmiech stifle; **∼k** m mil. silencer; mot. silencer Brt., muffler Am.
tłu|sty adj fat; **∼szcz** m fat; **∼ścioch** F m fatty F, fatso F
to pron it, this, that; **co** ∼ **za jeden?** F who's that guy?
toaleta f toilet; **∼owy** adj toilet ...
toast m toast (**za** to)
toczyć (kulać) roll; taczkę itp. wheel; tech. turn; **się** roll; fig. be* set, take* place
tok m course
toka|rka f lathe; **∼rz** m turner
toksyczny adj toxic
tolerować tolerate
tom m volume
ton m tone
tona f ton(ne)

tonacja f mus. key

tonąć ⟨u-⟩ drown; ⟨za-⟩ *statek*: sink*

topić ⟨u-⟩ drown; ⟨za-⟩ sink*; ⟨roz-⟩ melt; ~ **się** → **tonąć**, **topnieć**

topnieć ⟨s-⟩ melt, thaw

topola f poplar

topór m axe

tor m (**wyścigowy** race-) track; ~ **pocisku** trajectory

torba f (**na zakupy** shopping) bag

torebka f (hand)bag

tornister m satchel

torować ⟨u-⟩ **drogę** clear, pave

torsje pl vomiting; **mieć** ~ vomit

tort m (layer) cake

tortura f torture; fig. agony, torment

towar m article, commodity; ~**owy** adj pociąg itp.: goods ... Am., freight ... Am.; **dom** m ~**owy** department store

towarzy|ski adj sociable; ~**stwo** n (a. organizacja) society, company; **dotrzymywać komuś** ~**stwa** keep* s.o. company; ~**sz(ka** f) m companion; partyjny: comrade; ~**szyć** accompany

tożsamość f identity

tracić ⟨s-, u-⟩ lose

traf m luck; ~**i(a)ć** hit; (znajdować drogę) find* one's way (**do** to); (dostawać się) get*, land (**do więzienia** to jail); ~**i(a)ć się** happen; ~**ny**

adj apt, to the point

tragiczny adj tragic

trak|t m road; **w ~cie** during, in the course of

traktor m tractor

traktowa|ć ⟨po-⟩ treat; ~**nie** n treatment

trampolina f springboard

tramwaj m tram Brt., streetcar Am.

transformator m transformer

transfuzja f transfusion

transmi|sja f transmission; ~**tować** transmit

transparent m banner

transport m transport; ~**ować** transport, carry

tranzystor m transistor

tranzyt m transit

trapić (się) worry

trasa f route

tratować ⟨s-⟩ trample

tratwa f raft

trawa f grass

trawi|ć ⟨s-⟩ digest; ~**enie** n digestion

trawnik m lawn

trąb|a f trumpet; słoniowa: trunk; ~**ić** ⟨za-⟩ **trąbką**: blow a trumpet; klaksonem: hoot, toot; F (rozgłaszać) trumpet F

trąc|ać ⟨~**ić**⟩ jog, nudge; ~**ać** ⟨~**ić**⟩ **się kieliszkami**: clink

trąd m med. leprosy

trefl m clubs; **król** m ~ king of clubs

trema f stage fright

tren|er m trainer, coach; ~**ing** m training, practice; ~**ingo-**

wy *adj* training ...; **~ować ⟨wy-⟩** train

tres|ować ⟨wy-⟩ train; **~ura** training

treść *f* content

troch|ę a little, some; **ani ~ę** not at all; **po ~u** little by little

trofeum *n* trophy

tro|lić ⟨po-⟩ się triple; **~jaczki** *pl* triplets *pl*; **~jaki** threefold; **~je** *num* three (*children, people of different sexes*)

trolejbus *m* trolley(bus)

tron *m* throne

trop *m* trail, track; **~ić** trail, track

tropikalny *adj* tropical

tro|ska *f* care, worry; **~skliwy** *adj* caring, solicitous; **~szczyć się** care (o for)

trój|barwny *adj* three-coloured; **~ka** *f* (a) three; **~kąt** *m* triangle; **~skok** *m sp.* triple jump

tru|cizna *f* poison; **~ć ⟨o-⟩** poison

trud *m* toil; **~nić się czymś** do* s.th. for a living; **~ność** *f* difficulty; **~ny** *adj* difficult

trudzić się toil

trujący *adj* poisonous, toxic

trumna *f* coffin

trup *m* corpse, dead body

truskawka *f* strawberry

trwa|ć ⟨po-⟩ last, linger; **jak długo to będzie ~ło?** how long will it take?; **~ły** *adj* durable, lasting; **~nie** *n* duration

trwoga *f* fear, terror

trwonić ⟨roz-⟩ waste, squander

tryb *m* mode; *gr.* mood; *tech.* cog

trybuna *f (mównica)* rostrum; *sp.* (grand)stand; **~t** *m* tribunal

trys|kać ⟨~nąć⟩ gush, squirt, spurt; **radością, dumą itp.**: brim over with

trzask *m* crack, crackle; **~kać ⟨~nąć⟩** crack; bang

trząść ⟨po-, za-⟩ shake*; **~ się** shake*, shiver (**z zimna** with cold)

trzcina *f* reed; **~ cukrowa** sugarcane

trzeba *pred* one should/must; it is necessary; **do kłótni ~ dwóch** it takes two to make a quarrel; **nie ~** it is unnecessary

trzeci third; **~orzędny** *adj* third-rate

trzeć ⟨po-⟩ rub

trzepa|czka *f do dywanów*: (carpet) beater; *do jaj*: egg beater, whisk; **~ć skrzydłami**: flutter; **⟨wy-⟩ dywan** beat*

trzepnąć F *pf* slap

trzeszczeć ⟨za-⟩ creak

trzeź|wieć ⟨o-, wy-⟩ sober up; **~wy** *adj* fig. sober

trzęsienie *n*: **~ ziemi** earthquake

trzmiel *m* bumblebee

trzoda *f*: **~ chlewna** pigs *pl*

trzon *m* main part, stem; **~ek**

m shaft; **~owy** *adj*: **ząb ~**
~owy molar

trzpień *m* shank

trzustka *f med.* pancreas

trzy *num* three; **~dzieści** *num*
thirty

trzyma|ć *v/t* hold*; *kurczo-*
wo: clutch; *(utrzymywać)*
keep*; *v/i mróz*: last; *klej*:
hold*; **~ć się** hold*/hang*
on *(czegoś* to s.th.); *przepi-*
sów itp.: abide by; *(zachowy-*
wać kondycję) keep* well; **~j**
się! take care!

trzy|naście *num* thirteen;
~sta *num* three hundred

tu here; **~ i tam** here and there

tubka *f* tube

tulej(k)a *f tech.* sleeve

tulić ⟨*przy-*⟩ cuddle, hug; **~**
się nestle, snuggle *(do* to)

tulipan *m* tulip

tułów *m* trunk

tuman F *m fig.* nitwit, fathead

tunel *m* tunnel

tuńczyk *m* tuna (fish)

tup|ać ⟨*~nąć*⟩ tramp, stamp

tupet *m* nerve, cheek

tupot *m* tramp

tura *f* round

turban *m* turban

turbina *f* turbine

Tur|cja *f* Turkey; **~czynka** *f*
Turk; **2ecki** *adj* Turkish;
~ek *m* Turk

turkotać rattle

turniej *m* tournament

turyst|a *m* (**~ka** *f*) tourist;
~yczny *adj* tourist ...; **~yka** *f*
tourism

tusz *m* Indian ink; *mus.* flourish

tusza *f* corpulence

tuszować ⟨*za-*⟩ hush up

tut|aj → **tu**; **~ejszy** *adj* lo-
cal

tuzin *m* dozen

tuż *w przestrzeni*: close, near;
w czasie: just; **~ obok** close
by, hard by; **~ przed/po** just
before/after

tward|nieć ⟨*s-*⟩ harden;
~ość *f* toughness, hardness;
~y *adj przedmiot*: hard;
człowiek, mięso: tough

twarożek *m*, **twaróg** *m* cottage cheese

twarz *f* face; **do ~y ci w tej**
sukni this dress suits you;
~owy *adj* becoming

twierdza *f* fortress, strong-
hold

twierdz|enie *n* assertion, af-
firmation; **~ić** claim, maintain

twor|zyć ⟨*s-*⟩ create; ⟨*u-*⟩
form; **~wo** *n* material, substance; **~wo sztuczne** plastic

twój *pron* your(s)

twór *m* (*stworzenie*) creature;
(*wytwór*) creation; **~ca** *m*
creator; **~czość** *f* creation;
literacka itp.: production;
~czy *adj* creative

ty *pron* you

tyczk|a *f a. sp.* pole; **~rz** *m* pole
vaulter

tyczyć się refer, concern; **co**
się ~ as regards

tyć ⟨*u-*⟩ put on weight

tydzień *m* week; **Wielki** ♀ Holy Week

tyfus *m* typhus; → **dur**

tygodni|k *m* weekly; **~owy** *adj* weekly

tygrys *m* tiger

tyka *f* → **tyczka**

tykać¹ → **tknąć**; **tykać²** tick

tyle so as much, so/as many; **~kroć** so many times

tylko only; **~ co** just this moment

tylny *adj* siedzenie, drzwi: back; lampa, wejście: rear; noga: hind

tył *m* ciała, przedmiotu, sklepu: back; pojazdu, budynku: rear; **w tyle** at the back/rear; **od ~u, z ~u** from behind; **do ~u** backwards; **~ek** F *m* bottom, rear F, bum F Brt.

tymczas|em meanwhile, in the meantime; **~owy** *adj* temporary, provisional

tymianek *m* thyme

tynk *m* plaster; **~ować** ⟨o-⟩ plaster

typ *m* type; **~ować** ⟨wy-⟩ choose*, pick out; **~owy** *adj* typical (dla of)

tyran *m* tyrant; **~izować** tyrannize

tysiąc *num* thousand; **~lecie** *n* millennium

tytoń *m* tobacco

tytuł *m* title; **~ować** address, style; ⟨za-⟩ entitle, give a title; **~owy** *adj* title ...

U

u *prp* at; **~ dołu schodów** at the foot of the stairs; **~ nas** at our place; **~ Johna** at John's

uaktualni(a)ć update

ubezpiecz|ać insure (od against), **~enie** *n* (na życie life, od nieszczęśliwych wypadków accident, społeczne social) insurance; **~yć** pf → **ubezpieczać**

ubić pf → **ubijać**; **~ interes** F strike* a bargain

ubie|c pf anticipate (kogoś s.o.); **~gać się** apply (o for)

ubiegły *adj* last

ubierać (się) dress

ubijać ziemię ram; śmietanę whip, beat

ubikacja *f* toilet

ubiór *m* clothing

ubli|żać ⟨~yć⟩ insult, offend (komuś s.o.)

ubocz|e *n*: **na ~u** out of the way; **~ny** *adj* side; byproduct

ubogi *adj* poor

ubolew|ać be* sorry (nad for); ⟨żałować⟩ regret; **~anie** *n* regret; **godny ~ania** regrettable

ubóstwo *n* poverty

ubra|ć pf → **ubierać**; **~nie** *n* clothing; (garnitur) suit; **~ny** *adj* dressed (w coś in s.th.); wearing (w coś s.th.)

ubrudzić *pf* dirty, soil

uby(wa)ć decrease, dwindle

ucho *n* ear; (*uchwyt*) handle; *igły*: eye

ucho|dzić (*uciekać*) escape; *gaz itp.*: escape, leak; (*być poczytywanym*) pass (*za* for/ as); **~dźca** *m* refugee

uchronić *pf* protect; **~ się** guard oneself (*od* against)

uchwa|lać ⟨**~lić**⟩ *prawo* pass; *wniosek* carry; **~ła** *f* resolution

uchwy|cić *pf* → **chwytać**; **~t** *m* grip; (*rączka*) handle; **~tny** *adj* perceptible; *osoba*: available

uchybi(a)ć offend (**komuś** **czemuś** s.o./s.th.)

uchyl|ać ⟨**~ić**⟩ *kapelusza*: raise; *drzwi*: set ajar; *prawo* rescind, lift; **~ać** ⟨**~ić**⟩ **się** *od ciosu itp.*: dodge; *od odpowiedzialności*: shirk, evade (*od czegoś* s.th.); *od płacenia*: dodge (*od czegoś* s.th.); *od odpowiedzi*: decline

uciąć *pf* → **ucinać**

uciążliwy *adj* troublesome, strenuous

uciec *pf* → **uciekać**

uciecha *f* joy

ucie|czka *f* escape, flight; **~kać** escape; **~kinier** *m* fugitive

ucierpieć suffer

ucinać cut* off

ucisk *m* pressure; *fig.* oppression; **~ać** press; *fig.* oppress

ucisz|ać ⟨**~yć**⟩ silence, hush

uczcić *pf* honour; (*uświetnić*) celebrate

uczciw|ość *f* honesty; **~y** *adj* honest

ucze|lnia *f* college; university; **~lnica** *f* (**~ń** *m*) pupil, student *Am.*

uczesanie *n* hairstyle

uczestni|ctwo *n* participation; **~czka** *f* participant; **~czyć** participate, take* part (**w** in); **~k** *m* participant

uczęszczać attend

uczony *m* scholar, scientist

uczta *f* feast

uczuc|ie *n* feeling; **~owy** *adj* emotional

uczul|enie *n* med. allergy (**na** to); **~ony** *adj* allergic (**na** to)

uczyć teach*; **~ się** learn; *przed testem itp.*: study

uczyn|ek *m* deed; **~ić** *form.* (*zrobić*) do*; (*sprawić*) make*; **~ny** *adj* obliging, helpful

uda|ć *pf* → **udawać**; **~ny** *adj* succesful

udar *m med.*: **~ mózgu** stroke; **~ słoneczny** sunstroke

udaremni(a)ć frustrate, thwart

udawać *v/t* simulate; *v/i* pretend; **~ się** (*powieść się*) succeed; (*podążać*) proceed (**do** to)

uderz|ać ⟨**~yć**⟩ strike*, hit*; **~enie** *n* blow, hit, stroke

udławić się choke

udo *n* thigh

udogodnienie n facility, convenience

udoskonal|ać ⟨-ić⟩ perfect, improve; **-enie** n improvement

udostępni(a)ć make* accessible/available

udow|adniać ⟨-odnić⟩ prove, demonstrate

udręka f torment, anguish, agony

udusić pf strangle; **~ się** suffocate

udział m participation; (*wkład*) share; **brać ~** participate, take* part (**w** in); **-owiec** m partner, shareholder

udziel|ać ⟨-ić⟩ give*; *zezwolenia*: grant

udźwignąć pf → **dźwigać**

uf|ać ⟨za-⟩ trust (*komuś* s.o.); **~ność** f confidence; **~ny** adj trustful

uganiać się run (**za** after), chase (**za kimś** s.o.)

ugasić pf put* out, extinguish; *pragnienie* quench

ugi|nać ⟨-ać⟩ bend*; **~nać się** bend*; *pod ciężarem*: yield; fig. be* weighed down (**pod brzemieniem trosk** with cares)

ugoda f agreement, settlement

ugór m: **leżeć ugorem** lie* fallow

ugrzęznąć *samochód itp.*: get*/be* bogged (**w śniegu** in snow)

ujawni(a)ć disclose, reveal; **~ się** come* to light

ująć pf → **ujmować**

ujemny adj negative

uje|żdżać ⟨-ździć⟩ konia break in; **~żdżalnia** f riding school

ujma f discredit

ujmować ⟨chwycić⟩ grasp, seize; (*formułować*) formulate

ujmujący adj prepossessing

ujrzeć pf see*, catch* sight of

ujście n rzeki: mouth, estuary; **~ć** pf → **uchodzić**

ukarać punish

ukaz(yw)ać się a. książka: appear, come* out

uką|sić pf → **kąsać**; **~szenie** n bite, sting

uklęknąć pf → **klękać**

układ m (*ułożenie*) arrangement, set-up; (*system*) system (a. anat.); pol. treaty; *graficzny*: layout; **~ać ⟨kłaść⟩** lay, put* (in order); (*porządkować*) arrange; *plan* draw up; *włosy* set; **~anka** f jigsaw puzzle; **~y** pl negotiations pl; (*powiązania*) connections pl

ukłon m bow; **~y** pl a. regards pl; **~ić się** pf **~ kłaniać się**

ukochan|a f (**~y** m) darling, sweetheart

ukończyć complete, finish

uko|s m: **na ~s** diagonally, obliquely; **patrzeć z ~sa** look askew; **~śny** adj oblique

ukradk|iem adv by stealth, stealthily; **~owy** adj furtive

Ukrai|na f Ukraine; **~niec** m (**~nka** f) Ukrainian; **Ջński** adj Ukrainian

ukraść pf steal*

ukroić cut* off

ukry(wa)ć (się) hide*

ukształtować shape

ul m (bee)hive

ulatniać się leak, escape; F fig. disappear, vanish

ulatywać pf (**ulecieć**) fly* away

uleczalny adj curable

ule|gać ⟨~c⟩ (poddawać się) succumb; (podporządkować się) give* in, yield; zmianom itp.: undergo*, be* subject to; pokusie itp.: be* seized (czemuś with s.th.); **to nie ~ga wątpliwości** there is no doubt about it; **~gły** adj submissive

ulepsz|ać ⟨~yć⟩ improve; **~enie** n improvement

ulew|a f downpour; **~ny** adj torrential

ulg|a f relief; **~owy** adj reduced

uli|ca f street; **~czka** f (ślepa blind) alley; **~czny** adj street

ulotka f leaflet

ulotnić się → **ulatniać się**

ulubi|eniec m favourite; (a. zwierzę) pet; **~ony** adj favourite, pet ...

ulżyć lighten; ease

ułam|(yw)ać (się) break* off; **~ek** m (kawałek) frag-

ment; math. fraction

ułaskawi(a)ć pardon

ułatwi(a)ć make* easier, facilitate; **~enie** n facilitation

ułomn|ość f infirmity, handicap; **~y** adj infirm, disabled

ułożyć pf → **układać**

umacniać strengthen; mil. fortify

umarły adj dead, deceased

umarzać dług remit; jur. sprawę dismiss

umawiać się make* an appointment

umiar m moderation, restraint; **~kowany** adj moderate

umie|ć can*, be* able to; **~jętność** f skill; **~jętny** adj competent, skilful

umiejsc|awiać ⟨~owić⟩ locate

umierać die

umie|szczać ⟨~ścić⟩ place, put*

umknąć pf → **umykać**

umniejsz|ać ⟨~yć⟩ belittle, denigrate

umo|cnić pf → **umacniać**; **~cnienia** pl mil. fortifications pl; **~cow(yw)ać** fasten, secure

umorz|enie n remission; jur. dismissal; **~yć** pf → **umarzać**

umow|a f agreement; pol. treaty; **~a o pracę** contract (of employment); **~ny** adj contractual; (fikcyjny) fictional

umożliwi(a)ć make* possible

umówić się *pf* → **umawiać się**

umrzeć *pf* → **umierać**

umyć *pf* → **myć**

umykać escape, flee*

umysł *m* mind; **~owy** *adj* mental; **pracownik m ~owy** white-collar worker

umyślny *adj* deliberate; *jur.* premeditated

umywalka *f* washbasin

uncja *f* ounce

unia *f* union

uniemożliwi(a)ć make* impossible

unieruchomić *pf* immobilize

unieszkodliwi(a)ć render harmless, neutralize

unieść *pf* → **unosić się**

unieważni(a)ć invalidate; (*znosić*) annul

uniewinni(a)ć acquit; **~enie** *n* acquittal

uniezależni(a)ć się set* up on one's own

unik|ać ⟨**~nąć**⟩ avoid, evade

uniwersyte|cki *adj* university ..., academic; **~t** *m* university

unormować (**się**) normalize

unosić raise, lift; **~ się** rise; *zapach:* waft, be* wafted; **~ się gniewem** fly* into a rage

unowocześni(a)ć modernize

uodporni(a)ć inure (*na* to); immunize (*przeciw* against)

uogólni|(a)ć generalize; **~enie** *n* generalization

upa|dać fall*; *fig.* decay; **~dek** *m* fall

upa|lny *adj* sweltering, torrid; **~ł** *m* heat

upaństwowić *pf* nationalize

uparty *adj* stubborn, obstinate

upaść *pf* → **upadać**

upat|rywać ⟨**~rzyć**⟩ choose*, single out

upewni(a)ć assure; **~ się** make* sure

upić się *pf* → **upijać się**

upiec *pf* → **piec²**

upierać się insist (*przy* on), stick (*przy* to)

upiększ|ać ⟨**~yć**⟩ decorate; *a. fig.* embellish

upijać się get* drunk

upiór *m* ghost

upłynąć *pf* → **upływać**

upły|w *m czasu:* lapse; **~ krwi** loss of blood; **~ać** *czas:* lapse; *okres:* expire

upok|arzać ⟨**~orzyć**⟩ humiliate; **~orzenie** *n* humiliation

upom|inać rebuke, admonish; **~inać się** reproach, claim (*o coś* s.th.); **~inek** *m* gift, present; **~nieć** *pf* → **upominać**; **~nienie** *n* rebuke, reprimand

upor|ać się cope (*z* with); **~czywy** *adj* persistent

uporządkować *pf* arrange, tidy (up)

uposażenie *n* salary

upośledz|enie *n* handicap; **~ony** *adj* handicapped, disabled

upoważni|(a)ć authorize (*do*

to); ~**enie** n authorization
upowszechni(a)ć spread,
disseminate
upór n stubbornness, obstinacy
upraszczać simplify
upraw|a f cultivation; ~**iać**
cultivate; *sport* practise
uprawni(a)ć entitle (**do** to);
~**enie** n entitlement; *mst pl*
(**kwalifikacje**) qualification(s
pl)
uprościć pf → **upraszczać**
uprowadz|ać ⟨~**ić**⟩ **człowieka** abduct, kidnap; *samolot
itp.* hijack; ~**enie** n **człowieka**: abduction, kidnapping;
samolotu: hijacking
uprząż f harness
uprzeć się pf → **upierać się**
uprzedz|ać ⟨~**ić**⟩ (*ubiegać*)
forestall; (*ostrzec*) warn (**o**
of); ~**enie** n bias, prejudice
uprzejm|ość f politeness,
courtesy; ~**y** adj polite, courteous
uprzytomni(a)ć sobie realize
uprzywilejowany adj privileged
upuścić drop
uradować pf gladden
uratować pf save, rescue
uraz m injury; ~**a** f grudge;
~**ić** pf hurt*, offend
urlop m holiday; *macierzyński itp.* leave; ~**owicz** F m
holidaymaker
urna f urn; *wyborcza*: ballot
box

uroczy adj charming
uroczyst|ość f ceremony, celebration, festivity; ~**y** adj
solemn, festive
uroda f beauty
urodzaj m harvest; ~**ny** adj
fertile; *form.* fecund
urodz|enie n birth; **data** f
~**enia** date of birth; ~**ić** pf
give* birth; ~**ić się** be* born;
~**iny** pl birthday
urojenie n delusion
urok m charm; (*magia*) spell
urosnąć pf **grow***
urozmaic|enie n variety,
change; ~**ony** adj varied
uruch|amiać ⟨~**omić**⟩ start
(up)
urwać pf → **urywać**
urwis|ko n precipice; ~**ty** adj
precipitous, steep
uryw|ać tear* off; ~**ać się**
come* off; ~**ek** m fragment;
tekstu: excerpt, passage
urząd m (**stanu cywilnego** registry) office; ~ **zatrudnienia**
job centre
urządz|ać ⟨~**ić**⟩ arrange, organize; ~**enie** n device, appliance
urzeczywistni(a)ć realize
urzęd|niczka f (~**nik** m) *biurowy*: clerk; *wyższy*: official;
państwowy: civil servant;
form. office-holder; ~**ować**
(*pracować w urzędzie*) work;
(*sprawować urząd*) hold* office; ~**owanie** n: **godziny** pl
~**owania** office hours pl;
~**owy** adj document, język:

official; *ton*, *styl*: formal
uschnąć *pf* → **usychać**
usiąść *pf* → **siadać**
usilny *adj* insistent
usiłow|ać *pf* try, attempt, endeavour; **~anie** *n* attempt
uskarżać się complain (*na* about/of)
usłuchać *pf* obey (*kogoś* s.o.), listen (*kogoś* to s.o.)
usłu|ga *f* service; **~gi** *pl* services *pl*; **~giwać** serve, attend; **~gowy** *adj* service ...; **~żny** *adj* obliging
usłyszeć *pf* hear*
usnąć *pf* fall* asleep
uspok|ajać ⟨**~oić**⟩ calm; **~ajać się** calm down
usposobienie *n* disposition, nature
usprawiedliwi|a|ć excuse (**się** oneself); **~enie** *n* excuse
usprawni|a|ć improve, rationalize; **~enie** *n* improvement, rationalization
usta *pl* mouth
ustal|ać ⟨**~ić**⟩ (*wyznaczać*) fix, settle; (*stwierdzać*) ascertain; **~enie** *n* settlement
usta|nawiać ⟨**~nowić**⟩ impose, introduce; **~wa** *f* law, act
ustawi|a|ć put* up, set* up
ustawiczny *adj* incessant, continual
ustawodaw|ca *m* legislator; **~stwo** *n* legislation
ustawowy *adj* statutory
ustąpić *pf* → **ustępować**
usterka *f* fault, flaw

ustęp *m* (*urywek*) passage, excerpt; (*toaleta*) toilet
ustęp|liwy *adj* compliant; **~ować** *ze stanowiska*: resign; (*ulegać*) make* concessions, yield, give* in (*wobec czegoś* to s.th.); *ból*: wear* off; (*być gorszym*) be* inferior (*od* to); **~stwo** *n* concession
ustn|ik *m papierosa*: filter tip; *a. mus.* mouthpiece; **~y** *adj* oral
ustosunkować się *pf* take* a stand (*do* on)
ustrój *m* (*organizm*) organism; *kapitalistyczny itp.*: system; **~ państwowy** system of government, regime
usu|wać ⟨**~nąć**⟩ remove; *ząb* extract; *błąd* put* right; *usterkę* repair
usychać wither, wilt
usyp|iać *dziecko* lull; *zwierzę* put* to sleep, put* down
uszczel|ka *f tech.* gasket, seal; **~ni(a)ć** seal
uszczerbek *m* harm, damage
uszczęśliwi|a|ć make* happy
uszczyp|liwy *adj* cutting, biting; **~nąć** *pf* → **szczypać**
uszkadzać damage, impair
uszk|o *n kubka*: handle; *igły*: eye; **~a** *pl gastr.* ravioli
uszkodz|enie *n* damage; **~ić** *pf* → **uszkadzać**; **~ony** *adj* damaged
uścis|k *m* embrace; **~k dłoni**

handshake; **~kać, ~nąć** *pf* embrace

uśmiech *m* smile; *szeroki:* grin; *szyderczy:* smirk; **~ać ⟨~nąć⟩ się** smile

uśmierc|ać ⟨~ić⟩ kill

uśmierz|ać ⟨~yć⟩ *ból* relieve

uśpić *pf* → **usypiać**

uświad|amiać ⟨~omić⟩ enlighten; **~omić sobie** realize

utajony *adj* latent

utalentowany *adj* talented, gifted

utarty *adj* widespread, general

utk|nąć *pf* get* stuck/bogged; **~wić** *pf* oczy fix, fasten; *w pamięci:* stick

uto|nąć *pf człowiek*: drown, *statek*: sink*; **~pić (się)** *pf* drown

utracić *pf* lose*

utrata *f* loss

utrudni(a)ć make* difficult, impede

utrwal|ać ⟨~ić⟩ strengthen; *tech.* fix

utrzeć *pf* → **ucierać**

utrzym(yw)ać *v/t* hold*; *w czystości:* keep*; *rodzinę* maintain; *v/i (twierdzić)* maintain, claim; **~ się** make* a living (**z** from)

utw|orzyć *pf* create, form; *(ustanowić)* establish; **~ór** *m* composition, work

utykać limp

uwaga *f* attention, notice; *(spostrzeżenie)* remark; *w*

tekście: note; *(wymówka)* reprimand, rebuke; **brać coś pod ~ę** take s.th. into consideration; **~a!** look out!, caution!

uwalniać free *(się* oneself)

uwarunkow(yw)ać condition

uważać *v/i* pay attention; *(być ostrożnym)* be* careful, watch out; *(mniemać)* think*, be* of the opinion; *v/t* regard (**za** as), consider (**kogoś za coś** s.o. s.th.); **~ny** *adj* attentive

uwid|aczniać ⟨~ocznić⟩ show, reveal

uwielbi|ać adore; **~enie** *n* adoration

uwierzyć *pf* believe

uwieść *pf* → **uwodzić**

uwięzić *pf* imprison

uwikłać się *pf* get* involved/ entangled (**w** in)

uwłaczający *adj* derogatory, abusive

uwodzi|ciel(ka *f) m* seducer; **~ć** seduce

uwolnić *pf* → **uwalniać**

uwydatni(a)ć set* off; *(akcentować)* stress

uwzględni(a)ć take* into account

uzależni|enie *n* dependence *(od* to); *narkotyczne itp.*: addiction *(od* to); **~ony** *adj* addicted *(od* on)

uzasadni|a)ć *teorię itp.* justify (**coś** s.th.); *postępowanie itp.* give* reasons (**coś**

for s.th.); **~enie** n justification, reason

uzbr|ajać ⟨~oić⟩ (się) arm; **~ojenie** n armament, arms pl

uzdolni|enie m talent, gift; **~ony** adj talented, gifted

uzdr|awiać ⟨~owić⟩ heal; **~owiciel** m healer; **~owisko** n spa, watering place

uzg|adniać ⟨~odnić⟩ agree (on), co-ordinate

uziemienie n electr. earth

uzmysł|awiać ⟨~owić⟩ illustrate; → **uprzytomniać**

uzna|nie n recognition, acknowledgment; **~(wa)ć** recognize, acknowledge

uzupełni|(a)ć supplement, complete; **~enie** n supplement, complement

uzysk(iw)ać obtain, gain, receive

uży|cie n use; **~ć** pf → **używać**; **~teczny** adj useful; **~tek** m use; **~tkować** use, utilize; **~tkowanie** n use, utilization; **~tkownik** m user; **~wać** use; **~wany** adj used, second-hand

W

w prp in; **~ nocy** at night; **dzień ~ dzień** day after day, day in day out; **~ domu** at home; **we wtorek** on Tuesday; **grać ~ coś** play s.th.

wabić ⟨z-⟩ decoy

wachlarz m fan

wad|a f fault, defect; **~liwy** adj defective, faulty

wafel m wafer

waga f weight (a. fig.); (przyrząd) m (**restauracyjny** dining, **sypialny** sleeping) car

waha|ć się hesitate; **~dło** n pendulum; **~nie** n hesitation

wakacje pl holiday(s pl)

walc m waltz

walczyć fight

walec m roller; math. cylinder

walet m karciany: jack, knave

Walia f Wales sg

walić (uderzać) strike; F (bić) wallop; śnieg itp.: fall* heavily; serce: thump; → **obalać**, **zwalać**; **~ się** tumble (down)

Walij|czyk m Welshman; **~ka** f Welshwoman; **2ski** adj Welsh

walizka f (suit)case

walka f combat, fight; a. fig. struggle; **~ wręcz** hand-to-hand fight

walor m value, quality, merit

waluta f currency

wał m embankment; mil. rampart; tech. (napędowy drive) shaft; **~ek** m shaft, roller; maszyny do pisania: platen; **~ek do ciasta** rolling pin

wałęsać się roam

wałkować ⟨roz-⟩ *ciasto* roll out; F *temat itp.* harp on, rabbit on Brt.

wampir *m* vampire

wanilia *f* vanilla

wanna *f* bath, tub Am.

wap|ienny *adj* calcium ..., limy; **~ień** *m* limestone; **~no** *n* lime; **~ń** *m* calcium

warcaby *pl* draughts *pl*

warczeć snarl, growl

warga *f* lip

wari|actwo *n* lunacy, madness; **~at** *m* lunatic; *dom* **~atów** *a.* fig. madhouse; **~ować ⟨z-⟩** go* mad

warkocz *m* plait Brt., braid Am.

warkotać whirr, drone

warstwa *f* layer; *farby itp.*: coat; *(a. fig.)* stratum

warsztat *m* workshop; **~ samochodowy** garage

wart *adj* worth

warta *f (straż)* guard; *(wartownik)* sentry

wartki *adj* rapid, fast

warto *pred* it is worth(while); *to* **~ zobaczyć** it is worth seeing; **~ściowy** *adj* valuable; **~ść** *f* value, worth

wartownik *m* sentry, guard

warun|ek *m* condition; **~kowy** *adj a. tryb*: conditional

warzyw|ny *adj* vegetable ...; *sklep* **~ny** greengrocer's; **~o** *n* vegetable

wasz *pron* your(s)

wat *m* phys. watt

wata *f* cotton wool Brt., cotton Am.

waza *f* vase; *do zupy*: tureen

wazelina *f* Vaseline TM

wazon *m* vase

ważka *f* dragonfly

waż|ność *f* importance, significance; *dokumentu itp.*: expiry; *stracić* **~ność** expire; **~ny** *adj* important, significant; *paszport itp.*: valid; *osoba*: influential, important; **~na figura** F big shot F, big noise F; **~yć ⟨z-⟩** *a.* fig. weigh

wąchać smell

wąs *m (often* **~y** *pl)* moustache; **~aty** *adj* with a moustache

wąsk|i *adj* narrow; **~otorowy** *adj* narrow-gauge

wątek *m* thread, plot

wątły *adj* frail

wątp|ić doubt *(w coś* s.th.*)*; **~ienie** *n*: *bez* **~ienia** undoubtedly; **~liwość** *f* doubt; **~liwy** *adj* doubtful

wątroba *f* liver

wąwóz *m* ravine, gorge

wąż *m zo.* snake; *tech.* hose

wbić *pf* → **wbijać**

wbie|gać ⟨**~c**⟩ run* into; *(a. na górę)* run* up

wbijać knock into, drive *(w coś* into s.th.*)*

wbrew *prp* in spite of, counter to, against

wcale *adv*: **~ nie** not at all; **~ dobrze** quite well

wchłani|ać ⟨∼onąć⟩ absorb; *a. fig.* soak up

wchodzić enter, come* in; *na górę, na schody:* go* up, climb

wciąć *pf* → **wcinać**

wciąga|ć ⟨∼nąć⟩ drag in, draw* in; *podwozie* retract

w ciągu during, in the course of

wciąż *adv* still

wcielać incorporate, annex, *mil.* call up *Brt.*, conscript *Brt.*, draft *Am.*

wcierać rub in

wcięcie *n* incision, notch; *a. typ.* indentation

wcinać notch; *a. typ.* indent; F *(jeść)* tuck in F

wcis|kać ⟨∼nąć⟩ press in, push in

wczas|owicz *m* holidaymaker *Brt.*, vacationer *Am.*; **∼owy** *adj* holiday ...; **∼y** *pl* holiday(s *pl*), vacation *Am.*

wczesny *adj* early

wczoraj yesterday; **∼szy** *adj* yesterday('s) ...

wczu(wa)ć się empathize (*w* with)

wda(wa)ć się get* involved (*w* in)

wdepnąć step (*w* in); F *(odwiedzić)* drop in (*do kogoś* on s.o.)

wdow|a *f* widow; **∼iec** *m* widower; **słomiany ∼iec** grass widower

wdychać inhale, breathe in

wdzierać się force an entry (*do* into), break* into

wdzię|czność *f* gratitude; **∼czny** *adj* grateful; *ruchy:* graceful; **∼k** *m* grace, charm

we → **w**

według *prp* according to

wedrzeć się *pf* → **wdzierać się**

wejści|e *n* (*wchodzenie*) entrance, entry; (*miejsce*) entrance; *tech.* input; **∼a nie ma** no admittance; **∼owy** *adj* entrance ...

wejść *pf* → **wchodzić**

weksel *m econ.* bill of exchange

welon *m* veil

wełn|a *f* wool; **∼iany** *adj* woollen

weneryczn|y *adj:* **choroba ∼a** venereal disease

wentyla|cja *f* ventilation; **∼tor** *m* ventilator; *elektryczny:* fan

weranda *f* veranda(h)

werb|ować ⟨z-⟩ enlist, recruit; **∼unek** *m* enlistment, recruitment

werdykt *m* verdict

wersja *f* version

wesel|e *n* wedding; **∼ić się** rejoice; **∼ny** wedding ...

wesołość *f* merriness, cheerfulness, gaiety; **∼y** *adj* merry, cheerful, gay

wesprzeć *pf* → **wspierać**

westchn|ąć *pf* → **wzdychać**; **∼ienie** *n* sigh

wesz *f* louse

weterynarz *m* vet(erinary surgeon)

wetknąć pf → **wtykać**

wetrzeć pf → **wcierać**

wewn|ątrz adv inside, within; **do ~ątrz** inwards; **od ~ątrz** from the inside; **~ętrzny** adj choroby, handel: internal; ucho, życie: inner; kieszeń, tor: inside; **Ministerstwo Spraw ~ętrznych** Ministry of Internal Affairs, Home Office Brt.

wezwa|ć pf → **wzywać**; **~nie** n call; jur. summons

węch m smell

wędk|a f fishing rod; **~arski** adj fishing ...; **~arz** m angler; **~ować** angle

wędliny pl smoked meats, cold cuts, and sausages

wędrow|ać hike, ramble; **~iec** m hiker, rambler; **~ny** adj wandering; lud: nomadic; ptak: migratory

wędrówka f ramble, hike

wędz|ić ⟨u-⟩ smoke; **~ony** adj smoked

węgiel m coal; chem. carbon; **~ drzewny** charcoal; **~ny** adj: kamień **~ny** a. fig. cornerstone

Węgier|ka f) m Hungarian; **♀ski** Hungarian

węglowod|an m chem. carbohydrate; **~ór** m chem. hydrocarbon

węgorz m eel

Węgry pl Hungary

węszyć sniff

węz|eł m knot; **~łowy** adj fig. fundamental, crucial

wgiąć pf dent

wgłębi|a|ć się immerse oneself (w in); **~enie** n hollow, depression

wgnia|tać ⟨~eść⟩ dent

wiać blow*; F (uciekać) bolt

wiadomo it is known, everybody knows

wiadom|ość f (piece of) news, message; **podać do ~ości** announce, make* known; **~y** adj (znany) known; (pewien) certain

wiadro n bucket

wiara f belief; eccl. faith

wiarogodny adj reliable, credible

wiatr m wind; **~ak** m windmill; **~ówka** f windcheater; (broń) airgun

wiąza|ć ⟨z-⟩ tie, bind*; **~ć się** a. be* connected with; **~anie** n narciarskie: binding; **~ka** f bundle; światła: beam

wice- m vice-chief

wicher m gale

wichura f → **wicher**

wide|lec m fork; **~łki** pl teleph. cradle; rowerowe: forks pl

wideo n (urządzenie) video, VCR; (film) video; **~kaseta** f videotape

widły pl fork

wid|mo n phantom; wojny, bezrobocia: spectre; phys. spectrum; **~nokrąg** m horizon; **~ny** adj light; **~oczność** f visibility; **~oczny** adj visi-

ble; **~ok** *m* view, sight;
~okówka *f* postcard; **~owisko** *n* show, spectacle; **~ownia** *f* audience

widz *m* spectator; **~enie** *n*: **punkt** *m* **~enia** point of view; **do ~enia!** goodbye!, bye!; **~ialny** *adj* visible; **~ieć** see*

wiec *m* rally

wieczko *n* lid

wiecz|ność *f* eternity; **~ny** *adj* eternal, everlasting; → **pióro**

wieczor|ek *m* evening; **~em** in the evening; **dziś ~em** tonight; **~ny** *adj* tonight's ...; *każdego wieczora*: nightly; **~owy** *adj strój*: evening ...

wieczór *m* evening; **dobry ~!** good evening!

wiedz|a *f* knowledge; **~ieć** know*

wiedźma *f* witch

wiejski *adj* rural, country ...

wiek *m* age; (*stulecie*) century; **~owy** *adj* aged, ancient; *grupa*: age ...

wielbiciel(ka *f*) *m* admirer, fan

wielbłąd *m* camel

wiele 1. *adj ludzi*: many, a lot, a great deal; **2.** *adv* much, a great deal; **o ~ lepszy** much/far better; **tego już za ~!** that's a bit thick!

Wielkanoc *f* Easter; **na ~** at Easter; **2ny** *adj* Easter ...

wielk|i *adj* large, big, great; *fig. a.* grand; **2a Brytania** Great Britain; **2i Piątek** Good Friday; **2i Tydzień** Holy Week; **~ość** *f* size; *fig.* greatness

wielokrotny *adj* repeated

wieloryb *m* whale

wielostronny *adj* multilateral

wieloznaczny *adj* equivocal, ambiguous

wieniec *m* wreath

wieńcowy *adj med.* coronary

wieprz *m* hog; **~owina** *f* pork; **~owy** *adj* pork ...

wiercić drill, bore; **~ się** wriggle

wiern|ość *f* faithfulness, loyalty; **~y 1.** *adj* faithful, loyal, true; **2.** *m* the faithful, believer

wiersz *m* poem; verse; (*linia*) line

wiert|arka *f* drill; **~ło** *n* drill bit; **~niczy** *adj* drilling, boring

wierzący *m* believer → *a.* **wierny** 2

wierzba *f* willow

wierzch *m* upper part, top, surface; **na ~** on top; **~ni** *adj* top, outer; **~ołek** *m* top; *góry*: summit, peak; **~owiec** *m* mount

wierzy|ciel *m* creditor; **~ć** believe (**w** in); **~telności** *pl* liabilities *pl*

wiesz|ać hang*; *człowieka* hang; **~ak** *m* (coat) hanger; (*mebel*) coatrack; (*haczyk*) hook

wieś *f* village

wie|ść 1. *f* news; (*pogłoska*) rumour; **2.** *v/t* lead; **~ść się**:

jak ci się ~dzie? how are you getting along?, how are things?

wieśnia|czka f (**~k** m) villager

wietrz|ny adj windy; **~yć** air, ventilate

wiewiórka f squirrel

wieźć ⟨od-, za-⟩ carry, transport

wież|a f tower; szachowa: rook, castle; **~owiec** m high-rise building

więc so, therefore; **a ~** przy wyliczaniu: namely

więcej more; **mniej ~** more or less

więdnąć ⟨z-⟩ wither, wilt

większ|ość f majority; **~y** adj bigger, larger

więzi|ć hold*/keep* prisoner; **~enie** n prison, jail; **~eń** m prisoner

więzy pl bonds pl

wigilia f eve; **2 Bożego Narodzenia** Christmas Eve

wiklin|a f osier; **~owy** adj wicker

wilgo|ć f moisture; w powietrzu: humidity; **~tny** adj moist, powietrze: humid, damp

wilk m wolf

wina f guilt, fault, blame

winda f lift Brt., elevator Am.

wini|ak m brandy; **~arnia** f wine bar

wini|ć blame; **~en, ~na:** ile jestem ci **~en?** how much do I owe you?; → a. **winny²**

winnica f vineyard

winny¹ adj vine-, vinous

winny² adj guilty; → a. **winien**

wino n wine; **~branie** n vintage; **~grona** pl grapes pl; **~rośl** f vine

winszować ⟨po-⟩ congratulate

wiolonczela f cello

wioska f village

wiosło n krótkie: paddle; długie i pojedyncze: oar; **~wać** na kajaku: paddle; na łodzi: row

wiosna f spring

wioślar|ski adj rowing; **~stwo** n rowing; **~rz** m oarsman

wir m whirlpool

wiraż m curve, bend

wir|nik m tech. rotor; **~ować** rotate, revolve, spin*; **~ówka** f centrifuge

wirus m virus

wis|ieć hang*; **~zący** adj pendent; **most m ~zący** suspension bridge

wiśni|a f cherry; **~owy** adj cherry; **~ówka** f kirsch, cherry vodka

witać ⟨po-⟩ greet, welcome; **~ się ⟨przy-⟩** greet (z kimś s.o.), say hello (z to)

witamina f vitamin

witraż m stained glass (window)

witryna f shop window

wiza f visa

wizj|a f vision; **~er** m phot.

viewfinder; *mil.* sight(s *pl*)

wizyt|a *f* visit; **~ówka** *f* card

wjazd *m* approach, entrance, entry; (*droga*) driveway; **~owy** *adj* entrance ...

wje|żdżać ⟨**~chać**⟩ enter, drive* in; (*najeżdżać*) run* (*na słup* into a post); *windą itp.*: go* up

wkle|jać ⟨**~ić**⟩ paste in

wklęsły *adj* concave

wkład *m* (*w pieniądze itp.*): contribution; *długopisowy*: refill; **~ać** insert, put* in; (*nakładać*) put* on; **~ka** *f* insert

wkoło *prp* round

wkraczać enter; (*najeżdżać*) invade; *fig.* step in

wkra|dać ⟨**~ść**⟩ **się** skulk

wkrę|cać ⟨**~cić**⟩ screw in; **~t** *m* screw; **~tak** *m* screwdriver

wkroczyć *pf* → **wkraczać**

wkrótce *adv* soon, shortly

wkuwać F swot (up) F *Brt.*, grind F *Am.*

wlec drag, lug; **~ się** drag

wleźć *pf* → **włazić**

wlicz|ać ⟨**~yć**⟩ include, count in

wład|ać rule; (*dobrze*) **~ać angielskim** have* a (good) command of English; **~ca** *m* ruler; **~czy** *adj* imperious; **~ny** *adj* empowered, authorized (*coś zrobić* to do s.th.)

władza *f* (*rządzenie*) power, authority; *mst pl* (*instytucja*) authorities *pl*

włam|ać się *pf* → **włamywać**

się, **~anie** *n* burglary, break-in; **~ywacz** *m* burglar; **~ywać się** break* in(to)

własn|ość *f* property; **~y** *adj* own

właściciel(ka *f*) *m* owner, proprietor

właściw|ość *f* property, quality; **~y** *adj* proper, right; (*stosowny*) suitable, appropriate; (*charakterystyczny*) typical (*komuś* of s.o.); **~ie** *adv* actually; (*poprawnie*) properly

właśnie *adv* (*dokładnie*) exactly, just, precisely; *potwierdzająco*: exactly, just so

włazić get* into (*do czegoś* s.th.), clamber (*na* on)

włącz|ać ⟨**~yć**⟩ include; *światło itp.* switch on, turn on; **~ać się** join (*do czegoś* s.th.); **~nie** *adv* inclusive, including; *ze mną* **~nie** including me

Włoch *m* Italian; **~y** *pl* Italy

włochaty *adj* hairy

włos *m* hair

wło|ski *adj* Italian; ⒉**szka** *f* Italian

włożyć *pf* → **wkładać**

włóczęga *m* tramp

włóczka *f* yarn

włók|ienniczy *adj* textile ...; **~nisty** *adj* fibrous, stringy; **~no** *n* fibre

wmawiać ~ coś komuś make s.o. believe s.th., talk s.o. into believing s.th.

wódka

wmieszać *pf* mix in; (*wplątać*) involve; ~ **się** *pf* mingle (**w** with), involve o.s. (**w** in)

wmówić *pf* → **wmawiać**

wmu|szać ⟨~sić⟩: ~**szać coś komuś** force s.th. upon s.o.

wnęka *f* recess, niche

wnętrz|e *n* interior; **do ~a** inwards; ~**ości** *pl* bowels *pl*, entrails *pl*

wnieść *pf* → **wnosić**

wnik|ać ⟨~nąć⟩ penetrate; (*roztrząsać*) go* into; ~**liwy** *adj* penetrating

wnios|ek *m* (*wynik*) conclusion; (*propozycja*) motion; ~**kodawca** *m* mover; ~**kować ⟨wy-⟩** infer, conclude (**z** from)

wnosić carry in, bring* in; *fig.* submit

wnu|czka *f* granddaughter; ~**k** *m* grandson

woalka *f* veil

wobec *prp* in view of, considering; *kogoś*: towards; ~ **tego** in that case

woda *f* water

wodo|ciąg *m* waterworks *sg*, *pl*; ~**lot** *m* hydroplane; ~**odporny** *adj* waterproof; ~**rost** *m* seaweed; ~**spad** *m* waterfall; falls *pl*; ~**szczelny** *adj* waterproof, watertight; ~**trysk** *m* fountain; ~**wać** *mar.* launch; *aer.* land on the water; *pojazd kosmiczny* splash down

wodór *m* hydrogen

wojenny *adj* war ..., martial

województwo *n* voivodship; province

woj|na *f* war; ~**na domowa** civil war; ~**owniczy** *adj* militant, belligerent; ~**ownik** *m* warrior; ~**sko** *n* army, the military, troops *pl*, the forces *pl*; ~**skowy 1.** *adj* military; **2.** *m* serviceman, soldier

wokoło → **wkoło**

wol|a *f* will; **siła** *f* ~**i** willpower; ~**eć** prefer (*coś od czegoś* s.th. to s.th.)

wolno 1. *adv* slow(ly); **2.** *pred:* **czy ~?** may I?

wolnocłowy *adj* duty-free

wolnorynkowy *adj* market ...

woln|ość *f* freedom, liberty; ~**ość słowa/wyznania** freedom of speech/religion; ~**y** *adj* free; (*powolny*) slow

woła|ć ⟨za-⟩ cry (out), call out; ~**nie** *n* cry, call

wołow|ina *f* beef; ~**y** *adj* beef

woń *f* fragrance

wore|czek *m* bag, pouch; ~**czek żółciowy** *med.* gall bladder; ~**k** *m* sack, bag

wosk *m* wax; ~**ować** *v* wax

wotum *n:* ~ **zaufania** vote of confidence

wozić transport, carry; **wózkiem:** cart

woźnica *m* carter; *powozu:* coachman

woźny *m* caretaker *Brt.*, janitor *Am.*

wódka *f* vodka
...

wódz m chief; (*przywódca*) leader

wół m ox

wór m sack

wóz m cart; *kryty*: wagon; F (*samochód*) car; **~ek** m barrow, cart; *dziecinny*: pram *Brt.*, baby buggy *Am.*: *spacerowy*: pushchair *Brt.*, stroller *Am.*; *inwalidzki*: wheelchair

wpadać fall* in(to)/down; *rzeka*: flow into

wpajać inculcate, instil

wpakow|ywać stuff into; **~ się w kłopoty** get* into trouble

wpaść pf → wpadać

wpat|rywać ⟨~rzeć⟩ się stare (**w** at)

wpędz|ać ⟨~ić⟩ drive* in; *on mnie ~ i do grobu fig.* he will be the death of me

wpierw adv first

wpi|nać ⟨~ąć⟩ pin on

wpis m record, registration; **~owe** n fee; **~(yw)ać** register, record

wpła|cać ⟨~cić⟩ pay (in); **~ta** f deposit, payment

wpław adv: *przepłynąć rzekę ~* to swim a river

wpływ m influence, impact; *a. tech.* effect; **~ać ⟨~nąć⟩** influence (**na coś** s.th.); *statek*: put in; *poczta*: arrive; **~owy** adj influential

wpoić pf → wpajać

wpół adv (in) half; **~ do drugiej** half past one; *objąć kogoś ~* hold* s.o. round the waist; *zgiąć się ~* bend* double

wprawa f skill, practice

wprawdzie adv admittedly, to be sure

wpraw|i(a)ć *szybę* fix into; **~i(a)ć się** practise, train; **~ny** adj skilful

wprost adv straight; (*bezpośrednio*) directly; (*bez ogródek*) outright

wprowadz|ać ⟨~ić⟩ show in, usher; (*wsuwać*) introduce (**do** into); **~ić się** move (**do** into); **~enie** n introduction

wpu|szczać ⟨~ścić⟩ let* in, admit

wracać return, come*/get* back; **~ do domu** return home

wrak m wreck, wreckage

wrastać grow* in

wraz adv (**z**) with, along with

wrażenie n impression

wrażliw|ość f sensitivity; **~y** adj sensitive (**na** to)

wredny F adj mean, wicked

wreszcie adv at last, eventually, finally

wręcz adv outright; **~ prze- ciwnie** on the contrary; → *walka*

wręcz|ać ⟨~yć⟩ hand (in), present (**komuś coś** s.o. with s.th.)

wrodzony adj innate, inborn

wrogi adj hostile; *a. mil.* enemy ...

wrona f crow

wrosnąć pf → wrastać

wrotk|i *pl* roller skates *pl*; **~arz** *m* roller skater
wróbel *m* sparrow
wrócić *pf* → **wracać**
wróg *m* enemy
wróż|ba *f* omen, augury; **~ka** *f* (*czarodziejka*) fairy; (*kabalarka*) fortune-teller; **~yć ⟨po-⟩** tell fortunes, predict
wrzas|k *m* scream, shriek; **~nąć** *pf* → **wrzeszczeć**
wrzawa *f* uproar
wrzą|cy *adj* boiling; **~tek** *m* boiling water
wrze|ć boil; *fig. walka*: rage; **~nie** *n* boil; *fig.* ferment
wrzesień *m* September
wrzeszczeć scream, shriek, yell
wrzos *m* heather; **~owisko** *n* heath, moor
wrzód *m* ulcer
wrzuca|ć ⟨~ić⟩ throw* in(to)
wsadz|ać ⟨~ić⟩ put* (in)
wscho|dni *adj* east(ern); *wiatr, kierunek*: easterly; **~dzić** *słońce*: rise*; *ziarno*: germinate
wschód *m* east; 2 the Orient; **Bliski/Środkowy/Daleki** 2 the Near/Middle/Far East; **~ słońca** sunrise
wsi|adać ⟨~ąść⟩ get* on; *do samolotu itp.*: board; *na konia*: mount
wsiąk|ać ⟨~nąć⟩ soak, sink* in
wskaz|ać ⟨~ywać⟩: **~ania** *pl med.* indications *pl*; *tech.* readings *pl*; **~any** *adj*

advisable, desirable; **~ówka** *f* clue; *zegara*: hand; **~ywać** point out, show; (*świadczyć*) indicate
wskaźnik *m* indicator; index
wskoczyć *pf* → **wskakiwać**
wskutek *prp* as a result of, through; **~ tego** therefore
wspaniał|omyślny *adj* generous; **~y** *adj* splendid
wsparcie *n* support
wspiąć się *pf* → **wspinać się**
wspierać support
wspina|czka *f* mountaineering, mountain climbing; **~ć się** climb (*na górę* a mountain)
wspom|inać ⟨~nieć⟩ remember; (*wzmiankować*) mention (*o czymś* s.th.); **~niany** in question; **~nienie** *n* memory
wspólnie *adv* together
wspóln|iczka *f* (**~ik** *m*) partner; **~ota** *f* community, fellowship; (*organizacja*) commonwealth; **2ta Europejska** the European Community, EC; **~y** *adj* common, joint; **2y Rynek** the Common Market
współczesn|ość *f* the present day; **~y** *adj* contemporary, present-day
współczu|cie *n* sympathy, compassion; **~ć** sympathize (*komuś* with s.o.)
współczynnik *m* coefficient
współdziałanie *n* cooperation
współlokator *m* roommate

współprac|a f collaboration, cooperation; **~ować** collaborate, cooperate; **~ownik** m collaborator, co-worker

współudział m participation

współwłaściciel m joint owner, co-owner

współzawodni|ctwo n competition; **~k** m competitor

współżycie n coexistence

wsta(wa)ć z łóżka: get* up; z krzesła: stand* up

wstawi|(a)ć put* in, insert; **~(a)ć się** stand up (za for), intercede (za for); **~ennictwo** n intercession; **~ony** F adj drunk, plastered F

wstąpić pf → **wstępować**

wstążka f ribbon

wstecz adv back(wards); **~ny** adj retrograde; **bieg** m **~ny** reverse (gear)

wstęga f band, ribbon

wstęp m admission, admittance; (wprowadzenie) preface; **~ny** adj preliminary, introductory; **artykuł** m **~ny** editorial, leader Brt.; **egzamin** m **~ny** entrance examination; **~ować** do sklepu: call by; z wizytą: call on; (dołączać) join (do czegoś s.th.)

wstręt m repugnance, disgust; **~ny** adj repugnant, disgusting

wstrząs m shock; **~ać** ⟨**~nąć**⟩ shake*

wstrzemięźliwy adj moderate, restrained; w jedzeniu itp.: abstemious

wstrzyk|iwać ⟨**~nąć**⟩ inject

wstrzym(yw)ać hold* up, suspend; **~ się** refrain; od głosu: abstain

wsty|d m shame; **~dliwy** adj shy, bashful; **~dzić się** be ashamed (za of)

wsu|wać ⟨**~nąć**⟩ slip into, slide into

wsyp(yw)ać pour into

wszcz|ynać ⟨**~ąć**⟩ institute, start

wszechmocny adj omnipotent, all-powerful, almighty

wszechstronny adj versatile; comprehensive

wszechświat m universe

wszechwiedzący adj omniscient

wszelki adj every (possible), all (sorts of); **~mi siłami** by every possible means

wszerz adv across, crosswise; **wzdłuż i ~** all over

wszędzie adv everywhere

wszyscy pl all, everybody

wszystk|ie (**~ka, ~ko, ~kie** pl) adj all; **~ko** n all, everything; **przede ~kim** first of all

wścibski adj nosy

wście|kać ⟨**~c⟩ się** F go* mad, fly* into a rage; **~klizna** f rabies (pl.); **~kłość** f rage, fury; **~kły** adj furious

wśród prp among

wtajemnicz|ać ⟨**~yć**⟩ initiate (w into); **~ony** adj initiate

wtargnąć force an entry; (najechać) invade

wtedy then

wtem adv suddenly, all of a sudden

wt∥aczać ⟨~oczyć⟩ force into, cram into

wtorek m Tuesday

wtór∥ny adj secondary; ~y adj: **po raz ~y** for the second time; **po ~e** secondly

wtrąc∥ać ⟨~ić⟩ uwagę put* in; do więzienia: cast; ~ać się interfere; do rozmowy: put* in, cut* in

wtrys∥kiwać ⟨~nąć⟩ inject

wty∥czka f electr. plug; ~kać stick, push into

wuj(ek) m uncle

wulgarny adj vulgar

wulkan m volcano; ~izować ⟨z-⟩ vulcanize

ww∥ozić ⟨~ieźć⟩ bring* in; import; ~óz m import(ation)

wy pron you

wybacz∥ać ⟨~yć⟩ forgive*; ~alny adj pardonable; ~enie n forgiveness

wybaw∥ca m, ~iciel m saviour; il(a)ć save; eccl. redeem; ~ienie n rescue; eccl. redemption

wybić pf → **wybijać**

wybieg m dla zwierząt: run; (wykręt) excuse, evasion

wybierać select, choose*; osobę elect; ~ się (be* about to) go*, think* of going

wybi∥jać knock out; szybę break*; zegar: strike*; ~tny adj prominent, outstanding

wyblakły adj watery, faded

wyboisty adj rough, bumpy

wybor∥ca m voter; ~czy adj electoral, election ...; ~ny adj exquisite, delicious; ~owy adj choice, select; ~y pl election

wybój m pothole

wybór m choice, selection

wybrać pf → **wybierać**

wybredny adj fussy, fastidious

wybryk m prank; ~ **natury** freak of nature

wybrzeże n coast

wybuch m explosion; wojny: outbreak; ~ać ⟨~nąć⟩ explode; wojna: break* out; ~owy adj explosive

wybujały adj roślina: rank, rampant

wyceni∥ać price, estimate

wychodzić leave* (**z pokoju** the room), go* out (**z pokoju** of the room); książka: come* out; w kartach: lead*; okno itp.: face (**na ogród** the garden); ~ **za mąż** get* married

wychow∥ać pf → **wychowywać**; ~anek m ⟨~anica f⟩ ward; ~anie n upbringing, education; (ogłada) breeding; ~any adj: **dobrze ~any** well-bred, well-mannered; **źle ~any** ill-bred; ~awca m tutor; klasy: form master Brt.; ~awczyni f (female) tutor; klasy: form mistress Brt.; ~ywać bring* up, raise, rear; ~ywać się grow* up

wychyl|ać ⟨~ić⟩ put*/stick* out; *kieliszek* toss off; ~**ać się** lean out

wyciąć *pf* → **wycinać**

wyciąg *m* (*ekstrakt*, *wypis*) extract; *z konta*: statement; ~ **krzesełkowy** chair lift; ~**ać** ⟨~**nąć**⟩ pull out, extract; ~**ać się**/~**nąć się** stretch

wycie *n* howl

wyciec *pf* → **wyciekać**

wycieczk|a *f* trip, outing, excursion; ~**owicz** F *m* tripper

wyciek *m* leak(age); ~**ać** leak

wycier|aczka *f* doormat; *mot.* windscreen wiper; ~**ać** *nogi, nos* wipe; *gumką*: erase

wycię|cie *n* notch; (*dekolt*) neckline; ~**nać** cut* out, notch; *drzewa* cut* down, fell; ~**nanka** *f* cut-out; ~**nek** *m* segment, section; ~**nkowy** *adj* fragmentary

wycis|kać ⟨~**nąć**⟩ (*wyży-mać*) squeeze, press out; (*od-ciskać*) impress

wycof|(yw)ać withdraw*, retract; ~ **się** retreat, withdraw*; (*rezygnować*) resign

wyczek|(iw)ać expect, await; ~**ujący** *adj* expectant

wyczerp|ać *pf* → **wyczerpy-wać**; ~**anie** *n* exhaustion; ~**any** exhausted; *nakład*: out of print; ~**ujący** *adj* (*dokładny*) exhaustive; (*męczący*) exhausting; ~**ywać** *a. fig.* exhaust; ~**ywać się** (*kończyć się*) run* out

wyczu|(wa)ć sense; ~**walny** *adj* palpable

wyczyn *m* feat, achievement, performance; ~**owiec** *m* top athlete, professional, pro F; ~**owy** *adj* professional, competitive; *sport m* ~**owy** competitive sport

wyczyścić *pf* → **czyścić**

wyć howl

wydać *pf* → **wydawać**

wydaj|ność *f* productivity, efficiency; ~**ny** *adj* productive, efficient

wyda|lać ⟨~**lić**⟩ expel; ~**le-nie** *n* expulsion

wyda|nie *n książki*: edition; *na ~nie panna*: marriageable

wydarz|ać ⟨~**yć**⟩ **się** happen, occur; ~**enie** *n* event

wydat|ek *m* expense; ~**kować** *form.* expend

wydatny *adj* (*wystający*) prominent; (*znaczny*) considerable

wyda|wać *pieniądze* spend*; *wyrok* pass; (*zdradzać*) give* away; ~**wać się** appear, seem; ~**je** (*mi*) **się** it seems (to me); ~**wca** *m* publisher; ~**wnictwo** *n* (*instytucja*) publishing house; (*dzieło*) publication; ~**wniczy** *adj* publishing ...

wydech *m* exhalation, expiration; ~**owy** *adj*: *rura f* ~**owa** exhaust (pipe)

wydłuż|ać ⟨~**yć**⟩ lengthen, extend

wydma *f* dune

wydoby|cie *n* extraction; **~(wa)ć** extract, mine; **~(wa)ć się** *gaz*: escape

wydosta(wa)ć extricate; **~ się** extricate o.s.

wydra *f* otter

wydrąży|ć hollow; *jabłko* core

wydruk *m komputerowy*: print-out; **~ować** print out

wydrzeć *pf* → **wydzierać**

wydział *m* department; *uniwersytetu*: faculty; **~owy** *adj* departmental; *univ.* faculty ...

wydziel|ać ⟨**~ić**⟩ *zapach*: give off; *biol.* secrete; **~anie** *n* secretion; **~ina** *f* secretion

wydzierać tear* out; *włosy a.* pluck

wydzierżawi(a)ć lease out

wydrzeć *pf* → **wydzierać**

wydźwięk *m* undertone

wyga *m* F old hand

wygad|ać *pf* ⟨*wyjawić*⟩ blurt out, give* away; **~any** *adj* wordy, verbose

wyganiać *bydło* drive*/chase away; ⟨*wyrzucać*⟩ kick out, turn out

wyga|sać ⟨**~snąć**⟩ go* out; *fig.* die out; **~szać** ⟨**~sić**⟩ put* out; **~sły** *adj* extinct

wygi|ęty *adj* bent; **~nać** ⟨**~ąć**⟩ (się) bend*

wyginąć *pf* become* extinct, perish

wygląd *m* appearance, looks *pl*; **~ać** *przez okno*: look out; *(mieć określony wygląd)* look (like)

wygładz|ać ⟨**~ić**⟩ smooth out/down, plane

wygłaszać **~osić** *opinię* express; *wykład, mowę* deliver

wygłupi(a) się F play the fool, fool about/around

wygni|atać ⟨**~eść**⟩ squeeze; *ciasto* knead; **~eść się** become* crumpled

wygod|a *f fizyczna*: comfort; *(udogodnienie)* convenience; **~ny** *adj* comfortable

wygoić *pf* heal (up/over)

wygonić *pf* → **wyganiać**

wygórowany *adj* excessive, exorbitant

wygra|ć *pf* → **wygrywać**; **~na** *f* winnings *pl*, prize; *(zwycięstwo)* victory

wygrażać threaten; shake* one's fist

wygrywać win*

wygwizd(yw)ać boo, hiss

wyhodować *zwierzę* breed*; *roślinę* grow*

wyjaśni(a)ć explain; **~(a)ć się** become* clear; **~enie** *n* explanation

wyjawi(a)ć reveal

wyjazd *m (odjazd)* departure; *(podróż)* travel, journey

wyjąć *pf* → **wyjmować**

wyjąkać stammer

wyjąt|ek *m* exception; **~ek od reguły** exception to the rule; **z ~kiem** *Johna* with the exception of John, except for John; **~kowo** *adv* exceptionally, for once F; **~kowy**

exceptional; **stan** m **~kowy** state of emergency

wyje|żdżać ⟨~chać⟩ leave*, go*; (*wydostawać się*) come*/drive* out (**z** from)

wyjmować take* out (**z** of)

wyjrzeć pf → **wyglądać**

wyjści|e n exit; (*sposób*) way out; **punkt** m **~a** point of departure; **~owy** adj exit ...; (*początkowy*) initial

wyjść pf → **wychodzić**

wykałaczka f toothpick

wykańczać finish (off); F (*zabić*) finish off

wykaz m register, list; **~(yw)ać** (*udowadniać*) prove; (*przejawiać*) show, display; (*~yw)ać się** show

wykąpać pf bath; ~ **się** have* a bath Brt., bathe Am.

wykipieć pf boil over

wykl|inać ⟨~ąć⟩ curse; eccl. excommunicate

wyklucz|ać ⟨~yć⟩ exclude (**z** from)

wykład m lecture; **~ać** lay* out, display; (*nauczać*) lecture; **tapetą**: cover; **kamieniami**: pave; **~owca** m lecturer

wykładzina f **podłogowa**: fitted carpet, wall-to-wall carpeting

wykon|ać pf → **wykonywać**; **~alny** adj feasible; **~anie** n execution; a. mus. performance; **~awca** m **utworu**: performer; **testamentu**: executor; **~awczy** adj executive;

~ywać pracę carry out; **wyrok** execute (**na kimś** s.o.); mus. perform

wykończ|yć pf → **wykańczać**; **~enie** n finish

wykop m ditch, excavation; **~ać** pf → **wykopywać**; **~alisko** n excavation; **~ywać** excavate

wykorzeni|a⟨ć⟩ fig. root out

wykorzyst|(yw)ać use, utilize; fig. exploit; **~anie** n utilization

wykraczać exceed, go* beyond; jur. transgress (*przeciw czemuś* s.th.)

wykre|s m graph, chart, diagram; **~ślać ⟨~ślić⟩** draw*; (*skreślać*) cross out

wykrę|cać ⟨~cić⟩ screw off; **rękę** twist; (*wyżymać*) wring*; **~cać się** F (*wywijać się*) wriggle out; (*unikać*) shirk (**od czegoś** s.th.); **~t** m excuse, evasion; **~tny** adj evasive

wykrocz|enie n offence; **~yć** pf → **wykraczać**

wykrój m pattern

wykrwawi|a⟨ć⟩ się bleed* to death

wykry|cie n detection; **~(wa)ć** detect

wykrztusić pf stammer out

wykrzyk|iwać shout; **~nik** m exclamation mark Brt., exclamation point Am.

wykrzywi|a⟨ć⟩ twist, crook; **twarz** distort, contort

wykształc|ać ⟨~ić⟩ educate;

~enie n education; **~ony** adj educated

wykwalifikowany adj skilled

wykwintny adj exquisite, refined

wylać pf → **wylewać**

wylatywać fly* out; F fig. z pracy: get* the sack F; → **odlatywać**

wylądować pf land

wylecieć pf → **wylatywać**

wyleczyć pf cure; **~ się** be* cured (**z** of)

wylegitymować check (**kogoś** s.o.'s papers); **~ się** identify o.s., prove one's identity

wylew m outflow, overflow; med. h(a)emorrhage; **~ać** pour out/away; (rozlewać) spill; **~ać** overflow

wyliczać ⟨**~yć**⟩ enumerate

wylot m → **odlot**; m outlet, mouth; lufy: muzzle; **na ~** fig. inside out

wyludnienie n depopulation

wyład|ow(yw)ać unload; **~unek** m unloading

wyłam(yw)ać break* off; drzwi break* open

wyłaniać się loom, appear

wyławiać fish* out

wyłącz|ać ⟨**~yć**⟩ switch off, turn off, shut* off; (eliminować) exclude; **~nik** m switch; **~ny** adj sole, only

wyło|nić się pf → **wyłaniać się**; **~wić** ⟨pf → **wyławiać**; **~żyć** pf → **wykładać**

wyłu|dzać ⟨**~dzić**⟩ swindle (coś od kogoś s.o. out of s.th.)

wymaga|ć require, demand; **~jący** adj demanding, exacting; **~nie** n demand, requirement

wymarły adj extinct

wymawiać dźwięki pronounce; pracę dismiss (komuś s.o.)

wymiana f exchange

wymiar m dimension, size; **~ sprawiedliwości** dispensation of justice

wymiatać sweep* (out)

wymien|i(a)ć exchange; (zastępować) replace; (przytaczać) mention; **~ny** adj exchangeable, interchangeable, replaceable; **handel** m **~nny** barter

wymierać die out; gatunek itp.: become* extinct

wymie|rny adj measurable; **~rzać** ⟨**~rzyć**⟩ measure; karę administer; broń level (**w** at), aim (**w** at)

wymię n udder

wymig(iw)ać się shirk (od czegoś s.th.)

wymijać ⟨**~nąć**⟩ → **mijać**

wymiot|ować ⟨**z-**⟩ vomit, throw* up, be* sick Brt.; **~y** pl vomiting

wymknąć się steal* out

wymogi pl requirements pl

wymow|a f pronunciation; **~ny** adj spojrzenie itp.: meaning ...

wymóc extort (*coś na kimś* s.th. from s.o.)

wymów|ić *pf* → **wymawiać**; **~ienie** *n* (*zwolnienie*) notice; **~ka** *f* excuse

wymrzeć *pf* → **wymierać**

wymu|szać ⟨**~sić**⟩ *pf* → **wymóc**; **~szony** *adj* uśmiech: constrained

wymysł *m* invention; **~ślać** *v/i* (*ubliżać*) abuse; *v/t* ⟨**~ślić**⟩ *coś nowego* invent; *historię itp.* make* up; **~ślny** *adj* elaborate, ingenious

wynagr|adzać ⟨**~odzić**⟩ reward; *stratę* compensate, make* up for; **~odzenie** *n* pay

wynaj|ąć *pf* → **wynajmować**; **~em** *m*, **~ęcie** *n* hire; **do ~ęcia** to let, for hire; **~mować** (*brać w najem*) hire, rent; (*oddawać w najem*) hire out, let*

wynalaz|ca *m* inventor; **~ek** *m* invention

wynieść *pf* → **wynosić**

wynik *m* result, outcome; **~ać** ⟨**~nąć**⟩ result (*z* from); *z tego ~a że ...* it follows from this that ...

wyniosły *adj* (*wysoki*) towering; (*dumny*) haughty

wyniszcz|ać ⟨**~yć**⟩ devastate; **~ony** *adj osoba*: emaciated

wynosić *v/t* carry out, remove; (*utworzyć sumę*) amount to

wynotow(yw)ać note

wynurz|ać ⟨**~yć**⟩ *się z wody*: surface; (*ukazywać się*) emerge

wyobra|źnia *f* imagination; **~żać** ⟨**~zić**⟩ (*przedstawiać*) represent; **~żać sobie** imagine; **~żenie** *n* representation; (*mniemanie*) notion, idea

wyodrębni(a)ć separate, isolate

wyolbrzymi(a)ć magnify

wypa|czać ⟨**~czyć**⟩ *a. fig.* warp

wypad *m a. mil.* sortie

wypa|dać fall* out; *gwiazdka ~a w niedzielę* Christmas falls on a Sunday; (*nie*) *~a* it is (not) fitting/proper/becoming; **~ek** *m* event, incident; **~ek drogowy** road accident; *na wszelki ~ek* just in case

wypa|sać ⟨**~ść**⟩ graze, pasture

wypaść *pf* → **wypadać**

wypa|trywać look out (*kogoś* for s.o.); **~trzyć** *pf* → **wypatrywać**

wypchnąć *pf* → **wypychać**

wypełni(a)ć fill in; (*spełniać*) fulfil

wypę|dzać ⟨**~dzić**⟩ drive* out, turn out

wypić *pf* → **wypijać**

wypierać oust; **~ się** deny

wypijać drink* (up)

wypis *m* extract; **~(yw)ać** write* out

wyplatać weave

wypła|**cać** ⟨**~cić**⟩ pay; **~calny** adj solvent; **~ta** f pay

wypły|**wać** ⟨**~nąć**⟩ sail out; *rzeka*: rise*; (*wynurzać się*) surface, emerge

wypoczą|**ć** pf → **wypoczywać**

wypocz|**ynek** m rest; **~wać** rest

wypo|**gadzać** ⟨**~godzić**⟩ **się** clear up

wypo|**minać** ⟨**~mnieć**⟩ reproach (**komuś coś** s.o. for s.th.)

wyposa|**żać** ⟨**~żyć**⟩ equip, provide (**w** with); **~enie** n equipment

wypowi|**adać** ⟨**~edzieć**⟩ express; announce (*coś* cancel; **komuś pracę** give* s.o. notice; **~adać wojnę** declare war (**komuś** on s.o.); **~adać się** express one's opinion; **~edzenie** n utterance; (*zwolnienie*) notice; **~edź** f statement

wypożycz|**ać** ⟨**~yć**⟩ (*dawać*) lend*, hire (out); (*brać*) borrow, hire; **~alnia** f rental service; **~alnia f książek** lending library

wypracow|**anie** n composition, essay; **~(yw)ać** work out

wypraszać obtain by imploring; **~ć kogoś z pokoju** show s.o. the door; **~m sobie takie traktowanie** I won't stand for that sort of treatment

wyprawa f expedition

wyprawi(a)ć send; *przyjęcie* arrange, give*; *skórę* tan

wyprodukować produce, make*

wyprosić pf → **wypraszać**

wyprostow|**(yw)ać** → **prostować**; straighten (**się** up)

wyprowadz|**ać** ⟨**~ić**⟩ take* out, bring* out; **~ać ⟨~ić⟩ się** move

wypróbowany adj tried, tested

wypróżni(a)ć clear out, empty; **~ się** defecate

wyprzeda|**(wa)ć** sell* off; **~ż** f sale

wyprzedz|**ać** ⟨**~ić⟩** *biegnąc, a. fig.* outstrip; *samochodem:* overtake*

wypukły adj convex

wypu|**szczać** ⟨**~ścić⟩** drop; (*uwolnić*) let* out; *płytę itp.* release; **~ść** → **puszczać**; *zwierzę* stuff

wypychać *za drzwi:* push out; *zwierzę* stuff

wypyt(yw)ać question, interrogate

wyrabiać produce, make*

wyrachowany adj calculating, mercenary

wyrast|**ać** grow* (**na kogoś** into s.o.); *z czegoś itp.* grow* out (**z czegoś** of s.th.), outgrow* (**z czegoś** s.th.)

wyra|**z** m (**obcy** loan-) word; **~zić** pf → **wyrażać**; **~zisty** adj expressive; (*wyraźny*) clear-cut, distinct; **~źny** adj

distinct, clear; **~żać** express; **~żać się** speak* **(dobrze/źle o kimś** well/ill o s.o.); **~żenie** n expression, phrase
wyręcz|ać ⟨**~yć**⟩ *kogoś* help s.o. out
wyrobi|ć pf → **wyrabiać;** **~enie** n experience; *towarzyskie:* urbanity
wyrok m verdict; **~ skazujący** sentence; **~ uniewinniający** acquittal; **~ować** ⟨**~** pf (-)ware; **~oby ze srebra** silverware
wyros|nąć pf → **wyrastać; ~t** m: **na ~t** *ubranie:* meant to be grown into; *plany:* allowing for future modifications; **~tek** m stripling, youngster; *anat.* appendix
wyrośnięty adj overgrown
wyrozumiały adj lenient, forbearing; **~ość** f lenience, forbearance
wyr|ób m product; *rolniczy:* produce; **~oby** pl (-)ware; **~oby ze srebra** silverware
wyrówn|anie n compensation, equalization; *sp.* equalizer; **~(yw)ać** a. *sp.* equalize
wyróżni|(a)ć favour; (*rozróżniać*) distinguish; **~enie** n distinction
wyrusz|ać ⟨**~yć**⟩ set* off/out
wyr|wa f w murze: breach; w ziemi: crater; **~(y)wać** tear* out, pull (*coś z czegoś* s.th. out of s.th.); *zęby:* extract; **~(y)wać się** wrench free/away
wyrzą|dzać ⟨**~dzić**⟩ *zło, szkodę* do

wyrzec pf form. (*powiedzieć*) say*; **~** n sacrifice
wyrzeczenie n sacrifice
wyrze|kać ⟨**~c**⟩ **się** renounce, relinquish
wyrzu|cać ⟨**~cić**⟩ throw* away; *z domu itp.:* turn out; *ze szkoły itp.:* expel; F (*zwolnić*) sack F; (*robić wyrzuty*) reproach (*komuś coś* s.o. with s.th.); **~t** m (*rzut*) throw; (*zarzut*) reproach; **~ty ~ż sumienia** remorse, qualms pl, pangs pl of conscience; **~tnia** f launching pad, launcher
wyrzyna|ć cut* out, carve out; F (*zabijać*) massacre, slaughter; **~ć się: ~ją mu się zęby** he is cutting his teeth
wyrżnąć pf → **wyrzynać;** F bang
wysa|dzać ⟨**~dzić**⟩ pasażerów put* down; *most itp.* blow up
wysepka f islet; *na jezdni:* traffic island
wysi|adać ⟨**~ąść**⟩ z samochodu: get* out; z pociągu itp.: get* off; form. alight
wysied|lać ⟨**~lić**⟩ displace
wysi|lać ⟨**~lić**⟩ strain; **~lać się** exert oneself; **~łek** m effort
wys|kakiwać ⟨**~koczyć**⟩ jump/leap out
wysłać pf → **wysyłać, wyściełać; ~annik** m (**~anniczka** f) envoy, emissary
wysł|awiać ⟨**~owić**⟩ **się** express o.s.

wysłu|ga f: ~**ga lat** seniority; ~**żony** adj worn-out

wysmukły adj slender

wyso|ce adv form. highly, extremely; ~**ki** adj high; **człowiek, drzewo**: tall

wysokogórski adj alpine

wysokoprężny adj tech. high-pressure

wysokościomierz m altimeter

wysokościowiec m high-rise building

wysokość f height, altitude

wyspa f island, isle

wyspać się pf get* enough sleep

wysportowany adj sporty

wystający adj protruding, prominent

wystar|czać ⟨~**czyć**⟩ suffice, be* sufficient

wystaw|a f exhibition, display; ~**ać** protrude; ~**ca** m exhibitor; ~**i(a)ć** put* out; exhibit; **thea.** stage; ~**ny** adj sumptuous; ~**owy** adj exhibition ...; **okno** n **owe** shop window

wystąpi|ć pf → **występować**; ~**enie** n speech

występ m performance; skalny: shelf, ledge; ~ **gościnny** guest performance; **posuwać naprzód:** step out; (pojawiać się) occur, be* found; (wypisać się) leave*

wystraszyć pf frighten, scare; ~ **się** be* frightened, be* scared, chicken out F

wystrzał m shot

wystrzegać się beware (**czegoś** of s.th.)

wystrzelić pf fire (**z czegoś** s.th.), shoot*; **rakietę** launch; → **strzelać**

wystrzępić fray

wysuwać put* out, draw* out; **pomysł itp.** propose

wysyłać send*, dispatch; ~**ka** f dispatching

wysyłać pf → **wysyłać**

wysypiać się sleep* late

wysyp|ka f rash; ~**ywać** pour out, tip out

wyszarp|(yw)ać ⟨~**nąć**⟩ wrench out

wyszukany → **wytworny**; ~**(iw)ać** find*

wyszyć pf → **haftować**

wyszydzać jeer

wyszywać → **haftować**

wyście|lić pf, ~**łać** stuff, upholster

wyścig m race; ~ **zbrojeń** arms race; ~**i** pl **konne** horse race, the races pl; ~**owy** adj racing, race ...

wyśledzić pf track down

wyślizgnąć się pf slip out

wyśmienity adj exquisite

wyśmi(ew)ać mock, poke fun (**kogoś** at s.o.), ridicule (**coś** s.th.); ~ **się** mock, poke fun (**z kogoś** at s.o.)

wyświadcz|ać ⟨~**yć**⟩ **przysługę** render

wyświechtany adj shabby; **zwrot itp.**: hackneyed

wyświetl|ać ⟨~**ić**⟩ **film** show;

(*wyjaśniać*) clear up
wytaczać roll out; *tech.* turn; **~komuś proces** take* s.o. to court
wytapiać *tech.* smelt
wytarty *adj* (*wyświetlany*) shabby, worn-out
wytchnieni|e *n* rest; **chwila** *f* **~a** breathing space; **bez ~a** tirelessly
wytepi(a)ć → *tępić*
wytęż|ać ⟨~yć⟩ strain; **siły** exert; **~ony** *adj* strenuous
wytknąć → **wytykać**
wytł|aczać ⟨~oczyć⟩ *sok itp.* press; → *a. tłoczyć*
wytłumacz|enie *n* explanation; **~yć** explain
wyto|czyć *pf* → **wytaczać**
~pić *pf* → **wytapiać**
wytrawny *adj wino:* dry; *człowiek:* experienced, seasoned
wytrą|cać ⟨~cić⟩ *z ręki itp.:* knock out; **~cać kogoś z równowagi** throw* s.o. off balance
wytrwa|ć *pf* hold* out, endure, persevere; **~łość** *f* perseverance; **~ły** *adj* persevering
wytrych *m* skeleton key
wytrys|k *m* *med.* ejaculation; **~ać ⟨~nąć⟩** → *tryskać*
wytrząs|ać ⟨~nąć⟩ shake* out, empty
wytrzeć *pf* → **wycierać**
wytrzym|ać *pf* → **wytrzymywać**; **~ałość** *f* endurance; *u ludzi, koni:* stamina; *tech.*

strength, resistance; **~ały** *adj* tough; *materiał:* durable; → **wytrwały**; **~ywać** hold* out, stand*, put* up (**coś** with s.th.)
wytw|arzać ⟨~orzyć⟩ make*, produce, manufacture
wytworny *adj* refined, elegant
wytwór *m* product; → *twór*; **~ca** *f* manufacturer, producer; **~czy** *adj* productive; **~nia** *f* factory, plant; **filmowa:** film company
wytycz|ać ⟨~yć⟩ mark out; *palikami:* stake out; **~na** *f* guideline
wytykać reproach (**komuś coś** s.o. for s.th.)
wytypować choose*; (*mianować*) appoint
wywabi|acz *m* (**~acz plam**) stain remover; **~(a)ć plamy** remove
wywal|ać ⟨~ić⟩ chuck out; *z pracy:* fire
wywalcz|ać ⟨~yć⟩ win*, secure
wyważ|ać ⟨~yć⟩ *drzwi* force open; *tech.* balance; *fig.* weigh (up)
wywiad *m* interview; *pol.*, *mil.* intelligence; **~owca** *m* secret agent; **~owczy** *adj* intelligence ...
wywiąz(yw)ać się fulfil (**z czegoś** s.th.)
wywierać wpływ *itp.* exert; **wrażenie** make*
wywie|szać ⟨~sić⟩ post up; **~szka** *f* notice, sign

wywieść pf → **wywodzić**

wywietrz|nik m ventilator; **~yć** air, ventilate

wywieźć pf → **wywozić**

wywij|ać ⟨**~nąć**⟩ (**rękawy** itp.) roll down; (**machać**) wave; **bronią** itp.: brandish; **~jać się** fig. wriggle out

wywodzić się derive, be* descended (**z** from)

wywoła|ć pf → **wywoływać**; **~wczy** adj sygnał: call; **cena**: reserve; **~ywacz** m phot. developer; **~ywać** call out; (**duchy**) call up; (**powodować**) cause, result in; phot. develop

wyw|ozić take* away, remove; F export; **~ozowy** adj export ...; **~óz** m removal, disposal; (**eksport**) export

wywr|acać ⟨**~ócić** (**się**)⟩ → **przewracać** (**się**); **~ótka** f dump(er) truck; F (**upadek**) fall; **~otowy** adj subversive; **~ócić** pf → **wywracać**

wywyższ|ać ⟨**~yć**⟩ **się** give* o.s. airs

wyzby(wa)ć się get* rid (**czegoś** of s.th.), shake off

wyzdrowieć pf recover

wyznać pf → **wyznawać**

wyznacz|ać ⟨**~yć**⟩ mark out; **datę** itp. fix, assign; **osobę** appoint

wyzna|nie n confession; eccl. religion; **~wać** confess; religię profess; **~wca** m believer; (**zwolennik**) adherent

wyzwać pf → **wyzywać**

wyzwala|cz m phot. shutter release; **~ć** liberate

wyzwanie n challenge

wyzwisko n term of abuse

wyzwol|enie n liberation; **~eńczy** adj liberation ...; **~ony** adj liberated

wyzysk m exploitation; **~(iw)ać** exploit; **~iwacz** m exploiter

wyzywa|ć challenge; (**wymyślać komuś**) call s.o. names; **~jący** adj provocative

wyż m high, anticyclone

wyżąć pf → **wyżymać**

wyżej adv comp higher, above; **jak ~** as above; **~ wymieniony** above-mentioned

wyżł|abiać ⟨**~obić**⟩ hollow out; **~obienie** n groove

wyższ|ość f superiority; **~y** adj comp higher; **człowiek**, **budynek**: taller

wyżyć pf survive

wyżyma|czka f wringler; **~ć** wring*

wyżyn|a f upland, uplands pl; **~ny** adj upland ...

wyżywi|ć rodzinę maintain; **~enie** n food, board

wzajemn|ie adv one another, each other, mutually; **~y** adj mutual, reciprocal

wzbog|acać ⟨**~cić**⟩ enrich; **~cić się** get* rich

wzbr|aniać ⟨**~onić**⟩ forbid*; **~aniać się** be* unwilling (**przed czymś** to do s.th.); **~oniony** adj forbidden; pa-

lenie ~onione no smoking

wzbudz|ać ⟨~ić⟩ arouse,
awake; *zainteresowanie a.* excite

wzburz|enie *n* ferment, unrest; ~ony *adj* agitated; *morze*: rough, heavy; ~yć agitate, perturb

wzdłuż *adv* lengthways; *prp* along

wzdrygnąć się start

wzdychać sigh

wzdymać się puff out;
brzuch: distend; *żagle*: swell* (out)

wzejść *pf* → **wschodzić**

wzgard|a *f* disdain, contempt; ~dzać ⟨~dzić⟩ disdain, scorn

wzgl|ąd *m* regard, consideration; ~ędy *pl (powody)* reasons *pl*; **pod każdym** ~**ędem** in every respect; ~**ędnie** *adv* relatively, comparatively; ~**ędny** *adj* relative

wzgó|rek *m* hillock, hummock, mound; ~rze *n* hill

wziąć *pf* → **brać**

wzię|cie *n (popularność)* popularity; ~ty *adj* popular

wzmacnia|cz *m* amplifier; ~ć strengthen, reinforce;
dźwięk amplify

wzmagać (się) intensify

wzmianka *f* mention

wzmocnić *pf* → **wzmacniać**

wzmożony *adj* intensive, increasing

wzmóc *pf* → **wzmagać**

wznak *adv*: **na** ~ on one's back

wznawiać resume; *thea. itp.* revive

wzn|iesienie *n* hill, height; ~**ieść** *pf* → **wznosić**; ~**iosły** *adj* lofty, high-sounding; ~**osić** raise, lift; *toast* propose; ~**osić się** rise

wznowi|ć *pf* → **wznawiać**; ~**enie** *n* revival

wzorcowy *adj* model, standard

wzorow|ać się imitate (**na** *czymś* s.th.), pattern o.s. (**na** upon); ~**y** *adj* exemplary

wzór *m* pattern; model; *math., chem.* formula

wzrastać grow* up

wzrok *m* eyesight; *(spojrzenie)* gaze

wzro|snąć *pf* → **wznosić**; ~**t** *m* height; *cen itp.*: rise

wzrusz|ać move, touch; *ramionami*: shrug; ~**ający** *adj* moving, touching; ~**enie** *n* emotion; *ramionami*: shrug; ~**yć** *pf* → **wzruszać**

wzwyż *adv* up, upwards; → **skok**

wzywać call, summon

Z

z, ze *prp* punkt wyjścia: from; ~ **Londynu** from London; *punkt wyjścia* a.: off; **spaść** ~ **krzesła** fall off the chair; *przyczyna*: out of; ~ **ciekawości** out of curiosity; *towarzyszenie*: with; ~ **tobą** with you; ~ **przyjmnością** with pleasure; *(około)* about, more or less; ~ **godzinę** about an hour; ~ **lekka** slightly; ~ **nazwiska** by name; ~ **widzenia** by sight

za 1. *prp* miejsce: behind, beyond; ~ **nami** behind us; ~ **górami** beyond the mountains; *czas*: in; ~ **2 tygodnie** in two weeks' time; *(podczas)* during; ~ **panowania** during the reign of; kolejność: after; ~ **moich czasów** during my time; kolejność: after; ~ **jeden** – **drugim** one after another; ~ **stołem** at table; ~ **pomocą** by means of; ~ **rękę** by the hand; ~ **rogiem** round the corner; **2.** *adv* too; ~ **młody** too young

zaawansowany *adj* advanced

zabarwienie *n* colour, tinge

zabaw|a *f* game, play; *(impreza)* party; ~ **a taneczna** dance; **~i(a)ć** entertain; **~i(a)ć się** amuse o.s.; **~ka** *f* toy; **~ny** *adj* funny, amusing

zabezpiecz|ać ⟨**~yć**⟩ se-

cure; **~enie** *n (ochrona)* protection **(przed** against); *(gwarancja)* security; **~ony** *adj* secured

zabić *pf* → **zabijać**

zabieg *m med. (minor)* surgery; *pl (starania)* efforts *pl*; **~ać** *court (o coś* s.th.)

zabierać take* away; *czas itp.* take* up; ~ **głos** take* the floor; ~ **się** begin* **(do czegoś** to do s.th.), set* about **(do czegoś** doing s.th.)

zabij|ać ⟨**się**⟩ kill (o.s.); **~aka** *m* thug; **~ty** *adj* dead, killed

zabłą|dzić *pf* **~kać się** *pf* get* lost, stray; **~kany** *adj* stray

zabobonny *adj* superstitious

zabor|ca *m* invader; **~czy** *adj* greedy

zabój|ca *m* killer; **~czy** *adj* lethal; **~stwo** *n* murder; *jur.* manslaughter; *form.* homicide

zab|ór *m* annexation; **~rać** → **zabierać**

zabr|aniać ⟨**~onić**⟩ forbid*, prohibit

zabrudz|ać ⟨**~ić**⟩ dirty

zabudowa *f (budowanie)* building; **~nia** *pl* buildings *pl*; **~ny** *adj*: **teren** *m* **~any** built-up area

zaburzenie *n mst pl* disorder

zabyt|ek m monument; **~ko-wy** adj antique, historical
zachcianka f whim
zachęc|ać ⟨**~cić**⟩ encourage; **~ta** f encouragement
zachłanny adj greedy
zachmurz|yć się pf → **chmurzyć się**, **~ony** adj cloudy, overcast
zacho|dni adj west(ern); *wiatr, kierunek*: westerly; **~dzić** ⟨zdarzać się⟩ set*, go down; ⟨odwiedzać⟩ drop in, call on; ⟨zdarzać się⟩ happen, occur; **~dzić na siebie** overlap; **~dzić w ciążę** become* pregnant
zachorować pf fall* ill, be taken ill (**na** with)
zachow|anie n behaviour; **~(yw)ać** keep, retain; **~(yw)ać się** behave
zachód m west; ♀ the West; *Dziki* ♀ the Wild West; **~ słońca** sunset
zachrypnięty adj hoarse
zachwalać praise
zachwy|cać ⟨**~cić**⟩ delight; **~cać się** be* enchanted (*czymś* by/with s.th.); **~cający** ravishing, delightful; **~t** m delight
zaciąć pf → **zacinać**
zaciąg|ać ⟨**~nąć**⟩ pull, drag; *zasłony* draw*; *pożyczkę* contract; ⟨do wojska⟩: enlist; *dymem* inhale
zaciekawi|ać arouse curiosity; **~enie** n curiosity
zaciekły adj ardent, zealous

zacierać *ślady* cover up; **~ ręce** rub one's hands; **~ się** *silnik*: seize up
zacieśni(a)ć tighten; *fig.* strengthen
zacię|cie n F ⟨uzdolnienie⟩ flair; **~tość** f doggedness; **~ty** adj dogged; *opór*: stiff
zacinać v/t ⟨skaleczyć⟩ cut*; *batem*: whip; v/i *deszcz*: lash; **~ się** cut* (o.s.); *maszyna*: seize up, jam
zacis|k m clamp, clasp; **~kać** ⟨**~nąć**⟩ clamp, clasp; *śrubę itp.* tighten; *zęby* clench
zacisz|e n shelter, nook; *domowe*: privacy; jam; **~ny** adj secluded
zacofan|ie n backwardness; **~y** adj backward
zaczaić się lie* in wait (**na** for)
zaczarowa|ć cast* a spell (*kogoś* over s.o.); **~ny** adj magic
zacząć pf → **zaczynać**
zaczep m catch; **~i(a)ć** attach, hook; F *kogoś* accost; *natarczywie*: pester; **~ny** adj truculent; *broń*: offensive
zaczerp|ywać ⟨**~nąć**⟩ scoop, ladle out; *powietrza*: breathe in, take* a breath
zaczerwienić się redden; *na twarzy* a.: blush
zaczynać (się) begin*, start
zaćmienie n ⟨słońca solar⟩ eclipse
zad m rump
zada|ć pf → **zadawać**; **~nie** n

task; *szkolne:* exercise; *matematyczne:* problem

zadatek *m* deposit, down payment

zadawać give*, assign; *pytanie* ask; *ból itp.* inflict

zadłuż|enie *n* indebtedness; **~ony** *adj* indebted

zadośćuczynić ǁ compensate (**za** for); **~enie** *n (rekompensata)* compensation

zadow|alać satisfy, please, gratify; **~alać się** content o.s. (**czymś** with s.th.); **~alający** *adj* satisfactory; **~olenie** *n* satisfaction; **~olić** *pf* → **zadowalać**; **~olony** *adj* satisfied, pleased, content

zadra *f* splinter; **~p(yw)ać** scratch

zadrzeć *pf* → **zadzierać**

zaduch *m* fustiness, fug F

zaduma *f* thoughtfulness, pensiveness; **~ny** *adj* thoughtful, pensive

Zaduszki *pl* All Souls' Day

zadymka *f* blizzard

zadzierać *v/t* głowę crane; *spódnicę itp.* pull up; **~nosa** put* on airs; *v/i (pokłócić się)* fall* foul (**z kimś** of s.o.)

zadziwi|ać amaze, baffle; **~ający** *adj* amazing

zagadk|a *f* riddle, puzzle; **~owy** *adj* mysterious, puzzling

zagadnienie *n* problem, issue

zagajnik *m* copse, coppice

zagarn|iać ⟨**~ąć**⟩ sweep*;

(przywłaszczać) appropriate

zagę|szczać ⟨**~ścić**⟩ condense, thicken

zagi|ąć *pf* → **zaginać**; **~ęcie** *n* fold; **~nać** bend, crook

zagin|ąć *pf* be* missing; → **przepadać**; **~iony** *adj* missing

zaglądać peep (**do środka** inside); *(odwiedzać)* pop in, drop in (**do kogoś** on s.o.)

zagłada *f* extermination

zagłębi|(a)ć się penetrate, plunge in; *w fotelu:* sink*; *w pracy itp.:* be* absorbed, pore (**w czytaniu** over a book); **~e** *n (węglowe* coal)field; **~enie** *n* depression

zagłówek *m* headrest

zagłusz|ać ⟨**~yć**⟩ drown (out); *tech.* jam

zagmatwany *adj* complicated

zagnie|żdżać ⟨**~ździć⟩ się** nest; *robactwo:* infest

zagoić się heal up/over

zagorzały *adj* fanatic, ardent

zagotować boil; **~ się** boil, start boiling

zagrać *pf* → **grać**

zagrodzić bar, block; *(ogradzać)* fence

zagranic|a *f* foreign countries *pl;* **z ~cy** from abroad; **~czny** *adj* foreign

zagrażać threaten; → **grozić**

zagro|da *f (miejsce ogrodzone)* enclosure; *(gospodarstwo)* farm, farmstead *Am.;* **~dzić** *pf* → **zagradzać**

zagro|zić pf → **zagrażać**; **~żenie** n threat, menace

zagrzać pf → **zagrzewać**

zagrzewać heat (up), warm up; fig. spur

zahacz|ać ⟨~yć⟩ v/t hook; v/i catch; **~yć się** catch*, get* caught

zahamowanie n inhibition

zahartowany adj hardened

zaimek m pronoun

zainteresowan|ie n interest; **~y** adj interested (**czymś** in s.th.)

zajadł|ość f bitterness; **~y** adj bitter, fierce; → **zapamiętały**

zajazd m inn

zając m hare

zająć pf → **zajmować**

zaje|żdżać ⟨~chać⟩ arrive

zajęc|ie n occupation; pl univ. class; **~ty** adj occupied, busy

zajm|ować occupy; **~ować się** occupy o.s. (**czymś** in s.th.), busy o.s. (**czymś** with s.th.); **~ujący** adj interesting

zajrzeć pf → **zaglądać**

zajś|cie n incident, event; **~ć** pf → **zachodzić**

zakamar|ek m recess; **~ki** pl nooks and crannies

zakańczać pf → **kończyć**

zakatarzony adj: **być ~m** have* a cold

zakaz m ban, prohibition; **~ postoju** no parking; **~any** adj forbidden

zaka|zać pf → **zakazać**; **~zić się** be* infected; form. con-

tract (**czymś** s.th.)

zakaz(yw)ać forbid*, prohibit

zaka|źny adj infectious, contagious; **oddział m ~źny** isolation ward; **~żać** infect; **~żenie** n infection; **~żenie krwi** blood poisoning

zakąska f appetizer, hors d'oeuvre; snacks to follow up a glass of vodka

zakątek m nook, corner

zakle|jać ⟨~ić⟩ stick, glue; **kopertę** seal

zaklęcie n incantation; **~ty** adj magic

zaklinać (błagać) entreat; **węże** charm; **~ się** swear*

zakład m (przedsiębiorstwo) enterprise; **produkcyjny**: works sg, pl; (instytucja) institution; (umowa) bet; **~ać** found, establish; **okulary** itp. put* on; (instalować) install; **~ać się** bet; **~ka** f bookmark; **~niczka** f ⟨**~nik** m⟩ hostage; **~owy** adj works ..., company ..., factory ...

zakłamany adj hypocritical

zakłopotan|ie n embarrassment; **~y** adj embarrassed

zakłóc|ać ⟨~ić⟩ disturb; **~enie** n disturbance; pl TV itp. interference

zakochać się fall* in love; **~ny** adj in love (**w kimś** with s.o.)

zakomunikować announce, inform (**coś komuś** s.o. of s.th.)

zakon *m* order; **~nica** *f* nun; **~nik** *m* monk; **~ny** *adj* monastic

zakończ|**yć** *pf* → **kończyć**; **~enie** *n* end, ending

zakop(yw)ać bury

zakorzeni(**a**)**ć się** *a. fig.* take* root

zakra|**dać** ⟨**~ść**⟩ **się** sneak, steal*

zakres *m* scope, range

zakreśl|**ać** ⟨**~ić**⟩ mark; *koło itp.* describe

zakrę|**cać** ⟨**~cić**⟩ *v/t* (*obracać w koło*) turn; *kurek itp.* turn off; *pokrywkę itp.* screw on; *v/i* (*brać zakręt*) turn, take a turning; *droga*: curve; **~t** *m* bend, curve; **~tka** *f* cap

zakrwawiony *adj* bloody, covered with blood

zakryć → **zakrywać**

zakrystia *f* vestry, sacristy

zakrywać cover

zakrztusić się *pf* choke

zakulisowy *adj a. fig.* backstage

zakup *m* purchase; *robić ~y* do* the shopping; **~ywać** ⟨**~ić**⟩ buy*, purchase

zakurzony *adj* dusty

zakwaterowanie *n* lodging(s *pl*); *mil.* billet

zala|**ć** → **zalewać**; **~ny** *adj* F plastered F, sloshed F

załążek *m fig.* germ

zalec|**ać** ⟨**~ić**⟩ recommend; **~ać się** court, woo (*do kogoś* s.o.); **~enie** *n* recommendation

zaledwie *adv* barely, hardly, only just

zaleg|**ać** be* in arrears (*z* with); **~łość** *f mst pl* arrears *pl*; **~ły** *adj* oustanding, overdue

zalepi(**a**)**ć** seal up

zaleta *f* advantage, virtue

zalewać flood, pour over; **~ się** F (*upijać się*) get* plastered; **~ się** *łzami* burst into tears

zależ|**eć** depend (*od kogoś/ czegoś* on s.o./s.th.); *to ~y od ciebie* it's up to you; **~nie** *adv* depending (*od* on); according (*od* to); **~ność** *f* dependance; *~ny adj* dependent (*od* on); *mowa f ~na gr.* reported speech

zalicz|**ać** number (*do* as); **~ać się** number, be* numbered (*do* among); rank (*do* as); **~enie** *n univ.* credit *mst Am.*; *za ~eniem* COD; **~ka** *f* advance; **~yć** *pf* → **zaliczać**

zalotny *adj* flirtatious, coquettish

zaludni(**a**)**ć** populate; *gęsto ~ony* densely populated; **~enie** *n* population

załad|**ow(yw)ać** load; **~unek** *m* loading

załam|**anie** *n światła*: refraction; *~anie nerwowe* nervous breakdown; **~(yw)ać** bend, fold; *phys.* refract; *~(yw)ać ręce* wring* one's hands; **~(yw)ać się** collapse; *fig.* break* down

załatwi|**(a)ć** settle, fix; **~enie** n: **mam coś do ~enia** I have s.th. to attend to

załącz|**ać** ⟨**~yć**⟩ enclose; **~enie** n: **w ~eniu** enclosed; **~nik** m enclosure

załog|**a** f crew; **~owy** adj manned

założ|**enie** n foundation, establishment; (teza) assumption; **~yciel**(**ka** f) m founder; **~yć** pf → **zakładać**

zamach m udany: assassination; attempt (**na czyjeś życie** on s.o.'s life); **~ stanu** coup (d'état); **~owiec** m assassin

zamar|**zać** ⟨**~znąć**⟩ freeze* (over); (umrzeć) freeze* to death

zamaszysty adj sweeping, vigorous

zamawiać order; miejsca, pokój itp. book

zamaz(**yw**)**ać** smear; fig. blur

zamążpójście n (woman's) marriage

zamek m castle; u drzwi: lock; **~ błyskawiczny** zip (fastener) Brt., zipper Am.

zamęcz|**ać** ⟨**~yć**⟩ torment; fig. pester

zamęt m confusion

zamężna adj kobieta: married

zamglony adj hazy, misty

zamian: **~ za** in exchange for; **~a** f exchange

zamiar m intention

zamiast prp instead (**kogoś/ czegoś** of s.o./s.th.)

zamiatać sweep*

zamieć f blizzard

zamiejscow|**y** adj visiting; **rozmowa** f **~a** long-distance call

zamien|**i**(**a**)**ć** exchange; **~ny** adj exchangeable; **części** pl **~ne** spare parts pl, spares pl Brt.

zamierać życie itp.: decay, waste away; dźwięk itp.: die away, fade away

zamierzać intend (**coś robić** to do s.th.)

zamierzchły adj immemorial, ancient

zamie|**rzenie** n intention, **~rzyć** pf → **zamierzać**

zamieszan|**ie** n zamęt: **~y** adj involved (**w coś** in s.th.), mixed up (**w coś** in s.th.)

zamieszcz|**ać** ⟨**umieszczać**⟩: ogłoszenie put* (**do gazety** in a paper)

zamieszk|**ać** pf → **zamieszczać**

zamieszki pl unrest, riot

zamieścić pf → **zamieszczać**

zamiłowan|**ie** n fondness, liking, passion (**do** for); **~y** adj keen

zamkn|**ąć** pf → **zamykać**; **~ięcie** n do drzwi itp.: fastening; zebrania, fabryki itp.: closure; **~ięty** adj closed

zamordować murder

zamorski adj overseas

zamożny adj well-off, affluent

zapewne

zamówi|ć pf → **zamawiać**;
~enie n order

zamraża|ć freeze*; **~rka** f
freezer, deep freeze

zamrozić pf → **zamrażać**

zamrzeć pf → **zamierać**

zamsz m suede; **~owy** adj
suede ...

zamyka|ć (się) close, shut*;
na klucz: lock

zamy|sł m intention; **~ślać**
⟨**~ślić**⟩ intend; **~ślić się** pf
fall* to thinking; **~ślony** adj
thoughtful

zanadto adv too, unduly

zaniechać abandon, drop F

zanieczy|szczać ⟨**~ścić**⟩
wodę, powietrze pollute;
żywność, wodę contaminate

zaniedb(yw)ać neglect

zaniemówić pf become*
speechless, be* struck dumb

zaniepokojenie n concern,
alarm

zanieść pf → **zanosić**

zanik m decay; a. med. atrophy; **~ać** ⟨**~nąć**⟩ decay,
fade; med. atrophy

zanim cj before

zanosić carry, take*; **~ się**
(zapowiadać się) look like,
be* imminent

zanurz|ać ⟨**~yć**⟩ dip; **~ać się**
dip, sink*; łódź podwodna:
submerge; **~enie** n submer-
sion

zaokrąglony adj round,
rounded

zaopat|rywać ⟨**~rzyć**⟩ pro-
vide, supply, stock (up);

~rzenie n supply

zaostrz|ać ⟨**~yć⟩ (się)** shar-
pen

zaoszczędzić pf save

zapach m smell, fragrance

zapad|ać sink*; noc: fall*;
decyzja: be* made; **~ać się**
droga, budynek: subside;
dach: fall* in; **~ły** adj
out-of-the-way, remote; po-
liczki: sunken, hollow

zapal|ać light*; silnik: start;
~ać się light*; catch* fire;
fig. become* enthusiastic
(do about); **~czywy** adj
hot-headed, impetuous;
~enie n med. inflammation;
~ić pf → **zapalać**; **~niczka** f
lighter; **~nik** m fuse; **~ny** adj
inflammable; punkt m **~ny**
trouble spot; **~ony** adj keen

zapał m enthusiasm, keen-
ness, zeal

zapałka f match

zapamięta|ć pf remember,
keep* in mind; **~ły** adj pas-
sionate

zaparz|ać ⟨**~yć⟩** infuse; F
make* (tea, coffee)

zapas m supply, stock; **~y** pl
provisions pl, reserves pl; pl.
wrestling; **~owy** adj spare ...

zapaść 1. f med. collapse; **2.**
pf → **zapadać**

zapaśnik m wrestler

zapatrywa|ć view (na coś
s.th.); **~nie** n view, opinion

zapełni(a)ć fill

zapewne adv form. (chyba)
presumably; (niewątpliwie)

surely; **~ni(a)ć** (*twierdzić*) assure (*kogoś o czymś* s.o. of s.th.); (*gwarantować*) secure (*komuś coś* s.o. s.th.)

zapędz|ać ⟨~ić⟩ (*zaganiać*) drive*; (*przynaglać*) urge

zapiąć pf → **zapinać**

zapie|kać ⟨~c⟩ roast; **~kan-ka** f casserole

zapinać *guziki* button (up), do* up; *pas* fasten, buckle

zapis m record; *jur.* legacy; *pl* enrolment, registration; **~ać** pf → **zapisywać**; **~ek** m mst pl note; **~ywać** record; *na kurs itp.*: register, enrol, sign up (*na* for); *lekarstwo*: prescribe; *jur.* bequeath; **~ywać się** enrol, register, sign up; *do partii*: join

zaplą|tać się tangle (up); *a. fig.* become* entangled; *fig.* get* mixed up (*w* in)

zaplecze n (*baza*) base; *sklepu:* back

zapleść pf → **zaplatać**

zapładniać ⟨~odnić⟩ fertilize

zapłata f pay

zapłodnienie n fertilization

zapłon m ignition

zapobie|gać ⟨~c⟩ prevent, ward off; **~gawczy** adj preventive; **~gliwy** adj provident, thrifty

zapoczątkow(yw)ać begin*, start

zapo|minać ⟨~mnieć⟩ forget*

zapomoga f benefit

zapora f barrier; *wodna:* dam

zapotrzebowanie n demand

zapowi|adać ⟨~edzieć⟩ announce; **~edź** f announcement; **ogłosić ~edzi** publish the banns

zapozna(wa)ć acquaint (z with); **~ się** get*/become* acquainted

zapożycz|ać ⟨~yć⟩ borrow; **~yć się** get* into debts

zapracow(yw)ać earn; **~** → **zarabiać**

zapraszać invite

zapraw|a f tech. mortar; *gastr.* seasoning; *sp.* work-out; **~i(a)ć** season

zapro|sić pf → **zapraszać**; **~szenie** n invitation

zaprowadz|ać ⟨~ić⟩ lead*, conduct; **~ić porządek** establish order

zaprzecz|ać ⟨~yć⟩ deny; **~enie** n negation

zaprzesta(wa)ć cease (*robienia czegoś* doing s.th.), discontinue

zaprzęg m team; **~ać ⟨~nąć⟩** harness

zaprzysi|ęgać ⟨~ąc⟩ (*zobowiązać się*) swear; (*zobowiązać kogoś*) swear in

zapu|szczać ⟨~ścić⟩ plunge in, dip into; *brodę itp.* grow*; **~ szczać korzenie** fig. put* down roots

zapyt|anie n: znak m **~ania** question mark; **~(yw)ać** → **pytać**

zarabiać v/t *pieniądze* earn; v/i (*pracować zarobkowo*) make*/earn one's living (**czymś** from s.th.)

zaradczy adj remedial

zaradny adj resourceful

zaradzić pf remedy

zaraz adv at once; (*wkrótce*) soon

zaraz|**a** f plague; **~ek** m germ; **~źliwy** adj contagious, infectious (a. fig.); **~żać** ⟨**~zić**⟩ infect (**czymś** with s.th.); **~zić się** contract, be* infected; **~żony** adj infected

zardzewiały adj rusty

zaręcz|**ać** ⟨**~yć**⟩ → **ręczyć**; guarantee; **~yć się** become* engaged (**z** to); **~ynowy** adj engagement ...; **~yny** pl engagement

zarob|**ek** m (*wynagrodzenie*) earnings pl; (*zarabianie*) livelihood; **~ić** pf → **zarabiać**; **~kowy** adj *praca*: paid

zarod|**ek** m (*wynagrodzenie*) *stłumić coś w ~ku* fig. nip s.th. in the bud

zaro|**st** m growth, stubble; **~śla** pl thicket

zarozumiały adj conceited

zarówno adv: **~ ... jak i ~** both ... and ...

zarumienić się pf flush, blush

zarys m outline; **~ow(yw)ać się** become* scratched; fig. arise

zarząd m board, management

zarządz|**ać** ⟨**~ić**⟩ order; *impf* manage; **~anie** n management; **~enie** n directive, instruction, order

zarzu|**cać** ⟨**~cić**⟩ throw on/ over; *wędkę* cast; (*pokrywać*) cover; (*rozrzucać*) scatter; (*obwiniać*) blame (**komuś coś** s.o. for s.th.); **~t** m reproach, blame; **bez ~tu** faultless, irreproachable

zasad|**a** f principle, rule; *chem.* base; **~ → a. reguła**; **~niczy** adj fundamental, basic; (*gruntowny*) radical; **~owy** adj chem. alkaline

zasadz|**ać** ⟨**~ić**⟩ plant

zasadzka f ambush

zasądz|**ać** ⟨**~ić**⟩ sentence (**kogoś** s.o.); *odszkodowanie itp.* adjudge

zasi|**adać** ⟨**~ąść**⟩ be* seated; *w parlamencie itp.*: have* a seat

zasięg m range, reach; **~ać** ⟨**~nąć**⟩ *informacji* inquire; *rady* ask

zasila|**cz** m power module; **~ć** ⟨**~lić**⟩ supply; **~łek** m benefit; **~łek chorobowy** sick pay, sickness benefit; **~łek dla bezrobotnych** unemployment benefit, dole F; **na ~łku** on the dole F

zaskak|**iwać** surprise; **~ujący** adj surprising

zaskarż|**ać** ⟨**~yć⟩** sue (**kogoś za coś** s.o. for s.th.); *wyrok* appeal against

zaskocz|**enie** n surprise;

~ony adj surprised; **~yć** pf → **zaskakiwać**

zaskroniec m grass snake

zasł|aniać ⟨~onić⟩ cover; *oczy itp.* screen; *widok* block off, be* in the way; **~ona** f curtain; **~ona dymna** mil. smokescreen

zasłu|ga f merit; **~giwać** ⟨~żyć⟩ deserve (**na coś** s.th.); **~żony** adj well-earned; *człowiek*: distinguished

zasnąć pf → **zasypiać**

zasob|nik m container; **~ny** adj wealthy; *człowiek*: well off; **~y** pl resources pl

zasób m store, supply; **~ słów** vocabulary

zaspa f snowdrift

zaspa|ć pf oversleep*; **~ny** adj sleepy

zaspok|ajać ⟨~oić⟩ satisfy, appease; *pragnienie* quench

zastać pf → **zastawać**

zastan|awiać ⟨~owić⟩ **się** wonder, think* (**nad** about), ponder (**nad** upon)

zastaw m pledge, security; *za butelkę*: deposit; **oddać w ~** pawn; **~a** f service; **~ać** ⟨~i(a)ć⟩ pawn; **~ka** f med. valve

zastąpić pf → **zastępować**

zastęp|ca m substitute, (*wice*) deputy; **~czy** adj substitute; **~ować** replace, substitute; **~stwo** n replacement, substitution

zastosow|anie n application, use; **~(yw)ać** apply, use

zastój m stagnation, recession

zastrasz|ać ⟨~yć⟩ intimidate; **~ający** adj alarming

zastrze|gać ⟨~c⟩ reserve (**sobie prawo do** the right to)

zastrzelić pf shoot* (dead)

zastrzeż|enie n reservation, provision, proviso; **~ony** adj reserved

zastrzyk m injection, shot f; **~iwać** ⟨~nąć⟩ inject

zasu|w(k)a f bolt; **~wać** ⟨~nąć⟩ push; *zasłonę* draw*

zasypiać fall* asleep

zasyp|ka f powder; **~(yw)ać** fill up

zaszczy|cać ⟨~cić⟩ honour; **~t** m honour, privilege; **~tny** adj honourable

zaślubi(a)ć marry

zaświadcz|ać ⟨~yć⟩ certify; **~enie** n certificate

zataczać koło describe a circle; **~ się** stagger

zata|jać ⟨~ić⟩ conceal (**coś przed kimś** s.th. from s.o.)

zatapiać sink*; (*zalać*) flood

zatarg m clash, conflict

zatem adv therefore

zatk|ać pf → **zatykać**; **~nąć** pf → **wtykać**

zatłoczony adj crowded

zato|czyć pf → **zataczać**; **~ka** f geogr. bay, gulf; *anat.* sinus

zato|nąć pf sink; **~pić** pf → **zatapiać**

zator m jam; med. embolism
zatru|cie n poisoning; *środowiska*: pollution; **∼ć** *pf → zatruwać*
zatrudni|(a)ć employ; **∼enie** n employment; **∼ony** m employee
zatruwać poison; *środowisko* pollute, contaminate
zatrzas|k m latch; **∼kiwać** ⟨**∼nąć**⟩ *drzwi* latch, leave* on the latch
zatrzeć *pf → zacierać*
zatrzym|(yw)ać stop; *samochodem a.*: pull up; (*aresztować*) arrest; **∼ się** stop; *w hotelu itp.*: put* up
zatwardzenie n med. constipation
zatwierdz|ać ⟨**∼ić**⟩ confirm, ratify; **∼enie** n confirmation
zaty|czka f plug; **∼kać** plug, clog, stop (up); **∼kać się** get* clogged/stopped
zaufa|ć trust; **∼nie** n confidence, trust; **∼ny** *adj* reliable, trustworthy, confidential
zaułek m alley
zauważ|ać ⟨**∼yć**⟩ notice
zawadz|ać be* in the way; ⟨**∼ić**⟩ brush, graze (*o coś* s.th.)
zawa|lać ⟨**∼lić**⟩ (*zasypać*) cover; (*zatarasować*) block; F *sprawę* screw up F; **∼lić się** collapse, fall* down; **∼ł** m med. coronary (thrombosis)
zawdzięcz|ać *owe* (*komuś coś* s.th. to s.o.)

zawezwać *pf → wzywać*
zawiad|amiać ⟨**∼omić**⟩ notify, inform, let* (s.o.) know; **∼omienie** n notification
zawiadowca m station master
zawias m hinge
zawieja f snowstorm, blizzard
zawierać contain, comprise; *umowę* enter into, contract; *związek małżeński* marry
zawie|sić *pf → zawieszać*; **∼sisty** *adj* sos: thick; **∼szać** hang (up); (*wstrzymywać*) suspend; **∼szenie** n suspension (*a. tech.*); **∼szenie broni** armistice, cease-fire; **wyrok** m **z ∼szeniem** suspended sentence
zawie|ść *pf → zawodzić*; **∼źć** *pf → zawozić*
zawi|jać *v/i* (*pakować*) wrap (in/up); (*podwijać*) wrap *v/i statek*: put* in; **∼ły** *adj* intricate; **∼nąć** *pf → zawijać*
zawinić *pf* be* guilty
zawi|stny *adj* envious; **∼ść** f envy
zawodni|czka f (**∼k** m) competitor, contestant
zawodny *adj* unreliable
zawod|owiec m professional, pro F; **∼owy** *adj* professional; **∼y** *pl* contest, competition, event, games *pl*
zawodzić (*sprawić zawód*) disappoint, frustrate; (*nie udać się*) fail; (*lamentować*) wail

zawozić take*, carry; *samochodem*: drive*

zawód¹ m occupation

zawód² m disappointment

zawór m valve

zawr|acać ⟨**ócić**⟩ turn back; **~otny** adj high: dizzy, giddy; *szybkość itp.*: terrific; **~ót** m: **~ót głowy** dizziness, giddiness, vertigo

zawrzeć pf → **zawierać**

zawsze adv always; **na** ~ for ever, for good, for keeps F

zazdro|sny adj jealous (**o kogoś/coś** of s.o./s.th.); **~ścić** be* jealous/envious (**czegoś** of s.th.), envy (**komuś czegoś** s.o. s.th.); **~ść** f jealousy, envy

zazębi(a)ć się mesh, interlock

ziębi|(a)ć się catch* (a) cold; **~enie** n cold

zaznacz|ać ⟨**~yć**⟩ mark; *(stwierdzać)* point out; *(podkreślać)* stress

zaznaj|amiać ⟨**omić**⟩ acquaint (**z** with); **~amiać się** become* acquainted

zazwyczaj adv usually

zażalenie n complaint

zażarty adj intense, keen; *zwolennik itp.*: diehard; *bój*: stiff

zażenowany adj embarrassed

zażyłość f familiarity

zaży(wa)ć *lekarstwo* take*

ząb m (**mądrości** wisdom, **mleczny** milk) tooth

zbaczać deviate (**z** from)

zbadać pf → **badać**

zbaw|ca m saviour; **2iciel** eccl. the Saviour; **~ienie** n salvation (a. eccl.); **~ienny** adj salutary, beneficial

zbędny adj superfluous, redundant; → a. **zbyteczny**

zbić pf give* a spanking/licking (**kogoś** to s.o.); *(stłuc)* break*; → **zbijać**

zbie|c pf flee*, run* away, escape; → **zbiegać**; **~g¹** m fugitive, runaway; **~g²** m ulic: intersection; **~g okoliczności** coincidence; **~gać ze schodów** itp. run* down; **~gać się** flock; *w czasie*: coincide; *tkanina*: shrink*; *drogi*: converge; **~gowisko** n crowd

zbierać collect, gather; *grzyby itp.* pick; ~ **się** gather, assemble

zbieżny adj convergent

zbijać nail (together); ~ **z nóg** knock down; ~ **z tropu** confuse

zbiornik m container, tank; **~owiec** m tanker

zbiorow|isko n collection; *ludzkie*: crowd; **~y** adj collective, group ...

zbiór m collection; **~ka** f assembly; *pieniężna*: collection

zbliż|ać bring* closer; **~ać się** approach; **~enie** n phot. close-up; *fizyczne*: intercourse; **~ony** adj similar (**do** to)

złaźnić się *pf* make* a fool of o.s.

zbocze *n* slope

bocz|enie *n med.* perversion; **~eniec** *m* pervert; **~yć** *pf* → **zbaczać**

zboże *n* cereal, grain

zbrodni|a *f* crime; **~arz** *m* criminal; **~czy** *adj* criminal

zbroić → **uzbrajać**; *pf* → **broić**

zbroj|a *f* (suit of) armour; **~enie** *n* armament; → **wyścig**; **~ny** *adj* armed

zbutwiały *adj* decayed, rotten

zbyt **1.** *adv* too; **2.** *m* sale, sales *pl*

zbyt|eczny *adj* needless, superfluous; **~ni** *adj* undue, excessive

zdać *pf* egzamin: pass; (*zwrócić*) return; → **zdawać**

zdaln|y *adj*: **~e sterowanie** *n* remote control

zdanie *n* sentence, clause; (*opinia*) opinion; **moim ~m** in my opinion, to my mind

zdarz|ać ⟨**~yć**⟩ **się** happen, occur; **~enie** *n* event

zdatny *adj* fit, suitable (**do** for), **-able**; **~ do picia** drinkable

zdawać hand over; egzamin: take*; **~ się** trust (**na** to); (*wydawać się*) seem; → **wydawać się**

zdąż|ać → **nadążać, podążać**; *pf* head (**do** for); **~yć** *pf* be* in time; na pociąg: catch*; **nie ~yć na pociąg** miss

zdechnąć *pf* → **zdychać**

zdecydowan|ie 1. *n* determination; **2.** *adv* decidedly; **~y** *adj* resolute, firm

zdejmować take* off, remove

zdenerwowany *adj* nervous, irritated

zderz|ać ⟨**~yć**⟩ **się** collide, crash; **~ak** *m* bumper; **~enie** *n* collision, crash

zdjąć *pf* → **zdejmować**; **~ęcie** *n* photo(graph), picture, shot

zdobić ⟨**o-**⟩ decorate

zdoby|cz *m* capture; zwierzęcia: prey; **~(wa)ć** capture, win*; wiedzę itp. acquire; bramkę: score; **~wca** *m* conqueror; nagrody: winner

zdoln|ość *f* ability, faculty; **~y** *adj* able, capable (**do** of); (*bystry*) able, gifted, talented

zdra|da *f* treachery; (*stanu* high) treason; **~da małżeńska** unfaithfulness; **~dzać** ⟨**~dzić**⟩ betray; partnera: be* unfaithful; **~dziecki** *adj* treacherous; **~jca** *m* (**~jczyni** *f*) traitor

zdrętwieć *pf* go* numb

zdrobni|ały *adj* diminutive; **~enie** *n* diminutive

zdrowie *n* health; **na ~!** cheers!; *po kichnięciu:* bless you!

zdrowy *adj* healthy, sound, fit, well

zdrów → **zdrowy**

zdumi|enie *n* amazement,

astonishment; **~e(wa)ć** amaze, astonish; **~e(wa)ć się be*** astonished/amazed; **~ewający** adj astonishing, amazing; **~ony** adj amazed

zdwajać ⟨~oić⟩ redouble

zdychać F die, rot

zdyskwalifikować pf disqualify

zdzierać tear* off; buty itp. wear* out

zdziwić pf surprise, astonish; **~ć się be*** surprised; **~ony** adj surprised

ze → z

zebra f zebra

zebra|ć pf → **zbierać**; **~nie** n meeting

zecer m compositor

zechcieć pf care, want

zedrzeć pf → **zdzierać**

zegar m clock; **~ek** m watch; **~mistrz** m watchmaker

zejść pf → **schodzić**

zel|ować ⟨pod-⟩ sole; **~ówka** f sole

zemdleć pf faint

zemsta f vengeance, revenge

zepsu|cie n moralne: depravity, corruption; **~ty** adj broken, out of order; (zdemoralizowany) corrupt; → **psuć**

zer|o n zero, nought; sp. nil, love; **poniżej ~a** below zero

zerwać pf → **zrywać**

zesła|ć pf → **zsyłać**; **~nie** n banishment, exile; **~niec** m exile

zespal|ać ⟨~olić⟩ (się) join, unite; **~olowy** adj joint, col-

lective, team ...; **~ół** m team

zestarzeć się pf age, grow* old

zestaw m set; **~i(a)ć** take* down; (łączyć) set*; med. knit; (porównywać) confront; **~ienie** n (kompozycja) composition; (wykaz) list, specification

zestrzelić shoot* down

zeszłoroczny adj last year's; **~y** adj last

zeszyt m exercise book

ześli|zgiwać ⟨~znąć⟩ **się** slide down, slip

zetknąć się pf → **stykać się**

zetrzeć pf → **ścierać**

zew m call

zewn|ątrz adv outside; **z ~ątrz** from the outside; **na ~ątrz** (on the) outside; **~ętrzny** adj outside

zewsząd adv from all sides/directions, from far and wide

zez m squint; **mieć ~a** squint

zezna|(wa)ć testify, give* evidence; **~nie** n testimony

zezować squint; **~ty** adj cross-eyed

zezw|alać ⟨~olić⟩ → **pozwalać**

zęb|aty adj toothed; **koło ~ate** cog(wheel); **~owy** adj dental; **~y** pl → **ząb**

zgad|ywać ⟨~nąć⟩ guess

zgadzać się agree (na to, z with); concur; **~ nie ~** disagree

zgaga f heartburn

zganić pf criticize, censure

zgarn|iać ⟨~ąć⟩ rake

zgas|ić *pf* put* out, switch off; **~nąć** *pf* go* out

zgę|szczać ⟨~ścić⟩ thicken, condense

zgiełk *m* din

zginać ⟨zgiąć⟩ (się) bend

zginąć *pf* → **ginąć**

zgładzić *pf* kill, put* to death

zgł|aszać ⟨~osić⟩ submit; **~aszać się** report (**na/do** to)

zgłoszenie *n* application

zgni|atać ⟨~eść⟩ crush; *fig.* suppress

zgni|lizna *f* decay, rot; *fig.* corruption; **~ły** *adj* rotten, putrid

zgod|a *f* agreement, harmony, concord, consent; **~ność** *f* compatibility; **~dny** *adj* complaisant; (*jednomyślny*) unanimous; (*niesprzeczny*) compatible, consistent (**z** with); **~dny z prawdą** truthful; **~dzić się** *pf* → **zgadzać się**

zgolić *pf* shave off

zgon *m* decease; **akt** *m* **~u** death certificate

zgorsz|enie *n* depravity; **ze ~eniem** with indignation; **~ony** *adj* scandalized, shocked

zgrabny *adj* shapely

zgromadz|ać ⟨~ić⟩ → **gromadzić**; **~enie** *n* assembly, meeting

zgroza *f* horror

zgrubi|ały *adj* calloused, roughened; **~enie** *n* med. callus

zgryźliwy *adj* spiteful

zgrzyt *m* rasp; **~ać** ⟨~nąć⟩ rasp; **zębami**: grind*

zgub|a *f* lost property; (*zagłada*) ruin, downfall; **~ić** *pf* lose*; **~ić się** get* lost; **~ny** *adj* disastrous, fatal

zgwałcić *pf* rape

ziarn|isty *adj* grainy, granular; **~o** *n* grain, seed; *kawy*: bean

ziele *n* herb

zziele|nić ⟨za-⟩ *drzewo*: come* into leaf; **~nieć** turn/go* green; **~ń** *f* green

zielon|y *adj* green (*a. fig.*); **2e Świątki** Whitsun

ziemi|a *f* earth; (*kraina*) land; (*grunt*) ground; (*gleba*) soil; **upaść na ~ę** fall* to the ground; **pod ~ą** underground; **2 the Earth**

ziemniak *m* potato

ziemn|y *adj* earth ...; **~ski** *adj* earth ...; land ...; (*doczesny*) earthly; **kula** *f* **~ska** the globe

ziewać ⟨~nąć⟩ yawn

zięć *m* son-in-law

zim|a *f* winter; **~no** *n, adv* cold; **~nokrwisty** *adj* cold-blooded; **~ny** *adj* cold; **~ować** ⟨prze-⟩ winter; *zwierzę*: hibernate; **~owy** *adj* winter ...

ziołowy *adj* herb ..., herbal

zjadać *v/t* eat*

zjadliwy *adj* malicious, spiteful

zjaw|a *f* phantom; **~i(a)ć się** show up, turn up, appear;

~isko *n* occurrence; *(fenomen)* phenomenon

zjazd *m* congress; *rodzinny itp.:* reunion; *sp.* downhill (race)

zje|chać *pf* → **zjeżdżać**; **~dnać** *pf* → **zjednywać**

zjednocz|enie *n* unification; **~yć** unite

zjednywać win*, gain

zjeść → **zjadać**

zjeżdżać go*/run*/race downhill; *winda:* go* down, descend; **~ się** arrive; *(gromadzić się)* gather, assemble

zlać *pf* F *(zbić)* beat* up, give* a spanking/licking *(kogoś* to s.o.);* **~ się** F wet o.s.; → **zlewać**

zlec|ać ⟨**~ić**⟩ commission; **~enie** *n* commission; **~eniodawca** *m* customer

zlew *m* sink; **~ać** pour (off), decant; *(polewać)* drench; *wężem:* hose; **~ać się** mingle, mix; **~ozmywak** *m* sink

zleźć *m* → **złazić**

zlęknąć się *pf* take* fright

złagodzić *pf* alleviate, ease; *karę* commute

złama|ć break*; **~nie** *n med.* fracture; *przepisów itp.:* breach; **~ny** *adj* broken; *(przygnębiony)* prostrate, broken-hearted

złapać *pf* → **łapać**

złazić F *z łóżka itp.:* get* off; *z drabiny itp.:* come* down; *farba:* peel off

złącz|e *n tech.* joint; *kompu-*

terowe: interface; **~yć** *pf* → **łączyć**

zło *n* evil

złoci|ć ⟨**po-**⟩ gild; **~sty** *adj* gold(en)

złodziej|(ka *f) m* thief

złom *m* scrap (metal)

złoś|cić ⟨**roz-**⟩ irritate, annoy; **~cić się** be* irritated; **~ć** *f* irritation, annoyance; **~liwy** *adj* malicious, spiteful; *med.* malignant

złot|nik *m* goldsmith; **~o** *n* gold; **~y 1.** *adj* gold(en); **2.** *m* zloty

złowić *pf* catch*

złowrogi *adj* ominous, portentous

złoże *n* deposit, layer

złoż|ony *adj* complex, compound, composite; *(skomplikowany)* intricate; **~yć** *pf* → **składać**

złu|dny *adj* illusory, deceiving; **~dzenie** *n* illusion

zły *adj* bad, evil; *(rozgniewany)* angry, cross; *(niewłaściwy)* wrong

zmagać się cope (**z** with)

zmarł|y 1. *adj* deceased, dead; *form.*late; **2.** *m* the deceased

zmarnować *pf* waste

zmarszcz|ka *f* wrinkle; **~yć** *pf* → **marszczyć**

zmartwi|ć *pf* → **martwić**; **~enie** *n* worry

zmartwychwstanie *n eccl.* the Resurrection

zmarznąć *pf* → **marznąć**

zmęcz|enie *n* fatigue, tired-

zniesławi(a)ć

ness; ~ony *adj* tired; ~yć *pf*
tire; ~yć się get* tired

zmiana *f* change; *nocna itp.:*
shift

zmiatać sweep*

zmien|i(a)ć (się) change, alter, vary; ~ny *adj* variable, changeable

zmierzać make* (do for), head (do for); *fig.* aim (do at)

zmierzch *m* twilight; dusk; ~ać darken

zmieszany *adj* confused, embarrassed

zmie|ścić *pf* → mieścić; ~ść *pf* → zmiatać

zmiękcz|ać ⟨~yć⟩ soften

zmniejsz|ać ⟨~yć⟩ (się) diminish, decrease, lessen

zmowa *f* plot, conspiracy

zmrok *m* → zmierzch, mrok

zmu|szać ⟨~sić⟩ force (kogoś do czegoś s.o. to do s.th.), make* (kogoś do czegoś s.o. to do s.th.)

zmyć *pf* → zmywać

zmykać scurry, scuttle

zmylić *pf* mislead*

zmysł *m* sense; ~owy *adj* sensual

zmyśl|ać ⟨~ić⟩ invent, make* up; ~ny *adj* ingenious; ~ony *adj* imaginary

zmywa|cz *m* remover; ~ć wash up; ~lny *adj* washable

znacz|ek *m* mark; (odznaka) badge; *pocztowy:* stamp; ~enie *n* meaning, sense; (ważność) importance, significance; ~ny *adj* considera-

ble; ~yć (zawierać znaczenie) mean; (znakować) mark

znać know*; dać komuś ~ let* s.o. know; ~ się be* acquainted, know* each other; (być znawcą) be* an expert (na czymś at s.th.)

znajdować find*; ~ się be*

znajom|ość *f* acquaintance; (wiedza) knowledge; ~y **1.** *adj* familiar; **2.** *m* acquaintance

znak *m* sign, mark

znakomity *adj* (wybitny) eminent; (doskonały) excellent

znal|azca *m* finder; ~eziony *adj*: biuro *n* rzeczy ~ezionych lost-property office; ~eźć *pf* → znajdować; ~eźne *n* reward

znamienny *adj* significant, symptomatic

znamię *n* birthmark, mole

zna|ny *adj* known; ~wca *m* expert, connoisseur

znęcać się bully, torment (nad kimś s.o.)

znicz *m*: ~ olimpijski the Olympic torch

zniechęc|ać ⟨~ić⟩ discourage, deter (do from); ~ać się be* discouraged

zniecierpliwienie *n* impatience

znieczul|ać ⟨~ić⟩ anaesthetize; ~enie *n* anaesthetic

zniedołężniały *adj* infirm, senile

znienacka *adv* all of a sudden

zniesławi|(a)ć libel, slander;

~enie *n* libel, slander, defamation

znieść *pf* → **znosić**

zniewa|ga *f* insult, offence, affront; **~żać ⟨~żyć⟩** insult, offend, affront

znik|ać ⟨~nąć⟩ disappear, vanish

znikomy *adj* slender

zniszcz|enie *n* destruction, devastation; **~ony** *adj* devastated, destroyed

zniweczyć *pf* plany itp. frustrate

zniż|ać ⟨~yć⟩ lower; **~ka** *f* reduction; **~kowy** *adj* reduced

zno|sić take*/bring* down; *jajka* lay*; *(unieważniać)* cancel, repeal; *ból* bear*, stand*; **nie ~szę go** I can't stand the sight of him; **~śny** *adj* tolerable, bearable

znowu, znów *adv* again

znudzenie *n* boredom; **aż do ~a** ad nauseam

znużony *adj* tired, weary **(czymś** of s.th.)

zobacz|enie *n*: **do ~enia!** see you!, so long!; **~yć** see*; **~ się** meet* **(z kimś** s.o.)

zobojętnieć *pf* become* indifferent

zobowiąz|anie *n* obligation, commitment; **~(yw)ać** oblige, bind*; **~(yw)ać się** commit o.s. **(do** to)

zodiak *m* zodiac

zoo *n* zoo

zorza *f*: **~ poranna** (red light

of) dawn; **~ wieczorna** afterglow; **~ polarna** northern lights *pl*

zosta(wa)ć remain, stay; *(pozostawać)* be* left; *(stawać się)* become*

zostawi(a)ć leave*

zran|ić *pf* wound; *a. fig.* hurt*; **~ć się** hurt* o.s.; **~enie** *n* injury

zrastać się *rana*: heal up; *kość*: knit (together)

zraż|ać ⟨~zić⟩ alienate; *(zniechęcać)* discourage; **~żać się** take* a dislike **(do** to); *(zniechęcać się)* become* discouraged

zrealizować *pf* realize, carry* into effect

zreszta *adv* besides, after all

zrezygnować *pf* give* up, resign, quit **(z czegoś** s.th.)

zręczn|ość *f* dexterity; skill; **~y** *adj* adroit, dexterous, skilful

zrobić *pf* → **robić**

zrozpaczony *adj* desparate

zrosnąć się *pf* → **zrastać się**

zrozumi|ały *adj* understandable, comprehensible; *(uzasadniony)* justifiable; **~eć** *pf* → **rozumieć**; **~enie** *n* understanding

zrówn|oważony *adj* composed, serene; **~(yw)ać ziemię** *pl*; **~(yw)ać** ziemię *n*) ... ; *(traktować jednakowo)* equalize

zrujnować *pf* ruin *(a. fig.)*

zryć *pf* → **ryć**

zrywać tear* off; *kwiaty itp.*

pick; *stosunki itp.* break* off; ~ **się** *sznur itp.*: snap, break*; (*wstawać*) spring* to one's feet

zrze|kać ⟨~**c**⟩ **się** relinquish, renounce (*czegoś* s.th.)

zrzu|cać ⟨~**cić**⟩ throw* off; *z samolotu:* drop; **~t** *m* drop

zsią|dać ⟨**zsiąść**⟩ get* off, dismount; **~ły** *adj:* **~łe mleko** *n* sour milk

zsu|wać ⟨~**nąć**⟩ **się** slip (down)

zsyłać *form. z nieba:* send*; (*deportować*) exile, banish

zsyp *m* (rubbish) chute

zszy|wacz *m* stapler; ⟨~**(wa)ć** stitch together; *ranę* suture; **~wka** *f* staple

zubożały *adj* impoverished

zuch *m w harcerstwie:* cub, brownie; **~walstwo** *n*, **~wałość** *f* impudence, audacity; **~wały** *adj* impertinent; (*odważny*) bold, cheeky

zupa *f* soup

zupełn|ie *adv* completely; **~y** *adj* complete, utter

zuży|cie *n* consumption; **~tkować** *pf* utilize; **~ty** *adj* worn-out; **~(wa)ć** *pf* use up

zwać call; ~ **się** be* called

zwal|ać ⟨~**ić**⟩ heap, pile up; (*przewracać*) knock down; **~ać winę** put* the blame (**na kogoś** on s.o.); **~ić się** fall*, tumble

zwalczać fight*; **~yć** *pf* overcome*

zwalniać slow down; (*luzo-*

wać) loosen; (*uwalniać*) release; *pokój* vacate; ~ **kogoś z pracy** dismiss s.o.

zwarcie *n electr.* short circuit

zwariowa|ć *pf* go* mad; **~ny** *adj* mad, crazy

zwarty *adj* dense, compact

zważa|ć consider; pay* attention (**na** to); *nie* ~ **jąc na** ... regardless of ..., heedless of ...

zważyć *pf* weigh

zwąchać *pf* nose out

zwątpienie *n* doubt

zwędzić *pf* F (*ukraść*) pinch F

zwę|żać narrow; *spodnie itp.* take* in; **~żać się** narrow

zwiać *pf* → **zwiewać**

zwiad *m* reconnaissance; **~owca** *m* scout

związ|ek *m* connection, relationship; (*zrzeszenie*) union, association; **~ek zawodowy** trade union; **~(yw)ać** tie, bind*

zwichnąć *pf* sprain; **~ięcie** *n* sprain

zwiedz|ać ⟨~**ić**⟩ tour, visit; **~anie** *n* sightseeing

zwierciadło *n* mirror, looking-glass

zwierz|ać ⟨~**yć**⟩ **się** confide (**komuś** in s.o.)

zwierzchni *adj* superior; **~czka** *f* (**~k** *m*) superior

zwierzę *n* animal; **~cy** *adj* animal (*a. fig.*); **~yna** *f* game

zwie|szać ⟨~**sić**⟩ hang* down

zwietrzały *adj* stale; *piwo:*

flat; *skała*: weathered
zwiewać blow* away; F
(*uciekać*) make* off, bunk off
zwiększ|ać ⟨~yć⟩ enlarge,
increase
zwięzły *adj* concise
zwijać roll up, wind* up
zwilż|ać ⟨~yć⟩ moisten, damp
zwinąć *pf* → **zwijać**
zwinny *adj* nimble, agile
zwis|ać ⟨~nąć⟩ hang*, droop
zwlekać hesitate; *nie* ~*jąc*
without delay
zwłaszcza *adv* especially,
chiefly, above all
zwłoka *f* delay
zwłoki *pl* corpse
zwodz|ić delude; ~*ony adj*:
most ~*ony* drawbridge
zwolenni|czka *f* ⟨~k *m*⟩ advo-
cate, adherent
zwolni|ć *pf* → **zwalniać**;
~*enie n jur.* exemption; *z
pracy*: dismissal; (*uwolnienie*) release; ~*enie lekarskie*
sick leave; (*dokument*) doctor's certificate
zwoł|ywać ⟨~ać⟩ call, summon
zwój *m* roll, scroll
zwracać give* back; (*wymio-
tować*) vomit, throw* up;

(*odwracać*) turn; ~ *czyjąś
uwagę* catch*/attract one's
attention; *nie* ~ *uwagi* pay*
no attention (*na* to); ~ *się*
address (*do kogoś* s.o.)
zwrot *m* turn; *językowy*: expression, phrase; *prawniczy
itp.*: term; ~*ka f verse*; ~*nica
f* point(s *pl*) *Brt.*, switch *Am.*;
~*nik m* tropic; ~*nikowy adj*
tropical; ~*ny adj* (*zwinny*)
agile; *samochód*: manoeu-
vrable; *gram.* reflexive;
punkt ~ *ny* turning point
zwycię|ski *adj* victorious; ~
stwo n victory; *sp. a.* win; ~
zca m winner; ~*żać* ⟨~*żyć*⟩
win*; ~*żczyni f* winner
zwyczaj *m* custom, practice;
~*ny adj* ordinary, common-
place
zwyk|le *adv* usually; ~*ły adj*
ordinary, regular
zwyżka *f* rise
zysk *m* profit, gain; ~(*iw*)*ać*
gain, profit; ~*owny adj* profitable
zza from behind
zży(wa)ć się get* accustomed (*z* to)

Ź

źdźbło *n* stalk, blade
źle *adv* badly, wrongly; ~ *się
zachowywać* misbehave; ~
się czuć feel* ill at ease; ~ *z
nim* he is in a bad way

źreb|ak *m*, ~*ię n* foal
źrenica *f* pupil
źród|lany *adj* spring ...; ~*ło n*
spring; *a. fig.* source; ~*łowy
adj* source ...

Ż

żaba f frog

żad|en (**~na, ~ne**) (*ani jeden*) no, no one; *z wielu*: none; *z dwóch*: neither

żagiel m sail; **~łowiec** m sailing ship; **~łowy** adj sailing, sail ...; **~łówka** f sailboat, sailing boat, sail ...

żakiet m jacket

żal m sorrow, grief; ~ *mi* I'm sorry; ~ *mi go* I am/feel sorry for him; **~ić** ⟨**po-**⟩ **się** complain

żaluzja f Venetian blind

żało|ba f mourning; **~bny** adj funeral; **marsz** m **~bny** dead march; **msza** f **~bna** requiem; **~sny** adj pathetic; **~wać** ⟨**po-**⟩ regret, be*/feel* sorry, pity

żar m glow; (*upał*) heat

żarcie n F grub F, chow F

żarliwy adj ardent

żarło|czny adj voracious, gluttonous; **~k** m glutton

żarówka f bulb

żart m joke, jest; **~obliwy** adj jocular, jesting; **~ować** ⟨**po-, za-**⟩ joke, jest; **~owniś** m joker

żarzyć się glow

żąda|ć ⟨**za-**⟩ demand, claim; **~nie** n demand, claim

żądło n sting

żądza f lust

że that; *dlatego*, ~ because

żebra|czka f beggar; **~ć** beg; **~k** m beggar

żebro n rib

żeby (in order) to

żegl|arski adj sailing, yacht ...; **~arstwo** n sailing, yachting; **~arz** m sailor, yachtsman; **~ować** sail; **~uga** f navigation, shipping

żegna|ć ⟨**po-**⟩ **się** say* goodbye (**z** to); ⟨**prze-**⟩ **się** cross o.s.

żelatyna f gelatine

żelaz|ko n iron; **~ny** adj iron; **~o** n iron

żenić ⟨**o-**⟩ (**się**) marry

żeński adj female

żerdź f perch

żłobek m crèche; *eccl.* crib *Brt.*, crèche *Am.*

żłób m manger

żmija f viper

żmudny adj strenuous, arduous

żniw|a pl harvest; **~iarka** f (*kobieta, maszyna*) harvester

żołąd|ek m stomach; **~kowy** adj stomach ..., gastric

żołądź f acorn

żołd m pay

żołnierz m soldier

żona f wife; **~ty** adj o *mężczyźnie*: married

żongler m juggler; **~ować** juggle

żółć f bile; **~ciowy** adj bile ...,

gall ...; **~knąć** ⟨**po-**⟩ yellow, turn yellow; **~taczka** f med. jaundice; **~tawy** adj yellowish; **~tko** n yolk; **~ty** adj yellow

żółw m tortoise; *wodny:* turtle

żr|ący adj corrosive; **~eć** ⟨**po-, ze-**⟩ F gobble F

żubr m zo. European bison

żu|cie n: **guma** f **do ~cia** (chewing) gum; **~ć** ⟨**prze-**⟩ chew

żuk m beetle

żur(ek) m a kind of sour soup

żuraw m zo., tech. crane

żużel m slag; (*popiół*) cinder; F *sp.* speedway

żwawy adj brisk

żwir m gravel; **~ownia** f gravel pit

życi|e n life; **~orys** m CV, curriculum vitae; **~owy** adj vital; (*praktyczny*) practical

życz|enie n wish; **~liwość** f

f kindness, friendliness; **~li-wy** adj friendly, warm-hearted, kind, benevolent; **~yć** wish

żyć live

Żyd m Jew; **&owski** adj Jewish; **~ówka** f Jew

żyletka f razor blade

żył|a f vein; **~ka** f wędkarska: fishing line; *fig.* flair

żyrafa f giraffe

żyt|ni adj rye ...; **~niówka** f rye vodka; **~o** n rye; F rye vodka

żyw|cem adv alive; **~ica** f resin; **~iciel(ka** f) m breadwinner; **~ić** ⟨**wy-**⟩ feed*

żywioł m elements pl; **~owy** adj spontaneous

żywność f food

żyw|ot m form. life; **~otność** f vitality; **~otny** adj vivacious, lively; **~y** adj living, live; pred alive

żyzny adj fertile

A

a [ə, *when stressed* eɪ], *before vowel:* **an** [ən, *when stressed* æn] (*przedimek nieokreślony*) jeden; jakiś, pewien; *with name:* niejaki

abandon [ə'bændən] zaniechać; *hope etc.* porzucać ‹-cić›

abbreviation [əbriːvɪeɪʃn] skrót *m*

ABC [eɪbiː'siː] elementarz *m*

abdicate ['æbdɪkeɪt] abdykować; *right etc.* zrzekać ‹zrzec› się

abdom|en ['æbdəmen] brzuch *m*; **~inal** [‿'dɒmɪnl] brzuszny

abduct [əb'dʌkt] por(y)wać

abhor [əb'hɔː] czuć wstręt (**s.th.** do czegoś)

ability [ə'bɪlətɪ] zdolność *f*

able ['eɪbl] zdolny; **be ~ to** być w stanie, móc

abnormal [æb'nɔːml] nienormalny

aboard [ə'bɔːd] na pokład(zie)

abolish [ə'bɒlɪʃ] znosić ‹znieść›

abortion [ə'bɔːʃn] (sztuczne) poronienie *n*

about [ə'baʊt] **1.** *prp contents:* o; *What ~ doing that?* Może

byśmy to zrobili?; *I had no money ~ me* nie miałem przy sobie pieniędzy; **2.** *adv* (*around*) tu i tam; *with figures, time:* mniej więcej, około; **be ~ to do s.th.** mieć coś właśnie zrobić

above [ə'bʌv] **1.** *prp* ponad, nad; **~ all** nade wszystko; **2.** *adv* powyżej, na górze; **3.** *adj* powyższy

abroad [ə'brɔːd] za granicą, za granicę

abrupt [ə'brʌpt] nagły; *person:* obcesowy

absence ['æbsəns] nieobecność *f*, brak *m*

absent ['æbsənt] nieobecny; **be ~** brakować; **~'minded** roztargniony

absolute ['æbsəluːt] absolutny

absorb [əb'sɔːb] ‹za›absorbować; **~ed in** pogrążony w; **~ent** wchłaniający, higroskopijny; **~ent cotton** *Am.* wata *f*

abstain [əb'steɪn] wstrzym(yw)ać się (**from** od)

abstract 1. ['æbstrækt] *adj* abstrakcyjny; **2.** [‿'strækt] streścić

absurd [əb'sɜːd] absurdalny

abundan|ce [ə'bʌndəns] obfitość *f*; **~t** obfity

abus|e 1. [ə'bjuːs] nadużycie *n*; (*insult*) obelgi *pl*; **2.** [~z] nadużyw(a)ć; (*insult*) znieważać <-żyć>; **~ive** [~sɪv] znieważający, obraźliwy

academ|ic [ækə'demɪk] akademicki; **~y** [ə'kædəmɪ] akademia *f*

accelerat|e [ək'seləreɪt] przyspieszać <-szyć>; *mot.* do-da(wa)ć gazu; **~or** pedał *m* gazu

accent ['æksənt] akcent *m*

accept [ək'sept] przyjmować <-jąć>, <za>akceptować

access ['ækses] *a. computer:* dostęp *m* (*to* do); **~ible** [ək'sesəbl] dostępny

accident ['æksɪdənt] przypadek *m*; (*collision etc.*) wypadek *m*; *by* ~ przypadkiem; ~**al** [~'dentl] przypadkowy

accommodat|e [ə'kɒmədeɪt] przyzwyczajać <-czaić> (*to* do); **~e s.o.** pogodzić (*to* do); **~e s.o.** pogodzić kogoś; da(wa)ć nocleg; ~**ion** [~'deɪʃn] (*Am. pl*) mieszkanie *n*

accompany [ə'kʌmpənɪ] towarzyszyć

accomplish [ə'kʌmplɪʃ] osiągać <-gnąć>; *a.* ~**ed** utalentowany

accord [ə'kɔːd] **1.** przyzwolenie *n*; *of one's own* ~ z własnej woli, sam z siebie; *with one* ~ jednomyślnie; **2.** zgadzać <zgodzić> się (*with*); ~**ance** in ~ance with zgodnie z; ~**ing:** ~**ing to** według

~ingly stosownie do tego

account [ə'kaʊnt] **1.** *banking:* konto *n* (*with* w), rachunek *m*; *pl in companies:* księgowość *f*; (*story*) relacja *f*; *on no* ~ pod żadnym pozorem; *on* ~ *of* wskutek; *take into* ~ wziąć pod uwagę; **2.** <wy>tłumaczyć (*for* s.th. coś); **~ant** księgowy *m* (-wa *f*)

accumulate [ə'kjuːmjʊleɪt] <z>gromadzić

accura|cy ['ækjʊrəsɪ] ścisłość *f*; **~te** [~rət] ścisły, wierny

accus|ation [ækjuː'zeɪʃn] *jur.* oskarżenie *n*; **~e** [ə'kjuːz] *jur.* oskarżać <-żyć> (*s.o. of* kogoś o); zarzucać <-cić> (*s.o. of s.th.* komuś coś); **~ed:** *the* ~**ed** oskarżony *m*, oskarżeni *pl*

accustom [ə'kʌstəm] przyzwyczajać <-czaić> (*to* do); *get* ~**ed to** przyzwyczajać <-czaić> się do; ~**ed** przyzwyczajony

ace [eɪs] as *n* (*a. fig.*)

ache [eɪk] **1.** boleć; **2.** ból *m*

achieve [ə'tʃiːv] *v/t* osiągać <-gnąć>; *v/i* odnieść <-nosić> sukces; ~**ment** osiągnięcie *n*

acid ['æsɪd] **1.** kwaśny; *fig.* cierpki; **2.** kwas *m*

acknowledge [ək'nɒlɪdʒ] uzna(wa)ć; *receipt* potwierdzać <-dzić>; ~**ment** potwierdzenie *n*; *pl in books etc.:* podziękowania *pl*

acquaint [ə'kweɪnt] zaznajamiać <-jomić>; *be* ~**ed with**

s.o. znać kogoś; **~ance** znajomość f; znajomy m (-ma f)
acquire [ə'kwaɪə] naby(wa)ć
acquit [ə'kwɪt] uniewinni(a)ć
across [ə'krɒs] **1.** prp przez; na drugą stronę; **2.** adv w poprzek, na krzyż; intn after measurements: ... szerokości; street, river: po drugiej stronie
act [ækt] **1.** działać; (behave) postępować; thea. grać; **~ as** funkcjonować jako; **2.** czyn m, uczynek m; jur. ustawa f; thea. akt m; (show) występ m; **~ion** czyn m, działanie m; tech. mechanizm m; jur. proces m; mil. akcja f
active [ˈæktɪv] aktywny; **~ity** [~'tɪvətɪ] działalność f; (occupation) czynność f
act|or [ˈæktə] aktor m; **~ress** [~trɪs] aktorka f
actual [ˈæktʃʊəl] faktyczny, konkretny
acute [ə'kjuːt] przenikliwy; med. ostry (a. fig.)
ad [æd] F → advertisement
adapt [ə'dæpt] dostosow(yw)ać; text (za)adaptować; **~er**, **~or** [ə'dæptə] złączka f
add [æd] doda(wa)ć
addict [ˈædɪkt] nałogowiec m, osoba f uzależniona; **~ed** [ə'dɪktɪd] uzależniony (to od)
addition [ə'dɪʃn] dodatek m; math. dodawanie n; **in ~** na dodatek, ponadto; **~al** dodatkowy

address [ə'dres] **1.** ⟨za⟩adresować; words etc. ⟨s⟩kierować (to do); zwracać ⟨-rócić⟩ się (s.o. do kogoś); **2.** adres m; (speech) przemowa f; **~ee** [ædre'siː] adresat(ka f) m
adequate [ˈædɪkwət] wystarczający, stosowny
adhe|re [əd'hɪə] **~re to** przylegać ⟨-lgnąć⟩ do; fig. trzymać się (to sth. czegoś); **~sive** [~'hiːsɪv] klej m; **~sive plaster** przylepiec m; **~sive tape** taśma f klejąca; Am. przylepiec m
adjacent [ə'dʒeɪsənt] przylegający (to do)
adjoin [ə'dʒɔɪn] sąsiadować, stykać się (sth. z czymś)
adjourn [ə'dʒɜːn] zakańczać ⟨-kończyć⟩ (obrady)
adjust [ə'dʒʌst] dostosow(yw)ać się; tech. ⟨pod⟩regulować, ⟨do⟩stroić; **~able** dający się regulować
administ|er [əd'mɪnɪstə] administrować; drugs zaordynować; justice wymierzać ⟨-rzyć⟩; **~ration** [~'streɪʃn] administracja f; esp. Am. rząd m; **~rative** [~'mɪnɪstrətɪv] administracyjny; **~rator** [~treɪtə] zarządca m
admirable [ˈædmərəbl] godny podziwu, zachwycający
admiral [ˈædmərəl] admirał m
admir|ation [ædmə'reɪʃn] podziw m; **~e** [əd'maɪə]

dziwiać; **~er** [~rə] wielbiciel(ka f) m

admiss|ible [əd'mɪsəbl] dopuszczalny; **~ion** [~'mɪʃn] (entry) wstęp m; (acknowledgement) przyznanie n się; (admittance) przyjęcie m, **~ion free** wstęp m wolny

admit [əd'mɪt] (confess) przyzna(wa)ć (się); (let in) wpuszczać ⟨wpuścić⟩

adopt [ə'dɒpt] (assume) przyb(ie)rać, przyjmować ⟨-jąć⟩

adore [ə'dɔː] uwielbiać

adult [ˈædʌlt] **1.** adj dojrzały, dorosły; **2.** (człowiek) dorosły m

advance [əd'vɑːns] **1.** v/t awansować; argument wysuwać ⟨-sunąć⟩, przedstawi(a)ć; money wypłacać ⟨-cić⟩ zadatkiem; v/i posuwać ⟨-sunąć⟩ się do przodu; **2.** (development) postęp m; money: zaliczka f; mil. natarcie n; **in ~** z góry; **~ payment** opłata f z góry; **~d** wyższy, zaawansowany

advantage [əd'vɑːntɪdʒ] korzyść f; (supremacy) przewaga f; **take ~ of** wykorzyst(yw)ać; **~ous** [ædvən'teɪdʒəs] korzystny

adventure [əd'ventʃə] przygoda f

advertise ['ædvətaɪz] da(wa)ć ogłoszenie (**for** o); (publicize) ⟨za⟩reklamować; **~ement** [əd'vɜːtɪsmənt] for

job etc.: ogłoszenie n; for product: reklama f; **~ing** ['ædvətaɪzɪŋ] reklamowanie n, reklama f

advice [əd'vaɪs] (po)rada f; **take s.o.'s ~** pójść za czyjąś radą

advis|able [əd'vaɪzəbl] wskazany; **~e** [~z] (po)radzić; **~er** doradca

aerial ['eərɪəl] esp. Brt. antena f

aero|bics [eə'rəʊbɪks] aerobik m; **~plane** ['eərəpleɪn] Brt. samolot m

affair [ə'feə] sprawa f; love: romans m

affect [ə'fekt] oddzia(ływ)ać, mieć wpływ (**s.o./s.th.** na kogoś/coś); med. zaatakować, dotykać ⟨-tknąć⟩

affection [ə'fekʃn] uczucie n, przywiązanie n; **~ate** [~ʃnət] kochający, czuły

affirmative [ə'fɜːmətɪv] **1.** adj twierdzący; **2.** **answer in the ~** odpowiadać ⟨-wiedzieć⟩ twierdząco

affluent ['æfluənt] zamożny

afford [ə'fɔːd] pozwalać ⟨-wolić⟩ sobie (**s.th.** na coś); **I can't ~ it** nie stać mnie na to

afraid [ə'freɪd]: **be ~** bać się (**of s.th.** czegoś)

African ['æfrɪkən] **1.** afrykański; **2.** Afrykanin m (-nka f)

after ['ɑːftə] **1.** prp space: za, po; time, fig.: po; **~ all** jakby nie było; **~ that** potem; **2.** cj

gdy już; **~'noon** popołudnie
n; *in the* **~noon** po południu;
this ~noon (dziś) po południu; **good ~noon** *after 12
o'clock*: dzień dobry; **~-
ward(s** *Brt.*) ['~wəd(z)] później, następnie, potem
again [ə'gen] znów, jeszcze
raz
against [ə'genst] przeciw
age [eɪdʒ] **1.** wiek *m*; *at the ~
of ...* w wieku ... lat; *of ~*
pełnoletni; *under ~* niepełnoletni; *for ~s* F lata całe;
2. ⟨po⟩starzeć (się); **~d**
['eɪdʒd] stary; *~ ...* ['eɪdʒd] w
wieku ... lat
agency ['eɪdʒənsɪ] agencja *f*
agenda [ə'dʒendə] porządek
m dzienny
agent ['eɪdʒənt] przedstawiciel *m*; *intelligence:* agent *m*
aggress|ion [ə'greʃn] *psych.*
agresja *f*; *esp. mil.* napaść *f*;
~ive [~sɪv] napastliwy, agresywny
agitate ['ædʒɪteɪt] *(stir)*
⟨wy⟩mieszać; *(upset)* poruszyć, wyprowadzać ⟨-dzić⟩ z
równowagi; **~ion** [~'teɪʃn]
poruszenie *n*
ago [ə'gəʊ] *time:* ...temu: *5
minutes ~* 5 minut temu;
long ~ dawno temu
agony ['ægənɪ] udręka *f*, katusze *pl*
agree [ə'griː] *v/i* zgadzać
⟨zgodzić⟩ się *(to, with* na, z),
wyrażać ⟨-razić⟩ zgodę *(to*
na); *(reach consent)* porozu-

mieć się; *food:* ⟨po-⟩służyć
(with s.o. komuś); *v/t* uzgodnić; **~able** [~ɪ-] przyjemny;
~ment [~ː-] zgodność *f*; porozumienie *n*, układ *m*, umowa *f*
agricultur|al [ægrɪ'kʌltʃərəl]
rolny, rolniczy; **~e** ['~ʃə] rolnictwo *n*
ahead [ə'hed] *(forward)* naprzód; *(in front/advance)* z
przodu, na przedzie; *~ of*
przed
aid [eɪd] **1.** pomagać; **2.** pomoc *f*
aim [eɪm] **1.** *v/i* ⟨wy⟩celować
⟨wy⟩mierzyć *(at* w, do); *v/t*
weapon wycelować *(at* w); **2.**
cel *m*
air¹ [eə] **1.** powietrze *n*; *by ~*
samolotem; *in the open ~* na
(otwartym) powietrzu; *on
the ~* na antenie; **2.** *room*
⟨wy⟩wietrzyć; *dog* wyprowadzać ⟨-dzić⟩ na spacer
air² [~] *(attitude)* postawa *f*;
(atmosphere) nastrój *m*, atmosfera *f*
'air|-conditioned klimatyzowany; **'~-conditioning** klimatyzacja *f*; **'~craft** *(pl
-craft)* samolot *m*; **'~field**
lotnisko *n*; **~ force** lotnictwo
n; **~ hostess** stewardesa *f*;
'~line linia *f* lotnicza; **'~mail**
poczta *f* lotnicza; **'~plane**
Am. samolot *m*; **'~port** port
m lotniczy, lotnisko *n*;
'~space przestrzeń *f* powietrzna; **~ terminal** dwo-

rzec *m* lotniczy; '**~tight** hermetyczny; '**~traffic control** kontrola *f* naziemna; '**~y** przewiewny

aisle [aɪl] przejście *n* między ławkami *itd.*; *arch.* nawa *f* boczna

alarm [ə'lɑ:m] **1.** urządzenie *n* alarmowe; (*a.* **~ clock**) budzik *m*; (*anxiety*) trwoga *f*, niepokój *m*; **give/raise the ~** podnieść alarm; *fig.* bić na trwogę; **2.** zaniepokoić, zatrwożyć

alcohol ['ælkəhɒl] alkohol *m*; **~ic** [~'hɒlɪk] **1.** *adj* alkoholowy; **2.** alkoholik *m* (-liczka *f*)

ale [eɪl] *rodzaj angielskiego piwa bezchmielowego*

alert [ə'lɜ:t] **1.** *adj* czujny; **2.** alarm *m*; (*signal*) sygnał *m* alarmowy; **3.** (za)alarmować

alien ['eɪljən] **1.** *adj* obcy, cudzoziemski; **2.** cudzoziemiec *m* (-mka *f*)

alike [ə'laɪk] **1.** *adv* podobnie, jednakowo; **2.** *adj* podobny, jednakowy

alimony ['ælɪmənɪ] alimenty *pl*

alive [ə'laɪv] żywy, żyjący

all [ɔ:l] **1.** *adj* cały, wszystek; *with pl nouns*: wszyscy/ wszystkie *pl*; **2.** *adv* całkiem, zupełnie; *with pl nouns* wszyscy; **at once** nagle; **~ but** wszyscy oprócz; **~ of us** my wszyscy;

~ over wszędzie; **~ right** w porządku; **~ the better** tym lepiej; **~ the time** (przez) cały czas; **not ... at ~** wcale nie; **not at ~!** nic nie szkodzi, nie ma za co dziękować!; **for ~ I care** jeżeli o mnie chodzi; **for ~ I know** o ile wiem; **two ~** *sp.* dwa - dwa

alleged [ə'ledʒd] rzekomy, domniemany

allerg|ic [ə'lɜ:dʒɪk] uczulony (**to** na); **~y** ['ælədʒɪ] alergia *f*, uczulenie *n*

alley ['ælɪ] (boczna) uliczka *f*; *with trees on both sides*: aleja *f*; *bowling*: tor *m* kręglarski

alliance [ə'laɪəns] sojusz *m*, przymierze *n*; **~ied** [(attr 'ælaɪd] sprzymierzony (**with, to** z)

allocate ['æləkeɪt] *funds* (wy)asygnować; *people* przydzielać ⟨-lić⟩

allow [ə'laʊ] pozwalać ⟨-wolić⟩, dopuszczać ⟨-puścić⟩ (do); *sum, amount* przeznaczać ⟨-czyć⟩; *time* da(wa)ć; **~ for** brać ⟨wziąć⟩ poprawkę na; **be ~ed** móc, mieć pozwolenie; **~ance** asygnowane fundusze *pl*; *maternity, fuel etc.*: dodatek *m* (do pensji); (*pocket money*) kieszonkowe *n*

alloy ['ælɔɪ] stop *m*

'all-purpose uniwersalny, ogólnego zastosowania; **~'round** wszechstronny, uniwersalny

ally 1. [ə'laɪ] ~ **o.s.** sprzymierzyć się (**with** z); **2.** ['ælaɪ] sprzymierzeniec *m*, sojusznik *m*

almond ['ɑːmənd] migdał *m*

almost ['ɔːlməʊst] prawie

alone [ə'ləʊn] sam, samotnie; *let* ~ nie mówiąc już o

along [ə'lɒŋ] **1.** *prp* wzdłuż, po; **2.** *adv* naprzód, dalej; ~ **with** razem z; *all* ~ od samego początku

aloud [ə'laʊd] na głos, głośno

alphabet ['ælfəbet] alfabet *m*; ~**ical** [~'betɪkl] alfabetyczny

alpine ['ælpaɪn] alpejski

already [ɔːl'redɪ] już

also ['ɔːlsəʊ] także, też, również

altar ['ɔːltə] ołtarz *m*

alter ['ɔːltə] zmieni(a)ć (się); ~**ation** [~'reɪʃn] zmiana *f*

alternat|e 1. ['ɔːltəneɪt] (*use in turn*) używać na przemian; (*occur in turn*) występować naprzemiennie; **2.** [~'tɜːnət] naprzemienny; '~**ing current** prąd *m* zmienny; ~**ive** [~'tɜːnətɪv] alternatywny, inny

although [ɔːl'ðəʊ] chociaż

altitude ['æltɪtjuːd] wysokość *f*

altogether [ɔːltə'geðə] całkiem, całkowicie, zupełnie

always ['ɔːlweɪz] zawsze

am [æm] *1 pers. sg pres of* **be**

amateur ['æmətə] **1.** amator(ka *f*) *m*; **2.** amatorski

amaz|e [ə'meɪz] zadziwi(a)ć, zdumie(wa)ć; ~**ing** zadziwiający

ambassador [æm'bæsədə] *pol.* ambasador *m*

amber ['æmbə] bursztyn *m*; *at* ~ na żółtym świetle

ambiguous [æm'bɪgjʊəs] dwuznaczny, niejasny

ambiti|on [æm'bɪʃn] ambicja *f*; ~**ous** [~'∫əs] ambitny

ambulance ['æmbjʊləns] karetka *f* (pogotowia)

amend [ə'mend] poprawi(a)ć się; *v/t* poprawi(a)ć, napraw(i)ać; ~**ment** poprawa *f*; *parl.* poprawka *f*; ~**s** odszkodowanie *n*, rekompensata *f*

America [ə'merɪkə] Ameryka; ~**n** [ə'merɪkən] **1.** amerykański; **2.** Amerykanin *m* (-nka *f*)

ammunition [æmjʊ'nɪʃn] amunicja *f*

amnesty ['æmnəstɪ] amnestia *f*

among(st) [ə'mʌŋ(st)] wśród, pośród, (po)między

amount [ə'maʊnt] **1.** ilość *f*, kwota *f*, suma *f*; **2.** ~ *to* równać się, wynosić ~-nieść

ample ['æmpl] obfity, dostatni; (*sufficient*) wystarczający

ampli|fier ['æmplɪfaɪə] wzmacniacz *m*; ~**y** ['~faɪ] wzmacniać ~-mocnić)

amputate ['æmpjuteɪt] amputować

amus|e [ə'mjuːz] rozbawi(a)ć, rozweselać ~-lić)

~ement rozrywka f; **~ement arcade** salon m gier zręcznościowych; **~ement park** Am. wesołe miasteczko n; **~ing** zabawny

an [ən, *when stressed* æn] (*przedimek nieokreślony*) jakiś, pewien; (*one*) jeden

analyse, Am. **~ze** ['ænəlaɪz] ⟨prze⟩analizować; **~sis** [ə'næləsɪs] (*pl* **-ses** [~siːz]) analiza f

anatomy [ə'nætəmɪ] anatomia f

ancestor ['ænsestə] przodek m

anchor ['æŋkə] **1.** kotwica f; **2.** ⟨za⟩kotwiczyć

ancient ['eɪnʃənt] starożytny

and [ænd] i, oraz

angel ['eɪndʒəl] anioł m

anger ['æŋgə] **1.** gniew m, złość f; **2.** ⟨roz⟩gniewać

angle¹ ['æŋgl] kąt m

angle² ['~] wędkować; '**~r** wędkarz

angry ['æŋgrɪ] gniewny, zły

anguish ['æŋgwɪʃ] udręka f, ból m

angular ['æŋgjʊlə] kanciasty

animal ['ænɪml] **1.** zwierzę n; **2.** zwierzęcy

animate 1. ['ænɪmeɪt] ożywiać; **2.** ['~mət] *adj* ożywiony; ' **~ed cartoon** film m rysunkowy; **~ion** [~'meɪʃn] ożywienie n; animacja f

ankle ['æŋkl] *anat.* kostka f

annex 1. [ə'neks] ⟨za⟩anektować, przyłączać ⟨-czyć⟩;

2. *a.* **~e** ['æneks] *s* pawilon m, oficyna f

anniversary [ænɪ'vɜːsərɪ] rocznica f

announce [ə'naʊns] ogłaszać ⟨-łosić⟩, oznajmi(a)ć; *TV etc.*: zapowiadać ⟨-wiedzieć⟩; **~ment** ogłoszenie n; *TV etc.*: zapowiedź f; **~r** *TV etc.*: spiker(ka f) m

annoy [ə'nɔɪ] ⟨z⟩irytować, ⟨roz⟩gniewać, ⟨z⟩denerwować; *be* **~ed** być złym/zirytowanym; **~ance** irytacja f; **~ing** denerwujący

annual ['ænjʊəl] (co)roczny, doroczny

anonymous [ə'nɒnɪməs] anonimowy

another [ə'nʌðə] (*different*) inny; (*one more*) jeszcze jeden

answer ['ɑːnsə] **1.** odpowiedź f; **2.** odpowiadać ⟨-wiedzieć⟩ (*s.th.* na coś); *the bell/ door* otwierać ⟨-worzyć⟩ (*komuś*); *the telephone* odbierać ⟨-debrać⟩ telefon; **~ for** odpowiadać za

ant [ænt] mrówka f

antenna [æn'tenə] (*pl* **-nas**) *esp. Am.* antena f

anthem ['ænθəm] hymn m

anti... [æntɪ] przeciw..., anty...; **~biotic** [æn'tɒtɪk] antybiotyk m; **~body** przeciwciało n

anticipate [æn'tɪsɪpeɪt] przewidywać ⟨-widzieć⟩, uprzedzać ⟨-dzić⟩ (*wypadki*) (*look forward to*) cieszyć się (*s.th.* na coś); oczekiwanie *n*; uprzedzenie *n* (w wypadk*m*)

anticlockwise [ænti'klɒk-waɪz] w kierunku przeciwnym do ruchu wskazówek zegara

antipathy [æn'tɪpəθɪ] antypatia *f*, niechęć *f*

antiquated ['æntɪkweɪtɪd] przestarzały

antiqu|e [æn'tiːk] **1.** stary, starożytny, antyczny; 2. antyk *m*; **∼ity** [ˌkwətɪ] starożytność *f*

antisocial [ˌæntɪ'səʊʃl] *person*: nietowarzyski; *behaviour*: aspołeczny

anxiety [æŋ'zaɪətɪ] niepokój *m*, lęk *m*; troska *f*

anxious ['æŋkʃəs] niespokojny; pragnący (*for s.th.* czegoś)

any ['enɪ] **1.** *adj* and *pron* jakiś, jakikolwiek, którykolwiek; *not ∼* żaden; *at ∼ time* kiedykolwiek; **2.** *adv* (*in negative sentences*) wcale, ani trochę, nic a nic; '∼**body** każdy, ktokolwiek; *in questions*: ktoś; '∼**how** tak czy owak; '∼**one** → **anybody**; '∼**thing** coś; ∼ *but* wszystko tylko nie...; ∼ *else?* (czy) coś jeszcze?; *not ... ∼* nic; '∼**way** → **anyhow**; '∼**where** gdziekolwiek; *not ... ∼* nigdzie

apart [ə'pɑːt] (*away*) z dala; (*separately*) osobno; ... ∼ ...

od siebie; ∼ *from* poza, oprócz, prócz

apartment [ə'pɑːtmənt] *Am.* mieszkanie *n*; *pl* apartament *m*

apathetic [æpə'θetɪk] apatyczny

ape [eɪp] małpa *f*

apolog|ize [ə'pɒlədʒaɪz] przepraszać ⟨-rosić⟩; ∼**y** przeprosiny *pl*

appal(**l**) [ə'pɔːl] przerażać ⟨-razić⟩; ∼**ling** przerażający

apparent [ə'pærənt] oczywisty, widoczny; (*seeming*) pozorny

appeal [ə'piːl] **1.** *jur.* składać ⟨złożyć⟩ apelację; ⟨za⟩apelować; zwracać ⟨-rócić⟩ się (*to* do, *for* o); **2.** *jur.* apelacja *f*, odwołanie *n*; (*call*) apel *m*, wezwanie *n*; (*charm*) urok *m*

appear [ə'pɪə] zjawi(a)ć się, ukaz(yw)ać się; (*seem*) wyda(wa)ć się; *TV etc.*: występować ⟨-tąpić⟩; ∼**ance** [-rəns] pojawienie *n* się; (*looks*) wygląd *m*; *mst pl* pozór *m*

appendix [ə'pendɪks] (*pl -dixes, -dices* [-dɪsiːz]) *book*: załącznik *m*, aneks *m*; *med.* wyrostek *m* robaczkowy

appe|tite ['æpɪtaɪt] apetyt *m* (*for* na); żądza *f* (*for s.th.* czegoś); ∼**tizing** ['-zɪŋ] apetyczny

applau|d [ə'plɔːd] *v/i* klaskać; *v/t* oklaskiwać; ∼**se** [-z] oklaski *pl*, aplauz *m*

apple ['æpl] jabłko n; ~ **pie** szarlotka f

appliance [ə'plaɪəns] przyrząd m, urządzenie n

application [æplɪ'keɪʃn] (use) zastosowanie n; in writing: podanie n; in studies: pilność f; lotion etc.: smarowanie n

apply [ə'plaɪ] zwracać ⟨-rócić⟩ się, składać ⟨złożyć⟩ podanie (**for** o); (be relevant) ⟨za⟩stosować się, odnosić ⟨-nieść⟩ się (**to** do); (use) ⟨za⟩stosować (**to** do); lotion etc. ⟨po⟩smarować (**to s.th.** coś)

appoint [ə'pɔɪnt] person mianować; time wyznaczać ⟨-czyć⟩; ~**ment** umówione spotkanie n; person: mianowanie n, wybór m na stanowisko, form. nominacja f

appreciate [ə'priːʃɪeɪt] cenić, uznać wartość; (understand) rozumieć

apprehen|d [æprɪ'hend] zatrzymać, aresztować; nature etc. rozumieć sens; ~**sion** [~ʃn] (misgiving) obawa f; (understanding) zrozumienie n; form. (arrest) aresztowanie n; ~**sive** [~sɪv] pełen obaw (**of** że)

approach [ə'prəʊtʃ] 1. v/i zbliżać ⟨-żyć⟩ się, nadchodzić ⟨-dejść⟩; v/t podchodzić ⟨-dejść⟩ do; 2. podejście n

appropriate [ə'prəʊprɪət] stosowny, odpowiedni

approv|al [ə'pruːvl] aprobata f; formal: zatwierdzenie n; ~**e** [~v] ⟨za⟩aprobować, pochwalać ⟨-lić⟩; formally: zatwierdzać ⟨-dzić⟩

approximate [ə'prɒksɪmət] przybliżony

apricot ['eɪprɪkɒt] morela f

April ['eɪprəl] kwiecień m

apron ['eɪprən] fartuch m

apt [æpt] remark etc.: trafny; person: skłonny (**to do** do (z)robienia)

Arab ['ærəb] 1. Arab(ka f) m; 2. adj arabski; ~**ic** [~ɪk] esp. ling. arabski

arbi|trary ['ɑːbɪtrərɪ] arbitralny, samowolny; ~**rate** ['~treɪt] rozsądzać ⟨-dzić⟩, rozstrzygać ⟨-gnąć⟩

arbo(u)r ['ɑːbə] altan(k)a f

arcade [ɑː'keɪd] arkady pl, podcienia pl; hala f targowa

arch [ɑːtʃ] 1. łuk m; 2. wyginać ⟨-giąć⟩ (się) w łuk

arch(a)eology [ɑːkɪ'ɒlədʒɪ] archeologia f

archaic [ɑː'keɪɪk] archaiczny, przestarzały

archbishop [ɑːtʃ'bɪʃəp] arcybiskup m

archeology Am. → **archaeology**

archer ['ɑːtʃə] łucznik m (-niczka f); ~**y** [~rɪ] łucznictwo n

architect ['ɑːkɪtekt] architekt m (f); ~**ure** [~ktʃə] architektura f

are [ɑː] pl and 2 pers. sg pres of **be**

area ['eərɪə] *math.* powierzchnia *f*; (*district etc.*) okolica *f*; (*field*) obszar *m*, pole *n*; **~ code** *Am. teleph.* numer *m* kierunkowy

argue ['ɑːgjuː] argumentować, dowodzić; (*quarrel*) sprzeczać się

argument ['ɑːgjʊmənt] argument *m*; (*quarrel*) spór *m*

arise [ə'raɪz] (*arose, arisen*) powsta(wa)ć; (*appear*) ukaz(yw)ać się; (*happen*) nadarzać się; (*result*) wynikać ⟨-knąć⟩; **~n** [ə'rɪzn] *pp of* **arise**

arithmetic [ə'rɪθmətɪk] arytmetyka *f*

arm¹ [ɑːm] ramię *n*, ręka *f*; *furniture*: poręcz *f*; *mil.* broń *f*

arm² [~] uzbrajać ⟨-broić⟩ (się)

armchair ['ɑːmtʃeə] fotel *m*

armo(u)r ['ɑːmə] **1.** *hist.* zbroja *f*; *mil., zo.* pancerz *m*; **2.** opancerzać ⟨-rzyć⟩

'armpit pacha *f*

arms [ɑːmz] *pl* broń *f*; (*family sign*) herb *m*

army ['ɑːmɪ] armia *f*; *institution*: wojsko *n*; wojska *pl* lądowe

arose [ə'rəʊz] *past of* **arise**

around [ə'raʊnd] **1.** *adv* wokoło, naokoło, dookoła; **2.** *prp* dokoła

arouse [ə'raʊz] *interest etc.*: pobudzać ⟨-dzić⟩; *sexually*: podniecać ⟨-cić⟩

arrange [ə'reɪndʒ] (*organize*) ⟨z⟩organizować; (*lay out*) ustawi(a)ć, układać ⟨ułożyć⟩; **~ment** załatwienie *n*; (*deal*) układ *m*; (*agreement*) umowa *f*

arrears [ə'rɪəz] *pl* zaległości *pl*

arrest [ə'rest] **1.** aresztowanie *n*; **2.** ⟨za⟩aresztować; (*check*) wstrzym(yw)ać

arriv|al [ə'raɪvl] przybycie *n*; *by train/car etc.*: przyjazd *m*; **~e** [~v] przyby(wa)ć; *by train/car etc.*: przyjeżdżać ⟨-jechać⟩

arrogant ['ærəgənt] arogancki, wyniosły

arrow ['ærəʊ] strzała *f*

art [ɑːt] sztuka *f*; *pl* (*education*) nauki *pl* humanistyczne

artery ['ɑːtərɪ] *med.* tętnica *f*; *mot.* arteria *f* komunikacyjna

article ['ɑːtɪkl] *newspaper*: artykuł *m*; *jur. etc.* paragraf *m*; *gram.* przedimek *m*

articulate 1. [ɑː'tɪkjʊleɪt] ⟨wy⟩artykułować; **2.** [~lət] wyraźny; *person*: elokwentny

artificial [ɑːtɪ'fɪʃl] sztuczny

artisan [ɑːtɪ'zæn] rzemieślnik *m*

artist ['ɑːtɪst] artysta *m* (-tka *f*); **~ic** [ɑː'tɪstɪk] artystyczny

as [æz] **1.** *adv* (tak) jak; jako; **2.** *cj* jako że, ponieważ, skoro; **~ ... ~** tak ... jak; **~ for** jeśli chodzi o

ascend [ə'send] *lift etc.*:

uda(wa)ć się do góry; (*climb*)
wstępować ⟨-tąpić⟩ (*s.th.* na
coś); **~t** [~t] *path*: podejście n;
(*climbing*) wspinaczka f

ash¹ [æʃ] jesion m

ash² [~] *a.* **~es** popiół m; 2
Wednesday Popielec m

ashamed [ə'ʃeɪmd] zawstydzony; **be ~ of** wstydzić się

ash|bin, ~can Am. → *dustbin*

ashore [ə'ʃɔː] na brzeg(u); *go
~* schodzić ⟨zejść⟩ na ląd

ashtray popielniczka f

Asia [ˈeɪʃə] Azja; **1.**
azjatycki; **2.** Azjata m (-tka
f); *an* [ˈeɪʃn] jesion m

aside [ə'saɪd] na bok(u)

ask [ɑːsk] *v/t s.o.* ⟨s⟩pytać;
(*request*) prosić (**for** o); (*demand*) wymagać (**of** od); *~ a
question* zadać pytanie; *v/i*
⟨po⟩prosić (**for** o)

asleep [ə'sliːp]: **be** (*fast,
sound*) (mocno, głęboko)
spać; *fall ~* zasnąć

asparagus [ə'spærəɡəs] szparag m

aspect [ˈæspekt] aspekt m

asphalt [ˈæsfælt] **1.** asfalt m;
2. ⟨wy⟩asfaltować

ass [æs] osioł m; *fig.* dureń m

assassin [ə'sæsɪn] *pol.* zabójca m, zamachowiec m;
~ate [~eɪt] *esp. pol.* zamordować; **~ation** [~'neɪʃn] *esp.
pol.* zabójstwo n, mord m

assault [ə'sɔːlt] **1.** *mil.* atak m,
szturm m; *fig.* atak m; *jur.*
napaść f; **2.** ⟨za⟩atakować

assemb|le [ə'sembl] ⟨z⟩gromadzić (się); *tech.* ⟨z⟩montować; **~y** zgromadzenie n,
zebranie n; *tech.* montaż m;
2. wyrazić zgodę (**to** na)

assert [ə'sɜːt] (*declare*)
stwierdzać ⟨-dzić⟩; (*demand*) domagać się

assess [ə'ses] *situation etc.*
oceni(a)ć; *value* ⟨o⟩szacować (**at** na)

asset [ˈæset] zaleta f; *pl econ.*
aktywa *pl*; *pl jur.* majątek m;
fig. person: mocny punkt m

assign [ə'saɪn] przydzielać
⟨-lić⟩; (*appoint*) wyznaczać
⟨-czyć⟩; **~ment** (*task*) zadanie n; (*appointment*) przydział m

assist [ə'sɪst] pomagać
⟨-móc⟩ (*s.o.* komuś); **~ance**
pomoc f; **~ant** pomocnik m
(-nica f); (*shop*) ~ *Brt.* sprzedawca m (-wczyni f)

associat|e [ə'səʊʃɪeɪt] obcować, trzymać się (**with** *s.o.*
kogoś); *psych.* ⟨s⟩kojarzyć;
2. [~ʃɪət] współpracownik m
(-nica f); **~ion** [~'eɪʃn] stowarzyszenie n, związek m

assorted [ə'sɔːtɪd] różnorodny

assume [ə'sjuːm] zakładać
⟨założyć⟩; przyjmować
⟨-jąć⟩

assur|ance [ə'ʃɔːrəns] (*assertion*) zapewnienie n; (*confidence*) wiara f; (*insurance*)
esp. Brt. ubezpieczenie n na
życie; **~e** [ə'ʃɔː] *s.o.* zapew-

audience

ni(a)ć; *esp. Brt.* life ubezpieczać ⟨-czyć⟩; **~ed** (*confident*) pewny; (*insured*) *esp. Brt.* ubezpieczony (na życie)

astonish [ə'stɒnɪʃ] zdumieć; **be ~ed** ⟨z⟩dziwić się (*at s.th.* czemuś); **~ing** zdumiewający; **~ment** zdumienie *n*

astronomy [ə'strɒnəmɪ] astronomia *f*

asylum [ə'saɪləm] *med.* szpital *m* psychiatryczny; *pol.* azyl *m*

at [æt] *prp place*: w, u, przy, na; *direction*: w (kierunku); *occupation*: przy, w trakcie; *price*: za; *time*: o; *age*: w wieku; **~ the cleaner's** w pralni; **~ my grandmother's** u mojej babci; **~ the door** przy drzwiach; **~ 10 pounds** za 10 funtów; **~ 5 o'clock** o piątej; **~ 18** w wieku lat 18; **not ... ~ all** wcale nie

ate [et] *past of* **eat**

athlet|e ['æθliːt] sportowiec *m*; **~ic** [~'letɪk] wysportowany; **~ics** *sg* lekka atletyka *f*

Atlantic [ət'læntɪk] atlantycki

atmosphere ['ætməsfɪə] atmosfera *f*

atom ['ætəm] atom *m*; **~ bomb** bomba *f* atomowa

atomic [ə'tɒmɪk] atomowy, jądrowy

atomizer ['ætəʊmaɪzə] rozpylacz *m*

atroci|ous [ə'trəʊʃəs] okrutny, nieludzki; **~ty** [~ɒsətɪ] okrucieństwo *n*

attach [ə'tætʃ] (*to*) przymocow(yw)ać; *importance etc.* przywiąz(yw)ać; **be ~ed to** być przywiązanym do

attack [ə'tæk] **1.** ⟨za⟩atakować; **2.** atak *m*

attempt [ə'tempt] **1.** usiłować; **2.** próba *f*

attend [ə'tend] *v/t* doglądać ⟨-znąć⟩; *lecture etc.* być (obecnym) na; *school etc.* uczęszczać ⟨pójść⟩ do czegoś; *v/i* **~ to** załatwi(a)ć, zajmować ⟨-jąć⟩ się; (*at a restaurant etc.*) obsługiwać ⟨-łużyć⟩ (*to s.o.* kogoś); **~ance** frekwencja *f*, obecność *f*; (*serving*) obsługa *f*; **~ant** osoba *f* z obsługi; *park, zoo*: dozorca *m*; *cinema, theatre*: bileter(ka *f*) *m*

attention [ə'tenʃn] uwaga *f*; **~ive** [~tɪv] uważny

attic ['ætɪk] strych *m*

attitude ['ætɪtjuːd] stosunek *m*, podejście *n* (*to(wards)* do)

attract [ə'trækt] *attention* przyciągać ⟨-gnąć⟩; *person* pociągać ⟨-gnąć⟩; **~ion** [~kʃn] powab *m*; **~ive** pociągający, atrakcyjny

attribute [ə'trɪbjuːt] przypisać (*to* do)

auction ['ɔːkʃn] **1.** aukcja *f*; **2.** *mst* **~ off** sprzedać na aukcji

audience ['ɔːdjəns] publiczność *f*; *radio*: słuchacze *pl*; *thea., cinema*: widzowie *pl*

August ['ɔ:gəst] sierpień *m*

aunt [ɑ:nt] ciotka *f*

austere [ɔ'stɪə] surowy, srogi

Australia [ɒ'streɪljə] *f* Australia *f*; **∼n** [ɒ'streɪljən] **1.** australijski; **2.** Australijczyk *m* (-jka *f*)

Austria ['ɒstrɪə] *f* Austria *f*; **∼n** ['ɒstrɪən] **1.** austriacki; **2.** Austriak *m* (-riaczka *f*)

authentic [ɔ:'θentɪk] autentyczny

author ['ɔ:θə] autor(ka *f*) *m*

authority [ɔ:'θɒrɪtɪ] (*power*) władza *f*; (*permission*) upoważnienie *n*; (*expert*) autorytet *m*; *mst pl* władze *pl*; **∼ze** ['ɔ:θəraɪz] *v/t* upoważnia(ć; *s.th.* ⟨u⟩sankcjonować, zgadzać ⟨zgodzić⟩ się na

automatic [ɔ:tə'mætɪk] automatyczny

autumn ['ɔ:təm] jesień *f*

auxiliary [ɔ:g'zɪljərɪ] pomocniczy, posiłkowy

available [ə'veɪləbl] dostępny; *econ.* do nabycia, dostępny na rynku

avalanche ['ævəlɑ:ntʃ] lawina *f*

avenge [ə'vendʒ] pomścić (*s.o.*, *s.th.* kogoś, coś), wziąć odwet (*s.o.* na kimś)

avenue ['ævənju:] ulica *f*; (*alley*) aleja *f*

average ['ævərɪdʒ] **1.** średnia

f, przeciętna *f*; **2.** średni, przeciętny

avert [ə'vɜ:t] odwracać ⟨-wrócić⟩

aviation [eɪvɪ'eɪʃn] lotnictwo *n*

avoid [ə'vɔɪd] unikać ⟨-knąć⟩

awake [ə'weɪk] **1.** przebudzony, nie śpiący; **2.** (*awoke or awaked, awoken or awaked*) *v/t* ⟨o⟩budzić, ⟨z⟩budzić; *v/i* ⟨o⟩budzić się; **∼n** [∼ən] → **awake** 2

award [ə'wɔ:d] **1.** nagroda *f*, wyróżnienie *n*; **2.** *prize etc.* przyznać

aware [ə'weə]: *be ∼ of s.th.* być świadomym czegoś, mieć świadomość czegoś

away [ə'weɪ] *adv and adj z* dala, w oddaleniu; (*travelling*) poza domem, w podróży

awe [ɔ:] **1.** (*bezbrzeżny*) podziw *m*, respekt *m*; (*dread*) groza *f*; **2.** wzbudzać ⟨-dzić⟩ lęk

awful ['ɔ:fʊl] straszny

awkward ['ɔ:kwəd] *person*, *movement*: niezdarny, niezgrabny; *time etc.*: niezręczny

awoke [ə'wəʊk] *past of* **awake** 2; *∼n past of* **awake** 2

ax(e) [æks] siekiera *f*, topór *m*

axis ['æksɪs] *pl* (*axes* ['∼si:z]) *mat.* oś *f*

axle ['æksl] oś *f* (koła)

B

baby ['beɪbɪ] **1.** dziecko *n*, niemowlę *n*; **2.** dziecięcy; **~car-riage** *Am.* wózek *m* dziecięcy; '**~sit** (-*sat*) pilnować dziecka; '**~sitter** opiekun(ka *f*) *m* do dziecka

bachelor ['bætʃələ] kawaler *m*

back [bæk] **1.** *s anat.* plecy *pl*, grzbiet *m*; *book:* grzbiet *m*; *chair etc.:* oparcie *n*; *paper:* odwrotna strona *f*; *(rear)* tył *m*; *sp.* obrońca *m*; **2.** *adj* tylni; **3.** *adv* w tył, do tyłu, wstecz; *with movement:* z powrotem; **4.** *v/t a.* **~ up** popierać ⟨-przeć⟩; cofać ⟨-fnąć⟩, wycofyw(ać) się; *v/i of-ten* **~ up** cofać ⟨-fnąć⟩ się, wycofyw(ać się; '**~bone** kręgosłup *m*; '**~fire** nie powieść się, dać efekt przeciwny do zamierzonego; '**~ground** tło *n*; '**~ing** poparcie *n*; '**~pack** *esp. Am.* plecak *m*; **~ seat** tylne siedzenie *n*; '**~space** (**key**) *typewriter, computer:* cofacz *m*; '**~up** poparcie *n*, *tech.* rezerwa *f*; *computer:* kopia *f* bezpieczeństwa; '**~ward** ['-wəd] **1.** *adj country:* zacofany; *child:* niedorozwinięty; **2.** *adv a.* **~wards** ['-wədz] do tyłu, w tył

bacon ['beɪkən] bekon *m*

bad [bæd] *smell, etc.:* rzykry; *food:* zepsuty; *wound:* paskudny; *accident:* fatalny; *language:* wulgarny; *money:* fałszywy

bade [beɪd] *past of* **bid** 1

badge [bædʒ] odznaka *f*

badger ['bædʒə] borsuk *m*

'**badly** *want, need:* strasznie, bardzo; *(poorly)* niedobrze, kiepsko; *hurt:* paskudnie, fatalnie; *he is* **~ off** kiepsko mu się wiedzie

baffle ['bæfl] zbi(ja)ć z tropu

bag [bæg] torba *f*; *lady's:* torebka *f*; *under eye:* worek *m*

baggage ['bægɪdʒ] *esp. Am.* bagaż *m*; '**~car** *Am. rail.* wagon *m* bagażowy; '**~ check** *Am.* kwit *m* bagażowy; '**~room** *Am.* przechowalnia *f* bagażu

baggy ['bægɪ] workowaty; *trousers:* powypychany

bail [beɪl] **1.** kaucja *f*; **2. ~ s.o. out** zapłacić za kogoś kaucję

bait [beɪt] przynęta *f* (*a. fig.*)

bak|e [beɪk] ⟨u⟩piec (się); *bricks* wypalać ⟨-lić⟩; '**~er** piekarz *m*; '**~ery** ['-ərɪ] piekarnia *f*; '**~ing powder** proszek *m* do pieczenia

balance ['bæləns] **1.** waga *f*; równowaga *f* (*a. fig.*); *econ.* bilans *m*; *econ.* saldo *n*; *econ.* reszta *f*, pozostałość *f*; **2.** *v/t*

⟨z⟩równoważyć; *accounts etc.* ⟨z⟩bilansować; *v/i* balansować; być w równowadze; *accounts:* zgadzać się; **~d** zrównoważony; **~ sheet** bilans *m*; zestawienie *n* bilansowe

balcony ['bælkənɪ] balkon *m*

bald [bɔːld] łysy

ball [bɔːl] *in games:* piłka *f*; *(sphere)* kula *f*; *billiards etc.:* bila *f*

ballad ['bæləd] ballada *f*

ball bearing [bɔːl'beərɪŋ] łożysko *n* kulkowe

ballet ['bæleɪ] balet *m*

balloon [bə'luːn] balon *m*; *children's:* balonik *m*

ballpoint (pen) ['bɔːlpɔɪnt] długopis *m*

ban [bæn] **1.** zakaz *m*; **2.** zakaz(yw)ać

banana [bə'nɑːnə] banan *m*

band [bænd] **1.** opaska *f*, przepaska *f*; *pattern:* pasek *m*; *tech.* pasmo *n*; *jazz, rock etc.:* zespół *m*, orkiestra *f*

bandage ['bændɪdʒ] **1.** bandaż *m*; **2.** bandażować

'Band-Aid *TM Am.* plaster *m* (z gazą)

bang [bæŋ] **1.** huk *m*, trzask *m*, łoskot *m*; **2.** trzaskać ⟨-snąć⟩, huknąć

bank¹ [bæŋk] **1.** *econ., a. blood, data etc.:* bank *m*; **2.** *v/t money* wpłacić do banku; *v/i* mieć konto (**with** w)

bank² [~] *river etc.:* brzeg *m*; *sand:* nasyp *m*, wał *m*

bank| account konto *n* bankowe; **~book** książeczka *f* oszczędnościowa; **~er** bankier *m*; **~ holiday** *Brt.* dzień *m* wolny od pracy; **~ note** banknot *m*; **~ rate** stopa *f* procentowa

bankrupt ['bæŋkrʌpt] **1.** zbankrutowany; **go ~** ⟨z⟩bankrutować; **2.** doprowadzać ⟨-dzić⟩ do bankructwa; **~cy** [-ptsɪ] bankructwo *n*

banner ['bænə] transparent *m*; *(flag)* sztandar *m*

bapti|sm ['bæptɪzəm] chrzest *m*; **~ze** [~'taɪz] ⟨o⟩chrzcić

bar [bɑː] **1.** pręt *m*, szlaban *m*; *pl* krata *f*; *(gold etc.)* sztaba *f*; *mus.* takt *m*; bar *m*; *hotel:* bar *m*; **~ of chocolate** tabliczka *f* czekolady, baton *m*; **~ of soap** kostka *f* mydła; **2.** *door* ⟨za⟩ryglować; *way* ⟨za⟩grodzić; *use* zakaz(yw)ać; *people* nie wpuszczać ⟨wpuścić⟩ (**from** do)

barbecue [bɑː'bɪkjuː] *(grill)* ruszt *m* ogrodowy; *(dish)* pieczeń *f* itp. z rusztu

barbed wire [bɑːbd'waɪə] drut *m* kolczasty

barber ['bɑːbə] fryzjer *m* (męski)

bare [beə] **1.** nagi, goły; **2.** odnażać ⟨-żyć⟩, ogołacać ⟨-łocić⟩; **~foot 1.** *adj* bosy; **2.** *adv* boso; **~ly** ledwo, ledwie

bargain ['bɑːgɪn] **1.** interes *m*, transakcja *f*; okazja *f* (handlowa), udany zakup *m*; **2.** targować się; układać się

bark[^1] ['bɑːk] kora *f*

bark[^2] [~] **1.** szczekać (-knąć); **2.** szczeknięcie *n*

barley ['bɑːlɪ] jęczmień *m*

barn [bɑːn] stodoła *f*

barracks ['bærəks] *sg* koszary *pl*

barrel ['bærəl] baryłka *f*; *gun*: lufa *f*

barricade [bærɪ'keɪd] barykada *f*

barrier ['bærɪə] bariera *f*, szlaban *m*; *fig.* przeszkoda *f*

barrister ['bærɪstə] *Brt.* adwokat *m*; obrońca *m*

barter ['bɑːtə] handel *m* wymienny

base[^1] [beɪs] nikczemny, niski, podły

base[^2] [~] **1.** podstawa *f*; *mil.* baza *f*; **2.** opierać (**on, upon** na); ~**ment** suterena *f*

bashful ['bæʃfʊl] nieśmiały, wstydliwy

basic ['beɪsɪk] **1.** podstawowy; **2.** *pl* podstawy *pl*; ~**ally** w zasadzie

basin ['beɪsn] miednica *f*; *wash*: umywalka *f*

basis ['beɪsɪs] (*pl* -**ses** ['~siːz]) podstawa *f*

basket ['bɑːskɪt] kosz(yk) *m*; ~**ball** koszykówka *f*

bass [beɪs] *mus.* bas *m*

bastard ['bɑːstəd] nieślubne

dziecko *n*, bękart *m* V; V sukinsyn *m* V

bat[^1] [bæt] *zo.* nietoperz *m*

bat[^2] [~] *sport.* kij *m* (do krykieta *itp.*); rakietka *f* (do ping-ponga)

batch [bætʃ] *goods*: partia *f* (towaru); *people*: turnus *m*; *computer*: plik *m* wsadowy

bath [bɑːθ] **1.** (*pl* **baths** [~ðz]) kąpiel *f* (w wannie); *havel take a* ~ brać (wziąć) kąpiel, (wy)kąpać się; **2.** (wy)kąpać (w wannie)

bathe [beɪð] **1.** *v/t wound etc.* przemy(wa)ć; *v/i* kąpać się (w rzece *itp.*), pływać; *Am.* brać (wziąć) kąpiel; **2.** kąpiel *f* (w rzece *itp.*)

bathing ['beɪðɪŋ]: ~ **costume**, ~ **suit** strój *m* kąpielowy; *go* ~ iść (pójść) popływać

bath|robe płaszcz *m* kąpielowy; *Am.* szlafrok *m*, podomka *f*; ~**room** łazienka *f*; *Am.* toaleta *f*, ubikacja *f*; ~ **towel** ręcznik *m* kąpielowy

battery ['bætərɪ] bateria *f*; *mot.* akumulator *m*

battle ['bætl] bitwa *f* (**of** pod); ~**field**, ~**ground** pole *n* bitwy

bay [beɪ] zatoka *f*

bazaar [bə'zɑː] bazar *m*

be [biː] (*was or were, been, pres am, is, are*) być; *you may be wrong* możesz nie mieć racji; *she is reading* ona czyta; *it is me* F to ja; *how much is (are)* ...? ile

[^1]:
[^2]:

kosztuje (-ją) ...?; *there is, there are* jest, są

beach [biːtʃ] plaża *f*; '~**wear** strój *m* plażowy

beak [biːk] dziób *m*

beaker ['biːkə] kubek *m* (plastikowy)

beam [biːm] **1.** belka *f*; *light:* promień *m* (światła); **2.** uśmiechać ⟨-chnąć⟩ się radośnie

bean [biːn] fasola *f*

bear¹ [beə] niedźwiedź *m*

bear² [~] (*bore, borne* or *born*); (*carry*) ⟨nieść⟩; (*stand*) znosić ⟨znieść⟩; *child* ⟨u⟩rodzić; **~able** ['~rəbl] znośny

beard [bɪəd] broda *f*

bearer ['beərə] posiadacz(ka *f*) *m* (*np.* paszportu), okaziciel(ka *f*) *m*

bearing ['beərɪŋ] wpływ *m* (*on* na); postawa *f*

beast [biːst] zwierzę *n*; bestia *f*

beat [biːt] **1.** (*beat, beaten* or *beat*) pobić; *eggs etc.* ubi(ja)ć; *drum* bębnić w; ~ *it!* F spieprzaj! F; ~u pobić; **2.** uderzenie *n*; *mus.* takt *m*; *drum:* bębnienie *n*; '~**en** *pp* of *beat* 1

beauti|ful ['bjuːtəfʊl] piękny; '~**y** piękno *n*

beaver ['biːvə] bóbr *m*

became [bɪ'keɪm] *past* of *become*

because [bɪ'kɒz] ponieważ; ~ *of* z powodu

becom|e [bɪ'kʌm] (*became, become*) zostać, stać się (*a. of s.o.* z kimś); ~**ing** twarzowy

bed [bed] łóżko *n*; *animal:* legowisko *n*; *agr.* grządka *f*; ~ *and breakfast* pokój *m* ze śniadaniem; '~**clothes** *pl* bielizna *f* pościelowa; '~**ding** pościel *f*; '~**ridden** obłożnie chory; '~**room** sypialnia *f*; '~**sit** F, ~'**sitter** *Brt.* kawalerka *f*

bee [biː] pszczoła *f*

beech [biːtʃ] buk *m*

beef [biːf] wołowina *f*

'beehive ul *m*

been [biːn] *pp* of *be*

beer [bɪə] piwo *n*

beet [biːt] burak *m*

beetle ['biːtl] żuk *m*, chrząszcz *m*

beetroot ['biːtruːt] burak *m* ćwikłowy

before [bɪ'fɔː] **1.** *adv space:* na przedzie, z przodu; *time:* przedtem, poprzednio; **2.** *cj* zanim; **3.** *prp* przed; ~**hand** z góry

beg [beg] żebrać; błagać

began [bɪ'gæn] *past of begin*

beggar ['begə] żebrak *m*

begin [bɪ'gɪn] (*began, begun*) zaczynać ⟨-cząć⟩; rozpoczynać ⟨-cząć⟩; '~**ner** początkujący *m*; '~**ning** początek *m*

begun [bɪ'gʌn] *pp* of *begin*

behalf [bɪ'hɑːf]: *on* ~ of (*Am. a. in*) ~ of w imieniu

behav|e [bɪ'heɪv] zachow(yw)ać się; **~io(u)r** [~vjə] zachowanie *n*

behind [bɪ'haɪnd] **1.** *prp* za; **2.** *adv* z tyłu, w tyle; **3.** *s* F tyłek *m* F

being ['bi:ɪŋ] bycie *n*, istnienie *n*; *human:* istota *f*

Belgian ['beldʒən] belgijski; **2.** Belg(ijka *f*) *m*; **~um** [~əm] Belgia *f*

belief [bɪ'li:f] wiara *f* (**in** w)

believe [bɪ'li:v] ⟨u⟩wierzyć (**in** w); **~r** wierny *m*, (człowiek) wierzący *f*

bell [bel] dzwon(ek) *m*

belly ['belɪ] F brzuch *m*

belong [bɪ'lɒŋ] należeć (**to** do); **~ings** *pl* dobytek *m*

beloved [bɪ'lʌvd] **1.** ukochany; **2.** ukochany *m* (-na *f*)

below [bɪ'ləʊ] **1.** *adv* na dole, pod spodem, poniżej; **2.** *prp* pod, poniżej

belt [belt] pas(ek) *m*

bench [bentʃ] ławka *f*

bend [bend] **1.** wygięcie *n*; *in road:* zakręt *m*; **2.** (**bent**) zginać ⟨zgiąć⟩ (się)

beneath [bɪ'ni:θ] **1.** *adv* poniżej, pod spodem, na dole; **2.** *prp* pod

beneficial [benɪ'fɪʃl] korzystny, zbawienny

benefit ['benɪfɪt] **1.** pożytek *m*, korzyść *f*; *social etc.:* świadczenie *n*; *unemployment*, *child:* zasiłek *m*; **2.** przynosić ⟨-nieść⟩ korzyść; **~ by/from** ⟨s⟩korzystać na

bent [bent] *past and pp of*

bend 2

beret ['bereɪ] beret *m*

berry ['berɪ] jagoda *f*

berth [bɜ:θ] *mar.* miejsce *n* postoju; *mar.* koja *f*; *rail.* kuszetka *f*

beside [bɪ'saɪd] *prp* przy, obok; **be ~ o.s.** nie posiadać się (**with** z); → **point** 1; **~s** [~z] **1.** *adv* poza tym, prócz tego; **2.** *prp* oprócz, poza

best [best] **1.** *adj* najlepszy; **2.** *adv* najlepiej; **at ~** w najlepszym razie; **do one's ~** da(wa)ć z siebie wszystko; **make the ~ of** ⟨z⟩robić jak najlepszy użytek z; **~ man** (*pl* - **men**) drużba *m*

bet [bet] **1.** zakład *m*; **2.** (**bet** *or* **betted**) zakładać ⟨założyć⟩ się; **you** ~ F jeszcze jak!

betray [bɪ'treɪ] zdradzać ⟨-dzić⟩; **~al** zdrada *f*

better ['betə] **1.** *adj* lepszy; **he is ~** lepiej mu; **2.** *adv* lepiej

between [bɪ'twi:n] **1.** *adv* pośrodku, między (*jednym a drugim*); **2.** *prp* między, pomiędzy

beverage ['bevərɪdʒ] napój *m*

beware [bɪ'weə] strzec/wystrzegać się (**of s.th./s.o.** kogoś/czegoś)

bewilder [bɪ'wɪldə] ⟨z⟩dezorientować; oszołamiać ⟨-łomić⟩

beyond [bɪ'jɒnd] **1.** *adv* dalej (położony); **2.** *prp* za, poza

bias ['baɪəs] (*prejudice*) uprzedzenie *n*; (*inclination*) skłon-

ność f; **~(s)ed** uprzedzony,
stronniczy

Bible ['baibl] Biblia f; **ℓical**
['biblikl] biblijny

bicycle ['baisikl] rower m

bid [bid] **1.** (**bid** or **bade, bid**
or **bidden**) składać
⟨złożyć⟩ ofertę (**s.th.** na
coś); **2.** econ. oferta f; cards:
odzywka f; **'~den** pp of **bid** 1

big [big] duży

bike [baik] motocykl m; F (bicycle) rower m

bilateral [bai'lætərəl] dwustronny

bilberry ['bilbəri] czarna jagoda f

bill¹ [bil] dziób m

bill² [] rachunek m; (poster)
plakat m; pol. projekt m
ustawy; Am. banknot m; **~ of**
exchange econ. weksel m;
'~board Am. plansza reklamowa; **'~fold** Am. portfel m

billiards ['biljədz] sg bilard m

billion ['biljən] miliard m

bin [bin] pojemnik m; rubbish:
kubeł m

bind [baind] (**bound**) (tie)
wiązać; together:
związ(yw)ać; to s.th. przy-
wiąz(yw)ać; (oblige) zobo-
wiąz(yw)ać; **'~er** (a. **book~**)
introligator m; (string) sznurek m; covers: skoroszyt m;
'~ing 1. adj wiążący; **2.** book:
oprawa f, okładka f; skiing:
wiązanie n narciarskie

binoculars [bi'nɒkjuləz] pl
lornetka f

biography [bai'ɒgrəfi] bio-
grafia f

biolog|**ical** [baiəu'lɒdʒikl]
biologiczny; **~y** ['ɒlədʒi]
biologia f

birch [bɜːtʃ] brzoza f

bird [bɜːd] ptak m

biro ['baiərəu] TM Brt.
długopis m

birth [bɜːθ] urodzenie n, urodziny pl; **give ~ to** urodzić;
date of ~ data f urodzenia;
~ certificate metryka f urodzenia; **~ control** antykon-
cepcja f, planowanie n rodziny; **'~day** urodziny pl; **hap-**
py ~! wszystkiego najlepsze-
go!; **'~place** miejsce n urodzenia; **'~rate** przyrost m
naturalny

biscuit ['biskit] Brt. herbatnik
m

bishop ['biʃəp] biskup m;
chess: goniec m

bit¹ [bit] kawałek m; **a ~**
troszkę

bit² [] computer: bit m

bit³ [] past of **bite** 2

bitch [bitʃ] suka f (a. fig. V)

bite [bait] **1.** food: kęs m;
wound: ukąszenie n, ugryzie-
nie n; **2.** (**bit, bitten**) kąsać
⟨ukąsić⟩, ⟨u⟩gryźć; pepper:
palić

bitten ['bitn] pp of **bite** 2

bitter ['bitə] **1.** gorzki; fig.
zgorzkniały; **2.** pl nalewka f
na żołądek, żołądkowa

black [blæk] **1.** czarny; **2.**
⟨po⟩czernić; **~ out** zaciem-

ni(a)ć; **3.** *colour*: czerń f; *person*: czarny m (-na f), Murzyn(ka f) m; '**~berry** jeżyna f; '**~bird** kos m; '**~board** tablica f; **~en** poczernić; ⟨s⟩czernieć, ⟨po⟩ciemnieć; **~ ice** gołoledź f; '**~mail 1.** szantaż m; **2.** szantażować; '**~mailer** szantażysta m (-tka f); **~ market** czarny rynek m; '**~out** (*power cut*) wyłączenie n prądu; (*loss of consciousness*) utrata f przytomności

bladder [blædə] *anat.* pęcherz m

blade [bleid] *grass*: źdźbło n; *knife*: ostrze m; *sword*: głownia f; *oar*: pióro n (wiosła); *propeller*: łopata f śmigła

blame [bleim] **1.** winić, obwini(a)ć; **~ s.o. for s.th.** obciążać ⟨-żyć⟩ kogoś odpowiedzialnością za coś; **2.** wina f, odpowiedzialność f

blank [blæŋk] **1.** czysty, niezapisany; *econ.* nie wypełniony, in blanco; **2.** puste/wolne miejsce n; *mil.* ślepy nabój m; *lottery*: pusty los m

blanket ['blæŋkit] **1.** koc m; **2.** pokry(wa)ć

blare [bleə] *radio etc.*: wyć, drzeć się; *trumpet*: ⟨za⟩grzmieć, ⟨za⟩trąbić

blast [blɑːst] **1.** wybuch m, podmuch m; **2.** v/t wysadzać ⟨-dzić⟩ w powietrze; v/i **~ off** *rocket*: startować; **F ~ it!** a niech to szlag! F; '**~furnace** piec m hutniczy; '**~off**

rocket: start m

blaze [bleiz] **1.** płomienie pl, ogień m; **2.** *fire*: płonąć; *light*: świecić

bleach [bliːtʃ] wybielać ⟨-lić⟩

bled [bled] *past and pp of* **bleed**

bleed [bliːd] (*bled*) krwawić; *fig.* F puszczać, farbować; '**~ing** krwawienie n

blend [blend] **1.** ⟨z⟩mieszać; **2.** mieszanka f; *tea* mikser m

bless [bles] (*blessed or blest*) ⟨po⟩błogosławić; (*God*) **~ you!** na zdrowie!; **~ me!**, **my soul!** coś podobnego!; **~ed** ['~id] błogosławiony; '**~ing** błogosławieństwo n

blest [blest] *past and pp of* **bless**

blew [bluː] *past of* **blow²**

blind [blaind] **1.** *adj* ślepy (*fig.* **to** na); **2.** roleta f, żaluzja f; **the ~** pl niewidomi pl; *fig.* zaślepi(a)ć; **~ alley** ślepa uliczka f; '**~fold s.o.** zawiązać komuś oczy

blink [bliŋk] v/t *eyes* mrugać ⟨-gnąć⟩; v/i *eyes* mrugać oczyma; *lights*: ⟨za⟩migotać

bliss [blis] błogość f, szczęście n

blister ['blistə] pęcherz m, bąbel m

blizzard ['blizəd] zamieć f

block [blɒk] **1.** *stone*: blok m; *psych.* blokada f; *esp. Am.* (*row of houses*) kwartał m; *a.* **~ of flats** Brt. blok m mieszkalny; **2.** *a.* **~ up**

⟨za⟩blokować ⟨się⟩; *pipes:* zapychać ⟨-pchać⟩ ⟨się⟩
block letters *pl* drukowane litery *pl*

bloke [bləʊk] *Brt.* F facet *m* F

blond [blɒnd] blond; **~e** blondynka *f*

blood [blʌd] krew *f*; **in cold ~** z zimną krwią; **~donor** dawca *m* krwi; **~group** grupa *f* krwi; **~less** bezkrwawy; **~poisoning** zakażenie *n* krwi; **~pressure** ciśnienie *n* krwi; **~relation, ~relative** krewny *m* (-na *f*); **~shed** rozlew *m* krwi; **~y** krwawy; *Brt.* F cholerny F

bloom [bluːm] **1.** kwiat *m*; **2.** ⟨za⟩kwitnąć

blossom ['blɒsəm] *esp. on trees:* **1.** kwiecie *n*, kwiat *m*; **2.** ⟨za⟩kwitnąć, rozkwitać ⟨-tnąć⟩

blot [blɒt] **1.** kleks *m*; *fig.* plama *f*; **2.** ⟨wy⟩suszyć

blouse [blaʊz] bluzka *f*

blow[1] [bləʊ] cios *m*, uderzenie *n*

blow[2] [~] *(blew, blown)* dmuchać ⟨-chnąć⟩, ⟨za⟩dąć; *mus. flute etc.* ⟨za⟩grać na; *fuse:* przepalać ⟨-lić⟩ ⟨się⟩; **~ one's nose** wycierać ⟨wytrzeć⟩ nos; **~ up** *v/t* wysadzać ⟨-dzić⟩ w powietrze; *phot.* powiększać *f*; *balloon* nadmuch(iw)ać *f*; *v/i* wybuchać ⟨-chnąć⟩ *(a. fig.)*, wylecieć w powietrze; **~-dry** suszyć suszarką; **~n** *pp of*

blow[2]; **~out:** *they had a **~out** mot.* złapali gumę F; **~-up** wybuch *m*; *phot.* powiększenie *n*

blue [bluː] niebieski; F smutny; **~bell** *bot.* dzwonek; **~print** plan *m*, schemat *m*

bluff [blʌf] **1.** blef *m*, blaga *f*; **2.** ⟨za⟩blefować

blunder ['blʌndə] **1.** głupstwo *n*; **2.** ⟨z⟩robić głupstwo

blunt [blʌnt] tępy; *fig.* otwarty, szczery; **~ly** bez ogródek

blur [blɜː] **1.** (niewyraźna) plama *f*; **2.** zamaz(yw)ać; **~red** *phot.* nieostry

blush [blʌʃ] **1.** rumieniec *m*; **2.** ⟨za⟩rumienić ⟨się⟩

boar [bɔː] knur *m*; *wild:* dzik *m*

board [bɔːd] **1.** *wooden:* deska *f*; *(meals)* wikt *m*; *chess:* szachownica *f*; *chopping:* deska *f* do krojenia; *diving:* trampolina *f*; *notice:* tablica *f*; **~ and lodging** zakwaterowanie *n* z wyżywieniem; **~ (of directors)** zarząd *m*; **on ~** na pokładzie; *w pociągu/auto-busie;* **2.** stołować się (with u); **~er** stołownik *m*, pensjonariusz(ka *f*) *m*; **~ing card/pass** *aer.* karta *f* pokładowa; **~ing house** pensjonat *m*; **~ing school** szkoła *f* z internatem

boast [bəʊst] **1.** przechwałka *f*; **2.** chwalić/szczycić się **(s.th.** czymś)

boat [bəʊt] łódka *f*; *(ship)* statek *m*

bossy

bodily ['bɒdɪlɪ] **1.** *adj* cielesny; **2.** *adv* cieleśnie

body ['bɒdɪ] ciało *n*; (*often **dead** ~*) zwłoki *pl*; gremium *n*; gros *n*, główna część *f*; *mot. a.* (*~work*) nadwozie *n*, karoseria *f*; '**~guard** ochrona *f* osobista, ochroniarz *m* F

bog [bɒg] bagno *n*, moczary *pl*

boil¹ [bɔɪl] czyrak *m*

boil² [bɔɪl] **1.** *v*/*u* gotować (się); '**~er** kocioł *m*; **~er suit** kombinezon *m*

bold [bəʊld] śmiały; ~ **type** tłusty druk *m*

bolt [bəʊlt] **1.** śruba *f*; zasuwa *f*; **2.** ~ **upright** *adv* prosto jakby kij połknął; **3.** *v*/*t* przyśrubow(yw)ać; (za)ryglować; *v*/*i* zwi(ew)ać, pryskać ⟨-snąć⟩ F

bomb [bɒm] **1.** bomba *f*; **2.** ⟨z⟩bombardować

bond [bɒnd] *econ.* obligacja *f*, list *m* zastawny; *pl fig.* więzi *pl*

bone [bəʊn] kość *f*

bonnet ['bɒnɪt] *Brt.* maska *f* (samochodu)

bonus ['bəʊnəs] premia *f*

book [bʊk] **1.** książka *f*, książeczka *f*, księga *f*; *pl a.* księgowość *f*; **2.** ⟨za⟩rezerwować, wynajmować ⟨-jąć⟩; ~ **in** *esp. Brt.* zameldować się (w hotelu); **~ed up** obłożony, pełny, brak miejsc; '**~case** biblioteczka *f*; '**~ing clerk** kasjer(ka *f*) *m*

na dworcu; '**~ing office** kasa *f* biletowa; '**~keeping** księgowość *f*; **~let** ['~lɪt] książeczka *f*; '**~shop** księgarnia *f*

boom¹ [buːm] *econ.* boom *m*, rozkwit *m*; (*noise*) huk *m*, grzmot *m*

boom² [~] ⟨za⟩grzmieć

boost [buːst] *esp. econ. and tech.* podnosić ⟨-nieść⟩, zwiększać ⟨-szyć⟩; *fig.* rozreklamować; **2.** wzrost *m*, skok *m*

boot [buːt] (wysoki) but *m*; *Brt. mot.* bagażnik *m*

booth [buːð] *market etc.*: budka *f*, stoisko *n*; *telephone*: budka *f*, kabina *f*

booze [buːz] F **1.** chlać F; **2.** gorzała *f* F

border ['bɔːdə] **1.** granica *f*; **2.** graniczyć (*on z*)

bore¹ [bɔː] **1.** *tech.* kaliber *m*; **2.** ⟨wy⟩wiercić

bore² [~] **1.** nudziarz *m*; *esp. Brt.* F przykrość *f*; **2.** ⟨z⟩nudzić; *be* ~*d* nudzić się

bore³ [~] *past of* **bear**²

boring ['bɔːrɪŋ] nudny

born [bɔːn] **1.** *pp of* **bear**²; **2.** *adj* urodzony; *I was* ~ *in Scotland* urodziłem się w Szkocji

borne [bɔːn] *pp of* **bear**²

borrow ['bɒrəʊ] pożyczać ⟨-czyć⟩

bosom ['bʊzəm] pierś *f*, łono *n*

boss [bɒs] szef *m*; '**~y** apodyktyczny

botch [bɒtʃ] spaprać

both [bəʊθ] obaj, obydwie, oboje; ~ **of them** obaj, obydwie, oboje; ~ ... **and** zarówno ... jak i

bother ['bɒðə] **1.** kłopot *m*, przykrość *f*, zawracanie *n* głowy; *v/t s.o.* męczyć, gnębić; *v/i* przejmować się; *don't* ~ **!** daj spokój!

bottle ['bɒtl] **1.** butelka *f*, butla *f*; **2.** butelkować

bottom ['bɒtəm] dno *n* spód *m*; F tyłek *m*

bought [bɔːt] *past and pp of* **buy**

bound[1] [baʊnd] **1.** *past and pp of* **bind**; **2.** *adj:* **be ~ to do s.th.** na pewno coś zrobić, musieć coś zrobić

bound[2] [~] w drodze (**for** do)

bound[3] [~] **1.** (pod)skok *m*, sus *m*; **2.** odbi(jać) się, odskakiwać ⟨-koczyć⟩

bound[4] [~] **1.** *mst pl* granica *f*; **2.** ograniczać ⟨-czyć⟩; '**~ary** granica *f*; '**~less** bezgraniczny

bouquet [bʊ'keɪ] bukiet *m*

bow[1] [baʊ] **1.** ukłon *m*; **2.** *v/i* kłaniać ⟨ukłonić⟩ się (**to s.o.** komuś); *v/t* zginać ⟨-giąć⟩; *head* skłaniać ⟨-łonić⟩, skinąć

bow[2] [~] *mar.* dziób *m* (statku)

bow[3] [baʊ] *weapon:* łuk *m*; *knot:* kokarda *f*

bowel [baʊəl] jelito *n*, kiszka *f*; *pl* wnętrzności *pl*

bowl[1] [baʊl] (*small container*)

miseczka *f*; (*large container*) półmisek *m*; *toilet:* miska *f*; (*a. sugar ~*) cukierniczka *f*

bowl[2] [~] **1.** *bowling:* kula *f*; **2.** *bowling:* rzucać ⟨-cić⟩; *cricket:* ⟨za⟩serwować; '**~ing** kręgle *pl*

box[1] [bɒks] pudełko *n*, pudło *n*, skrzynka *f*; skrytka *f* pocztowa; Brt. F telewizor *m*; *tech.* obudowa *f*; Brt. kabina *f* telefoniczna; *jur.* miejsce *n* dla świadka; *thea.* loża *f*; *in print:* ramka *f*; ~ **office** *thea.* etc. kasa *f* biletowa

box[2] [~] boksować; ~ **s.o.'s ears** dać komuś po uszach; '**~er** bokser *m*; '**~ing** boks *m*; **Qing Day** Brt. drugi dzień świąt Bożego Narodzenia

boy [bɔɪ] chłopiec *m*

'**boy|friend** chłopak *m*, sympatia *f*; '**~ish** chłopięcy; '**~ scout** harcerz *m*

bra [brɑː] biustonosz *m*

brace [breɪs] **1.** tech. klamra *f*, zwora *f*; *for teeth:* dentystyczna klamra *f* korekcyjna; *pl* Brt. szelki *pl*; **2.** tech. ściągać ⟨-gnąć⟩/spinać ⟨spiąć⟩ klamrą; ~ **s. up** zbierać ⟨zebrać⟩ siły, brać ⟨wziąć⟩ się w garść

bracelet ['breɪslɪt] bransoleta *f*

bracket ['brækɪt] podpórka *f*; tech. krokszyn *m*; print. klamra *f*

brag [bræg] chełpić/chwalić się

brain [breɪn] *anat.* mózg *m*; *often pl fig.* pomyślunek *m F*; **'~storming** burza *f* mózgów; **'~washing** pranie *n* mózgu; **'~wave** genialny pomysł *m*

brake [breɪk] **1.** hamulec *m*; **2.** ⟨za⟩hamować

bramble ['bræmbl] jeżyna *f*

branch [brɑːntʃ] **1.** *a. fig.* gałąź *f*; *company etc.:* filia *f*; **2.** *often* **~ off** odgałęzi(a)ć się

brand [brænd] znak *m* firmowy; *commodity:* gatunek *m*, marka *f*

brand-'new nowiut(eń)ki

brass [brɑːs] mosiądz *m*; **~ band** orkiestra *f* dęta

brassière ['bræsɪə] biustonosz *m*

brat [bræt] bachor *m*

brave [breɪv] dzielny

brawl [brɔːl] burda *f*, awantura *f*

bread [bred] chleb *m*

breadth [bretθ] szerokość *f*

break [breɪk] **1.** *school etc.:* przerwa *f*; F szansa *f:* **give s.o. a** ~ da⟨wa⟩ć komuś szansę; **take a** ~ ⟨z⟩robić przerwę; **at the** ~ **of day** o świcie; **lucky** ~ F fart *m* F, uśmiech *m* losu; **2.** (**broke, broken**) *v/t* ⟨z⟩łamać; *a.* ~ **in** *horse* ujeżdżać ⟨ujeździć⟩; *code etc.* ⟨z⟩łamać; *news* zakomunikować; *v/i* ⟨z⟩łamać się *a.* ⟨z⟩łamywać się (*a. fig.*); pękać ⟨-knąć⟩, ⟨s⟩tłuc się;

weather: zmieni(a)ć się; *day:* ⟨za⟩świtać; ~ **away** uciekać ⟨uciec⟩, wyr(y)wać się; ~ **down** ⟨po⟩psuć się; *mot.* zepsuć się; ~ **in** włam(yw)ać się; *conversation:* wtrącać ⟨-cić⟩ się; *door* wyłam(yw)ać; ~ **off** zrywać ⟨zerwać⟩; ~ **out** uciekać ⟨uciec⟩; *war:* wybuchać ⟨-chnąć⟩; ~ **up** rozchodzić ⟨-zejść⟩ się, rozpraszać ⟨-roszyć⟩ się; *marriage etc.:* rozpadać ⟨-paść⟩ się; **'~down** załamanie *n*; *mot.* defekt *m*

breakfast ['brekfəst] **1.** śniadanie *n*; **have** ~ a **2.** śniadać, ⟨z⟩jeść śniadanie

breast [brest] pierś *f*

breath [breθ] oddech *m*

breathe [briːð] oddychać ⟨odetchnąć⟩

breath|less ['breθlɪs] zadyszany, bez tchu; **'~taking** zapierający dech w piersi

bred [bred] *past and pp of* **breed** 2

breed [briːd] **1.** rasa *f*; **2.** (**bred**) rozmnażać ⟨-nożyć⟩ się; *animals etc.* hodować; **'~er** hodowca *m*; **'~ing** *animals:* hodowla *f*; (*upbringing*) wychowanie *n*

breeze [briːz] wietrzyk *m*

brew [bruː] *beer* warzyć; *tea etc.* ⟨-rzyć⟩; **~ery** ['bruːərɪ] browar *m*

bribe [braɪb] **1.** łapówka *f*; **2.** przekupywać ⟨-pić⟩; **~ry** ['~ərɪ] łapownictwo *n*

brick [brɪk] cegła f; klocek m;
'**~layer** murarz m

bride [braɪd] panna f młoda;
~groom ['~grʊm] pan m
młody

bridge [brɪdʒ] most m; (game)
brydż m

brief [bri:f] **1.** krótki, zwięzły;
2. zrobić odprawę, zorientować; '**~case** aktówka f

briefs [bri:fs] majtki pl

bright [braɪt] colour: żywy;
day, room: jasny; light: jaskrawy; (brainy) bystry; '**~en**,
a. ~ **up** rozjaśni(a)ć (się);
ożywi(a)ć się; '**~ness** jaskrawość f, żywość f

brilliant ['brɪljənt] lśniący; career: świetny, błyskotliwy;
colour: jasny, jaskrawy;
idea: znakomity; person:
błyskotliwy, uzdolniony

brim [brɪm] hat: rondo n;
glass: krawędź f

bring [brɪŋ] (brought) przynosić ⟨-nieść⟩; przyprowadzać ⟨-dzić⟩; (persuade) nakłaniać ⟨-łonić⟩ (to
do do zrobienia); ~ **about**
⟨s⟩powodować; ~ **round**, ~
to ⟨o⟩cucić; ~ **up** question
etc. poruszać ⟨-szyć⟩; child
wychow(yw)ać

British ['brɪtɪʃ] **1.** brytyjski; **2.**
Brytyjczyk m (-jka f); **the** ~ pl
Brytyjczycy pl

broad [brɔ:d] szeroki; accent:
silny; field: rozległy; hint:
wyraźny; in ~ **daylight** w
biały dzień; '**~cast 1.** (~cast

or ~casted) radio, TV: nada(wa)ć; **2.** radio, TV: audycja f, program m; '**~en**
poszerzać ⟨-rzyć⟩; ~ **jump**
Am. sp. skok m w dal; '**~minded** światły, o szerokich horyzontach

brochure ['brəʊʃə] broszura f

broke [brəʊk] **1.** past of **break**
2; **2.** F spłukany, bez grosza;
'**~n 1.** pp of **break 2;** **2.** rozbity, złamany (a. fig.);
~n-'hearted zrozpaczony

broker ['brəʊkə] makler m,
pośrednik m

bronchitis [brɒŋ'kaɪtɪs] med.
zapalenie n oskrzeli

bronze [brɒnz] **1.** brąz m, spiż
m; **2.** spiżowy

brooch [brəʊtʃ] broszka f

brook [brʊk] strumyk m

broom [bru:m] miotła f

brother ['brʌðə] brat m; **~s
and sisters** pl rodzeństwo n;
~-in-law ['~rɪnlɔ:] szwagier
m; '**~ly** braterski

brought [brɔ:t] past and pp of
bring

brow [braʊ] czoło n; brew m

brown [braʊn] **1.** brązowy; **2.**
v/t przyrumieni(a)ć; v/i
⟨z⟩brązowieć

bruise [bru:z] **1.** siniak m; **2.**
posiniaczyć, kontuzjować

brush [brʌʃ] **1.** szczotka f;
paint: pędzel m; **2.**
⟨wy⟩szczotkować; ~ **up**
knowledge odświeżać ⟨-żyć⟩

Brussels sprouts [brʌsl-
'spraʊts] brukselka f

brutal [ˈbruːtl] brutalny; **~ity** [~ˈtælətɪ] brutalność *f*

brute [bruːt] bydlę *n* (*a. fig.*)

bubble [ˈbʌbl] **1.** *air etc.*: bańka *f*, bąbel *m*; **2.** *wine*: musować; *water*: bulgotać

buck [bʌk] *Am. sl.* dolar *m*, dolec *F*

bucket [ˈbʌkɪt] wiadro *n*

buckle [ˈbʌkl] **1.** klamra *f*; **2.** ~ **on** przypiąć

bud [bʌd] **1.** pączek *m*; **2.** pączkować; *fig.* rozwijać się

buddy [ˈbʌdɪ] *F* kumpel *m* F

budget [ˈbʌdʒɪt] budżet *m*

buff [bʌf] maniak *m*, zapaleniec *m*

bug [bʌg] **1.** *zo.* pluskwa *f*, *Am.* insekt *m*, robak *m*; *tech.* F pluskwa *f* F; *computer*: błąd *m* w programie; **2.** założyć podsłuch; **be ~ged** być na podsłuchu

build [bɪld] **1.** (**built**) ⟨z⟩budować; ⟨wy⟩budować; **2.** budowa (*ciała*); **~er** murarz *m*, budowniczy *m*; **~ing 1.** budynek *m*; **2.** *adj* budowlany

built [bɪlt] *past and pp of* **build** 1; **~'in** wbudowany; **~'up area** *mot.* teren *m* zabudowany

bulb [bʌlb] cebulka *f*; *electr.* żarówka *f*

bulge [bʌldʒ] **1.** wybrzuszenie *n*; **2.** wydymać się, wybrzuszać się; *fig.* pękać (**with** od)

bulk [bʌlk] (*majority*) przeważająca część *f*; (*mass*) masa *f*; (*fat body*) cielsko *n*; **~y** objętościowo duży; (*cumbersome*) nieporęczny

bull [bʊl] byk *m*; **~doze** wyrówn(yw)ać (spychaczem)

bullet [ˈbʊlɪt] kula *f*

bulletin [ˈbʊlətɪn] biuletyn *m*; *radio*: komunikat *m*; **~ board** *Am.* tablica *f* ogłoszeń

bully [ˈbʊlɪ] **1.** tyran *m*; **2.** tyranizować, terroryzować

bump [bʌmp] **1.** guz *m*; *mot.* stłuczka *f*; *pl on road*: wyboje *pl*; **2.** walnąć/stuknąć (*into/against* w); (*collide*) zderzyć się (*into/against* z); (*meet by accident*) natknąć się (*s.o.* na kogoś); **~er** zderzak *m*; **~y** wyboisty

bun [bʌn] (*słodka*) bułeczka *f*; *hair*: kok *m*

bunch [bʌntʃ] pęk *m*, wiązka *f*; *kids etc.*: F paczka *f*, banda *f*; *flowers*: bukiet *m*; *grapes*: kiść *f*

bundle [ˈbʌndl] **1.** tobołek *m*, zawiniątko *n*; **2.** *a.* **~ up** zbierać ⟨zebrać⟩ do kupy

bungalow [ˈbʌŋgələʊ] domek *m* (parterowy); *rodzaj domku kempingowego*

bungle [ˈbʌŋgl] spaprać, spartaczyć

burden [ˈbɜːdn] **1.** ciężar *m*, *fig. a.* brzemię *n*; **2.** obciążać ⟨-żyć⟩

burger [ˈbɜːgə] *gastr.* hamburger *m*

burglar [ˈbɜːglə] włamywacz

m; **~arize** ['~raɪz] *Am.* → **burgle**; **~ary** ['~rɪ] włamanie *n*; **~e** ['~gl] włam(yw)ać się (**s.th.** do czegoś)

burial ['berɪəl] pogrzeb *m*

burn [bɜːn] **1.** oparzenie *n*; **2.** *(burnt* or *burned)* ⟨s⟩palić; *food* przypalać ⟨-lić⟩; **~t** [~t] *past* and *pp* of **burn 2**

burst [bɜːst] **1.** *(burst)* *v/i* pękać ⟨-knąć⟩; *v/t* rozsadzać ⟨-dzić⟩; **~ into tears** wybuchnąć płaczem; **2.** pęknięcie *n*; *(explosion)* wybuch *m*; *fig.* wybuch *m*, ...

bury ['berɪ] ⟨po⟩grzebać

bus [bʌs] autobus *m*

bush [buʃ] krzak *m*

business ['bɪznɪs] interes *m*, zajęcie *n*; *on* ~ służbowo; *that's none of your* ~ to nie twój interes; → *mind* **2**; ~ **hours** *pl* godziny *pl* handlu/urzędowania; **~like** rzeczowy, oficjalny; **~man** *(pl -men)* człowiek *m* interesu; biznesmen *m* F; ~ **trip** podróż *f* służbowa; **~woman** *(pl -women)* kobieta *f* interesu

bus stop przystanek *m* autobusowy

busy ['bɪzɪ] **1.** zajęty; *street:* ruchliwy; *day:* pracowity; *Am. teleph.* zajęty; *be* ~ *doing s.th.* być czymś robieniem czegoś; **2.** ~ **o.s. with/in/about s.th.** zajmować ⟨-jąć⟩ się czymś

but [bʌt] **1.** *cj* ale, lecz; jednak; *he could not* ~ *laugh* mógł się tylko ⟨za⟩śmiać; **2.** *prp* oprócz, poza; *all* ~ *him* wszyscy oprócz niego; *the last* ~ *one* przedostatni; *nothing* ~ ... nic tylko ...

butcher ['butʃə] rzeźnik *m*

butter ['bʌtə] **1.** masło *n*; **2.** ⟨po⟩smarować masłem; **~fly** motyl *m*

buttocks ['bʌtəks] *pl* pośladki *pl*, siedzenie *n*

button ['bʌtn] **1.** guzik *m*; **2.** *mst* ~ *up* zapinać ⟨-piąć⟩ (na guziki)

buy [baɪ] *(bought)* kupować ⟨-pić⟩; **~er** kupujący *m*, nabywca *m*

buzz [bʌz] **1.** brzęczenie *n*, buczenie *n*; *voices:* gwar *m*; **2.** ⟨za⟩brzęczeć, bzykać ⟨-knąć⟩

buzzer ['bʌzə] brzęczyk *m*

by [baɪ] **1.** *prp spatial:* przy, u; *temporal:* (najpóźniej) do ...; *watch:* według; *source, reason:* przez; *distance:* o; *math. razy:* przez; *surface:* na; *math. divided:* przez; *side* ~ *side* obok siebie; ~ *day* za dnia; ~ *night* nocą; ~ *bus* autobusem; ~ *the dozen* na tuziny; ~ *my watch* według mojego zegarka; *a play* ~ sztuka (napisana przez) ...; *an inch* co tyle; cal; **2.** ~ **4** 2 razy 4; *2m* ~ *4m* 2m na 4m; **6** ~ **3** 6 przez 3; ~ *o.s.* sam; **2.** *adv* obok, mimo; w pobliżu; → *put by*

bye [baɪ], a. ~'**bye** int pa!, cześć!

'**by|-election** dodatkowe wybory pl; '~**gone** 1. miniony; 2. let ~**gones** be ~**gones** co się stało to się nie odstanie;

'~**pass** 1. mot. obwodnica f; med. bypass m; 2. obstacle omijać ⟨ominąć⟩; issue ⟨z⟩ignorować; '~**product** produkt m uboczny

byte [baɪt] computer: bajt m

C

cab [kæb] dorożka f; (taxi) taksówka f; ~ **rank**, '~**stand** postój m taksówek

cabbage ['kæbɪdʒ] kapusta f

cabin ['kæbɪn] chata f; mar. a. kabina f, kajuta f

cabinet ['kæbɪnɪt] pol. gabinet m; medicine: szafk(a f) f; (cupboard) kredens m

cable ['keɪbl] 1. kabel m (a. electr.); (telegram) telegram m; 2. ⟨za⟩telegrafować; TV okablow(yw)ać; ~ **car** kolejka f linowa

café ['kæfeɪ] kawiarnia f

cafeteria [kæfɪ'tɪərɪə] bar m (samoobsługowy)

cage [keɪdʒ] klatka f

cake [keɪk] (pastry) ciastko n; soap: kostka f

calculat|e ['kælkjuleɪt] obliczać ⟨-czyć⟩, wyliczać ⟨-czyć⟩; ~**ion** [ˌ~'leɪʃn] wyliczenie n, wyrachowanie n; '~**or** kalkulator m

calendar ['kælɪndə] kalendarz m

calf[1] [kɑːf] (pl calves [~vz]) cielę n

calf[2] [~] (pl calves [~vz]) łyd-

ka f

calibre, Am. **-ber** ['kælɪbə] kaliber m

call [kɔːl] 1. wołanie n, krzyk m; teleph. rozmowa f; visit: (krótka) wizyta f; on ~ gotowy na wezwanie; **make a** ~ ⟨za⟩telefonować; 2. v/t naz(y)wać; (cry) ⟨za⟩wołać, wykrzykiwać ⟨-knąć⟩; (summon) przywoł(yw)ać; teleph. zadzwonić do; attention zwrócić (to na); v/i teleph. ⟨za⟩telefonować; be ~**ed** nazywać się; ~ **s.o. names** ⟨na⟩wymyślać komuś; ~ **at** wstępować ⟨-tąpić⟩ do, odwiedzać ⟨-dzić⟩ (miejsce); rail. ⟨przy⟩stawać; harbour zawijać ⟨-winąć⟩ do; teleph. oddzwaniać ⟨-wonić⟩; ~ **for** wzywać ⟨wezwać⟩; (demand) wymagać; ~ **off** odwoł(yw)ać; ~ **on s.o.** odwiedzać ⟨-dzić⟩; ~**box** automat m telefoniczny; '~**er** osoba f telefonująca; (visitor) gość m

callous ['kæləs] zrogowaciały; fig. gruboskórny, nieczuły

calm [kɑːm] **1.** cichy; spokojny; **2.** cisza *f*, spokój *m*; **3.** *often* ~ **down** *wind*: uciszać ⟨-szyć⟩ się; *person*: uspokajać ⟨-koić⟩ się

calves [kɑːvz] *pl of* **calf**[1],[2]

came [keɪm] *past of* **come**

camel ['kæml] wielbłąd *m*

camera ['kæmərə] aparat *m* fotograficzny; *(ciné)* kamera *f*

camouflage ['kæməflɑːʒ] **1.** kamuflaż *m*, maskowanie *n*; **2.** ⟨za⟩maskować

camp [kæmp] **1.** obóz *m*; **2.** obozować

camp chair krzesło *n* składane

campaign [kæm'peɪn] **1.** kampania *f*; **2.** prowadzić kampanię

camper ['kæmpə] obozowicz(ka *f*) *m*; *Am.* mikrobus *m* kempingowy; **~ground** *esp. Am.* → **campsite**; **~ing** obozowanie *n*; **~site** pole *n* namiotowe

can[1] [kæn] *v/aux (past could)* móc

can[2] [~] **1.** puszka *f*; **2.** puszkować

Canadian [kə'neɪdjən] **1.** kanadyjski; **2.** Kanadyjczyk *m* (-jka *f*)

canal [kə'næl] kanał *m*

canary [kə'neəri] kanarek *m*

cancel ['kænsl] *flight, concert etc.* odwoł⟨yw⟩ać; *ticket etc.* anulować, unieważni⟨a⟩ć

cancer ['kænsə] *med.* rak *m*

candid ['kændɪd] szczery, otwarty

candidate ['kændɪdət] kandydat(ka *f*) *m*

candle ['kændl] świeca *f*; **~stick** lichtarz *m*

cando(u)r ['kændə] szczerość *f*, otwartość *f*

candy ['kændɪ] *esp. Am.* słodycze *pl*; cukierek *m*

cane [keɪn] laska *f*; *bot.* trzcina *f*

canned [kænd] ... w puszkach, ... w konserwie; *beer*: puszkowy

cannon ['kænən] *(pl ~, ~s)* armata *f*

cannot ['kænɒt] nie mogę/ możesz *itd.*

canoe [kə'nuː] czółno *n*

can opener *esp. Am.* → **tin opener**

can't [kɑːnt] F → **cannot**

canteen [kæn'tiːn] stołówka *f*; *(flask)* manierka *f*

canvas ['kænvəs] płótno *n*

cap [kæp] czapka *f*, kaszkiet *m*; *part of uniform*: czepek *m*; *on bottle*: zakrętka *f*

capability [keɪpə'bɪlətɪ] zdolność *f*; **~le** zdolny (**of** do)

capacity [kə'pæsətɪ] *(volume)* pojemność *f*; *(output)* wydajność *f*

cape [keɪp] przylądek *m*

capital ['kæpɪtl] **1.** *(city)* stolica *f*; *(letter)* duża litera *f*; *econ.* kapitał *m*; **2.** *econ.* kapitałowy; F kapitalny; *jur.* *punishment*: główny

capital letter duża litera *f*; **~ punishment** kara *f* śmierci

capsize [kæp'saɪz] przewracać ⟨-rócić⟩ (się) do góry dnem

captain ['kæptɪn] kapitan *m*

caption ['kæpʃn] *cartoon:* podpis *m; film:* napis *m*

captivate ['kæptɪveɪt] ujmować ⟨-jąć⟩; *fig.* urzekać ⟨-rzec⟩; **~e** jeniec *m;* **~ity** [~'tɪvətɪ] niewola *f*

capture ['kæptʃə] chwytać ⟨-wycić⟩, pojmać, brać ⟨wziąć⟩ do niewoli

car [kɑː] samochód *m; rail.* wagon *m*

caravan ['kærəvæn] *Brt.* przyczepa *f* kempingowa

caraway ['kærəweɪ] kminek *m*

carbohydrate [kɑːbəʊ'haɪdreɪt] węglowodan *m*

carbu|ret(t)er, **~ret(t)or** [kɑːbə'retə] *mot.* gaźnik *m*

card [kɑːd] karta *f;* **~board** tektura *f*, karton *m*

cardigan ['kɑːdɪgən] sweter *m* rozpinany

cardinal ['kɑːdɪnl] **1.** zasadniczy, kardynalny; **2.** kardynał *m;* **~ number** liczebnik *m* główny

card index kartoteka *f*

care [keə] **1.** opieka *f*, troska *f; (attention)* uwaga *f;* **~ of** *(abbr. c/o) address:* na adres ..., u ...; **take ~** uważać; **take ~ of** zajmować ⟨-jąć⟩ się; **with ~!** ostrożnie!; **2.** niepokoić się (**about** o); lubić (**for** s.o. kogoś); dbać, troszczyć

się (**~ for** o); *I don't* **~!** nic mnie to nie obchodzi!

career [kə'rɪə] kariera *f* zawodowa

'care|free beztroski; **'~ful** ostrożny; **be ~!** uważaj!; **'~less** niedbały, nieostrożny

caress [kə'res] **1.** pieszczota *f;* **2.** pieścić

'caretaker dozorca *m* (-rczyni *f*)

cargo ['kɑːgəʊ] *(pl* **-go(e)s)** ładunek *m*

carnation [kɑː'neɪʃn] goździk *m*

carol ['kærəl] kolęda *f*

car park *Brt.* parking *m*

carpet ['kɑːpɪt] dywan *m*

carriage ['kærɪdʒ] powóz *m; Brt. rail.* wagon *m;* koszt(y) *m (pl)* transportu

carrier ['kærɪə] przewoźnik *m; med.* nosiciel *m; bicycle:* bagażnik *m;* **~ bag** *esp. Brt.* (papierowa/plastikowa) torba *f*

carrot ['kærət] marchew *f*

carry ['kærɪ] nosić ⟨nieść⟩; *(have on one)* nosić/mieć przy sobie; *(transport)* przewozić ⟨-wieźć⟩; **~ on** kontynuować; **~ out** wykon(yw)ać, wcielać ⟨-lić⟩ w życie; **~through** przeprowadzać ⟨-dzić⟩; **~cot** *Brt.* rodzaj torby-łóżeczka do przenoszenia dziecka

cart [kɑːt] wóz *m*

cartoon [kɑː'tuːn] *(drawing)* dowcip *m* rysunkowy; *(cari-*

cature) karykatura *f; Brt. (comic strip)* komiks *m; film:* film *m* rysunkowy

cartridge ['kɑːtrɪdʒ] nabój *m; phot.* kaseta *f; record-player:* wkładka *f; tech.* wkład *m*

carv|e [kɑːv] *meat* ⟨u⟩kroić; *in wood etc.:* wycinać ⟨-ciąć⟩, ⟨wy⟩rzeźbić; **'~er** snycerz *m*

car wash myjnia *f (*samochodowa)

case¹ [keɪs] skrzynka *f; violin etc.:* futerał *m; glass:* gablotka *f*

case² [~] przypadek *m; jur.* sprawa *f; in ~ (that)* na wypadek

cash [kæʃ] **1.** gotówka *f; ~ down* (zapłata) w gotówce; *in ~* gotówką; *~ in advance* opłata (gotówką) z góry; *~ on delivery (abbr. COD)* za pobraniem (pocztowym); *short of ~* bez gotówki; **2.** *cheque etc.* podejmować ⟨-djąć⟩; *~ desk dep. store etc.:* kasa *f; ~ dispenser* automat *m* bankowy; **'~ier** [~ʃɪə] kasjer(ka *f*) *m*

cassette [kə'set] kaseta *f; ~ radio* radiomagnetofon *m; ~ recorder* magnetofon *m* kasetowy

cast [kɑːst] **1.** rzut *m; tech.* odlew *m; med.* opatrunek *m* gipsowy; *thea., film:* obsada *f;* **2.** *(cast)* tech. odlewać ⟨-lać⟩; *~ iron* żeliwo *n; thea., film:* obsadzać ⟨-dzić⟩

castle ['kɑːsl] zamek *m; chess:* wieża *f*

casual ['kæʒʊəl] przypadkowy, nie planowany *; remark:* zdawkowy; *smile:* niewymuszony; *~ wear* niedbały strój *m; ~ty* ['~tɪ] nieszczęście *n,* wypadek *m; mil.* zabity/ranny *m; casualties pl* ofiary *pl* (wypadku); *mil.* straty *pl* w ludziach; *a. ~ ward* oddział *m* urazowy

cat [kæt] kot *m*

catalogue, *Am.* **-log** ['kætəlɒɡ] **1.** katalog *m;* **2.** ⟨s⟩katalogować

catalytic converter [kætə'lɪtɪk kən'vɜːtə] *mot.* katalizator *m*

catastrophe [kə'tæstrəfɪ] nieszczęście *n,* katastrofa *f; (esp. natural ~)* klęska *f* żywiołowa

catch [kætʃ] **1.** *fish:* połów *m; door, window:* zatrzask *m,* haczyk *m; lock:* zapadka *f; (hidden difficulty)* haczyk *m,* pułapka *f;* **2.** *(caught) (seize)* ⟨z⟩łapać, chwytać ⟨-wycić⟩; *(get stuck in)* zahaczać ⟨-czyć⟩, zaczepi(a)ć (się); *~ (a) cold* przezięb(i)ać się; *~ up (with)* doganiać ⟨-gonić⟩

category ['kætəɡərɪ] kategoria *f*

cater ['keɪtə] zaopatrywać ⟨-trzyć⟩, aprowizować *(for s.o./s.th.* coś/kogoś), ⟨za⟩dbać (*for* o); **~er** ['~ə] dostawca *m* żywności

caterpillar ['kætəpilə] gąsienica f

cathedral [kə'θiːdrəl] katedra f

Catholic ['kæθəlik] **1.** katolicki; **2.** katolik m (-liczka f)

cattle ['kætl] bydło n

caught [kɔːt] past and pp of **catch** 2

cauliflower ['kɒliflauə] kalafior m

cause [kɔːz] **1.** przyczyna f; **2.** ⟨s⟩powodować

caution ['kɔːʃn] **1.** ostrożność f; ~! uwaga!; **2.** ostrzegać ⟨-rzec⟩, przestrzegać ⟨-rzec⟩

cautious ['kɔːʃəs] ostrożny

cave [keɪv] jaskinia f, grota f

CD [siː'diː] (abbr. for **compact disc**) recording: płyta f kompaktowa; player: odtwarzacz m kompaktowy

cease [siːs] ⟨za⟩przesta(wa)ć; **~ fire** zawieszenie n broni

ceiling ['siːlɪŋ] sufit m; tech., fig. pułap m

celebr|ate ['selibreɪt] świętować, obchodzić; **~ity** [sɪ'lebrəti] person: sława f, znakomitość f

celery ['seləri] seler m

cell [sel] komórka f

cellar ['selə] piwnica f

cello ['tʃeləʊ] wiolonczela f

cellular phone [seljələ 'fəʊn] telefon m komórkowy

cement [sɪ'ment] **1.** cement m; (glue) spoiwo n; **2.**

⟨za/s⟩cementować; (glue together) zespajać ⟨-poić⟩; (glue) przyklejać ⟨-leić⟩

cemetery ['semitri] cmentarz m

cent [sent] Am. cent m

center Am. → **centre**

centi|grade ['sentigreɪd]: **10 degrees ~** 10 stopni Celsjusza; **'~metre**, Am. **~meter** centymetr m

central ['sentrəl] środkowy, centralny; **~ heating** centralne ogrzewanie n; **~ize** ⟨s⟩centralizować; **~ processing unit** (abbr. **CPU**) computer: procesor m (główny)

centre, Am. **-ter** ['sentə] środek m, fig. centrum n, ośrodek m

century ['sentʃʊri] wiek m

ceramics [sɪ'ræmiks] ceramika f

cereal ['sɪərɪəl] **1.** zbożowy; **2.** zboże n; processed food: płatki pl (owsiane, kukurydziane itp.)

ceremony ['serɪmənɪ] uroczystość f, ceremonia f

certain ['sɜːtn] pewny, pewien; **a ~ Mr S.** niejaki pan S.; **'~ly** na pewno, z pewnością; answer: naturalnie, oczywiście; **'~ty** pewność f

certi|ficate [sə'tɪfɪkət] zaświadczenie n, świadectwo n; **~ficate of birth** metryka f urodzin; **~fy** ['sɜːtɪfaɪ] zaświadczać ⟨-czyć⟩, poświadczać ⟨-czyć⟩

chain [tʃeɪn] **1.** łańcuch *m*; **2.** przykuwać ⟨-kuć⟩

chair [tʃeə] krzesło *n*; *fig.* katedra *f*; **~ lift** wyciąg *m* krzesełkowy; **~man** (*pl* **-men**) przewodniczący *m*, prezes *m*; **~woman** (*pl* **-women**) przewodnicząca *f*, prezeska *f*

chalk [tʃɔːk] kreda *f*

challenge ['tʃælɪndʒ] **1.** wyzwanie *n*; **2.** wyz(y)wać, rzucać ⟨-cić⟩ wyzwanie

chamber ['tʃeɪmbə] izba *f*, sala *f*; **~maid** pokojówka *f*

champagne [ʃæm'peɪn] szampan *m*

champion ['tʃæmpjən] orędownik *m*; *sp.* mistrz(yni *f*) *m*; **~ship** mistrzostwa *pl*

chance [tʃɑːns] **1.** traf *m*, przypadek *m*, (*opportunity*) szansa *f*, okazja *f* (*of* do); *by* **~** przypadkiem; *take a* **~** ryzykować; *take no* **~s** nie ryzykować; **2.** zaryzykować; **3.** *adj* przypadkowy

chandelier [ʃændə'lɪə] żyrandol *m*

change [tʃeɪndʒ] **1.** zmieni(a)ć ⟨się⟩; *clothes* przeb(ie)rać się; *money* wymieni(a)ć; *trains, planes etc.* przesiadać ⟨-siąść⟩ się; **2.** zmiana *f*, odmiana *f*; *travelling*: przesiadka *f*; *money*: drobne *pl*; *for a* **~** dla odmiany

channel ['tʃænl] *geogr.*, *radio*, *TV*: kanał *m*

chaos ['keɪɒs] chaos *m*; **~tic**

[**~**'ɒtɪk] chaotyczny

chap [tʃæp] gość *m*, facet *m* F

chapel ['tʃæpl] kaplica *f*

chapter ['tʃæptə] *book*: rozdział *m*; *cathedral*: kapituła *f*

character ['kærəktə] charakter *m*; litera *f*, czcionka *f*; *novel etc.*: postać *f*; **~istic** ['~'rɪstɪk] **1.** charakterystyczny (*of* dla); **2.** właściwość *f*, cecha *f* charakterystyczna, **~ize** [~'raɪz] ⟨s⟩charakteryzować

charge [tʃɑːdʒ] **1.** *battery etc.* ⟨na⟩ładować; *s.o.* oskarżyć (*with* o ⟨a. *jur.*⟩; *econ.* ~ so. obciążyć; *money* ⟨za⟩żądać; zaatakować (*at s.th.* coś); **2.** *electr.*, *mil.* ładunek *m*; *money*: opłata *f*; *attack*: szarża *f*; *person*: podopieczny *m*; *a. jur.* oskarżenie *n*; *free of* ~ nieodpłatnie; *be in* **~** *of* odpowiadać za

charit|able ['tʃærətəbl] dobroczynny; **~y** miłosierdzie *n*; *organization*: organizacja *f* dobroczynna

charm [tʃɑːm] **1.** urok *m*, wdzięk *m*; (*amulet*) amulet *m*; **2.** oczarować; ' **~ing** czarujący

chart [tʃɑːt] mapa *f*; wykres *m*; *pl* lista *f* przebojów

chase [tʃeɪs] **1.** gonić, ścigać; **2.** pościg *m*, gonitwa *f*

chassis ['ʃæsɪ] (*pl* ['~sɪz]) podwozie *n*

chat [tʃæt] **1.** gawędzić; **2.** pogawędka f; **~ show** program z gości w studiu

chatter ['tʃætə] **1.** gadać, trajkotać; *teeth*: szczękać; **2.** *people*: paplanina f; *machines*: terkot m, szczęk m; '**~box** gaduła m

cheap [tʃiːp] tani

cheat [tʃiːt] **1.** oszukiwać ⟨-kać⟩; **2.** oszustwo n; oszust m

check [tʃek] **1.** kontrola f, sprawdzenie n; *Am.* czek m; *Am.* kwit m kasowy, rachunek m; *Am.* kwit m bagażowy; *Am.* numerek m z szatni; *pattern*: krata; **hold or keep in ~** *fig.* trzymać w ryzach; **keep ~** mieć pod obserwacją (**on s.o.** kogoś); **2.** zatrzym(yw)ać; **~ in** *hotel*: ⟨za⟩meldować się; *aer.* załatwi(a)ć formalności przed lotem; **~ out** *hotel*: wymeldow(yw)ać się; **~ up** zasięgać ⟨-gnąć⟩ informacji (**on s.o.** o kimś); (*restrain*) przytrzym(yw)ać; (*examine*) sprawdzać ⟨-dzić⟩, ⟨s⟩kontrolować; *Am.* on a list: odhaczać ⟨-czyć⟩; '**~book** *Am.* książeczka f czekowa; **~ card** *Am.* karta f bankowa; **~ed** kraciasty, w kratę

checker/board ['tʃekəbɔ:d] *Am.* szachownica f; '**~ed** *Am.* → **chequered**; '**~s** *sg Am.* warcaby *pl*

'**check-in** *hotel*: zameldowanie n; *aer.* odprawa f przed lotem; **~ counter** *aer.* recepcja f na lotnisku; '**~mate 1.** (szach) mat m; **2.** dać mata; '**~out** *hotel*: wymeldowanie n się; '**~point** punkt m kontrolny; '**~room** *Am.* szatnia f; *Am.* przechowalnia f bagażu; '**~up** *med.* F badanie f lekarskie

cheek [tʃiːk] policzek m; (*impudence*) tupet m; '**~y** bezczelny

cheer [tʃɪə] **1.** aplauz m, wiwaty *pl*; **~s!** *Brt.* F na zdrowie!; **2.** *v/t* poprawić humor; *a.* **~ on** dopingować; *a.* **~ up** rozweselać ⟨-lić⟩; *v/i* wiwatować; *a.* **~ up** rozchmurzyć się; **~ up!** głowa do góry!; '**~ful** ochoczy, wesoły, pogodny; '**~io** ['tʃɪr'əʊ] *int Brt.* F cześć!; '**~less** posępny, ponury

cheese [tʃiːz] ser m

chef [ʃef] szef m kuchni

chemical ['kemɪkl] **1.** chemiczny; **2.** *pl* chemikalia *pl*

chemist ['kemɪst] chemik m; *dispensing*: aptekarz m; **~'s (shop)** apteka f; **~ry** ['-trɪ] chemia f

cheque [tʃek] *Brt.* czek m; '**~book** *Brt.* książeczka f czekowa; **~ card** *Brt.* karta f bankowa

chequered ['tʃekəd] *esp. Brt.* kraciasty, w kratę; *fig.* burzliwy

cherry ['tʃerɪ] wiśnia f; *sweet*: czereśnia f

chess [tʃes] szachy *pl*; **'~board** szachownica *f*

chest [tʃest] skrzynia *f*; (*trunk*) kufer *m*; *anat.* klatka *f* piersiowa; **~ of drawers** komoda *f*

chestnut ['tʃesnʌt] kasztan *m*

chew [tʃuː] żuć; **'~ing gum** guma *f* do żucia

chicken ['tʃɪkɪn] kurczę *n*; *as food*: kurczak *m*; **~ pox** [pɒks] ospa *f* wietrzna

chicory ['tʃɪkərɪ] cykoria *f*

chief [tʃiːf] **1.** wódz *m*; **2.** główny, naczelny; **'~ly** głównie, zwłaszcza, przede wszystkim

child [tʃaɪld] (*pl* **children** ['tʃɪldrən]) dziecko *n*; **'~birth** poród *m*; **'~hood** ['~hʊd] dzieciństwo *n*; **'~ish** dziecinny; **'~less** bezdzietny; **'~like** dziecinny; **~ren** ['tʃɪldrən] *pl* of **child**

chill [tʃɪl] **1.** chłód *m*, ziąb *m*; *illness*: przeziębienie *n*; (*shiver*) dreszcz *m*; **2.** ⟨s⟩chłodzić, ochładzać ⟨-łodzić⟩, ⟨o⟩studzić; **3.** *adj* → **'~y** chłodny, zimny

chimney ['tʃɪmnɪ] komin *m*

chimpanzee [tʃɪmpæn'ziː] szympans *m*

chin [tʃɪn] podbródek *m*

china ['tʃaɪnə] porcelana *f*

Chinese [tʃaɪ'niːz] **1.** chiński; **2.** Chińczyk *m*, Chinka *f*

chip [tʃɪp] **1.** (*fragment*) odłamek *m*; *on glass etc.*: szczerba *f*; *in gambling*:

żeton *m*; *computer*: obwód *m* scalony; kość *f* *F*; *pl* *Brt.* frytki *pl*; *pl Am.* czipsy *pl*; **2.** wyszczerbić (się)

chive(s *pl*) [tʃaɪv(z)] szczypiorek *m*

chlorine ['klɔːriːn] chlor *m*

chocolate ['tʃɒkələt] czekolada *f*; **'~s** *pl* czekoladki *pl*

choice [tʃɔɪs] **1.** wybór *m*; **2.** wyborowy, doborowy, luksusowy

choir ['kwaɪə] chór *m*

choke [tʃəʊk] **1.** dusić (się); **2.** *mot.* ssanie *n*

choose [tʃuːz] (**chose, chosen**) wybierać ⟨-brać⟩

chop [tʃɒp] **1.** uderzenie *n* (siekierą *itp.*); *pork, lamb*: kotlet *m*; **2.** ⟨po⟩ciachać ⟨-chnąć⟩; **~ down** ściąć ⟨ścinać⟩; **'~per** tasak *m*; *aer.* F helikopter *m*; **'~stick** pałeczka *f* do jedzenia

chord [kɔːd] *mus.* akord *m*

chore [tʃɔː] niewdzięczna praca *f* *F*; czarna robota *f* F

chorus ['kɔːrəs] chór *m*; *in a song*: refren *m*; *revue*: chór *m*

chose [tʃəʊz] *past of* **choose**; **'~n** *pp of* **choose**

Christ [kraɪst] Chrystus *m*

christen ['krɪsn] ⟨o⟩chrzcić

Christian ['krɪstʃən] **1.** chrześcijański; **2.** chrześcijanin *m* (*-janka f*); **~ity** [ˌtrɪæntɪ] chrześcijaństwo *n*; **~ name** imię *n*

Christmas ['krɪsməs] Boże Narodzenie *n*; **at ~** na Boże

Narodzenie; → **merry**; **~ Day** pierwszy dzień świąt Bożego Narodzenia; **~ Eve** wigilia f Bożego Narodzenia

chronic ['krɒnɪk] chroniczny

chronicle ['krɒnɪkl] kronika f

chubby ['tʃʌbɪ] pucołowaty

chuck [tʃʌk] F wyrzucać ‹-cić›

church [tʃɜːtʃ] kościół m; **'~yard** cmentarz m

cider ['saɪdə] jabłecznik m (napój)

cigar [sɪ'gɑː] cygaro n

cigarette [sɪgə'ret] papieros m, Am. a. **-ret** [sɪgə'ret] papieros m

cine|camera ['sɪnɪkæmərə] kamera f filmowa; **'~film** taśma f filmowa

cinema ['sɪnəmə] Brt. kino n

cinnamon ['sɪnəmən] cynamon m

circle ['sɜːkl] **1.** koło n, krąg m; thea. galeria f (2-go piętra); fig. środowisko; **2.** okrążać ‹-żyć›

circuit ['sɜːkɪt] obieg m, okrążenie f; electr. obwód m; **short ~** zwarcie n;

circulat|e ['sɜːkjʊleɪt] puszczać ‹puścić› w obieg; **~ion** [~'leɪʃn] krążenie n; econ. obieg m

circumstance ['sɜːkəmstəns] wydarzenie n, wypadek m; mst pl: okoliczние f; **in** or **under no ~s** w żadnym wypadku; **in** or **under the ~s** w zaistniałej sytuacji

circus ['sɜːkəs] cyrk m; Brt.

okrągły plac m

citizen ['sɪtɪzn] obywatel(ka f) m; **'~ship** obywatelstwo n

city ['sɪtɪ] miasto n; **the ~** londyńskie City n; **~ centre** Brt. centrum n (miasta); **~ hall** ratusz m

civil ['sɪvl] obywatelski; (polite) uprzejmy; jur. cywilny

civilian [sɪ'vɪljən] **1.** cywil m; **2.** cywilny

civiliz|ation [sɪvɪlaɪ'zeɪʃn] cywilizacja f; **~e** ['~laɪz] ‹u›cywilizować

civil| rights pl prawa pl obywatelskie; **~ servant** urzędnik m państwowy; **~ service** administracja f państwowa; **~ war** wojna f domowa

claim [kleɪm] **1.** (demand) żądanie n; jur. roszczenie pl; **2.** (maintain) utrzymywać, twierdzić; (demand) ‹za›żądać; right: rościć sobie prawo

clamp [klæmp] zacisk m, klamra f

clap [klæp] **1.** hands: klaśnięcie n; on the back etc.: klepnięcie n; **2.** hands klaskać ‹-snąć›; s.o. on the back etc.: klepać ‹-pnąć›

clarity ['klærətɪ] jasność f, czystość f

clash [klæʃ] **1.** starcie n, potyczka f, utarczka f; cultures etc.: zderzenie n; metal: szczęk m; **2.** ścierać ‹zetrzeć› się; events: zbiec się w czasie; me-

tal: szczekać ⟨-knąć⟩; *colours*: gryźć się F

class [klɑːs] *school*: klasa *f*; *university*: zajęcia *pl*; *Am. graduates etc.*: rocznik *m*

classic ['klæsɪk] **1.** klasyk *m*; *example*: klasyczny przykład *m*; **2.** klasyczny; **~al** klasyczny

classification [klæsɪfɪ'keɪʃn] klasyfikacja *f*; **~fied** ['~faɪd] *mil., pol.* tajny; **~fied ad**(*vertisement*) ogłoszenie *n* drobne; **~fy** ['~faɪ] ⟨s⟩klasyfikować

class|mate kolega *m*/koleżanka *f* z klasy; **~room** klasa *f*, sala *f* szkolna

clause [klɔːz] *jur.* klauzula *f*; *gr.* zdanie *n*

claw [klɔː] **1.** pazur *m*; *bird*: szpon *m*; *crab*: szczypce *pl*; **2.** drapać ⟨-pnąć⟩ pazurami, szarpać ⟨-pnąć⟩ pazurami

clay [kleɪ] glina *f*

clean [kliːn] **1.** *adj* czysty; *sl.* nie biorący już narkotyków; **2.** *adv* całkowicie, zupełnie; **3.** *v/t* ⟨o⟩czyścić; *v/i* sprzątać ⟨-tnąć⟩; **~ out** oczyścić; **~ up** oczyścić, dokładnie sprzątnąć, wysprzątać; **~er** czyściciel *m*, czyścicielka *m*; → *dry cleaner*('*s*)

cleanse [klenz] ⟨o⟩czyścić; **~r** płyn *m* czyszczący

clear [klɪə] **1.** *adj statement*: jasny; *picture*: wyraźny; *con-*

science, water: czysty; (*not touching*) wolny (**of** od) (*a. fig.*); *econ.* netto, czysty; **2.** *adv* jasno, wyraźnie; *z* dala (**of** od); **3.** *v/t* (*often* **~ away**) uprzątać ⟨-tnąć⟩; *v/i* usuwać ⟨-sunąć⟩ się; *sky*: rozchmurzyć się; *fog*: podnieść się; **~ off!** F zjeżdżaj! F; **~ out** F wynosić ⟨-nieść⟩ się F; **~ up** *mystery etc.* wyjaśnić, wyświetlić; *weather*: przejaśni⟨a⟩ć się; **~ance** ['~rəns] oczyszczenie *n*; *formalities*: załatwienie *n* formalności; (*consent*) zgoda *f*, pozwolenie *n*; **~ing** ['~rɪŋ] polana *f*; **~ly** wyraźnie; (*obviously*) najwyraźniej

clench [klentʃ] zaciskać ⟨-cisnąć⟩

clergy ['klɜːdʒɪ] duchowieństwo *n*; **~man** (*pl* **-men**) duchowny *m*

clerk [klɑːk] urzędnik *m* (-niczka *f*); *Am.* recepcjonista *m* (-tka *f*)

clever ['klevə] sprytny, mądry

click [klɪk] **1.** *lock etc.*: szczęknięcie *n*; *tongue*: mlaśnięcie *n*; **2.** *lock*: szczękać ⟨-knąć⟩

cliff [klɪf] skała *f*

climate ['klaɪmɪt] klimat *m*

climax ['klaɪmæks] punkt *m* kulminacyjny

climb [klaɪm] wspinać ⟨-piąć⟩ się; *in the air/sky*: wznosić ⟨-nieść⟩ się; **~er** wspinacz *m*; *bot.* pnącze *n*

coach

cling [klɪŋ] (**clung**) (**to**) przylegać (-lgnąć) (do)

clinic ['klɪnɪk] klinika f; '**~al** kliniczny

clip¹ [klɪp] **1.** wycinać ⟨-ciąć⟩; przycinać ⟨-ciąć⟩; **2.** wycinek m; *film etc.*: urywek m filmu; *video*: teledysk m

clip² [~] **1.** spinacz m; *hair*: klamerka f; *ear*: klips m; **2.** a. **~ on** przypinać ⟨-piąć⟩ klamerkę *itp.*

cloakroom ['kləʊkruːm] toaleta f; *esp. Brt.* szatnia f, garderoba f

clock [klɒk] **1.** *wall, grandfather, tower*: zegar m; **2.** *tech.* licznik m (zegarowy); **~ in, ~ on** wybi(ja)ć godzinę przyjścia na karcie zegarowej; **~ out, ~ off** wybi(ja)ć godzinę wyjścia na karcie zegarowej; '**~wise** w kierunku wskazówek zegara; '**~work** mechanizm m (zegarowy)

clog [klɒg] **1.** chodak m; **2.** a. **~ up** zatykać ⟨-tkać⟩ (się), zapychać ⟨-pchać⟩ się

close 1. [kləʊs] *adj* bliski; *friend*: serdeczny, bliski; *inspection etc.*: szczegółowy, gruntowny; *atmosphere*: duszny, parny; *print etc.*: gęsty, zwarty; **2.** [kləʊs] *adv* blisko; **~ by** w pobliżu; **~ at hand** pod ręką; **3.** [kləʊz] *v/t* zamykać ⟨-mknąć⟩; *meeting etc.* zakańczać ⟨-kończyć⟩; *v/i* zamykać ⟨-mknąć⟩ się; **~ down** *station, channel* za-

kończyć nadawanie; **~ in** *darkness, night*: zbliżać się; **~ up** *people*: ścieśni(a)ć się

closet ['klɒzɪt] *esp. Am.* szaf(k)a f

close-up ['kləʊsʌp] *phot. etc.* zbliżenie n

cloth [klɒθ] materiał m, tkanina f

clothe [kləʊð] odzi(ew)ać, ub(ie)rać

clothes [kləʊðz] odzież f, ubranie n

cloud [klaʊd] **1.** chmura f, obłok m; **2.** *sky*: zachmurzyć (się); *glass*: zamglić (się); *liquid*: zmącić się; '**~burst** oberwanie p chmury; '**~y** pochmurny

clove [kləʊv] *spice*: goździk m

club [klʌb] **1.** klub m; (*stick*) pałka f; *sp.* kij m do golfa; *cards*: trefl m; **2.** uderzać ⟨-rzyć⟩ (pałką)

clue [kluː] trop m, ślad m, wskazówka f

clump [klʌmp] bryłk(a) f; *trees*: kępa f

clumsy ['klʌmzɪ] niezdarny, niezgrabny

clung [klʌŋ] *past and pp of* **cling**

clutch [klʌtʃ] **1.** chwyt m; *mot.* sprzęgło n; **2.** trzymać (kurczowo), ściskać ⟨-snąć⟩ w rękach

coach [kəʊtʃ] **1.** powóz m; *Brt. mot.* autokar m; *Brt. rail.* wagon m; *sp.* trener m; **2.** dawać korepetycje (**s.o.**

komuś); *sp.* trenować (**s.o.** kogoś)

coal [kəʊl] węgiel *m*

coarse [kɔːs] *cloth:* szorstki, chropowaty; *person:* nieokrzesany

coast [kəʊst] wybrzeże *n;* '**~al** przybrzeżny

coat [kəʊt] **1.** płaszcz *m,* palto *n;* (*layer*) warstwa *f;* **2.** *with paint etc.:* pokry(wa)ć; '**~ing** warstwa *f,* powłoka *f;* **~ of arms** herb *m*

coax [kəʊks] *v/t* nakłaniać ⟨-łonić⟩ (pochlebstwem *itp.*) (**s.o. into doing s.th.** kogoś do zrobienia czegoś); *v/i* przymilać się

cobweb ['kɒbweb] pajęczyna *f*

cock [kɒk] **1.** *zo.* kogut *m;* **2.** (*lift*) podnosić ⟨-nieść⟩; *mil.* odwieść kurek (**s.th.** u czegoś)

'**cockpit** kokpit *m,* kabina *f* pilota

cockroach ['kɒkrəʊtʃ] karaluch *m*

cocoa ['kəʊkəʊ] kakao *n*

cod [kɒd] dorsz *m*

code [kəʊd] **1.** kod *m;* (*rules*) kodeks *m;* **2.** ⟨za⟩kodować

coffee ['kɒfɪ] kawa *f;* **~ bar** *Brt.* kawiarnia *f*

coffin ['kɒfɪn] trumna *f*

coherent [kəʊ'hɪərənt] spójny, logiczny

coil [kɔɪl] **1.** *v/t a.* **~ up** zwijać ⟨zwinąć⟩; *v/i* okręcać ⟨-cić⟩ się, owijać ⟨owinąć⟩ się; **2.** zwój *m; electr.* cewka *f; med.*

spirala *f*

coin [kɔɪn] **1.** moneta *f;* **2.** *word* (u)tworzyć

coincide [kəʊɪn'saɪd] zbiec się; '**~nce** [~'ɪnsɪdəns] zbieg *m* okoliczności

cold [kəʊld] **1.** zimny; *I'm* (*feeling*) **~** zimno mi; → *blood;* **2.** zimno *n;* (*illness*) przeziębienie *n*

collaborate [kə'læbəreɪt] współpracować

collapse [kə'læps] **1.** zawalać się; (*faint*) ⟨za⟩słabnąć; **2.** upadek *m,* krach *m;* '**~ible** składany

collar ['kɒlə] kołnierz(yk) *m; dog:* obroża *f;* '**~bone** obojczyk *m*

colleague ['kɒliːg] kolega *m*

collect [kə'lekt] **1.** *v/t* (*pick up*) odbierać ⟨odebrać⟩; (*gather*) ⟨z⟩gromadzić, zbierać ⟨zebrać⟩; *money* ⟨za⟩inkasować; *v/i* zbierać ⟨zebrać⟩ się; kwestować, zbierać ⟨zebrać⟩ na tacę; **2.** *adv: a.* **~ on delivery** (*abbr.* **COD**) *Am.* za pobraniem, za zaliczeniem pocztowym; *call* **~** *Am.* zamówić rozmowę na koszt odbiorcy; **~ call** *Am.* rozmowa *f* na koszt odbiorcy *f;* **~ed** *fig.* opanowany, skupiony; **~ion** [~'kʃn] zbiór *m,* kolekcja *f;* (*picking up*) odbiór *m; econ.* inkaso *n; eccl.* kwesta *f;* **~ive** zbiorowy, zbiorczy

college ['kɔlɪdʒ] uczelnia f; *rodzaj szkoły wyższej; form.* kolegium n

collide [kə'laɪd] zderzać ⟨-rzyć⟩ się

collision [kə'lɪʒn] zderzenie n

colloquial [kə'ləʊkwɪəl] potoczny

colonel ['kɜːnl] pułkownik m

colony ['kɔlənɪ] kolonia f

colo(u)r ['kʌlə] **1.** kolor m, barwa f; *pl mil.* sztandar m, *mar.* bandera f; **2.** *v/t* ⟨u⟩farbować; *v/i person:* ⟨za⟩czerwienić się; **'~blind** nie rozróżniający kolorów; **'~ed 1.** barwny, kolorowy; **2.** kolorowy (-wa *f*); *pl* kolorowi *pl;* **'~fast** o trwałych kolorach; **'~ful** *a. fig.* barwny

column ['kɔləm] kolumna f; *print.* szpalta f

comb [kəʊm] **1.** grzebień m; **2.** ⟨u⟩czesać (się)

combat ['kɔmbæt] **1.** bój m; **2.** zwalczać

combination [kɔmbɪ'neɪʃn] połączenie n; kombinacja f; **~e** [kəm'baɪn] ⟨po⟩łączyć (się)

come [kʌm] (*came, come*) przyby(wa)ć; *on foot a.:* przychodzić ⟨przyjść⟩; *riding, driving etc. a.:* przyjeżdżać ⟨-jechać⟩; *~ across* natykać ⟨-tknąć⟩ się na; *person:* ⟨z⟩robić wrażenie; *~ along* nadchodzić ⟨-dejść⟩ się; (*join*) przyłączać ⟨-czyć⟩ się

(*with* do); *~ apart* rozpadać ⟨-paść⟩ się, rozłatywać ⟨-lecieć⟩ się; *~ by* wejść w posiadanie; *visitor:* zachodzić ⟨zajść⟩, wpadać ⟨wpaść⟩; *~ in!* wejść!; *~ off* button etc.: odpadać ⟨-paść⟩; *~ on!* dalej(że)!; *~ round visitor:* wpadać ⟨wpaść⟩, zaglądać ⟨zajrzeć⟩; *~ to* przychodzić ⟨przyjść⟩ do siebie

comedian [kə'miːdjən] komik m; **~y** ['kɔmədɪ] komedia f

comfort ['kʌmfət] **1.** wygoda f; (*consolation*) pociecha f; **2.** pocieszać ⟨-szyć⟩; **'~able** wygodny

comic(al) ['kɔmɪk(əl)] komiczny; **~s** *pl* komiksy *pl*

command [kə'mɑːnd] **1.** rozkaz m; *mil.* dowództwo n; **2.** rozkaz(yw)ać; *mil.* dowodzić; **~er** dowódca m; **~er in chief** [~ɜːrɪn'tʃiːf] naczelny wódz m; **~ment** przykazanie n

commemorate [kə'meməreɪt] ⟨u⟩czcić (pamięć)

comment ['kɔment] **1.** komentarz m, uwaga f (*on s.th.* na temat czegoś); *no ~!* bez komentarzy!; **2.** ⟨s⟩komentować (*on s.th.* coś)

commerce ['kɔmɜːs] handel m

commercial [kə'mɜːʃl] **1.** handlowy, komercyjny; *product:* (ogólnie) dostępny na rynku; **2.** *radio, TV:* reklama f

commission [kəˈmɪʃn] **1.**
work of art etc.: zamówienie
n; *econ.* prowizja *f*; (*committee*) komisja *f*; *mil.* patent *m*
oficerski; **2.** zamawiać
〈**~er** 〈-mówić〉, *mil.* mianować
oficerem; **~er** [~ʃnə] komisarz *m*, pełnomocnik *m*
commit [kəˈmɪt] poświęcać
〈-cić〉 (**to s.th.** czemuś);
crime popełni(a)ć; **~ o.s.** zobowiąz(yw)ać się (**to** do);
~ment poświęcenie *n* się;
(*obligation*) zobowiązanie *n*;
~tee [~tɪ] komitet *m*
common [ˈkɒmən] wspólny;
(*ordinary*) pospolity; **have**
s.th. in ~ mieć coś wspólnego; **2 Market** Wspólny Rynek *m*; *pl the* **2s** *GB parl.*
Izba Gmin; **~ sense** zdrowy
rozsądek *m*; **~place** pospolity, banalny
commotion [kəˈməʊʃn] tumult *m*, zamieszanie *n*
communal [ˈkɒmjʊnl]
wspólny, społeczny; (*municipal*) komunalny
communicat|e [kəˈmjuːnɪkeɪt] *v/t* przekaz(yw)ać; *v/i*
porozumiewać 〈-mieć〉 się;
~ion [~ˈkeɪʃn] porozumienie
n; *pl* łączność *f*; **~ive**
[kəˈmjuːnɪkətɪv] rozmowny,
towarzyski
communis|m [ˈkɒmjʊnɪzəm]
komunizm *m*; **~t** [~ɪst] **1.** komunista *m* (-tka *f*); **2.** komunistyczny
community [kəˈmjuːnətɪ]

społeczność *f*
commute [kəˈmjuːt] *rail. etc.*
dojeżdżać; **~r** dojeżdżający
m; **~r train** pociąg *m* podmiejski
compact 1. [ˈkɒmpækt] *s* puderniczka *f*; **2.** [kəmˈpækt]
adj zwarty, spoisty; (*small*)
niewielkich rozmiarów;
style: zwięzły; **~ disc** → **CD**
companion [kəmˈpænjən] towarzysz(ka *f*) *m* (podróży
itp.), osoba *f* towarzysząca
company [ˈkʌmpənɪ] towarzystwo *n*; *econ.* firma *f*,
przedsiębiorstwo *n*; *mil.*
kompania *f*; *theat.* trupa *f*;
keep s.o. ~ dotrzym(yw)ać
komuś towarzystwa
compar|able [ˈkɒmpərəbl]
porównywalny; **~ative**
[kəmˈpærətɪv] *adj* względny;
study: porównawczy; **~e**
[~ˈpeə] *v/t* porówn(yw)ać; *v/i*
da(wa)ć się porównać; **~ison**
[~ˈpærɪsn] porównanie *n*
compartment [kəmˈpɑːtmənt] przegródka *f*; *rail.*
przedział *m*
compass [ˈkʌmpəs] kompas
m; *pl. a.* **pair of ~es** cyrkiel *m*
compatible [kəmˈpætəbl]
możliwy do pogodzenia,
zgodny; **be ~** pasować do
siebie (**with** z); *computer etc.*:
być kompatybilnym (**with** z)
compensat|e [ˈkɒmpenseɪt]
s.o. wynagrodzić (komuś);
(*balance*) wyrówn(yw)ać;
~ion [~ˈseɪʃn] odszkodowa-

nie *n*, rekompensata *f*
compete [kəm'pi:t] ubiegać
się (**for** o); współzawodni-
czyć; *sp.* uczestniczyć w za-
wodach
competen|ce [ˈkɒmpɪ-
təns, ˈ⸝sɪ] competency *f*; znajomość *f* rzeczy, kompeten-
cja *f*; **⸝t** [ˈ⸝nt] fachowy, kom-
petentny
competit|ion [kɒmpɪ'tɪʃn]
współzawodnictwo *n*; *econ.*
konkurencja *f*; *sp.* zawody
pl; **⸝ive** [kəm'petɪtɪv] kon-
kurujący ze sobą; *person:*
zdolny/chętny do współza-
wodnictwa; **⸝or** [⸝tə] *sp.*
współzawodnik *m* (-niczka
f); *econ.* konkurent(ka *f*) *m*
complain [kəm'pleɪn]
⟨po⟩skarżyć się (**about/of
s.th.** na coś, **to s.o.** komuś),
narzekać (**about/of** na);
(**protest formally**) składać
⟨złożyć⟩ skargę; **⸝t** [⸝t] skarga *f*; *med.* dolegliwość *f*
complete [kəm'pli:t] **1.**
całkowity, zupełny, kom-
pletny; **2.** ⟨u⟩kończyć, zakańczać ⟨-kończyć⟩
complexion [kəm'plekʃn] cera *f*
complicated [ˈkɒmplɪkeɪtɪd]
skomplikowany
compliment 1. [ˈkɒmplɪ-
mənt] komplement *m*; **2.**
[ˈ⸝ment] *s.o.* powiedzieć
komplement; (**congratulate**)
pogratulować (**on s.th.** czegoś)

component [kəm'pəʊnənt]
składnik *m*
compos|e [kəm'pəʊz]
składać ⟨złożyć⟩; *mus.*
⟨s⟩komponować; **be ⸝ed of**
składać się z; **⸝e o.s.** uspokajać ⟨-koić⟩ się, opa-
now(yw)ać się; **⸝ed** spokojny, opanowany; **⸝er** *m*; **⸝ition**
[kɒmpə'zɪʃn] kompozycja *f*;
(**essay**) wypracowanie *n*;
⸝ure [kəm'pəʊʒə] zimna
krew *f*, spokój *m*
compound 1. [kəm'paʊnd]
⟨z⟩mieszać, ⟨po⟩łączyć; **2.**
[ˈkɒmpaʊnd] *adj* złożony;
med. fracture: skomplikowany; **3.** [ˈkɒmpaʊnd] połączenie *n*; *chem.* związek *m*
comprehen|d [kɒmprɪ'hend]
pojmować ⟨-jąć⟩; **⸝sion**
[⸝ʃn] zrozumienie *n*; **beyond
⸝sion** nie do pojęcia, nie-
pojęty; **⸝sive** [⸝sɪv] **1.** obszerny, wyczerpujący; **2.** *a.*
⸝sive school *Brt.* typ szkoły
o szerokim profilu
compress [kəm'pres]
⟨s⟩kondensować, sprężać
⟨-ży⟩
compromise [ˈkɒmprəmaɪz]
1. kompromis *m*; **2.** *v/t*
⟨s⟩kompromitować; *v/i* zawierać ⟨-wrzeć⟩ kompro-
mis/ugodę
compuls|ion [kəm'pʌlʃn]
przymus *m*; **⸝ive** [⸝sɪv]
nałogowy; (**irresistible**) taki,
od którego nie sposób się

oderwać; **~ory** [~sərɪ] przymusowy, obowiązkowy

computer [kəm'pju:tə] komputer m; **~ science** informatyka f

conceal [kən'si:l] ukryć

conceit [kən'si:t] zarozumiałość f, zadufanie n; **~ed** zarozumiały

conceiv|able [kən'si:vəbl] możliwy do wyobrażenia; **~e** [~'si:v] v/t wyobrażać sobie (**of s.th.** coś); v/t pojmować ⟨-jąć⟩; child poczynać ⟨-cząć⟩

concentrate ['kɒnsəntreit] ⟨s⟩koncentrować się; skupi(a)ć się (**on** na)

concern [kən'sɜ:n] **1.** care troska f; (business) zainteresowanie n; econ. firma f, przedsiębiorstwo n; **2.** ⟨do⟩tyczyć; **~ o.s. with** interesować się (anxious) zaniepokojony, niespokojny; (involved) zainteresowany

concert ['kɒnsət] koncert m; **~o** [kən'tʃeətəʊ] mus. piece: koncert m

concession [kən'seʃn] ustępstwo n

conclu|de [kən'klu:d] doprowadzać ⟨-dzić⟩ do końca; agreement zawrzeć; **~sion** [~'u:ʒn] koniec m, ukończenie n; **~sive** [~sɪv] ostateczny, rozstrzygający

concrete¹ ['kɒŋkri:t] konkretny

concrete² ['~] beton m

condemn [kən'dem] potępi(a)ć; (sentence) skaz⟨yw⟩ać; **~ation** [kɒndem'neɪʃn] potępienie n

condescend [kɒndɪ'send] raczyć (**to do** coś zrobić); to people: zniżać ⟨-żyć⟩ się do poziomu; **~ing** protekcjonalny

condition [kən'dɪʃn] **1.** stan m; sp. forma f; pl warunki pl; **on ~ that** pod warunkiem że; **2.** uwarunkować; (mould) wychow⟨yw⟩ać; **~al** [~ʃənl] warunkowy

condole [kən'dəʊl] wyrażać ⟨-razić⟩ współczucie (**with s.o.** komuś); **~nce** mst pl kondolencje pl

condom ['kɒndəm] prezerwatywa f

conduct 1. ['kɒndʌkt] zachowanie n, prowadzenie n; **2.** [kən'dʌkt] prowadzić; phys. przewodzić; mus. dyrygować; **~or** [~'dʌktə] konduktor m; mus. dyrygent m; phys. przewodnik m

confection [kən'fekʃn] wyrób m cukierniczy; **~er** [~ʃnə] cukiernik m; **~ery** [~ʃnərɪ] słodycze pl; business: cukiernictwo n

confer [kən'fɜ:] v/t title etc. nada⟨wa⟩ć; v/i naradzać ⟨-dzić⟩ się; **~ence** ['kɒnfərəns] konferencja f

confess [kən'fes] wyzna⟨wa⟩ć; **~ion** [~'feʃn] wyznanie n; (*admission of guilt*) przyznanie n się (do winy); *eccl.* spowiedź f

confide [kənˈfaɪd] powierzać ⟨-rzyć⟩; zwierzać ⟨-rzyć⟩ się (**in** s.o. komuś)

confiden|ce [ˈkɒnfɪdəns] zaufanie n; (*self-assurance*) pewność f siebie; **⁓t** ufny, pewny (siebie); **⁓tial** [⁓ˈdenʃl] poufny

confine [kənˈfaɪn] zamykać ⟨-mknąć⟩, ⟨u⟩więzić; ograniczać ⟨-czyć⟩; **be ⁓d** ograniczać się (**to** do); **be ⁓ed to bed** być przykutym do łóżka; **⁓ment** ⟨u⟩więzienie n

confirm [kənˈfɜːm] potwierdzać ⟨-dzić⟩; **⁓ation** [kɒnfəˈmeɪʃn] potwierdzenie n

conflict 1. [ˈkɒnflɪkt] konflikt m; **2.** [kənˈflɪkt] kolidować (**with** z)

conform [kənˈfɔːm] dostosow(yw)ać się (**to** do)

confront [kənˈfrʌnt] stawiać ⟨postawić⟩ przed; *problem etc.* stawi(a)ć czoła

confus|e [kənˈfjuːz] ⟨po⟩mylić; (*bewilder*) ⟨z⟩dezorientować; (*complicate*) ⟨s⟩komplikować; **⁓ed** zdezorientowany; **⁓ing** mylący, dezorientujący; **⁓ion** [⁓ʒn] (*chaos*) zamieszanie n

congest|ed [kənˈdʒestɪd] zatłoczony, przeciążony; **⁓ion** [⁓tʃən] a. **traffic ⁓ion** zator m

congratulat|e [kənˈgrætʃʊleɪt] ⟨po⟩gratulować; **⁓ion** [⁓ˈleɪʃn] gratulacje pl; **⁓s!** gratuluję!

congregation [kɒŋgrɪˈgeɪʃn] *eccl.* parafia f, parafianie pl

congress [ˈkɒŋgres] kongres m, zjazd m

conjur|e [ˈkʌndʒə] ⟨wy⟩czarować; [kənˈdʒʊə] zaklinać, błagać; **⁓er, ⁓or** [ˈkʌndʒərə] magik m, sztukmistrz m

connect [kəˈnekt] ⟨po⟩łączyć; *electr.* podłączać ⟨-czyć⟩ (**to** do); *rail. etc.* korespondować (**with** z); **⁓ed** powiązany, związany; *electr.* podłączony; **⁓ion** *transport:* połączenie n; (*association*) związek m

conque|r [ˈkɒŋkə] zdoby(wa)ć, podbi(ja)ć; **⁓ror** [⁓rə] zdobywca m; **⁓st** [ˈkɒŋkwest] podbój m

conscien|ce [ˈkɒnʃəns] sumienie n; **⁓tious** [kɒnʃɪˈenʃəs] sumienny

conscious [ˈkɒnʃəs] świadomy; **⁓ness** świadomość f

conscript [kənˈskrɪpt] *mil.* powoł(yw)ać do wojska; **2.** [ˈkɒnskrɪpt] *mil.* poborowy m; pobór m; służba f wojskowa

consent [kənˈsent] **1.** zgoda f, przyzwolenie n; **2.** zgadzać ⟨zgodzić⟩ się

consequen|ce [ˈkɒnsɪkwəns] skutek m, następstwo n; **⁓tly** [ˈ⁓tlɪ] wskutek tego

conserv|ation [kɒnsəˈveɪʃn]
environment: ochrona f przyrody; *art*: konserwacja f; **~ationist** [~ʃnɪst] ekolog m F; **~ative** [kənˈsɜːvətɪv] **1.** konserwatywny; **2.** *pol.* mst ♀ członek/zwolennik partii konserwatywnej; **~e** [ˈsɜːv] oszczędzać ‹-dzić›

consider [kənˈsɪdə] (*believe*) uważać; (*contemplate*) rozważać ‹-żyć›; **~able** [~rəbl] znaczny; **~ably** znacznie; **~ate** [~rət] *person*: delikatny; **~ation** [~ˈreɪʃn] (*deliberation*) rozważenie n; (*factor*) kwestia f; (*thoughtfulness*) wzgląd m; **~ing** [~ˈsɪdərɪŋ] zważywszy na

consist [kənˈsɪst] składać się (*of s.th.* z czegoś); **~ence**, **~ency** [~ənsɪ], **~nsɪ] konsekwencja f; *substance*: konsystencja f; **~ent** konsekwentny

consol|ation [kɒnsəˈleɪʃn] pociecha f; **~e** [kənˈsəʊl] pocieszać ‹-szyć›

conspicuous [kənˈspɪkjʊəs] rzucający się w oczy, wyraźny

constable [ˈkʌnstəbl] *Brt.* posterunkowy m

constant [ˈkɒnstənt] stały

constituency [kənˈstɪtjʊənsɪ] okręg m wyborczy

constitute [ˈkɒnstɪtjuːt] stanowić; (*make up*) składać ‹złożyć› się na

constitution [kɒnstɪˈtjuːʃn]

pol. konstytucja f; *health*: konstytucja f (fizyczna); **~al** [~ʃənl] konstytucyjny

construct [kənˈstrʌkt] ‹s›konstruować; *building* ‹z›budować; **~ion** [~kʃn] budowa f, konstrukcja f; *under* **~ion** w budowie; **~ion site** budowa f, plac m budowy; **~ive** konstruktywny; **~or** konstruktor m

consul [ˈkɒnsl] konsul m; **~ate** [ˈsjʊlət] konsulat m

consult [kənˈsʌlt] *v/t* ‹po›radzić się, zasięgać ‹-gnąć› porady u; *book etc.* zaglądać ‹zajrzeć› do; *v/i* naradzać ‹-dzić› się; **~ant** doradca m; *Brt.* lekarz-specjalista m; **~ation** [kɒnsəl-ˈteɪʃn] konsultacja f-(cje pl); **~ing hour** (zamówiona) wizyta f u lekarza; **~ing room** gabinet m lekarski

consum|e [kənˈsjuːm] zuży(wa)ć; *food* ‹s›konsumować; **~er** konsument m; (*user*) użytkownik m; **~er goods** pl artykuły pl konsumpcyjne; **~ption** [~ˈsʌmpʃn] konsumpcja f; *energy etc.*: zużycie n

contact [ˈkɒntækt] **1.** kontakt m; **2.** ‹s›kontaktować się (*s.o.* z kimś); **~ lens** szkło n kontaktowe

contagious [kənˈteɪdʒəs] *med.* zakaźny; *fig.* zaraźliwy

contain [kənˈteɪn] (*hold*) zawierać; (*restrain*) ‹za›pano-

control

wać nad; **~er** pojemnik *m*; *shipping*: kontener *m*

contaminat|e [kənˈtæmɪnet] zanieczyszczać ⟨-czyścić⟩; (*irradiate*) skażać ⟨-skazić⟩; **~ion** [~ˈneɪʃn] zanieczyszczenie *n*, *with radiation*: skażenie *n*

contemplate [ˈkɒntemplet] (*consider*) rozważać *m*; (*look*) przyglądać się

contemporary [kənˈtempərərɪ] **1.** współczesny; **2.** człowiek *m* dzisiejszy/ współczesny

contempt [kənˈtempt] pogarda *f*; **~ible** godny pogardy; **~uous** [~tʃʊəs] pogardliwy

content¹ [ˈkɒntent] *m. pl* zawartość *f*

content² [kənˈtent] **1.** zadowalać ⟨-wolić⟩; zaspokajać ⟨-koić⟩; **2.** zadowolony; *~ o.s. with* zadowolić się, poprzestać na; **~ed** zadowolony, zaspokojony

contest 1. [ˈkɒntest] *beauty:* konkurs *m*; (*struggle*) rywalizacja *f*; **2.** [kənˈtest] ubiegać się o; *jur.* podważać ⟨-żyć⟩; **~ant** [kənˈtestənt] współzawodnik *m* (-niczka *f*); rywal(ka *f*) *m*

continent [ˈkɒntɪnənt] kontynent *m*; *the* 2 *Brt.* Europa *f* (*poza Wlk. Brytanią*); **~al** [~ˈnentl] kontynentalny

continua|l [kənˈtɪnjuəl] nieustanny; **~ation** [~ˈeɪʃn] kontynuacja *f*; **~e** [~ˈtɪnjuː] *v/t*

s.th. kontynuować; *to do s.th.* robić co dalej; *to be ~ed* ciąg dalszy nastąpi; *v/i* trwać (dalej), ciągnąć się; **~ity** [kɒntɪˈnjuːətɪ] ciągłość *f*; **~ous** [kənˈtɪnjuəs] ciągły

contracep|tion [kɒntrəˈsepʃn] antykoncepcja *f*, zapobieganie *n* ciąży; **~ive** [~tɪv] *adj* and *s* (środek *m*) antykoncepcyjny

contract 1. [ˈkɒntrækt] umowa *f*, kontrakt *m*; **2.** [kənˈtrækt] zawierać ⟨-wrzeć⟩ umowę; (*shirk*) ⟨s⟩kurczyć się; *disease* zarażać ⟨-razić⟩ się; **~or** [kənˈtræktə] *a. building ~or* przedsiębiorca *m* budowlany

contradict [kɒntrəˈdɪkt] sprzeciwia(ć) się; **~ion** [~kʃn] sprzeczność *f*; **~ory** [~tərɪ] sprzeczny

contrary [ˈkɒntrərɪ] **1.** *adj* przeciwny; *person:* przekorny; **2.** *adv* wbrew (**to s.th.** czemuś); **3.** *s* przeciwieństwo *n*; *on the ~* wręcz przeciwnie

contrast 1. [ˈkɒntrɑːst] kontrast *m*; (*opposite*) przeciwieństwo *n*; **2.** [kənˈtrɑːst] *v/t* przeciwstawi(a)ć; *v/i* kontrastować (**with** z)

contribut|e [kənˈtrɪbjuːt] przyczyni(a)ć się (*to* do), mieć wkład (*to* w); **~ion** [kɒntrɪˈbjuːʃn] wkład *m*

control [kənˈtrəʊl] **1.** (*check*) panować nad; (*govern*) kierować, kontrolować; *(master)* opanow(yw)ać; sterować; **2.** *(power)* władza *f;* *(mastery)* panowanie *n; pl price etc.:* regulacja *f; tech.* sterowanie *n; mst pl tech.* przyrządy *pl* kontrolne/sterownicze; *be in ~ of* panować nad; *bring (or get) under ~* zapanować nad; *get out of ~* wymykać ⟨-mknąć⟩ się spod kontroli; *lose ~ of* ⟨s⟩tracić panowanie/kontrolę nad; **~ centre** *(Am. center)* centrala *f;* **~ desk** pulpit *m* kontrolny; **~er** główny inspektor *m; accounts:* rewident *m;* **~ panel** deska *f* rozdzielcza; **~ tower** *aer.* wieża *f* kontrolna

controvers|ial [kɒntrə'vɜ:ʃl] sporny, kontrowersyjny; **~y** ['kɒntrəvɜ:sɪ] spór *m,* kontrowersja *f; press:* polemika *f*

conveni|ence [kən'vi:njəns] wygoda *f; Brt.* toaleta *f* publiczna; *all (modern)* **~ces** *z* wszelkimi wygodami; **~t** wygodny, dogodny

convent ['kɒnvənt] klasztor *m* (żeński)

convention [kən'venʃn] *(assembly)* zjazd *m; (agreement)* konwencja *f; (custom)* konwenans *m;* **~al** [~ʃənl] konwencjonalny; *(standard)* standardowy

conversation [kɒnvə'seɪʃn] rozmowa *f*

convert [kən'vɜ:t] *(transform)*

przemieni(a)ć (się); *(adapt)* przerabiać ⟨-robić⟩; *math.* przeliczać ⟨-czyć⟩; *eccl.* nawracać ⟨-wrócić⟩; **~ible** **1.** przeliczalny; *currency:* wymienialny; **2.** *mot.* kabriolet *m*

convey [kən'veɪ] przekaz(yw)ać; *idea etc.* ⟨za⟩komunikować; **~or (belt)** przenośnik *m* taśmowy

convict 1. [kən'vɪkt] *jur.* skaz(yw)ać *(of za);* **2.** ['kɒnvɪkt] skazaniec *m;* **~ion** [kən'vɪkʃn] przekonanie *n; jur.* skazanie *n*

convinc|e [kən'vɪns] przekon(yw)ać; **~ing** przekonujący

cook [kʊk] **1.** kucharz *m* ⟨-charka *f⟩;* **2.** ⟨u⟩gotować; **~book** *esp. Am.* książka *f* kucharska; **~er** *Brt.* kuchenka *f;* **~ery book** *esp. Brt.* książka *f* kucharska; **~ie** *Am.* herbatnik *m*

cool [ku:l] **1.** chłodny, orzeźwiający; *fig.* opanowany; **2.** ochładzać ⟨-łodzić⟩

cooperative [kəʊ'ɒpərətɪv] skłonny do współdziałania/ współpracy

cop [kɒp] F *(police(wo)man)* glina *m* F

cope [kəʊp]: *~ with* ⟨po⟩radzić sobie; *(contend)* borykać się

copier ['kɒpɪə] kopiarka *f*

copper ['kɒpə] miedź *f*

copy ['kɒpɪ] **1.** kopia f; book etc.: egzemplarz m; print. rękopis m, maszynopis m; **fair** ~ czystopis m; **rough** ~ brudnopis m; ⟨s⟩kopiować; in writing: przepis(yw)ać; '~**right** n. prawo n autorskie; **2.** chroniony prawem autorskim

coral ['kɒrəl] koral m

cord [kɔːd] **1.** sznur m (a. electr.), przewód m (cloth) sztruks m; **2.** sztruksowy; '~**uroy** ['kɔːdərɔɪ] sztruks m; pl spodnie pl ze sztruksowe

core [kɔː] rdzeń m, jądro n (a. fig.)

cork [kɔːk] **1.** korek m; **2.** ⟨za⟩korkować; '~**screw** korkociąg m

corn¹ [kɔːn] zboże n; Am. kukurydza f

corn² [~] med. odcisk m

corner ['kɔːnə] **1.** street: narożnik m, róg m; room: kąt m; esp. mot. zakręt m; football: róg m; fig. (a. **tight** ~) ślepa uliczka f, kozi róg m; **2.** adj narożny; **3.** fig. przypierać ⟨-przeć⟩ do muru; animal osaczać ⟨-czyć⟩; ~ **kick** football: rzut m rożny

coronary ['kɒrənərɪ] F ~ **thrombosis** (pl -ses [-siːz]) zawał m serca

corporat|e ['kɔːpərət] zbiorowy; business: ... biznesu; '~**ion** [-ə'reɪʃn] jur. osoba f prawna; business: korporacja f; Am. spółka f akcyjna;

Brt. władze pl miejskie

corpse [kɔːps] trup m

correct [kə'rekt] **1.** prawidłowy, poprawny; time a.: dokładny; **2.** poprawi(a)ć; ~**ion** [~kʃn] poprawka f

correspond [kɒrɪ'spɒnd] odpowiadać (sobie) (exchange letters) korespondować (**with, to** z); ~**ence** zgodność f; (letters) korespondencja f; ~**ing** odpowiednio

corridor ['kɒrɪdɔː] korytarz m

corro|de [kə'rəʊd] ⟨s⟩korodować; relationship etc. (powoli, stopniowo) niszczyć; ~**sion** [~ʒn] korozja f

corrupt [kə'rʌpt] **1.** zdeprawowany; (dishonest) skorumpowany; text: zniekształcony; **2.** ⟨z⟩deprawować; with money: ⟨s⟩korumpować; text zniekształcić; ~**ion** [~pʃn] demoralizacja f; (dishonesty) korupcja f

cosmetic [kɒz'metɪk] **1.** kosmetyczny; **2.** kosmetyk m

cost [kɒst] **1.** koszty pl; (price) cena f; **2.** (cost) kosztować; '~**ly** kosztowny, drogi; ~ **of living** koszty pl utrzymania

cosy ['kəʊzɪ] przytulny

cot [kɒt] łóżeczko n dziecięce; Am. łóżko n polowe

cottage ['kɒtɪdʒ] wiejski domek m parterowy; ~ **cheese** twaróg m

cotton ['kɒtn] bawełna f; ~ **wool** Brt. wata f

couch [kaʊtʃ] tapczan m; in

surgery: leżanka *f*

cough [kɒf] **1.** kaszel *m;* **2.**
⟨za⟩kaszleć

could [kʊd] *past of* **can'**

council ['kaʊnsl] rada *f;* Brt.
rada *f* miejska; **~ flat** Brt.
mieszkanie *n* kwaterunkowe; **~(l)or** ['kaʊnsələ] radny *m*
(-na *f*)

counsel ['kaʊnsl] **1.** (*advice*)
(po)rada *f; lawyer:* adwokat
m; **2.** doradzać ⟨-dzić⟩;
~(l)or ['kaʊnslə] doradca *m;*
Am. adwokat *m*

count' [kaʊnt] ⟨po⟩liczyć; **~
on** liczyć na

count² [kaʊnt] hrabia *m*

counter' ['kaʊntə] tech. licznik
m; games: żeton, żeton *m*

counter² ['kaʊntə] *café:* kontuar *m;*
shop: lada *f*

counter³ ['kaʊntə] ⟨od⟩parować
(cios), odpierać ⟨odeprzeć⟩
(atak)

counter|act [kaʊntə'rækt] *in-
fluence* przeciwdziałać; *taste*
⟨z⟩neutralizować; **~bal-
ance 1.** ['kaʊntəbæləns] przeciw-
waga *f;* **2.** [kaʊntə'bæləns]
⟨z⟩równoważyć, ⟨s⟩kom-
pensować; **~clockwise** *Am.
→* **anticlockwise; ~espio-
nage** [-r'espjənɑːʒ] kontr-
wywiad *m;* **~feit** ['kaʊntə-
fɪt] **1.** *adj* fałszywy, sfałszo-
wany; *card* fałszywy *m;* **2.**
money etc. ⟨s⟩fałszować; **3.**
~foil odcinek *m* kontrolny;
~part odpowiednik *m*

countess ['kaʊntɪs] hrabina *f*

'countless niezliczony

country ['kʌntrɪ] kraj *m; in
the* **~** na wsi; **~man** (*pl
-men*) rodak *m;* (*peasant*)
wieśniak *m;* **~side** wieś *f,*
okolica *f* wiejska; **~woman**
(*pl -women*) rodaczka *f;*
(*peasant*) wieśniaczka *f*

county ['kaʊntɪ] Brt. hrabst-
wo *n; Am.* okręg *m*

couple ['kʌpl] **1.** para *f; a* **~ of**
F parę; **2.** ⟨po⟩łączyć

courage ['kʌrɪdʒ] odwaga *f;*
~ous [kə'reɪdʒəs] odważny

courier ['kʊrɪə] pilot *m* (wy-
cieczek); (*messenger*) kurier *m*

course [kɔːs] (*route*) kurs *m;
action:* tryb *m* postępowania; *racing:* tor *m; golf:* pole
n; meal: danie *n; training:*
kurs *m;* **of** **~** oczywiście, naturalnie

court [kɔːt] **1.** *jur.* sąd *m; royal
etc.:* dwór *m; tennis:* kort
m; **2.** zalecać się (s.o. do kogoś)

courte|ous ['kɜːtjəs] grzecz-
ny; **~sy** ['kɜːtɪsɪ] grzeczność *f*

'courtyard podwórze *n*

cousin ['kʌzn] kuzyn(ka *f*) *m,*
brat *m* cioteczny *siostra *f*
cioteczna

cover ['kʌvə] **1.** *tech.* osłona *f;
bedclothes:* przykrycie *n; furniture etc.:* pokrowiec *m;
book:* okładka *f; spying:*
przykrywka *f; mil.* schronienie *n;* **2.** przy-
kry(wa)ć, pokry(wa)ć; *di-*

stance: przeby(wa)ć; *mil.* ubezpieczać; *econ.* stanowić zabezpieczenie; *media*: relacjonować; ~**up** 〈za〉tuszować; ~**age** ['ʌrɪdʒ] *media*: relacjonowanie *n*, transmisja *f*

cow [kaʊ] krowa *f*

coward ['kaʊəd] tchórz *m*; ~**ice** ['ʌɪs] tchórzostwo *n*; '~**ly** tchórzliwy

coy [kɔɪ] (pozornie) nieśmiały

crack [kræk] **1.** *s noise*: trzask *m*; (*slit*) pęknięcie *n*, szczelina *f*; **2.** *adj* doborowy; **3.** *v/i* pękać 〈-knąć〉, trzaskać 〈-snąć〉; *voice*: załam(yw)ać się; *fig.* (*a.* ~ **up**) załam(yw)ać się; *v/t* 〈z〉łamać, 〈s〉tłuc; *nut* 〈u〉tłuc; *code* 〈z〉łamać; *safe* 〈roz〉pruć; '~**er** *gastr.* (słone) ciasteczko *n*; *toy*: cukierek-petarda *f*

cradle ['kreɪdl] **1.** kołyska *f*; **2.** ostrożnie trzymać

craft [krɑːft] rzemiosło *n*; *aer.* samolot *g pl m*; *mar.* (*boat*) łódź *f*, (*ship*) okręt *m*, *-y pl*; '~**sman** (*pl -men*) rzemieślnik *m*; '~**y** przebiegły

cramp [kræmp] skurcz *m*

cranberry ['krænbəri] żurawina *f*

crane [kreɪn] *zo.* and *tech.* żuraw *m*

crank [kræŋk] korba *f*; F *person*: oszołom *m*, czubek *m* F

crash [kræʃ] **1.** rozbi(ja)ć się; (*strike*) uderzyć, grzmotnąć;

mot. mieć wypadek; *aer.* rozbi(ja)ć się; **2.** łomot *m*, grzmot *m*; *econ.* krach *m*; *mot.*, *aer.* kraksa *f*; ~**course** kurs *m* błyskawiczny; ~**diet** dieta-cud *f*; ~**helmet** kask *m*

crate [kreɪt] *beer, milk etc.*: skrzynka *f*

crave [kreɪv] (*desire*) pragnąć; (*long*) tęsknić (**for** za)

crawl [krɔːl] **1.** pełzać 〈-znąć〉 〈po〉czołgać się; **2.** *swimming*: kraul *m*

crayon ['kreɪən] kredka *f*

craz|e [kreɪz] szał *m*, mania *f*; '~**y** szalony

cream [kriːm] **1.** krem *m*; *liquid*: śmietana *f*; *fig.* śmietanka *f*; **2.** *gastr.* ubi(ja)ć; ~**cheese** serek *m* twarogowy; '~**y** zawierający dużo śmietany; *colour*: kremowy

crease [kriːs] **1.** fałda *f*, zmarszczka *f*; **2.** 〈po〉miąć (się)

creat|e [kriːˈeɪt] 〈s〉tworzyć; ~**ion** twórczość *f*; ~**ive** twórczy; ~**or** twórca *m*; ~**ure** ['kriːtʃə] stworzenie *n*; *imaginary*: stwór *m*

crèche [kreɪʃ] żłobek *m*

credible ['kredəbl] wiarygodny

credit ['kredɪt] **1.** zaufanie *n*, wiara *f*; (*merit*) zasługa *f*; *econ.* kredyt *m*; **2.** przypis(yw)ać; *econ.* udzielać 〈-lić〉 kredytu; *econ.* przelewać 〈-lać〉 na konto; '~**able** wiarygodny zaszczytny, chlubny; **~ card** karta *f* kredytowa; **'~or** wierzyciel *m*

credulous ['kredjʊləs] łatwowierny

creek [kri:k] *Brt.* zato(cz)ka *f*; *Am.* potok *m*

creep [kri:p] (*crept*) skradać się, podkradać ⟨-raść⟩ się; (pod)pełzać powoli; **'~er** pnącze *n*; **'~y** przyprawiający o dreszcze

crept [krept] *past and pp of creep*

crescent ['kresnt] półksiężyc *m*; *street*: (półkolista) uliczka *f*

crevice ['krevɪs] szczelina *f*, rysa *f*

crew [kru:] załoga *f*

crib [krɪb] **1.** *Am.* łóżeczko *n* dziecięce; *school*: ściąga *f* F; **2.** *school*: ściągać F

cricket ['krɪkɪt] *zo.* świerszcz *m*; *sp.* krykiet *m*

crime [kraɪm] przestępstwo *n*; (*murder etc.*) zbrodnia *f*

criminal ['krɪmɪnl] **1.** *act*: przestępczy; *offence*: kryminalny; *law*: karny; **2.** przestępca *m* (-pczyni *f*)

crimson ['krɪmzn] amarantowy, purpurowy

cripple ['krɪpl] **1.** kaleka *m*; **2.** okaleczyć; *fig.* ⟨s⟩paraliżować

crisis ['kraɪsɪs] (*pl* **-ses** ['~si:z]) kryzys *m*

crisp [krɪsp] **1.** chrupiący; *vegetables*: świeży; *air etc.*:

rześki; **2.** *pl Brt.* czipsy *pl*

critic ['krɪtɪk] krytyk *m*; **~al** krytyczny; **~ism** ['~sɪzəm] krytyka *f*; **~ize** ['~saɪz] ⟨s⟩krytykować

crook [krʊk] **1.** zgięcie *n*, zakrzywienie *n*; F oszust *m*; **2.** zginać ⟨zgiąć⟩; **~ed** ['~ɪd] krzywy, zakrzywiony, zgięty; F *person*: nieuczciwy

crop [krɒp] **1.** plon *m*; **2.** *hair* ścinać ⟨ściąć⟩ na krótko

cross [krɒs] **1.** *s* krzyż *m*; *biol.* krzyżówka *f*; **2.** *v/i* ⟨s⟩krzyżować się, przecinać ⟨-ciąć⟩ się; **3.** *v/t* przecinać ⟨-ciąć⟩; *street* przechodzić ⟨przejść⟩ na drugą stronę; *biol.* ⟨s⟩krzyżować; **~ off**, **~ out** wykreślać ⟨-lić⟩; **~ o.s.** ⟨prze⟩żegnać się; **~ one's legs** założyć nogę na nogę; **keep one's fingers ~ed** trzymać kciuki; **4.** *adj* zły, rozgniewany; **~breed** *biol.* mieszaniec *m*; **~'country** przełajowy; **~examine** brać ⟨wziąć⟩ w krzyżowy ogień pytań; **~eyed** zezowaty; **~ing** przejazd *m* kolejowy; *Brt.* przejście *n* dla pieszych; *mar.* podróż *f* morska; **~roads** *pl or sg* skrzyżowanie *n*, krzyżówka *f* F; *fig.* rozdroże *n*; **~section** przekrój *m*; **~walk** *Am.* przejście *n* dla pieszych; **~word (puzzle)** krzyżówka *f*

crow¹ [krəʊ] wrona *f*

crow² [~] ⟨za⟩piać

cure

crowd [kraʊd] **1.** tłum *m*; **2.** tłoczyć się; '~ed załoczony (**with** *instr.*)

crown [kraʊn] **1.** korona *f*; *career etc.*: zwieńczenie *n*; **2.** *a. fig.* ⟨u⟩koronować

crucial ['kruːʃl] decydujący, przełomowy

crude [kruːd] surowy, nie wykończony, zgrubny; *fig.* nieokrzesany

cruel [kroəl] okrutny; '~ty okrucieństwo *n*

cruise [kruːz] **1.** krążyć *f*, rejs *m* wycieczkowy

crumb [krʌm] okruch *m*, okruszek *m*; '~le ['~bl] *v/t* rozkruszyć; *v/i* ⟨po⟩kruszyć się, rozsyp(yw)ać się

crunch [krʌntʃ] *v/t* (*eat*) chrupać; (*crush*) rozgnieść z trzaskiem; *v/i* chrzęścić

crush [krʌʃ] **1.** *crowd*: tłum *m*; F pociąg *m* (**on** s.o. do kogoś); **2.** ⟨z⟩miażdżyć, zgniatać ⟨-nieść⟩ (się)

crust [krʌst] skorup(k)a *f*; *bread*: skórka *f*

cry [kraɪ] **1.** żądać, domagać się (**out**) **for** s.th. czegoś); **2.** ⟨o⟩krzyk *m*

crystal ['krɪstl] kryształ *m*; (*a. ~ glass*) szkło *n* kryształowe, kryształ *m*; '~lize ['~təlaɪz] ⟨wy⟩krystalizować się

cube [kjuːb] *ice etc.*: kostka *f*; *figure*: sześcian *m*

cubic ['kjuːbɪk] sześcienny, kubiczny; '~le ['~kl] kabina *f*

cuckoo ['kʊkuː] kukułka *f*

cucumber ['kjuːkʌmbə] ogórek *m*

cuddle ['kʌdl] ⟨przy⟩tulić (się)

cue [kjuː] wskazówka *f*; (*signal*) sygnał *m*; *sp.* kij *m* bilardowy

cuff [kʌf] mankiet *m*; **~ link** spinka *f* do mankietów

cul-de-sac ['kʌldəsæk] ślepa uliczka *f*

cult [kʌlt] kult *m*

cultivat|e ['kʌltɪveɪt] *land* uprawiać; *talent* rozwijać ⟨-winąć⟩ w sobie; *people* zjednywać sobie, hołubić; '~ion [~'veɪʃn] *crops*: uprawa *f*; *tastes etc.*: rozwijanie *n* (**in** w); *people*: zjednywanie *n* sobie

cultur|al ['kʌltʃərəl] kulturowy; *activities*: kulturalny; '~e [~tʃə] kultura *f*; (*animals*) hodowla *f*

cumbersome ['kʌmbəsəm] nieporęczny, niewygodny

cup [kʌp] filiżanka *f*; *egg*: kieliszek *m*; *bra*: miseczka *f*; *sp.* puchar *m*; **~board** ['kʌbəd] kredens *m*, szafka *f*; **~ final** finały *pl* pucharowe

curable ['kjʊərəbl] uleczalny

curb [kɜːb] **1.** ograniczać ⟨-czyć⟩, ukrócić; *s.o.* przywoł(yw)ać do porządku; **2.** *Am.* krawężnik *m*

cure [kjʊə] **1.** kuracja *f*; (*remedy*) lekarstwo *n*; **2.** *s.o.* uzdrawiać ⟨-rowić⟩; *s.th. a.* wyleczyć

curi|osity [kjʊərɪˈɒsətɪ] *quality:* ciekawość *f; thing:* osobliwość *f,* ciekawostka *f;* **~ous** [ˈ~əs] ciekawy; (*peculiar*) osobliwy, niezwykły

curl [kɜːl] **1.** lok *m,* pukiel *m;* **2.** *v/t hair* skręcać ⟨-cić⟩ w loki; *v/i* zwijać ⟨zwinąć⟩ się, skręcać ⟨-cić⟩ się; *hair:* kręcić się; **~ up** *person:* zwinąć się w kłębek; **~er** wałek *m* do włosów; **~y** *hair:* kręcony

currant [ˈkʌrənt] porzeczka *f; dried:* rodzynek *m*

curren|cy [ˈkʌrənsɪ] *econ.* waluta *f;* **foreign ~cy** dewizy *pl;* **~t** [ˈ~nt] **1.** aktualny; *month, issue, account:* bieżący; **2.** prąd *m,* nurt *m; electr.* a. natężenie *n* prądu

curriculum [kəˈrɪkjʊləm] (*pl* **-la** [ˈ~lə]**, -lums**) program *m* (*nauczania, studiów*); **~ vitae** [ˈ~viːtaɪ] życiorys *m*

curse [kɜːs] **1.** przekleństwo *n;* **2.** *v/i* ⟨za⟩kląć; *v/t* przeklinać ⟨-kląć⟩; **~d** [ˈ~ɪd] przeklęty

curtain [ˈkɜːtn] zasłona *f,* kotara *f; lace:* firanka *f; thea.* kurtyna *f*

curve [kɜːv] **1.** łuk *m;* (*bend*) zakręt *m; diagram:* krzywa *f;* **2.** wyginać ⟨-giąć⟩ się; *car, rocket:* zakręcać ⟨-cić⟩

cushion [ˈkʊʃn] **1.** poduszka *f;* **2.** wyściełać ⟨wysłać⟩; *shock:* ⟨z⟩amortyzować, osłabi(a)ć

custody [ˈkʌstədɪ] areszt *m; jur.* opieka *f* nad dzieckiem

custom [ˈkʌstəm] zwyczaj *m,* obyczaj *m; econ.* stałe zaopatrywanie się w danej firmie; **~ary** zwyczajowy; **~er** klient(ka *f*) *m*

customs [ˈkʌstəmz] *pl* cło *n,* urząd *m* celny; **~ clearance** odprawa *f* celna; **~ officer** celnik *m* (-niczka *f*)

cut [kʌt] **1.** (na)cięcie *n; wound:* skaleczenie *n; clothes:* krój *m; meat:* porcja *f; precious stones:* szlif *m; prices, wages:* obniżka *f;* **2.** (*cut*) ucinać ⟨uciąć⟩; *grass* ścinać ⟨ściąć⟩; *expenditure* obcinać ⟨-ciąć⟩; (*hurt*) skaleczyć; *taxes, expenditure* obniżać ⟨-żyć⟩; *mot. corner* ścinać ⟨ściąć⟩; **she's ~ting a tooth** wyrzyna jej się ząb; **~ down** ograniczać ⟨-czyć⟩; *tree* ścinać ⟨ściąć⟩; **~ in on s.o.** *mot.* zajechać komuś drogę; **~ off** odcinać ⟨-ciąć⟩; *electricity* wyłączać ⟨-czyć⟩; **~ out** wycinać ⟨-ciąć⟩; *dress etc.* wykrajać ⟨-kroić⟩

cute [kjuːt] sprytny; *esp. Am.* pretty: śliczny, ładniutki

cutlery [ˈkʌtlərɪ] sztućce *pl*

cut|-'price *Brt.,* **~-'rate** *Am.* przeceniony

cycl|e [ˈsaɪkl] **1.** cykl *m;* **2.** ⟨po⟩jechać na rowerze; **~ing** jeżdżenie *n* na rowerze; *sp.* kolarstwo *n;* **~ist** rowe-

date

rzysta *m* (-tka *f*)
cylinder ['sılındə] *tech.* cylinder *m*; *math.* walec *m*

cynical ['sınıkl] cyniczny
Czech [tʃek] **1.** Czech *m*, Czeszka *f*; **2.** czeski

D

dab [dæb] *from s.th.* wycierać ⟨wytrzeć⟩ *s.th.* (lekko) ⟨po⟩smarować
dad [dæd] F **~dy** tata *m* F
daft [dɑːft] F głupi; stuknięty
daily ['deılı] **1.** (co)dzienny; **2.** dziennik *m*, gazeta *f*; *a.* **~ help** *Brt.* kobieta *f* do sprzątania
dairy ['deərı] mleczarnia *f*
damage ['dæmıdʒ] **1.** uszkodzenie *n*, szkoda *f*; *pl jur.* odszkodowanie *n*; **2.** uszkadzać ⟨-kodzić⟩, nadwyrężać ⟨-żyć⟩
damn [dæm] *a.* **~ed** przeklęty; **~ it!** F cholera! F
damp [dæmp] **1.** wilgotny; **2.** wilgoć *f*; **3.** *a.* **~en** zwilżać ⟨-żyć⟩
danc|e [dɑːns] **1.** ⟨za⟩tańczyć; **2.** taniec *m*; **~er** tancerz *m* (-cerka *f*)
dandruff ['dændrʌf] łupież *m*
Dane [deın] Duńczyk *m*, Dunka *f*
danger ['deındʒə] niebezpieczeństwo *n*; **~ous** ['~dʒərəs] niebezpieczny
Danish ['deınıʃ] duński
dar|e [deə] śmieć, mieć śmiałość; **how ~ you!** jak

śmiesz!; **~ing** ['~rıŋ] odważny
dark [dɑːk] **1.** *colour*: ciemny; *room etc. a.*: mroczny; *fig.* posępny; **2.** zmrok *m*; **after ~** po zmroku; **~en** ['~ən] ściemnieć, pociemnieć; **~ness** ciemność *f*
darling ['dɑːlıŋ] **1.** ukochany *m* (-na *f*); **2.** ukochany
dart [dɑːt] **1.** *game*: strzałka *f*; **2.** rzucać ⟨-cić⟩ się do przodu
dash [dæʃ] **1.** ⟨po⟩pędzić; (*throw*) ciskać ⟨-snąć⟩; *hopes etc.* ⟨z⟩druzgotać; **2.** (*sudden movement forward*) rzut *m* do przodu, wypad *m*; (*small quantity*) odrobina *f*; *rum etc.*: kropelka *f*; *salt etc.*: szczypta *f*; **make a ~ for** rzucić się do; **~board** deska *f* rozdzielcza; **~ing** olśniewający
data ['deıtə] *pl* (*often sg*) dane *pl* (*a. computer*): dane *pl*; **~ base** baza *f* danych; **~ processing** przetwarzanie *n* danych
date¹ [deıt] daktyl *m*
date² [~] **1.** data *f*; (*appointment*) (umówione) spotkanie *n*; F randka *f* F; *esp. Am.* osoba, z którą ma się randkę; **out**

of ~ nieaktualny; (*obsolete*) przestarzały; **up to** ~ aktualny; (*modern*) nowoczesny; 2. *v/i* datować się (**from** z); (*age*) starzeć się; *v/t* datować; *esp. Am.* chodzić (**s.o.** z kimś) F; **'~d** przestarzały

daughter ['dɔːtə] córka *f*; **'~-in-law** ['~rɪnlɔː] synowa *f*

dawn [dɔːn] **1.** świt *m*; **2.** ⟨za⟩świtać

day [deɪ] dzień *m*; ~ **off** wolny dzień; **by** ~ za dnia; ~ **after** ~ dzień po dniu; ~ **in,** ~ **off** dzień w dzień; **in those** ~**s** w owych czasach; **one** ~ któregoś dnia; **the other** ~ onegdaj, któregoś dnia; **the** ~ **after tomorrow** pojutrze; **the** ~ **before yesterday** przedwczoraj; **let's call it a** ~ na dzisiaj dość!; **'~break** brzask *m*, świt *m*; **'~dream** śnić na jawie; **'~light** światło *n* dnia

dazed [deɪzd] oszołomiony

dead [ded] **1.** nieżywy, umarły, martwy, (*insensitive*) nieczuły/obojętny (**to** na); ~ **tired** śmiertelnie zmęczony; **2. the** ~ *pl* umarli *pl*; **~en** ['dedn] przytępi(a)ć; (*the* ~ ostateczny/nieprzekraczalny termin *m*; **'~lock** martwy punkt *m*, impas *m*; **'~ly** śmiertelny

deaf [def] głuchy; **'~and-'dumb** głuchoniemy; **~en** ['defn] ogłuszyć; **'~ening** ogłuszający; **~'mute** głuchoniemy

deal [diːl] **1.** (**dealt**) *cards* rozda(wa)ć; *blow* zada(wa)ć; *often* ~ **out** rozdzielać ⟨-lić⟩, rozda(wa)ć; ~ **in s.th.** econ. handlować czymś; ~ **with s.th.** zajmować ⟨-jąć⟩ się (czymś); econ. sie. robić interesy z (kimś); **2.** F interes *m*, handel *m* F; *big* ~! no i co z tego!; **it's a** ~! zrobione!, zgoda!; **a good** ~ sporo (**of s.th.** czegoś); **a great** ~ mnóstwo (**of s.th.** czegoś); **'~er** econ. handlowiec *m*, dealer *m*; *antiques, drugs:* handlarz *m*; **~t** [delt] *past and pp of* **deal** 1

dear [dɪə] **1.** (*expensive*) drogi; *address:* drogi, kochany; 2 *Sir* (*in letters*) Szanowny Panie!; **2.** kochanie, mój drogi *m*/ moja droga *f*; **3.** *int* (**oh**) ~!, ~ **me!** o jeju

death [deθ] śmierć *f*

debate [dɪ'beɪt] **1.** dyskusja *f*, debata *f*; **2.** roztrząsać, dyskutować

debris ['deɪbriː] gruzy *pl*

debt [det] dług *m*; **be in** ~ mieć dług(i); **'~or** dłużnik *m* (-niczka *f*)

decade [dekeɪd] dziesięciolecie *n*, dekada *f*

decay [dɪ'keɪ] **1.** niszczeć; *biol.* próchnieć, rozkładać *f*; *tooth:* psuć się; **2.** rozkład *m*; *med.* próchnica *f*

deceit [dɪ'siːt] oszustwo *n*

deceive [dɪ'siːv] oszuk(iw)ać, okłam(yw)ać

December [dɪ'sembə] grudzień m

decen|cy ['di:snsɪ] przyzwoi-
tość f; **~t** przyzwoity

deception [dɪ'sepʃn] oszu-
kaństwo n; (trick) podstęp
m; **~ive** [~tɪv] zwodniczy,
złudny

decide [dɪ'saɪd] ⟨z⟩decydo-
wać (się), zadecydować; **~d**
ewidentny; views: zdecydowany

decis|ion [dɪ'sɪʒn] decyzja f,
postanowienie n; **~ive** [dɪ-
'saɪsɪv] decydujący; person:
stanowczy, zdecydowany

deck [dek] mar. pokład m;
esp. Am. talia f (kart);
~chair leżak m

declar|ation [deklə'reɪʃn]
oświadczenie n, deklaracja f;
~e [dɪ'kleə] v/i oświadczyć
(announce) deklarować ⟨-ło-
sić⟩; v/t ⟨za⟩deklarować

decline [dɪ'klaɪn] 1. (diminish) spadać ⟨spaść⟩; (refuse)
odmawiać ⟨-mówić⟩ (to do
s.th. zrobienia czegoś); 2.
spadek m; (fall) upadek m,
schyłek m

decompose [di:kəm'pəuz]
rozkładać ⟨-złożyć⟩ się

decorat|e ['dekəreɪt] ozda-
biać ⟨-dobić⟩; flat etc.
⟨wy⟩remontować; (award)
⟨u⟩dekorować; **~ion**
[~'reɪʃn] ozdoba f, dekoracja
f; (medal) odznaczenie n;
~ive ['~rətɪv] ozdobny; **~or**
['~reɪtə] malarz m (pokojo-

wy) or tapeciarz m

decrease 1. ['di:kri:s] spadek
m; **2.** [di:'kri:s] spadać
⟨spaść⟩, zmniejszać ⟨-szyć⟩
się

dedicat|ed ['dedɪkeɪtɪd] od-
dany (to s.th. czemuś); **~ion**
[~'keɪʃn] poświęcenie n

deduct [dɪ'dʌkt] odciągać
⟨-gnąć⟩ (from od), potrącać
⟨-cić⟩ (from z); **~ion** [~kʃn]
dedukcja f; (subtraction)
potrącenie n

deep [di:p] głęboki (a. fig.);
~en pogłębi(a)ć (się) (a.
fig.); **~freeze 1.** zamrażarka f; **2.** (-froze, -frozen)
zamrażać ⟨-mrozić⟩; **~fry**
⟨u⟩smażyć w tłuszczu

deer [dɪə] male: jeleń m; female: sarna f; collectively:
zwierzyna f płowa

defeat [dɪ'fi:t] **1.** po-
kon(yw)ać, pobić; **2.** klęska
f, porażka f

defect ['di:fekt] brak m, man-
kament m; **~ive** [dɪ'fektɪv]
wadliwy, mający braki

defence [dɪ'fens] obrona f

defend [dɪ'fend] ⟨o⟩bronić;
~ant jur. oskarżony m (-na f)

defens|e [dɪ'fens] Am. → de-
fence, department; ~ive 1.
obronny; **2.** gotowość f do
obrony

deficien|cy [dɪ'fɪʃnsɪ] (lack)
brak m; (shortage) niedobór
m, niedostatek m; **~t** nieodpowiedni; (short of) mający
niedobór

defin|e [dɪ'faɪn] określać ‹-lić›, ‹z›definiować; **~ite** ['defɪnɪt] zdecydowany, jasno określony/sprecyzowany; **~itely** zdecydowanie, stanowczo; **~ition** [˷'nɪʃn] definicja f; (quality): wyrazistość f; phot., TV etc. rozdzielczość f; **~itive** [dɪ'fɪnɪtɪv] ostateczny, rozstrzygający

deform [dɪ'fɔːm] zniekształcić; **~ity** zniekształcenie n, deformacja f

degenerate 1. [dɪ'dʒenəreɪt] popadać ‹-paść›, przerodzić się (w coś gorszego); **2.** [˷rət] adj zwyrodniały, zdegenerowany

degrade [dɪ'greɪd] s.o. upadlać ‹upodlić›, poniżać ‹-żyć›; s.th. (s)powodować degradację f

degree [dɪ'griː] stopień m; **by ~s** stopniowo

delay [dɪ'leɪ] **1.** v/t opóźni(a)ć (s.th. coś); v/i zwlekać (s.th. z czymś); **be ~ed** rail., etc. mieć opóźnienie; **2.** zwłoka f; rail., etc. opóźnienie n

delegat|e 1. ['delɪɡət] delegat(ka f) m; **2.** ['˷ɡeɪt] duties, power przekaz(yw)ać; s.o. ‹od›delegować; **~ion** [˷'ɡeɪʃn] delegacja f; duties etc.: przekazanie n

delete [dɪ'liːt] usuwać ‹usunąć›; computer: ‹s›kasować

deliberate [dɪ'lɪbərət] celowy, rozmyślny; **~ly** celowo, umyślnie

delica|cy ['delɪkəsɪ] delikatność f; (food) delikates m; **~te** ['˷ət] delikatny; person: wątły; **~tessen** [˷'tesn] sg shop: delikatesy pl; pl food: smakołyki pl

delicious [dɪ'lɪʃəs] wyborny; (delightful) zachwycający

delight [dɪ'laɪt] **1.** zachwyt m; (great pleasure) rozkosz f; **2.** zachwycać ‹-cić›; rozkoszować się (in s.th. czymś); **~ful** czarujący, cudowny, rozkoszny

deliver [dɪ'lɪvə] dostarczać ‹-czyć›; letters doręczać ‹-czyć›; speech wygłaszać ‹-łosić›; **~y** [˷rɪ] dostawa f; post: doręczenie n; med. poród m; **~ cash.**, **~y van** samochód m dostawczy

demand [dɪ'mɑːnd] **1.** żądanie n, wymaganie n; (need) zapotrzebowanie n (for na); pl wymagania pl (on w stosunku do); econ. popyt m (for na); **on ~** na żądanie; **2.** wymagać, ‹za›żądać; domagać się; **~ing** wymagający

democra|cy [dɪ'mɒkrəsɪ] demokracja f; **~t** ['deməkræt] demokrata m (-tka f); **~tic** [˷'krætɪk] demokratyczny

demonstrat|e ['demənstreɪt] ‹za›demonstrować; (prove) dowodzić ‹-wieść›, wykaz(yw)ać; **~ion** [˷'streɪʃn] demonstracja f; **~or** uczestnik *m* (-niczka *f*) demonstracji

denial [dɪ'naɪəl] zaprzeczenie *n*; (*refusal*) odmowa *f*

denims ['denɪmz] *pl* dżinsy *pl*

Denmark ['denmɑːk] Dania *f*

dens|e [dens] gęsty; **~ity** ['~ətɪ] gęstość *f*

dent [dent] **1.** wgięcie *n*; *fig.* szczerba *f*; **2.** wginać ⟨wgiąć⟩; *fig.* nadwerężać ⟨-żyć⟩

dent|al [dentl] zębowy; **'~ist** dentysta *m* (-tka *f*); **~ure** ['~tʃə] *mst pl* sztuczna szczęka *f*

deny [dɪ'naɪ] zaprzeczać ⟨-czyć⟩; (*refuse*) odmawiać ⟨-mówić⟩

depart [dɪ'pɑːt] odchodzić ⟨-dejść⟩; *by car, train etc.*: odjeżdżać ⟨-jechać⟩; *aer.* odlatywać ⟨-lecieć⟩ (*from* z)

department [dɪ'pɑːtmənt] oddział *m*; *univ.* instytut *m*, (*faculty*) wydział *m*; (*ministry*) ministerstwo *n*; ⁓ **of Defense/of the Interior** Ministerstwo Obrony/ Spraw Wewnętrznych; ⁓ **of State** *USA* Departament *m* Stanu; ⁓ **store** dom *m* towarowy

departure [dɪ'pɑːtʃə] odejście *n*; *train, coach*: odjazd *m*; *plane*: odlot *m*; ⁓ **lounge** poczekalnia *f* dla odlatujących

depend [dɪ'pend] zależeć (*on s.th.* od czegoś); polegać (*on s.o.* na kimś); *that* ⁓*s* to za-

leży; **~ant** osoba *f* na utrzymaniu; **~ence** uzależnienie *n* (*on* od); **~ent** uzależniony (*on* od)

deplor|able [dɪ'plɔːrəbl] godny ubolewania; **~e** [~ɔː] boleć/ubolewać (*s.th.* nad czymś)

deposit [dɪ'pɒzɪt] **1.** składać ⟨złożyć⟩ (*leave*) zostawi(a)ć; *passengers* wysadzać ⟨-dzić⟩; *bank*: wpłacać ⟨-cić⟩; *for safekeeping*: składać ⟨złożyć⟩ w depozyt; **2.** *chem.* osad *m*; *geol.* a. złoże *n*; *bank*: wkład *m* (długoterminowy); (*down payment*) pierwsza wpłata *f*

depress [dɪ'pres] naciskać ⟨-snąć⟩, przyciskać ⟨-snąć⟩; (*bring down*) obniżać ⟨-żyć⟩; (*sadden*) przygnębi(a)ć; **~ed** przygnębiony, zniechęcony; **~ion** [~ʃn] zastój *m*, stagnacja *f (a. econ.)*; *psych.*: depresja *f*; (*sadness*) przygnębienie *n*; *meteor.* niż *m*

deprive [dɪ'praɪv] pozbawić (*s.o. of s.th.* kogoś czegoś); **~d** ubogi; *area*: niedorozwinięty (*np.* ekonomicznie)

depth [depθ] głębia *f*; *distance*: głębokość *f*

deputy ['depjʊtɪ] zastępca *m* (-pczyni *f*), wice-...; *Am.* zastępca *m* szeryfa

derive [dɪ'raɪv] *v/t* czerpać (*from* z); *v/i* pochodzić, brać ⟨wziąć⟩ się (*from* z)

descen|d [dɪ'send] schodzić

⟨zejść⟩, zstępować ⟨-tąpić⟩; *(fall)* zapadać ⟨-paść⟩; **be ~ded** pochodzić *(from* od); **~dant** potomek *m;* **~t** [dɪ'sent] zejście *n,* zstąpienie *n;* *(slope)* spadek *m;* *aer.* obniżenie *n* lotu

descri|be [dɪ'skraɪb] opis(yw)ać; *(label)* określać ⟨-lić⟩; **~ption** [~'skrɪpʃn] opis *m;* *(kind)* rodzaj *m*

desert¹ ['dezət] pustynia *f*

desert² [dɪ'zɜːt] porzucać ⟨-cić⟩, opuszczać ⟨opuścić⟩; *mil.* ⟨z⟩dezerterować **(s.th.** z czegoś)

deserve [dɪ'zɜːv] zasługiwać ⟨-służyć⟩ **(s.th.** na coś)

design [dɪ'zaɪn] **1.** ⟨za⟩projektować; *tech.* ⟨s⟩konstruować; **2.** projekt *m;* *tech.* konstrukcja *f;* **~er** [dɪ'zaɪnə] projektant(ka *f) m;* *tech.* konstruktor *m*

desir|able [dɪ'zaɪərəbl] pożądany, wskazany; **~e** [~aɪə] **1.** życzyć sobie; pragnąć; *s.o.* pożądać; **2.** życzenie *n,* pragnienie *n; for s.o.:* pożądanie *n*

desk [desk] biurko *n; school:* ławka *f; restaurant etc.:* kasa *f; hotel:* recepcja *f*

despair [dɪ'speə] **1.** rozpacz **(at** z powodu); nie mieć nadziei **(of** na); **2.** rozpacz *f*

desperate ['despərət] rozpaczliwy; *person:* zdesperowany; **~ion** [~'reɪʃn] desperacja *f*

despise [dɪ'spaɪz] gardzić

despite [dɪ'spaɪt] pomimo

dessert [dɪ'zɜːt] deser *m*

destin|ation [destɪ'neɪʃn] cel *m* podróży; *s.th.* miejsce *n* przeznaczenia; **~e** [~ɪn] przeznaczać ⟨-czyć⟩; **~y** los *m*

destroy [dɪ'strɔɪ] ⟨z⟩niszczyć

destruction [dɪ'strʌkʃn] ⟨z⟩niszczenie *n; building:* ⟨z⟩burzenie *n;* **~ive** [~ɪv] niszczycielski; *feeling, emotion:* zgubny

detach [dɪ'tætʃ] odłączać ⟨-czyć⟩; **~ oneself** odseparow(yw)ać się; *mil.* odkomenderow(yw)ać; **~ed house:** wolno stojący

detail ['diːteɪl] szczegół *m,* detal *m*

detect [dɪ'tekt] wykry(wa)ć; **~ion** wykrycie *n,* wykrywanie *n;* **~ive** wywiadowca *m; private:* detektyw *m;* **~ive novel/story** powieść *f* kryminalna, kryminał *m f;* **~or** wykrywacz *m,* detektor *m*

detention [dɪ'tenʃn] *jur.* areszt *m; school:* zostawienie *n* po lekcjach

deter [dɪ'tɜː] odstraszać ⟨-szyć⟩

deteriorate [dɪ'tɪərɪəreɪt] pogarszać ⟨-gorszyć⟩ (się)

determin|ation [dɪtɜːmɪ'neɪʃn] determinacja *f; s.th.* ustalenie *n,* określenie *n;* **~e** [dɪ'tɜːmɪn] określać ⟨-lić⟩, wyznaczać ⟨-czyć⟩; *(resolve)*

postanowić (**to do s.th.** coś
zrobić); **~ed** zdecydowany,
stanowczy

deterrent [dɪ'terənt] **1.** odstraszający, zapobiegawczy;
2. środek m zapobiegawczy/
odstraszający

detest [dɪ'test] nie cierpieć,
nienawidzieć

detour ['diːtʊə] nadłożenie n
drogi; Am. objazd m

devalu|ation [diːvæljʊ'eɪʃn]
dewaluacja f; **~e** [ˌ'væljuː]
⟨z⟩dewaluować

devastat|e ['devəsteɪt] ⟨s⟩pu-
stoszyć, ⟨z⟩niszczyć; **~ing**
niszczycielski; (upsetting)
załamujący; (stunning) za-
bójczy F

develop [dɪ'veləp] rozwijać
⟨-winąć⟩ się; **~er** phot. wy-
woływacz m; **~ment** rozwój
m; (event) obrót m sprawy

device [dɪ'vaɪs] urządzenie n

devil ['devl] diabeł m; **~ish**
diabelski

devise [dɪ'vaɪz] wymyślać
⟨-lić⟩, obmyślać ⟨-lić⟩

devote [dɪ'vəʊt] poświęcać
⟨-cić⟩ (**to s.th.** czemuś); **~d**
oddany; research etc.:
wytężony

devour [dɪ'vaʊə] pochłaniać
⟨-łonąć⟩

devout [dɪ'vaʊt] pobożny;
(staunch) gorliwy, gorący

diabetes [daɪə'biːtiːz] cukrzy-
ca f

diagram ['daɪəɡræm] wykres
m, diagram m

dial ['daɪəl] **1.** tarcza f; (indicator) wskaźnik m; teleph.
tarcza f; **2.** teleph. wykręcać
⟨-cić⟩; **~ tone** Am. teleph.
wolny sygnał m

dialect ['daɪəlekt] dialekt m

dialling code ['daɪəlɪŋ] Brt.
teleph. numer m kierunko-
wy; **~tone** Brt. teleph. wolny
sygnał m

dialogue, Am. **-log** ['daɪəlɒɡ]
dialog m

diameter [daɪ'æmɪtə] średni-
ca f

diamond ['daɪəmənd] brylant
m, diament m; cards: karo n

diaper ['daɪəpə] Am. pieluszka f

diary ['daɪərɪ] dziennik m, pamiętnik m; for appointments
etc.: terminarz m

dictat|e [dɪk'teɪt] ⟨po⟩dykto-
wać; fig. narzucać ⟨-cić⟩
swoją wolę; **~ion** dyktando
n; fig. dyktat m; **~or** dykta-
tor m; **~orship** dyktatura f

dictionary ['dɪkʃənrɪ] słownik
m

did [dɪd] past of do

die¹ [daɪ] umierać ⟨umrzeć⟩
(**of** z.); **~ away** wind: ucisząć
⟨-szyć⟩ się; sound: zamierać
⟨-mrzeć⟩; light: ⟨z⟩gasnąć;
~ down → **~ away**; excitement: uspokajać ⟨-koić⟩ się;
~ out wymierać ⟨-mrzeć⟩

die² [~] matryca f; Am. kostka
f (do gry)

diet ['daɪət] **1.** dieta f; **2.** odchudzać się

differ ['dɪfə] *things*: różnić się; *people*: mieć różne zdanie; **~ence** ['dɪfrəns] różnica *f*; *opinions*: różnica *f* zdań; **'~ent** odmienny, inny; (*separate*) różny; **~entiate** [~'renʃɪeɪt] rozróżni(a)ć, odróżni(a)ć

difficult ['dɪfɪkəlt] trudny; **'~y** trudność *f*

dig [dɪg] ⟨wy⟩kopać

digest 1. [dɪ'dʒest] ⟨s⟩trawić, ⟨prze⟩trawić; **2.** ['daɪdʒest] streszczenie *n*; **~ible** [dɪ'dʒestəbl] strawny; **~ion** [dɪ'dʒestʃn] trawienie *n*

digit ['dɪdʒɪt] *math.* cyfra *f*; **'~al** cyfrowy

dignified ['dɪgnɪfaɪd] pełen godności, dystyngowany; **~ty** ['~əti] godność *f*

digs [dɪgz] *pl Brt.* stancja *f*

diligent ['dɪlɪdʒənt] pilny, pracowity

dilute [daɪ'ljuːt] rozcieńczać ⟨-czyć⟩

dime [daɪm] *Am.* dziesięciocentówka *f*

dimension [dɪ'menʃn] wymiar *m*

diminish [dɪ'mɪnɪʃ] *v/i* zmniejszać ⟨-szyć⟩ się; *v/t* pomniejszać ⟨-szyć⟩, zmniejszać ⟨-szyć⟩; **~utive** [~jʊtɪv] drobny

dine [daɪn] ⟨z⟩jeść (późny) obiad; **'~er** *in restaurant*: gość *m*; *Am.* bar *m* szybkiej obsługi; *rail.* wagon *m* re-

-stauracyjny; **~ing car** ['daɪn-

-ɪŋ] wagon *m* restauracyjny; **~ing room** jadalnia *f*, pokój *m* jadalny

dinner ['dɪnə] (późny) obiad *m*; **~ jacket** smoking *m*; **~ party** proszony obiad *m*; **'~time** pora *f* obiadowa

dip [dɪp] **1.** zanurzać ⟨-rzyć⟩ (się), zamaczać ⟨-moczyć⟩ (się); (*descend*) opaść, obniżyć się; *head*: pochylić się; **~ the headlights** *esp. Brt. mot.* skracać ⟨-rócić⟩ światła; **2.** zanurzenie *n*; (*descent*) obniżenie *n*, nachylenie *n*; (*swim*) kąpiel *f*

diploma [dɪ'pləʊmə] dyplom *m*

diplomacy [dɪ'pləʊməsɪ] dyplomacja *f*; **~t** ['dɪpləmæt] dyplomata *m*; **~tic** [~ə'mætɪk] dyplomatyczny

dire [daɪə] straszny, ponury

direct [dɪ'rekt] **1.** kierować; (*instruct*) nakaz(yw)ać; *film etc.*: ⟨wy⟩reżyserować; *letter etc.*: ⟨za⟩adresować; *s.o.*: skierować (*to* do); **2.** bezpośredni; **~ current** prąd *m* stały; **~ion** kierunek *m*; *film etc.*: reżyseria *f*; *pl* wskazówki *pl*; **~s** (*for use*) *pl* instrukcja *f*; **~ly** wprost, bezpośrednio; **~or** dyrektor *m*; *film etc.*: reżyser *m*; **~ory** [~tərɪ] spis *m*

dirt [dɜːt] brud *m*, błoto *n*; *fig.* plugastwo *n*; **~cheap** tani jak barszcz; **'~y 1.** brudny, zabłocony; *fig.* plugawy,

disguise

sprośny; **2.** ⟨za⟩brudzić

disabled [dɪs'eɪbld] upośledzony, kaleki

disadvantage [dɪsəd'vɑːntɪdʒ] wada f; *situation:* niekorzystna sytuacja f; *to one's* ~ na czyjąś niekorzyść; ~**ous** [dɪsædvə'nteɪdʒəs] niekorzystny, niemiły; ~**ment** [~'griːmənt] różnica f zdań

disagree [dɪsə'griː] nie zgadzać ⟨-godzić⟩ się (*with* z); *food:* ⟨za⟩szkodzić (*with s.o.* komuś); ~**able** [~'grɪəbl] nieprzyjemny, niemiły; ~**ment** [~'griːmənt] różnica f zdań

disappear [dɪsə'pɪə] znikać ⟨-knąć⟩; ~**ance** [~rəns] zniknięcie n

disappoint [dɪsə'pɔɪnt] rozczarow(yw)ać; ~**ment** rozczarowanie n

disapprove [dɪsə'pruːv] nie pochwalać (*of s.th.* czegoś)

disarm [dɪs'ɑːm] rozbrajać ⟨-roić⟩ (*a. pol.*); ~**ament** [~əmənt] rozbrojenie n (*a. pol.*)

disast|er [dɪ'zɑːstə] katastrofa f; ~**rous** [~strəs] fatalny, katastrofalny, zgubny

disbe|lief [dɪsbɪ'liːf] niedowierzanie n; *in ~lief* z niedowierzaniem; ~**lieve** [~'liːv] nie wierzyć

disc [dɪsk] krążek m (*record*) płyta f (gramofonowa); *computer* → **disk**

disclose [dɪs'kləuz] wyjawi(a)ć, odsłaniać ⟨-łonić⟩

discolo(u)r [dɪs'kʌlə] odbar-

dis'comfort niewygoda f

disconnect rozłączać ⟨-czyć⟩, odłączać ⟨-czyć⟩; *mains etc.* wyłączać ⟨-czyć⟩

discontent [dɪskən'tent] niezadowolenie n; ~**ed** niezadowolony, rozgoryczony

discotheque ['dɪskəutek] dyskoteka f

discount ['dɪskaunt] rabat m

discourage [dɪ'skʌrɪdʒ] zniechęcać ⟨-cić⟩

discover [dɪ'skʌvə] odkry(wa)ć; ~**y** [~rɪ] odkrycie n

discredit [dɪs'kredɪt] **1.** ⟨s⟩kompromitować, ⟨z⟩dyskredytować; **2.** kompromitacja f

discreet [dɪ'skriːt] dyskretny

discretion [dɪ'skreʃn] dyskrecja f

discriminate [dɪ'skrɪmɪneɪt] dyskryminować (*against s.o.* kogoś)

discuss [dɪ'skʌs] omawiać ⟨omówić⟩; (*talk over*) ⟨prze⟩dyskutować; ~**ion** [~ʃn] omówienie n; (*debating*) dyskusja f

disease [dɪ'ziːz] choroba f

disgrace [dɪs'greɪs] **1.** hańba f, wstyd m; *in* ~ w niełasce; **2.** przynosić ⟨-nieść⟩ wstyd; ~**ful** haniebny, sromotny

disguise [dɪs'gaɪz] **1.** przebierać ⟨-brać⟩ (*o.s.* się); *voice* zmieni(a)ć, *s.th.* ⟨za⟩maskować; (*hide*) ukry(wa)ć; **2.** przebranie n

disgust

disgust [dɪs'gʌst] **1.** wstręt *m*, odraza *f*; **2.** budzić wstręt/ odrazę; **~ing** obrzydliwy, wstrętny

dish [dɪʃ] danie *n*; *crockery*: naczynie *n*; **the ~es** *pl* naczynia *pl*; **'~cloth** ścier(ecz)ka *f* do naczyń

dishonest [dɪs'ɒnɪst] nieuczciwy; **~y** nieuczciwość *f*

dishono(u)r [dɪs'ɒnə] hańba *f*, niesława *f*

'dish|washer zmywarka *f* do naczyń; **'~water** pomyje *pl*

disillusion [dɪsɪ'luːʒn] rozczarow(yw)ać

disinfect [dɪsɪn'fekt] ⟨z⟩dezynfekować; **~ant** środek *m* dezynfekujący/odkażający

disintegrate [dɪs'ɪntɪgreɪt] rozpadać ⟨-paść⟩ się

disinterested [dɪs'ɪntrɪstɪd] bezinteresowny; (*impartial*) bezstronny

disk [dɪsk] *esp. Am.* → *disc*; *computer*: dysk *m*; **~ drive** stacja *f* dysków; **~ette** [dɪs'ket] dyskietka *f*

dislike [dɪs'laɪk] **1.** niechęć *f*; **2.** nie lubić, czuć niechęć

dismantle [dɪs'mæntl] rozmontow(yw)ać

dismiss [dɪs'mɪs] odprawi(a)ć; *problem etc.* pomijać ⟨-minąć⟩; *employee*: zaniechać; **~al** (*sacking*) zwolnienie *n*

dis|obedience [dɪsə'biːdjəns] nieposłuszeństwo *n*; **~obedient** nieposłuszny; **~obey**

nie ⟨po⟩słuchać

disorder [dɪs'ɔːdə] nieład *m*; (*riots*) zamieszki *pl*; *med.* zaburzenia *pl*; **~ly** bezładny, niechlujny; *jur.* zakłócający porządek publiczny

disorganized [dɪs'ɔːgənaɪzd] źle zorganizowany

dispatch [dɪ'spætʃ] wysy(ł)ać

dispense [dɪ'spens] rozda(wa)ć, rozdzielać ⟨-lić⟩; **~ with** oby(wa)ć się bez; **~r** *tech.* dozownik *m*

disperse [dɪ'spɜːs] rozpraszać ⟨-roszyć⟩ (się)

displace [dɪs'pleɪs] przesuwać ⟨-sunąć⟩, przestawi(a)ć; *people* przesiedlać ⟨-lić⟩

display [dɪ'spleɪ] **1.** pokaz(yw)ać; *goods* wystawi(a)ć; **2.** wystawa *f*; *tech.* wskaźnik *m*

displease [dɪs'pliːz] nie ⟨s⟩podobać się

dispos|able [dɪ'spəuzəbl] jednorazowego użytku; **~al** usuwanie *n*; *garbage*: wywóz *m*; **be/put at s.o.'s ~al** być/ oddać do czyjejś dyspozycji; **~e** [~z] pozby(wa)ć się (*of s.th.* czegoś); **~ed** skłonny; **~ition** [~pə'zɪʃn] usposobienie *n*; (*inclination*) skłonność *f*; (*arrangement*) układ *m*

disprove [dɪs'pruːv] obalać ⟨-lić⟩, odpierać ⟨odeprzeć⟩

dispute 1. [dɪ'spjuːt] *v/i* spierać się; *v/t* ⟨za⟩kwestionować; **2.** [~, 'dɪspjuːt] spór *m*

disqualify [dɪs'kwɒlɪfaɪ] ⟨z⟩dyskwalifikować

disregard [dɪsrɪ'gɑːd] pomijać ⟨-minąć⟩

disrespectful [dɪsrɪs'pektfʊl] lekceważący

disrupt [dɪs'rʌpt] *meeting* zrywać ⟨zerwać⟩; *process* zakłócać ⟨-cić⟩

dissatis|faction ['dɪssætɪs'fækʃn] niezadowolenie *n*; **~fied** [~'sætɪsfaɪd] niezadowolony

dissolve [dɪ'zɒlv] rozpuszczać ⟨-puścić⟩ (się); *jur.*, *pol.* rozwiąz⟨yw⟩ać

distan|ce ['dɪstəns] odległość *f*; *sp.*, *psych.* dystans *m*; *at/from a ~ce* z dala; *from a ~ce* z oddali; **~t** odległy; *person:* z rezerwą

distinct [dɪ'stɪŋkt] różny (*from* od); (*clear*) wyraźny; *as ~ from* w odróżnieniu od; **~ion** rozróżnienie *n*; (*difference*) różnica *f*; (*honour*) wyróżnienie *n*; **~ive** charakterystyczny

distinguish [dɪ'stɪŋgwɪʃ] rozróżni(a)ć (*between* między); odróżni(a)ć (*from* od); **~ed** wybitny; (*dignified*) dystyngowany

distort [dɪ'stɔːt] zniekształcać ⟨-cić⟩; *face:* wykrzywi(a)ć (się); *argument* przekręcać ⟨-cić⟩

distract [dɪ'strækt] *s.o.* odrywać ⟨oderwać⟩; *attention* rozpraszać ⟨-roszyć⟩; **~ed**

rozkojarzony; **~ion** rozpraszanie/odciąganie *n* uwagi; (*amusement*) rozrywka *f*

distress [dɪ'stres] **1.** strapienie *n*; (*hardship*) niedola *f*; *emergency:* rozpaczliwe położenie *n*; **2.** ⟨z⟩martwić, przygnębi(a)ć

distribut|e [dɪ'strɪbjuːt] rozdzielać ⟨-lić⟩, rozda(wa)ć; **~ion** [~'bjuːʃn] podział *m*, rozdział *m*; *math.* rozkład *m*, rozrzut *m*

district ['dɪstrɪkt] okręg *m*, obwód *m*; *city:* dzielnica *f*

distrust [dɪs'trʌst] **1.** nieufność *f*, niedowierzanie *n*; **2.** nie dowierzać/ufać

disturb [dɪ'stɜːb] przeszkadzać ⟨-kodzić⟩; (*bother*) ⟨za⟩niepokoić; **~ance** zakłócenie *n* spokoju

ditch [dɪtʃ] rów *m*

dive [daɪv] **1.** ⟨za⟩nurkować; *with hand:* sięgać ⟨-gnąć⟩; (*rush*) rzucić się (*for* za); **2.** skok *m* do wody; *aer.* pikowanie *n*; **~r** nurek *m*

divers|e [daɪ'vɜːs] rozmaity; **~ion** [~ʃn] (*amusement*) rozrywka *f*; (*distraction*) odwrócenie *n* uwagi; *Brt.* objazd *m*; **~ity** [~səti] różnorodność *f*

divide [dɪ'vaɪd] **1.** *v/t* ⟨po⟩dzielić *math.* (*by* przez); *v/i* dzielić się *math.* (*by* przez); **2.** podział *m*

divis|ible [dɪ'vɪzəbl] podzielny; **~ion** [~ʒn] podział *m* *mil.* dywizja *f; math.* dzielenie *n*

divorce [dɪˈvɔːs] **1.** rozwód *m;* **get a ~** rozwieść się (**from** *z);* **2.** *jur.* rozwodzić ⟨-wieść⟩ się (**s.o.** z kimś); **get ~d** rozwieść się

dizzy [ˈdɪzɪ] oszołomiony

do [duː] (**did, done**) *v/t* ⟨z⟩robić, ⟨u⟩czynić; *room* ⟨po⟩sprzątać; *dishes* ⟨po⟩zmywać, zmy⟨wa⟩ć; *distance etc.* pokon⟨yw⟩ać; *sentence* F odsiedzieć; **have one's hair done** zrobić sobie fryzurę; *v/i* wystarczać ⟨-czyć⟩: *that will* ~ (to) wystarczy; mieć się, wieść się: ~ **well** mieć się dobrze; *on introduction:* **how ~ you ~** bardzo mi miło, jak się Pan(i) ma; *v/aux in interrogative sentences:* ~ **you know him?** (czy) znasz go?; *in negative sentences:* **I don't know** nie wiem; *for emphasis:* ~ **be quick** pospiesz się, proszę!; *substitute verb to avoid repetitions:* ~ **you like London?** – **I** ~ podoba ci się Londyn? – tak; *in question tags:* **he works hard, doesn't he?** (on) ciężko pracuje, nieprawdaż?; ~ **away with** pozby⟨wa⟩ć się; **I'm done in** F jestem wykończony F; ~ **up** *dress etc.* zapinać ⟨-piąć⟩ *f; hair* upinać ⟨-piąć⟩; *house etc.* ⟨wy⟩remontować; *package* ⟨za⟩pakować;

I could ~ with ... przydałby mi się ...; ~ **without** obchodzić ⟨obejść⟩ się bez

dock¹ [dɒk] **1.** basen *m* portowy, dok *m;* ława *f* oskarżonych; **2.** *v/t* ship dokować, wprowadzać ⟨-dzić⟩ do portu; *v/i* zawijać ⟨-winąć⟩ do portu/przystani

doctor [ˈdɒktə] doktor *m,* lekarz *m* (*-karka f*)

document 1. [ˈdɒkjumənt] dokument *m;* **2.** [ˈ~ment] udokumentować; **~ary** [~ˈmentərɪ] film *m* dokumentalny

dog [dɒg] pies *m;* **~gie, ~gy** [ˈdɒgɪ] psina *f*

dog-'tired zmordowany

do-it-yourself [duːɪtjɔːˈself] **1.** majsterkowanie *n;* **2.** ...dla majsterkowiczów

dole [dəʊl] **1.** *Brt.* F zasiłek *m* (dla bezrobotnych); **be on the** ~ być na zasiłku; **2.** ~ **out** wydzielać ⟨-lić⟩ po trochu

doll [dɒl] lalka *f*

dollar [ˈdɒlə] dolar *m*

dome [dəʊm] kopuła *f*

domestic [dəˈmestɪk] **1.** domowy; *concerning the country:* krajowy; **2.** służący *m* (*-ca f*); ~ **animal** zwierzę *n* domowe; **~ate** [~keɪt] *animals* udomowić ⟨-mowić⟩, oswajać ⟨-woić⟩; **be ~ated** być domatorem

dominant [ˈdɒmɪnənt] dominujący, przeważający; ~ **ate** [ˈ~neɪt] ⟨z⟩dominować;

~ation [~'neɪʃn] dominacja f, panowanie n; **~eering** [~'nɪərɪŋ] apodyktyczny, despotyczny

done [dʌn] pp of **do**; zrobiony; (finished, ready) gotowy; **well** ~ gastr. dobrze wypieczony/wysmażony

donkey ['dɒŋkɪ] osioł m

donor ['dəʊnə] dawca m (-wczyni f)

door [dɔː] drzwi pl; **'~bell** dzwonek m (do drzwi); **'~handle** klamka f; **'~keeper** portier(ka f) m, dozorca m (-rczyni f); **'~mat** wycieraczka f; **'~step** próg m

dope [dəʊp] 1. F narcotic: narkotyk m; information: cynk m F; sl. dureń m; 2. odurzać ⟨-rzyć⟩

dormitory ['dɔːmətrɪ] Am. dom m studencki

dose [dəʊs] dawka f

dot [dɒt] kropka f; **on the** ~ F co do sekundy; **~ted line** linia f kropkowana

dote [dəʊt]: ~ **on s.o.** świata nie widzieć poza kimś

double [dʌbl] 1. adj podwójny; 2. adv podwójnie; 3. s sobowtór m; film, TV: dubler(ka f) m; 4. v podwajać ⟨-doić⟩ (się); ~ **up** zginać ⟨zgiąć⟩ się **with pain z** bólu; **~'check** dokładnie sprawdzać ⟨-dzić⟩; **~'cross** F przechytrzyć; **~'decker** autobus m piętrowy, piętrus m F; **~'park** ⟨za⟩parkować

„na drugiego" (tj. blokując komuś wyjazd); **~'quick** 1. adj: in ~-**quick time** →; 2. adv F błyskawicznie, „piorunem" F; **~ room** pokój m dwuosobowy; **~s** (pl ~) tennis: debel m

doubt [daʊt] 1. wątpić; 2. wątpliwość f; **no** ~ niewątpliwie; **'~ful** wątpliwy; person: niepewny, całkowity; **'~less** bez wątpienia

dough [dəʊ] ciasto n; sl. (money) szmal m sl.; **'~nut** rodzaj pączka

down¹ [daʊn] 1. adv w dół; powalać ⟨-lić⟩; aer. strącać ⟨-cić⟩; drink wychylać ⟨-lić⟩; ~ **the street** po ulicy

down² [~] puch m, meszek m

'down|hill 1. z góry, z górki; skiing: zjazdowy; ~ **payment** zadatek m, pierwsza rata f; **'~pour** ulewa f; **'~right** zupełny, całkowity; **~stairs** 1. [daʊn'steəz] adv na/w dół; 2. ['~steəz] adj na dole, poniżej; **~-to-'earth** przyziemny, konkretny, praktyczny; **~-town** esp. Am. 1. [~'taʊn] śródmiejski; 2. ['~taʊn] śródmieście n

doze [dəʊz] 1. drzemać; ~ **off** zdrzemnąć się, przysnąć; 2. drzemka f

dozen ['dʌzn] tuzin m

drab [dræb] bury; (dreary) nieciekawy, monotonny

draft [drɑːft] 1. brudnopis m, szkic m; econ. weksel m; Am.

mil. pobór *m*; *Am.* →
draught; **2.** ⟨na⟩szkicować,
⟨na⟩pisać na brudno; *Am.*
mil. powoł(yw)ać; **~ee** [~'ti:]
Am. poborowy *m*

drag [dræg] wlec ⟨się⟩,
ciągnąć ⟨się⟩; **~ on** *fig.*
ciągnąć/wlec się

drain [dreɪn] **1.** *v/t* osuszać
⟨-szyć⟩; (*empty*) opróż-
ni(a)ć; *v/i*: **~ off** *or* **away** wyciekać ⟨-ciec⟩; **2.** odpływ *m*,
ściek *m*; **~age** ['~ɪdʒ] osusza-
nie *n*, drenowanie *n*; **~pipe**
rura *f* odpływowa

drama ['drɑːmə] dramat *m*;
~tic [drə'mætɪk] dramatycz-
ny; **~list** ['dræmətɪst] drama-
topisarz *m* (-sarka *f*); **~tize**
['dræmətaɪz] adaptować (na
scenę); *fig.* dramatyzować

drank [dræŋk] *past of* **drink** 1

drastic ['dræstɪk] drastyczny

draught [drɑːft] (*Am.* **draft**)
przeciąg *m*; *liquid*: haust *m*,
łyk *m*; *of* warcaby *pl*; **beer on
~**, **~ beer** piwo *n* beczkowe;
'~board *Brt.* szachownica *f*;
'~sman (*pl* **-men**) *esp. Brt.*
kreślarz *m*; (*cartoonist*) ry-
sownik *m*; **'~y** *esp. Brt.* pełen
przeciągów

draw [drɔː] **1.** (**drew**, **drawn**)
v/t ⟨na⟩rysować; (*pull*)
⟨po⟩ciągnąć; *attention* przyciągać ⟨-gnąć⟩; *breath* brać
⟨wziąć⟩; *curtains* zaciągać
⟨-gnąć⟩ *or* rozsuwać ⟨-nąć⟩;
knife, gun wyciągać ⟨-gnąć⟩;
money, cheque podejmować

⟨-djąć⟩; *tooth* wyr(yw)ać;
water pobierać ⟨-brać⟩; *v/i*
chimney: ciągnąć ⟨-nąć⟩; *tea etc.*:
naciągać ⟨-gnąć⟩; *sp.* ⟨z⟩re-
misować; **~ back** cofać
⟨-fnąć⟩ się; **~ out** *money* podejmować ⟨-djąć⟩; *fig.* przeciągać ⟨-gnąć⟩; **~ up** *writing*
⟨na⟩szkicować, ⟨na⟩pisać
na brudno; *car etc.*: zatrzy-
mać się; **2.** pociągnięcie *n*;
lottery: ciągnienie *n*, lo-
sowanie *n*; *sp.* remis *m*;
fig. atrakcja *f*; **'~back** wada *f*

drawer [drɔː] szuflada *f*; *of*
garment: majtki *pl*

drawing ['drɔːɪŋ] rysunek *m*;
~ board rysownica *f*, deska *f*
kreślarska; **~ pin** *Brt.* pinezka *f*; **~ room** salon *m*

drawn [drɔːn] *pp of* **draw** 1

dread [dred] **1.** bać/lękać się;
2. strach *m*, przerażenie *n*;
'~ful straszny

dream [driːm] **1.** marzenie *n*;
while sleeping: sen *m*; **2.**
(**dreamed** *or* **dreamt**) marzyć; *while sleeping*: śnić;
~er marzyciel(ka *f*) *m*; **~t**
[dremt] *past and pp of* **dream**
2; **'~y** rozmarzony, marzy-
cielski; (*fantastic*) jak ze snu

drench [drentʃ] zmoczyć; *s.o.*
przemoczyć

dress [dres] **1.** strój *m*, ubiór
m; *woman's*: suknia *f*; **2.**
ubierać ⟨ubrać⟩ (się); *salad*
przyprawi(a)ć; *hair* układać ⟨ułożyć⟩, ⟨u⟩czesać,

⟨u⟩fryzować; *wound etc.* opatrywać ⟨-trzyć⟩; **get** ⟨**ed**⟩ ubrać się

dressing ['dresɪŋ] toaleta *f*; *med.* opatrunek *m*; *salad:* sos *m* do sałatki; *gastr.* marsz *m*; **~ gown** szlafrok *m*; **~ room** *sp.* szatnia *f*; **~ table** toalet(k)a *f*

dress|maker ['dresmeɪkə] krawcowa *f*, krawiec *m* damski; **~ rehearsal** *thea.* próba *f* generalna

drew [druː] *past of* draw 1

drier ['draɪə] → **dryer**

drift [drɪft] **1.** *v/i* dryfować, unosić się z prądem; *fig.* być biernym; *snow, sand:* ⟨na⟩gromadzić się; *v/t* ⟨stream⟩ nieść; **2.** *river:* prąd *m*; (*a.* **snow** ~) zaspa *f*; *fig.* wątek *m*, sens *m* wypowiedzi

drill [drɪl] **1.** świder *m*, wiertarka *f*; (*exercise*) ćwiczenie *n*; *mil.* musztra *f*; **2.** ⟨wy⟩wiercić; (*practise*) ⟨prze⟩ćwiczyć

drink [drɪŋk] **1.** (*drank, drunk*) ⟨wy⟩pić; **2.** napój *m*; *alcohol:* drink *m f*; **~ing water** woda *f* do picia

drip [drɪp] **1.** kapać ⟨-pnąć⟩, ciec; **2.** kapanie *n*; *med.* kroplówka *f*; **~·dry** nie wymagający prasowania; **~ping** tłuszcz *m* spod pieczeni

drive [draɪv] **1.** (*drove, driven*) ⟨po⟩jechać; **~e s.o. somewhere** zawozić ⟨-wieźć⟩ kogoś dokądś; *car*

kierować; *animals etc.* ⟨po⟩pędzić; **~e s.o. mad** doprowadzić ⟨-dzić⟩ kogoś do szału; **2.** przejażdżka *f tech.*, *computer:* napęd *m*; *psych.* popęd *m*; *fig.* przedsiębiorczość *f*; *left/right-hand* **~e** z kierownicą po lewej/prawej stronie; **'~·in** dla zmotoryzowanych; **~en** [drɪvn] *pp of* drive 1; **~er** ['draɪvə] kierowca *m*; **~er's license** *Am.* prawo *n* jazdy; **~eway** podjazd *m*; **~ing** ['draɪvɪŋ] prowadzenie *n* samochodu; *tech.* napędowy; **~ing force** siła *f* napędowa; **~ing licence** *Brt.* prawo *n* jazdy; **~ing test** egzamin *m* na prawo jazdy

drizzle ['drɪzl] **1.** mżyć; **2.** mżawka *f*, kapuśniaczek *m*

drop [drɒp] **1.** kropla *f*; *aer.* zrzut *m*; *altitude:* a. *fig.:* spadek *m*; **2.** *v/i* spadać ⟨spaść⟩ (*a. prices etc.*); *ground:* opadać ⟨opaść⟩; *v/t* upuszczać ⟨upuścić⟩, zrzucać ⟨-cić⟩; *remark etc.* rzucać ⟨-cić⟩; *passenger etc.* wysadzać ⟨-dzić⟩, podrzucać ⟨-cić⟩; *voice* zniżać ⟨-żyć⟩; **~ s.o. a few lines** skreślić ⟨-ć⟩ parę słów; **~ in** wpadać ⟨wpaść⟩; **~ out** ⟨wy⟩cofać się ⟨-cić⟩ (*of s.th.* coś); **'~out** osoba, która przerwała naukę

drove [drəʊv] *past of* drive 1

drown [draʊn] ⟨u⟩topić się,

⟨u⟩tonąć; *be* ~*ed* ⟨u⟩tonąć

drug [drʌg] **1.** lekarstwo *n*; *(narcotic)* narkotyk *m*; *be on* ~*s* narkotyzować się; **2.** narkotyzować się, poda(wa)ć narkotyk; ~ *addict* narkoman(ka *f*) *m*; ~*gist* ['~ɪst] *Am.* aptekarz *m*; '~*store* *Am.* apteka *f*

drum [drʌm] **1.** bęben *m*, *anat.* bębenek *m*; *pl mus.* perkusja *f*; **2.** bębnić; ~*mer* perkusista *m*

drunk [drʌŋk] **1.** *pp of* drink 1; **2.** *adj* pijany; *get* ~ upi(ja)ć się; **3.** pijak *m* (-jaczka *f*); ~*ard* ['~əd] pijak *m*; '~*en* pijany; ~*en driving* prowadzenie *n* samochodu po pijanemu

dry [draɪ] **1.** suchy; *wine etc.*: wytrawny; **2.** suszyć (się); *dishes* wycierać ⟨wytrzeć⟩; ~ *up* wysychać ⟨-schnąć⟩; '~*clean* ⟨u⟩prać chemicznie; ~ *cleaner('s) business:* pralnia *f* chemiczna; '~*er a. drier* suszarka *f*

dual ['dju:əl] dwojaki; *(double)* podwójny; ~ *carriageway* *Brt.* dwupasmówka *f f*

dubious ['dju:bjəs] wątpliwy, dwuznaczny; *person:* pełen wątpliwości

duck [dʌk] **1.** kaczka *f*; **2.** uchylać ⟨-lić⟩ się *(s.th.* przed czymś⟩

due [dju:] **1.** *adj* należny, zasłużony; *(proper)* stosowny, odpowiedni; *econ.* płat-

ny; *train, etc.*: oczekiwany; ~ *to* z powodu; *be* ~ *to* (do s.th.) mieć (coś zrobić); **2.** *adv* w kierunku; ~ *east* w kierunku wschodnim; **3.** *s pl* należność *f* ⟨-ności *pl*⟩

duel ['dju:əl] pojedynek *m*

dug [dʌg] *past and pp of* dig

duke [dju:k] książę *m*

dull [dʌl] **1.** *(boring)* nudny, nieciekawy; *blade etc.*: tępy; *sound:* głuchy, stłumiony; *weather:* pochmurny; **2.** stępi(a)ć, przytępi(a)ć

dumb [dʌm] niemy, oniemiały; *esp. Am.* F głupi

dump [dʌmp] **1.** ⟨z⟩rzucać ⟨-cić⟩; *s.o.* rzucać ⟨-cić⟩; *econ.* sprzeda(wa)ć po cenie dumpingowej; **2.** wysypisko *n*

dumpling ['dʌmplɪŋ] klucha *f*; *(pudding)* jabłko *n* w cieście, knedel *m*

dungarees [dʌŋgə'ri:z] *pl* (spodnie-)ogrodniczki *pl*

duplicate 1. ['dju:plɪkət] wtórny, identyczny; **2.** [~] duplikat *m*, kopia *f*; **3.** [~keɪt] po-wielać ⟨-lić⟩, ⟨s⟩kopiować

dura|ble ['djuərəbl] trwały; ~*tion* [~'reɪʃn] trwanie *n*

during ['djuərɪŋ] podczas

dusk [dʌsk] zmierzch *m*

dust [dʌst] **1.** kurz *m*, pył *m*; **2.** *v/t* odkurzać ⟨-rzyć⟩; *v/i* ścierać kurze; '~*bin* *Brt.* kubeł/pojemnik *m* na śmieci; '~*er* ścier(ecz)ka *f* do kurzu; '~*man* (*pl* -*men*) *Brt.* śmieciarz *m*; '~*y* zakurzony

Dutch [dʌtʃ] **1.** holenderski; **2.** *the* ~ *pl* Holendrzy *pl*

duty ['dju:tɪ] obowiązek *m*, zadanie *n*; *mil.*, *police*: służba *f*; *econ.* cło *n*, opłata *f* celna; *on* ~ na służbie; *off* ~ po służbie, wolny od służby;

~'**free** bezcłowy

dye [daɪ] ⟨u⟩farbować ~ *black* ufarbować na czarno

dying ['daɪɪŋ] umierający; *species etc.*: wymierający

dynamic [daɪ'næmɪk] dynamiczny; ~**s** *sg* dynamika *f*

E

each [i:tʃ] **1.** *adj*, *pron* każdy; ~ *other* się (nawzajem); *to* ~ *other* sobie nawzajem, jeden drugiemu/drugiemu; **2.** *adv* ... na osobę, ... za sztukę

eager ['i:gə] chętny

eagle ['i:gl] orzeł *m*

ear [ɪə] ucho *n*

earl [ɜ:l] (brytyjski) hrabia *m*

early ['ɜ:lɪ] (za) wcześnie

earn [ɜ:n] *money* zarabiać ⟨-robić⟩; *reputation etc.* zyskać sobie

earnest ['ɜ:nɪst] **1.** szczery, poważny; (*conscientious*) sumienny; **2.** *in* ~ na poważnie, (na) serio, szczerze

earnings ['ɜ:nɪŋz] *pl* zarobki *pl*

'**ear**|**phones** *pl* słuchawki *pl*; '~**ring** kolczyk *m*; '~**shot**: *out of* ~**shot** poza zasięgiem słuchu; *within* ~**shot** w zasięgu słuchu

earth [ɜ:θ] **1.** ziemia *f*; *Brt. electr.* uziemienie *n*; **2.** *Brt. electr.* uziemiać(ać); ~**en** ['ɜ:θən] gliniany; '~**enware** wyroby *pl* garncarskie; '~**ly**

ziemski; '~**quake** trzęsienie *n* ziemi; '~**worm** dżdżownica *f*

ease [i:z] **1.** łatwość *f*; (*comfort*) wygoda *f*; *at* (*one's*) ~ spokojny, nieskrępowany; na luzie *V*; *be* or *feel at* ~ czuć się swobodnie; *be* or *feel ill at* ~ czuć się nieswojo; **2.** (delikatnie) wsuwać ⟨wsunąć⟩; *tension etc.* rozładow(yw)ać; *pains* uśmierzać ⟨-rzyć⟩

easily ['i:zɪlɪ] z łatwością, łatwo

east [i:st] **1.** *s* wschód *m*; **2.** *adj* wschodni; **3.** *adv direction*: na wschód; *location*: na wschodzie

Easter ['i:stə] Wielkanoc *f*

easy ['i:zɪ] łatwy; *take it* ~! spokojnie!, nie przejmuj się!; ~ *chair* fotel *m*

eat [i:t] (*ate, eaten*) ⟨z⟩jeść; *animals a.*: ⟨ze⟩żreć; ~**en** ['i:tn] *pp* of *eat*

eavesdrop ['i:vzdrɒp] podsłuch(iw)ać (*on s.o.* kogoś)

ecolog|ical [i:kə'lɒdʒɪkl] ekologiczny; **~y** [i:'kɒlədʒɪ] ekologia *f*

econom|ic [i:kə'nɒmɪk] gospodarczy, ekonomiczny; **~ical** oszczędny, ekonomiczny; **~ics** *sg* ekonomia *f*; **~ist** [ɪ'kɒnəmɪst] ekonomista *m* (-tka *f*); **~ize** oszczędzać (*on* na sing) *f* gospodarka *f*

edge [edʒ] 1. krawędź *f*, obrzeże *n*, brzeg *m*; *on* **~e → ~y** edgy; 2. obrzeżać <-żyć>; *movement:* posuwać <-suwać> się po trochu; **~y** nerwowy

edible ['edɪbl] jadalny

edit ['edɪt] *text* <z>redagować; *newspaper etc.* wyda(wa)ć; **~ion** [ɪ'dɪʃn] wydanie *n*; **~or** ['edɪtə] redaktor *m*; *newspaper, magazine:* wydawca *m*; **~orial** [edɪ'tɔ:rɪəl] artykuł *m* wstępny

educat|e ['edʒukeɪt] <wy>kształcić; **~ed** wykształcony; **~ion** [~'keɪʃn] wykształcenie *n*, *form.* edukacja *f*; *system:* oświata *f*; **~ional** oświatowy

effect [ɪ'fekt] 1. (*result*) skutek *m*, rezultat *m*; (*impact*) działanie *n*, wpływ *m*; *take* **~** wchodzić <wejść> w życie; (*work*) zadziałać; 2. przeprowadzać <-dzić>; **~ive** skuteczny

efficien|cy [ɪ'fɪʃənsɪ] sprawność *f*, skuteczność *f*; *industry:* wydajność *f*; **~t** sprawny, skuteczny; *industry:* wydajny

effort ['efət] wysiłek *m*; **~less** łatwy, nie wymagający wysiłku

egg [eg] jajko *n*

eight [eɪt] osiem; **~een** [eɪ'ti:n] osiemnaście; **~h** [eɪtθ] ósmy; **~y** ['eɪtɪ] osiemdziesiąt

either ['aɪðə, *Am.* 'i:ðə] który-kolwiek (*z dwóch*); **~ ... or** albo ... albo; *not ... ~* też nie, ani też ...

eject [ɪ'dʒekt] wyrzucać <-cić>; (*expel*) wydalać <-lić>

elaborate 1. [ɪ'læbərət] wymyślny, skomplikowany, zawiły; 2. [~eɪt] opis(yw)ać szczegółowo

elastic [ɪ'læstɪk] 1. elastyczny; 2. *Brt. a.* **~ band** taśma *f* gumowa, gum(k)a *f*

elbow ['elbəʊ] 1. łokieć *m*; *tech.* kolano *n*; 2. <u>torować sobie drogę (łokciami)

elder ['eldə] *brother, sister etc.:* starszy

elde|rly ['eldəlɪ] starszy; **~st** [~ɪst] *brother, sister etc.:* najstarszy

elect [ɪ'lekt] 1. wybierać <-brać>; 2. nowo obrany; **~ion** [~kʃn] wybory *pl*; **~or** wyborca *m*; **~orate** [~rət] wyborcy *pl*

electric [ɪ'lektrɪk] elektryczny; **~al** elektryczny; **~ian** [~'trɪʃn] elektryk *m*; **~ity** [~'trɪsətɪ] elektryczność *f*

electronic [ɪlek'trɒnɪk] elektroniczny; **~ data proces-**

sing elektroniczne przetwarzanie *n* danych; **~s** *sg* elektronika *f*

elegan|ce ['elɪgəns] elegancja *f*; **'~t** elegancki

element ['elɪmənt] element *m*; *weather*: żywioł *m*; *chem*. pierwiastek *m*; **~ary** [.~'mentərɪ] podstawowy, elementarny; **~ary school** *Am*. szkoła *f* podstawowa

elephant ['elɪfənt] słoń *m*

elevator ['elɪveɪtə] *Am*. dźwig *m*, winda *f*

eleven [ɪ'levn] jedenaście; **~th** [~θ] jedenasty

eligible ['elɪdʒəbl] nadający się, spełniający warunki; *be* **~** kwalifikować się

eliminat|e [ɪ'lɪmɪneɪt] ⟨wy⟩eliminować, usuwać ⟨-sunąć⟩; **~ion** [~'neɪʃn] eliminacja *f*

else [els] jeszcze; *anything* **~** czy jeszcze coś?; *no one* **~** nikt więcej; *or* **~** albo też; **~'where** gdzie indziej

embark [ɪm'bɑːk] załadować na statek, zaokrętować (się); **~** *(up)on* rozpoczynać ⟨-cząć⟩

embarrass [ɪm'bærəs] ⟨za⟩żenować, zawstydzać ⟨-dzić⟩; **~ed** zażenowany; **~ing** żenujący; **~ment** zażenowanie *n*

embassy ['embəsɪ] ambasada *f*

embrace [ɪm'breɪs] **1.** obejmować ⟨objąć⟩; **2.** uścisk *m*

embroider [ɪm'brɔɪdə] ⟨wy⟩haftować; *fig*. ubarwi(a)ć; **~y** [~rɪ] haft *m*

emerge [ɪ'mɜːdʒ] wyłaniać ⟨-łonić⟩ się; *truth etc*.: wychodzić ⟨wyjść⟩ na jaw

emergency [ɪ'mɜːdʒənsɪ] sytuacja *f* wyjątkowa, nagły wypadek *m*; *in an* **~** w nagłym wypadku, w razie niebezpieczeństwa; **~ exit** wyjście *n* awaryjne; **~ landing** *aer*. lądowanie *n* awaryjne; **~ number** numer *m* alarmowy

eminent ['emɪnənt] wybitny, znakomity

emotion [ɪ'məʊʃn] uczucie *n*, wzruszenie *n*; **~al** emocjonalny; *person, attitude*: uczuciowy

emperor ['empərə] cesarz *m*

empha|sis ['emfəsɪs] (*pl* **-ses** [~sɪz]) nacisk *m*; **'~size** podkreślać ⟨-lić⟩; **'~tic** [ɪm'fætɪk] dobitny

empire ['empaɪə] cesarstwo *n*

employ [ɪm'plɔɪ] zatrudni(a)ć; **~ee** [emplɔɪ'iː] pracownik *m* (-nica *f*); **~er** [ɪm'plɔɪə] pracodawca *m* (-wczyni *f*); **~ment** zatrudnienie *n*

empress ['empris] cesarzowa *f*

empt|iness ['emptɪnɪs] pustka *f* (*a. fig.*); **~y 1.** pusty, próżny; **2.** wypróżni(a)ć, opróżni(a)ć

enable [ɪ'neɪbl] umożliwi(a)ć

enamel [ɪˈnæml] emalia *f*; *pottery*: glazura *f*; *nails*: lakier *m* do paznokci

enclos|e [ɪnˈkləʊz] ograniczać ⟨-rodzić⟩; *in parcel*: ⟨o⟩pakować; *in letter*: załączać ⟨-czyć⟩; **~ure** [⟨-ʒə⟩] ogrodzenie *n*; *letter*: załącznik *m*

encounter [ɪnˈkaʊntə] **1.** spotykać ⟨-tkać⟩ *etc.* napotykać ⟨-tkać⟩; **2.** spotkanie *n*; *mil.* potyczka *f*

encourag|e [ɪnˈkʌrɪdʒ] zachęcać ⟨-cić⟩; **~ement** zachęta *f*; **~ing** [ɪnˈkʌrɪdʒɪŋ] zachęcający

end [end] **1.** koniec *m*, kres *m*; *in the* **~** w końcu; *stand on* **~** *hair*: stawać ⟨stanąć⟩ dęba; **2.** ⟨za⟩kończyć (się); **~ up** skończyć, wylądować F

endeavo(u)r [ɪnˈdevə] **1.** usiłować, usilnie próbować; **2.** próba *f*, usiłowanie *n*; *pl* starania *pl*

ending [ˈendɪŋ] *gr.* końcówka *f*

endless bezustanny, nie kończący się

endur|ance [ɪnˈdjʊərəns] (*stamina*) wytrzymałość *f*; (*patience*) cierpliwość *f*; **~ance test** próba *f* wytrzymałości; **~e** [⟨-ʊə⟩] wytrzym(yw)ać

enemy [ˈenəmɪ] **1.** wróg *m*; **2.** wrogi

energ|etic [enəˈdʒetɪk] energiczny; **~y** energia *f*; **~y-saving** energooszczędny

engage [ɪnˈgeɪdʒ] *v/t* zajmować ⟨-jąć⟩; (*hire*) ⟨za⟩angażować; *tech.* włączać ⟨-czyć⟩; *v/i tech.* sprzęgać ⟨-rząc⟩ się; **~ in** zajmować ⟨-jąć⟩ się; **~d** zajęty (*a. seat, toilet, Brt. teleph.*); *to get* **~** zaręczać ⟨-czyć⟩ się (*to z*); **~d tone** sygnał *m* zajętej linii; **~ment** zaręczyny *pl*

engine [ˈendʒɪn] silnik *m*; *rail.* lokomotywa *f*; **~ driver** maszynista *m*

engineer [endʒɪˈnɪə] inżynier *m*; (*repairer*) technik *m*; *Am.* maszynista *m*; *mil.* saper *m*; **~ing** [⟨-rɪŋ⟩] technika *f*; *civil* **~ing** inżynieria *f*

Engl|and [ˈɪŋglənd] Anglia *f*; **~ish** [ˈɪŋglɪʃ] **1.** angielski; **2.** the **~ish** *pl* Anglicy *pl*; '**~ishman** (*pl* **-men**) Anglik *m*; '**~ishwoman** (*pl* **-women**) Angielka *f*

enjoy [ɪnˈdʒɔɪ] znajdować ⟨znaleźć⟩ przyjemność (*s.th.* w czymś); *did you* **~** *it?* podobało ci się?; **~ o.s.** dobrze się bawić; **~able** przyjemny; **~ment** zabawa *f*, uciecha *f*

enlarge [ɪnˈlɑːdʒ] powiększać ⟨-szyć⟩; **~ment** powiększenie *n*

enormous [ɪˈnɔːməs] ogromny, olbrzymi

enough [ɪˈnʌf] dosyć, dość

enquire, enquiry → *inquire, inquiry*

enrol(l) [ɪnˈrəʊl] zapis(yw)ać się

ensure [ɪn'ʃɔː] zapewni(a)ć
enter ['entə] v/t wchodzić
⟨wejść⟩ (*s.th.* do czegoś);
mar. wpływać ⟨-łynąć⟩
(*s.th.* do czegoś); *rail.*
wjeżdżać ⟨-jechać⟩ (*the station etc.* na stację *itp.*);
wpis(yw)ać, wciągać ⟨-gnąć⟩
(*names* nazwiska na listę);
sp. zgłaszać ⟨-łosić⟩; v/i
wchodzić ⟨wejść⟩; *sp.* zgłaszać ⟨-łosić⟩ swój udział
(*for* w); ~ ... *thea.* wchodzi
...

enterpris|e ['entəpraɪz] (*com-
pany*) przedsiębiorstwo *n*;
(*venture*) przedsięwzięcie *n*;
~ing przedsiębiorczy

entertain [entə'teɪn] zaba-
wi(a)ć; **~er** artysta *m* w kaba-
retowy; **~ment** rozrywka *f*

enthusias|m [ɪn'θjuːzɪæzm]
entuzjazm *m*, zapał *m*; **~t**
[~st] entuzjasta *m* (-tka *f*);
~tic [~'æstɪk] entuzjastyczny,
zapalony

entire [ɪn'taɪə] całkowity; **~ly**
całkowicie

entitle [ɪn'taɪtl] uprawni(a)ć
(*to* do)

entrance ['entrəns] *door*:
wejście *n*; *gate*: wjazd *m*; ~
fee opłata *f* za wstęp

entry ['entrɪ] wstęp *m*; (*entrance*) wejście *n*; *lexicon*:
hasło *n*; *list*: pozycja *f*; *sp.*
zgłoszenie *n*; ~ **form** formularz *m*; ~ **visa** wiza *f* wjazdowa

envelop [ɪn'veləp] owijać

⟨owinąć⟩, okry(wa)ć; **~e**
['envələʊp] koperta *f*

envi|able ['envɪəbl] godny
pozazdroszczenia; **~ous** za-
wistny, zazdrosny

environment [ɪn'vaɪərən-
mənt] środowisko *n*; **~al**
[~'mentl] środowiskowy; **~al
pollution** zatrucie *n* środowiska; **~al protection** o-
chrona *f* środowiska; **~alist**
[~'təlɪst] ekolog *m*

envy ['envɪ] **1.** zawiść *f*, zazdrość *f*; **2.** zazdrościć (*s.o.
s.th.* komuś czegoś)

epidemic [epɪ'demɪk] epide-
mia *f*

episode ['epɪsəʊd] epizod *m*;
radio, TV: odcinek *m*

equal ['iːkwəl] **1.** *adj* równy;
be ~ to czuć się na siłach,
task: dorastać ⟨-rosnąć⟩
(*s.th.* do czegoś); **2.** *s* osoba *f*
równa (innej); **3.** równać się;
person: dorówn(yw)ać *itp.*;
~ity [ɪ'kwɒlətɪ] równość *f*;
~ize [~'iːkwəlaɪz] zrówn(yw)ać,
wyrówn(yw)ać; **~ly** równie

equat|e [ɪ'kweɪt] utożsa-
mi(a)ć; **~ion** [~ʒn] *math.*
równanie *n*; **~or** [ɪ'kweɪtə]
równik *m*

equilibrium [iːkwɪ'lɪbrɪəm]
równowaga *f*, zrówno-
ważenie *n*

equip [ɪ'kwɪp] wyposażać
⟨-żyć⟩; **~ment** wyposażenie
n, sprzęt *m*

equivalent [ɪ'kwɪvələnt] **1.**
równoważny (**to** *s.th.* cze-

muś); **be ~** odpowiadać (**to s.th.** czemuś); **2.** odpowiednik *m*

erase [ɪ'reɪz] ⟨z⟩mazać, ścierać ⟨zetrzeć⟩; *sound* ⟨s⟩kasować; **~r** gumka *f*

erect [ɪ'rekt] **1.** wyprostowany; **2.** wznosić ⟨-nieść⟩; **~ion** [~k]n] budowa *f*, wzniesienie *n*; *physiol.* erekcja *f*

erotic [ɪ'rɒtɪk] erotyczny

err [ɜː] ⟨z⟩błądzić

errand ['erənd] polecenie *n*, zadanie *n*; **run ~s** załatwiać polecenia

erratic [ɪ'rætɪk] nierówny, niekonsekwentny; *pattern*: przypadkowy

error ['erə] błąd *m*

escalate ['eskəleɪt] rozszerzać ⟨-rzyć⟩ (się), powiększać ⟨-szyć⟩ (się), rozrastać ⟨-rosnąć⟩ się; **~ion** [~'leɪʃn] eskalacja *f*; **~or** schody *pl* ruchome

escape [ɪ'skeɪp] **1.** *v/t duty etc.* unikać ⟨-knąć⟩; *attention* umykać ⟨umknąć⟩; *v/i* uciekać ⟨uciec⟩, umykać ⟨umknąć⟩; *gas, liquid*: wyciekać ⟨-ciec⟩; **2.** ucieczka *f*; **have a narrow ~** ledwo ujść z życiem

escort 1. ['eskɔːt] *police etc.*: eskorta *f*; (*companion*) osoba *f* towarzysząca; (*hired companion*) (wynajęta) towarzyszka *f*; **2.** [ɪ'skɔːt] odprowadzać ⟨-dzić⟩; *mil., police*: eskortować

especial [ɪ'speʃl] specjalny, szczególny; **~ly** specjalnie, szczególnie, zwłaszcza

espionage ['espɪənɑːʒ] szpiegostwo *n*

essay ['eseɪ] esej *m*; *school*: wypracowanie *n*

essential [ɪ'senʃl] **1.** (*vital*) istotny; (*fundamental*) podstawowy, zasadniczy; **2.** *mst pl* rzeczy *pl* niezbędne/istotne; **~ly** zasadniczo

establish [ɪ'stæblɪʃ] ustanawiać ⟨-nowić⟩; *organization, company* zakładać ⟨założyć⟩; **~ o.s.** wyrabiać ⟨-robić⟩ sobie pozycję; **~ment** założenie *n*, ustanowienie *n*; (*business*) zakład *m*

estate [ɪ'steɪt] posiadłość *f*; *Brt.* osiedle *n*; *Brt.* dzielnica *f* przemysłowa; *jur.* mienie *n*; **~ agent** pośrednik *m* w handlu nieruchomościami; **~ car** *Brt.* samochód *m* kombi

estimate 1. ['estɪmeɪt] ⟨o⟩szacować, oceni⟨a⟩ć; **2.** ['estɪmət] szacunkowe dane *pl*; *person*: ocena *f*; *job*: kosztorys *m*; **~ion** [~'meɪʃn] wyliczenie *n*; *person*: ocena *f*

Estonia [e'stəʊnɪə] Estonia *f*; **~n 1.** *adj* estoński; **2.** Estończyk *m*, Estonka *f*

etern|al [ɪ'tɜːnl] (od)wieczny; **~ity** [~nətɪ] wieczność *f*

European [jʊərə'piːən] **1.** europejski; **2.** Europejczyk *m* (-jka *f*)

evade [ɪ'veɪd] (*dodge*) unikać

⟨-knąć⟩ (*s.th.* czegoś); (*escape*) umykać ⟨umknąć⟩ (*s.th./s.o.* czemuś/komuś)

evaluate [ɪ'væljʊeɪt] oceni(a)ć

evaporate [ɪ'væpəreɪt] *v/i* wyparow(yw)ać; *v/t* odparow(yw)ać

evasi|on [ɪ'veɪʒn] unikanie *n*; uchylanie *n* się od; **~ve** [~sɪv] wykrętny

even ['iːvn] **1.** *adv* nawet; **2.** *adj* równy, gładki; *math.* parzysty; *get* **~ with s.o.** policzyć się z kimś, wyrównać z kimś rachunki

evening ['iːvnɪŋ] wieczór *m*; *in the* **~** wieczorem, *regularly:* wieczorami; *this* **~** dziś wieczór/wieczorem; *good* **~** dobry wieczór

event [ɪ'vent] wydarzenie *n*; (*planned occasion*) impreza *f*; *sp.* konkurencja *f*, dyscyplina *f*; *at all* **~s** w każdym wypadku; *in the* **~** *of* w przypadku

eventually [ɪ'ventʃʊəlɪ] w końcu

ever ['evə] kiedykolwiek; **~** *since* odkąd tylko; '**~green** roślina *f* wiecznie zielona; *mus.* złoty przebój *m*, niezapomniany utwór *m*; '**~lasting** wieczny, wiekuisty

every ['evrɪ] każdy; **~** *other day* (w) co drugi dzień; **~** *now and then* od czasu do czasu; '**~body → everyone**; '**~day** codzienny; '**~one**

każdy (człowiek); '**~thing** wszystko; '**~where** wszędzie

eviden|ce ['evɪdəns] *jur.* dowody *pl*; (*testimony*) zeznanie *n*; *give* **~ce** zeznawać; '**~t** oczywisty, ewidentny

evil ['iːvl] **1.** zły, podły; **2.** zło *n*

evoke [ɪ'vəʊk] wywoł(yw)ać

evolution [iːvə'luːʃn] ewolucja *f*

evolve [ɪ'vɒlv] rozwijać ⟨-winąć⟩ (się)

ex- [eks] były

exact [ɪg'zækt] **1.** dokładny; **2.** wymagać; **~ly** dokładnie; *int* właśnie

exaggerat|e [ɪg'zædʒəreɪt] przesadzać ⟨-dzić⟩; **~ion** [~'reɪʃn] przesada *f*

exam [ɪg'zæm] F egzamin *m*

examin|ation [ɪgzæmɪ'neɪʃn] egzamin *m*; *jur.* przesłuchanie *n*; *med.* badanie *n*; **~e** [~'zæmɪn] ⟨z⟩badać; *school:* ⟨prze⟩egzaminować (*in* z; *on* na temat); *jur.* przesłuch(iw)ać; **~er** *school:* egzaminator(ka *f*) *m*

example [ɪg'zɑːmpl] przykład *m*; *for* **~** na przykład

exceed [ɪk'siːd] przekraczać ⟨-roczyć⟩, przewyższać ⟨-szyć⟩; **~ingly** nadzwyczajnie, niezmiernie

excel [ɪk'sel] celować (*in/at* w); '**~lent** doskonały, świetny

except [ɪk'sept] **1.** wyłączać

⟨-czyć⟩, wykluczać ⟨-czyć⟩; **2.** z wyjątkiem; **~ for** poza; **~ion** [-ʌpʃn] wyjątek *m*; **~io-nal(ly)** wyjątkowo

excess [ɪk'ses] nadmiar *m*, nadwyżka *f*; *behaviour:* nieumiarkowanie *n*; *pl acts:* wybryki *pl*; **in ~ of** powyżej; **~ baggage** *aer.* nadwyżka *f* bagażu; **~ fare** dopłata *f* do biletu; **~ive** nadmierny; **~ luggage** *esp. Brt. aer.* nadwyżka *f* bagażu

exchange [ɪks'tʃeɪndʒ] **1.** zamieni(a)ć (**for** na), wymieni(a)ć (**for** na); (*swap*) zamienić się (**s.th.** czymś); *money* wymieni(a)ć; **2.** zamiana *f*, wymiana *f*; *teleph.* centrala *f*; *econ.* giełda *f*; *econ.* kantor *m* wymiany; **rate of ~, ~ rate** kurs *m* (wymiany); **~ bill of exchange, foreign exchange**

Exchequer [ɪks'tʃekə]: **the ~** *GB* Ministerstwo *n* Finansów

excit|able [ɪk'saɪtəbl] pobudliwy; **~e** [-aɪt] pobudzać ⟨-dzić⟩, ożywi(a)ć; podniecać ⟨-cić⟩; **~ed** pobudzony, ożywiony, podniecony; **~ement** podniecenie *n*; **~ing** interesujący

exclaim [ɪk'skleɪm] wykrzykiwać ⟨-knąć⟩

exclamation [eksklə'meɪʃn] okrzyk *m*; **~ mark**, *Am. a.* **~ point** wykrzyknik *m*

exclu|de [ɪk'skluːd] wyłączać ⟨-czyć⟩; **~sion** [-ʒn] wyłączenie *n*; **~sive** [-sɪv] wyłączny; (*select*) ekskluzywny

excursion [ɪk'skɜːʃn] wycieczka *f*

excuse 1. [ɪk'skjuːz] (*justify*) ⟨wy⟩tłumaczyć; (*pardon*) wybaczać ⟨-czyć⟩; **~ me!** przepraszam!; **2.** [-uːs] wytłumaczenie *n*; *insincere:* wymówka *f*

execut|e ['eksɪkjuːt] dokon(yw)ać egzekucji (**s.o.** na kimś); *mus. etc., plan* wykon(yw)ać; **~ion** [-'kjuːʃn] egzekucja *f*; *mus. etc.* wykonanie *n*; **~ive** [ɪg'zekjʊtɪv] **1.** *pol.* wykonawczy; **2.** *pol.* władza *f* wykonawcza; *party:* egzekutywa *f*; *econ.* samodzielny pracownik *m* firmy

exercise ['eksəsaɪz] **1.** ćwiczenie *n*; **take ~** zaży(wa)ć ruchu; **2.** ⟨po⟩ćwiczyć; *rights etc.* ⟨s⟩korzystać (**s.th.** z czegoś); **~ book** zeszyt *m*

exhaust [ɪg'zɔːst] **1.** wyczerp(yw)ać; **2.** *a.* **~ fumes** spaliny *pl*; **~ed** wyczerpany; **~ion** wyczerpanie *n*

exhibit [ɪg'zɪbɪt] **1.** wystawi(a)ć (na pokaz); *fig.* okaz(yw)ać, wykaz(yw)ać; **2.** eksponat *m*; *jur.* dowód *m* rzeczowy; **~ion** [eksɪ'bɪʃn] wystawa *f*

exile ['eksaɪl] **1.** wygnanie *n*;

person: wygnaniec *m*; **2.** wygnać

exist [ɪg'zɪst] istnieć; (*survive*) utrzymywać się przy życiu; **~ence** istnienie *n*, egzystencja *f*; **~ing** obecny, istniejący

exit ['eksɪt] wyjście *n*; *mot.* zjazd *m*

exotic [ɪg'zɒtɪk] egzotyczny

expan|d [ɪk'spænd] *v/i* wzrastać ⟨-rosnąć⟩; (*grow*) rozszerzać ⟨-rzyć⟩ się; *v/t* rozszerzać ⟨-rzyć⟩ się; *institution* rozbudow(yw)ać; **~se** [~ns] przestrzeń *f*, przestwór *m*; **~sion** wzrost *m*, ekspansja *f*

expect [ɪk'spekt] spodziewać się, oczekiwać; *be ~ing* F być przy nadziei; **~ation** [ekspek'teɪʃn] oczekiwanie *n*

expedition [ekspɪ'dɪʃn] wyprawa *f*, ekspedycja *f*; (*excursion*) wycieczka *f*; wypad *m* F

expel [ɪk'spel] wydalać ⟨-lić⟩ (*from z*); wysiedlać ⟨-lić⟩

expen|diture [ɪk'spendɪtʃə] wydatki *pl*; (*outlay*) wydatkowanie *n*; **~se** [~ns] koszty *pl*; *at the ~se of s.th.* czegoś; *at s.o.'s ~se* na czyjś koszt; **~sive** drogi

experience [ɪk'spɪəriəns] **1.** przeżycie *n*; (*practice*) doświadczenie *n*; **2.** przeży(wa)ć, doświadczać ⟨-czyć⟩; **~d** doświadczony

experiment 1. [ɪk'sperɪmənt] eksperyment *m*; *phys.*, *chem.* *a.* doświadczenie *n*; **2.**

[~mənt] ⟨za⟩eksperymentować

expert ['ekspɜːt] **1.** *s* ekspert *m*, rzeczoznawca *m*; (*skilled person*) fachowiec *m*; **2.** *adj* biegły

expir|e [ɪk'spaɪə] (*run out*) wygasać ⟨-snąć⟩; ⟨s⟩tracić ważność; (*pass away*) wyzionąć ducha; **~y** [~ərɪ] wygaśnięcie *n* (ważności)

expl|ain [ɪk'spleɪn] wyjaśni(a)ć; **~anation** [eksplə'neɪʃn] (wy)tłumaczenie *n*, wyjaśnienie

explicit [ɪk'splɪsɪt] sprecyzowany, jasny, wyraźnie określony

explode [ɪk'spləud] eksplodować, wybuchać ⟨-chnąć⟩

exploit [ɪk'splɔɪt] wyzyskiwać; *s.o.* wykorzyst(yw)ać

explor|ation [eksplɔ'reɪʃn] badania *pl*; **~e** [ɪk'splɔː] ⟨z⟩badać; **~er** [~rə] badacz(ka *f*) *m*

explosi|on [ɪk'spləuʒn] wybuch *m*, eksplozja *f*; **~ve** [~sɪv] **1.** wybuchowy; **2.** materiał *m* wybuchowy

export 1. [ɪk'spɔːt] ⟨wy⟩eksportować; **2.** ['ekspɔːt] eksport *m*; (*commodity*) towar *m* eksportowany; *pl* eksport *m*; **~er** [ɪk'spɔːtə] eksporter *m*

expose [ɪk'spəuz] odsłaniać ⟨-łonić⟩; *phot.* naświetlić; *fig.* ujawni(a)ć; *s.o.* ⟨z⟩demaskować; **~ to** wystawi(a)ć na; *danger etc.*: narażać ⟨-razić⟩ na

express [ık'spres] **1.** *v/t* wyrażać ⟨-razić⟩; **~ o.s.** wysławiać ⟨-łowić⟩ się; **2.** *s* rail., *esp. Brt. post.* ekspres *m*; **3.** *adv esp. Brt.* ekspresem; **4.** *adj* ekspresowy; **~ion** [∼ʃn] wyrażenie *n*; **~ive** [∼sıv] wyrazisty; **~ train** pociąg *m* ekspresowy; **~way** *Am.* autostrada *f*

extend [ık'stend] ciągnąć się, sięgać ⟨-gnąć⟩ (*stick out*) wystawiać ⟨-wić⟩; *hand etc.* wyciągać ⟨-gnąć⟩; *econ., jur. etc.* rozszerzać ⟨-rzyć⟩ (**to** na); *passport etc.* przedłużać ⟨-żyć⟩; **~sion** [∼ʃn] przedłużenie *n*; *arch.* nadbudówka *f*, dobudówka *f*; *teleph.* numer *m* wewnętrzny; **~sive** [∼sıv] szeroki, obszerny; **~t** zasięg *m*; (*dimension*) miara *f*; (*degree*) stopień *m*

exterior [ık'stıərıə] **1.** zewnętrzny; **2.** *human:* powierzchowność *f*; *things:* część *f* zewnętrzna

external [ık'stɜːnl] zew-

nętrzny

extinguish [ık'stıŋgwıʃ] ⟨z⟩gasić; **~er** gaśnica *f*

extra ['ekstrə] **1.** dodatkowy; **~ charge** dodatkowa opłata *f*; **2.** dodatek *m*; *pl esp. mot.* wyposażenie *n* dodatkowe; *film:* statysta *m* (-tka *f*)

extract 1. [ık'strækt] wydostawać; *tooth* usuwać ⟨usunąć⟩; *tech. oil etc.* wydobywać; **2.** ['ekstrækt] ekstrakt *m*

extraordinary [ık'strɔːdnrı] nadzwyczajny

extravagan|ce [ık'strævəgəns] rozrzutność *f*; **~t** rozrzutny; (*exaggerated*) przesadny; (*elaborate*) ekstrawagancki

extreme [ık'striːm] **1.** najdalszy; *fig.* skrajny; **2.** skrajność *f*; **~ly** nadzwyczajnie; szalenie F

eye [aı] oko *n*; '**~brow** brew *f*; '**~lash** rzęsa *f*; '**~lid** powieka *f*; '**~liner** kredka *f* do oczu; '**~shadow** cień *m* do powiek; '**~sight** wzrok *m*; '**~witness** naoczny świadek *m*

F

fabric ['fæbrık] tkanina *f*; *fig.* struktura *f*

fabulous ['fæbjʊləs] bajeczny

face [feıs] **1.** twarz *f*; (*expression*) mina *f*; (*front*) prawa/

czołowa strona *f*; *clock:* tarcza *f*; **~ to ~** oko w oko; **2.** stawać ⟨stanąć⟩ w obliczu; (*cope with*) stawi⟨ać⟩ czoła

facil|itate [fə'sılıteıt] ułat-

fantastic

wi(a)ć; **~ity** łatwość f (**for s.th.** czegoś); pl at home etc.: udogodnienia pl

fact [fækt] fakt m; **in ~, as a matter of ~** właściwie, prawdę powiedziawszy

factor ['fæktə] czynnik m

factory ['fæktərı] fabryka f

faculty ['fæklti] umiejętność f, zdolność f; univ. wydział m; Am. univ. wykładowcy pl

fade [feɪd] zanikać ⟨-knąć⟩, ⟨z⟩gasnąć; colours: ⟨wy⟩blaknąć, ⟨wy⟩płowieć

fail [feɪl] v/t zawodzić ⟨-wieść⟩; candidate, exam oblewać ⟨-lać⟩ F; v/i attempt: nie powieść się; **~ure** ['~jə] niepowodzenie n, fiasko n; tech. defekt m

faint [feɪnt] **1.** adj słaby, nikły; light: blady; **2.** ⟨ze⟩mdleć

fair¹ [feə] jarmark m; econ. targi pl

fair² [~] (just) sprawiedliwy, słuszny; idea, guess: dość dobry; candidate, amount, size, degree: spory; hair: jasny, blond; skin: biały; school: dostateczny; **play ~** grać przepisowo; fig. postępować uczciwie; **'~ly** (pretty) dość; (equally) sprawiedliwie; **'~ness** sprawiedliwość, uczciwość f

faith [feɪθ] wiara f; '**~ful** wierny

fake [feɪk] **1.** fałszerstwo n; podróbka f F; **2.** (forge) ⟨s⟩fałszować; (feign)

uda(wa)ć

fall [fɔːl] **1.** upadek m; Am. season: jesień f; pl wodospad m; **2.** (fell, fallen) upadać ⟨upaść⟩, spadać ⟨spaść⟩; night, curtain: zapadać ⟨-paść⟩; **~ back on s.th.** ⟨po⟩ratować się czymś; **~ for s.o.** F ⟨s⟩tracić dla kogoś głowę; **~ ill, ~ sick** zachorować; **~ in love with** zakoch⟨iw⟩ać się w; '**~en** pp of **fall** 2

false [fɔːls] fałszywy

fame [feɪm] sława f

familiar [fə'mıljə] znajomy (**to s.o.** komuś); obeznany (**with** z); '**~rity** [fə'ærəti] obeznanie n (**with s.th.** z czymś), znajomość f (**with s.th.** czegoś); (intimacy) zażyłość f

family ['fæməli] rodzina f; **~ doctor** lekarz m domowy; **~ name** nazwisko n

famous ['feɪməs] sławny

fan¹ [fæn] wachlarz m; electric: wentylator m

fan² [~] sp. kibic m; muz. fan m

fanatic [fə'nætɪk] fanatyk m (-tyczka f); **(~al)** fanatyczny

fancy ['fænsı] **1.** pociąg m, upodobanie n; (imagination) fantazja f; **2.** wymyślny, fantazyjny; **3.** mieć ochotę (**s.th.** na coś), czuć pociąg (**s.o.** do kogoś); (imagine) wyobrażać ⟨-razić⟩ sobie; '**~free** niezależny, bez zobowiązań

fantastic [fæn'tæstɪk] (unusual) niezwykły; (incredible) nieprawdopodobny; (*wonderful*) fantastyczny F

fantasy ['fæntəsɪ] (*dream*) marzenie *n*; (*misconception*) wymysł *m*; (*unreality*) fantazja *f*

far [fɑ:] **1.** *adj* daleki, odległy; **2.** *adv* daleko; **~ away**, **~ off** hen, daleko; **as ~ as** o ile

fare [feə] (*money*) opłata *f* (za przejazd); (*price*) cena *f* (biletu); **~! well 1.** int żegnaj!; **2.** pożegnanie *n*

farfetched [fɑ:'fetʃt] nieprawdopodobny

farm [fɑ:m] **1.** gospodarstwo *n* rolne; *poultry*, *mink*, *etc.*: ferma *f*; **2.** *v/i* prowadzić gospodarstwo; *v/t* uprawiać; **~er** rolnik *m*, gospodarz *m*; **~house** zagroda *f*

farsighted [fɑ:'saɪtɪd] dalekowzroczny; **be ~** *esp. Am. med.* być dalekowidzem

farthe|r ['fɑ:ðə] *comp of* **far**, **~st** ['~ɪst] *sup of* **far**

fascinat|e ['fæsɪneɪt] ⟨za⟩fascynować; **~ing** fascynujący

fashion ['fæʃn] moda *f*; **in ~** w modzie, modny; **out of ~** niemodny; **~able** modny

fast [fɑ:st] szybki, prędki; *phot.* czuły; *colour*: trwały; **~ food** potrawy *pl* na szybko; **~ lane** *mot.* pas *m* szybkiego ruchu; **~ train** pociąg *m* pospieszny; **be ~ clock**: spieszyć się

fasten ['fɑ:sn] przymocow(yw)ać, przytwierdzać

⟨-dzić⟩, umocow(yw)ać (**to** do); **seat-belt** zapinać ⟨-piąć⟩; **~er** (*zip*) zamek *m* błyskawiczny; (*clasp*) klamerka *f*

fat [fæt] **1.** tłusty; *person a.*: gruby; **2.** tłuszcz *m*

fatal ['feɪtl] śmiertelny

fate [feɪt] los *m*

father ['fɑ:ðə] ojciec *m*; **~hood** ojcostwo *n*; **~in-law** ['~rɪnlɔ:] teść *m*; **~ly** ojcowski

fatigue [fə'ti:g] **1.** zmęczenie *n* (*a. tech.*); **2.** ⟨z⟩męczyć

faucet ['fɔ:sɪt] *Am.* kurek *m*, kran *m*

fault [fɔ:lt] wina *f*; *character*: wada *f*; (*defect*) defekt *m*; (*error*) błąd *m*; **find ~ with** krytykować; czepiać się F; **~less** bez zarzutu; **~y** wadliwy

favo(u)r ['feɪvə] **1.** przysługa *f*; (*approval, sympathy*) przychylność *f*, względy *pl*; **in ~ of** na korzyść; **do s.o. a ~** oddawa⟨ć sobie⟩przysługę, coś dla kogoś ⟨z⟩robić; **2.** faworyzować (**s.o** kogoś), sprzyjać (**s.o.** komuś); (*support*) popierać ⟨-przeć⟩; **~able** *response, people*: przychylny; *moment*: korzystny; **~ite** ['~rɪt] **1.** ulubieniec *m* (-nica *f*), faworyt(ka *f*) *m*; **2.** ulubiony

fax [fæks] **1.** (tele)faks *m*; **2.** ⟨prze⟩faksować

fear [fɪə] **1.** lęk *m*, strach *m* (**of**

przed); **2.** lękać się, obawiać się; '**~ful** straszny, nieprzyjemny; *person:* bojaźliwy; '**~less** nieustraszony

feature ['fiːtʃə] **1.** cecha *f*, właściwość *f*; *pl face:* rysy *pl*; *newspaper etc.:* (duży) artykuł *m*; *a.* **~ film** film *m* pełnometrażowy; **2.** przedstawi(a)ć; (*promote*) wyróżni(a)ć, uwypuklać ⟨-lić⟩

February ['februərɪ] luty *m*

fed [fed] *past and pp of* feed 2

federa∣l ['fedərəl] *pol.* federalny, związkowy; **~tion** [~'reɪʃn] federacja *f*

fee [fiː] honorarium *n*; *entrance, registration etc.:* opłata *f*

feed [fiːd] **1.** *animal:* pasza *f*; **2.** (*fed*) *v/t* ⟨na⟩karmić; *family* ⟨wy⟩żywić; *data* wprowadzić; **be fed up with s.th./s.o.** mieć czegoś/kogoś po uszy; *v/i* żywić się; '**~back** *electr.* sprzężenie *n* zwrotne; *information etc.:* odzew *m*, reakcja *f*

feel [fiːl] (*felt*) *v/i* czuć się; *v/t* odczu(wa)ć, wyczu(wa)ć; (*touch*) ⟨po⟩macać; **it ~s …** wydaje się …; **~ like** mieć ochotę (**s.th.** na coś); '**~ing** czucie *n*

feet [fiːt] *pl of* foot

fell [fel] **1.** *past of* fall 2; **2.** powalić; *tree* ścinać ⟨ściąć⟩

fellow ['feləʊ] facet *m*; gość *m* F; **~ citizen** współobywa-

tel(ka *f*) *m*; **~ countryman** (*pl* **-men**) rodak *m* (-daczka *f*)

felt¹ [felt] *past and pp of* feel

felt² [~] filc *m*; **~ tip**, **~tip(ped) pen** pisak *m*, mazak *m*

female ['fiːmeɪl] **1.** żeński; **2.** *zo.* samica *f*

femini∣ne ['femɪnɪn] kobiecy; '**~st** feministka *f*

fence [fens] **1.** płot *m*, ogrodzenie *n*; **2.** *v/t* (*a.* **~ in**) ogradzać ⟨-rodzić⟩; *v/i* fechtować się, uprawiać szermierkę; '**~ing** szermierka *f*

fender ['fendə] *Am.* błotnik *m*

ferry ['ferɪ] **1.** prom *m*; **2.** wozić tam i z powrotem; *on river etc.:* przeprawi(a)ć promem

fertil∣e ['fɜːtaɪl] żyzny, **~ity** [fə'tɪlətɪ] płodność *f*; **~ize** ['fɜːtəlaɪz] nawozić ⟨-wieźć⟩; '**~izer** *esp. artificial:* nawóz *m*

festiv∣al ['festəvl] festiwal *m*; *eccl.* święta *pl*; **~e** ['~ɪv] świąteczny, odświętny; **~ity** [~'stɪvətɪ] święto *n*; *pl* uroczystości *pl*

fetch [fetʃ] przynosić ⟨-nieść⟩

fever ['fiːvə] gorączka *f*; **~ish** ['~rɪʃ] gorączkujący, rozgorączkowany

few [fjuː] mało, niewiele, niewielu; *a* **~** parę, paru

fiancé [fi'ɒnseɪ] narzeczony *m*; **~e** [~] narzeczona *f*

fib∣re, *Am.* **~er** ['faɪbə] włókno *n*

ficti|on ['fɪkʃn] proza f; (*invention*) fikcja f; **~tious** [fɪk-'tɪʃəs] fikcyjny

fiddle ['fɪdl] **1.** skrzypce n; **2.** (*twiddle*) majstrować (**with s.th.** przy czymś); (*fidget*) bawić się (bezmyślnie) (**with s.th.** czymś); a. **~ about** *or* **around** marnować czas; '**~r** skrzypek m

fidelity [fɪ'delətɪ] wierność f

field [fiːld] pole n; sp. boisko n; **~ events** pl sp. konkurencje pl nie-biegowe; **~ glasses** pl lornetka f

fierce [fɪəs] srogi; *battle etc.*: zawzięty

fif|teen [fɪf'tiːn] piętnaście; **~th** [fɪfθ] piąty; **~ty** pięćdziesiąt; **~ty-'fifty** F pół na pół

fight [faɪt] **1.** walka f (**for** o); (*brawl*) bójka f; (*quarrel*) kłótnia f; **2.** (**fought**) walczyć (**for s.th.** o coś); zwalczać (**s.th., s.o.** coś, kogoś); (*brawl*) bić się; (*quarrel*) kłócić się; '**~er** bojownik m (-niczka f); aer. myśliwiec m; sp. bokser m

figure ['fɪgə] **1.** postać f; figura f; *math.* (*digit*) cyfra f; (*number*) liczba f; (*illustration*) ilustracja f; **2.** występować ⟨-tąpić⟩; *Am.* myśleć, uważać; a. **~ out** obliczać ⟨-czyć⟩; **~ skating** łyżwiarstwo n figurowe

file¹ [faɪl] **1.** kartoteka f; akta

pl; *computer*: plik m; **on ~** w kartotece; **2.** a. **~ away** *letters etc.* wkładać ⟨włożyć⟩ do kartoteki, ⟨z⟩archiwizować

file² [~] **1.** pilnik m; **2.** ⟨s⟩piłować

fill [fɪl] napełni(a)ć; **~ in** *names* wpis(yw)ać; *form etc.* (*Am.* a. **~ out**) wypełni(a)ć; **~ up** napełni(a)ć (się); *tank* ⟨za⟩tankować

fillet, *Am.* **filet** ['fɪlɪt] filet m

filling ['fɪlɪŋ] nadzienie n; *tooth*: plomba f; **~ station** stacja f benzynowa

film [fɪlm] **1.** film m; *phot.* błona f, film m F; *plastic*: folia f; **2.** ⟨s⟩filmować

filter ['fɪltə] **1.** filtr m; **2.** ⟨prze⟩filtrować; **~ tip** filtr m papierosowy; → '**~-tipped cigarette** papieros m z filtrem

filth [fɪlθ] brud m; *fig.* plugastwo n, sprośności pl; '**~y** brudny; *fig.* plugawy, sprośny

final ['faɪnl] **1.** końcowy, ostateczny; **2.** sp. finał m, finały pl; mst pl egzamin m końcowy; '**~ly** ['~nəlɪ] w końcu

financ|e [faɪ'næns] **1.** finanse pl; **2.** ⟨s⟩finansować; **~ial** [~nʃl] finansowy

find [faɪnd] **1.** (**found**) znajdować ⟨-naleźć⟩; a. **~ out** dowiadywać ⟨-wiedzieć⟩ się; (*discov-*

er) odkry(wa)ć; **2.** znalezisko *n*

fine¹ [faɪn] **1.** *adj* (*beautiful*) piękny; (*thin*) cienki; (*dainty*) delikatny; *sand, powder*: drobny; *I'm ~* u mnie wszystko dobrze, czuję się znakomicie; **2.** *adv* bardzo dobrze, wspaniale

fine² [~] **1.** grzywna *f*, kara *f* pieniężna; **2.** (u)karać grzywną

finger ['fɪŋgə] **1.** palec *m*; **2.** (po)macać; *instrument, etc.* przebierać palcami (*s.th.* po czymś); **'~nail** paznokieć *m*; **'~print** odcisk *m* palca

finish ['fɪnɪʃ] **1.** (s)kończyć (się); *a. ~ off* zakończyć; *~ up* or *off* zjeść/wypić do końca; **2.** wykończenie *n*; *sp.* meta *f*, (*end*) finisz *m*; **'~ing line** linia *f* mety

Finn [fɪn] Fin(ka *f*) *m*; **'~ish** fiński

fir [fɜː] jodła *f*

fire [faɪə] **1.** ogień *m*; *disaster*: pożar *m*; *be on ~* palić się; *catch ~* zapalić <-lić> się; *set on ~, set ~ to* podpalać <-lić>; **2.** *v/t pottery* wypalać <-lić>; (*sack*) wyrzucać <-cić> z pracy; *weapon* strzelać <-lić> z (*s.th.* z czegoś); *shot* odda(wa)ć; *v/i* strzelać <-lić>; *mot.* zaskoczyć, zapalić; **~ alarm** alarm *m* przeciwpożarowy; **~arms** ['~rɑːmz] *pl* broń *f* palna; **~**

brigade *Brt.*, **~ department** *Am.* straż *f* pożarna; **~ escape** schody *pl* przeciwpożarowe; **~ extinguisher** gaśnica *f*; **'~man** (*pl -men*) strażak *m*; **'~place** kominek *m*; **'~proof** ogniotrwały; **~wood** drewno *n* opałowe

firm¹ [fɜːm] firma *f*

firm² [~] *body etc.*: twardy; *friendship etc.*: trwały; *decision etc.*: stanowczy; *belief etc.*: mocny

first [fɜːst] **1.** *adj* pierwszy; *at ~ hand* z pierwszej ręki; **2.** *adv* najpierw, początkowo; *~ of all* przede wszystkim; **3.** *s* at *~* z początku; *~ aid* pierwsza pomoc *f*; **~ aid box** or **kit** apteczka *f*; **~ class** pierwszorzędny; **~ floor** *Brt.* pierwsze piętro *n*; *Am.* parter *m*; **~ hand** z pierwszej ręki; **~ly** po pierwsze; **~ name** imię *n*; **~ rate** pierwszorzędny

fish [fɪʃ] **1.** (*pl ~, fish species: ~es*) ryba *f*; **2.** łowić ryby; **'~bone** ość *f*; **~erman** ['~əmən] (*pl -men*) rybak *m*; **'~ing** rybołówstwo *n*; (*angling*) wędkarstwo *n*; **'~ing rod** wędka *f*; **'~y** F podejrzany

fist [fɪst] pięść *f*

fit¹ [fɪt] atak *m*

fit² [~] **1.** nadający się, odpowiedni; (*healthy*) w dobrej kondycji; **2.** *v/i* pasować; *v/t* dopasow(yw)ać; *tech.* (za)montować, (za)instalować; '**~ness** stosowność *f*, nadawanie *n* się; (*health*) dobra kondycja *f*; '**~ted** nadający się; *clothes*: dopasowany; **~ted carpet** wykładzina *f* dywanowa; '**~ter** monter *m*; '**~ting 1.** pasujący; **2.** *by tailor*: przymiarka *f*; (*installation*) instalacja *f*; **2l** wyposażenie *n* wnętrza, instalacje *pl*

five [faɪv] pięć

fix [fɪks] przyczep(i)a(ć), przymocow(yw)ać; *attention etc.* ⟨s⟩koncentrować; *eyes* utkwić (**on** w); *price etc.* ustalać ⟨-lić⟩; *esp. Am. meal* ⟨z⟩robić, przyrządzać ⟨-dzić⟩; **~ed** stały; **~ture** ['~stʃə] część *f* wyposażenia

flag [flæg] flaga *f*, chorągiew *f*

flak|e [fleɪk] **1.** płatek *m*; **2.** *a. ~e off* łuszczyć się; '**~y** płatkowaty; *paint*: łuszczący się; **~y pastry** ciasto *f* francuskie

flame [fleɪm] **1.** płomień *m*; **2.** ⟨za⟩płonąć

flammable ['flæməbl] *Am. or tech.* → **inflammable**

flannel ['flænl] flanela *f*; *Brt.* ściereczka *f* frotowa; *pl* spodnie *pl* flanelowe

flash [flæʃ] **1.** błysk *m*; *radio etc.*: wiadomość *f* z ostatniej chwili; **2.** błyskać ⟨-snąć⟩, migać ⟨-gnąć⟩; '**~back** (nagłe) wspomnienie *n*; '**~bulb** żarówka jednorazowego użytku do lampy błyskowej; '**~er** *mot.* kierun-

kowskaz *m*; '**~light** flesz *m*; *esp. Am.* latarka *f*; **~ of lightning** błyskawica *f*; **~y** efekciarski; szpanerski *sl.*

flask [flɑːsk] piersiówka *f*; (*Thermos*) termos *m*

flat¹ [flæt] **1.** płaski; *battery*: wyładowany; *drink*: zwietrzały; *refusal*: kategoryczny; *tyre*: bez powietrza; *mus.* z bemolem; **2.** nizina *f*; *esp. Am. tyre*: guma *f* F

flat² [~] *Brt.* mieszkanie *n*

flatter ['flætə] pochlebi(a)ć; '**~y** ['~ərɪ] pochlebstwa *pl*

flavo(u)r ['fleɪvə] **1.** smak *m*; *fig.* posmak *m*; **2.** ... **~ed** o smaku ...; '**~ing** ['~rɪŋ] przyprawa *f*

flaw [flɔː] *character*: wada *f*; *in glass etc.*: skaza *f*; '**~less** nieskazitelny

flee [fliː] *past and pp of* **flee**

flee [fliː] (**fled**) uciekać ⟨uciec⟩

fleet [fliːt] flota *f*

flesh [fleʃ] mięso *n*; *fig.* ciało *n*; '**~y** mięsisty

flew [fluː] *past of* **fly³**

flexible ['fleksəbl] elastyczny

flicker ['flɪkə] ⟨za⟩migotać

flight [flaɪt] lot *m*; **~ of stairs** kondygnacja *f* (schodów)

fling [flɪŋ] **1.** rzut *m*; *fig.* romansik *m*, przygoda *f*; **2.** (**flung**) rzucać ⟨-cić⟩; **~ o.s.** rzucać ⟨-cić⟩ się

float [fləʊt] **1.** *tech.* pływak *m*; *lorry*: platforma *f* (na kołach); **2.** unosić się, pływać

flock [flɒk] **1.** *sheep, birds*: stado *n*; *people*: gromada *f*; *fig.* tłoczyć się

flood [flʌd] **1.** *disaster*: powódź *f*; *fig.* zalew *m*; *a.* ~ **tide** przypływ *m*; **2.** zalewać ⟨-lać⟩; **~light** reflektor *m*; **~lit** jaskrawo oświetlony

floor [flɔː] **1.** podłoga *f*; *(storey)* piętro *n*; *disco etc.*: parkiet *m*; *ocean etc.*: dno *n*; **2.** układać ⟨ułożyć⟩ podłogę **(s.th.** w czymś); *s.o.* powalać ⟨-lić⟩ na ziemię; *fig.* zatkać f

flop [flɒp] **1.** opadać ⟨opaść⟩; *with noise*: klapnąć, plasnąć; **2.** plaśnięcie *n*; *fig.* klapa *f*; **~py disk** dyskietka *f*

florist [ˈflɒrɪst] kwiaciarz *m* (-ciarka *f*); *or* **~'s** kwiaciarnia *f*

flour [ˈflaʊə] mąka *f*

flourish [ˈflʌrɪʃ] bujnie rosnąć; *fig. a.* kwitnąć, rozwijać się, być u szczytu (kariery)

flow [fləʊ] **1.** ⟨po⟩płynąć; **2.** strumień *m*, potok *m*

flower [ˈflaʊə] **1.** kwiat *m* (a. *fig.*); **2.** ⟨roz⟩kwitnąć

flown [fləʊn] *pp of* **fly³**

flu [fluː] F grypa *f*

fluent [ˈfluːənt] *language*: płynny, biegły; *style*: potoczysty

fluff [flʌf] kłaczki *pl*; *cloth*: puszek *m*, meszek *m*; **~y** mechaty, puszysty

fluid [ˈfluːɪd] **1.** ciekły, płynny; **2.** ciecz *f*, płyn *m*

flung [flʌŋ] *past and pp of* **fling** 2

flush [flʌʃ] **1.** *(blush)* rumieniec *m*; *(surge)* przypływ *m*; *flood*: obfitość *f*; **2.** ⟨za⟩rumienić (się); *a.* ~ **out** buchać ⟨-chnąć⟩, tryskać ⟨-snąć⟩; ~ **down** spłuk(iw)ać; ~ **the toilet** spuszczać ⟨spuścić⟩ wodę

flute [fluːt] flet *m*

fly¹ [flaɪ] mucha *f*

fly² [~] rozporek *m*

fly³ [~] **(flew, flown)** ⟨po⟩lecieć, latać; *plane* pilotować; **~over** *Brt.* wiadukt *m* (drogowy)

foam [fəʊm] **1.** piana *f*; **2.** ⟨s⟩pienić się; ~ **rubber** pianka *f* (gumowa); **~y** pienisty; *(foam-like)* piankowaty

focus [ˈfəʊkəs] **1.** *(pl* **-cuses**, **-ci** [ˈ~saɪ]) ośrodek *m*; *opt., phot.* ognisko *f*; *phot.* ostrość *f*; **2.** skupi(a)ć (się), ⟨s⟩koncentrować (się); *opt., phot.* nastawi(a)ć ostrość

fog [fɒg] mgła *f*; **~gy** mglisty

foil [fɔɪl] folia *f* (metalowa)

fold [fəʊld] **1.** *often* ~ **up** składać ⟨złożyć⟩; *arms* zakładać ⟨założyć⟩; **2.** fałda *f*

fold|er skoroszyt *m*, teczka *f*; **~ing** składany

folk [fəʊk] **1.** *pl* ludzie *pl*; **2.** ludowy

follow [ˈfɒləʊ] chodzić ⟨pójść⟩ **(s.o.** za kimś), *(tail)* śledzić (**s.o.** kogoś); (*come after*) następować ‹-tąpić› (**s.th.** po czymś); **as ~s** co/ jak następuje; **'~er** zwolennik *m* (-niczka *f*)

fond [fɒnd] czuły; **be ~ of** lubić; **~le** ['-dl] pieścić; **'~ness** (*affection*) czułość *f*; (*inclination*) zamiłowanie *n*, pociąg *m* (**for** do)

food [fuːd] pożywienie *n*, jedzenie *n*, pokarm *m*; *collectively:* żywność *f*

fool [fuːl] **1.** głupiec *m*; **make a ~ of o.s.** ośmieszać ‹-szyć› kogoś, wystrychnąć kogoś na dudka; **2.** oszuk(iw)ać, wystrychnąć na dudka; (*joke*) żartować; **~ about** *or* **around** (*lark about*) błaznować, wygłupiać się; (*do nothing*) próżnować; **'~hardy** nieroztropny, lekkomyślny; **'~ish** głupi, niemądry; **'~proof** *plan etc.:* niezawodny

foot [fʊt] (*pl* **feet** [fiːt]) *anat.* stopa *f*; (*at a foot*) stopa *f* (30.48 *cm*); dół *m*; **on ~** piechotą; **'~ball** piłka *f* nożna; **'~hold** oparcie *n*, stopień *m*; **'~ing** oparcie *n*; *fig.* poziom *m*, stopa *f*; **'~note** przypis *m*; **'~print** ślad *m* (stopy), odcisk *m* (stopy)

for [fɔː] **1.** *prp* dla; *purpose, destination:* po; **what's this tool ~?** do czego służy to narzędzie?; (*on the occasion of*) na; **~ Christmas** na

gwiazdkę; *shows payment, price:* za; **~ £ 2** za dwa funty; *send etc.:* po; (*considering*) jak na, zważywszy; **he's young ~ a doctor** jest młody jak na lekarza; *length of time:* **~ three days** na trzy dni; *przez trzy dni; of three days;* *distance:* **walk ~ a mile** przejść milę; **what ~?** po co?; **2.** *cj* ponieważ, gdyż

forbad(e) [fə'bæd] *past of* **forbid**

forbid [fə'bɪd] (**-bade** *or* **-bad**, **-bidden** *or* **-bid**) zakazywać ‹-zać›, zabraniać ‹-ronić›; **~den** *pp of* **forbid**; **~ding** odpychający; ponury, groźny

force [fɔːs] **1.** siła *f*, moc *f*; (*violence*) przemoc *f*; *the* (*police*) policja *f*; *pl* (*a. armed ~s*) *mil.* siły *pl* zbrojne; **by ~** siłą, przemocą; **come** *or* **put into ~** wchodzić ‹wejść› *or* wprowadzać ‹-dzić› w życie; **2.** *s.o.* zmuszać ‹-sić›; *s.th.* narzucać ‹-cić›; wymuszać ‹-sić›; **~ open** *door etc.* wyważać ‹-żyć›, wyłam(yw)ać; **~d** przymusowy; wymuszony; **~d landing** przymusowe lądowanie *n*; **'~ful** silny

fore [fɔː] przedni; *mar.* dziobowy; przed...; **~arm** ['-rɑːm] przedramię *n*; **~cast** ‹-cast‹ed›› przewidzieć; *weather* przepowiadać ‹-wiedzieć›; **'~fathers** *pl* przodkowie *pl*; **'~finger**

palec *m* wskazujący; '**~ground** pierwszy plan *m*; **~head** ['fɔrɪd] czoło *n*

foreign ['fɔrən] obcy; zagraniczny, cudzoziemski; **~ affairs** *pl* polityka *f* zagraniczna; **~ currency** waluta *f* obca; '**~er** cudzoziemiec *m*, obcokrajowiec *m*; **~ exchange** *money*: dewizy *pl*; *buying and selling*: obrót *m* dewizami; **~ language** język *m* obcy; 2 **Office** *Brt.* Ministerstwo *n* Spraw Zagranicznych; **~ policy** polityka zagraniczna *f*; 2 **Secretary** *Brt.* minister spraw zagranicznych *m*

'**fore|most 1.** *adj* czołowy; **2.** *adv first and ~most* przede wszystkim; '**~see** (*-saw, -seen*) przewidywać ⟨-dzieć⟩; '**~sight** dalekowzroczność *f*, przewidywanie *n*

forest ['fɔrɪst] las *m*; '**~er** leśniczy *m*; '**~ry** leśnictwo *n*

'**fore|taste** przedsmak *m*; **~tell** (*-told*) przepowiadać ⟨-wiedzieć⟩; wywróżyć

foreword przedmowa *f*

forge [fɔːdʒ] **1.** kuźnia *f*; **2.** kuć; (*counterfeit*) ⟨s⟩fałszować, podrabiać ⟨-drobić⟩; '**~r** fałszerz *m*; **~ry** [-ərɪ] fałszerstwo *n*; *document, banknote etc.*: falsyfikat *m*

forget [fəˈget] (*-got, -gotten*) zapominać ⟨-mnieć⟩; '**~ful** zapominalski; **~me-not**

niezapominajka *f*

forgive [fəˈgɪv] (*-gave, -given*) przebaczać ⟨-czyć⟩

fork [fɔːk] **1.** widelec *m*; widły *pl*; rozwidlenie *n*; **2.** spulchni(a)ć; rozwidlać ⟨-lić⟩ się

form [fɔːm] **1.** forma *f*; kształt *m*; (*document*) formularz *m*; *esp. Brt. school*: klasa *f*; **2.** ⟨u⟩kształtować (się), ⟨u⟩formować (się), ⟨u⟩tworzyć (się)

formal ['fɔːml] formalny; (*official*) oficjalny; **~ity** [~'mælətɪ] formalność *f*

forma|tion [fɔːˈmeɪʃn] tworzenie (się) *n*, powstawanie *n*; (*arrangement*) formacja *f*; **~ive** [-ˈmətɪv] kształtujący

former ['fɔːmə] **1.** poprzedni, dawny, miniony; **2. the ~** pierwszy (z dwu); '**~ly** dawniej

formidable ['fɔːmɪdəbl] potężny; (*frightening*) straszny

formula ['fɔːmjolə] (*pl -las, -lae* [-liː]) wzór *m*; (*recipe*) przepis *m*; **~te** ['-leɪt] ⟨s⟩formułować; (*frame*) wyrażać ⟨-razić⟩

for|sake [fəˈseɪk] (*-sook, -saken*) opuścić, porzucić

forth [fɔːθ] dalej, naprzód; '**~coming** nadchodzący, przyszły

fortieth ['fɔːtɪɪθ] czterdziesty

fortnight ['fɔːtnaɪt] dwa tygodnie; *in a ~* za dwa tygodnie

fortunate ['fɔːtʃnət] szczęśliwy; pomyślny; '**~ly** szczęśliwie, na szczęście

fortune ['fɔːtʃn] *(money)* majątek *m*, fortuna *f*; *(fate)* los *m*, traf *m*

forty ['fɔːtɪ] czterdzieści

forward ['fɔːwəd] **1.** *adv (a.* **~s)** naprzód, do przodu; **2.** *adj* przedni; *(too confident)* bezczelny; **3.** *s ssp.* napastnik *m*; **4.** *v/t* wysłać; przesłać (dalej)

foster| child ['fɒstətʃaɪld] *(pl* **-children)** wychowanek *m*; **~ parents** *pl* przybrani rodzice *pl*

fought [fɔːt] *past and pp of* **fight** 2

foul [faul] **1.** ohydny, wstrętny; *fig. a.* ordynarny, sprośny; *food:* zgniły; *weather:* brzydki; *sp.* nieprzepisowy; *sp.* faul *m*; **3.** zanieczyszczać ⟨-czyścić⟩; *sp.* ⟨s⟩faulować

found[1] [faund] *past and pp of* **find** 1

found[2] [~] zakładać ⟨założyć⟩

foundation [faun'deɪʃn] założenie *n*; *(organization)* fundacja *f*; *fig.* podstawa *f*; '**~s** *pl a.* fig. fundament *m*

'**founder** założyciel *m*

fountain ['fauntɪn] fontanna *f*; **~ pen** wieczne pióro *n*

four [fɔː] cztery, czterej; '**~teen** [~'tiːn] czternaście; **~th** [~θ] czwarty

fowl [faul] drób *m*

fox [fɒks] lis *m*

fract|ion ['frækʃn] *math.* ułamek *m*; **~ure** ['~ktʃə] złamanie *n*

fragile ['frædʒaɪl] kruchy

fragment ['frægmənt] fragment *m*; okruch *m*

fragran|ce ['freɪgrəns] zapach *m*, woń *f*; '**~t** aromatyczny

frame [freɪm] **1.** ram(k)a *f*; *of glasses:* oprawka *f*; *film:* klatka *f*; **~ of mind** usposobienie *n*, nastrój *m*; **2.** *picture:* oprawi(a)ć; *s.o.* *F* wrabiać ⟨wrobić⟩ kogoś; '**~work** *tech. a.* fig. szkielet *m*, struktura *f*

France [frɑːns] Francja *f*

frank [fræŋk] **1.** *adj* szczery; **2.** *letters:* ⟨o⟩frankować; '**~ly** szczerze

frantic ['fræntɪk] oszalały; szalony

fraud [frɔːd] oszustwo *n*; *(person)* oszust *m*

freak [friːk] dziwoląg *m*; dziw *m* natury; *(fan)* miłośnik *m*, maniak *m*

freckle ['frekl] pieg *m*

free [friː] **1.** wolny, swobodny; **~ and easy** beztroski; **set ~** uwalniać ⟨uwolnić⟩; **2.** *(freed)* uwalniać ⟨uwolnić⟩; '**~dom** wolność *f*; '**~lance** niezależny; '**²mason** wolnomularz *m*; '**~way** *Am.* autostrada *f*

freez|e [friːz] **1.** *(froze, frozen)* *v/i* ⟨za⟩marznąć, zamarzać; *v/t* zamrażać ⟨-rozić⟩; **2.** mróz *m*; *econ., pol.* zam-

fuel

rożenie *n*; **wage ~** zamrożenie *n* płac; **'~er** (*a. deep freeze*) zamrażarka *f*; **'~ing** mroźny; **~ing compartment** zamrażalnik *m*

freight [freɪt] (*cargo*) przewóz *m*; (*charge*) opłata *f* za przewóz; **~car** *Am.* wagon *m* towarowy; **~er** frachtowiec *m*; samolot *m* towarowy; **~train** *Am.* pociąg *m* towarowy

French [frentʃ] **1.** *adj* francuski; **2. the ~** *pl* Francuzi *pl*; **~doors** *pl esp. Am.* → **French window(s)**; **~ fries** *pl esp. Am.* frytki *pl*; **'~man** (*pl -men*) Francuz *m*; **~ window(s** *pl*) oszklone drzwi *pl*; **'~woman** (*pl -women*) Francuzka *f*

frequen|cy ['friːkwənsɪ] częstość *f*; *electr., phys.* częstotliwość *f*; **~t 1.** ['~nt] *adj* częsty; **2.** [frɪ'kwent] często bywać, uczęszczać

fresh [freʃ] świeży; (*new*) nowy; **~en** *wind:* ochładzać <-łodzić> się; **~** (*o.s.*) **up** odświeżać <-żyć> się; **'~ness** świeżość *f*; **~water** słodkowodny

friction ['frɪkʃn] tarcie *n*

Friday ['fraɪdɪ] piątek *m*

fridge [frɪdʒ] lodówka *f*

friend [frend] przyjaciel *m*, przyjaciółka *f*; **make ~s with s.o.** zaprzyjaźni(a)ć się z kimś; **'~ly** przyjazny; **'~ship** przyjaźń *f*

fright [fraɪt] strach *m*; **'~en**

przestraszyć; **be ~ened** bać się (**of s.th.** czegoś); **'~ful** przerażający

frigid ['frɪdʒɪd] *a. fig.* zimny, lodowaty

fringe [frɪndʒ] frędzla *f*

frog [frɒg] żaba *f*

from [frɒm] z, od; **~ 9 to 5 (o'clock)** od dziewiątej do piątej

front [frʌnt] **1.** przód *m*, przednia część *f*; front *m* (*a. mil.*); **in ~** z przodu; **in ~ of** przed; **2.** stać frontem (**onto** do); **~ door** drzwi *pl* frontowe/wejściowe; **~ entrance** wejście *n* frontowe/główne

frontier ['frʌntɪə] granica *f*

frost [frɒst] **1.** szron *m*; (*freeze*) mróz *m*; **2.** pokry(wa)ć się szronem; **'~bite** odmrożenie *n*

frown [fraʊn] <z>marszczyć brwi

froze [frəʊz] *past of* **freeze**; **'~n 1.** *pp of* **freeze** 1; **2.** (za)mrożony; **~ food** mrożonki *pl*

fruit [fruːt] owoc *m*, owoce *pl*; **'~ful** owocny; **~y** owocowy

frustrate [frʌ'streɪt] <s>frustrować

fry [fraɪ] <u>smażyć; **fried eggs** *pl* jajka *pl* sadzone; **fried potatoes** *pl* smażone ziemniaki *pl*; **'~ing pan** patelnia *f*

fuel [fjʊəl] **1.** paliwo *n*; opał *m*; **2.** (za)tankować; *fig.* podsycać <-cić>

fugitive ['fju:dʒətɪv] zbieg *m*

fulfil, *Am. a.* **-fill** [fʊl'fɪl] wypełni(a)ć, spełni(a)ć; **~ment** spełnienie *n*, wywiązanie *n* się

full [fʊl] **1.** *adj (filled completely)* pełny; *(whole)* cały; **~ of s.th.** pełny/pełen czegoś; **2.** *adv* do pełna; *(straight)* prosto; **~'grown** dorosły; **~ moon** pełnia *f*; **~ stop** kropka *f*; **~'time** na cały etat

fume [fju:m] wściekać się; **~s** *pl* opary *pl*, wyziewy *pl*

fun [fʌn] zabawa *f*; **for ~** dla zabawy/żartu; **make ~** wyśmiewać (**of s.o.** z kogoś)

function ['fʌŋkʃn] **1.** funkcja *f*; **2.** funkcjonować; **~al** funkcjonalny

fund [fʌnd] fundusz *m*; *fig.* zapas *m*, zasób *m*

fundamental [fʌndə'mentl] zasadniczy, podstawowy

funeral ['fju:nərəl] pogrzeb *m*

funfair *esp. Brt.* wesołe miasteczko *n*

funny ['fʌnɪ] zabawny

fur [fɜ:] futro *n*; *(covering)* nalot *m*

furious ['fjʊərɪəs] wściekły

furl [fɜ:l] zwinąć

furnish ['fɜ:nɪʃ] ⟨u⟩meblować; zaopatrywać ⟨-rzyć⟩

furniture ['fɜ:nɪtʃə] meble *pl*

furrow ['fʌrəʊ] **1.** *a. fig.* bruzda *f*; **2.** ⟨wy⟩żłobić, ⟨po⟩bruździć

further ['fɜ:ðə] **1.** *adv* dalej; *(more)* więcej; **2.** *adj* dalszy; *(additional)* dodatkowy; **3.** *v/t* popierać ⟨-przeć⟩, wspierać ⟨wesprzeć⟩

furtive ['fɜ:tɪv] ukradkowy, potajemny

fury ['fjʊərɪ] furia *f*, wściekłość *f*

fuse [fju:z] **1.** lont *m*, zapalnik *m*; *electr.* bezpiecznik *m*; **2.** *phys.*, *tech.* stapiać ⟨stopić⟩ się; *electr.* przepalać ⟨-lić⟩ się

fuss [fʌs] **1.** zamieszanie *n*; awantura *f*; **2.** *v/i* zawracać głowę; *v/i* przejmować się (drobiazgami); **~y** kapryśny, drobiazgowy; *clothes*: wymyślny

futile ['fju:taɪl] daremny, próżny

future ['fju:tʃə] **1.** przyszłość *f*; *gr.* czas *m* przyszły; **2.** *adj* przyszły

fuzzy ['fʌzɪ] *hair*: kędzierzawy; *picture*: niewyraźny

G

gadget ['gædʒɪt] przyrząd *m*, F patent *m* F

gag [gæg] **1.** knebel *m*; F gag *m*; **2.** ⟨za⟩kneblować

gaiety ['geɪətɪ] wesołość *f*; **~ly** radośnie, wesoło

gain [geɪn] **1.** zysk(iw)ać; zdoby(wa)ć; *experience* naby(wa)ć; *clock:* śpieszyć się; **~ ground** zyskiw)ać na popularności; **~ on** doganiać; **~ 10 pounds** przytyć 10 funtów; **2.** zysk *m;* wzrost *m*

gale [geɪl] wichura *f*

gall [gɔːl] żółć *f;* **'~ bladder** [~blædə] woreczek *m* żółciowy

gallery ['gælərɪ] *a.* arch. galeria *f*

gallon ['gælən] galon *m* (*Brt.* 4,546 *l, Am.* 3,785 *l*)

gallop ['gæləp] **1.** cwał *m;* **2.** cwałować

gallows ['gæləʊz] (*pl* **~**) szubienica *f*

gallstone ['gɔːlstəʊn] *med.* kamień *m* żółciowy

gamble ['gæmbl] **1.** uprawiać hazard; **2.** ryzyko *n,* ryzykowne przedsięwzięcie *n;* **'~er** hazardzista *m;* **'~ing** hazard *m*

game [geɪm] gra *f;* zabawa *f; bridge:* partia *f; tennis:* gem *m; pl sp.* zawody *pl,* igrzyska *pl;* (*animal meat*) dziczyzna *f,* (*animals*) zwierzyna *f* łowna

gang [gæŋ] **1.** gang *m,* banda *f;* (*friends*) paczka *f* F; (*workers*) brygada *f;* **~ up** zmówić się (*on/against* przeciwko)

gap [gæp] szpara *f,* luka *f; fig. a.* przepaść *f*

gap|e [geɪp] gapić się; **'~ing** *wound:* otwarty; *abyss:* ziejący

garage ['gærɑːʒ] garaż *m;* (*service station*) warsztat *m* samochodowy

garbage ['gɑːbɪdʒ] *esp. Am.* śmieci *pl;* **~ can** *Am.* → **dustbin**

garden ['gɑːdn] ogród *m;* **'~er** ogrodnik; **'~ing** ogrodnictwo *n*

gargle ['gɑːgl] płukać gardło

garlic ['gɑːlɪk] czosnek *m*

garment ['gɑːmənt] część *f* garderoby

garret ['gærət] poddasze *n*

garter ['gɑːtə] podwiązka *f*

gas [gæs] gaz *m; Am.* F benzyna *f*

gasket ['gæskɪt] *tech.* uszczelka *f*

gasoline ['gæsəʊliːn] (*a.* **-lene**) *Am.* benzyna *f*

gasp [gɑːsp] sapnąć, syknąć; **~ for breath** łapać powietrze

gas| pedal *Am.* pedał *m* gazu; **~ station** *Am.* stacja *f* benzynowa; **'~works** *sg* gazownia *f*

gate [geɪt] brama *f; aer.* wyjście *n* do samolotu; **'~crash** wpraszać ⟨-rosić⟩ się; **'~way** brama *f* wjazdowa

gather ['gæðə] *v/t* zbierać ⟨zebrać⟩; ⟨z⟩gromadzić; *fig.* ⟨wy⟩wnioskować, ⟨z⟩rozumieć (*from* z); **~ speed** nab(ie)rać szybkości; *v/i* zbierać ⟨zebrać⟩ się, ⟨z⟩gromadzić się; **'~ing** ['~rɪŋ] zgromadzenie *n*

gauge [geɪdʒ] **1.** przyrząd *m* pomiarowy, wskaźnik *m*; **2.** ⟨z⟩mierzyć

gave [geɪv] *past of* **give**

gay [geɪ] **1.** *adj* radosny, wesoły; **2.** F pedał *m* F

gaze [geɪz] **1.** przyglądać się, przypatrywać się; **2.** (uporczywe) spojrzenie *n*

gear [gɪə] *mot.* przekładnia *f*; bieg *m*; (*tools*) sprzęt *m*, ekwipunek *m*; (*mechanism*) układ *m*, mechanizm *m*; **~box** *mot.* skrzynia *f* biegów; **~ lever**, *Am. a.* **~shift** dźwignia *f* biegów

geese [giːs] *pl of* **goose**

gem [dʒem] kamień *m* szlachetny

gene [dʒiːn] *biol.* gen *m*

general ['dʒenərəl] **1.** *adj* ogólny, powszechny; **2.** *mil.* generał *m*; **~ election** wybory *pl* powszechne; **~ization** [dʒenərəlaɪ'zeɪʃn] uogólnienie *n*; **'~ize** uogólni(a)ć; **'~ly** zwykle, na ogół; (*by most people*) ogólnie, powszechnie; **~ practitioner** lekarz *m* ogólny f

generat|e ['dʒenəreɪt] wytwarzać ⟨-worzyć⟩, ⟨wy⟩produkować; **~ion** [‿'reɪʃn] pokolenie *n*; **~or** ['‿reɪtə] generator *m*; *mot.* prądnica *f*

gener|osity [dʒenə'rɒsɪtɪ] hojność *f*, szczodrość *f*; **~ous** ['‿rəs] hojny, szczodry

genius ['dʒiːnjəs] geniusz *m*

gentle [dʒentl] (*soft*) łagod-

ny, delikatny; (*kind*) miły; **'~man** (*pl* -**men**) dżentelmen *m*; *address:* pan *m*

genuine ['dʒenjuɪn] prawdziwy, autentyczny

geograph|ic(al) [dʒɪə'græfɪk(l)] geograficzny; **~y** [‿'ɒgrəfɪ] geografia *f*

geolog|ic(al) [dʒɪəʊ'lɒdʒɪk(l)] geologiczny; **~ist** [‿'ɒlədʒɪst] geolog *m*; **~y** geologia *f*

geometr|ic(al) [dʒɪəʊ'metrɪk(l)] geometryczny; **~y** [‿'ɒmətrɪ] geometria *f*

germ [dʒɜːm] zarazek *m*; *fig.* zarodek *m*

German ['dʒɜːmən] **1.** *adj* niemiecki; **2.** Niemiec *m* (-mka *f*); **'~y** Niemcy *pl*

gesticulate [dʒe'stɪkjuleɪt] gestykulować

gesture ['dʒestʃə] gest *m*

get [get] (**got, got** *or Am.* **gotten**) *v/t* (*receive*) dost(aw)ać, otrzym(yw)ać; (*bring*) przynosić ⟨-nieść⟩, poda(wa)ć; (*catch*) ⟨z⟩łapać; (*understand*) ⟨z⟩rozumieć; **~ one's hair cut** dać się ostrzyc; **~ s.th. ready** przygotow(yw)ać coś; **have got** mieć; **have got to** musieć; *v/i* (*become*) sta(wa)ć się; (*go*) dosta(wa)ć się; *with pp or adj:* **~ tired** zmęczyć się; **~ drunk** upić się; **it's ... ing late/cold** robi się późno/zimno; **~ to know s.o.** pozn(aw)ać kogoś bliżej; **~**

about ruszać się; *news etc.*: rozchodzić ⟨rozejść⟩ się; ~ *along* (*manage*) da(wa)ć sobie radę; (*get on*) zgadzać się (*with* z); ~ *away* uciekać ⟨uciec⟩; ~ *away with* unikać ⟨-knąć⟩ odpowiedzialności; ~ *back* wracać ⟨wrócić⟩; ~ *in* (*arrive*) przyjeżdżać ⟨-je-chać⟩; (*call*) wzywać ⟨we-zwać⟩; ~ *off* wysiadać ⟨-siąść⟩; (*remove*) usuwać ⟨usunąć⟩; ~ *on* wsiadać ⟨wsiąść⟩; (*put on*) wkładać ⟨włożyć⟩; (*continue*) kontynuować; ~ *on with s.o.* zgadzać się z kimś; ~ *out* wydosta(wa)ć się; *information*: rozchodzić ⟨-zejść⟩ się; ~ *over* przychodzić ⟨przyjść⟩ do siebie; ~ *together* zebrać ⟨zbierać⟩ się; ~ *up* wsta(wa)ć

ghost [gəʊst] duch *m*; '.**ly** upiorny

giant ['dʒaɪənt] **1.** olbrzym *m*; **2.** *adj* olbrzymi

gidd|iness ['gɪdɪnɪs] zawrót *m* głowy; '.**y** oszołomiony; zawrotny

gift [gɪft] prezent *m*; (*talent*) dar *m*, talent *m*; '.**ed** utalentowany

gigantic [dʒaɪ'gæntɪk] olbrzymi, gigantyczny

giggle ['gɪgl] **1.** chichotać; **2.** chichot *m*

gin [dʒɪn] dżin *m*

gipsy ['dʒɪpsɪ] Cygan(ka *f*) *m*

giraffe [dʒɪ'rɑːf] (*pl* ~s, ~)

żyrafa *f*

girl [gɜːl] dziewczyn(k)a *f*; '.**friend** dziewczyna *f*; ~ **guide** *Brt.*, ~ **scout** *Am.* harcerka *f*

give [gɪv] (**gave**, **given**) *v/t* da(wa)ć; *orders etc.* wyda(wa)ć; *help* udzielać ⟨-lić⟩; *time* poświęcać ⟨-cić⟩; *idea, clue* podsuwać ⟨-sunąć⟩; nasuwać ⟨-sunąć⟩; ~ *her my love* pozdrów ją ode mnie; *v/i* podda(wa)ć się ustępować ⟨-tąpić⟩; ~ *away* rozda(wa)ć; *secret* wyda(wa)ć; ~ *back* odda(wa)ć; ~ *in* podda(wa)ć się; *paper etc.* odda(wa)ć; ~ *off smoke etc.* wydzielać ⟨-lić⟩; ~ *out* rozda(wa)ć; *supply etc.*: wyczerp(yw)ać się; *machine etc.*: ⟨ze⟩psuć się; ~ *up smoking etc.* rzucać; ~ *up* poddawać się, zaprzesta(wa)ć; ~ *o.s. up* poświęcić się (*to s.th.* czemuś); '.**n** *pp of* give

glacier ['glæsjə] lodowiec *m*

glad [glæd] zadowolony; *be* ~ cieszyć się; '.**ly** chętnie

glamo|rous ['glæmərəs] olśniewający, czarujący; '.**o(u)r** czar *m*, urok *m*

glance [glɑːns] **1.** spojrzeć (*at* na); **2.** spojrzenie *n*

gland [glænd] gruczoł *m*

glare [gleə] oślepiać, razić blaskiem; ~ *at s.o.* przeszy(wa)ć/piorunować kogoś wzrokiem

glass [glɑːs] szkło *n*; *container*: szklanka *f*, kieliszek *m*; '**~es** *pl* okulary *pl*; '**~house** *Brt.* szklarnia *f*; '**~ware** szkło *n*, wyroby *pl* szklane

glaze [gleɪz] **1.** ⟨o⟩szklić; *f* glazura *f*; **~ier** ['~jə] szklarz *m*

glide [glaɪd] **1.** ślizgać się; *bird*: szybować; **2.** ślizg *m*; *aer.* lot *m* ślizgowy; '**~er** szybowiec *m*; '**~ing** szybownictwo *n*

glimpse [glɪmps] **1.** zobaczyć/ujrzeć w przelocie; **2.** przelotne spojrzenie *n*

glisten ['glɪsn] lśnić, błyszczeć

glitter ['glɪtə] **1.** błyszczeć; **2.** blask *m*

globe [gləʊb] kula *f*; (*spherical model*) globus *m*; (*the Earth*) kula *f* ziemska

gloom [gluːm] półmrok *m*; *fig.* przygnębienie *n*; '**~y** *day*: mroczny; *person*: ponury; *future*: przygnębiający

glorify ['glɔːrɪfaɪ] gloryfikować; '**~ious** *victory*: chlubny; (*splendid*) wspaniały; '**~y** chwała *f*, chluba *f*; '**~ious** (*splendid appearance*) wspaniałość *f*

glossary ['glɒsərɪ] słowniczek *m*

glossy ['glɒsɪ] lśniący, połyskujący

glove [glʌv] rękawiczka *f*

glow [gləʊ] **1.** żarzyć się; **2.** żar *m*

glue [gluː] **1.** klej *m*; **2.**

go [gəʊ] **1.** (*pl goes*) próba *f*; *it's my* ~ F moja kolej; *all the* ~ F ostatni krzyk mody; *have a* ~ F spróbować (*at s.th.* czegoś); **2.** (*went, gone*) chodzić, iść; *jechać* (*to do*); *road etc.*: iść, prowadzić (*to* do); *bus etc.*: jechać; *tech.* chodzić, funkcjonować, poruszać się; ~ *swimming* iść ⟨pójść⟩ popływać; *it is ~ing to rain* będzie padać; *I must be ~ing* muszę iść; ~ *for a walk* chodzić ⟨pójść⟩ na spacer; ~ *to school* chodzić do szkoły; ~ *to see s.o.* odwiedzić ⟨-dzić⟩ kogoś; *let* ~ puszczać ⟨puścić⟩; ~ *at* rzucać ⟨-cić⟩ się na; ~ *away* odchodzić ⟨odejść⟩; ~ *back* wracać ⟨wrócić⟩; ~ *back on* cofać ⟨-fnąć⟩, wycof⟨yw⟩ać się z; ~ *by* kierować się (*s.th.* czymś); *time*: upływać ⟨-łynąć⟩; ~ *down* obniżać ⟨-żyć⟩ się; *sun*: zachodzić; *ship*: zatonąć; ~ *for* atakować; ~ *in sun*: ⟨s⟩chować się; ~ *in for* brać ⟨wziąć⟩ udział w; zajmować ⟨-jąć⟩ się; ~ *off* wybuchać ⟨-chnąć⟩; *machine, light*: ⟨ze⟩psuć się, wysiadać ⟨-siąść⟩; ~ *on* kontynuować, nie prze⟨ry⟩wać; (*happen*) dziać się; ~ *out* ⟨z⟩gasnąć; ~ *through* przejść ⟨przechodzić⟩; ~ *up* podnosić ⟨-nieść⟩ się, ⟨pod⟩skoczyć

goal [gəul] cel m; *sp.* bramka f; '**~keeper** bramkarz m

goat [gəut] koza f

'go-between pośrednik m (-niczka f)

god [gɒd] bóg m; (*eccl.* 2) Bóg m; thank 2! dzięki Bogu!; '**~child** (pl **-children**) chrześniak m (-niaczka f); '**~father** (ojciec) chrzestny m; '**~mother** (matka) chrzestna f

gold [gəuld] 1. złoto n; 2. złoty; '**~en** colour: złoty, złocisty; '**~smith** złotnik m

golf [gɒlf] 1. golf m; 2. grać w golfa; **~ club** klub m golfowy; stick: kij m golfowy; **~ course** pole n golfowe; '**~er** gracz m w golfa

gone [gɒn] 1. pp of go 2. adj miniony

good [gud] 1. adj dobry; (*suitable*) odpowiedni; (*kind*) miły; (*well-behaved*) grzeczny; a **~ many** wiele, dużo; for **~** na dobre; **~by(e)** [~'bai]; 1. say **~by(e)** to s.o., wish s.o. **~by(e)** pożegnać się z kimś; 2. int do widzenia!, *teleph.* do usłyszenia!; 2 Friday Wielki Piątek m; '**~hu-mo(u)red** dobroduszny; '**~-looking** przystojny; **~'na-tured** pogodny, życzliwy; '**~ness** dobro n

goods [gudz] (*possessions*) dobra pl; (*articles*) towary pl, wyroby pl

goose [gu:s] (pl geese [gi:s]) gęś f; '**~berry** ['guz~] agrest m; '**~bumps**, '**~ pimples** pl gęsia skórka f

gorgeous ['gɔ:dʒəs] wspaniały

gorilla [gə'rilə] goryl m

gospel ['gɒspl] *mst* 2 Ewangelia f

gossip ['gɒsip] 1. plotka f; *person:* plotkarz m (-rka f); 2. plotkować

got [gɒt] past and pp of get

gotten ['gɒtn] *Am. pp of* get

govern ['gʌvn] rządzić; '**~ment** rząd m; **~or** ['~ənə] gubernator m

gown [gaun] suknia f wieczorowa; toga f

grab [græb] chwytać 〈-wycić〉

grace [greis] wdzięk m, gracja f; (*tact*) poczucie n przytomności; (*delay*) zwłoka f, odroczenie n; '**~ful** pełen wdzięku; wdzięczny

gracious ['greiʃəs] 1. łaskawy, miłosierny; 2. int good(ness)~! o Boże!

grade [greid] stopień m; (*quality*) gatunek m, jakość f; *Am. school:* klasa f; *esp. Am.* (*mark*) stopień m, ocena f; 2. **~ crossing** *Am.* przejazd m kolejowy

gradual ['grædʒuəl] stopniowy

graduate 1. ['grædʒuət] absolwent(ka f) m; *Am.* abiturient(ka f) m; 2. ['~eit] zosta(wa)ć absolwentem, ⟨u⟩kończyć studia; *Am.* ⟨u⟩kończyć szkołę; **~ion** [~'eɪʃn] podziałka *f*; *univ.* absolutorium *n*; *Am.* ukończenie *n* szkoły

graft [grɑ:ft] *med.* przeszczepi(a)ć; *bot.* szczepić

grain [greɪn] ziarno *n*; zboże *n*; *sand etc.*: ziarnko *n*; *fig.* szczypta *f*, źdźbło *n*

gramma|r ['græmə] gramatyka *f*; **~tical** [grə'mætɪkl] gramatyczny

gramme [græm] gram *m*

grand [grænd] *adj* (*impressive*) wspaniały; *person:* dostojny; **~child** [~'tʃ-] (*pl -children*) wnuk *m*, wnuczka *f*; **~daughter** wnuczka *f*; **~father** ['~d-] dziadek *m*; **~mother** ['~nm-] babcia *f*; **~parents** *pl* dziadkowie *pl*; **~ piano** *mus.* fortepian *m*; **~son** wnuk *m*; **~stand** ['~d-] trybuna *f*

granite ['grænɪt] granit *m*

grant [grɑ:nt] **1.** przyzna(wa)ć; *wish etc.* spełni(a)ć; **take s.th. for ~ed** zakładać ⟨założyć⟩ coś z góry; przyjmować ⟨-jąć⟩ coś za oczywistość; **2.** stypendium *n*

grape [greɪp] winogrono *n*; **~fruit** grejpfrut *m*; **~ sugar** cukier *m* gronowy; **~vine** winorośl *f*

graph [grɑ:f, græf] wykres *m*; **~ic** ['græfɪk] **1.** *adj* graficzny; **2.** *mst* **~ics** *pl* grafika *f*

grapple ['græpl] mocować się (**with** *z*)

grasp [grɑ:sp] **1.** chwycić, złapać; *fig.* pojąć, zrozumieć; **2.** (u)chwyt *m*; *fig.* zdolność *f* pojmowania

grass [grɑ:s] trawa *f*; '**~hopper** konik *m* polny; **~ widow** słomiana wdowa *f*; **~ widower** słomiany wdowiec *m*; '**~y** trawiasty

grate¹ [greɪt] krata *f*; ruszt *m*

grate² [~] ucierać ⟨utrzeć⟩

grateful ['greɪtfʊl] wdzięczny

grater ['greɪtə] tarka *f*

grati|fication [grætɪfɪ'keɪʃn] satysfakcja *f*; **~fy** ['~faɪ] zadowalać ⟨-wolić⟩, zaspokajać ⟨-koić⟩

gratitude ['grætɪtjuːd] wdzięczność *f*

grave¹ [greɪv] grób *m*

grave² [~] poważny

gravel ['grævl] żwir *m*

grave|stone nagrobek *m*; '**~yard** cmentarz *m*

gravi|tation [grævɪ'teɪʃn] grawitacja *f*; '**~ty** ['~vəti] powaga *f*; *phys.* grawitacja *f*

gravy ['greɪvɪ] sos *m* (mięsny)

gray [greɪ] *Am.* → **grey**

graze [greɪz] *v/t* paść, wypasać; *v/i* paść się

grease [griːs] **1.** tłuszcz *m*; *tech.* smar *m*; **2.** [~z] ⟨na⟩smarować; **~y** ['~zɪ] tłusty; usmarowany

great [greɪt] wielki, duży; (*important*) znaczący; (*splendid*) F świetny, znakomity;

~'**grandchild** (pl -**children**) prawnuk m (-nuczka f); ~'**grandfather** pradziadek m; ~'**grandmother** prababcia f; '**.ly** znacząco, znacznie; '**.ness** wielkość f

Gree|ce [griːs] Grecja f; ~**k** [griːk] **1.** adj grecki; **2.** Grek m, Greczynka f

greed [griːd] chciwość f, zachłanność f; '**.y** zachłanny, chciwy; łapczywy

green [griːn] **1.** adj a. fig. zielony; **2.** zieleń f; '**.grocer** esp. Brt. kupiec m warzywny; '**.house** szklarnia f

greet [griːt] pozdrawiać ⟨-rowić⟩ ⟨po⟩witać; '**.ing** pozdrowienie n, powitanie n; (good wish) życzenia pl

grenade [grɪ'neɪd] granat m

grew [gruː] past of **grow**

grey [greɪ] szary; '**.haired** siwy; '**.hound** zo. chart m

grief [griːf] smutek m, żal m

grill [grɪl] **1.** piec na ruszcie; **2.** ruszt m

grim [grɪm] groźny; ponury

grimace [grɪ'meɪs] **1.** grymas m; **2.** ⟨s⟩krzywić się

grin [grɪn] **1.** ⟨wy⟩szczerzyć się, ⟨wy⟩szczerzyć zęby; **2.** szeroki uśmiech m

grind [graɪnd] (**ground**) ⟨ze⟩mleć, ucierać ⟨utrzeć⟩; knive etc. ⟨na⟩ostrzyć

grip [grɪp] **1.** chwytać ⟨-wycić⟩; **2.** chwyt m, uścisk m

groan [grəʊn] **1.** jęczeć; **2.** jęk m

grocer ['grəʊsə] właściciel(ka f) m sklepu spożywczego; at the ~'**s** (**shop**) w sklepie spożywczym; **.ies** ['~rɪz] pl artykuły pl spożywcze; ~**y** ['~rɪ] sklep m spożywczy

groin [grɔɪn] anat. pachwina f

groove [gruːv] rowek m

gross [grəʊs] (total) brutto; error etc.: rażący; (vulgar) ordynarny; (fat) tłusty

ground[1] [graʊnd] **1.** past and pp of **grind**; **2.** adj mielony; ~ meat mielone mięso n

ground[2] [~] **1.** ziemia f; in water: dno n; (land) teren m; Am. electr. uziemienie n; pl (reason) przyczyna f, powód m, podstawy pl; (area) tereny pl; **2.** mar. osiadać ⟨osiąść⟩ na mieliźnie; Am. electr. uziemi(a)ć; fig. opierać ⟨oprzeć⟩ się (on, in o); ~ **floor** esp. Brt. parter m; '**.less** bezzasadny; '**.nut** orzeszek m ziemny

group [gruːp] **1.** grupa f; **2.** grupować (się)

grow [grəʊ] (**grew, grown**) ⟨u⟩rosnąć; ~ **up** dorastać ⟨-rosnąć⟩

growl [graʊl] warczeć ⟨-rknąć⟩

grown [grəʊn] pp of **grow**; ~**-up 1.** ['~ʌp] adj dorosły, dojrzały; **2.** ['~ʌp] dorosły m

growth [grəʊθ] a. fig. wzrost m

grub [grʌb] larwa f

grudg|e [grʌdʒ] **1.** żałować

(s.o. s.th. komuś czegoś); zazdrościć; **2.** uraza *f*; **'~ing** niechętny

guarant|ee [gærən'tiː] **1.** gwarancja *f*; **2.** ⟨za⟩gwarantować; **~'ı'**\~ty] *jur.* rękojmia *f*, poręka *f*

guard [gaːd] **1.** ⟨u⟩chronić, ⟨u⟩pilnować; zabezpieczać ⟨-czyć⟩ się (**against** przed); **2.** warta *f*, straż *f*; (*person*) strażnik *m*; *Brt. rail.* konduktor *m*; **be on one's ~** być czujnym, mieć się na baczności; **off one's ~** nie przygotowany; **~ed** ostrożny; **~ian** ['~ʃən] *jur.* opiekun *m*; *f*; **'~ianship** *jur.* kuratela *f*

guess [ges] **1.** zgadywać ⟨-dnąć⟩; *esp. Am.* sądzić; **2.** domysł *m*, domniemanie *n*

guest [gest] gość *m*; **'~house** pensjonat *m*; **'~room** pokój *m* gościnny

guidance ['gaɪdns] kierownictwo *n*, poradnictwo *n*; *mil.* naprowadzanie *n*

guide [gaɪd] **1.** ⟨po⟩kierować, ⟨po⟩prowadzić; **2.** przewodnik *m*; *fig.* wskazówka *f*; (*book*) przewodnik *m*; **'~book** przewodnik *m*; **'~d** kierowany; **~d missile** pocisk *m* kierowany; **'~lines** *pl* wskazówki *pl*

guilt [gɪlt] wina *f*; **'~y** winny (**of s.th.** czegoś)

guinea pig ['gɪnɪ] świnka *f* morska; *fig.* królik *m*

doświadczalny

guitar [gɪ'taː] gitara *f*

gulf [gʌlf] zatoka *f*; *fig.* przepaść *f*

gull [gʌl] mewa *f*

gulp [gʌlp] **1.** *often* **~ down** połykać ⟨-łknąć⟩; **2.** łyk *m*, łyknięcie *n*

gum¹ [gʌm] *mst pl* dziąsło *n*

gum² [~] **1.** guma *f*; (*resin*) żywica *f*; (*adhesive*) klej *m*; **2.** ⟨przy⟩kleić

gun [gʌn] (*weapon*) broń *f* (*palna*); (*cannon*) armata *f*, działo *n*; (*pistol*) rewolwer *m*, pistolet *m*; : **'~powder** proch *m* strzelniczy; **'~shot** strzał *m*

gurgle ['gɜːgl] ⟨za⟩bulgotać; ⟨za⟩gruchać

gush [gʌʃ] **1.** tryskać ⟨-snąć⟩, chlustać ⟨-snąć⟩; **2.** wytrysk *m*

gust [gʌst] podmuch *m*

gut [gʌt] jelito *n*; *mus.* struna *f*; *pl* wnętrzności *pl*; *pl* (*bravery*) F odwaga *f*

gutter ['gʌtə] *pipe:* rynna *f*; *ditch:* ściek *m*; *a. fig.* rynsztok *m*

guy [gaɪ] F facet *m* F

gym [dʒɪm] F → **gymnasium**, **gymnastics**; **'~ shoes** *pl* tenisówki *pl*; **~nasium** [~'neɪzjəm] sala *f* gimnastyczna; **~nast** ['~næst] gimnastyk *m*; **~nastics** [~'næstɪks] *sg* gimnastyka *f*

gyn(a)ecologist [gaɪnə'kɒl-ədʒɪst] ginekolog *m*

H

habit ['hæbɪt] nawyk *m*, zwyczaj *m*; *bad*: nałóg *m*; *monk's*: habit; **~ual** [hə'bɪtʃʊəl] nawykowy, nałogowy; *(customary)* zwyczajowy

had [hæd] *past and pp of* **have**

h(a)emorrhage ['hemərɪdʒ] *med.* krwotok *m*

hair [heə] włos *m*, włosy *pl*; **'~brush** szczotka *f* do włosów; **'~cut** strzyżenie *n*; *(hairstyle)* fryzura *f*; **'~do** F fryzura *f*; **'~dresser** fryzjer(ka *f*) *m*; *at the* **~dresser's** u fryzjera; **'~dryer** (*a.* **hairdrier**) suszarka *f* do włosów; **'~less** bezwłosy, pozbawiony włosów; **'~pin** spinka *f* do włosów; **'~-raising** mrożący krew w żyłach; **~ slide** wsuwka *f*; **'~-splitting** drobiazgowy; **'~style** uczesanie *n*

half [hɑːf] **1.** *s* (*pl* **halves** [hɑːvz]) połowa *f*; **~ past ten**, *Am. a.* **~ after ten** wpół do jedenastej; **2.** *adj* pół; **~ an hour** pół godziny; **~ a pound** pół funta; **3.** *adv* na pół, do połowy, częściowo; **~'hearted** niezdecydowany, pozbawiony entuzjazmu; **~ time** *sp.* przerwa *f*; **~way** w połowie drogi

hall [hɔːl] hall *m*, korytarz *m*;

(room) sala *f*; *(townhall)* ratusz *m*

hallucination [həluːsɪ'neɪʃn] halucynacja *f*

halt [hɔːlt] **1.** przystanek *m*, postój *m*; **2.** zatrzym(yw)ać się

halve [hɑːv] przepoławiać ⟨-łowić⟩; zmniejszać ⟨-szyć⟩ o połowę; **~s** [~vz] *pl of* **half** l

ham [hæm] szynka *f*

hamburger ['hæmbɜːgə] *gastr.* hamburger *m*

hammer ['hæmə] **1.** młotek *m*; **2.** uderzać ⟨-rzyć⟩/ wbi(ja)ć młotkiem; *(hit)* walić, tłuc

hammock ['hæmək] hamak *m*

hamster ['hæmstə] *zo.* chomik *m*

hand [hænd] **1.** ręka *f*; *clock*: wskazówka *f*; *(handwriting)* pismo *n*; *(help)* pomoc *f*; *(worker)* pomocnik *m*; *cards*: ręka *f*, karty *pl*; **at** ~ blisko, pod ręką; **at first** ~ z pierwszej ręki; **by** ~ ręcznie; **on the one** ~ ..., **on the other** ~ ... z jednej strony..., z drugiej strony; **on the right** ~ z prawej strony; **~s off!** precz z rękami!, ręce precz!; **~s up!** ręce do góry!; **change** ~s przechodzić ⟨przejść⟩ w inne ręce; **shake ~s** przywitać się, uścisnąć dłoń (**with s.o.** komuś); 2. wręczać ‹-czyć›, poda(wa)ć; **~ down** przekaz(yw)ać; **~ over** odda(wa)ć, przekaz(yw)ać; **'~bag** torebka f; **'~book** podręcznik m; poradnik m; **'~brake** hamulec m ręczny; **'~cuffs** pl kajdanki pl

handicap ['hændɪkæp] 1. handicap m, upośledzenie n; sp. a. for m; med. upośledzenie n; 2. utrudni(ać), przeszkadzać ‹-kodzić›

handi|craft ['hændɪkrɑːft] rzemiosło n, rękodzieło n; **'~work** praca f ręczna, rękodzieło n; fig. dzieło n, sprawka f

handkerchief ['hæŋkətʃɪf] chusteczka f

handle ['hændl] 1. rączka f, uchwyt m; knife: rękojeść f; hammer: trzonek m; door: klamka f; 2. dotykać, manipulować; (treat) traktować, obchodzić się z; (deal with) załatwi(ać)

hand| luggage bagaż m podręczny; **~'made** ręcznie robiony; **~'rail** poręcz f; **'~shake** uścisk m dłoni

handsome ['hænsəm] esp. man: przystojny; sum etc.: znaczny, pokaźny

'hand|writing charakter m pisma; kaligrafia f; **'~written** odręczny; **'~y** poręczny, wygodny w użyciu, dogodny

hang¹ [hæŋ] (hung) wieszać ‹powiesić›, zawieszać ‹-sić›; wisieć; head zwieszać ‹zwiesić›; wallpaper ‹wy›tapetować

hang² [~] (hanged) wieszać ‹powiesić› (na szubienicy); **~ o.s.** wieszać ‹powiesić› się; **~ about, ~ around** wałęsać się bezczynnie; **~ on** trzymać się kurczowo (**to s.th.** czegoś); **~ on!** poczekaj no!

hangar ['hæŋə] hangar m

'hanger wieszak m

hang| glider lotnia f; **~ gliding** lotniarstwo n; **'~man** kat m; **'~over** kac m F

haphazard [hæp'hæzəd] przypadkowy

happen ['hæpən] zdarzać ‹-rzyć› się, przytrafi(ać) się; **~ing** ['hæpnɪŋ] wydarzenie n; art: happening m

happ|ily ['hæpɪlɪ] szczęśliwie; **'~iness** szczęście n; **'~y** szczęśliwy

harbo(u)r ['hɑːbə] 1. port m; przystań f; 2. da(wa)ć schronienie; grudge etc. żywić

hard [hɑːd] (firm) twardy; (difficult) trudny; fig: ciężki; winter: srogi, (severe) surowy; **~ of hearing** przygłuchy; **~ up** F spłukany F; **'~back** book: książka f w twardej oprawie; **'~cover = hardback**; **~ disk** computer: dysk m twardy; **~en** ['hɑːdn] v/t utwardzać ‹-dzić›; v/i ‹s›twardnieć; **~headed**

praktyczny, trzeźwy; '**.ly**
prawie (nie/nikt/nigdy), ledwo, mało (kto/co); '**.ness**
twardość f; wytrzymałość f;
'**.ship** trud m, niedostatek
m; '**.ware** towary pl żelazne; F żelastwo n; *computer*:
sprzęt m komputerowy; '**.y**
odporny, twardy

hare [heə] zając m

harm [hɑːm] **1.** krzywda f; **2.**
⟨s⟩krzywdzić; '**.ful** szkodliwy; '**.less** nieszkodliwy

harmon|ious [hɑːˈməʊnjəs]
harmonijny; zgodny; '**.ize**
[ˈ.ənaɪz] harmonizować

harpoon [hɑːˈpuːn] **1.** harpun
m; **2.** trafić harpunem

harsh [hɑːʃ] surowy; *voice*:
chrapliwy, szorstki

harvest [ˈhɑːvɪst] **1.** żniwa pl,
zbiory pl; plon m; **2.** zbierać
⟨zebrać⟩, sprzątać ⟨-tnąć⟩
(zboże itp.)

has [hæz] ma; → **have**

haste [heɪst] pośpiech m; **.en**
[ˈ.sn] przyspieszać ⟨-pieszyć⟩; pospieszyć; '**.y** pospieszny; (*rash*) pochopny

hat [hæt] kapelusz m

hat|e [heɪt] **1.** nienawidzić; **2.**
nienawiść f; '**.red** [ˈ.rɪd] nienawiść f

haul [hɔːl] ciągnąć, wlec, holować; (*transport*) przewozić

haunt [hɔːnt] nawiedzać,
straszyć; *fig.* prześladować;
(*visit*) uczęszczać, często odwiedzać; **this place is .ed** tu
straszy

have [hæv] (*had*) v/t mieć, posiadać; ~ **breakfast** ⟨z⟩jeść
śniadanie; *with inf*: musieć; **I
~ to go** muszę iść; *with object
and pp*: kazać, życzyć sobie; **I
had my hair cut** kazać sobie
obciąć włosy; ~ **on** mieć na
sobie; *fig.* nab(ie)rać; v/aux
forms perfect tenses:; **I ~
lived here for 5 years** mieszkam tu od 5 lat

hawk [hɔːk] jastrząb m (*a.
pol.*)

hay [heɪ] siano n; ~ **fever** katar m sienny; '**.stack** stóg m
siana

hazard [ˈhæzəd] **1.** ryzyko n;
2. ⟨za⟩ryzykować; '**.ous** ryzykowny

haze [heɪz] mgiełka f

hazel [ˈheɪzl] **1.** leszczyna f; **2.**
adj colour: orzechowy; '**.nut**
orzech m laskowy

hazy [ˈheɪzɪ] zamglony; *fig.*
niejasny, mglisty

he [hiː] **1.** *pron* on; **2.** s on m;
3. *adj zo. in compounds*: samiec m

head [hed] **1.** s głowa f; *plant,
nail*: główka f; (*top*) góra f;
(*front*) przód m; (*person*) kierownik m, szef m; **£ 15 a/per
~** 15 funtów na głowę; **20** ~ pl
(*of cattle*) 40 sztuk (bydła);
~**s or tails?** coin: orzeł czy
reszka?; **at the** ~ na czele (*of
s.th.* czegoś); ~ **over heels**
na łeb na szyję; ~ **over heels
in love** zakochany po uszy;
lose one's ~ stracić głowę; **2.**

adj główny, naczelny; **3.** *v/t* (*lead*) prowadzić, być na czele; (*be in charge*) kierować; *football:* główkować; *v/i* kierować się, iść (*for* do); **~ache** ból *m* głowy; **~light** reflektor *m*; **~line** nagłówek *m*; **~master** *school:* dyrektor *m* szkoły; **~ office** centrala *f*; **~ on** *collision:* czołowo, czołowy; **~phones** słuchawki *pl*; **~quarters** *pl, sg mil.* kwatera *f* główna, punkt *m* dowodzenia; **~rest** zagłówek *m*; **~strong** uparty

heal [hi:l] (*a.* **~ up/over**) (za)goić się

health [helθ] zdrowie *n*; **your ~!** na zdrowie!; **~ food** zdrowa żywność *f*; **~ insurance** ubezpieczenie *n* zdrowotne; **~ resort** uzdrowisko *n*; **~ service** służba *f* zdrowia; **~y** zdrowy

heap [hi:p] **1.** stos *m*, sterta *f*; **2.** (*a.* **~ up**) układać ⟨ułożyć⟩ stos, ⟨na⟩gromadzić

hear [hɪə] (**heard**) słuchać ⟨u⟩słyszeć; **~d** [hɜːd] *past and pp of* **hear**; **~ing** ['~rɪŋ] słuch *m; esp. pol.* przesłuchanie *n; jur.* rozprawa *f; within/out of ~ing* w zasięgu/poza zasięgiem głosu; **~ing aid** aparat *m* słuchowy

heart [hɑːt] serce *n* (*a. fig.*); serdeczny *m; fig.* centrum *n; cards:* kier *m; by ~* na pa-

mięć; **~ attack** atak *m* serca; **~breaking** rozdzierający serce; **~burn** zgaga *f*; **heart|less** nieczuły, bez serca; **~ transplant** transplantacja *f* serca; **~y** serdeczny; *meal:* obfity

heat [hi:t] **1.** upał *m*, żar *m; phys.* ciepło *n; fig.* uniesienie *n;* podniecenie *n;* **2.** (*a.* **~ up**) podgrzew(a)ać; **~ed** podgrzewany; *fig.* ożywiony, gorący; **~er** grzejnik *m*

heath [hi:θ] wrzosowisko *f*

heathen ['hi:ðn] **1.** poganin *m* (-nka *f*); **2.** *adj* pogański

heather ['heðə] wrzos *m*

heat|ing ['hi:tɪŋ] ogrzewanie *n;* **~stroke** udar *m* słoneczny; **~ wave** fala *f* upałów

heaven ['hevn] niebo *n;* **~ly** niebiański

heavy ['hevɪ] ciężki; (*difficult*) trudny; *traffic etc.:* intensywny; *rain:* rzęsisty

Hebrew ['hi:bru:] hebrajski

hectare ['hektɑː] hektar *m*

hedge [hedʒ] żywopłot *m*; **~hog** jeż *m*

heel [hi:l] pięta *f; shoe:* obcas *m*

height [haɪt] wysokość *f; fig.* wzrost *m; fig.* punkt *m* kulminacyjny, szczyt *m,* pełnia *f; ~en* ['~tn] podwyższać ⟨-ższyć⟩

heir [eə] spadkobierca *m*

held [held] *past and pp of* **hold**

helicopter ['helɪkɒptə] śmigłowiec *m,* helikopter *m*

hell [hel] piekło n; *what the ~
...?* F co, do diabła, ...?

hello [hə'ləʊ] *int* cześć; *teleph.*
halo

helm [helm] ster m

helmet ['helmɪt] hełm m, kask
m

help [help] **1.** pomoc f; **2.** pomagać ⟨-móc⟩; ~ **o.s.**
⟨po⟩częstować się; *I can't ~
it* nic na to nie poradzę; *I
couldn't ~ laughing* nie
mogłem powstrzymać się od
śmiechu; '**~er** pomocnik m;
'**~ful** pomocny, przydatny;
'**~less** bezradny

hen [hen] kura f; *bird*: samiczka f

her [hɜː] jej, ją

herb [hɜːb] zioło n

herd [hɜːd] stado n

here [hɪə] tu(taj); *~'s to you!*
twoje zdrowie!; *~ you are!*
proszę!

hereditary [hɪ'redɪtərɪ] dziedziczny

heritage ['herɪtɪdʒ] dziedzictwo n, spuścizna f

hermetic [hɜː'metɪk] hermetyczny, szczelny

hero ['hɪərəʊ] (*pl -oes*) bohater m; *~ic* [hɪ'rəʊɪk] bohaterski

heroin ['herəʊɪn] heroina f

herring ['herɪŋ] (*pl -s, ~*) śledź
m

hers [hɜːz] jej

herself [hɜː'self] *reflexive*: się,
siebie, sobie; *emphasis*: (ona)
sama

hesitat|e ['hezɪteɪt] wahać się;
~ion [~'teɪʃn] wahanie n

hi [haɪ] *int* F cześć F

hiccup ['hɪkʌp] **1.** (*a. hic-
cough*) czkawka f; **2.** mieć
czkawkę, czkać ⟨czknąć⟩

hid [hɪd] *past and pp* '**~den** *pp
of* **hide¹**

hide [haɪd] (*hid, hidden or
hid*) ukry(wa)ć (się); ⟨s⟩chować (się)

high [haɪ] **1.** *adj* wysoki; *voice*:
cienki; *meat*: zepsuty; F *on
drugs*: naćpany F; *in ~ spirits*
w świetnym humorze; *it is ~
time* najwyższy czas; **2.** *meteor.* wyż m; *~'class* luksusowy; *~fidelity* hi-fi, wysoka wierność f odtwarzania; *~'jump sp.* skok m wzwyż;
~'light **1.** atrakcja f; **2.** uwydatni(a)ć; *'~ly fig.* wysoce,
wysoko; *think ~ of s.o.* mieć
wysokie mniemanie o kimś;
'**²ness** *title*: Wysokość f;
~'pitched tone: wysoki;
roof: spadzisty; *~'powered*
o dużej mocy; *fig.* dynamiczny; *'~rise* wieżowiec m;
'**~road** *esp. Brt.* szosa f; ~
school *Am.* szkoła f średnia;
'**~street** *Brt.* główna ulica f; ~
tech [~'tek] supernowoczesny; *~ technology* zaawansowana technologia f;
~'tension electr. wysokie
napięcie n; '**~way** *esp. Am.*
szosa f

hijack ['haɪdʒæk] *plane* uprowadzać ⟨-dzić⟩, por(y)wać;

train etc. ⟨ob⟩rabować; '**~er** porywacz *m*

hike [haɪk] **1.** wędrować; **2.** wędrówka *f*, wycieczka *f* piesza; '**~r** wędrowiec *m*, turysta *f*

hilarious [hɪ'leərɪəs] komiczny, wesoły

hill [hɪl] wzgórze *n*, wzniesienie *n*; '**~side** stok *m*, zbocze *n*; '**~y** pagórkowaty, górzysty

him [hɪm] (je)go, (je)mu; '**~self** *reflexive:* się, siebie, sobie; *emphasis:* (on) sam

hind [haɪnd] tylny, zadni

hind|er ['hɪndə] przeszkadzać ⟨-kodzić⟩, utrudni(a)ć; **~rance** ['~drəns] przeszkoda *f*

hinge [hɪndʒ] zawias *m*

hint [hɪnt] **1.** wskazówka *f*; aluzja *f*; **2.** napomykać ⟨-mknąć⟩

hip [hɪp] *anat.* biodro *n*

hippopotamus [hɪpə'pɒtəməs] (*pl* **-muses, -mi** [~maɪ]) hipopotam *m*

hire ['haɪə] **1.** (*a.* **~ out**) *Brt. car etc.* wynajmować ⟨-jąć⟩, wypożyczać ⟨-czyć⟩; *plane etc.* ⟨wy⟩czarterować; *people* najmować ⟨-jąć⟩; **2.** wynajem *m*; **for** ~ do wynajęcia; *taxi:* wolna; ~ **purchase** *esp. Brt.* sprzedaż *f* ratalna

his [hɪz] jego

hiss [hɪs] **1.** syczeć ⟨syknąć⟩; **2.** syk *m*

histor|ian [hɪ'stɔːrɪən] historyk *m*; **~ic** [~'stɒrɪk] (*important*) historyczny; **~ical** historyczny; **~y** ['~ərɪ] historia *f*

hit [hɪt] **1.** (*hit*) (*strike*) uderzać ⟨-rzyć⟩; F (*reach*) docierać ⟨dotrzeć⟩; (*a.* ~ **on** or **upon**) natrafi(a)ć na, wymyśleć ⟨-lić⟩; **2.** uderzenie *n*; trafienie *n*; *song etc.:* przebój *m*

hitch [hɪtʃ] **1.** doczepi(a)ć ⟨u⟩wiązać (**to** do); ~ **up** podciągać ⟨-gnąć⟩; ~ **a ride** F złapać okazję; → **hitchhike**; **2.** szarpnięcie *n*; *mar.* węzeł *m*; *fig.* komplikacja *f*; **without a** ~ gładko, bez komplikacji; '**~hike** jeździć autostopem; '**~hiker** autostopowicz *m*

hive [haɪv] ul *m*; (*bees*) rój *m*

hoarse [hɔːs] chrapliwy, ochrypły

hobby ['hɒbɪ] hobby *n*, '**~horse** konik *m* (*a. fig.*)

hockey ['hɒkɪ] *esp. Brt.* hokej *m* na trawie; *esp. Am.* hokej *m* na lodzie

hog [hɒg] wieprz *m*

hoist [hɔɪst] **1.** podnosić ⟨-dnieść⟩; **2.** dźwig *m*

hold [həʊld] **1.** (*held*) *v/t* trzymać; (*conduct*) odby(wa)ć; *fire, breath etc.* wstrzym(yw)ać; (*keep*) utrzym(yw)ać; *position* zajmować; (*contain*) mieścić; *shares etc.* posiadać; (*de-*

fend) bronić; *(think)* uważać *(that* że); ~ *s.th. against s.o.* wymawiać komuś coś; ~ **responsible** *v/t* obciążać ⟨-żyć⟩ odpowiedzialnością; *v/i* trzymać się; *(last)* utrzym⟨yw⟩ać się; *(a. ~ the line)* *teleph.* czekać (przy telefonie); ~ **on** trzymać się *(to s.th.* czegoś); *teleph.* czekać (przy telefonie); ~ **out** wytrzym⟨yw⟩ać; *supplies etc.:* wystarczać; ~ **up** zatrzym⟨yw⟩ać; *bank etc.* ⟨ob⟩rabować; fig. stawiać za wzór; **2.** (u)chwyt m, trzymanie n; *(control)* kontrola f, władza f *(on, over* nad); *have a (firm)* ~ *on s.o.* mieć władzę nad kimś; *catch (get, take)* ~ *of s.th.* złapać; zdobyć; ~ **up** *traffic:* zator m; *(stickup)* napad m

hole [həʊl] **1.** dziura f, otwór m; **2.** przedziurawi⟨a⟩ć

holiday ['hɒlɪdeɪ] święto n; *mst pl esp. Brt.* wakacje pl, urlop m; *take a* ~ wziąć wolny dzień; ~**maker** ['hɒlɪdɪ-] urlopowicz m, wczasowicz m

Holland ['hɒlənd] Holandia f

hollow ['hɒləʊ] **1.** wgłębienie n; **2.** adj pusty, wydrążony; **3.** often ~ out wydrążać ⟨-żyć⟩

holocaust ['hɒləkɔːst] zagłada f

holster ['həʊlstə] kabura f

holy ['həʊlɪ] święty; ♀ **Week** Wielki Tydzień m

home [həʊm] **1.** s dom m, miejsce n zamieszkania; fig. ojczyzna f; *at* ~ w domu; *make o.s. at* ~ rozgościć się; *at* ~ *and abroad* w kraju i za granicą; **2.** adj domowy; krajowy, lokalny; sp. miejscowy; **3.** adv do domu; w domu; **4.** v/i: ~ *in missile:* naprowadzać ⟨-dzić⟩ się *(on s.th.* na coś); ~ **address** adres m domowy; ~ **computer** komputer m domowy; '~**less** bezdomny; '~**ly** swojski; *food:* prosty; *Am.* pospolity, nieładny; ~**made** własnej/domowej roboty; ♀ **Office** *Brt.* Ministerstwo n Spraw Wewnętrznych; ♀ **Secretary** *Brt.* minister m spraw wewnętrznych; '~**sick**: *be* ~*sick* tęsknić za domem; ~ **town** miasto n rodzinne; ~**ward** ['~wəd] powrotny; ~**wards** ku domowi, do domu; '~**work** praca f domowa, zadanie n domowe

homicide ['hɒmɪsaɪd] *jur.* zabójstwo n

homosexual [hɒməʊ'sekʃʊəl] **1.** adj homoseksualny; **2.** homoseksualista m (-tka f)

honest ['ɒnɪst] uczciwy; '~**y** uczciwość f

honey ['hʌnɪ] miód m; esp. *Am.* ~! kochanie!, skarbie!; '~**moon** miesiąc m miodowy

honorary ['ɒnərərɪ] honorowy

hono(u)r ['ɒnə] **1.** honor *m*, cześć *f*; zaszczyt *m*; **2.** zaszczycać ⟨-cić⟩; *bill etc.* honorować; **~able** ['ˌɒrəbl] zaszczytny; poważany

hood [hud] kaptur *m*; *car, pram*: bud(k)a *f*; *Am.* maska *f* samochodu

hoof [hu:f] (*pl* **~s, hooves** [~vz]) kopyto *n*

hook [huk] **1.** ha(cz)yk *m*; **2.** zahaczać ⟨-czyć⟩, zaczepi(a)ć

hooligan ['hu:lɪɡən] chuligan *m*

hoot [hu:t] ⟨za⟩trąbić; ⟨za⟩hukać

hoover ['hu:və] *TM often* 2 **1.** odkurzacz *m*; **2.** odkurzać ⟨-rzyć⟩ odkurzaczem

hop¹ [hɒp] **1.** *v/t* przeskakiwać ⟨-koczyć⟩; *v/i* skakać ⟨skoczyć⟩; **2.** (pod)skok *m*

hop² [~] chmiel *m*

hope [həup] **1.** mieć nadzieję (*for* na); *I* ~ *so* mam nadzieję, że tak; **2.** nadzieja *f*; **~ful** pełen nadziei; (*promising*) obiecujący; **~fully** z nadzieją; (*spicy*) ostry

horizon [hə'raɪzn] horyzont *m*; **~tal** [hɒrɪ'zɒntl] poziomy, horyzontalny

horn [hɔ:n] *a. mus.* róg *m*; *mot.* klakson *m*

horoscope ['hɒrəskəup] horoskop *m*

horr|ible ['hɒrəbl] straszny, okropny; (*promising*) **~ify** ['~ɪfaɪ] przerażać ⟨-razić⟩; **~or** prze-

rażenie *n*, groza *f*

horse [hɔ:s] koń *m*; **~back: on ~back** na koniu, konno; **~power** koń *m* mechaniczny; **~ race** wyścigi *pl* konne; **~radish** chrzan *m*; **~shoe** podkowa *f*

hose [həuz] wąż *m* (strażacki *itp.*)

hospitable ['hɒspɪtəbl] gościnny

hospital ['hɒspɪtl] szpital *m*

hospitality [hɒspɪ'tælətɪ] gościnność *f*

host [həust] gospodarz *m*, pan *m* domu

hostage ['hɒstɪdʒ] zakładnik *m*

hostel ['hɒstl] *esp. Brt.* dom *m* akademicki, internat *m*; *mst* **youth ~** schronisko *n* młodzieżowe

hostess ['həustɪs] gospodyni *f*, pani *f* domu; *aer.* (*a.* **air ~**) stewardesa *f*

hostile ['hɒstaɪl] wrogi; **~ity** [~'stɪlətɪ] wrogość *f*

hot [hɒt] gorący; (*spicy*) ostry

hotel [həu'tel] hotel *m*

hot|house cieplarnia *f*; **~spot** *esp. pol.* punkt *m* zapalny

hour ['auə] godzina *f*; **~ly** godzinny

house [haus] **1.** (*pl* **houses** ['~zɪz]) dom *m*; **2.** [~z] zapewni(a)ć schronienie, umieszczać ⟨umieścić⟩; **~breaking** włamanie *n*; **~hold** domownicy *pl*; **~keeper**

właściciel *m* (domu), najemca *m*; '**~keeping** gospodarstwo *n* domowe, gospodarowanie *n*; ♀ **of Commons** *Brt. parl.* Izba *f* Gmin; ♀ **of Lords** *Brt. parl.* Izba *f* Lordów; ♀ **of Representatives** *Am. parl.* Izba *f* Reprezentantów; '**~wife** (*pl* -**wives**) gospodyni *f* domowa

hover ['hɒvə] unosić się w powietrzu; '**~craft** (*pl* ~(**s**)) poduszkowiec *m*

how [hau] jak; ~ **are you?** jak się masz?; ~ **about ...?** a może by tak...?; ~ **much/many?** ile?; ~ **much is it?** ile to kosztuje?; ~**ever** jakkolwiek; jednakże

howl [haul] **1.** wycie *n*, ryk *m*; **2.** ⟨za⟩wyć

hug [hʌg] **1.** ⟨przy⟩tulić; **2.** uścisk *m*

huge [hjuːdʒ] ogromny

human ['hjuːmən] **1.** *adj* ludzki, człowieczy; **2.** (*a.* ~ **being**) człowiek *m*, istota *f* ludzka; **~e** [~'meɪn] humanitarny; **~itarian** [~mænɪ'teərɪən] działacz *m* na rzecz dobra ludzkości; **~ity** [~'mænəti] człowieczeństwo *n*; ludzkość *f*

humble ['hʌmbl] **1.** pokorny, uniżony; **2.** upokarzać ⟨~korzyć⟩

humid ['hjuːmɪd] wilgotny; **~ity** [~'mɪdətɪ] wilgotność *f*

humiliat|e [hjuː'mɪlɪeɪt] poniżać ⟨~żyć⟩; **~ion** [~mɪlɪ'eɪʃn] poniżenie *n*

humility [hjuː'mɪlətɪ] pokora *f*

humo(u)r ['hjuːmə] **1.** humor *m*; **2.** pobłażać, dogadzać ⟨~godzić⟩

hump [hʌmp] garb *m*; '**~back** garb *m*; *contp.* (*person*) garbus *m*

hunch [hʌntʃ] **1.** → *hump*; przeczucie *n*; **2.** ⟨z⟩garbić; '**~back** garb *m*

hundred ['hʌndrəd] sto

hung [hʌŋ] *past and pp of* **hang**

Hungar|ian [hʌŋ'geərɪən] **1.** *adj* węgierski; **2.** Węgier(ka *f*) *m*; **~y** Węgry *pl*

hunger ['hʌŋgə] **1.** głód *m* (*a. fig.*); **2.** *fig.* łaknąć, pożądać (**for**/**after** *s.th.* czegoś)

hungry ['hʌŋgrɪ] głodny

hunt [hʌnt] **1.** polować; **2.** polowanie *n*, (*search*) poszukiwanie *n*; '**~er** myśliwy *m*; '**~ing** polowanie *n*, łowiectwo *n*

hurdle ['hɜːdl] płotek *m*; *fig.* przeszkoda *f*; ~ **race** *sp.* bieg *m* przez płotki

hurl [hɜːl] ciskać ⟨~snąć⟩

hurricane ['hʌrɪkən] huragan *m*

hurried ['hʌrɪd] pośpieszny

hurry ['hʌrɪ] **1.** *v/t* dostarczać ⟨~czyć⟩, spiesznie przywozić ⟨~wieźć⟩; *often* ~ **up** przyspieszyć ⟨~szać⟩, ponaglać ⟨~glić⟩; *v/i* spieszyć się; ~ **up!** pospiesz się!; **2.** pośpiech *m*

hurt [hɜːt] (**hurt**) *v/t* ⟨z⟩ranić;

⟨s⟩kaleczyć; *fig.* urazić; *v/i* boleć

husband ['hʌzbənd] mąż *m*

hush [hʌʃ] **1.** *int* cicho!; **2.** uciszać ⟨-szyć⟩, uspokajać ⟨-koić⟩; ~ *up* ⟨za⟩tuszować; **3.** cisza *f*

husky ['hʌskɪ] *voice*: ochrypły

hut [hʌt] chata *f*

hydraulic [haɪ'drɔːlɪk] hydrauliczny; ~**s** *sg* hydraulika *f*

hydro... [haɪdrəʊ] hydro..., wodno...; ~**carbon** węglowodór *m*; ~**foil** wodolot *m*

hydrogen ['haɪdrədʒən] wodór *m*; ~ **bomb** bomba *f* wodorowa

hyena [haɪ'iːnə] hiena *f*

hygien|e ['haɪdʒiːn] higiena *f*; ~**ic** [~'dʒiːnɪk] higieniczny

hyper... [haɪpə] nad..., hiper...; ~**market** *Brt.* megasam *m*; ~**tension** nadciśnienie *n*

hyphen ['haɪfn] *gr.* łącznik *m*

hypno|sis [hɪp'nəʊsɪs] (*pl* -ses [~siːz]) hipnoza *f*; ~**tize** ['~nətaɪz] ⟨za⟩hipnotyzować

hypo|crisy [hɪ'pɒkrəsɪ] obłuda *f*, hipokryzja *f*; ~**crite** ['hɪpəkrɪt] obłudnik *m*, hipokryta *m*; ~**critical** [~əʊ'krɪtɪkl] dwulicowy, obłudny

hypothesis [haɪ'pɒθɪsɪs] (*pl* -ses [~siːz]) hipoteza *f*

hysteri|a [hɪ'stɪərɪə] histeria *f*; ~**cal** [~'sterɪkl] histeryczny; ~**cs** [~'sterɪks] *mst sg* histeria *f*

I

I [aɪ] ja

ice [aɪs] **1.** lód *m*; **2.** oziębia(ć)ć; *mst* ~ *up* or *over* zamarzać ⟨-znąć⟩; ~**berg** ['~bɜːg] góra *f* lodowa; ~**breaker** *mar.* lodołamacz *m*; ~ **cream** lody *pl*; ~**d** mrożony; ~ **hockey** hokej *m* na lodzie; ~ **rink** (sztuczne) lodowisko *n*

icy ['aɪsɪ] *a. fig.* lodowaty

idea [aɪ'dɪə] pomysł *m*; (*conception*) pojęcie *n*, idea *f*; (*guess*) wrażenie *n*, przeświadczenie *n*

ideal [aɪ'dɪəl] idealny

identical [aɪ'dentɪkl] identyczny, taki sam (**to**, **with** jak); ~ **twins** *pl* bliźnięta *pl* jednojajowe

identi|fication [aɪdentɪfɪ'keɪʃn] identyfikacja *f*; ~ (*papers pl*) dowód *m* tożsamości; ~**fy** [~'dentɪfaɪ] rozpozna(wa)ć; ~**fy o.s.** ⟨wy⟩legitymować się

identity [aɪ'dentətɪ] tożsamość *f*; ~ **card** dowód *m* tożsamości

ideology [aɪdɪ'ɒlədʒɪ] ideologia *f*

idiom ['ɪdɪəm] idiom *m*

idiot ['ɪdɪət] idiota *m*; **~ic** [~'ɒtɪk] idiotyczny

idle ['aɪdl] **1.** bezczynny; (*lazy*) leniwy; *talk*: czczy; *tech.* jałowy; **2.** próżnować; *tech.* chodzić na wolnych obrotach; *mst* **~ away time** ⟨z⟩marnować czas

if [ɪf] jeśli, jeżeli; *~* **I were you** gdybym był na twoim miejscu

ignit|e [ɪg'naɪt] *v/i* zapalać ⟨-lić⟩ się; *v/t* zapalać ⟨-lić⟩; **~ion** [~'nɪʃn] zapłon *m*; **~ion key** kluczyk *m* (zapłonu)

ignor|ance ['ɪgnərəns] ignorancja *f*, nieznajomość *f* (*of s.th.* czegoś); **~ant** nieuczony, ciemny; nieświadomy; **~e** [~'nɔː] ⟨z⟩ignorować

ill [ɪl] **1.** *adj* (*unwell*) chory; (*bad*) zły; *fall* **~, be taken ~** zachorować; *→* **ease; 2.** *often pl* nieszczęście *n*, zło *n*; **~-advised** nierozważny, nierozsądny; **~-bred** grubiański, źle wychowany

illegal [ɪ'liːgl] nielegalny, bezprawny

il'legible [ɪ'ledʒəbl] nieczytelny

illegitimate [ɪlɪ'dʒɪtɪmət] nieprawny; *child*: nieślubny

illiterate [ɪ'lɪtərət] niepiśmienny

ill-'mannered [ɪl'mænəd] niegrzeczny, grubiański; **~'natured** złośliwy

'illness choroba *f*

ill-'tempered [ɪl'tempəd] zły, złośliwy

illuminat|e [ɪ'luːmɪneɪt] oświetlać ⟨-lić⟩; **~ion** [~'neɪʃn] oświetlenie *n*

illus|ion [ɪ'luːʒn] złudzenie *n*, iluzja *f*; **~ive** [~sɪv], **~ory** [~sərɪ] złudny, iluzoryczny

illustrat|e ['ɪləstreɪt] ⟨z⟩ilustrować; **~ion** [~'streɪʃn] ilustracja *f*

image ['ɪmɪdʒ] wizerunek *m*, podobizna *f*; (*reflection*) odbicie *n*; (*conception*) wyobrażenie *n*

imagin|able [ɪ'mædʒɪnəbl] wyobrażalny; **~ary** urojony, zmyślony; **~ation** [~'neɪʃn] wyobraźnia *f*, fantazja *f*; **~ative** [ɪ'mædʒɪnətɪv] obdarzony wyobraźnią; **~e** [~ɪn] wyobrażać ⟨-brazić⟩ sobie; (*suppose*) przypuszczać

imitat|e ['ɪmɪteɪt] naśladować; **~ion** [~'teɪʃn] naśladownictwo *n*; imitacja *f*

immature [ɪmə'tjʊə] niedojrzały

immediate [ɪ'miːdjət] natychmiastowy; (*near*) bezpośredni; *family etc.*: najbliższy; **~ly** natychmiast; (*directly*) bezpośrednio; (*when*) skoro, jak tylko

immense [ɪ'mens] ogromny

immerse [ɪ'mɜːs] zanurzać ⟨-rzyć⟩; *~* **o.s.** zagłębia(ć)ć się (*in s.th.* w czymś)

immigra|nt ['ɪmɪgrənt] imigrant(ka *f*) *m*; **~te** [~eɪt] imigrować; **~tion** [~'greɪʃn] imigracja *f*

imminent ['ɪmɪnənt] nadciągający, bliski

immoral amoralny, niemoralny

immortal nieśmiertelny

immun|e [ɪˈmjuːn] *a. med.* odporny (*to* na); **~ity** odporność *f*

impact [ˈɪmpækt] uderzenie *n*, zderzenie *n*; *fig.* wpływ *m*

impair [ɪmˈpeə] osłabi(a)ć, nadwerężać ⟨-żyć⟩

im'partial bezstronny

impatien|ce niecierpliwość *f*; **~t** niecierpliwy

imped|e [ɪmˈpiːd] ⟨za⟩hamować, utrudni(a)ć; **~iment** [~ˈpedɪmənt] przeszkoda *f*, utrudnienie *n*

imperative [ɪmˈperətɪv] **1.** *adj* naglący, konieczny; **2.** *gr.* tryb *m* rozkazujący

imperfect [ɪmˈpɜːfɪkt] niedoskonały, wadliwy; *gr.* niedokonany

im'peril narażać ⟨-razić⟩ na niebezpieczeństwo

impersona|l bezosobowy; **~te** [ɪmˈpɜːsənet] uosabiać ⟨-sobić⟩; wcielać ⟨-lić⟩ się (**s.o.** w kogoś)

impertinen|ce [ɪmˈpɜːtɪnəns] impertynencja *f*; **~t** impertynencki

implant [ɪmˈplɑːnt] med. wszczepi(a)ć; **2.** [ˈ~] wszczep *m*

implement [ˈɪmplɪmənt] narzędzie *n*

implicat|e [ˈɪmplɪkeɪt] wpląt(yw)ać; **~ion** [~ˈkeɪʃn]

implikacja *f*

implicit [ɪmˈplɪsɪt] ukryty; (*unquestioning*) bezwarunkowy

implore [ɪmˈplɔː] błagać (*for* o)

imply [ɪmˈplaɪ] sugerować, implikować

impolite [ɪmpəˈlaɪt] niegrzeczny, nieuprzejmy

import 1. [ɪmˈpɔːt] importować; **2.** [ˈ~] import *m*; (*commodity*) towar *m* importowany

importan|ce [ɪmˈpɔːtns] znaczenie *n*, ważność *f*; **~t** ważny

importer [ɪmˈpɔːtə] importer *m*

impos|e [ɪmˈpəʊz] *v/t* narzucać ⟨-cić⟩, nakładać ⟨nałożyć⟩; *v/i* **~e on s.o.** narzucać się komuś; **~ing** okazały, imponujący

impossible niemożliwy

impoten|ce [ˈɪmpətəns] niedolność *f*; *med.* impotencja *f*; **~t** nieudolny; *med.* cierpiący na impotencję

impoverish [ɪmˈpɒvərɪʃ] zubożać ⟨-żyć⟩

im'practicable niewykonalny

impregnate [ˈɪmpregneɪt] impregnować

impress [ɪmˈpres] ⟨za⟩imponować, wywierać ⟨-wrzeć⟩ wrażenie; (*press*) odciskać ⟨-snąć⟩; **~ s.o.** zwracać ⟨-rócić⟩ czyjąś uwagę (*with s.th.* na coś); **~ion** [~ˈpreʃn] wrażenie n; (imprint) odcisk m; **~ive** [~'presɪv] imponujący

imprint 1. [ɪm'prɪnt] odciskać ⟨-snąć⟩; **2.** ['~] odcisk m

imprison [ɪm'prɪzn] uwięzić; **~ment** uwięzienie n

im'probable nieprawdopodobny

im'proper niewłaściwy, niestosowny

improve [ɪm'pruːv] ulepszać ⟨-pszyć⟩, udoskonalać ⟨-lić⟩; **~ment** ulepszenie n, udoskonalenie n; poprawa f

improvise ['ɪmprəvaɪz] improwizować

impudent ['ɪmpjʊdənt] bezczelny, zuchwały

impuls|e ['ɪmpʌls] impuls m, odruch m; (urge) bodziec m; **~ive** [~'pʌlsɪv] impulsywny

in [ɪn] **1.** prp (within) w, we, na; **~ London** w Londynie; **~ the street** na ulicy; (into) do; **put it ~ your pocket** włóż to do kieszeni; time: za, w; **~ two hours** za dwie godziny; **~ a week** za tydzień; **one ~ ten** jeden na dziesięć; **~ (the year) 1999** w r. 1999; **~ a week** za tydzień; (by means of) **~ ink** atramentem; **~ English** po angielsku; **dressed ~ blue** ubrana na niebiesko; **~ my opinion** w mojej opinii; **~ Shakespeare** u Szekspira; **three ~ all** razem trzy; **one ~ ten** jeden na dziesięć; **2.** adv w środku, do środka; **3.** adj F modny, w modzie

inability niezdolność f

inaccessible [ɪnæk'sesəbl] niedostępny

in'accurate niedokładny, nieścisły

in'active nieczynny

in'adequate nieodpowiedni

inappropriate nieodpowiedni, niewłaściwy

in'apt niestosowny

inaugural [ɪ'nɔːɡjʊrəl] inauguracyjny; **~te** [~eɪt] ⟨za⟩inaugurować

inborn [ɪn'bɔːn] wrodzony

in'capable niezdolny

incapaci|tate [ɪnkə'pæsɪteɪt] ⟨u⟩czynić niezdolnym; **~ty** niezdolność f

incentive [ɪn'sentɪv] bodziec m

incessant [ɪn'sesnt] nieustanny

incest ['ɪnsest] kazirodztwo n

inch [ɪntʃ] cal m (2,54 cm)

incident ['ɪnsɪdənt] incydent m, zajście n; **~al** [~'dentl] przypadkowy; **~ally** nawiasem mówiąc

incis|e [ɪn'saɪz] nacinać ⟨-ciąć⟩; **~ion** [~'sɪʒn] nacięcie n; **~ive** [~'saɪsɪv] dobitny; **~or** [~'saɪzə] anat. siekacz m

inclin|ation [ɪnklɪ'neɪʃn] skłonność f; (slope) stok m; **~e** [~'klaɪn] **1.** schylać ⟨-lić⟩; fig. skłaniać się; **2.** stok m

inclu|de [ɪn'kluːd] zawierać, obejmować; list: włączać ⟨-czyć⟩; **tax ~ded** z podatkiem; **~ding** włączając, łącznie; **~sive of...** łącznie z...

income ['ıŋkʌm] dochód *m*; **~ tax** ['~ɔmtæks] podatek *m* dochodowy

incompatible niezgodny

incompeten|ce nieudolność *f*, brak *m* kompetencji; **~t** nieudolny, niekompetentny

incomplete niekompletny, niezupełny

incomprehensible niezrozumiały

inconsiderable nieznaczny

inconsiderate bezmyślny

inconsistent niezgodny, sprzeczny

inconspicuous niezauważalny

inconvenien|ce 1. niewygoda *f*, kłopot *m*; **2.** sprawi(a)ć kłopot; **~t** niewygodny

incorporate 1. [ın'kɔ:pəreıt] włączać ⟨-czyć⟩, zawierać ⟨-wrzeć⟩; **2.** [~rət] *adj* → **~d** [~'reıtıd] *econ., jur.* zarejestrowany

incorrect niepoprawny, nieprawidłowy

increas|e 1. [ın'kri:s] *v/t* zwiększać ⟨-kszyć⟩; *prices* podnosić ⟨-dnieść⟩; *v/i* wzrastać ⟨-rosnąć⟩; **2.** ['ıŋkri:s] wzrost *m*; **~ingly** coraz bardziej

incredible niewiarygodny, niesamowity

in'curable nieuleczalny

indeed [ın'di:d] **1.** *adv* fak-

tycznie, naprawdę; **2.** *int* czyżby?, doprawdy?

indefinable niedokreślony, trudny do określenia

indefinite [ın'defınət] nieokreślony; **~ly** na czas nieokreślony

in'delicate niedelikatny, nietaktowny

independen|ce niepodległość *f*, niezależność *f*; **~t** niepodległy, niezależny

indeterminate [~'tɜ:mınət] nieokreślony

index ['ındeks] (*pl* -dexes, -dices ['~dısi:z]) indeks *m*; *math.* wykładnik *m*; **card ~** katalog *m*; **~ finger** palec *m* wskazujący

Indian ['ındjən] **1.** *adj from India:* hinduski; *from America:* indiański; **2.** *from India:* Hindus *m*; *from America:* Indianin *m*; **~ corn** kukurydza *f*; **~ summer** babie lato *n*

indicat|e ['ındıkeıt] wskaz(yw)ać; *mot.* mrugać (kierunkowskazem); **~ion** [~'keıʃn] wskazówka *f*, znak *m*; **~or** ['~dıkeıtə] *tech.* wskaźnik *m* (*a. fig.*); *mot.* kierunkowskaz *m*

indices ['ındısi:z] *pl* → **index**

indifferen|ce obojętność *f*; **~t** obojętny

indigestible niestrawny; **~ion** niestrawność *f*

indign|ant [ın'dıgnənt] oburzony; **~ation** [~'neıʃn] oburzenie *n*

in|dignity upokorzenie n; **~direct** pośredni

indis|creet niedyskretny; (*incautious*) nierozważny; **~cretion** niedyskrecja f; nierozwaga f

indispensable nieodzowny, konieczny

indispos|ed niedysponowany; **~ition** niedyspozycja f

indisputable bezsporny

individual [ɪndɪˈvɪdʒʊəl] **1.** poszczególny, odrębny; (*distinctive*) osobisty; **2.** osobnik m, jednostka f; **~ly** pojedyńczo, osobno

indolen|ce [ˈɪndələns] opieszałość f, lenistwo n; **~t** opieszały, leniwy

indoor [ˈɪndɔː] domowy; *pool:* kryty; *sp.* halowy; **~s** [-ˈdɔːz] (*inside*) pod dachem, w domu; (*into*) do środka

induce [ɪnˈdjuːs] skłaniać ⟨-łonić⟩

indulge [ɪnˈdʌldʒ] pobłażać; *whim etc.* zaspokajać ⟨-koić⟩; **~ in s.th.** pozwalać ⟨-wolić⟩ sobie na coś; **~nce** pobłażanie n; *self* pobłażliwy

industrial [ɪnˈdʌstrɪəl] przemysłowy; **~ estate** Brt., **~ park** Am. dzielnica f przemysłowa; **~ist** przemysłowiec m; **~ize** uprzemysławiać ⟨-słowić⟩

industri|ous [ɪnˈdʌstrɪəs] pracowity; **~y** [ˈɪndəstrɪ] przemysł m; (*diligence*) pracowitość f

in|effective, **~effectual** [ɪnɪˈfektʃʊəl] nieskuteczny

inefficient nieefektywny

inept [ɪˈnept] niestosowny; nieudolny

inestimable [ɪnˈestɪməbl] nieoceniony

inevitable [ɪnˈevɪtəbl] nieuchronny

inexpensive niedrogi

inexperienced niedoświadczony

infan|cy [ˈɪnfənsɪ] niemowlęctwo n; **~t** niemowlę n, (małe) dziecko n; **~tile** [ˈ-aɪl] infantylny

infantry [ˈɪnfntrɪ] *mil.* piechota f

infect [ɪnˈfekt] *food* zakażać ⟨-kazić⟩; *disease:* zarażać ⟨-razić⟩ (*a. fig.*); **~ion** [ˌ-kʃn] zakażenie n, infekcja f; **~ious** zakaźny

inferior [ɪnˈfɪərɪə] **1.** gorszy, niższy (*to* niż); *be* **~ to s.o.** ustępować komuś; **2.** podwładny m; **~ity** [ˌ-ˈɒrətɪ] niższość f

infertile [ɪnˈfɜːtaɪl] *soil:* nieurodzajny; *person:* bezpłodny

infidelity niewierność f

infinit|e [ˈɪnfɪnət] nieskończony; **~ive** [ˌ-ˈnɪtɪv] *gr.* bezokolicznik m; **~y** [ˌ-ətɪ] nieskończoność f

infirm [ɪnˈfɜːm] niedołężny; **~ary** szpital m; **~ity** niedołęstwo n

inflame [ɪnˈfleɪm] rozpalać ⟨-lić⟩

inflamma|ble [ɪn'flæməbl] (łatwo) palny; **~tion** [~'meɪʃn] med. zapalenie n

inflat|able [ɪn'fleɪtəbl] nadmuchiwany; **~e** [~eɪt] nadmuch(iw)ać; tyres etc. napompo(wy)wać; prices śrubować F; **~ion** econ. inflacja f

inflict [ɪn'flɪkt] narzucać ⟨-cić⟩ (s.th. on/upon sth. coś komuś); pain za-da(wa)ć; penalty nakładać ⟨nałożyć⟩

influen|ce ['ɪnfluəns] 1. wpływ m; 2. wpływać ⟨-lynąć⟩ na; **~tial** [~'enʃl] wpływowy

influenza [ɪnflu'enzə] grypa f

inform [ɪn'fɔːm] ⟨po⟩informować, zawiadamiać ⟨-domić⟩ (of, about o); **~ against/on** s.o. donosić ⟨-nieść⟩ na kogoś

informal [ɪn'fɔːml] nieoficjalny, nieformalny

inform|ation [ɪnfə'meɪʃn] informacja f, wiadomość f; **~ation technology** informatyka f, **~ative** [~'fɔːmətɪv] pouczający; **~er** informator m

infrared [ɪnfrə'red] tech. podczerwony

infrequent [ɪn'friːkwənt] rzadki

ingen|ious [ɪn'dʒiːnjəs] pomysłowy; **~uity** [~dʒɪ'njuːɪtɪ] pomysłowość f

ingratitude niewdzięczność f

ingredient [ɪn'griːdjənt] składnik m

inhabit [ɪn'hæbɪt] mieszkać, zamieszkiwać; **~ant** mieszkaniec m

inhale [ɪn'heɪl] wdychać; cigarette: zaciągać ⟨-gnąć⟩ się

inherent [ɪn'hɪərənt] nieodłączny

inherit [ɪn'herɪt] ⟨o⟩dziedziczyć; **~ance** spadek m

inhibit [ɪn'hɪbɪt] powstrzymywać; **~ion** [~'bɪʃn] psych. zahamowanie n

inhuman [ɪn'hjuːmən] nieludzki; **~e** [~'meɪn] niehumanitarny

initial [ɪ'nɪʃl] 1. adj początkowy, wstępny; 2. inicjał m; 3. parafować; **~ly** [~ʃəlɪ] początkowo

initiat|e [ɪ'nɪʃɪeɪt] zapoczątkow(yw)ać, ⟨za⟩inicjować; (give knowledge) wtajemniczać ⟨-czyć⟩ (into w); **~ion** [~'eɪʃn] inicjacja f, (start) zapoczątkowanie n; **~ive** [ɪ'nɪʃɪətɪv] inicjatywa f

inject [ɪn'dʒekt] med., tech. wtryskiwać ⟨-snąć⟩; **~ion** [~kʃn] med. zastrzyk m; tech. wtrysk m

injur|e [ɪn'dʒə] a. fig. ⟨z⟩ranić; **~ed** 1. adj zraniony; fig. urażony; 2. ranny m; **~y** ['~ərɪ] uraz m, kontuzja f

injustice niesprawiedliwość f

ink [ɪŋk] atrament m

inland 1. ['ɪnlænd] adj krajowy, śródlądowy; 2 Revenue

Brt. urząd *m* skarbowy; **2.** [ˈlænd] *adv* w głąb kraju, w głębi kraju

inmost [ˈɪnməʊst] najbliższy, najgłębiej położony; *fig.* najskrytszy

inn [ɪn] gospoda *f*

innate [ɪˈneɪt] wrodzony

inner [ˈɪnə] wewnętrzny; **'~most → inmost**

innocen|ce [ˈɪnəsəns] niewinność *f*; **~t** [ˌsnt] niewinny

innovation [ɪnəʊˈveɪʃn] innowacja *f*

innumerable [ɪˈnjuːmərəbl] niezliczony

inoculat|e [ɪˈnɒkjʊleɪt] ⟨za⟩szczepić; **~ion** [ˌleɪʃn] szczepienie *n*

¹input 1. *econ.* wkład *m; computer:* wejście *n; (data)* dane *pl* wejściowe; **2.** (*-putted* or *-put*); *computer:* wprowadzać ⟨-dzić⟩ dane

inquir|e [ɪnˈkwaɪə] dowiadywać się, pytać; badać (*into s.th.* coś); **~y** [ˌrɪ] zapytanie *n*, zasięganie *n* informacji; *(investigation)* dochodzenie *n*

insane [ɪnˈseɪn] obłąkany, szalony

insanity obłęd *m*

inscription [ɪnˈskrɪpʃn] napis *m*

insect [ˈɪnsekt] owad *m;* **~icide** [ˌsektɪsaɪd] środek *m* owadobójczy

insecure niepewny

inseminate [ɪnˈsemɪneɪt] zapładniać ⟨-łodnić⟩

insensi|ble *(senseless)* nieprzytomny; *(insensitive)* nieczuły (*to* na); **~tive** niewrażliwy (*to* na); *(uncaring)* nieczuły

insert [ɪnˈsɜːt] wkładać ⟨włożyć⟩, umieszczać ⟨umieścić⟩; **2.** [ˈ.sɜːt] wkładka *f*

inside 1. [ɪnˈsaɪd, ˈɪnsaɪd] wnętrze *n; turn ~ out* wywracać ⟨-wrócić⟩ na drugą stronę; **2.** [ˈ~] *adj* wewnętrzny; *information etc.:* poufny; **3.** [ˌˈsaɪd] *adv* wewnątrz, w środku; do wewnątrz, do środka; **4.** [ˌˈsaɪd] *prp* w, do; **~ the house** w domu

insight [ˈɪnsaɪt] wgląd *m* (*into* w)

insignificant znikomy, nieistotny

insincere nieszczery

insist [ɪnˈsɪst] nalegać (*on* na); upierać się (*on* przy); **~ent** uporczywy

inspect [ɪnˈspekt] ⟨z⟩badać; *troops* dokon(yw)ać przeglądu; **~ion** [ˌkʃn] inspekcja *f*, badanie *n*; **~or** *a. police:* inspektor *m*

inspir|ation [ɪnspəˈreɪʃn] natchnienie *n*, inspiracja *f*; **~e** [ˌˈspaɪə] natchnąć ⟨za⟩inspirować

instal(l) [ɪnˈstɔːl] *tech.* ⟨za⟩instalować; **~ation** [ˌleɪʃn] *tech.* instalacja *f; tech.* urządzenie *n*

instal(l)ment [ɪn'stɔːlmənt] *econ.* rata *f*; *story*: odcinek *m*; ~ **plan**: **on/by the ~ plan** *Am.* na raty

instance ['ɪnstəns] przykład; **for ~** na przykład

instant ['ɪnstənt] **1.** moment *m*, chwila *f*; **2.** *adj* natychmiastowy; *food*: błyskawiczny; ~ **camera** natychmiast aparat *fotograficzny*; ~ **coffee** kawa *f* rozpuszczalna; '**~ly** natychmiast

instead [ɪn'sted] zamiast (*of s.th.* czegoś)

instinct ['ɪnstɪŋkt] instynkt *m*; **~ive** [~'stɪŋktɪv] instynktowny

institute ['ɪnstɪtjuːt] **1.** zakładać ⟨założyć⟩; **2.** instytut *m*; **~ion** [~'tjuːʃn] instytucja *f*, zakład *m*

instruct [ɪn'strʌkt] ⟨po⟩instruować; polecić; **~ion** [~kʃn] szkolenie *n*; instrukcja *f*; polecenie *n*; **~s** *pl* **for use** instrukcja *f* obsługi; **~ive** pouczający; **~or** instruktor *m*

instrument ['ɪnstrʊmənt] narzędzie *n*, przyrząd *m*; *mus.* instrument *m*

insubordinate nieposłuszny

insufficient niewystarczający

insulate ['ɪnsjʊleɪt] *electr.*, *tech.* izolować; **~ion** [~'leɪʃn] *electr.*, *tech.* izolacja *f*

insult 1. [ɪn'sʌlt] znieważać ⟨~żyć⟩; **2.** ['~] zniewaga *f*

insurance [ɪn'ʃɔːrəns] *econ.* ubezpieczenie *n*; **~ance agent**

agent *m* ubezpieczeniowy; **~ance company** towarzystwo *n* ubezpieczeniowe; **~ance policy** polisa *f* ubezpieczeniowa; **~e** [~'ʃɔː] ubezpieczać ⟨-czyć⟩; **~ed** (*pl* ~ed) ubezpieczony *m*

intact [ɪn'tækt] nietknięty, nienaruszony

integrity [ɪn'tegrətɪ] prawość *f*

intellect ['ɪntəlekt] intelekt *m*; **~ual** [~'lektjʊəl] **1.** *adj* intelektualny; **2.** *s* intelektualista *m*

intelligence [ɪn'telɪdʒəns] inteligencja *f*; (*information*) informacje *pl* (wywiadu); (*a.* **~ence service**) wywiad *m*; **~ent** inteligentny; **~ible** zrozumiały

intend [ɪn'tend] zamierzać; przeznaczać ⟨-czyć⟩

intensle [ɪn'tens] silny; *person*: poważny; **~ify** [~sɪfaɪ] wzmacniać ⟨-mocnić⟩; **~ity** intensywność *f*; **~ive** intensywny; **~ive care unit** oddział *m* intensywnej terapii

intent [ɪn'tent] **1.** zamiar *m*, intencja *f*; **2.** *adj* skupiony; **be ~ on doing s.th.** być zdecydowanym na zrobienie czegoś; **~ion** zamiar *m*; **~ional** umyślny

intercede [ɪntə'siːd] wstawi(a)ć się (*for s.o. with s.o.* za kimś u kogoś)

intercept [~'sept] przechwytywać ⟨-cić⟩

intercession [~'seʃn] wstawiennictwo *n*

interchange 1. [ɪntə'tʃeɪndʒ] wymieni(a)ć; **2.** ['\~] wymiana f; mot. bezkolizyjne skrzyżowanie n

intercourse ['ɪntəkɔːs] (a. **sexual** \~) stosunek m płciowy

interest ['ɪntrɪst] **1.** zainteresowanie n; econ. procent m; (share) udział m; **take an** \~ **in s.th.** ⟨za⟩interesować się czymś; **2.** ⟨za⟩interesować (**in s.th.** czymś); '\~ed zainteresowany (**in s.th.** czymś); **be** \~**ed** interesować się (**in s.th.** czymś); '\~**ing** interesujący; \~ **rate** stopa f procentowa

interfere [ɪntə'fɪə] wtrącać ⟨-cić⟩ się; \~ **with** przeszkadzać ⟨-kodzić⟩; zakłócać ⟨-cić⟩; \~**nce** [\~'fɪərəns] mieszanie n się; tech. zakłócenia pl

interior [ɪn'tɪərɪə] **1.** adj wewnętrzny; **2.** wnętrze n; \~ **department**; \~ **decorator** (a. \~ **designer**) dekorator m wnętrz

interjection [ɪntə'dʒekʃn] gr. wykrzyknik m

intermedia|ry [ɪntə'miːdjərɪ] pośrednik m; mediator m; \~**te** [\~jət] pośredni

internal [ɪn'tɜːnl] wewnętrzny; \~**combustion engine** silnik m spalinowy; ♀ **Revenue** Am. urząd m skarbowy; \~**ly** wewnętrznie

international [ɪntə'næʃənl] międzynarodowy

interpret [ɪn'tɜːprɪt] tłuma-

czyć; \~**ation** [\~'teɪʃn] mus. etc. interpretacja f; (explanation) tłumaczenie n; \~**er** [\~'tɜːprɪtə] tłumacz m

interrogat|e [ɪn'terəgeɪt] przesłuch(iw)ać; \~**ion** [\~'geɪʃn] przesłuchanie n; \~**ion mark** → **question mark**

interrupt [ɪntə'rʌpt] prze-r(y)wać; \~**ion** [\~pʃn] przerwa f, przerwanie n

intersect [ɪntə'sekt] przecinać ⟨-ciąć⟩ się; \~**ion** [\~kʃn] przecięcie n; mot. skrzyżowanie n

interval ['ɪntəvl] przerwa f; Brt. antrakt m; mus. interwał m

interven|e [ɪntə'viːn] interweniować; ⟨w⟩mieszać się; \~**tion** [\~'venʃn] interwencja f

interview ['ɪntəvjuː] **1.** wywiad m; **2.** przeprowadzać ⟨-dzić⟩ wywiad; '\~**er** osoba f przeprowadzająca wywiad

intestine [ɪn'testɪn] jelito n; **large/small** \~ jelito n grube/cienkie

intima|cy ['ɪntɪməsɪ] intymność f; poufałość f, zażyłość f; \~**te** [\~ət] intymny; friend etc.: bliski; knowledge: dogłębny

intimidate [ɪn'tɪmɪdeɪt] zastraszać ⟨-szyć⟩

into ['ɪntʊ] prp do; w; na

intoler|able [ɪn'tɒlərəbl] nieznośny; \~**ant** nietolerancyjny

intricate ['ɪntrɪkət] zawiły

intrigue [ɪn'triːg] **1.** ⟨za⟩intrygować, zaciekawi(a)ć; **2.** intryga f

introduc|e [ɪntrə'djuːs] wprowadzać ⟨-dzić⟩; przedstawi(a)ć; **~tion** [~'dʌkʃn] wprowadzenie n; przedstawienie n; *book etc.*: wstęp m

intru|de [ɪn'truːd] niepokoić (*on s.o.* komuś); przeszkadzać (*on s.o.* komuś); **~der** intruz m

invade [ɪn'veɪd] dokon(yw)ać inwazji, najeżdżać ⟨-jechać⟩; **~r** najeźdźca m

invalid¹ ['ɪnvəlɪd] **1.** inwalida m; **2.** adj chory, kaleki

invalid² [ɪn'vælɪd] adj *passport etc.*: nieważny

invaluable nieoceniony, bezcenny

invariab|le niezmienny, stały; **~ly** niezmiennie; zawsze

invasion [ɪn'veɪʒn] inwazja f

invent [ɪn'vent] wynaleźć; wymyślać ⟨-lić⟩; **~ion** wynalazek m; **~ive** pomysłowy; **~or** wynalazca m

invert [ɪn'vɜːt] odwracać ⟨-rócić⟩; **~ed commas** pl cudzysłów m

invest [ɪn'vest] ⟨za⟩inwestować

investigat|e [ɪn'vestɪgeɪt] ⟨z⟩badać; *crime etc.* prowadzić śledztwo; **~ion** [~'geɪʃn] śledztwo n

invest|ment [ɪn'vestmənt] lokata f, inwestycja f; **~or** inwestor m

in'visible niewidzialny

invit|ation [ɪnvɪ'teɪʃn] zaproszenie n; **~e** [~'vaɪt] zapraszać ⟨-rosić⟩

involve [ɪn'vɒlv] wciągać ⟨-gnąć⟩, ⟨za⟩angażować; (*entail*) pociągać za sobą, wymagać

in'vulnerable nie do zaatakowania; niewrażliwy

inward ['ɪnwəd] **1.** adj wewnętrzny; skierowany do wewnątrz; **2.** adv Am. → **inwards**; **~ly** w duchu; **~s** [~z] do środka

Ireland ['aɪələnd] Irlandia f

iris ['aɪərɪs] anat. tęczówka f; bot. irys m

Irish ['aɪərɪʃ] **1.** adj irlandzki; **2. the ~** pl Irlandczycy pl; **~man** (pl -men) Irlandczyk m; **~woman** (pl -women) Irlandka f

iron ['aɪən] **1.** *metal*: żelazo n; *appliance*: żelazko n; **2.** adj żelazny; **3.** ⟨wy⟩prasować

ironic(al) [aɪ'rɒnɪk(l)] ironiczny

iron|ing prasowanie n; **~ing board** deska f do prasowania; **~works** pl. a. sg huta f żelaza

irony ['aɪərənɪ] ironia f

ir'rational nieracjonalny, irracjonalny

ir'regular nieregularny; (*uneven*) nierówny; (*illegal*) nieprzepisowy; (*odd*) dziwny

ir'relevant nieistotny, nie związany z tematem

irreplaceable niezastąpiony

irresistible nieodparty

irrespective: ~ of niezależnie od, bez względu na

irresponsible nieodpowiedzialny

irrigat|e ['ɪrɪgeɪt] nawadniać ⟨-wodnić⟩; **~ion** [~'geɪʃn] nawadnianie n

irrit|able ['ɪrɪtəbl] drażliwy; **~ate** ['~eɪt] irytować, (a. med.) podrażnić; **~ation** [~'teɪʃn] irytacja f, rozdrażnienie n; med. podrażnienie n

is [ɪz] sg pres of **be**

Islam ['ɪzlɑːm] islam m; **~ic** [~'læmɪk] muzułmański

island ['aɪlənd] wyspa f; mot. (a. traffic ~, Am. safety ~) wysepka f

isn't ['ɪznt] for **is not**

isolat|e ['aɪsəleɪt] odosobni(a)ć, izolować; **~ed** odosobniony; **~ion** [~'leɪʃn] odosobnienie n, izolacja f

Israel ['ɪzreɪl] Izrael m; **~i**

[~'reɪlɪ] **1.** adj izraelski; **2.** Izraelczyk m (-lka f)

issue ['ɪʃuː] s newspaper etc.: numer m, wydanie n; stamps: emisja f; (problem) temat m, kwestia f; (result) wynik m; **point at ~** punkt m sporny; **2.** v/t newspaper etc. wyda⟨wa⟩ć; banknotes etc. emitować; v/i wydosta⟨wa⟩ć

it [ɪt] to, ono

Ital|ian [ɪ'tæljən] **1.** adj włoski; **2.** Włoch m, Włoszka f; **~y** ['ɪtəlɪ] Włochy pl

itch [ɪtʃ] **1.** swędzenie n; **2.** swędzić

item ['aɪtəm] pozycja f, punkt m; (news) wiadomość f

its [ɪts] pron jego; jej; swój

it's [ɪts] for **it is, it has**

itself [ɪt'self] pron się; siebie; sobie (reflexive); strong form: sam; sama; samo

I've [aɪv] for **I have**

ivory ['aɪvərɪ] kość f słoniowa

ivy ['aɪvɪ] bluszcz m

J

jack [dʒæk] **1.** tech. lewarek m, podnośnik m; cards: walet m; **2. ~ up** mot. podnosić ⟨-nieść⟩ (lewarkiem)

jackal ['dʒækɔːl] szakal m

jacket ['dʒækɪt] marynarka f; book: obwoluta f

jack|knife (pl -knives) nóż m składany; **~pot** pula f

jail [dʒeɪl] **1.** więzienie n; **2.** ⟨u⟩więzić

jam¹ [dʒæm] dżem m

jam² [~] **1.** v/t wciskać ⟨-snąć⟩, stłaczać ⟨-łoczyć⟩; (a. ~ up) ⟨za⟩blokować; radio: zagłuszać ⟨-łuszyć⟩; v/i zacinać ⟨-ciąć⟩ się; brakes: ⟨za⟩blokować się; **2.** ścisk *m*; **traffic ~** korek *m* F; **be in a ~** F być w tarapatach

January ['dʒænjʊərɪ] styczeń *m*

Japan [dʒə'pæn] Japonia *f*; **~ese** [dʒæpə'niːz] **1.** *adj* japoński; **2.** Japończyk *m*, Japonka *f*

jar [dʒɑː] słój *m*, słoik *m*

jaundice ['dʒɔːndɪs] żółtaczka *f*

jaw [dʒɔː] *anat.* szczęka *f*

jazz [dʒæz] **1.** jazz *m*; **2. ~ up** ożywia(ć)

jealous ['dʒeləs] zazdrosny (**of** *o*); **~y** zazdrość *f*

jeans [dʒiːnz] *pl* dżinsy *pl*

jeep [dʒiːp] *TM* łazik *m*, dżip *m*

jeer [dʒɪə] **1.** wyśmi(ew)ać, wyszydzać ‹-dzić› (**at** *s.o.* kogoś); **2.** szyderstwo *m*

jell|ied ['dʒelɪd] w galarecie; **'~y** galareta *f*, galaretka *f*

'jellyfish meduza *f*

jeopardize ['dʒepədaɪz] narażać ‹-razić› na niebezpieczeństwo

jerk [dʒɜːk] szarpać ‹-pnąć›

jersey ['dʒɜːzɪ] sweter *m*

jest [dʒest] **1.** żart *m*, dowcip *m*; **2.** żartować

jet [dʒet] **1.** strumień *m*; *tech.* dysza *f*; *aer.* odrzutowiec *m*; **2.** tryskać ‹-snąć›; *aer.* F podróżować odrzutowcem; **~engine** silnik *m* odrzutowy

Jew [dʒuː] Żyd *m*, Żydówka *f*

jewel ['dʒuːəl] klejnot *m*; **~(l)er** jubiler *m*; **~(le)ry**

['ˌlrɪ] kosztowności *pl*, biżuteria *f*

Jew|ess ['dʒuːɪs] *contp.* Żydówka *f*; **'~ish** żydowski

jiffy ['dʒɪfɪ] F chwilka *f*; **in a ~** za chwilkę

jigsaw (puzzle) ['dʒɪgsɔː] układanka *f*

jingle ['dʒɪŋgl] **1.** brzęczeć, dzwonić; **2.** brzęk *m*

job [dʒɒb] praca *f*; (*piece of work*) robota *f*, zadanie *n*; **out of a ~** bezrobotny; **~cen-tre** *Brt.* urząd *m* zatrudnienia; **'~less** bezrobotny

jockey ['dʒɒkɪ] dżokej *m*

jog [dʒɒg] **1.** trącać ‹-cić›; *sp.* biegać, uprawiać jogging; **2.** szturchnięcie *m*; *sp.* trucht *m*

join [dʒɔɪn] **1.** *v/t* ‹po›łączyć, dołączać ‹-czyć›; *army etc.* wstępować ‹-tąpić›; **~ in** włączać ‹-czyć› się; **will you ~ me in a drink?** napijesz się ze mną?; *v/i* ‹po›łączyć się; **2.** spojenie *m*, połączenie *n*; **'~er** stolarz *m*

joint [dʒɔɪnt] **1.** złącze *n*; *anat.* staw *m*; **2. ~'stock compa-ny** *Brt.* spółka *f* akcyjna; **~ venture** *econ.* joint venture

jok|e [dʒəʊk] **1.** dowcip *m*, kawał *m*; **play a ~e on** *s.o.* zrobić komuś kawał *m*; **2.** ‹za›żartować; **'~er** żartowniś *m*, dowcipniś *m*; *cards:* dżoker *m*; **'~ing apart** żarty żartami, żarty na bok; **'~ing-ly** żartobliwie

jolly ['dʒɒlɪ] **1.** adj wesoły; **2.** adv Brt. F bardzo

jolt [dʒəʊlt] **1.** wstrząsać ⟨-snąć⟩, szarpać ⟨-pnąć⟩; vehicle: podskakiwać ⟨-skoczyć⟩; telepać się F; **2.** szarpnięcie n; fig. wstrząs m

jostle ['dʒɒsl] popychać ⟨-pchnąć⟩, szturchać ⟨-chnąć⟩

journal ['dʒɜːnl] czasopismo n; (diary) pamiętnik m, dziennik m; **'~ism** ['~əlɪzəm] dziennikarstwo n; **'~ist** dziennikarz m

journey ['dʒɜːnɪ] podróż f

joy [dʒɔɪ] radość f; **'~stick** aer. drążek m; computer: joystick m

jubilee ['dʒuːbɪliː] jubileusz m

judge [dʒʌdʒ] **1.** sędzia m; jur. sądzić; sp. etc. sędziować; fig. osądzać ⟨-dzić⟩; **'~(e)ment** jur. wyrok m, (opinion) zdanie n; ocena f; (discernment) wyczucie n; **the Last** 2**(e)ment**, 2**(e)ment Day, Day of** 2**(e)ment** eccl. Sąd Ostateczny

jug [dʒʌg] dzbanek m

juggle ['dʒʌgl] żonglować; **'~r** żongler m

juic|e [dʒuːs] sok m; **'~y** soczysty

July [dʒuːˈlaɪ] lipiec m

jump [dʒʌmp] **1.** v/i skakać ⟨skoczyć⟩, podskakiwać ⟨-koczyć⟩; v/t przeskakiwać ⟨-koczyć⟩; **2.** skok m

'jumper¹ sp. skoczek m

'jumper² esp. Brt. sweter m

'jumpy nerwowy

junction ['dʒʌŋkʃn] rail. węzeł m; skrzyżowanie n; **~ure** ['~ktʃə]: **at this ~ure** w tym momencie

June [dʒuːn] czerwiec m

jungle ['dʒʌŋgl] dżungla f

junior ['dʒuːnjə] s, adj młodszy; sp. junior m

junk [dʒʌŋk] rupieć m, rupiecie pl, grat m; **~ food** appr. niezdrowa żywność f; **'~ie, '~y** sl. ćpun m sl.; **~ shop** sklep m ze starzyzną

juror ['dʒʊərə] sędzia m przysięgły, ławnik m

jury ['dʒʊərɪ] jury n; jur. ława f przysięgłych

just [dʒʌst] **1.** adj sprawiedliwy; (fair) słuszny; **2.** adv (exactly) właśnie, dokładnie; (a short time ago) dopiero co; (only) tylko; **~ about** mniej więcej; **~ like that** właśnie tak; **~ now** właśnie teraz

justice ['dʒʌstɪs] sprawiedliwość f; wymiar m sprawiedliwości; (judge) sędzia m

justi|fication [dʒʌstɪfɪˈkeɪʃn] usprawiedliwienie n; **~fy** ['~faɪ] usprawiedliwi(a)ć

juvenile ['dʒuːvənaɪl] **1.** adj młodociany, małoletni, nieletni; **2.** form. młodzieniec m

K

kangaroo [kæŋɡəˈruː] kangur *m*

keen [kiːn] *competition etc.*: ostry; *wind*: przejmujący; (*eager*) zapalony; **be ~ on s.o./s.th.** interesować się kimś/czymś, szaleć za kimś/czymś

keep [kiːp] **1.** utrzymanie *n*; **for ~s** F na zawsze; **2.** (*kept*) *v/t* zatrzym(yw)ać; trzymać, mieć (**~ closed** *window etc.* trzymać/zatrzym(yw)ać zamknięte); *secret* zachow(yw)ać; *family* utrzym(yw)ać; *promise*, *word* dotrzym(yw)ać; *food* zachow(yw)ać świeżość; *v/i* (*remain*) pozosta(wa)ć; (*continue*) kontynuować, wciąż coś robić; **~ smiling!** uśmiechaj się!, bądź pogodny!; **~ (on) talking** mówić dalej; **~ (on) trying** wytrwale próbować; **~ s.o. company** dotrzym(yw)ać komuś towarzystwa; **~ s.o. waiting** kazać komuś czekać; **~ time** *clock*: chodzić punktualnie; **~ away** trzymać (się) z dala (*from* od), nie podchodzić; **~ (from)** powstrzym(yw)ać się (*doing s.th.* od zrobienia czegoś); **~ in** zatrzym(yw)ać; **~ off** nie dopuszczać 〈-puścić〉; **~ on** kontynuować, nie przeszkadzać; **~ out** nie wchodzić, nie przepuszczać; **~**

out! wstęp wzbroniony!; **~ to** trzymać się (**s.th.** czegoś); **~ up** podtrzym(yw)ać (*a. fig*); (*continue*) kontynuować; **~ up with** dotrzym(yw)ać kroku; **'~er** dozorca *m*, opiekun *m*

kennel ['kenl] psia buda *f*; *often pl* hodowla *f* psów, psiarnia *f*

kept [kept] *past and pp of keep* 2

kerb [kɜːb], **'~stone** *Brt.* krawężnik *m*

kettle ['ketl] czajnik *m*, kociołek *m*

key [kiː] **1.** klucz *m* (*a. fig.*); klawisz *m*; *mus.* tonacja *f*; **2. ~ in** *computer*: wstuk(iw)ać, wprowadzać 〈-dzić〉 dane; **'~board** klawiatura *f*; **'~hole** dziurka *f* od klucza

kick [kɪk] **1.** kopać 〈-pnąć〉; *horse*: wierzgać 〈-gnąć〉; **~ out** wyrzucać 〈-cić〉; **2.** kopnięcie *n*

kid [kɪd] **1.** koźlę *n*; F dzieciak *m*; **2.** F *v/t* nab(ie)rać; *v/i* żartować

kidnap ['kɪdnæp] (*-nap-*〈-p〉*ed*) por(y)wać, uprowadzać 〈-dzić〉; **'~(p)er** porywacz *m*; **'~(p)ing** por(y)wanie *n*

kidney ['kɪdnɪ] *anat.* nerka *f*

kill [kɪl] zabi(ja)ć; **'~er** zabójca *m*

labor

kilo ['ki:ləʊ] kilo *n*;
~gram(me) ['kɪləʊgræm] ki-
logram *m*; **'~metre,** *Am.*
'~meter kilometr *m*
kind¹ [kaɪnd] uprzejmy, życzliwy
kind² [~] rodzaj *m*; *all ~s of*
wszelkiego rodzaju; *nothing
of the ~* nic podobnego; *~ of*
F raczej; coś w rodzaju
kindergarten ['kɪndəgɑ:tn]
przedszkole *n*
kind-hearted [kaɪnd'hɑ:tɪd]
łagodny, dobrotliwy
'kind|ly uprzejmie; *(please)*
łaskawie, z łaski swojej;
'~ness uprzejmość *f*
king [kɪŋ] król *m*; **'~dom**
królestwo *n*
kiosk ['ki:ɒsk] kiosk *m*; *Brt.*
budka *f* telefoniczna
kiss [kɪs] **1.** pocałunek *m*; **2.**
⟨po⟩całować
kit [kɪt] zestaw *m*; *soldier's
etc.*: sprzęt *m*
kitchen ['kɪtʃɪn] kuchnia *f*; *~
sink* zlewozmywak *m*
kite [kaɪt] latawiec *m*
kitten ['kɪtn] kotek *m*
knee [ni:] kolano *n*
kneel [ni:l] *(knelt or kneeled)*
klękać ⟨klęcnąć⟩
knelt [nelt] *past and pp of kneel*

knew [nju:] *past of know*
knife [naɪf] **1.** (*pl knives* [~vz])
nóż *m*; **2.** pchnąć nożem
knight [naɪt] rycerz *m*; *chess:*
skoczek *m*
knit [nɪt] *(knitted or knit)*
⟨z⟩robić na drutach; *(a. ~
together)* ⟨po⟩łączyć; *bone:*
zrastać ⟨zrosnąć⟩ się; '~ting
robótka *f*; '~wear wyroby *pl*
dziewiarskie, dzianiny *pl*
knives [naɪvz] *pl of knife* 1
knob [nɒb] gałka *f*
knock [nɒk] **1.** uderzenie *n*,
stuknięcie *n*, pukanie *n*; **2.** *v/t*
uderzać ⟨-rzyć⟩; *v/i* pukać
⟨-knąć⟩; *~ down building
etc.* ⟨z⟩burzyć; *person*
przewracać ⟨-rócić⟩; *car:*
przejechać; *price* obniżać
⟨-żyć⟩; *~ out* powalić; *boxing:* ⟨z⟩nokautować; *~ over*
przewracać ⟨-rócić⟩
know [nəʊ] *(knew, known)* *v/t*
znać; *(have knowledge)*
umieć; *v/i* wiedzieć; *you never ~* nigdy nic nie wiadomo;
'~ing coś: porozumiewaw-
czy; '~ledge ['nɒlɪdʒ] wiedza
f; *to my ~ledge* o ile mi wiadomo; *have a good ~ledge*
znać się *(of s.th.* na czymś*)*;
~n 1. *pp of know*; **2.** *adj* znany

L

lab [læb] F laboratorium *n*
label ['leɪbl] **1.** etykietka *f*,
nalepka *f*; **2.** opatrywać

⟨-trzyć⟩ etykietką/nalepką
labor ['leɪbə] *Am.* → *labour
etc.*; *~ office Am.* urząd *m*

zatrudnienia; ~ **union** *Am.* związek *m* zawodowy

laboratory [ləˈbɒrətəri] laboratorium *n*

labour, *Am.* **-bor** [ˈleɪbə] **1.** (ciężka) praca *f*; *people*: siła *f* robocza; *med.* poród *m*; **2.** harować; *'≗* **Party** *pol.* Partia *f* Pracy

lace [leɪs] **1.** *cloth*: koronka *f*; *shoe*: sznurowadło *n*; **2.** (*a. ~ up*) ⟨za⟩sznurować

lack [læk] **1.** brak *m* (**of s.th.** czegoś); **2.** brakować, nie mieć; **be ~ing** brakować, nie mieć

lacquer [ˈlækə] **1.** lakier *m*, emalia *f*; **2.** ⟨po⟩lakierować

ladder [ˈlædə] drabina *f*

lady [ˈleɪdɪ] dama *f*, pani *f*; *≗ title*: lady *f*; jej lordowska mość; **'~bird**, *Am. a.* **'~bug** biedronka *f*

laid [leɪd] *past and pp of* **lay²**

lain [leɪn] *pp of* **lie¹** 1

lake [leɪk] jezioro *n*

lamb [læm] jagnię *n*

lame [leɪm] **1.** *adj* kulawy, *fig.* nieprzekonujący; **2.** okulawi(a)ć

lamp [læmp] lampa *f*; *street*: latarnia *f*; **'~post** słup *m* latarni; **'~shade** abażur *m*

land [lænd, *in comb. mst* lənd] **1.** ląd *m*; (*ground*) ziemia *f*; (*country*) kraj *m*; **by ~** drogą lądową; **2.** ⟨wy⟩lądować; *goods* wyładow(yw)ać

land|lady [ˈlænleɪdɪ] gospodyni *f*; **~lord** [ˈlæn-] gospo-

darz *m*; **~owner** [ˈlænd-] ziemianin *m*; **~scape** [ˈlænskeɪp] krajobraz *m*

lane [leɪn] dróżka *f*, uliczka *f*; *mot.* pas *m* ruchu; *sp.* tor *m*

language [ˈlæŋgwɪdʒ] język *m*; mowa *f*

lantern [ˈlæntən] latarnia *f*

lap¹ [læp] chłeptać

lap² [~] **1.** *sp.* okrążenie *n*; **2.** *sp.* ⟨z⟩dublować

lapel [ləˈpel] klapa *f* (marynarki)

large [lɑːdʒ] **1.** *adj* duży; **2.** *s*: **at ~** na wolności; ogólnie; **'~ly** w dużym stopniu

lark [lɑːk] skowronek *m*

larynx [ˈlærɪŋks] (*pl* **-ynges** [ləˈrɪndʒiːz]**, -ynxes**) *anat.* krtań *f*

laser [ˈleɪzə] laser *m*; **~ printer** *computer*: drukarka *f* laserowa

lash [læʃ] **1.** bat *m*, bicz *m*; *eye*: rzęsa *f*; **2.** smagać, chłostać

last¹ [lɑːst] **1.** *adj* (*final*) ostatni; (*recent*) ubiegły, zeszły; **~ but one** przedostatni; **~ night** wczoraj wieczorem; zeszłej nocy; **2.** *adv* na końcu; **~ but not least** co nie mniej ważne; **3.** *s* ostatni; reszta *f*; **at ~** w końcu, wreszcie

last² [~] *v/i* trwać

'lastly wreszcie, na koniec

latch [lætʃ] **1.** zasuwa *f*; **2.** zamykać ⟨-mknąć⟩ na zasuwę

late [leɪt] późny, spóźniony;

be ~ spóźni(a)ć się; *train etc.*: mieć spóźnienie; ~*r on* później; '~*ly* ostatnio

latitude ['lætɪtjuːd] *geogr.* szerokość *f* geograficzna

latter ['lætə] drugi *m* (z dwóch); (*recent*) ostatni

Latvia ['lætvɪə] Łotwa *f*; ~**n 1.** *adj* łotewski; **2.** Łotysz(ka *f*) *m*

laugh [lɑːf] **1.** śmiać się (*at* z); **2.** śmiech *m*; '~**ingstock** pośmiewisko *n*; '~**ter** śmiech *m*

launch [lɔːntʃ] **1.** *ship* wodować; *rocket* wystrzeli(wa)ć; *project etc.* zapoczątkow(yw)ać; **2.** *ship*: wodowanie *n*; *rocket*: wystrzelenie *n*; '~(**ing**) **pad** wyrzutnia *f*

launder ['lɔːndə] ⟨wy⟩prać; ~**ry** ['~drɪ] pranie *n*; (*place*) pralnia *f*

lavatory ['lævətərɪ] ubikacja *f*

law [lɔː] prawo *n*; (*rule*) ustawa *f*; ~ **court** sąd *m*; '~**ful** legalny; '~**less** bezprawny

lawn [lɔːn] trawnik *m*

law|**suit** ['lɔːsuːt] proces *m*; ~**yer** ['~jə] prawnik *m*

lay¹ [leɪ] *past of lie¹*

lay² [~] (*laid*) położyć ⟨kłaść⟩; *table* nakry(wa)ć; *eggs* znosić ⟨znieść⟩; *trap etc.* zastawi(a)ć; ~ *aside* odkładać ⟨odłożyć⟩ na bok; ~ *off* zwalniać ⟨zwolnić⟩ czasowo; ~ *out* ⟨za⟩projektować; rozkładać ⟨-złożyć⟩

lay³ [~] *adj* laicki

layer warstwa *f*

layman (*pl -men*) laik *m*

lazy ['leɪzɪ] leniwy

lead¹ [liːd] **1.** (*led*) ⟨po⟩prowadzić; *mil.* dowodzić; ~ *on fig.* nab(ie)rać; ~ *to fig.* doprowadzać ⟨-dzić⟩ (*s.th. do* czegoś); ~ *up to* być wstępem (*s.th. do* czegoś); **2.** prowadzenie *n*; przewaga *f* (*a. sp.*); (*hint*) wskazówka *f*; poszlaka *f*; *thea.* główna rola *f*; (*leash*) smycz *f*

lead² [led] *metal*: ołów *m*; *pencil*: grafit *m*; ~**en** ['~dn] *a. fig.* ołowiany

leader ['liːdə] przywódca *m*, lider *m*; *Brt.* artykuł *m* wstępny; '~**ship** przywództwo *n*

lead-free [led'friː] bezołowiowy

leading ['liːdɪŋ] główny, wiodący

leaf [liːf] **1.** (*pl leaves* [~vz]) liść *m*; *table*: klapa *f*; (*page*) kartka *f*; ~ *through* ⟨prze⟩kartkować; '~**let** [~lɪt] ulotka *f*

league [liːg] liga *f*

leak [liːk] **1.** przeciek *m*, wyciek *m*; **2.** *v/i liquid etc.*: przeciekać ⟨-ciec⟩; *gas etc.*: przepuszczać; ~ *i* celowo wyjawi(a)ć; ~ *out fig.* wyjść na jaw; '~**age** ['~ɪdʒ] przeciek *m*; '~**y** nieszczelny

lean¹ [liːn] (*leant or leaned*) pochylać ⟨-lić⟩ się; ~ *on* opierać ⟨oprzeć⟩ się

lean² [~] *adj* chudy

leant [lent] *past and pp of* **lean¹**

leap [li:p] **1.** (*leapt or leaped*) skakać ⟨skoczyć⟩; **2.** skok *m*; *~t* [lept] *past and pp of* **leap** 1; **~ year** rok *m* przestępny

learn [lɜːn] (*learned or learnt*) ⟨na⟩uczyć się; (*become informed*) ⟨do⟩wiedzieć się; **~ed** ['~ɪd] uczony; **~er** uczeń *m*, słuchacz *m*; **~t** [~t] *past and pp of* **learn**

lease [li:s] **1.** dzierżawa *f*; **2.** (*a. ~ out*) ⟨wy⟩dzierżawić

leash [li:ʃ] smycz *f*

least [li:st] **1.** *adj* najmniejszy; **2.** *adv* najmniej; **at ~** przynajmniej

leather ['leðə] skóra *f*

leave [li:v] **1.** (*left*) opuszczać ⟨opuścić⟩; zostawi(a)ć, pozostawi(a)ć; **~ alone** zostawi(a)ć w spokoju; **be left** zostawać, zostać; **there's nothing left** nic nie zostało; **2.** zezwolenie *n*; *sick*: zwolnienie *n*; (*holiday*) urlop *m*; **on ~** na urlopie

leaves [li:vz] *pl of* **leaf** 1

lecture ['lektʃə] **1.** wykład *m*; *fig.* kazanie *n*; **2.** wykładać; *fig.* prawić kazania; **~r** wykładowca *m*

led [led] *past and pp of* **lead¹**

left¹ [left] *past and pp of* **leave** 1

left² [~] **1.** *adj* lewy; **2.** *s* lewa strona *f*; **on the ~** po lewej stronie; **to the ~** w lewo; **3.** *adv* w lewo; **turn ~** skręcać ⟨-cić⟩ w lewo; **~-hand:** **~-hand bend** zakręt *m* w lewo; **~-hand drive** z kierownicą po lewej stronie; **~ turn** zakręt *m* w lewo; **~-handed** leworęczny; **~ luggage** (*office*) *Brt.* przechowalnia *f* bagażu

leg [leg] noga *f*; **pull s.o.'s ~** nabierać kogoś, żartować z kogoś

legacy ['legəsɪ] spadek *m*, dziedzictwo *n*

legal ['li:gl] prawny, prawniczy; (*lawful*) legalny

legend ['ledʒənd] *a. fig.* legenda *f*

legible ['ledʒəbl] czytelny

legislat|e ['ledʒɪsleɪt] ustanawiać ⟨-nowić⟩ prawo, uchwalać ⟨-lić⟩; **~ion** [~'leɪʃn] ustawodawstwo *n*; **~ive** ['~lətɪv] ustawodawczy

legitimate [lɪ'dʒɪtɪmət] prawowity

leisure ['leʒə] wolny czas *m*; **~ly** powolny, niespieszny

lemon ['lemən] cytryna *f*; **~ade** [~'neɪd] oranżada *f*

lend [lend] (*lent*) pożyczać ⟨-czyć⟩; **~ing library** wypożyczalnia *f*

length [leŋθ] długość *f*; **at ~** szczegółowo; **~en** przedłużać ⟨-żyć⟩, wydłużać ⟨-żyć⟩

lens [lenz] *anat.*, *opt.* soczewka *f*; *phot.* obiektyw *m*

lent [lent] *past and pp of* **lend**

less [les] **1.** *adv* mniej; **2.** *adj* mniejszy; **3.** *prp* mniej; **~en** ['\.sn] zmniejszać ⟨-szyć⟩

lesson ['lesn] lekcja *f*; *fig.* nauczka *f*

let [let] ⟨*let*⟩ pozwalać ⟨-wolić⟩; *esp.* Brt. wynajmować ⟨-jąć⟩; **~ alone** nie mówiąc już o; **~ down** zawieść ⟨-wieść⟩; **~ go** puszczać ⟨-puścić⟩

lethal ['li:θl] śmiertelny

letter ['letə] list *m*; litera *f*; '**\.box** *esp.* Brt. skrzynka *f* pocztowa

lettuce ['letis] sałata *f*

level ['levl] **1.** *adj* poziomy, równy; **~ with** równoległy, na wysokości/poziomie; **2.** *adv* **~ with** równo z, blisko; **s** poziom *m* (*a. fig.*), równia *f*; **4.** *v/t* wyrówn⟨yw⟩ać; (*pull down*) zrówn⟨yw⟩ać z ziemią; **~ crossing** Brt. przejazd *m* kolejowy

lever ['li:və] dźwignia *f*

liability [laɪə'bɪlətɪ] odpowiedzialność *f*; podatność *f* (**to** na); *jur.* zadłużenie *n*

liable ['laɪəbl] odpowiedzialny; podatny; **be ~ to** być narażonym/wystawionym na; *jur.* podlegać (**a fine** grzywnie)

liar ['laɪə] kłamca *m*

libel ['laɪbl] **1.** *jur.* oszczerstwo *n*, zniesławienie *n*; **2.** zniesławi(a)ć

liberal ['lɪbərəl] liberalny; tolerancyjny; (*generous*) hojny

liberate ['lɪbəreɪt] wyzwalać ⟨-wolić⟩

liberty ['lɪbətɪ] wolność *f*; **at ~** na wolności; **take the ~** pozwolić sobie (**of doing s.th.** zrobić coś)

librar|ian [laɪ'breərɪən] bibliotekarz *m* (-karka *f*); **~y** ['\.brərɪ] biblioteka *f*

lice [laɪs] *pl of* **louse**

licence, *Am.* **-cense** ['laɪsəns] licencja *f*, koncesja *f*; pozwolenie *n*; **driving ~** prawo *n* jazdy

license, *Am. a.* **-cence** ['\.~] upoważni(a)ć, udzielać ⟨-lić⟩ pozwolenia; **~ plate** *Am. mot.* tablica *f* rejestracyjna

lick [lɪk] ⟨po⟩lizać; F spuścić lanie; '**\.ing** F porażka *f*, lanie *n* F

lid [lɪd] pokryw(k)a *f*, wieko *n*

lie¹ [laɪ] **1.** (**lay, lain**) leżeć; **~ down** kłaść ⟨położyć⟩ się; **~ in** Brt. wylegiwać się (w łóżku); **2.** ułożenie *n*, układ *m*

lie² [\~] **1.** (**lied**) ⟨s⟩kłamać; **2.** kłamstwo *n*

lieutenant [lef'tenənt, *Am.* lu:'tenənt] porucznik *m*

life [laɪf] *pl* (**lives** [\.vz]) życie *n*; **~ belt** pas *m* ratunkowy; '**\.boat** łódź *f* ratunkowa; '**\.guard** ratownik *m*; **~ insurance** ubezpieczenie *n* na życie; **~ jacket** kamizelka *f* ratunkowa; '~less martwy; bez życia; '~like jak żywy; '~long trwający całe życie, dozgonny; '~saving ratownictwo n; '~time życie n

lift [lɪft] 1. podnosić ⟨-dnieść⟩ (się); ~ off ⟨wy⟩startować, wznosić ⟨-nieść⟩ się; F ⟨u⟩kraść; podniesienie n; Brt. winda f; give s.o. a ~ podwieźć kogoś; '~off aer. start m

light¹ [laɪt] 1. s światło n; (flame etc.) ogień m; fig. in the ~ of Brt., in ~ of Am. w świetle; 2. adj jasny; 3. (lighted or lit) v/t zapalać ⟨-lić⟩, oświetlać ⟨-lić⟩; (a. ~ up) rozświetlać ⟨-lić⟩; zapalać ⟨-lić⟩; v/i mst ~ up face etc.: rozjaśnić się

light² [~] adj lekki

light bulb żarówka f

lighten¹ ['laɪtn] v/t oświetlać ⟨-lić⟩, rozjaśni(a)ć

lighten² [~] v/t odciążać ⟨-życ⟩; v/i zelżeć

'lighter zapalniczka f

'light|house latarnia f morska; '~ing oświetlenie n

'lightly lekko

'lightness¹ jasność f

'lightness² lekkość f

lightning ['laɪtnɪŋ] błyskawica f; ~ conductor Brt., ~ rod Am. piorunochron m

light pen tech. pióro n świetlne

likable ['laɪkəbl] sympatyczny

like¹ [laɪk] 1. adj podobny; 2. prp jak; what is she ~? jaka ona jest?; 2. s taki sam; coś podobnego

like² [~] lubić; I ~ it to mi się podoba; I ~ her lubię ją; ona mi się podoba; I would ~ to know chciałbym wiedzieć; (just) as you ~ jak chcesz; '~able → likable

like|lihood ['laɪklɪhʊd] prawdopodobieństwo n; '~ly prawdopodobny; '~ness podobieństwo n

liking ['laɪkɪŋ] upodobanie n

limb [lɪm] anat. kończyna f; (branch) konar m

lime¹ [laɪm] wapno n

lime² [~] bot. lipa f

limit ['lɪmɪt] 1. granica f, kres m; off ~s esp. Am. zamknięty; that's the ~! F to przekracza wszelkie granice!; within ~s w pewnych granicach; 2. ograniczać ⟨-czyć⟩ (to do); ~ation [~'teɪʃn] a. fig. ograniczenie n; ~ed (liability) company spółka f z ograniczoną odpowiedzialnością

limp [lɪmp] utykać, kuleć

line [laɪn] 1. linia f, kreska f, (row) szereg m; (string) sznurek m; rail. tor m; teleph. linia f, połączenie n; the ~ is busy/engaged teleph. numer jest zajęty; hold the ~ teleph. proszę nie odkładać słuchawki; draw the ~ fig. nie posuwać się (at do); 2.

lobby

⟨po⟩liniować, ⟨po⟩kreskować; **~ up** ustawi(a)ć się w szereg

linen ['lɪnɪn] płótno *n*; *bed etc.*: bielizna *f*

lingerie ['lænʒəri:] bielizna *f* damska

link [lɪŋk] **1.** ogniwo *n* (*a. fig.*); *(connection)* połączenie *n*; *fig.* więź *f*; **2.** (*a.* **~ up**) ⟨po⟩łączyć (się)

lion ['laɪən] lew *m*; **~ess** ['~es] lwica *f*

lip [lɪp] warga *f*; **'~stick** szminka *f*

liqueur [lɪ'kjʊə] likier *m*

liquid ['lɪkwɪd] **1.** ciecz *f*; **2.** *adj* płynny

liquor ['lɪkə] *Am.* mocny alkohol *m*

lisp [lɪsp] seplenić

list [lɪst] **1.** lista *f*, spis *m*; **2.** spis(yw)ać, sporządzać ⟨-dzić⟩ listę/wykaz; *when speaking*: wymieni(a)ć

listen ['lɪsn] słuchać; **~ in** podsłuch(iw)ać; **~** ⟨po⟩słuchać; **'~er** *m* słuchacz *m*

lit [lɪt] *past and pp of* **light**[1] [3]

liter ['li:tə] *Am.* → **litre**

literal ['lɪtərəl] dosłowny

litera|ry ['lɪtərərɪ] literacki; **'~ture** ['~rətʃə] literatura *f*

Lithuania [lɪθjʊ'eɪnɪə] Litwa *f*; **~n** [1] *adj* litewski; **2.** Litwin(ka *f*) *m*

litre, *Am.* **-ter** ['li:tə] litr *m*

litter ['lɪtə] *esp. esp*: śmieci *pl*; **'~ basket**, **'~bin** kosz *m* na śmieci

little ['lɪtl] **1.** *adj* mały, niewielki; **2.** *adv* mało, niewiele; **3.** *s*: **a ~** trochę; **~ by ~** po trochu

live[1] [lɪv] żyć; mieszkać; **~ on** przetrwać; **~ up** żyć zgodnie (**to s.th.** z czyms) sprostać oczekiwaniom

live[2] [laɪv] **1.** *adj* żywy; *electr.* pod napięciem; *radio, TV*: bezpośredni; **2.** *adv* na żywo

live|lihood ['laɪvlɪhʊd] utrzymanie *n*; **'~ly** żywy, wesoły

liver ['lɪvə] wątroba *f*

lives [laɪvz] *pl of* **life**

living ['lɪvɪŋ] **1.** *adj* żywy, żyjący; **2.** życie *n*, utrzymanie *n*; **earn/make a ~** zarabiać na życie; **standard of ~**, **~ standard** stopa *f* życiowa; **~ room** salon *m*, bawialnia *f*

lizard ['lɪzəd] jaszczurka *f*

load [ləʊd] **1.** ładunek *m*, ciężar *m* (*a. fig.*); **2.** ⟨za⟩ładować; *gun* ⟨na⟩ładować

loaf [ləʊf] (*pl* **loaves** [~vz]) bochenek *m*

loan [ləʊn] **1.** pożyczka *f*; **on ~** wypożyczony; **2.** *esp. Am.* pożyczać ⟨-czyć⟩ (**s.o.** komuś)

loathe [ləʊð] czuć odrazę (**s.o./s.th.** do kogoś/czegoś); nie cierpieć (**s.o./s.th.** kogoś/czegoś)

loaves [ləʊvz] *pl of* **loaf**[1]

lobby ['lɒbɪ] hol *m*, westybul *m*; *pol.* lobby *n*, grupa *f* nacisku

lobster ['lɒbstə] homar *m*

local ['ləʊkl] lokalny, miejscowy; **~ call** teleph. rozmowa *f* miejscowa; **~ity** [~'kæləti] rejon *m*; **~ly** miejscowo; **~ time** czas *m* miejscowy

locat|e [ləʊ'keɪt] umiejscawiać ⟨-cowić⟩, ⟨z⟩lokalizować; **be ~ed** znajdować się; **~ion** położenie *n*, lokalizacja *f*; **on ~ion** film: w plenerze

lock [lɒk] **1.** zamek *m*; **2.** (a. **~ up**) zamykać ⟨-mknąć⟩ na klucz; tech. ⟨za⟩blokować się; **~ away** ⟨s⟩chować pod kluczem; **~ in** zamykać ⟨-mknąć⟩ (**s.o.** kogoś); **~ out** *v/t* nie wpuszczać ⟨wpuścić⟩; *v/i* zamykać ⟨-mknąć⟩ się; mot. etc. ⟨za⟩blokować się

locksmith ślusarz *m*

lodg|e [lɒdʒ] **1.** portiernia *f*; stróżówka *f*; hunting etc.: domek *m*, chata *f*; **2.** *v/i* wynajmować pokój (**with s.o.** u kogoś); bullet etc.: utkwić; *v/t* wynajmować pokoje; complaint etc. wnosić ⟨wnieść⟩; **~er** (sub)lokator *m*; **~ing** (wynajęte) mieszkanie *n*

loft [lɒft] strych *m*; poddasze *n*; **~y** wyniosły

log [lɒg] kłoda *f*, kloc *m*

logic ['lɒdʒɪk] logika *f*; **~al** logiczny

lollipop ['lɒlɪpɒp] lizak *m*

lone|liness ['ləʊnlɪnɪs] samotność *f*; **~ly** samotny

long¹ [lɒŋ] **1.** adj długi; **2.** adv długo; **as** or **so ~** as tak długo aż; **so ~!** F cześć!, na razie!; **3.** s: **before ~** wkrótce; for **~** długo; **take ~** długo trwać; **I won't take ~** nie zajmie mi to dużo czasu

long² [~] tęsknić (**for** za)

long-'distance międzymiastowy; sp. długodystansowy; **~ call** rozmowa *f* międzymiastowa

longing ['lɒŋɪŋ] tęsknota *f*

longitude ['lɒndʒɪtju:d] geogr. długość *f* geograficzna

long| jump skok *m* w dal; **~'range** dalekosiężny, dalekiego zasięgu; **~'sighted** dalekowzroczny; **~'term** długofalowy; **~ wave** fale *pl* długie

loo [lu:] Brt. F ubikacja *f*

look [lʊk] **1.** spojrzenie *n*, rzut *m* oka (**at** na); often *pl* wygląd *m*; **2.** patrzeć (**at** na); wyglądać; **~ after** opiekować się; **~ at** przyglądać się; **~ back** oglądać ⟨obejrzeć⟩ się za siebie; fig. wspominać; **~ down** fig. patrzeć z góry (**on** na); **~ for** szukać; **~ forward to** oczekiwać z niecierpliwością; **~ into** rozpatrywać ⟨-trzyć⟩; **~ on** uważać (**s.o. as** kogoś za); **~ out** wypatrywać (**for s.o.** kogoś); **~ out!** uważaj!; **~ over**

przeglądać ⟨przejrzeć⟩; ~ **round** rozglądać ⟨-zejrzeć⟩ się; ~ **through** przeglądać ⟨przejrzeć⟩; ~ **up** poprawiać się; *fig.* poważać (**to s.o.** kogoś); *word etc.* sprawdzać ⟨-dzić⟩, wyszuk(iw)ać

'**looking glass** lustro *n*

loom [luːm] krosno,*pl* krosna *f/pl*

loop [luːp] **1.** pętla *f*, oczko *n*; *computer*: pętla *f*; **2.** zrobić pętlę, oplatać ⟨-leść⟩

loose [luːs] luźny *adj.*; ~**n** ['~sn] poluźni(a)ć ⟨się⟩ (*w/v.*)

lord [lɔːd] pan *m*; *Brt.* lord *m*; **the** ⅋ (*a.* (**the**) ⅋) **God**) Pan *m* (Bóg); (**the** (**House of**) ⅋s *Brt.* Izba *f* Lordów; ⅋ **Mayor** *Brt.* burmistrz *m* Londynu

lorry ['lɒrɪ] *Brt.* ciężarówka *f*

lose [luːz] ⟨*lost*⟩ *parents etc.* ⟨s⟩tracić; *keys etc.* ⟨z⟩gubić; (*fail to win*) przegr(yw)ać; *watch, clock*: spóźniać się; ~ **o.s.** zabłądzić; '**~r** (człowiek) *m* przegrany/zwyciężony

loss [lɒs] strata *f*; zguba *f*; **be at a** ~ być w kropce, nie wiedzieć co począć

lost [lɒst] **1.** *past and pp of* **lose**; **2.** *adj* zgubiony, stracony; przegrany; ~**and**-'**found** (**office**) *Am.*,~ **property office** *Brt.* biuro *n* rzeczy znalezionych

lot [lɒt] los *m* (*a. fig.*); artykuł *m*, obiekt *m*; *esp. Am.* parcela *f*; (*set*) partia *f* (*towaru*); **the** ~ wszystko; *persons*: wszyscy; **a** ~ **of**, ~**s of** wiele, dużo, mnóstwo

lotion ['ləʊʃn] płyn *m*

loud [laʊd] głośny; *colour*: krzykliwy; '~**speaker** głośnik *m*

lounge [laʊndʒ] *esp. Brt.* salon *m*, bawialnia *f*; *hotel*: hol *m*, westybul *m*

lous|**e** [laʊs] (*pl* **lice** [laɪs]) wesz *f*; ~**y** ['~zɪ] zawszony; *fig.* marny, okropny

lovable ['lʌvəbl] sympatyczny, miły

love [lʌv] **1.** miłość *f*; *person*: ukochany *m*, ukochana *f*; **be in** ~ być zakochanym (**with** w); **fall in** ~ zakochać się (**with** w); **make** ~ kochać się; **2.** kochać; (*have a liking*) ~ **to do s.th.** uwielbiać ⟨z⟩robić coś z przyjemnością; '~**able** → **lovable**; '~**ly** śliczny, uroczy; *F* komity; '~**r** kochanek *m*; *music etc.*: miłośnik *m*

loving ['lʌvɪŋ] kochający

low [ləʊ] **1.** *adj* niski, niewysoki; *voice etc.*: cichy; *trick*: podły; **2.** *meteor.* niż *m*

lower ['ləʊə] **1.** *adj* niższy; **2.** obniżać ⟨-żyć⟩, zniżać ⟨-żyć⟩; *fig.* ~ **o.s.** zniżyć się (**by** do)

'**low**|**land** nizina *f*; '~**rise** *building*: niski, piętrowy

loyal ['lɔɪəl] lojalny, wierny; '~**ty** lojalność *f*, wierność *f*

luck [lʌk] traf *m*, szczęście *n*; powodzenie *n*; **bad/hard/ill**

~ pech *m*; **good** ~ powodzenie *n*, szczęśliwy traf *m*; **good** ~**!** powodzenia!; '~**ily** na szczęście; '~**y** mający szczęście; szczęśliwy; **be** ~**y** mieć szczęście

lug [lʌg] ⟨przy⟩wlec, ⟨przy⟩taszczyć

luggage ['lʌgɪdʒ] bagaż *m*; ~ **rack** półka *f* bagażowa; ~ **van** *Brt. rail.* wagon *m* bagażowy

lukewarm ['luːnə] letni

lull [lʌl] **1.** uspokajać ⟨-koić⟩, ⟨u⟩kołysać; **2.** (chwilowa) cisza *f*; '~**aby** ['~əbaɪ] kołysanka *f*

lunar ['luːnə] księżycowy

lunatic ['luːnətɪk] **1.** *adj* szalony; **2.** szaleniec *m*

lunch [lʌntʃ] **1.** lunch *m*; **2.** ⟨z⟩jeść lunch; ~ **hour** przerwa *f* na lunch; '~**time** pora *f* lunchu

lung [lʌŋ] *anat.* płuco *n*; **the** ~**s** *pl* płuca *pl*

lure [luə] **1.** wabik *m*; przynęta *f*; *fig.* pokusa *f*; **2.** ⟨z⟩wabić, ⟨z⟩nęcić

lust [lʌst] żądza *f*

luxur|ious [lʌɡ'ʒuərɪəs] luksusowy; ~**y** ['lʌkʃərɪ] luksus *m*, zbytek *m*

lying ['laɪɪŋ] **1.** *pres p of* **lie**[1] *and* **lie**[2] **1.**; **2.** *adj* kłamliwy, zakłamany

lynch [lɪntʃ] ⟨z⟩linczować

lynx [lɪŋks] ryś *m*

lyrics ['lɪrɪks] *pl* tekst *m*, słowa *pl* (piosenki)

M

machine [mə'ʃiːn] maszyna *f*; ~ **gun** karabin *m* maszynowy; ~**made** wykonany maszynowo; ~ **tool** obrabiarka *f*

machinery [mə'ʃiːnərɪ] maszyny *pl*; *a. fig* mechanizm *m*

mad [mæd] szalony, obłąkany; *esp. Am.* (angry) wściekły; zwariowany; **about s.th.** na punkcie czegoś; **drive s.o.** ~ doprowadzić kogoś do szału; **go** ~ zwariować, oszaleć

madam ['mædəm] *address*: proszę pani

made [meɪd] *past and pp of* **make**[1]

'**mad|man** (*pl* -**men**) szaleniec *m*; '~**ness** obłęd *m*, szaleństwo *n*

magazine [mægə'ziːn] czasopismo *n*; *gun*: magazynek *m*

magic ['mædʒɪk] **1.** magia *f* (*a. fig.*), czary *pl*; **2.** *adj* magiczny, czarodziejski; *fig.* czarowny; ~**ian** [mə'dʒɪʃn] magik *m*; czarodziej *m*

magnet ['mægnɪt] magnes *m*; ~**ic** [~'netɪk] magnetyczny

magnificen|ce [mæg'nɪfɪsns] świetność *f*, wspaniałość *f*; ~**t**

man

[~snt] wspaniały

magnify ['mægnıfaı] powiększać ⟨-kszyć⟩; **'~ing glass** szkło *n* powiększające; **~en** [~dn] panna *f*; **~en name** nazwisko *n* panieńskie

mail [meıl] **1.** poczta *f*; **2.** *esp.* Am. przes(y)łać pocztą; **'~box** Am. skrzynka *f* pocztowa; **~man** (*pl -men*) Am. listonosz *m*

main [meın] **1.** *adj* główny; **2.** *mst* *pl* sieć *f* zasilająca; **'~frame** *computer*: komputer *m* dużej mocy; **~land** ['~lənd] kontynent *m*; **~ly** głównie; **'~road** szosa *f*, **~ street** Am. główna ulica *f*

maintain [meın'teın] zachow(yw)ać, utrzym(yw)ać; (*assert*) twierdzić; *tech.* konserwować; *family etc.* utrzym(yw)ać

maintenance ['meıntənəns] utrzym(yw)anie *n*; *tech.* konserwacja *f*; *jur.* alimenty *pl*

maize [meız] kukurydza *f*

majestic [mə'dʒestık] majestatyczny; **~y** ['mædʒəstı] majestat *m*

major ['meıdʒə] **1.** *adj* główny, większy; *jur.* pełnoletni; *mus.* durowy; **C ~** C-dur; **2.** *s mil.* major *m*; *jur.* osoba *f* pełnoletnia; Am. *univ.* przedmiot *m* kierunkowy; **~ity** [mə'dʒɔrətı] większość *f*; *jur.* pełnoletność *f*

make [meık] **1.** (*made*) ⟨z⟩robić; (*produce*) wytwarzać ⟨-worzyć⟩, ⟨wy⟩produkować; *money* zarabiać ⟨-robić⟩; (*arrive*) docierać ⟨dotrzeć⟩; *mistake* popełni(a)ć; (*equal*) być, stanowić; *speech* wygłaszać ⟨-łosić⟩; (*force*) zmuszać ⟨-sić⟩; *I'll ~ you do it!* zmuszę cię do tego!; (*become*) okazać się, zostać; (*cause to be*) uczynić (*s.o. happy* kogoś szczęśliwym); *it* powieść się; *what do you ~ of it?* co sądzisz o tym?; *~ friends with* zaprzyjaźni(a)ć się; *~ believe* uda(wa)ć; *~ into* przerabiać ⟨-robić⟩; *~ off* uciekać ⟨uciec⟩; *~ over* przekaz(yw)ać; *~ up* wymyślać ⟨-lić⟩; *v/i* malować się; *~ up one's mind* zdecydować się; *be made up of* być zrobionym z; *~ up for* wynagradzać ⟨-grodzić⟩; *~ it up* pogodzić się; **2.** *mot.* marka *f*; **'~-believe** udawanie *n*; **'~-up** makijaż *m*

male [meıl] **1.** męski; **2.** mężczyzna *m*; *zo.* samiec *m*

malice ['mælıs] złośliwość *f*; **~ious** [mə'lıʃəs] złośliwy (*a. med.*)

malignant [mə'lıgnənt] złośliwy (*a. med.*)

maltreat [mæl'tri:t] ⟨z⟩maltretować

mammal ['mæml] ssak *m*

man 1. [mæn, *in comb.* mən] (*pl* **men** [men]) człowiek *m*, rodzaj *m* ludzki; *(human male)* mężczyzna *m*; **2.** [mæn] *mil. etc.* obsadzać ⟨-dzić⟩

manage ['mænɪdʒ] kierować, zarządzać; *(succeed)* da(wa)ć sobie radę; zdołać, ⟨po⟩radzić sobie; **'∼able** podatny; *task*: wykonalny; **∼ment** *econ.* zarządzanie *n*; kierownictwo *n*, zarząd *m*; **∼r** dyrektor *m*, kierownik *m*, menedżer *m*

mandarin ['mændərɪn] *(a. ∼ orange)* mandarynka *f*

mane [meɪn] grzywa *f*

manifest ['mænɪfest] **1.** *adj* jawny; **2.** ujawni(a)ć, ukaz(yw)ać

man|kind [mæn'kaɪnd] ludzkość *f*; **'∼ly** męski; **∼'made** sztuczny

manner ['mænə] sposób *m*; sposób *m* bycia; *pl* maniery *pl*

man(o)euvre [mə'nu:və] **1.** manewr *m*; *fig.* intryga *f*; **2.** manewrować

manor ['mænə] dobra *pl* ziemskie; **∼ (house)** dwór *m*, rezydencja *f*

mansion ['mænʃn] dwór *m*, rezydencja *f*

'manslaughter *jur.* zabójstwo *n*

manual ['mænjuəl] **1.** *adj* ręczny, manualny; *worker*: fizyczny; **2.** podręcznik *m*

manufacture [mænju'fæktʃə] **1.** ⟨wy⟩produkować; **2.** pro-

dukcja *f*; **∼r** [∼ərə] producent *m*

manure [mə'njuə] **1.** nawóz *m*; **2.** nawozić

manuscript ['mænjuskrɪpt] rękopis *m*, manuskrypt *m*

many ['menɪ] dużo, wiele; **∼ times** często; **a great ∼** bardzo dużo/wiele

map [mæp] mapa *f*; *town etc.*: plan *m*

maple ['meɪpl] klon *m*

marble ['mɑ:bl] marmur *m*; *ball*: szklana kulka *f*

March [mɑ:tʃ] marzec *m*

march [∼] **1.** maszerować; **2.** marsz *m*

mare [meə] klacz *f*, kobyła *f*

marg|arine [mɑ:dʒə'ri:n], *Brt. F a.* **∼e** [mɑ:dʒ] margaryna *f*

margin ['mɑ:dʒɪn] margines *m*; brzeg *m*, skraj *m*; *fig.* rezerwa *f*, margines *m*; **'∼al** marginesowy

marine [mə'ri:n] **1.** *adj* morski; **2.** żołnierz *m* piechoty morskiej

marjoram ['mɑ:dʒərəm] majeranek *m*

mark [mɑ:k] **1.** *on skin*: znamię *n*; *(stain)* plama *f*; *(sign)* znak *m*; *fig.* oznaka *f*; *school*: stopień *m*, ocena *f*; *(target)* cel *m*; **hit the ∼** trafić; **miss the ∼** spudłować; **2.** ⟨po⟩znaczyć, ⟨o⟩znaczyć; *(characterize)* cechować; *school*: oceni(a)ć; **∼ down** ⟨za⟩notować; *price* obniżać

⟨-niżyć⟩; **~ off** oddzielać ⟨-lić⟩; *on a list*: ⟨-czyć⟩ ⟨-czyć⟩; **~ out** przeznaczać ⟨-czyć⟩ *(for* do); **~ up** *price* podnosić ⟨-dnieść⟩

marke|d ['maːkt] wyraźny, znaczny; *~t* pisak *m*

market ['maːkɪt] **1.** rynek *m*; **2.** sprzeda(wa)ć

marmalade ['maːməleɪd] dżem *z owoców cytrusowych*

marriage ['mærɪdʒ] małżeństwo *n*; ślub *m*; **~ certificate** świadectwo *n* ślubu

married ['mærɪd] *man*: żonaty; *woman*: zamężna

marrow ['mærəʊ] *anat.* szpik *m* kostny

marry ['mærɪ] *v/t* poślubi(a)ć; *woman*: wychodzić ⟨wyjść⟩ za mąż; *man*: ⟨o⟩żenić się; *priest*: udzielać ⟨-lić⟩ ślubu; *daughter*: wydać za mąż, *son* ożenić; *v/i* (*a.* **get married**) brać ⟨wziąć⟩ ślub, pob(ie)rać się; ⟨o⟩żenić się; wychodzić ⟨wyjść⟩ za mąż

marshal ['maːʃl] *mil.* marszałek *m*; *Am.* szeryf *m*

martial ['maːʃl] wojenny, wojskowy

martyr ['maːtə] męczennik *m* (-nnica *f*)

marvel ['maːvl] **1.** cudo *n*; **2.** *v/t* podziwiać (*at s.o./s.th.* kogoś/coś); *v/i* dziwić się; **~(l)ous** cudowny, zdumiewający

mascara [mæ'skɑːrə] tusz *m* do rzęs

mascot ['mæskət] maskotka *f*

masculine ['mæskjʊlɪn] męski

mask [maːsk] **1.** maska *f*; **2.** ⟨za⟩maskować ⟨się⟩

mass [mæs] **1.** masa *f*; *eccl.* msza *f*; **2.** ⟨z⟩gromadzić się

massacre ['mæsəkə] **1.** masakra *f*; **2.** ⟨z⟩masakrować

massage ['mæsɑːʒ] **1.** masaż *m*; **2.** masować

massive ['mæsɪv] masywny, ciężki

mass| media *sg, pl* środki *pl* masowego przekazu; **~-produce** produkować masowo; **~ production** produkcja *f* masowa

mast [maːst] maszt *m*

master ['maːstə] **1.** *s* pan *m*; *dog etc.*: właściciel *m*; (*teacher*) nauczyciel *m*, pan *m*, profesor *m*; *art etc.*: mistrz *m*; **2.** *adj* mistrzowski; **3.** opanow(yw)ać; *fear etc.* pokon(yw)ać; **~ly** mistrzowski; **~piece** arcydzieło *n*; **~y** ['maːrɪ] biegłość *f*; panowanie *n* (*over/of* nad)

masturbate ['mæstəbeɪt] onanizować się

match¹ [mætʃ] zapałka *f*

match² [mætʃ] **1.** rzecz *f* do kompletu; *football etc.*: mecz *m*; *person*: godny przeciwnik *m*; **be a (no) ~ for s.o.** (nie) dorównywać komuś; *find/meet one's* **~** trafić na równego sobie; **2.** pasować, dopaso(wy)wać; (*be equal*) dorówn(yw)ać; '**~box** pudełko *n* zapałek

mate [meɪt] kolega *m*; *zo.* samiec *m*, samica *f*

material [mə'tɪərɪəl] **1.** *adj* materialny; (*essential*) istotny; ~ *damage* szkoda *f* materialna; **2.** materiał *m*; **~ize** ⟨z⟩materializować się

maternal [mə'tɜːnl] macierzyński, matczyny

maternity [mə'tɜːnətɪ] macierzyństwo *n*; ~ *leave* urlop *m* macierzyński; ~ *ward* oddział *m* położniczy

math [mæθ] *Am.* F matematyka *f*

mathematic|al [mæθə'mætɪkl] matematyczny; **~ian** [ˌmæθə'tɪʃn] matematyk *m* (-tyczka *f*); **~s** [ˌ'mætɪks] *mst sg* matematyka *f*

maths [mæθs] *mst sg Brt.* F matematyka *f*

matt [mæt] matowy

matter ['mætə] **1.** materia *f*, substancja *f*; *med.* ropa *f*; (*affair*) sprawa *f*; *a* ~ *of course* rzecz *f* naturalna, coś oczywistego; *as a* ~ *of fact* właściwie, w istocie; *a* ~ *of time* kwestia *f* czasu; *what's the* ~ (*with you*)? co się ⟨z tobą⟩ dzieje?; **2.** mieć znaczenie; *it doesn't* ~ to nie ma znaczenia, nie to nie szkodzi

mattress ['mætrɪs] materac *m*

mature [mə'tjʊə] **1.** *adj* dojrzały; **2.** dojrze(wa)ć

Maundy Thursday ['mɔːndɪ]

Wielki Czwartek *m*

May [meɪ] maj *m*

may [ˌ] *v/aux* (*past* **might**) móc; *wish:* oby; ~ *you be happy* obyś był szczęśliwy; '**~be** być może

mayonnaise [meɪə'neɪz] majonez *m*

mayor [meə] burmistrz *m*

maze [meɪz] labirynt *m*

me [miː] mnie, mi; ja

meadow ['medəʊ] łąka *f*

meal [miːl] posiłek *m*; '**~time** pora *f* posiłku

mean[1] [miːn] *adj* podły; (*ungenerous*) skąpy

mean[2] [ˌ] **1.** średnia *f*; *pl* (*a. sg*) środek *m*, (*income*) środki *pl*; *by all* ~*s* oczywiście!, bardzo proszę!; *by no* ~*s* w żadnym razie/wypadku; *by* ~*s of* przy użyciu/pomocy; **2.** *adj* średni, przeciętny

mean[3] [ˌ] (**meant**) znaczyć, oznaczać; (*intend*) mieć na myśli, zamierzać; ~ *well* chcieć dobrze

'**meaning 1.** znaczenie *n*, sens *m*; **2.** *adj look:* znaczący; '**~ful** znaczący, istotny; '**~less** bez znaczenia

meant [ment] *past and pp of* **mean**[3]

mean'time 1. tymczasem; **2.** *in the* ~*time* → ~'**while** tymczasem

measure ['meʒə] **1.** miara *f*; jednostka *f* miary; *fig.* krok *m*, środek *m* zaradczy; **2.** *height etc.* ⟨z⟩mierzyć;

clock: odmierzać; *(have size)*
mieć rozmiar; **'ment** rozmiar *m*, wymiar *m*; pomiar *m*

meat [mi:t] mięso *n*; **'ball**
klops *m*

mechanic [mɪ'kænɪk] mechanik *m*; **al** mechaniczny *(a. fig.)*; maszynowy

mechan|ism ['mekənɪzəm]
mechanizm *m*; **'ize** ⟨z⟩mechanizować

medal ['medl] medal *m*

media ['mi:djə] **1.** *pl of medium* 1; **2.** *sg, pl* media *pl*

mediat|e ['mi:dɪeɪt] pośredniczyć; **ion** [ˌ'eɪʃn] mediacja *f*; **or** mediator *m*

medical ['medɪkl] **1.** *adj* medyczny; **2.** badanie *n* lekarskie; **certificate** zaświadczenie *n* lekarskie

medicin|e ['medɪsɪn] leczniczy; **e** ['medsɪn] lekarstwo *n*; *science*: medycyna *f*

medieval [medɪ'iːvl] średniowieczny

mediocre [mi:dɪ'əʊkə] mierny

meditat|e ['medɪteɪt] medytować; **ion** [ˌ'teɪʃn] medytacja *f*

medium ['mi:djəm] **1.** *(pl dia* [ˌ'djə], *diums)* środek *m*; *radio, TV)* środki *pl* masowego przekazu; **2.** średni; **wave** *electr.* fale *pl* średnie

meek [mi:k] łagodny

meet [mi:t] *(met)* *v/t*
spot(y)kać (się); *(get to*

know) pozna(wa)ć; *needs
etc.* zaspokajać ⟨-koić⟩; *v/i
(join)* ⟨po⟩łączyć się, schodzić się; **with** spot(y)kać
się, napot(y)kać *(difficulties
etc.)*; **'ing** spotkanie *n*;
(gathering) zebranie *n*; *sp.*
mityng *m*

melancholy ['melənkəlɪ] **1.**
melancholia *f*, smutek *m*; **2.**
adj melancholijny, smutny

mellow ['meləʊ] **1.** *adj (ripe)*
dojrzały; *(gentle)* łagodny; **2.**
⟨z⟩łagodnieć

melod|ious [mɪ'ləʊdjəs] melodyjny; **y** ['melədɪ] melodia *f*

melt [melt] *ice*: ⟨s⟩topnieć;
sun etc.: ⟨s⟩topić; **down**
⟨s⟩topić *(metal)*

member ['membə] członek *m*
(a. anat.); **ship** członkostwo *n*, przynależność *f*

membrane ['membreɪn]
błona *f*, membrana *f*

memo ['meməʊ] notatka *f*

memorial [mə'mɔ:rɪəl] pomnik *m*

memor|ize ['meməraɪz] zapamięt(yw)ać; **y** pamięć *f (a.
computer)*; *(recollection)*
wspomnienie *n*

men [men] *pl of man* 1

mend [mend] ⟨z⟩reperować,
naprawi(a)ć

menstruation [menstru'eɪʃn]
menstruacja *f*

mental ['mentl] umysłowy;
(done in the thoughts) pamięciowy; **hospital** szpital

m dla umysłowo chorych; **~ity** [~'tælɪt] mentalność *f*, umysłowość *f*; **~ly** ['~təlɪ] umysłowo; **~ly handicapped** upośledzony umysłowo; **~ly ill** umysłowo chory

mention ['menʃn] 1. wspominać ⟨-mnieć⟩, wzmiankować; **don't ~ it** nie ma za co; 2. wzmianka *f*

menu ['menju:] menu *n*, karta *f* (dań); *computer:* menu *n*

merchan|dise ['mɜ:tʃəndaɪz] towary *pl*; **~t** ['~ənt] kupiec *m*

merci|ful ['mɜ:sɪful] miłosierny, litościwy; **~less** bezlitosny

mercury ['mɜ:kjʊrɪ] rtęć *f*

mercy ['mɜ:sɪ] miłosierdzie *n*, litość *f*, łaska *f*

mere [mɪə] zwykły; (*only*) tylko; **~ly** po prostu, jedynie

merge [mɜ:dʒ] ⟨po⟩łączyć się (*a. econ.*), zl(ew)ać się; **~r** *econ.* fuzja *f*

meridian [mə'rɪdɪən] południk *m*

merit ['merɪt] 1. zasługa *f*; 2. zasługiwać ⟨-łużyć⟩ (*s.th.* na coś)

merry ['merɪ] wesoły; ♀ **Christmas!** Wesołych Świąt!; **~-go-round** karuzela *f*

mess [mes] 1. bałagan *m*, nieład *m*; *fig.* kłopot *m*, tarapaty *pl*; 2.: **~ about, ~ around** próżnować; **~ up** nabałaganić; *fig.* zepsuć

message ['mesɪdʒ] wiado-

mość *f*; (*important idea*) przesłanie *n*

messenger ['mesɪndʒə] posłaniec *m*

messy ['mesɪ] brudny, niechlujny

met [met] *past and pp of* **meet**

metal ['metl] metal *m*; **~lic** [mɪ'tælɪk] metalowy; *colour, sound:* metaliczny

meter¹ ['mi:tə] licznik *m*

meter² [~] *Am.* → **metre**

method ['meθəd] metoda *f*; **~ical** [mɪ'θɒdɪkl] metodyczny, systematyczny

metre, *Am.* **-ter** ['mi:tə] metr *m*

Mexic|an ['meksɪkən] 1. *adj* meksykański; 2. Meksykanin *m* (-nka *f*); **~o** Meksyk *m*

miaow [mi:'aʊ] ⟨za⟩miauczeć

mice [maɪs] *pl of* **mouse**

micro... [maɪkrəʊ] mikro...; **~computer** mikrokomputer *m*; **~electronics** *sg* mikroelektronika *f*; **~film** mikrofilm *m*

microphone ['maɪkrəfəʊn] mikrofon *m*

microprocessor ['maɪkrəʊ-'prəʊsesə] mikroprocesor *m*

micro|scope ['maɪkrəskəʊp] mikroskop *m*; **~wave** mikrofala *f*; **~wave oven** kuchenka *f* mikrofalowa

mid [mɪd] środkowy, w środku; **~day** południe *n*

middle ['mɪdl] 1. *adj* środkowy; 2. środek *m*; *in the ~ of* w

mint

środku; **~'aged** w średnim wieku; ♀ **Ages** pl średniowiecze n; **~class(es** pl) klasa f średnia; ♀ **East** Bliski Wschód m

'mid|night północ f; **'~sum-mer** pełnia f lata; **~'way** w połowie drogi; **'~wife** (pl **-wives**) położna f

might [mait] past of **may**; **~y** potężny

migrate [mai'greit] migrować, wędrować

mild [maild] łagodny, delikatny

mildew ['mildju:] pleśń f

mildness ['maildnis] łagodność f

mile [mail] mila f (1,609 km)

military ['militəri] wojskowy

milk [milk] **1.** mleko n; **2.** ⟨wy⟩doić; **~chocolate** czekolada f mleczna; **'~man** (pl **-men**) dostawca m; **~tooth** (pl **-teeth**) ząb m mleczny

mill [mil] **1.** młyn m (factory) fabryka f; **2.** ⟨ze⟩mleć; **'~er** młynarz m

milli|gram(me) ['miligræm] miligram m; **'~metre**, Am. **-er** milimetr m

million ['miljən] milion m; **~aire** [~'neə] milioner m

mince [mins] ⟨po⟩siekać

mind [maind] **1.** umysł m; **be out of one's ~** być szalony!; **bear/keep s.th. in ~** pamiętać; **change one's ~** zmienia⟨ć⟩ zdanie; **make up one's ~** zdecydować się; **2.**

uważać, zważać; (look after) pilnować; **do you ~ if I smo-ke?, do you ~ my smoking?** pozwolisz, że zapalę?; **~ the step!** uwaga! stopień!; **~ your own business!** pilnuj swoich spraw!; **~ (you)** uważaj; zapamiętaj; **~I** uważaj!; **never ~!** nie szkodzi!; **I don't ~** nie mam nic przeciwko

mine¹ [main] mój

mine² [~] **1.** kopalnia f (a. fig.); mil. mina f; **2.** coal etc. wydobywać; mil. ⟨za⟩minować; **'~r** górnik m

mineral ['minərəl] minerał m; **~ water** woda f mineralna

mini... [mini] mini...; **~bus** mikrobus m; **~skirt** mini-spódniczka f

miniature ['minətʃə] miniatura f

mini|mal ['miniml] minimalny; **'~mize** ⟨z⟩minimalizować

mining ['mainiŋ] górnictwo n

minister ['ministə] minister m; eccl. pastor m

ministry ['ministri] ministerstwo n; eccl. duszpasterstwo n

mink [miŋk] zo. norka f

minor ['mainə] **1.** adj mniejszy, niewielki; jur. nieletni; mus. molowy, minorowy; **D ~** d-moll; **2.** jur. nieletni m; **~ity** ['nrəti] mniejszość f; jur. nieletniość f

mint¹ [mint] bot. mięta f

mint² [~] **1.** mennica f; **2.** bić monety

minus 364

minus ['maɪnəs] minus; mniej

minute ['mɪnɪt] minuta f; *fig.* chwila f; *pl* protokół m; **in a ~** za chwilę; **just a ~** chwileczkę

mirac|le ['mɪrəkl] cud m; **~ulous** [mɪ'rækjʊləs] cudowny, nadzwyczajny

mirror ['mɪrə] **1.** lustro n; **2.** odzwierciedlać ⟨-lić⟩, odbi(ja)ć

mis... [mɪs] nie..., źle...; **~apply** źle zastosować

misbehave źle się zachow(yw)ać

miscellaneous [mɪsə'leɪnjəs] różnorodny

mischie|f ['mɪstʃɪf] psota f, figiel m; (*harm*) szkoda f; **~vous** ['~vəs] psotny, figlarny; złośliwy

miser|able ['mɪzərəbl] (*unhappy*) nieszczęśliwy; (*pathetic*) marny, nędzny; **'~y** nieszczęście n, niedola f

mis'fortune pech m

mis'giving obawa f, złe przeczucie n

mis'handle źle obchodzić ⟨obejść⟩ się (z)

mis'judge źle ⟨o⟩sądzić

mis'lead (**-led**) wprowadzać ⟨-dzić⟩ w błąd

mis'place zapodziać; *feelings* źle ⟨u⟩lokować; **~d** źle umieszczony

miss¹ [mɪs] (*before a name 2*) panna f

miss² [~] **1.** (*fail to hit*) chybi(a)ć, nie trafi(a)ć; (*fail to*

hear) nie dosłyszeć; (*fail to see*) nie zauważyć; (*be late*) spóźni(a)ć się; (*avoid*) uniknąć; (*feel the lack*) tęsknić, odczuwać brak; **2.** chybienie n; pudło n F

missile ['mɪsaɪl] pocisk m

missing ['mɪsɪŋ] brakujący, zaginiony; **be ~** brakować

mission ['mɪʃn] misja f pol., eccl., mil. misja f

mist [mɪst] **1.** mgła f, mgiełka f; **2. ~ over** zaparować; **~ up** pokryć parą

mistake [mɪ'steɪk] **1.** (**-took**, **-taken**) źle zrozumieć, pomylić; **~ s.o. for s.o. else** wziąć kogoś za kogoś innego; **2.** pomyłka f, błąd m; **by ~** przez pomyłkę; **~n** w błędzie; **be ~n** być w błędzie, mylić się

mistress ['mɪstrɪs] pani f; (*teacher*) nauczycielka f; (*lover*) kochanka f

mistrust [mɪs'trʌst] **1.** nie ufać/dowierzać; **2.** nieufność f, brak m zaufania

misty ['mɪstɪ] mglisty, zamglony

misunderstand (**-stood**) źle zrozumieć; **~ing** nieporozumienie n

misuse 1. [mɪs'juːz] niewłaściwie uży(wa)ć; **2.** [~'juːs] złe użycie n

mitigate ['mɪtɪgeɪt] ⟨z⟩łagodzić

mix [mɪks] **1.** ⟨z⟩mieszać, wymieszać; (*combine*) mieszać się, łączyć się; ~ **up** pomylić (**s.o. with s.o.** kogoś z kimś); **be ~ed up** być zamieszanym (**in** w); 2. mieszanka *f*; ~**ed** mieszany (a. *feelings etc.*); '~**er** mikser *m*; ~**ture** ['~tʃə] mieszanina *f*, mikstura *f*

moan [məʊn] 1. jęk *m*; 2. jęczeć ⟨jęknąć⟩

mob [mɒb] motłoch *m*

mobile ['məʊbaıl] ruchomy, przenośny; ~**ity** [~'bılətı] ruchliwość *f*

mock [mɒk] 1. wyśmie(wa)ć, ⟨wy⟩kpić (**at** z); przedrzeźniać; 2. *adj* udawany, pozorowany; '~**ery** kpina *f*

mode [məʊd] tryb *m* (a. *gr., computer*)

model ['mɒdl] 1. model *m*, wzór *m*; *tech.* model *m*, typ *m*; (*person*) model(ka *f*) *m*; 2. ⟨wy⟩modelować; *clothes etc.* prezentować

moderate 1. ['mɒdərət] *adj* umiarkowany; 2. ['~eıt] *v/t* ⟨po⟩hamować, ⟨z⟩łagodzić; *v/i* ⟨z⟩łagodnieć; **~ion** [~'reıʃn] (*self-control*) umiarkowanie *n*; (*reduction*) złagodzenie *n*

modern ['mɒdən] (*up to date*) nowoczesny; (*not ancient*) współczesny; '~**ize** ⟨z⟩modernizować, unowocześni(a)ć

modest ['mɒdıst] skromny; '~**y** skromność *f*

modi|fication [mɒdıfı'keıʃn]

modyfikacja *f*, zmiana *f*; ~**fy** ['~faı] ⟨z⟩modyfikować

moist [mɔıst] wilgotny; ~**en** ['~sn] zwilżać ⟨-żyć⟩; ~**ure** ['~stʃə] wilgotność *f*

molar (**tooth**) ['məʊlə] (*pl teeth*) ząb *m* trzonowy

mole [məʊl] kret *m*

molest [məʊ'lest] molestować, napastować

moment ['məʊmənt] chwila *f*, moment *m*; **at the ~** w tej chwili, obecnie

monarch ['mɒnək] monarcha *m*; ~**y** monarchia *f*

monastery ['mɒnəstərı] klasztor *m*

Monday ['mʌndı] poniedziałek *m*

monetary ['mʌnıtərı] monetarny, pieniężny

money ['mʌnı] pieniądze *pl*; ~ **order** przekaz *m* pieniężny

monitor ['mɒnıtə] 1. monitor *m*; urządzenie *n* kontrolne; 2. kontrolować, nadzorować

monk [mʌŋk] mnich *m*

monkey ['mʌŋkı] małpa *f*; ~ **wrench** *tech.* klucz *m* francuski

monopol|ize [mə'nɒpəlaız] ⟨z⟩monopolizować; ~**y** monopol *m*

monoton|ous [mə'nɒtənəs] monotonny; ~**y** [~'tnı] monotonia *f*

monster ['mɒnstə] potwór *m*

month [mʌnθ] miesiąc *m*; '~**ly** 1. *adj* miesięczny; 2. miesięcznik *m*

monument ['mɔnjʊmənt] pomnik *m*

moo [mu:] *cow:* ryczeć

mood [mu:d] nastrój *m*; *be in the ~ for s.th.* mieć nastrój/ochotę do czegoś; **'~y** kapryśny, zmienne usposobienie

moon [mu:n] księżyc *m; once in a blue ~* F raz od wielkiego święta; **'~light** 1. światło *n* księżyca; 2. F pracować na czarno F; **'~lit** oświetlony światłem księżyca; **'~shine** *Am.* bimber *m*

moose [mu:s] (*pl ~*) łoś *m*

mop [mɔp] 1. szczotka *f* do mycia podłogi; zmywak *m*; 2. wycierać ⟨wytrzeć⟩; *~ up* zmy(wa)ć

moral ['mɔrəl] 1. *adj* moralny; 2. morał *m* (*opowieści*); *pl* moralność *f*, obyczaje *pl*; **~e** [mɒ'rɑ:l] morale *n*, duch *m*; **~ity** [mə'rælətɪ] moralność *f*; **~ize** ['mɔrəlaɪz] moralizować

more [mɔ:] 1. *adj* więcej; *some ~ tea* jeszcze trochę herbaty; 2. *adv* bardziej; *~ and ~* coraz bardziej; *~ important* ważniejszy; *~ often* częstszy; *~ or less* mniej więcej; *once ~* jeszcze raz; *a little ~* jeszcze trochę więcej; **'~over** [~'rəʊvə] ponadto

morgue [mɔ:g] kostnica *f*

morning ['mɔ:nɪŋ] rano *n*, (po)ranek *m*; przedpołudnie *n*; *in the ~* (jutro) rano; *this ~*

dzisiaj rano; *good ~* dzień dobry

mortal ['mɔ:tl] 1. *adj* śmiertelny; 2. śmiertelnik *m*; **~ity** [~'tælətɪ] śmiertelność *f*

mortgage ['mɔ:gɪdʒ] 1. hipoteka *f*; 2. oddać w zastaw hipoteczny

mortuary ['mɔ:tʃʊərɪ] kostnica *f*

mosaic [məʊ'zeɪk] mozaika *f*

Moslem ['mɒzləm] 1. *adj* muzułmański; 2. muzułmanin *m* (*-nka f*)

mosque [mɒsk] meczet *m*

mosquito [mə'ski:təʊ] (*pl -to⟨e⟩s*) moskit *m*; komar *m*

moss [mɒs] mech *m*

most [məʊst] 1. *adj* najwięcej; bardzo; *for the ~ part* przeważnie; *~ people* większość ludzi; 2. *adv* najbardziej; *~ of all* najbardziej; *the ~ important* najważniejszy; 3. *s* większość *f*; *at (the) ~* co najwyżej; *make the ~ of s.th.* wykorzystywać coś w pełni; **'~ly** przeważnie, najczęściej

moth [mɒθ] ćma *f*; *clothes:* mól *m*

mother ['mʌðə] 1. matka *f*; 2. matkować; **~hood** ['~hʊd] macierzyństwo *n*; **'~-in-law** ['~ɔːrɪnlɔː] teściowa *f*; **'~ly** matczyny, macierzyński; **~ tongue** język *m* ojczysty

motif [məʊ'ti:f] *art:* motyw *m*

motion ['məʊʃn] 1. ruch *m*; *parl.* wniosek *m*; *put/set in ~ a. fig.* wprawi(a)ć w ruch; 2.

skinąć; '**~less** nieruchomy; **~ picture** Am. film m

motiv|ate ['məʊtɪveɪt] ⟨u⟩motywować; **~e** [~ɪv] motyw m (działania)

motor ['məʊtə] silnik m, motor m; '**~bike** Brt. F motocykl m; '**~boat** motorówka f; '**~car** samochód m; '**~cycle** motocykl m; '**~cyclist** motocyklista m; '**~ist** [~ɔrɪst] kierowca m; '**~scooter** skuter m; '**~way** Brt. autostrada f

mount [maʊnt] 1. v/t exhibition etc. ⟨z⟩montować, ⟨z⟩organizować; (fix) osadzać ⟨-dzić⟩, oprawi⟨a⟩ć; (climb) wspinać ⟨-piąć⟩ się; horse dosiadać ⟨-siąść⟩; v/i (rise) narastać; podnosić się; 2. rzeczowa f, stojak m; (horse) wierzchowiec m

mountain ['maʊntɪn] góra f; **~eer** [~'nɪə] wspinacz m; **~eering** [~'nɪərɪŋ] wspinaczka f; **~ous** górzysty

mourn [mɔːn] v/t opłakiwać; v/i płakać (In, over nad); '**~er** żałobnik m; '**~ful** żałobny; '**~ing** żałoba f

mouse [maʊs] (pl mice [maɪs]) mysz f

moustache [mə'stɑːʃ] wąsy pl

mouth [maʊθ] (pl **~s** [~ðz]) usta pl; animal: pysk m; river: ujście n; '**~ful** łyk m, kęs m; '**~organ** harmonijka f ustna; '**~piece** ustnik m; teleph. mikrofon m

move [muːv] 1. v/t ruszać

⟨-szyć⟩; przesuwać ⟨-sunąć⟩; form. wzruszać ⟨-ruszyć⟩; **~ house** przeprowadzać ⟨-dzić⟩ się; przeprowadzać ⟨-dzić⟩ się; chess: ⟨z⟩robić ruch; ruszać się; parl. etc. stawiać ⟨postawić⟩ wniosek; **~ in** wprowadzać ⟨-dzić⟩ się; **~ on** ruszać ⟨-szyć⟩ naprzód/dalej; **~ out** wyprowadzać ⟨-dzić⟩ się; 2. ruch m; fig. krok m; chess: ruch m, posunięcie n; get a **~ on!** F ruszaj!; '**~ment** ruch m; poruszenie n; mus. część f

movie ['muːvɪ] esp. Am. film m; pl kino n

moving ['muːvɪŋ] ruchomy; fig. wzruszający; **~ staircase** ruchome schody pl

mow [məʊ] (mowed, mowed or mown) ⟨s⟩kosić; '**~er** kosiarka f; **~n** pp of mow

much [mʌtʃ] 1. adj dużo, wiele; 2. adv dużo, wiele; how **~?** ile?; 3. s: nothing **~** nic szczególnego

mud [mʌd] błoto n

muddle ['mʌdl] 1. bałagan m; 2. (a. **~ up**) ⟨po⟩mieszać, ⟨po⟩plątać

mud|dy ['mʌdɪ] zabłocony, błotnisty; '**~guard** błotnik m

mug [mʌg] kubek m

mule [mjuːl] muł m

multiple ['mʌltɪpl] wielokrotny, wieloraki, wielostronny

multi|plication [mʌltɪplɪ'keɪʃn] mnożenie n; **~plication table** tabliczka f mnożenia; **~ply**

['ʌplaɪ] ⟨po⟩mnożyć (**by** przez); *animals*: rozmnażać ⟨-nożyć⟩ się; **~'storey** wielopiętrowy; **~storey car park** parking m wielopoziomowy

multitude ['mʌltɪtjuːd] mnóstwo n; **the ~(s** pl) masy pl

mum [mʌm] *Brt.* F mamusia f

mumble ['mʌmbl] ⟨wy⟩mruczeć, ⟨wy⟩mamrotać

mummy ['mʌmɪ] mumia f

municipal [mjuː'nɪsɪpl] miejski, komunalny

murder ['mɜːdə] 1. morderstwo n, mord m; 2. ⟨za⟩mordować; **~er** ['~rə] morderca m; **~ous** ['~rəs] morderczy

murmur ['mɜːmə] 1. mruczenie n, pomruk m; 2. ⟨za⟩mruczeć; (*complain*) szemrać (**at/against** na)

musc|le ['mʌsl] mięsień m; **~ular** ['~kjʊlə] mięśniowy; (*strong*) muskularny

museum [mjuː'zɪəm] muzeum n

mushroom ['mʌʃrʊm] grzyb m

music ['mjuːzɪk] muzyka f; nuty pl; **~al** 1. adj muzyczny; *person*: muzykalny; 2. musical m; **~ hall** esp. Brt. wodewil m; **~ian** [~'zɪ[n] muzyk m

must [mʌst] 1. v/aux musieć; **I ~ not** nie wolno mi; 2. konieczność f

mustache [mə'staːʃ] Am. → **moustache**

mustard ['mʌstəd] musztarda f

mute [mjuːt] 1. adj niemy; 2. niemowa m; mus. tłumik m

mutilate ['mjuːtɪleɪt] okaleczyć

mutiny ['mjuːtɪnɪ] 1. bunt m; 2. ⟨z⟩buntować się

mutter ['mʌtə] 1. mruczeć, mamrotać; (*complain*) szemrać; 2. mruczenie n, pomruk m

mutton ['mʌtn] baranina f

mutual ['mjuːtʃʊəl] wzajemny; (*equally shared*) wspólny

muzzle ['mʌzl] 1. pysk m; kaganiec m; mil. wylot m lufy; 2. a. fig. nakładać ⟨nałożyć⟩ kaganiec

my [maɪ] mój

myself [maɪ'self] reflexive: się, siebie, sobie; emphasis: (ja) sam(a)

myster|ious [mɪ'stɪərɪəs] tajemniczy; **~y** ['~stərɪ] tajemnica f

mystify ['mɪstɪfaɪ] ⟨za⟩intrygować

myth [mɪθ] mit m; **~ology** [~'θɒlədʒɪ] mitologia f

N

nag [næg] zrzędzić, marudzić; **'~ging** dokuczliwy

nail [neɪl] **1.** *anat.* paznokieć *m*; *for hammering*: gwóźdź *m*; **2.** przybi(ja)ć; **~ polish, ~ varnish** lakier *m* do paznokci

naked ['neɪkɪd] nagi, goły

name [neɪm] **1.** nazwa *f*; *first*: imię *n*; (*surname*) nazwisko *n*; *what's your ~?* jak się nazywasz?; *call s.o. ~s* (na)wymyślać komuś; **2.** naz(y)wać, nada(wa)ć imię; (*identify*) wymieni(a)ć; **'~ly** mianowicie; **'~sake** imiennik *m*

nanny ['nænɪ] niania *f*

nap [næp] **1.** drzemka *f*; *have/ take a ~* **2.** zdrzemnąć się

napkin ['næpkɪn] serwetka *f*; *Brt.* **~py** *Brt.* pieluszka *f*

narcotic [nɑːˈkɒtɪk] **1.** narkotyk *m*; **2.** *adj* narkotyczny

narrate [nəˈreɪt] opowiadać ⟨-wiedzieć⟩; **~ion** narracja *f*; **~or** [nəˈreɪtə] narrator *m*

narrow ['nærəʊ] **1.** *adj* wąski; *fig.* ograniczony; **2.** zwężać ⟨zwęzić⟩ się; **~ly** o włos; **~'minded** ograniczony

nasty ['nɑːstɪ] nieprzyjemny; *smell*: przykry; (*malicious*) złośliwy; *accident etc.*: groźny

nation ['neɪʃn] naród *m*

national ['næʃənl] **1.** *adj* narodowy; **2 Health Service** *Brt.* państwowa służba *f* zdrowia; **2 Insurance** *Brt.* system *m* ubezpieczeń społecznych; **~ park** park *m* narodowy; **2.** obywatel *m*; **~ity** [~ˈnælətɪ] narodowość *f*; **~ize** [ˈ~nəlaɪz] ⟨z⟩nacjonalizować

native ['neɪtɪv] **1.** *adj* ojczysty; **~ country** ojczyzna *f*; **~ language** język *m* ojczysty; **2.** krajowiec *m*

natural ['nætʃrəl] naturalny; (*innate*) wrodzony; **~ gas** gaz *m* ziemny; **~ize** naturalizować; *bot., zo.* aklimatyzować; **~ science** nauki *pl* przyrodnicze

nature ['neɪtʃə] natura *f*, przyroda *f*

naughty ['nɔːtɪ] niegrzeczny

nautical ['nɔːtɪkl] morski, żeglarski; **~ mile** mila *f* morska

navel ['neɪvl] pępek *m*

naviga|ble ['nævɪgəbl] żeglowny; **~te** [ˈ~eɪt] sterować; pilotować; **~tion** [~ˈgeɪʃn] nawigacja *f*

navy ['neɪvɪ] marynarka *f* wojenna

near [nɪə] **1.** *adj* bliski, niedaleki; **2.** *adv* blisko; **3.** *prp* obok, u; **4.** *v/t* zbliżać ⟨-żyć⟩ się (do); **~by 1.** [ˈ~baɪ] *adj* pobliski; **2.**

[~'baɪ] *adv* nieopodal, w pobliżu; '**~ly** prawie; **~'sighted** krótkowzroczny

neat [niːt] schludny, czysty; *whisky etc.*: czysty, nierozcieńczony

necessar|ily ['nesəsərəlɪ] koniecznie; *not* **~ily** niekoniecznie; **~y** ['~sərɪ] konieczny, nieodzowny, niezbędny

necessit|ate [nɪ'sesɪteɪt] wymagać; **~y** [~'sesətɪ] konieczność *f*

neck [nek] szyja *f*; *shirt*: kołnierzyk *m*; *bottle*: szyjka *f*; **~lace** ['~lɪs] naszyjnik *m*; '**~line** dekolt *m*; '**~tie** *Am.* krawat *m*

need [niːd] **1.** potrzebować, wymagać; (*have to*) musieć; **2.** potrzeba *f*; (*poverty*) bieda *f*; (*reason*) powód *m*; *it ~ be* w razie potrzeby; *in ~* w potrzebie; *be in ~ of s.th.* potrzebować czegoś

needle ['niːdl] igła *f*

negat|e [nɪ'geɪt] ⟨za⟩negować, ⟨za⟩przeczyć; **~ion** negacja *f*, zaprzeczenie *n*; **~ive** ['negətɪv] **1.** *adj answer etc.*: przeczący; *results etc.*: negatywny; (*less than zero*) ujemny; **2.** przeczenie *n*; *phot.* negatyw *m*

neglect [nɪ'glekt] zaniedb(yw)ać

neglig|ence ['neglɪdʒəns] niedbalstwo *n*; **~ent** niedbały; '**~ible** nieistotny, bez znaczenia

negotiat|e [nɪ'gəʊʃɪeɪt] *v/i* pertraktować; *v/t* ⟨wy⟩negocjować; **~ion** [~'eɪʃn] negocjacja *f*; **~or** [~'gəʊʃɪeɪtə] negocjator *m*

Negro ['niːgrəʊ] (*pl -groes*) Murzyn *m*

neighbo(u)r ['neɪbə] sąsiad(ka *f*) *m*; '**~hood** sąsiedztwo *n*; dzielnica *f*

neither ['naɪðə, *Am.* 'niːðə] **1.** *adj, pron* żaden (z dwóch); **2.** *cj*: **~ ... nor** ani... ani; **3.** *adv* też nie

nephew ['nevjuː] bratanek *m*, siostrzeniec *m*

nerve [nɜːv] *anat., bot.* nerw *m*; (*courage*) zimna krew *f*; F tupet *m*; '**~-racking** F denerwujący, szarpiący nerwy

nervous ['nɜːvəs] nerwowy; (*worried*) zdenerwowany, niespokojny

nest [nest] **1.** gniazdo *n*; **2.** ⟨za⟩gnieździć się

net [net] **1.** siatka *f*; **~ curtain** firanka *f*

network ['netwɜːk] *radio, roads etc.*: sieć *f*

neutral ['njuːtrəl] **1.** *adj* neutralny; *electr.* obojętny; **2.** państwo *n* neutralne; *mot.* luz *m*; **~ity** [~'trælətɪ] neutralność *f*; **~ize** ['~trəlaɪz] unieszkodliwi(a)ć

never ['nevə] nigdy; '**~-ending** [~ər~] nie kończący się; **~theless** [~ðə'les] niemniej, jednak

new [njuː] nowy; świeży; *po-*

tatoes: młody; **nothing** ~ nic nowego; **'~born** nowo narodzony; **'~comer** przybysz *m*; **'~ly** *adv* nowo; dopiero co; ~ **moon** nów *m*

news [nju:z] *sg* wiadomości *pl*; ~ **agency** agencja *f* informacyjna; **'~agent** *Brt.* kioskarz *m* (-rka *f*); **'~cast** *radio, TV*: dziennik *m*; **'~caster** lektor(ka *f*) *m* dziennika; ~ **dealer** *Am.* → *newsagent*; **'~letter** biuletyn *m*; **'~paper** gazeta *f*; **'~reader** *Brt.* → *newscaster*; **'~reel** kronika *f* filmowa; **'~stand** kiosk *m*

new year nowy rok *m*; *Happy 2!* Szczęśliwego Nowego Roku!; *2's Day* Nowy Rok *m*; *2's Eve* Sylwester *m*

next [nekst] **1.** *adj* następny; *week etc.*: przyszły; ~ **door** obok; ~ **but one** przedostatni; **2.** *adv* następnie; potem, później; ~ **to** obok; **'~door** sąsiedni; najbliższy

nice [naɪs] miły, przyjemny; **'~ly** *adv* miło, przyjemnie

nickname ['nɪkneɪm] **1.** przydomek *m*, przezwisko *n*; **2.** przezwać

niece [ni:s] bratanica *f*, siostrzenica *f*

niggard ['nɪgəd] *contp.* skąpiec *m*, sknera *m*, *f*; **'~ly** skąpy

night [naɪt] noc *f*; (*evening*) wieczór *m*; *at* ~, *by* ~, *in the* ~ nocą, w nocy; *good* ~ dobra-

noc; **'~club** klub *m* nocny; **'~dress** koszula *f* nocna; **'~fall**: *at* ~*fall* o zmroku; **'~gown** koszula *f* nocna; **~ingale** ['~ɪŋgeɪl] słowik *m*; **'~ly 1.** *adj* conocny; cowieczorny; **2.** *adv* co noc; co wieczór; **~mare** ['~meə] koszmar *m*; ~ **school** nocna szkoła *f* wieczorowa; ~ **shift** nocna zmiana *f*; **'~shirt** koszula *f* nocna; **'~time**: *at* ~*time*, *in the* ~*time* w nocy, nocą

nine [naɪn] dziewięć; **~teen** [~'ti:n] dziewiętnaście; **'~ety** dziewięćdziesiąt; **~th** [naɪnθ] dziewiąty

nipple ['nɪpl] *anat.* sutek *m*, brodawka *f* (piersiowa)

nitrogen ['naɪtrədʒən] azot *m*

no [nəʊ] **1.** *adv* nie; **2.** *adj* żaden; ~ **one** nikt

nobility [nəʊ'bɪlətɪ] szlachetność *f*; (*aristocracy*) szlachta *f*

noble ['nəʊbl] szlachetny; *family etc.*: szlachecki

nobody ['nəʊbədɪ] nikt

nod [nɒd] **1.** skinąć głową; ~ *off* przysnąć; **2.** skinienie *n* (głowy)

noise [nɔɪz] hałas *m*, dźwięk *m*; *radio etc.*: szum *m*; **'~less** bezszelestny, bezgłośny

noisy ['nɔɪzɪ] hałaśliwy

nomin|al ['nɒmɪnl] nominalny; *payment*: symboliczny; **~ate** ['~eɪt] mianować; (*appoint*) wysuwać ⟨-sunąć⟩ kandydaturę; **~ation** [~'neɪʃn] nominacja *f*

non... [nɒn] nie..., bez...

nonalcoholic bezalkoholowy

noncommissioned officer podoficer *m*

none [nʌn] **1.** *pron* żaden; **2.** *adv* (wcale) nie; **~theless** [ˌðəˈles] → *nevertheless*

nonexistent nie istniejący

non(in)flammable niepalny

non-'iron niemnący się

no-'nonsense rzeczowy

nonsense [ˈnɒnsəns] absurd *m*, niedorzeczność *f*

non'stop nieprzerwany, non stop; *train etc.*: bezpośredni

noodle [ˈnuːdl] kluska *f*; makaron *m*

noon [nuːn] południe *n*; *at* **~** w południe

nor [nɔː] → *neither* **2**; też nie

norm [nɔːm] norma *f*; **~al** normalny; **~alize** ⟨z⟩normalizować; **~ally** *adv* normalnie; zwykle

north [nɔːθ] **1.** północ *f*; **2.** *adj* północny; **3.** *adv* na północ; **~erly** [ˈˌðəlɪ], **~ern** [ˈˌðn] *adj* północny; **~ward(s)** [ˈˌwəd(z)] *adv* na północ

Nor|way [ˈnɔːweɪ] Norwegia *f*; **~wegian** [ˈwiːdʒən] **1.** *adj* norweski; **2.** Norweg *m* (-eżka *f*)

nose [nəuz] nos *m*; węch *m*; *plane etc.*: dziób *m*

nostril [ˈnɒstrɪl] nozdrze *n*

nosy [ˈnəuzɪ] wścibski

not [nɒt] nie; **~ a** ani

notable [ˈnəutəbl] godny uwagi

notary [ˈnəutərɪ] *mst* **~ public** notariusz *m*

note [nəut] **1.** *often pl* notatka *f*; (*remark*) uwaga *f*; *diplomatic*: nota *f*; (*letter*) liścik *m*; (*money*) banknot *m*; *mus.* nuta *f*; *take* **~** *of s.th.* zwrócić uwagę na coś; **2.** zauważać ⟨-żyć⟩; *often* **~ down** ⟨za⟩notować; **~book** notes *m*; **~d** znany; **~pad** notatnik *m*

nothing [ˈnʌθɪŋ] nic; **~ but** tylko; **~ much** niewiele; *for* **~** na nic; (*free*) za darmo; *to say* **~** *of* nie mówiąc już o

notice [ˈnəutɪs] **1.** wiadomość *f*, ogłoszenie *n*; (*dismissal*) wypowiedzenie *n*; (*attention*) uwaga *f*; *at short* **~** w krótkim terminie, bez uprzedzenia; *until further* **~** aż do odwołania; *give s.o.* **~** przedzać ⟨-dzić⟩ kogoś; *four weeks'* **~** czterotygodniowe wypowiedzenie; *take* **~** *of s.th.* zwrócić uwagę na coś; **2.** zauważyć; **~able** widoczny, dostrzegalny

notify [ˈnəutɪfaɪ] zawiadamiać ⟨-domić⟩

notion [ˈnəuʃn] pojęcie *n*; (*whim*) kaprys *m*

notorious [nəuˈtɔːrɪəs] osławiony, znany (*for* z)

nought [nɔːt] *Brt.* zero *n*

noun [naun] *gr.* rzeczownik *m*

nourish [ˈnʌrɪʃ] ⟨wy⟩żywić, odżywiać ⟨-wić⟩; *fig.* żywić; **~ing** pożywny; **~ment** pożywienie *n*

novel ['nɒvl] **1.** powieść f; **2.** adj nowatorski; **~ist** ['~list] powieściopisarz m (-sarka f); **~ty** nowatorstwo n, nowość f

November [nəʊ'vembə] listopad m

novice ['nɒvɪs] nowicjusz(ka f) m (a. eccl.)

now [naʊ] teraz, obecnie; **~ and again, ~ and then** od czasu do czasu; **by ~** już; **from ~ on** odtąd; **just ~** dopiero co, przed chwilką

nowadays ['naʊədeɪz] w dzisiejszych czasach, obecnie

nowhere ['nəʊweə] nigdzie

nuclear ['nju:klɪə] jądrowy, nuklearny; **~ energy** energia f jądrowa; **~ physics** sg fizyka f jądrowa; **~ power** energia f jądrowa; **~ power station** elektrownia f jądrowa; **~ reactor** reaktor m jądrowy; **~ waste** odpady pl promieniotwórcze; **~ weapons** pl broń f jądrowa

nude [nju:d] **1.** adj nagi; **2.** art: akt m; **in the ~** nago

nuisance ['nju:sns] utrapienie n; **make a ~ of o.s.** być nieznośnym

numb [nʌm] **1.** adj a. fig. zdrętwiały, skostniały (**with** z); **2.** ⟨s⟩paraliżować

number ['nʌmbə] **1.** liczba f, cyfra f; (issue) numer m; **2.** v/t ⟨po⟩numerować; form. (include) zaliczać ⟨-czyć⟩; v/i liczyć, wynosić; **~less** niezliczony; **~plate** Brt. mot. tablica f rejestracyjna

numer|al ['nju:mərəl] liczebnik m; **~ous** liczny

nun [nʌn] zakonnica f

nurse [nɜ:s] **1.** pielęgniarka f; (nanny) opiekunka f; **2.** people pielęgnować; illness leczyć

nursery ['nɜ:səri] żłobek m; **~ rhyme** rymowanka f; **~ school** przedszkole n; **~ teacher** przedszkolanka f

nursing ['nɜ:sɪŋ] pielęgniarstwo n

nut [nʌt] orzech m; tech. nakrętka f; **~cracker(s** pl**)** dziadek m do orzechów

nuts [nʌts] F stuknięty F

'nut|shell skorupka f orzecha; **in a ~shell** w paru słowach, w (najwiekszym) skrócie; **~ty** orzechowy

nylon ['naɪlɒn] nylon m

O

o [əʊ] **1.** och!, ach!; **2.** teleph. zero n

oak [əʊk] dąb m

oar [ɔ:] wiosło n

oasis [əʊ'eɪsɪs] (pl **-ses** [~si:z]) oaza f (a. fig.)

oat [əʊt] mst pl owies m

oath [əʊθ] (pl **~s** [əʊðz]) przysięga f; **on / under ~** pod przysięgą

obedien|ce [ə'bi:djəns] posłuszeństwo n; **~t** posłuszny

obey [ə'beɪ] ⟨u⟩słuchać; *order etc.* spełni(a)ć (rozkaz); *law* przestrzegać

obituary [ə'bɪtʃʊərɪ] nekrolog m

object 1. ['ɒbdʒɪkt] przedmiot m, obiekt m; (*purpose*) cel m; *gr.* dopełnienie n; **2.** [əb'dʒekt] sprzeciwi(a)ć się; **~ion** [əb'dʒekʃn] sprzeciw m; zarzut m; **~ive 1.** *adj* obiektywny; **2.** cel m

obligation [ɒblɪ'geɪʃn] obowiązek m, zobowiązanie n; **~ory** [ə'blɪgətərɪ] obowiązkowy

oblig|e [ə'blaɪdʒ] zobowiąz(yw)ać; (*do a favour*) ⟨z⟩robić grzeczność; **much ~ed!** bardzo dziękuję!; **~ing** uprzejmy

oblique [ə'bli:k] skośny; (*indirect*) okrężny

oblong ['ɒblɒŋ] **1.** prostokąt m; **2.** *adj* podłużny

obscene [əb'si:n] sprośny

obscure [əb'skjʊə] **1.** *adj* mroczny; (*not known*) nieznany; *fig.* niejasny; **2.** zasłaniać ⟨-łonić⟩, zaciemni(a)ć

observa|nce [əb'zɜ:vns] przestrzeganie n; **~nt** [~nt] spostrzegawczy; **~tion** [ɒbzə'veɪʃn] obserwacja f; (*remark*) spostrzeżenie n;

~tory [əb'zɜ:vətrɪ] obserwatorium n

observe [əb'zɜ:v] spostrzegać ⟨-trzec⟩; (*watch*) obserwować; *law etc.* przestrzegać; **~r** obserwator m

obsess [əb'ses]: **~ed by/with s.th.** opętany przez coś; **~ion** obsesja f

obsolete ['ɒbsəli:t] przestarzały

obstacle ['ɒbstəkl] przeszkoda f

obstin|acy ['ɒbstɪnəsɪ] upór m; **~ate** [~ənət] uparty

obstruct [əb'strʌkt] ⟨za⟩tarasować, ⟨za⟩tamować; **~ion** [~kʃn] zator m; *pol., med.* obstrukcja f

obtain [əb'teɪn] uzysk(iw)ać, otrzym(yw)ać; **~able** do nabycia

obvious ['ɒbvɪəs] oczywisty

occasion [ə'keɪʒn] okazja f, sposobność f; (*event*) uroczystość f; **~al** sporadyczny; **~ally** czasami, niekiedy

occup|ant ['ɒkjʊpənt] mieszkaniec m, lokator m; **~ation** [~'peɪʃn] (*job, pastime*) zajęcie n; *mil.* okupacja f; **~y** ['~paɪ] zajmować ⟨-jąć⟩; *mil.* okupować

occur [ə'kɜ:] zdarzać ⟨-rzyć⟩ się; **it ~red to me** przyszło mi na myśl; **~rence** [ə'kʌrəns] zdarzenie n

ocean ['əʊʃn] ocean m

o'clock [ə'klɒk] godzina f; (**at**) **five ~** o piątej

one

October [ɒkˈtəʊbə] październik *m*

octopus [ˈɒktəpəs] ośmiornica *f*

odd [ɒd] dziwny; *number*: nieparzysty; **~s** *pl* szanse *pl*

of [ɒv, əv] *z* (*proud* ~); *od* (*north* ~); na (*die* ~); *o* (*speak* ~ *s.th.*); *the city ~ London* miasto Londyn; *the works ~ Dickens* dzieła Dikkensa; *your letter ~...* Pański list z...; *five minutes ~ twelve Am.* za pięć dwunasta

off [ɒf] **1.** *adv* precz; *light etc.*: wyłączony; (*cancelled*) odwołany; (*free*) wolny, nie pracujący; *food*: zepsuty; **2.** *prp z; od;* **3.** *adj* prawy

offen|ce, *Am.* **~se** [əˈfens] obraza *f; jur.* przestępstwo *n;* **~d** [~nd] obrażać ⟨-razić⟩, urażać ⟨urazić⟩; **~sive 1.** *adj* obraźliwy; *weapons*: ofensywny, zaczepny; **2.** ofensywa *f*

offer [ˈɒfə] **1.** oferta *f*, propozycja *f;* **2.** ⟨za⟩proponować; ⟨za⟩ofiarować

office [ˈɒfɪs] biuro *n;* gabinet *m;* urząd *m;* **~ block** biurowiec *m;* **~ hours** *pl* godziny *pl* urzędowania

officer [ˈɒfɪsə] funkcjonariusz *m;* mil. oficer *m*

official [əˈfɪʃl] **1.** *adj* urzędowy; oficjalny; **2.** (wyższy) urzędnik *m*

often [ˈɒfn] często

oil [ɔɪl] **1.** olej *m*, oliwa *f;* (*petroleum*) ropa *f;* **2.** ⟨na⟩oliwić; **~cloth** cerata *f;* **~painting** obraz *m* olejny; **~ well** szyb *m* naftowy; **~y** oleisty, tłusty

ointment [ˈɔɪntmənt] maść *f*

old [əʊld] stary; **~ age** podeszły wiek *m;* **~ age 'pension** renta *f* starcza; **~fashioned** staromodny

olive [ˈɒlɪv] oliwka *f;* (*tree*) drzewo *n* oliwne

Olympic Games [əʊˈlɪmpɪk] *pl* olimpiada *f*, igrzyska *pl* olimpijskie

omelet(te) [ˈɒmlɪt] omlet *m*

omi|ssion [əˈmɪʃn] pominięcie *n*, opuszczenie *n;* **~t** [əˈmɪt] opuszczać ⟨opuścić⟩, pomijać ⟨-minąć⟩

on [ɒn] **1.** *prp* na (~ *the table*); w (~ *a plane*); (*towards*) do, na; *time*: w (~ *Sunday*); o (~ *his arrival*); (*near*) przy, nad; (*about*) na temat; **2.** *adv, adj light etc.*: włączony; *clothes*: na (sobie, siebie); (*forward*) dalej; *thea. etc.* w programie; *and so* ~ i tak dalej; ~ *and* ~ bez końca

once [wʌns] **1.** *adv* raz; (*formerly*) niegdyś; ~ *again*, ~ *more* jeszcze raz; *at* ~ natychmiast; *all at* ~ nagle; *for* ~ choć raz; **2.** *cj* skoro

one [wʌn] *adj, pron, s* jeden; pewien; ktoś, ktoś; ten; ~ *day*, ~ *of these days* kiedyś, któregoś dnia; ~ *by* jeden po drugim; ~ **another** jeden drugiego, nawzajem; **which** ~? który?; ~'**self** pron się; sam; ~'**sided** jednostronny; ~'**way:** ~**way street** ulica f jednokierunkowa; ~**way ticket** Am. bilet m w jedną stronę

onion ['ʌnjən] cebula f

only ['əʊnlɪ] **1.** adj jedyny; **2.** adv tylko, jedynie; ~ **just** dopiero co

onto ['ɒntʊ, 'ɒntə] prp na

onward ['ɒnwəd] naprzód, do przodu; ~(**s**) naprzód; **from now** ~(s) odtąd

ooze [uːz] sączyć się

open ['əʊpən] **1.** adj otwarty; **in the** ~ **air** na otwartym powietrzu; **2.** v/t otwierać ⟨-worzyć⟩; v/i otwierać ⟨-worzyć⟩ się; ~**air** na wolnym powietrzu; ~**handed** szczodry, hojny; ~**ing** otwarcie n; otwór m; ~**ly** otwarcie; ~**minded** z otwartą głową

opera ['ɒpərə] opera f; ~ **glasses** pl lornetka f teatralna; ~ **house** opera f

operat|e ['ɒpəreɪt] v/t machine obsługiwać; v/i działać; med. ⟨z⟩operować (**on s.o.** kogoś); ~**ing system** computer: system m operacyjny; ~**ing theatre** sala f operacyjna; ~**ion** [~'reɪʃn] działanie n; med., tech. operacja f

opinion [ə'pɪnjən] opinia f,

zdanie n, pogląd m; **in my** ~ moim zdaniem

opponent [ə'pəʊnənt] przeciwnik m

opportun|e ['ɒpətjuːn] stosowny; ~**ity** [~'tjuːnətɪ] sposobność f, okazja f

oppos|e [ə'pəʊz] sprzeciwiać się; **be** ~**ed to** ... być przeciw(ko) ...; **as** ~**ed to** w przeciwieństwie do; ~**ite** ['ɒpəzɪt] **1.** adj przeciwny; **2.** adv naprzeciw(ko); **3.** s przeciwieństwo n; ~**ition** [ɒpə'zɪʃn] sprzeciw m; pol. opozycja f

oppress [ə'pres] uciskać, ciemiężyć; ~**ive** uciążliwy

optician [ɒp'tɪʃn] optyk m

optimism ['ɒptɪmɪzəm] optymizm m

option ['ɒpʃn] opcja f, option m; ~**al** ['ɒpʃənl] fakultatywny

or [ɔː] cj lub; albo; czy; ~ **else** bo; inaczej (bowiem)

oral ['ɔːrəl] ustny

orange ['ɒrɪndʒ] **1.** pomarańcza f; **2.** adj pomarańczowy

orbit ['ɔːbɪt] **1.** okrążać; **2.** orbita f

orchard ['ɔːtʃəd] sad m

orchestra ['ɔːkɪstrə] orkiestra f

ordeal [ɔː'diːl] ciężka próba f

order ['ɔːdə] **1.** kolejność f; (discipline) porządek m, ład m; econ. zamówienie m, zlecenie m; (command) rozkaz m; (distinction) order m, odznaczenie *n*; *eccl.* zakon *m*; **in ~ to** aby; **out of ~** nieczynny, zepsuty; **2.** (*command*) rozkaz(yw)ać; (*ask for*) zamawiać 〈-mówić〉; (*arrange*) 〈u〉porządkować; *med.* przepis(yw)ać, zalecać 〈-cić〉; **'~ly 1.** *adj* zdyscyplinowany, systematyczny; **2.** sanitariusz *m*

ordinary ['ɔːdnrɪ] zwykły; przeciętny

ore [ɔː] ruda *f*

organ ['ɔːɡən] narząd *m*, organ *m*; *mus.* organy *pl*; **~ic** [ɔː'ɡænɪk] organiczny

organiz|ation [ɔːɡənaɪ'zeɪʃn] organizacja *f*; **~e** ['~naɪz] 〈z〉organizować

orientate ['ɔːrɪenteɪt] 〈z〉orientowa(wa)ć, rozezna(wa)ć się

origin ['brɪdʒɪn] pochodzenie *n*; początek *m*; **~al** [ə'rɪdʒənl] **1.** *adj* pierwotny; (*unusual*) oryginalny, autentyczny; **2.** *art:* oryginał *m*; **~ality** [ərɪdʒə'nælɪtɪ] oryginalność *f*; **~ate** [ə'rɪdʒɪneɪt] pochodzić, zrodzić się

orphan ['ɔːfn] sierota *m*, *f*; **'~age** sierociniec *m*

ostrich ['bstrɪtʃ] struś *m*

other ['ʌðə] inny; drugi; **the ~ day** niedawno; **every ~ day** co drugi dzień; **~wise** ['~waɪz] poza tym; inaczej

otter ['ɒtə] wydra *f*

ought [ɔːt] *v/aux* powinien, trzeba; **you ~ to have done it**

powinieneś był/trzeba było to zrobić

ounce [aʊns] uncja *f* (*28,35 g*)

our ['aʊə], **~s** nasz; **~selves** [~'selvz] *reflexive:* się, siebie, sobie; *emphasis:* (my) sami, (my) same

out [aʊt] **1.** *adv* na zewnątrz; poza domem; (*completely*) całkiem; (*aloud*) głośno; *sp.* autowy; (*not fashionable*) niemodny; **2.** *prp:* **~ of** z; poza; bez; **be ~ of s.th.** nie mieć czegoś

'out|break, '~burst wybuch *m*

'outcome wynik *m*

out'dated przestarzały

out'do (**-did, -done**) prześcigać 〈-gnąć〉, przewyższać 〈-szyć〉

outdoor ['aʊtdɔː] na wolnym powietrzu; *dress:* wyjściowy; **~s** [~'dɔː] na (wolnym) powietrzu

outer ['aʊtə] zewnętrzny; **~ space** przestrzeń *f* kosmiczna

'outfit strój *m*; wyposażenie *n*

out'grow (**-grew, -grown**) wyrastać 〈-rosnąć〉 (**s.th.** z czegoś)

'outing wycieczka *f*

'out|line 1. zarys *m*, kontur *m*; **2.** 〈na〉szkicować

out'live przeżyć (**s.o.** kogoś)

'outlook widok *m*; perspektywa *f*; *weather:* prognoza *f*; (*point of view*) pogląd *m*

out'number przewyższać 〈-szyć〉 liczebnie

out-of-'date przestarzały; niemodny

'output produkcja f; *computer*: wyjście n

outrage ['autreɪdʒ] **1.** gwałt m, akt m przemocy; **2.** (za)szokować, oburzać ⟨-rzyć⟩; **~ous** [~'reɪdʒəs] skandaliczny, oburzający

outright 1. [aut'raɪt] adv całkowicie; (at once) na miejscu; (openly) bez ogródek, wprost; **2.** ['~] adj bezsporny

out'side 1. s zewnętrzna strona f; **2.** adj zewnętrzny; **3.** adv na zewnątrz, z zewnątrz; **4.** prp na zewnątrz, poza; **~'sider** autsajder m

'outskirts pl peryferie pl

out'spoken szczery

out'standing wybitny; *bills*: zaległy

outward ['~wəd] **1.** adj zewnętrzny; **2.** adv mst **~s** na zewnątrz; **~ly** na zewnątrz; na pozór

out'wit przechytrzyć

oval ['əʊvl] **1.** adj owalny; **2.** owal m

ovary ['əʊvərɪ] jajnik m

oven ['ʌvn] piekarnik m; piec m

over ['əʊvə] **1.** prp (po)nad; na; **2.** adv na dół/ziemię; na drugą stronę, przez; tam; **~** wszędzie; (all) **~ again** jeszcze raz, od początku; **~ and ~ again** wielokrotnie; **~all** ['əʊvərɔːl] **1.** adj całko-

wity; **2.** kitel m, fartuch m; pl kombinezon m; **'~cast** zachmurzony; **~'come** (-came, -come) przezwyciężać ⟨-żyć⟩; **~'crowded** przepełniony, załoczony; **~'do** (-did, -done) przesadzać ⟨-dzić⟩; **~'flow** przel(ew)ać się; **~'haul** tech. przeglądać ⟨-dnąć⟩; **~'head 1.** ['~hed] adv nad głową, powyżej; **2.** ['~hed] adj napowietrzny; **~'hear** (-heard) podsłuchać; **~'lap** zachodzić na siebie; **~'load** przeciążać ⟨-żyć⟩; **~'look** nie zauważyć, przeoczyć; **~'night 1.** adj nocny; **2.** adv przez noc, na noc; fig. z dnia na dzień, nagle; stay **~night** zostać na noc, przenocować; **~'rate** przeceni(a)ć; **~'rule** unieważni(a)ć; **~'run** (-ran, -run) przekroczyć czas, przedłużyć się; be **~run with s.th.** roić się od czegoś; **~'seas** zamorski; **~'see** (-saw, -seen) nadzorować; **~'seer** nadzorca m; **'~sight** przeoczenie n; **'~sleep** (-slept) zaspać; **~'take** (-took, -taken) wyprzedzać ⟨-dzić⟩; **~'throw 1.** ['~θrəʊ] (-threw, -thrown) obalać ⟨-lić⟩; **2.** [~'θrəʊ] przewrót m, obalenie n; **'~time** nadgodziny pl

overture ['əʊvətjʊə] uwertura f

over'turn przewracać ⟨-rócić⟩ (się); **~whelm**

[əʊvə'welm] przygniatać ⟨-gnieść⟩; **~work** ['əʊvəwɜːk] przepracowanie n; **2.** [~'wɜːk] przepraco(wy)wać się

owe [əʊ] być winnym (coś)

owing ['əʊɪŋ]: **~ to** wskutek

owl [aʊl] sowa f

own [əʊn] **1.** adj własny; **on one's ~** samotnie; samo-

dzielnie; **2.** posiadać

owner ['əʊnə] właściciel(ka f) m; **'~ship** własność f; prawo n własności

ox [ɒks] (pl **~en** ['~sən]) wół m

oxygen ['ɒksɪdʒən] tlen m

oyster ['ɔɪstə] ostryga f

ozone ['əʊzəʊn] ozon m; **~ hole** dziura f ozonowa; **~ layer** warstwa f ozonowa

P

pace [peɪs] **1.** krok m; tempo n; **2.** v/t odmierzać ⟨-rzyć⟩ krokami; v/i kroczyć; **'~ma-ker** med. stymulator m serca

pacify ['pæsɪfaɪ] uspokajać ⟨-koić⟩

pack [pæk] **1.** tłumok m; cards: talia f; esp. Am. cigarettes etc.: paczka f; **2.** v/t ⟨za⟩pakować, ⟨s⟩pakować; people ⟨s⟩tłoczyć; v/i ⟨s⟩pakować się; people: ⟨s⟩tłoczyć się; **'~age** paczka f, pakunek m; computer: pakiet m; **~et** ['~ɪt] paczka f, plik m

pact [pækt] pakt m

pad [pæd] **1.** podkładka f, wkładka f; film, na do pisania); **2.** wyściełać ⟨wysłać⟩

paddl|e ['pædl] **1.** wiosło n; **2.** wiosłować; (walk in water) brodzić, taplać się; **'~ing pool** brodzik m

padlock ['pædlɒk] kłódka f

pagan ['peɪgən] **1.** adj po-

gański; **2.** poganin m (-nka f)

page [peɪdʒ] book etc.: strona f; hotel: goniec m

paid [peɪd] past and pp of **pay** 2

pail [peɪl] wiadro n

pain [peɪn] ból m; pl starania pl; **take ~s** dokładać ⟨dołożyć⟩ starań; **'~ful** bolesny; **'~less** bezbolesny; **~staking** ['~zteɪkɪŋ] staranny

paint [peɪnt] **1.** farba f; **2.** ⟨na⟩malować, ⟨po⟩malować; **'~box** pudełko n z farbami; **'~brush** pędzel m; **'~er** malarz m (-larka f); **'~ing** malowanie n; art: malarstwo n; (picture) obraz m

pair [peə] para f; **a ~ of...** para...

pajamas [pə'dʒɑːməz] pl Am. piżama f

pal [pæl] F kumpel m, kompan m F

palace ['pælɪs] pałac m

pale [peɪl] blady

palm [pɑːm] dłoń *f*; (*tree*) palma *f*

pamphlet ['pæmflɪt] broszura *f*

pan [pæn] rondel *m*; *frying*: patelnia *f*; '**~cake** naleśnik *m*

pane [peɪn] szyba *f*

panic ['pænɪk] **1.** panika *f*; **2.** wpadać ⟨wpaść⟩ w panikę

pansy ['pænzɪ] *bot.* bratek *m*

pant [pænt] dyszeć, sapać

panties ['pæntɪz] *pl* majtki *f*

pant [pænt] *pl esp. Am.* spodnie *m*; *Brt.* majtki *pl*

panty hose ['pæntɪhəʊz] *Am.* rajstopy *pl*

paper ['peɪpə] **1.** papier *m*; (*newspaper*) gazeta *f*; (*exam*) egzamin *m* (pisemny); *conference*: referat *m*; *pl* dokumenty *pl*; **2.** ⟨wy⟩tapetować; '**~back** książka *f* w miękkiej okładce; **~ bag** torba *f* papierowa; **~ clip** spinacz *m*; **~ cup** kubek *m* papierowy

parachut|e ['pærəʃuːt] spadochron *m*; '**~ist** spadochroniarz *m*

parade [pə'reɪd] parada *f*; defilada *f*; **2.** paradować

paradise ['pærədaɪs] raj *m*

paragraph ['pærəɡrɑːf] akapit *m*

parallel ['pærəlel] **1.** *adj* równoległy; (*corresponding*) podobny; **2.** linia *f* równoległa; *fig.* podobieństwo *n*; *geogr.* równoleżnik *m*

paraly|se, *Am.* **-lyze** ['pærəlaɪz] ⟨s⟩paraliżować; **~sis** [pə'rælɪsɪs] (*pl* **-ses** [~siːz]) paraliż *m*

parasite ['pærəsaɪt] pasożyt *m*

parcel ['pɑːsl] paczka *f*

pardon ['pɑːdn] **1.** przebaczać ⟨-czyć⟩; *jur.* ułaskawi(a)ć; **2.** przebaczenie *n*; *jur.* ułaskawienie *n*; *I beg your* ~ przepraszam

parent ['peərənt] rodzic *m*; *pl* rodzice *pl*; **~al** [pə'rentl] rodzicielski

parish ['pærɪʃ] parafia *f*

park [pɑːk] **1.** park *m*; **2.** ⟨za⟩parkować

parking ['pɑːkɪŋ] parkowanie *n*; *place*: parking *m*; *no* ~ zakaz *m* parkowania; **~ garage** *Am.* parking *m* wielopoziomowy; **~ lot** *Am.* parking *m*; **~ meter** parkometr *m*; **~ place** parking *m*; **~ ticket** mandat *m* za złe parkowanie

parliament ['pɑːləmənt] parlament *m*; **~ary** [~'mentərɪ] parlamentarny

parquet ['pɑːkeɪ] parkiet *m*

parrot ['pærət] papuga *f*

parsley ['pɑːslɪ] pietruszka *f*

parson ['pɑːsn] pastor; '**~age** plebania *f*

part [pɑːt] **1.** *v/t* ⟨po⟩dzielić, rozdzielać ⟨-lić⟩; *v/i* rozsta(wa)ć się; **2.** część *f* (*a. tech.*); *thea.*, *fig.* rola *f*; *take ~ in s.th.* brać ⟨wziąć⟩ udział w czymś

partial ['pɑːʃl] częściowy; *(biased)* stronniczy; *be ~ to s.th.* lubić coś; **~ity** [-'ʃræləti] stronniczość *f*; zamiłowanie *n*, słabość *f*

particip|ant [pɑː'tɪsɪpənt] uczestnik *m* (-niczka *f*); **~ate** [-peɪt] brać 〈wziąć〉 udział, uczestniczyć; **~ation** [-'peɪʃn] uczestnictwo *n*, udział *m*

particle ['pɑːtɪkl] cząstka *f*, drobina *f*

particular [pə'tɪkjulə] **1.** adj szczególny, specyficzny; *(fussy)* wybredny; *in ~* szczególnie, w szczególności; **2.** szczegół *m*, detal *m*; *pl* personalia *pl*; dane *pl*; **~ly** szczególnie, zwłaszcza

'**partly** częściowo

partner ['pɑːtnə] partner(ka *f*) *m*, wspólnik *m* (-niczka *f*); '**~ship** współudział *m*; *(company)* spółka *f*

'**part-time** na pół etatu

party ['pɑːtɪ] *(reception)* przyjęcie *n*; *pol.* partia *f*; *(group)* grupa *f*

pass [pɑːs] **1.** *v/t* przechodzić 〈przejść〉, przejeżdżać 〈-jechać〉; mijać 〈minąć〉; *mot.* wymijać 〈-minąć〉; *time* spędzać 〈-dzić〉; *ball* podawać; *exam* zdać; *law* uchwalić; *judgment* wydawać; *v/i* mijać 〈minąć〉; przechodzić 〈przejść〉, przejeżdżać 〈-jechać〉; *cards*: 〈s〉pasować; *time*: mijać

〈minąć〉; **~ away** umrzeć; **~ for** uchodzić za, udawać; **~ over** pomijać 〈-minąć〉; **2.** przepustka *f*; *mountain*: przełęcz *f*; *sp.* podanie *n*; *school*: zdanie *n* egzaminu; *univ.* zaliczenie *n*

passage ['pæsɪdʒ] przejście *n*; *(corridor)* korytarz *m*; *of time*: upływ *m*; *(journey)* podróż *f* (morska)

passenger ['pæsɪndʒə] pasażer(ka *f*) *m*

passer-by [pɑːsə'baɪ] *(pl passers-by)* przechodzień *m*

passion ['pæʃn] namiętność *f*, pasja *f*; **~ate** ['-ət] namiętny

passive ['pæsɪv] bierny

pass|port ['pɑːspɔːt] paszport *m*; '**~word** hasło *n*

past [pɑːst] **1.** *s* przeszłość *f*; **2.** adj przeszły, ubiegły, miniony; **3.** adv obok; **4.** prp obok; po; *half ~ two* wpół do trzeciej

paste [peɪst] **1.** ciasto *n*; pasta *f*; *(glue)* klej *m*; **2.** 〈s〉kleić, naklejać 〈-leić〉; '**~board** tektura *f*

pastime ['pɑːstaɪm] rozrywka *f*

pastry ['peɪstrɪ] ciasto *n*

pasture ['pɑːstʃə] pastwisko *n*

patent ['peɪtənt] **1.** patent *m*; **2.** opatentować; adj patentowy; F oryginalny, swój własny

path [pɑːθ] *(pl ~s [-ðz])* ścieżka *f*; droga *f*

pathetic [pə'θetik] żałosny

patien|ce ['peɪʃns] cierpliwość f; '**~t 1.** adj cierpliwy; **2.** pacjent(ka f) m

patriot ['pætrɪət] patriota m (-tka f); **~ic** [ˌ~'ɒtɪk] patriotyczny

patrol [pə'trəul] **1.** patrol m; **2.** patrolować; **~ car** radiowóz m

pattern ['pætən] wzór m; wykrój m

pause [pɔːz] **1.** przerwa f; **2.** ⟨z⟩robić przerwę

pave [peɪv] ⟨wy⟩brukować; fig. way ⟨u⟩torować; '**~ment** chodnik m

paw [pɔː] łapa f

pawn [pɔːn] **1.** pionek m; **2.** zastawia(ć)

pay [peɪ] **1.** płaca f; **2.** (**paid**) a. fig. ⟨za⟩płacić (**for** za); spłacać ⟨-cić⟩; visit składać ⟨złożyć⟩; attention zwracać ⟨-rócić⟩; '**~able** płatny; '**~day** dzień m wypłaty; '**~ment** zapłata f, opłata f; '**~roll** lista f płac

pea [piː] groszek m

peace [piːs] pokój m; (calmness) spokój m; '**~ful** pokojowy; (calm) spokojny

peach [piːtʃ] brzoskwinia f

peacock ['piːkɔk] paw m

peak [piːk] szczyt m; cap: daszek m; **~ hours** pl godziny pl szczytu

peanut ['piːnʌt] orzeszek m ziemny

pear [peə] gruszka f

pearl [pɜːl] perła f

peasant ['peznt] chłop m, wieśniak m

peck [pek] dziobać ⟨-bnąć⟩

peculiar [pɪ'kjuːljə] osobliwy; (exclusive) specyficzny (**to** dla); **~ity** [ˌ~lɪ'ærətɪ] osobliwość f

pedal ['pedl] **1.** tech. pedał m; **2.** pedałować

pedestrian [pɪ'destrɪən] pieszy m; **~ crossing** przejście n dla pieszych; **~ precinct** deptak m

pedigree ['pedɪgriː] rodowód m, pochodzenie n

pee [piː] F siusiać

peel [piːl] **1.** skórka f; **2.** v/t ob(ie)rać; v/i ⟨z⟩łuszczyć się

peep [piːp] **1.** zerknięcie n; **2.** zerkać ⟨-knąć⟩

peer [pɪə] przyglądać ⟨-dnąć⟩ się

peg [peg] kołek m; wieszak m; (a. clothes **~**) klamerka f (do bielizny)

pen [pen] pióro n; długopis m

penalty ['penltɪ] kara f; (a. **~ty kick**) sp. rzut m karny

pence [pens] → **penny**

pencil ['pensl] ołówek m

penetrat|e ['penɪtreɪt] przenikać ⟨-knąć⟩; **~ion** [ˌ~'treɪʃn] przenikanie n, penetracja f

penguin ['peŋgwɪn] pingwin m

penholder obsadka f

peninsula [pə'nɪnsjulə] półwysep m

penis ['piːnɪs] penis m, prącie n

'pen|knife (*pl* **-knives**) scyzoryk *m*; **~name** pseudonim *m* literacki

penniless ['penɪlɪs] bez grosza, biedny

penny ['penɪ] (*pl* **pennies** or **pence** [pens]) pens *m*

pension ['penʃn] emerytura *f*; renta *f*; ~ **off** przenosić ⟨-nieść⟩ na emeryturę; **~er** ['~ənə] emeryt(ka *f*) *m*; rencista *m* (-tka *f*)

penthouse ['penthaʊs] *luksusowe* mieszkanie na dachu budynku

people ['piːpl] *pl* ludzie *pl*; są naród *m*

pepper ['pepə] **1.** pieprz *m*; paprzka *f*; **2.** ⟨po⟩pieprzyć; **~mint** mięta *f* pieprzowa; *sweet:* cukierek *m* miętowy

per [pɜː] na; od

perceive [pə'siːv] ⟨s⟩postrzegać

per| cent [pə'sent] procent *m*; **~'centage** (*proportion*) procent *m*

perceptible [pə'septəbl] dostrzegalny

percolator ['pɜːkəleɪtə] zaparzacz *m* do kawy

percussion [pə'kʌʃn] *mus.* perkusja *f*; ~ **instrument** instrument *m* perkusyjny

perfect 1. ['pɜːfɪkt] *adj* doskonały; (*complete*) zupełny, całkowity; **2.** [pə'fekt] ⟨u⟩doskonalić; **~ion** [~'fekʃn] perfekcja *f*; doskonałość *f*

perforate ['pɜːfəreɪt] przedziurawi(a)ć

perform [pə'fɔːm] wykon(yw)ać, dokon(yw)ać; *thea., mus.* wystawi(a)ć, zagrać; **~ance** wykonanie *n*; *thea., mus.* występ *m*, przedstawienie *n*; **~er** wykonawca *m*, odtwórca *m*

perfume ['pɜːfjuːm] perfumy *pl*; zapach *m*

perhaps [pə'hæps, præps] może

period ['pɪərɪəd] okres *m* (*a. physiol.*); *esp. Am.* kropka *f*; **~ic** [~'ɒdɪk] okresowy; **~ical 1.** *adj* okresowy; **2.** czasopismo *n*

peripheral [pə'rɪfərəl] **1.** *adj* peryferyjny; **2.** *computer:* urządzenie *n* peryferyjne

perish ['perɪʃ] zginąć

perm [pɜːm] trwała *f*; **~anent** ['~ənənt] trwały, stały

permi|ssion [pə'mɪʃn] pozwolenie *n*; **~t 1.** [~t] zezwalać ⟨-wolić⟩; umożliwi(a)ć; **2.** ['pɜːmɪt] pozwolenie *n*, zezwolenie *n*

perpetual [pə'petʊəl] wieczny; (*uninterrupted*) nieustanny

persecut|e ['pɜːsɪkjuːt] prześladować; **~ion** [~'kjuːʃn] prześladowanie *n*

persist [pə'sɪst] *weather:* utrzymywać się; *person:* upierać się, obstawać (*in/with* przy); **~ent** uparty

person ['pɜːsn] osoba *f*; **~al**

osobisty; (*private*) prywatny; **~al computer** komputer *m* osobisty; pecet *m* F; **~ality** [ˌ~sə'næləti] osobowość *f*; osobistość *f*; **~ify** [pə'sɒnɪfaɪ] ucieleśni(a)ć; personifikować

personnel [pɜːsə'nel] personel *m*; **~ manager** kierownik *m* działu kadr

persua|de [pə'sweɪd] przekon(yw)ać; **~sion** [ˌ~ʒn] perswazja *f*; **~sive** przekonywający

perver|se [pə'vɜːs] przekorny; (*annoying*) uparty; perwersyjny, nienaturalny; **~t 1.** [ˌ~'vɜːt] ⟨z⟩deprawować; wypaczać ⟨-czyć⟩; **2.** ['pɜːvɜːt] zboczeniec *m*

pessimism ['pesɪmɪzəm] pesymizm *m*

pest [pest] szkodnik *m*; zaraza *f*; F utrapienie *n*; **'~er** molestować, naprzykrzać się

pet [pet] **1.** zwierzę *n* domowe; **2.** pieścić

petition [pə'tɪʃn] **1.** petycja *f*; **2.** wnosić ⟨wnieść⟩ petycję *n*

pet name pieszczotliwe imię *n*

petrol ['petrəl] *Brt.* benzyna *f*; **~ ga(u)ge** wskaźnik *m* paliwa; **~ pump** pompa *f* paliwowa; **~ station** stacja *f* benzynowa

pet shop sklep *m* ze zwierzętami

pharmacy ['fɑːməsɪ] apteka *f*; *study:* farmacja *f*

phase [feɪz] faza *f*

pheasant ['feznt] bażant *m*

phenomenon [fə'nɒmɪnən] (*pl* **-na** [ˌ~nə]) zjawisko *n*; fenomen *m*

philosoph|er [fɪ'lɒsəfə] filozof *m*; **~y** filozofia *f*

phone [fəʊn] **1.** telefon *m*; **2.** ⟨za⟩telefonować; **~ card** karta *f* telefoniczna

phon(e)y ['fəʊnɪ] F; **1.** *adj* fałszywy; lipny F; **2.** oszust *m*

photo ['fəʊtəʊ] fotografia *f*; **'photocop|ier** fotokopiarka *f*; **'~y 1.** fotokopia *f*; **2.** ⟨z⟩robić fotokopie

photograph ['fəʊtəgrɑːf] **1.** fotografia *f*, zdjęcie *n*; **2.** ⟨s⟩fotografować; **~er** [fə'tɒgrəfə] fotograf(ik) *m*; **~y** [ˌ~'tɒgrəfɪ] fotografia *f*

phrase [freɪz] **1.** wyrażenie *n*, zwrot *m*; *mus.* fraza *f*; **2.** wyrażać ⟨-razić⟩; **'~book** rozmówki *pl*

physic|al ['fɪzɪkl] **1.** *adj* fizyczny; **~al handicap** kalectwo *n*; **2.** badanie *n* lekarskie; **~ian** [ˌ~'zɪʃn] lekarz *m* (*-karka f*); **~ist** [ˌ~sɪst] fizyk *m*; **'~s** *sg* fizyka *f*

piano [pɪ'ænəʊ] fortepian *m*, pianino *n*

pick [pɪk] **1.** wybór *m*; **2.** wyb(ie)rać; *flowers etc.* zrywać ⟨zerwać⟩, zbierać ⟨zebrać⟩; *nose* dłubać; **~ out** wyb(ie)rać; wypatrzeć, dostrzec; **~ up** podnosić

⟨dnieść⟩; ⟨po⟩zbierać; F podłapać, nauczyć się; F *girl* podrywać ⟨derwać⟩; (*collect*) odbierać ⟨odebrać⟩

'pick|pocket kieszonkowiec *m*; **'~up** półciężarówka *f*

picnic ['pɪknɪk] piknik *m*

picture ['pɪktʃə] **1.** (*painting*) obraz *m*; (*photograph*) zdjęcie *n*; (*film*) film *m*; pl kino *n*; **2.** wyobrażać ⟨brazić⟩ sobie

pie [paɪ] placek *m*

piece [piːs] kawałek *m*, część *f*; (*coin*) moneta *f*; *mus.* utwór *m*; *chess etc.*: kamień *m*; **~ by ~** po kawałku; *in* **~s** w częściach; **to ~s** na kawałki; **'~meal** po kawałku

pier [pɪə] molo *n*, pomost *m*

pierce [pɪəs] przedziurawi(a)ć, przebi(ja)ć

pig [pɪg] świnia *f*

pigeon ['pɪdʒɪn] gołąb *m*; **'~hole** przegródka *f*

pig|headed uparty; **'~tail** warkocz *m*

pike [paɪk] (*pl* **~, ~s**) szczupak *m*

pile [paɪl] **1.** stos *m*, sterta *f*; **2.** *often* **~ up** układać ⟨ułożyć⟩ (w stos)

pilgrim ['pɪlgrɪm] pielgrzym *m*

pill [pɪl] pastylka *f*; *the* **~** pigułka *f* antykoncepcyjna

pillar ['pɪlə] kolumna *f*; **~ box** *Brt.* typ skrzynki pocztowej

pillow ['pɪləʊ] poduszka *f*; **'~case**, **'~slip** poszewka *f*

pilot ['paɪlət] **1.** pilot *m*; **~ scheme** projekt *m* próbny; **2.** pilotować

pimple ['pɪmpl] pryszcz *m*

pin [pɪn] **1.** szpilka *f*; **2.** przypinać ⟨piąć⟩

pincers ['pɪnsəz] *pl* (*a. a pair of* **~**) szczypce *pl*, obcążki *pl*

pinch [pɪntʃ] **1.** uszczypnięcie *n*; *salt etc.*: szczypta *f*; **2.** *v/t* szczypać ⟨uszczypnąć⟩; *v/i shoe*: uwierać

pine [paɪn] sosna *f*; **'~apple** ananas *m*

pink [pɪŋk] różowy

pint [paɪnt] pół kwarty (*Brt.* 0,57 *l*, *Am.* 0,47 *l*)

pioneer [paɪə'nɪə] pionier *m*

pious ['paɪəs] pobożny

pipe [paɪp] **1.** rura *f*; fajka *f*; **2.** *water etc.* przes(y)łać rurami; **'~line** rurociąg *m*

pirate ['paɪərət] **1.** pirat *m*; **2.** rozpowszechniać bez praw autorskich

pistol ['pɪstl] pistolet *m*

piston ['pɪstən] tłok *m*

pit [pɪt] **1.** dół *m*; (*mine*) kopalnia *f*; **2.** wystawi(a)ć (*against* przeciw)

pitch [pɪtʃ] **1.** *min.* smoła *f*; *Brt.* boisko *n*; (*degree*) natężenie *n*, *mus.* wysokość *f*; **2.** *tent* rozbi(ja)ć; (*throw*) ciskać ⟨snąć⟩; *mus.* nastrajać ⟨roić⟩; *mar.* kołysać; **~'black** czarny jak smoła

pitfall *fig.* pułapka *f*

piti|ful ['pɪtɪfʊl] żałosny; **'~less** bezlitosny

pity ['pɪtɪ] **1.** litość *f*; *it's a ~ szkoda*; *what a ~!* jaka szkoda!; **2.** litować się, współczuć

pivot ['pɪvət] **1.** *tech.* oś *f*; *fig.* sedno *n*; **2.** *v/i* obracać ⟨-rócić⟩ się

place [pleɪs] **1.** miejsce *n*; *in ~ of* zamiast; *out of ~* nie na miejscu; *take ~* mieć miejsce; zdarzać ⟨-rzyć⟩ się; *in the first/second ~* po pierwsze/ drugie; **2.** umieszczać ⟨umieścić⟩, umiejscawiać ⟨-cowić⟩; *order* składać ⟨złożyć⟩

plague [pleɪg] **1.** dżuma *f*, plaga *f*; **2.** gnębić

plain [pleɪn] **1.** *adj* prosty; *(clear)* zrozumiały; *(frank)* szczery; **2.** *mst pl* równina *f*; **~ chocolate** gorzka czekolada *f*

plait [plæt] **1.** warkocz *m*; **2.** zaplatać ⟨-leść⟩

plan [plæn] **1.** plan *m*; **2.** ⟨za⟩planować

plane [pleɪn] **1.** *adj* płaski; **2.** samolot *m*; *math.* płaszczyzna *f*; *fig.* poziom *m*; *tech.* strug *m*

planet ['plænɪt] planeta *f*

plank [plæŋk] deska *f*

plant [plɑ:nt] **1.** roślina *f*; *tech.* fabryka *f*; *(machinery)* urządzenia *pl* mechaniczne; **2.** ⟨za⟩sadzić; F podrzucać ⟨-cić⟩, podkładać ⟨-łożyć⟩; **~ation** [plæn'teɪʃn] plantacja *f*

plaster ['plɑ:stə] **1.** gips *m*;

tynk *m*; *med.* plaster *m*; **2.** ⟨o⟩tynkować; **~ cast** odlew *m* gipsowy; *med.* gips *m*; **~ of Paris** gips *m*

plastic ['plæstɪk] **1.** *mst pl* tworzywo *n* sztuczne; **2.** *adj* plastikowy; *(easily formed)* plastyczny; **~ bag** torba *f* plastikowa; **~ surgery** chirurgia *f* plastyczna; operacja *f* plastyczna

plate [pleɪt] *(dish)* talerz *m*; płyt(k)a *f*, tablica *f*, tabliczka *f*; *book*: plansza *f*

platform ['plætfɔ:m] platforma *f*, podwyższenie *n*; *rail.* peron *m*

plausible ['plɔ:zəbl] wiarogodny

play [pleɪ] **1.** gra *f*, zabawa *f*; *thea.* sztuka *f*; *tech.* luz *m*; **2.** bawić się; *sp.*, *thea.*, *mus.* ⟨za⟩grać; **~ down** pomniejszać ⟨-szyć⟩; **~ s.o. off** napuszczać ⟨-puścić⟩ kogoś *(against s.o.* na kogoś); **~ up** podkreślać ⟨-lić⟩; **'~er** gracz *m*; instrumentalista *m* (-tka *f*); **'~ful** żartobliwy; **'~ground** boisko *n*; **'~ing field** boisko *n*; **'~mate** towarzysz *m* zabaw; **~wright** ['~raɪt] dramaturg *m*

pleasant ['pleznt] przyjemny

please [pli:z] zadowalać ⟨-wolić⟩; chcieć; *~!* proszę!; **~ yourself** rób jak chcesz; **~d** zadowolony

pleasure ['pleʒə] przyjemność *f*

plent|iful ['plentɪfʊl] obfity; **'~y** obfitość f; **~y of** mnóstwo

pliers ['plaɪəz] pl (a. **a pair of ~**) szczypce pl

plimsolls ['plɪmsɔlz] pl Brt. tenisówki pl

plot [plɔt] **1.** parcela f; (plan) zmowa f, spisek m; story: fabuła f; **2.** spiskować; nakreślać ⟨-lić⟩; **'~ter** computer: ploter m

plough, Am. **plow** [plaʊ] **1.** pług m; **2.** ⟨za⟩orać

plug [plʌg] **1.** zatyczka f; electr. wtyczka f; mot. świeca f; **2.** zat(y)kać; **~ in** electr. włączać ⟨-czyć⟩ do kontaktu

plum [plʌm] śliwka f

plumb [plʌm] zgłębi(a)ć; **~ in** podłączać ⟨-czyć⟩; **'~er** hydraulik m

plump [plʌmp] pulchny

plunder ['plʌndə] ⟨s⟩plądrować

plunge [plʌndʒ] zanurzać ⟨-rzyć⟩ (się), zagłębi(a)ć (się)

plural ['plʊərəl] gr. liczba f mnoga

plus [plʌs] **1.** plus z. **plus** m pneumatyczny; **~ drill** młot m pneumatyczny

pneumatic [njuːˈmætɪk] pneumatyczny; **~ drill** młot m pneumatyczny

pneumonia [njuːˈməʊnjə] zapalenie n płuc

poach [pəʊtʃ] kłusować, uprawiać kłusownictwo; **'~er** kłusownik m

P.O. Box [piː əʊ 'bɒks]

skrzynka f pocztowa

pocket ['pɒkɪt] **1.** kieszeń f; **2.** wkładać ⟨włożyć⟩ do kieszeni; **3.** adj kieszonkowy; **'~book** notesik m; książka f (małego formatu); **'~knife** (pl -knives) scyzoryk m; **~ money** kieszonkowe n

poem ['pəʊɪm] wiersz m

poet ['pəʊɪt] poeta m (-tka f); **~ic(al)** [~'etɪk(l)] poetyczny; **~ry** ['~ɪtrɪ] poezja f

point [pɔɪnt] **1.** ostrze n, czubek m; geogr. cypel m; kropka f, math. przecinek m; a. sp. punkt m; fig. kwestia f, sedno n sprawy; (moment) chwila f, moment m; pl rail. zwrotnica f; **be beside the ~** nie mieć nic do rzeczy, nie wiązać się ze sprawą; **be on the ~ of** mieć właśnie (inf-ing etc.) wyjść itp.); **to the ~** trafny, do rzeczy; **2.** wskaz(yw)ać; **~ at** gun ⟨wy⟩celować; **~ out** zwracać ⟨-rócić⟩ uwagę; **~ to s.o./ s.th.** wskaz(yw)ać na kogoś/ coś; **'~ed** spiczasty; fig. uszczypliwy; **'~er** wskazówka f, strzałka f; **'~less** bezsensowny; **~ of view** punkt m widzenia

poison ['pɔɪzn] **1.** trucizna f; **2.** otruć; zatru(wa)ć; **'~er** truciciel m; **'~ous** trujący

poke [pəʊk] wetknąć ⟨wtykać⟩; szturchać ⟨-chnąć⟩; **'~r** pogrzebacz m

Poland ['pəʊlənd] Polska f

polar ['pəʊlə] polarny; **~ bear**
  niedźwiedź *m* polarny

Pole [pəʊl] Polak *m* (-lka *f*)

pole[1] [pəʊl] biegun *m*

pole[2] [~] słup *m*, drąg *m*, tyka *f*

police [pə'liːs] policja *f*; **~man**
  (*pl* **-men**) policjant *m*; **~ officer** policjant(ka *f*) *m*; **~ station** komisariat *m*; **~woman**
  (*pl* **-women**) policjantka *f*

policy ['pɒləsɪ] polityka *f*; *insurance*: polisa *f*

Polish ['pəʊlɪʃ] polski

polish ['pɒlɪʃ] **1.** pasta *f* do
  polerowania; połysk *m*; *fig.*
  polor *m*, ogłada *f*; **2.**
  ⟨wy⟩polerować; *shoe* ⟨wy⟩-
  czyścić

polite [pə'laɪt] uprzejmy;
  ~ness uprzejmość *f*

politic|al [pə'lɪtɪkl] politycz-
  ny; **~ian** [pɒlɪ'tɪʃn] polityk
  m; **~s** ['pɒlɪtɪks] *sg, pl* polityka *f*

poll [pəʊl] **1.** ankieta *f*; *pol.*
  głosowanie *n*, wybory *pl*; **2.**
  votes zdobyć, zebrać; (*question*) ankietować

pollen ['pɒlən] pyłek *m*

pollut|e [pə'luːt] zanieczysz-
  czać ⟨-niczyścić⟩; **~ion** za-
  nieczyszczenie *n*, skażenie *n*

polo ['pəʊləʊ] polo *n*; **~ neck**
  esp. Brt. golf *m*

pomp [pɒmp] pompa *f*, przepych *m*; **~ous** napuszony,
  pompatyczny

pond [pɒnd] staw *m*

ponder ['pɒndə] rozważać
  ⟨-żyć⟩

pony ['pəʊnɪ] kucyk *m*; **~tail**
  hairstyle: koński ogon *m*

pool [puːl] **1.** basen *m*; (*puddle*) kałuża *f*; **2.** *money*
  składać ⟨złożyć⟩ się; **~s** *pl*
  totalizator *m* sportowy

poor [pɔː] biedny; słaby; **~ly**
  słabo

pop [pɒp] **1.** trzask *m*; pu-
  knięcie *n*; *music*: pop *m*; **2.**
  pękać ⟨-knąć⟩, przebija⟨ją⟩ć;
  ~ in (*visit*) wpadać ⟨wpaść⟩

Pope [pəʊp] papież *m*

poplar ['pɒplə] topola *f*

poppy ['pɒpɪ] *bot.* mak *m*

popul|ar ['pɒpjʊlə] popular-
  ny; (*widespread*) rozpowszechniony; **~arity** [~'lærətɪ]
  popularność *f*; **~ate** ['~eɪt] zamieszkiwać; **~ation** [~'leɪʃn]
  ludność *f*, populacja *f*

porcelain ['pɔːslɪn] porcelana
  f

porch [pɔːtʃ] ganek *m*; *Am.*
  weranda *f*

pork [pɔːk] wieprzowina *f*

porridge ['pɒrɪdʒ] owsianka *f*

port [pɔːt] port *m*; *mar.* lewa
  burta *f*; *computer*: port *m*

portable ['pɔːtəbl] przenośny; **~ radio** radio *n* prze-
  nośne

porter ['pɔːtə] portier *m*; *rail.*
  bagażowy *m*

portion ['pɔːʃn] część *f*, porcja
  f, udział *m*; *food*: porcja *f*,
  racja *f*

portrait ['pɔːtreɪt] portret *m*

portray [pɔː'treɪ] przedsta-
  wi(a)ć

Portu|gal ['pɔːtʃʊgəl] Portugalia f; **~guese** [ˌ~'giːz] **1.** adj portugalski; **2.** Portugalczyk m (-lka f)

position [pə'zɪʃn] **1.** pozycja f; (job) posada f; (place) położenie n; **2.** ⟨u⟩lokować, umieszczać ⟨umieścić⟩

positive ['pɒzɪtɪv] pozytywny; (sure) przekonany; math. dodatni; (definite) jednoznaczny

possess [pə'zes] posiadać; **~ion** posiadanie n; majątek m

possib|ility [pɒsə'bɪlɪtɪ] możliwość f; **~le** ['pɒsəbl] możliwy, prawdopodobny; **~ly** możliwie, ewentualnie

post [pəʊst] **1.** poczta f; (pole) słup m; (position) posada f; mil. posterunek m; **2.** letter etc. nada(wa)ć; sign etc. wywieszać ⟨-wiesić⟩; **~age** opłata f pocztowa; **~al** pocztowy; **~al order** przekaz m pocztowy; **~box** esp. Brt. skrzynka f pocztowa; **~card** kartka f pocztowa; **~code** Brt. kod m pocztowy

poster ['pəʊstə] plakat m

post|man (pl -men) esp. Brt. listonosz m, doręczyciel m; **~mark** stempel m pocztowy; **~ office** urząd m, urząd m pocztowy

postpone [pəʊst'pəʊn] odkładać ⟨odłożyć⟩, odraczać ⟨-roczyć⟩

posture ['pɒstʃə] postawa f; pozycja f

postwar powojenny

pot [pɒt] dzbanek m; for plants: doniczka f; cooking: garnek m

potato [pə'teɪtəʊ] (pl -toes) ziemniak m

potential [pə'tenʃl] **1.** adj potencjalny; **2.** potencjał m

pothole wybój m, dziura f

potter ['pɒtə] garncarz m (-carka f); **~y** [ˈ~ərɪ] garncarstwo n; wyroby pl garncarskie; garncarnia f

poultry ['pəʊltrɪ] drób m

pound [paʊnd] **1.** weight: funt m (454 g); money: funt m; **2.** walić; ⟨s⟩tłuc

pour [pɔː] lać (się); nal(ew)ać; it's **~ing** (with rain) leje (deszcz)

poverty ['pɒvətɪ] bieda f

powder ['paʊdə] **1.** proszek m; puder m; proch m; **2.** ⟨po⟩pudrować

power ['paʊə] **1.** siła f, moc f; pol. władza f; electr. prąd m; **2.** napędzać; **~-driven** tech. mechaniczny; **~ful** potężny; **~less** bezsilny; **~ station** elektrownia f

practi|cable ['præktɪkəbl] wykonalny; **~cal** praktyczny; **~ce** [ˈ~tɪs] **1.** praktyka f; wprawa f; **2.** Am. → **~se** ćwiczyć; praktykować; **~tioner** [ˌ~'tɪʃnə]: general **~tioner** lekarz m ogólny

praise [preɪz] **1.** (po)chwała f; **2.** chwalić; **~worthy** godny pochwały

pram [præm] wózek *m* dziecięcy

prank [præŋk] psota *f*; kawał *m*

prawn [prɔ:n] krewetka *f*

pray [preɪ] ⟨po⟩modlić się; **~er** [preə] modlitwa *f*

preach [pri:tʃ] wygłaszać ⟨-łosić⟩ kazanie; F prawić kazania; zalecać ⟨-cić⟩

precaution [prɪ'kɔ:ʃn] środek *m* ostrożności; **~ary** zapobiegawczy, prewencyjny

precede [pri:'si:d] poprzedzać ⟨-dzić⟩; **~nce** ['presɪdəns] pierwszeństwo *n*; **~nt** precedens *m*

precinct [pri:sɪŋkt] teren *m*; *Am.* obwód *m*; *Am.* rejon *m*; **pedestrian** ~ deptak *m*

precious ['preʃəs] cenny; drogocenny, szlachetny

precise [prɪ'saɪs] dokładny; **~ion** [prɪ'sɪʒn] dokładność *f*

predecessor ['pri:dɪsesə] poprzednik *m* ⟨-niczka *f*⟩; przodek *m*

predict [prɪ'dɪkt] przepowiadać ⟨-wiedzieć⟩; **~ion** przepowiednia *f*

predomina|nt [prɪ'dɒmɪnənt] dominujący; **~te** [~eɪt] przeważać ⟨-żyć⟩

preface ['prefɪs] wstęp *m*

prefer [prɪ'fɜ:] woleć; **~ably** najlepiej; **~ence** ['prefərəns] preferencja *f*; skłonność *f*

pregnan|cy ['pregnənsɪ] ciąża *f*; **~t** w ciąży

prejudice ['predʒudɪs] **1.** u-

przedzenie *n* (*against* do); **2.** uprzedzać ⟨-dzić⟩ (*for* or *against* do); ⟨za⟩szkodzić; **~d** uprzedzony

preliminary [prɪ'lɪmɪnərɪ] wstępny

prelude ['prelju:d] wstęp *m*; *mus.* preludium *n*

premises ['premɪsɪz] *pl* teren *m*; posesja *f*; siedziba *f*

preoccupied [pri:'ɒkjupaɪd] zaabsorbowany; zajęty

prepar|ation [prepə'reɪʃn] przygotowanie *n*; **~e** [prɪ'peə] przygoto⟨wy⟩wać

prescri|be [prɪ'skraɪb] *a. med.* zalecać ⟨-cić⟩, przepis⟨yw⟩ać; **~ption** [~'skrɪpʃn] *med.* recepta *f*

presence ['prezns] obecność *f*; **~ of mind** przytomność *f* umysłu

present¹ ['preznt] **1.** obecny; **at ~** obecnie; **2.** prezent *m*; podarunek *m*

present² [prɪ'zent] wręczyć ⟨-czać⟩ (*s.o. with s.th.* komuś coś); przedstawi⟨a⟩ć

presentation [prezən'teɪʃn] prezentacja *f*; pokaz *m*; *thea.* inscenizacja *f*

present-day ['preznt] współczesny; **~ly** niedługo (potem); wkrótce; *esp. Am.* obecnie

preserv|ation [prezə'veɪʃn] przechowywanie *n*; ochrona *f*; **~e** [prɪ'zɜ:v] **1.** ⟨za⟩konserwować, zaprawi⟨a⟩ć; ochraniać ⟨-ronić⟩; **2.** kon-

serwa f; konfitura f; strefa f
zastrzeżona, rezerwat m

preside [prɪ'zaɪd] przewodniczyć

president ['prezɪdənt] prezydent m; dyrektor m

press [pres] **1.** prasa f (drukarska); drukarnia f; **the** ~
prasa f; **go to** ~ iść ⟨pójść⟩
do druku; **2.** (hand to chest)
przyciskać ⟨-snąć⟩; **button**
naciskać ⟨-snąć⟩; **shirt**
⟨wy⟩prasować; zgniatać
⟨-nieść⟩; ~ **s.b. to do s.th.**
nalegać by ktoś coś zrobił; ~
for domagać się (s.th. czegoś); '~**ing** pilny; ~ **conference** konferencja f prasowa

pressure ['preʃə] ciśnienie n

presum|ably [prɪ'zju:məblɪ]
przypuszczalnie; **~e** [~m]
zakładać ⟨założyć⟩, przypuszczać ⟨-puścić⟩;
⟨wy⟩wnioskować

preten|ce, Am. **-se** [prɪ'tens]
pozór m; udawanie n;
wykręt m; **~d** udawać; mieć
aspiracje (to do); **~sion** aspiracje pl, ambicje pl (to do)

pretty ['prɪtɪ] **1.** adj ładny; **F**
niezły; **2.** adv całkiem; dość

prevent [prɪ'vent] zapobiegać
⟨-biec⟩; ~ **s.b. from doing
s.th.** powstrzymać kogoś od
⟨z⟩robienia czegoś; **~ion** zapobieganie n; **~ive** zapobiegawczy

previous ['pri:vjəs] poprzedni; ~ **to** przed; '~**ly** poprzednio

prewar [pri:'wɔː] przedwojenny

prey [preɪ] zdobycz f; łup m;
beast of ~ drapieżnik m; **bird
of** ~ ptak m drapieżny

price [praɪs] cena f; '~**less**
bezcenny

prick [prɪk] **1.** (feeling)
ukłucie n; (hole) nakłucie n;
2. ukłuć, nakłu(wać); **~le**
['~kl] (sharp point) kolec m;
(feeling) ukłucie n

pride [praɪd] duma f; (group)
stado n

priest [pri:st] ksiądz m;
kapłan m

primar|ily ['praɪmərəlɪ] przede wszystkim; '~**y** podstawowy; najważniejszy; **~y
school** szkoła f podstawowa

prime [praɪm] pierwszy,
główny; znakomity, pierwszorzędny; ~ **minister** premier m

primeval [praɪ'mi:vl] prehistoryczny, prastary; pierwotny

primitive ['prɪmɪtɪv] prymitywny

prince [prɪns] książę m; **~ss**
[~'ses, attr '~ses] księżna f;
księżniczka f

princip|al ['prɪnsəpl] **1.** główny; **2.** dyrektor m szkoły;
'~**ally** głównie; **~le** ['prɪnsəpl] zasada f; prawo n; zasada f działania; reguła f;
on ~**le** z zasady; **in** ~**le** w zasadzie

print [prɪnt] **1.** druk m; odcisk

m; reprodukcja *f*; *phot.* odbitka *f*; **out of ~** wyczerpany; **2.** ⟨wy⟩drukować, ⟨o⟩publikować; *phot.* ⟨z⟩robić odbitki; **~ out** *computer*: sporządzać ⟨-dzić⟩ wydruk; **'~er** drukarz *m*; *computer*: drukarka *f*; **'~out** *computer*: wydruk *m*

prior ['praɪə] **1.** *adj* wcześniejszy; ważniejszy; **2.** *adv* **~ to** (the war etc.) przed (wojną *itd.*); **~ity** [~'ɒrəti] pierwszeństwo *n*; priorytet *m*

prison ['prɪzn] więzienie *n*; **'~er** więzień *m*; **~er of war** jeniec *m* wojenny; **take s.o. ~er** uwięzić kogoś

privacy ['prɪvəsɪ] spokój *m*; samotność *f*, zacisze *n*

private ['praɪvɪt] **1.** prywatny, osobisty; **2.** szeregowiec *m*; **in ~** na osobności

privilege ['prɪvɪlɪdʒ] przywilej *m*; **'~d** uprzywilejowany

prize [praɪz] **1.** nagroda *f*, wygrana *f*; zdobycz *f*, trofeum *n*; **2.** wysoko cenić; **'~winner** laureat(ka *f*) *m*

pro [prəʊ] **1.** za; **2.** zawodowiec *m*; **3. the ~s and cons** *pl* za i przeciw

probab|ility [prɒbə'bɪlətɪ] prawdopodobieństwo *n*; ewentualność *f*; **'~le** możliwy, prawdopodobny; **'~ly** prawdopodobnie

problem ['prɒbləm] problem

m; kłopot *m*

procedure [prə'si:dʒə] procedura *f*; sposób *m* postępowania

proceed [prə'si:d] kontynuować; przystępować ⟨-tąpić⟩ **(to** do), zaczynać ⟨-cząć⟩; postępować; wynikać ⟨-knąć⟩ **(from** z); **~ings** *pl* protokół *m*, sprawozdanie *n*; *jur.* postępowanie *n*; proces *m*

process ['prəʊses] **1.** proces *m*; przebieg *m*; proces *m* produkcyjny; **2.** przetwarzać ⟨-worzyć⟩ (*a. computer*); podda(wa)ć obróbce, konserwować; *phot.* wywoł(yw)ać; **in the ~** (of doing s.th.) w trakcie (robienia czegoś); **~ion** [prə'seʃn] procesja *f*; parada *f*; **~or** ['prəʊsesə] *computer*: procesor *m*; **word ~or** edytor *m* (tekstu)

procla|im [prə'kleɪm] ogłaszać ⟨-łosić⟩; **~mation** [prɒklə'meɪʃn] obwieszczenie *n*, ogłoszenie *n*

produce 1. [prə'dju:s] ⟨wy⟩produkować; wyjmować ⟨-jąć⟩; ⟨s⟩tworzyć; *fig.* wywoł(yw)ać; *thea.* wystawi(a)ć; **2.** ['prɒdju:s] *agr.* płody *pl* rolne; towary *pl* spożywcze; **~r** [prə'dju:sə] wytwórca *m*; producent *m* (*a. film, thea.*)

product ['prɒdʌkt] produkt *m*; **~ion** [prə'dʌkʃn] produkcja *f*; *thea.* inscenizacja *f*;

~ive [~'dʌktɪv] produktywny, wydajny; **~ivity** [prɒdʌk'tɪvɪtɪ] wydajność *f*

profess [prə'fes] oświadczać ⟨-czyć⟩; udawać; ⟨s⟩twierdzić; wyzna(wa)ć; **~ion** zawód *m*; grupa *f* zawodowa; **~ional 1.** zawodowy; profesjonalny; fachowy; **2.** zawodowiec *m*; fachowiec *m*; **~or** profesor *m*, nauczyciel *m* akademicki

proficien|cy [prə'fɪʃnsɪ] biegłość *f*, sprawność *f*; **~t** biegły

profile ['prəʊfaɪl] profil *m*

profit ['prɒfɪt] **1.** zysk *m*; pożytek *m*; **2.** ~ *by*, ~ *from* ⟨s⟩korzystać *z*; zysk(iw)ać na; czerpać zysk *z*; **~able** dochodowy; pożyteczny

profound [prə'faʊnd] głęboki; poważny

program ['prəʊɡræm] **1.** *computer* program *m*; *Am.* → *programme* 1; **2.** *computer*: ⟨za⟩programować; *Am.* → *programme* 2; '**~me** *Brt.* **1.** program *m*; **2.** ⟨za⟩programować; '**~(m)er** programista *m* (-tka *f*)

progress 1. ['prəʊɡres] postęp(y *pl*) *m*; *in* ~ w toku; **2.** [~'ɡres] posuwać ⟨-sunąć⟩ się; rozwijać ⟨-winąć⟩ się; **~ive** [~'ɡresɪv] postępowy; postępujący

prohibit [prə'hɪbɪt] zabraniać ⟨-ronić⟩; **~ion** [prəʊ'bɪʃn] zakaz *m*

project 1. ['prɒdʒekt] przedsięwzięcie *n*; **2.** [prə'dʒekt] projektować; **~ion** [~'dʒekʃn] część *f* wystająca; (*estimate*) prognoza *f*; *film*: projekcja *f*; **~or** [~'dʒektə] projektor *m*; *slide*: rzutnik *m*

prolong [prəʊ'lɒŋ] przedłużać ⟨-żyć⟩

prominent ['prɒmɪnənt] wybitny; wyróżniający się, widoczny; wystający

promis|e ['prɒmɪs] **1.** obietnica *f*; (dobra) prognoza *f*; nadzieja *f*; **2.** obiec(yw)ać; przyrzekać ⟨-rzec⟩; (dobrze) zapowiadać się; '**~ing** obiecujący

promote [prə'məʊt] pobudzać, krzewić; awansować (*kogoś*); *econ.* lansować, reklamować; **~ter** organizator *m*, promotor *m*; popularyzator *m*; **~tion** promocja *f*, kampania *f* reklamowa; popularyzacja *f*; awans *m*

prompt [prɒmpt] **1.** natychmiastowy, szybki; punktualny; **2.** skłaniać ⟨-łonić⟩ (*s.o. to do s.th.* kogoś do zrobienia czegoś); ⟨s⟩powodować; '**~ly** bezzwłocznie; punktualnie

prone [prəʊn]: *be ~ to* być podatnym na

pronounce [prə'naʊns] wymawiać ⟨-mówić⟩; **~unciation** [~nʌnsɪ'eɪʃn] wymowa *f*

proof [pruːf] **1.** dowód *m*; korekta *f*; *print.*, *phot.* odbitka *f*; **2.** odporny; **~ against** s.th. odporny na coś, zabezpieczony przed czymś

propaga|te ['prɒpəgeɪt] rozpowszechni(a)ć; rozmnażać ⟨-nożyć⟩ (się); **~tion** [ˌ'ɡeɪʃn] rozpowszechnianie *n*; rozmnażanie *n* (się)

propel [prə'pel] napędzać, poruszać ⟨-szyć⟩, pchać ⟨pchnąć⟩; **~ler** *aeroplane:* śmigło *n*; *ship:* śruba *f* napędowa

proper ['prɒpə] porządny, prawdziwy; właściwy; dokładny; prawidłowy; *esp. Brt.* F poprawny, stosowny; **'~ty** właściwość *f*, cecha *f*; własność *f*; nieruchomość *f*

prophe|cy ['prɒfɪsɪ] proroctwo *n*; **~sy** [ˌ'aɪ] ⟨wy⟩prorokować; **~t** ['~ɪt] prorok *m*

proportion [prə'pɔ:ʃn] proporcja *f*; procent *m*; liczba *f*; proporcja *f*; *pl* wymiary *pl*; **in ~ to** w stosunku do; **~al** proporcjonalny

propos|al [prə'pəʊzl] propozycja *f*, projekt *m*; oświadczyny *pl*; **~e** [ˌ'z] ⟨za⟩proponować; oświadczać ⟨-czyć⟩ się (**to** s.o. komuś); **~ition** [prɒpə'zɪʃn] wniosek *m*; teza *f*, pogląd *m*; przedsięwzięcie *n*

prose [prəʊz] proza *f*

prosecut|e ['prɒsɪkju:t] ścigać sądownie; zaskarżać ⟨-żyć⟩; **~ion** [ˌ'kju:ʃn] wy-

toczenie *n* sprawy sądowej; proces *m* sądowy; strona *f* oskarżająca; **'~or** oskarżyciel *m*; **public ~or** prokurator *m*

prospect ['prɒspekt] widok *m* (*a. fig.*); perspektywa *f*, prawdopodobieństwo *n*; **~ive** [prə'spektɪv] przyszły; niedoszły

prosper ['prɒspə] (dobrze) prosperować, kwitnąć; **~ity** [ˌ'sperətɪ] pomyślność *f*; **~ous** [ˌ'ərəs] (dobrze) prosperujący

prostitute ['prɒstɪtju:t] prostytutka *f*

protect [prə'tekt] ⟨o⟩chronić; **~ion** opieka *f*, ochrona *f*; osłona *f*; zabezpieczenie *n*; **~ive** ochronny; **~or** obrońca *m*; opiekun *m*; osłona *f*

protein ['prəʊtiːn] białko *n*

protest 1. ['prəʊtest] protest *m*; sprzeciw *m*; **2.** [prə'test] ⟨za⟩protestować; ⟨za⟩oponować; **~ant** ['prɒtɪstənt] **1.** protestancki; **2.** protestant *m*

protrude [prə'truːd] wystawać

proud [praʊd] dumny (**of** z)

prove [pruːv] (**proved**, **proved** or *Am. also* **proven**) udowadniać ⟨-wodnić⟩, dowodzić ⟨-wieść⟩, potwierdzać ⟨-dzić⟩; ukaz⟨yw⟩ać; okaz⟨yw⟩ać się; **~n 1.** sprawdzony; udowodniony; **2.** *esp. Am. pp of* **prove**

proverb ['prɒvɜːb] przysłowie *n*

provide [prə'vaɪd] dostarczać ⟨-czyć⟩, zapewni(a)ć; przewidywać ⟨-widzieć⟩; ~ *against* zabezpieczać ⟨-czyć⟩ się przed; ~ *for* utrzym(yw)ać; brać ⟨wziąć⟩ pod uwagę, uwzględni(a)ć; zezwalać ⟨-wolić⟩ na; ~ *providing (that)* pod warunkiem *że*

province ['prɒvɪns] okręg *m*, prowincja *f*

provision [prə'vɪʒn] zaopatrzenie *n*; zapewnienie *n*; wsparcie *n*, pomoc *f*; ~al tymczasowy

provo|cation [prɒvə'keɪʃn] prowokacja *f*; ~cative [prə'vɒkətɪv] prowokacyjny; ~ke [prə'vəʊk] ⟨s⟩prowokować

pseudonym ['sjuːdənɪm] pseudonim *m*

psychiatr|ist [saɪ'kaɪətrɪst] psychiatra *m*; ~y psychiatria *f*

psychic(al) ['saɪkɪk(l)] psychiczny; umysłowy

psycho|analysis [saɪkəʊ-ə'næləsɪs] psychoanaliza *f*; ~logical [~kə'lɒdʒɪkl] psychologiczny; ~logist [~'kɒlədʒɪst] psycholog *m*; ~logy [~'kɒlədʒɪ] psychologia *f*; ~path [~'kəʊpæθ] psychopata *m*; ~'therapy psychoterapia *f*

pub [pʌb] pub *m*

puberty ['pjuːbətɪ] pokwitanie *n*

public ['pʌblɪk] **1.** społeczny, ogólny; publiczny; oficjalny; **2.** społeczeństwo *n*; środowisko *n*, grupa *f* społeczna; *in* ~ publicznie; ~ation [~'keɪʃn] publikacja *f*; wydanie *n*; ~ *convenience* toaleta *f* publiczna

publicity [pʌb'lɪsətɪ] reklama *f*

public| opinion opinia *f* publiczna; ~*school* Brt. szkoła *f* prywatna; Am. szkoła *f* państwowa; ~ *transport* komunikacja *f*

publish ['pʌblɪʃ] ⟨o⟩publikować; *book etc. a.* wyd(awa)ć; ~*er* wydawca *m*; ~*ing* działalność *f* wydawnicza; ~*ing company*, ~*ing house* wydawnictwo *n*

pudding ['pʊdɪŋ] Brt. deser *m*; pudding *m*

puddle ['pʌdl] kałuża *f*

puff [pʌf] **1.** *cigarette:* zaciągnięcie *n* się; podmuch *m*; dmuchnięcie *n*; **2.** *cigarette:* zaciągać ⟨-gnąć⟩ się (*s.th.* czymś); sapać; dmuchać; *out of* ~ bez tchu; ~*y* spuchnięty

pull [pʊl] **1.** pociągnięcie *n*, szarpnięcie *n*; przyciąganie *n*; wysiłek *m*; **2.** ⟨po⟩ciągnąć; ~ *back* wycof(yw)ać się; ~ *down* ⟨z⟩burzyć; ~ *in* zatrzym(yw)ać się; *train:* przyjeżdżać ⟨-jechać⟩; ~ *off* zjeżdżać ⟨zjechać⟩; ruszać ⟨-szyć⟩ w drogę; dokon(yw)ać; ~ **out** wyjeżdżać ⟨-jechać⟩; *train:* odjechać; *(withdraw)* wycof(yw)ać (się); ~ **o.s. together** brać ⟨wziąć⟩ się w garść; ~ **up** *car:* zatrzym(yw)ać się; przyciągać ⟨-gnąć⟩

pullover ['pʊləʊvə] sweter *m*
puls|ate [pʌl'seɪt] pulsować; **~e** [pʌls] puls *m*, tętno *n*
pump [pʌmp] **1.** pompa *f*, pompka *f*; **2.** ⟨na⟩pompować; ~ **s.o. about s.th.** wyciągać ⟨-gnąć⟩ z kogoś informacje o czymś; **~s** *pl* tenisówki *pl*
punch [pʌntʃ] **1.** cios *m* (pięścią); *tech.* dziurkacz *m*, perforator *m*; **2.** uderzać ⟨-rzyć⟩ pięścią; wystuk(iw)ać na (klawiaturze); ⟨prze⟩dziurkować; ~ **line** pointa *f*
punctual ['pʌnktʃʊəl] punktualny
puncture ['pʌnktʃə] przebicie *n*
pungent ['pʌndʒənt] cierpki; ostry
punish ['pʌnɪʃ] ⟨u⟩karać; **'~ment** kara *f*; męczarnia *f*
pupil¹ ['pju:pl] *school:* uczeń *m*, uczennica *f*
pupil² ['~] źrenica *f*
puppet ['pʌpɪt] kukiełka *f*; *fig.* marionetka *f*
puppy ['pʌpɪ] szczeniak *m*
purchas|e ['pɜ:tʃəs] **1.** zakup

m; nabytek *m*; **2.** naby(wa)ć, zakupywać ⟨-kupić⟩; **~ing power** siła *f* nabywcza
pure [pjʊə] czysty; **~ly** całkowicie; najzwyczajniej
puri|fy ['pjʊərɪfaɪ] oczyszczać ⟨oczyścić⟩ (*a. fig.*); **~ty** ['~rəti] czystość *f*
purple ['pɜ:pl] purpurowy, fioletowy
purpose ['pɜ:pəs] cel *m*; zadanie *n*; funkcja *f*; stanowczość *f*; **on** ~ celowo, umyślnie; **'~ful** celowy; **'~ly** celowo
purse [pɜ:s] portmonetka *f*; *Am.* torebka *f*
pursue [pə'sju:] *aim* zmierzać, dążyć (**s.th.** do czegoś); *subject* zajmować ⟨-jąć⟩ się (czymś); *activity* wykonywać, oddawać się (czemuś); *thief* ścigać (*a. fig.*); **~er** ścigający *m*; **~it** [~'sju:t] pogoń *f* (**of s.th.** za czymś); dążenie *n* (**of s.th.** do czegoś); oddawanie się (**of s.th.** czemuś)
push [pʊʃ] **1.** pchnięcie *n*; naciśnięcie *n*; dążanie *n*; energia *f*, determinacja *f*; **2.** pchać ⟨pchnąć⟩, popychać ⟨-pchnąć⟩; pchać się, przepychać ⟨-pchnąć⟩ się; *button* naciskać ⟨-snąć⟩; ~ **along** *lub* **off** F odchodzić ⟨odejść⟩, znikać ⟨-knąć⟩ F; ~ **on** ⟨po⟩jechać dalej (*a. fig.*); **'~chair** spacerówka *f*; **'~y** F nachalny
puss [pʊs], **'~y(cat)** kotek *m*, kicia *f*

put [pʊt] (*put*) kłaść ⟨położyć⟩, stawiać ⟨postawić⟩, wkładać ⟨włożyć⟩; *question* zada(wa)ć; *idea* wyrażać ⟨-razić⟩; *proposal* przedstawi(a)ć; ~ **away** odkładać ⟨odłożyć⟩ (na miejsce); ~ **back** opóźni(a)ć, przesuwać ⟨-sunąć⟩ (w czasie); *clock* cofać ⟨-fnąć⟩; ~ **down** kłaść ⟨położyć⟩; *hand* opuszczać ⟨opuścić⟩; *words* zapis(yw)ać; *riot* ⟨s⟩tłumić; (*ridicule*) ośmieszać ⟨-szyć⟩; *animal* usypiać ⟨uśpić⟩; ~ **forward** *clock* posunąć do przodu; *proposal etc.* ⟨za⟩proponować; ~ **in** wkładać ⟨włożyć⟩; *request* składać ⟨złożyć⟩; *comment* wtrącać ⟨-rącić⟩; ~ **off** odkładać ⟨odłożyć⟩; odmawiać ⟨-mówić⟩; ~ **on** *clothes* zakładać ⟨założyć⟩; *play* wystawi(a)ć; (*turn on*) włączać ⟨-czyć⟩, nastawi(a)ć; ~ **on weight** przyb(ie)rać na wadze; ~ **out** ogłaszać ⟨-łosić⟩; wyciągać ⟨-gnąć⟩; wypuszczać ⟨-puścić⟩; wys(y)łać; *fire* ⟨u⟩gasić; *light* ⟨z⟩gasić; ~ **through** *teleph.* połączyć (**to** z); ~ **together** składać ⟨złożyć⟩; ~ **up** podnosić ⟨-nieść⟩; *tent* rozbi(ja)ć; *wall* wznosić ⟨-nieść⟩, ⟨z⟩budować; *guest* przenocować; *resistance*, *fight* ⟨z⟩organizować; *price* podnosić ⟨-nieść⟩; ~ **up for sale** wystawi(a)ć na sprzedaż; ~ **up with** znosić ⟨znieść⟩

puzzl|**e** ['pʌzl] **1.** zagadka *f* (*a. fig.*); łamigłówka *f*, układanka *f*; **2.** zaskakiwać ⟨-skoczyć⟩, zadziwi(a)ć; łamać sobie głowę (**over** nad)

pyjamas [pə'dʒɑːməz] *pl* Brt. piżama *f*

pyramid ['pɪrəmɪd] piramida *f*

Q

quadruple ['kwɒdrʊpl] **1.** cztery razy większy; **2.** zwiększać ⟨-szyć⟩ (się) czterokrotnie; ~**ts** ['~plɪts] *pl* czworaczki *pl*

quake [kweɪk] **1.** trząść się; **2.** F trzęsienie *n* ziemi

quali|**fications** [kwɒlɪfɪ-'keɪʃnz] *pl* kwalifikacje *pl*; ~**fied** ['~faɪd] wykwalifikowany, dyplomowany; ~**fy** ['~faɪ] otrzym(yw)ać dyplom (**as s.o.** kogoś), zdoby(wa)ć kwalifikacje; zakwalifikować się (**for** do); ~**ty** (wysoka) jakość *f*; cecha *f*; zaleta *f*; gatunek *m*

quantity ['kwɒntətɪ] ilość *f*

quarrel ['kwɒrəl] **1.** kłótnia *f*; **2.** ⟨po⟩kłócić się; ~**some**

kłótliwy

quarter ['kwɔːtə] **1.** ćwiartka f; kwartał m; Am. ćwierć f dolara; ćwierć f funta; dzielnica f; pl kwatera f (a. mil.); usu. pl fig. kręgi pl; **a ~ of an hour** kwadrans m; **a ~ to l past** (Am. **a ~ of l after**) za kwadrans l kwadrans po; **2.** ⟨po⟩kroić ⟨po⟩dzielić na cztery części; da(wa)ć schronienie; mil. ⟨roz⟩kwaterować; **~'final** sp. ćwierćfinał m; '**~ly 1.** raz na kwartał, kwartalnie; **2.** kwartalny; **3.** kwartalnik m

queen [kwiːn] królowa f; cards: dama f; chess: hetman m

query ['kwɪərɪ] **1.** zapytanie n, zakwestionowanie n; znak m zapytania; **2.** sprawdzać ⟨-dzić⟩, ⟨za⟩kwestionować (esp. Am.) ⟨za⟩pytać

question ['kwestʃən] **1.** ⟨za⟩kwestionować; wypyt(yw)ać; jur. przesłuch(iw)ać; **2.** pytanie n; wątpliwość f; niepewność f; problem m, zadanie n; **in ~** wspomniany, o którym mowa; **that is out of the ~** to wykluczone, to nie wchodzi w rachubę; **~able** niejasny; wątpliwy;

'**~ing 1.** przesłuchanie n; **2.** pełen niepewności; **~ mark** znak m zapytania; **~naire** [~'neə] kwestionariusz m

queue [kjuː] **1.** kolejka f; (a. **~ up**) czekać w kolejce; ustawiać się w kolejkę

quick [kwɪk] szybki, prędki; bystry; krótki; **be ~!** pospiesz się; '**~en** przyspieszać ⟨-szyć⟩; **~'tempered** porywczy

quid [kwɪd] pl ~ Brt. F funt m (szterling), funciak m F

quiet ['kwaɪət] **1.** spokojny; cichy; **2.** cisza f; '**~en** usu. **~ down** uspokajać ⟨-koić⟩ (się)

quilt [kwɪlt] kołdra f

quit [kwɪt] (**quit**) przesta(wa)ć; job F rzucać ⟨-cić⟩

quite [kwaɪt] całkiem, dość; zupełnie; **~ (so)!** właśnie!

quiz [kwɪz] **1.** quiz m; school: sprawdzian m; **2.** wypyt(yw)ać

quotation [kwəʊ'teɪʃn] cytat m; oferta f cenowa, stawka f; econ. notowanie n; **~ marks** pl cudzysłów m

quote [kwəʊt] **1.** cytat m; F cudzysłów m; **2.** ⟨za⟩cytować; przytaczać ⟨-toczyć⟩; price pod(aw)ać

R

rabbit ['ræbɪt] królik m
race¹ [reɪs] rasa f
race² [~] **1.** wyścig m (a. fig.);

bieg m; **a ~ against time** wyścig z czasem; **the ~s** pl wyścigi pl konne; **2.** ścigać się (**s.o.** *or* **against s.o.** z kimś); ⟨po⟩pędzić, ⟨po⟩mknąć; **'.course** *Brt.* tor *m* wyścigów konnych; **~horse** koń *m* wyścigowy; **'.track** tor *m* wyścigowy

racial ['reɪʃl] rasowy; **~equality** równość *f* rasowa

racing ['reɪsɪŋ] **1.** wyścigi *pl* konne; **2.** wyścigowy

racis|m ['reɪsɪzəm] rasizm *m*; **'.t 1.** rasista *m* (-tka *f*) ; **2.** rasistowski

rack [ræk] **1.** półka *f* s *clothes*: stojak *m*, wieszak *m*; *roof*: bagażnik *m* (dachowy); **2.** dręczyć, prześladować; **~ one's brains** *fig.* łamać sobie głowę

racket ['rækɪt] rakieta *f* (tenisowa)

radar ['reɪdɑ:] radar *m*

radi|ant ['reɪdjənt] rozpromieniony, promienny; rozjarzony; **~ate** ['~ieɪt] rozchodzić się promieniście; promieniować; *emotion*: tryskać (**s.th.** czymś); **~ate** *from* emanować; **~ation** [~'eɪʃn] promieniowanie *n*; **~ator** ['~ieɪtə] kaloryfer *m*, grzejnik *m*; *mot.* chłodnica *f*

radical ['rædɪkl] podstawowy; gruntowny; radykalny

radio ['reɪdɪəʊ] **1.** radio *n*; odbiornik *m* radiowy; **by ~** przez radio, drogą radiową; **on the ~** w radiu; **2.** nad(aw)ać drogą radiową

radish ['rædɪʃ] rzodkiewka *f*

raft [rɑ:ft] tratwa *f*; materac *m* nadmuchiwany; **~er** krokiew *f*

rag [ræg] szmat(k)a *f*; *Brt.* F *newspaper*: brukowiec *m*; **~s** *pl* łachmany *pl*

rage [reɪdʒ] **1.** wściekać się (**about** / **at** na); *wind, disease etc.*: szaleć; **2.** wściekłość *f*, szał *m*

ragged ['rægɪd] *person*: obdarty; *clothes*: podarty, poszarpany; *edge*: nierówny

raid [reɪd] **1.** nalot *m*; napad *m*; obława *f*; **2.** napadać ⟨-paść⟩ (**s.th.** na coś); zrobić obławę (**s.th.** na coś); ⟨s⟩plądrować

rail [reɪl] poręcz *f*, balustrada *f*; szyna *f*; *towel*: wieszak *m*; *mar.* reling *m*; szyn|a *f*; **by ~** koleją; **'.road** *Am.* → **'.way** *Brt.* kolej *f*; **~way line** linia *f* kolejowa; **~way station** dworzec *m* kolejowy

rain [reɪn] **1.** padać; deszcz *m*; *it is ~ing* pada deszcz; *the ~s pl* pora *f* deszczowa; **'.bow** tęcza *f*; **'.coat** płaszcz *m* przeciwdeszczowy; **'.drop** kropla *f* deszczu; **'.fall** opad(y *pl*) *m* deszczu; **'.y** deszczowy; **for a ~y day** na czarną godzinę

raise [reɪz] **1.** podnosić ⟨-nieść⟩; *rent etc. a.* podwyższać ⟨-szyć⟩; *money* zbierać ⟨zebrać⟩; *children* wychow(yw)ać; *animals* ⟨wy⟩hodować; *plants* uprawiać; *ban* etc. znosić ⟨znieść⟩; **2.** *Am.* podwyżka *f* (wynagrodzenia)

raisin ['reɪzn] rodzynek *m*

rake [reɪk] **1.** grabie *pl*; **2.** ⟨za⟩grabić; zgarniać ⟨-nąć⟩ (grabiami); (*search*) przeszuk(iw)ać

rally ['rælɪ] **1.** zlot *m*, wiec *m*; *mot.* rajd *m*; *tennis:* wymiana *f* (piłek); **2.** ⟨z⟩gromadzić (się); zbierać ⟨zebrać⟩ (się); **~ round** *s.o.* przychodzić ⟨przyjść⟩ komuś z pomocą

ram [ræm] **1.** *zo.* baran *m*; *tech.* kafar *m*; taran *m*; **2.** ⟨s⟩taranować; wbi(ja)ć; wpychać ⟨wepchnąć⟩

ramp [ræmp] rampa *f*, podjazd *m*; garb *m*

ran [ræn] *past of run* 1

ranch [rɑːntʃ, *Am.* ræntʃ] rancho *n*; ferma *f*

random ['rændəm] **1.** *at* ~ na chybił trafił; **2.** losowy, przypadkowy

range [reɪndʒ] **1.** zakres *m*; zasięg *m*; odległość *f*; *mountain:* łańcuch *m*; *price* etc.: przedział *m*; *rifle:* strzelnica *f*; *missile:* poligon *m*; *econ.* gama *f*, zestaw *m*; pastwisko *n*; **2.** *v/i* oscylować, wahać się (**from ... to ...** *or* **between ... and ...** od ... do ...) (*a. prices*); *writing* etc.: rozciągać się, mieć zasięg; *it books* etc. ustawi(a)ć; *forces* zjednoczyć; *~r* strażnik *m* leśny;

Am. komandos *m*

rank [ræŋk] **1.** stopień *m*, ranga *f* (*a. mil.*); klasa *f*; szereg *m*; *taxi:* postój *m*; **2.** zaliczać się; ~ **among** zaliczać się do; ~ **as** *s.o.* być traktowanym jako ktoś

ransom ['rænsəm] okup *m*; **hold to** ~ więzić żądając okupu; *fig.* przypierać do muru

rape [reɪp] **1.** gwałt *m*; **2.** ⟨z⟩gwałcić

rapid ['ræpɪd] szybki; **~ity** [rə'pɪdətɪ] szybkość *f*; **~s** *pl* bystrzyna *f*, progi *pl*

rar|e [reə] rzadki; *steak:* krwisty; *air:* rozrzedzony; **~ity** ['reərətɪ] rzadkość *f*

rash[1] [ræʃ] pochopny

rash[2] [~] wysypka *f*; seria *f*

rasher ['ræʃə] plasterek *m*

rat [ræt] szczur *m*

rate [reɪt] **1.** tempo *n*; szybkość *f*; wskaźnik *m*, współczynnik *m*; *econ.* stopa *f*, wysokość *f*; **at any** ~ w każdym bądź razie; **at this** ~ jeśli tak dalej pójdzie; **exchange** ~, ~ **of exchange** kurs *m* wymiany (waluty); **interest** ~ stopa *f* procentowa; **2.** oceni(a)ć; uzn(aw)ać (**as** za); mieć dobre zdanie (**s.th.** o czymś); zasługiwać (**s.th.** na coś)

rather ['rɑːðə] dość, dosyć; raczej; **~!** *F* jeszcze jak

ration ['ræʃn] **1.** przydział *m*; porcja *f*; **2.** racjonować

rational ['ræʃənl] racjonalny,

rozsądny; rozumny; **~ize** ['\nəlaız] uzasadni(a)ć; ⟨z⟩racjonalizować

rattle ['rætl] **1.** grzechotka *f*; grzechot *m*; stukot *m*, stukanie *n*; **2.** stukać; grzechotać; **~snake** grzechotnik *m*

raw [rɔ:] surowy; nieprzetworzony, w postaci naturalnej; bolesny; niedoświadczony; *weather*: mokry i zimny; **~ material** surowiec *m*

ray [reı] promień *m*; *hope etc.*: promyk *m*

razor ['reızə] brzytwa *f*; maszynka *f* do golenia; **~ blade** żyletka *f*

re [ri:] *econ.* w nawiązaniu do

re- [ri:] powtórny; powtórnie

reach [ri:tʃ] **1.** *v/t place* docierać ⟨dotrzeć⟩ do; *object* sięgać ⟨-gnąć⟩; *person* ⟨s⟩kontaktować się z; *shelf* dosięgać ⟨-gnąć⟩ (do); *level* osiągać ⟨-gnąć⟩; *v/i* sięgać ⟨-gnąć⟩ **for** po; **~ out** wyciągać ⟨-gnąć⟩ rękę; **2.** zasięg *m*, **out of ~** poza zasięgiem; **within easy ~** w pobliżu

react [rı'ækt] ⟨za⟩reagować (**to** na); ⟨s⟩prawdzi(a)ć się (**against s.th.** czemuś); **~ion** reakcja *f*; **~ionary** [\ʃənrı] reakcyjny; **~or** reaktor *m*

read 1. [ri:d] (**read** [red]) *v/t* ⟨prze⟩czytać; *subject* studiować; (*interpret*) odczyt(yw)ać; (*interpret*) odczyt(yw)ać; *book*: czytać się; *instrument*: wskaz(yw)ać; **~ to s.o.** czytać

komuś; **2.** [red] *past and pp of* **read** 1

readi|ly ['redılı] chętnie; łatwo; **~ness** gotowość *f*; chęć *f*

reading ['ri:dıŋ] czytanie *n*; lektura *f*; interpretacja *f*; *by meter etc.*: odczyt *m*

ready ['redı] gotowy (**for** do); natychmiastowy; **~ cash** (żywa) gotówka *f*; **get ~** przygotow(yw)ać się; **~made** gotowy (do spożycia, użycia)

real [rıəl] prawdziwy, autentyczny, rzeczywisty; *income*: realny; **for ~** naprawdę; **the ~ thing** oryginał *m*; **~ estate** nieruchomość *f*, nieruchomości *pl*; **~istic** [\'lıstık] realistyczny; **~ity** [rı'ælətı] rzeczywistość *f*; prawdziwość *f*; **~ization** [rıəlaı'zeıʃn] *hopes*: spełnienie *n*, realizacja *f* (*a. econ.*); *mistakes*: zrozumienie *n*; **~ize** zda(wa)ć sobie sprawę (**s.th.** z czegoś); **~ly** w rzeczywistości; naprawdę, rzeczywiście; **~!, well ~!** coś takiego!; **not ~** nie zupełnie

realm [relm] dziedzina *f*; królestwo *n* (*a. fig.*)

rear [rıə] **1.** tylny wycho(wy)wać; *cattle etc.* ⟨wy⟩hodować; *horse*: (*a.* **~ up**) stawać ⟨stanąć⟩ dęba; **2.** *usu.* **the ~** tył *m*; *queue*: *usu.* **the ~** koniec *m*; F tyłek *m* F; **3.** tylny

rearrange [rıə'reındʒ] *furni-*

ture przestawi(a)ć; *appointment* przesuwać ⟨-sunąć⟩

'**rear-view mirror** *mot.* lusterko *n* wsteczne

reason ['ri:zn] **1.** przyczyna *f*; powód *m*; rozum *m*; (zdrowy) rozsądek *m*; **for some ~** nie wiadomo dlaczego; **within ~** w granicach zdrowego rozsądku; **2.** myśleć; rozumować; argumentować; **~ with** przekonywać; '**~able** rozsądny; racjonalny; *price*: znośny, uczciwy

reassure [ri:ə'ʃɔ:] uspokajać ⟨-koić⟩, pocieszać ⟨-szyć⟩

rebel 1. ['rebl] rebeliant *m*, powstaniec *m*; buntownik *m*; **2.** [rɪ'bel] ⟨z⟩buntować się (**against** przeciwko); **~lion** [rɪ'beljən] rebelia *f*, rewolta *f*; bunt *m*; **~lious** [rɪ'beljəs] buntowniczy

recall [rɪ'kɔ:l] przypominać ⟨-mnieć⟩ sobie; **as I ~** jak pamiętam

receipt [rɪ'si:t] pokwitowanie *n*, kwit *m*; odbiór *m*; *pl* przychody *pl*

receive [rɪ'si:v] otrzym(yw)ać; *criticism etc.* spot(y)kać się z; *signals* odbierać ⟨odebrać⟩; *guests, new members* przyjmować ⟨-jąć⟩; **~r** odbiornik *m*; *teleph.* słuchawka *f*

recent ['ri:snt] ostatni; niedawny; '**~ly** ostatnio; niedawno

reception [rɪ'sepʃn] przyjęcie *n*; *radio*: odbiór *m*; *hotel*: recepcja *f*; **~ desk** *hotel*: recepcja *f*; **~ist** recepcjonista *m*, recepcjonistka *f*

recipe ['resɪpɪ] przepis *m* (kulinarny)

recipient [rɪ'sɪpɪənt] odbiorca *m*

recit|al [rɪ'saɪtl] *mus.* recital *m*; **~e** [~'saɪt] ⟨wy⟩recytować; *list* wymieni(a)ć

reckless ['reklɪs] lekkomyślny

reckon ['rekən] F uważać, sądzić

reclaim [rɪ'kleɪm] odzysk(iw)ać (*a. tech.*); *baggage* ~ odbiór *m* bagażu

recogni|tion [rekəg'nɪʃn] rozpoznanie *n*, identyfikacja *f*; uznanie *n*; **beyond ~tion** nie do rozpoznania; **~ze** ['~naɪz] rozpozn(aw)ać; doceni(a)ć; spostrzegać ⟨-rzec⟩

recollect [rekə'lekt] przypominać ⟨-mnieć⟩; **~ion** wspomnienie *n*, obraz *m* w pamięci; przypomnienie *n* sobie

recommend [rekə'mend] polecać ⟨-cić⟩; zalecać ⟨-cić⟩; **~ation** [~'deɪʃn] rekomendacja *f*; zalecenie *n*

reconcil|e ['rekənsaɪl] pogodzić; być pogodzić się z kimś; **~e oneself to s.th.** pogodzić się z czymś; **~iation** [~sɪlɪ'eɪʃn] pojednanie *n*, zgoda *f*

reconsider [riːkənˈsɪdə] (powtórnie) przemyśleć

reconstruct [riːkənˈstrʌkt] odbudow(yw)ać; ⟨z⟩reorganizować; ⟨z⟩rekonstruować; **~ion** odbudowa *f*; reorganizacja *f*; rekonstrukcja *f*

record 1. [ˈrekɔːd] zapis *m*; rejestr *m*; protokół *m*; płyta *f* (gramofonowa); (*past career*) osiągnięcia *pl*, przeszłość *f*; *sp*. rekord *m*; *off the* ~ poza protokołem, nieoficjalnie; **2.** [rɪˈkɔːd] ⟨za⟩rejestrować, zapis(yw)ać; ⟨za⟩notować; *on tape etc.*: nagr(yw)ać; **~er** [~kˈ-] magnetofon *m*; *mus.* flet *m* prosty; **~ player** [ˈrekɔːd] gramofon *m*

recover [rɪˈkʌvə] wyzdrowieć, wracać ⟨-cić⟩ do zdrowia (*from* po); przychodzić ⟨przyjść⟩ do siebie (*from* po); *money* odzysk(iw)ać; *econ.* wychodzić ⟨wyjść⟩ z kryzysu; **~y** [~ərɪ] powrót *m* do zdrowia, poprawa *f*; *property etc.*: odzyskanie *n*; *econ.* powrót *m* koniunktury

recruit [rɪˈkruːt] **1.** rekrut *m*; *fig.* nowicjusz(ka *f*) *m*; **2.** ⟨z⟩werbować, zatrudni(a)ć (*for* do)

rectangle [ˈrektæŋgl] prostokąt *m*

recycl|e [riːˈsaɪkl] przetwarzać ⟨-worzyć⟩ powtórnie; **~ing** powtórna przeróbka *f*

red [red] czerwony; *hair*: ru-

dy; **⁀** **Cross** Czerwony Krzyż *m*; **~den** [ˈredn] ⟨po⟩czerwienieć; ⟨za⟩czerwienić się

reduc|e [rɪˈdjuːs] zmniejszać ⟨-szyć⟩, ⟨z⟩redukować; zmuszać ⟨-sić⟩ (*to* do); *sauce etc.* odparow(yw)ać; **~tion** [~ˈdʌkʃn] zmniejszanie *n*, redukcja *f*; ograniczenie *n*

redundan|cy [rɪˈdʌndənsɪ] zwolnienie *n* (z pracy); bezrobocie *n*; zbyteczność *f*; **~cy payment** zasiłek *m* dla bezrobotnych; **~t** bezrobotny; zbyteczny

reed [riːd] trzcina *f*; *mus.* stroik *m*

reef [riːf] rafa *f*

reel [riːl] **1.** *thread*: szpulka *f*; *magnetic tape*: szpula *f*; *film, adhesive tape etc.*: rolka *f*; *for angling*: kołowrotek *m*; **2.** zataczać się; chwiać się; **~ in** wyciągać ⟨-gnąć⟩ z wody

refer [rɪˈfɜː]: ~ *to* nawiąz(yw)ać do; określać (*as* jako); *notes*: zaglądać do; *literature*: odsyłać do

referee [refəˈriː] sędzia *m*; osoba *f* polecająca

reference [ˈrefrəns] aluzja *f*, wzmianka *f*, konsultacja *f*; referencja *f*, list *m* polecający; odwołanie *n* (do literatury); nota *f* bibliograficzna; *with* ~ *to* w nawiązaniu do; **~ book** informator *m*; publikacja *f* encyklopedyczna

refill 404

refill 1. ['riːfil] F dolewka *f*; *pen*: wkład *m*; **2.** [ˌ'fil] powtórnie napełni(a)ć

refine [riˈfain] oczyszczać 〈oczyścić〉, rafinować; doskonalić 〈-nalić〉; **~d** wytworny, dystyngowany; dopracowany; *tech.* rafinowany, oczyszczony; **~ry** [ˌ'~əri] rafineria *f*

reflect [riˈflekt] odzwierciedlać 〈-lić〉; przedstawi(a)ć; odbi(ja)ć (się); zastanawiać 〈-nowić〉 się; *fig.* wpływać 〈-łynąć〉 (*on* na opinię *v*); **~ion** odbicie *n*, odzwierciedlenie *n*; zaduma *f*; spostrzeżenie *n* (*on* co do); **on ~ion** po zastanowieniu

reflex ['riːfleks] odruch *m*; *pl* refleks *m*; **~ive** odruchowy

reform [riˈfɔːm] **1.** reforma *f*; **2.** 〈z〉reformować; poprawi(a)ć się

refrain [riˈfrein] **1.** powstrzym(yw)ać się (*from* od); **2.** refren *m*

refresh [riˈfreʃ]: **~** (*o.s.*) odświeżać 〈-żyć〉 (się); **~ s.o.'s memory** przypomnieć komuś

refrigerator [riˈfridʒəreitə] lodówka *f*

refuge ['refjuːdʒ] schronienie *n*; *take* **~** 〈s〉chronić się; **~e** [ˌ'dʒiː] uchodźca *m*

refund 1. [riˈfʌnd] zwracać 〈-rócić〉, 〈z〉refundować; **2.** ['riːfʌnd] zwrot *m*;

refus|al [riˈfjuːzl] odmowa *f*;

odpowiedź *f* odmowna; odrzucenie *n*; **~e 1.** [riˈfjuːz] odmawiać 〈-mówić〉; odrzucać 〈-cić〉; **2.** ['refjuːs] odpadki *pl*

regain [riˈgein] *health etc.* odzysk(iw)ać

regard [riˈgɑːd] **1.** uznanie *n* (*for* dla); (*kind*) **~s** (serdeczne) pozdrowienia; **with ~, in ~ to** co się tyczy; **without ~ for** nie zważając na; **2.** uznawać (*as* za); myśleć (*s.o., s.th. with* o kimś, czymś *z*); *as* **~s** co się tyczy; **~ing** odnośnie; **~less** niezależnie (*~ of* od); bez względu na okoliczności

region ['riːdʒən] region *m*, okręg *m*; *knowledge etc.*: dziedzina *f*; **~s** *pl* prowincja *f*

register ['redʒistə] **1.** wykaz *m*, rejestr *m* (*a. mus.*), lista *f*; *Am.* kasa *f* sklepowa; **2.** *v/i* 〈za〉rejestrować się, 〈za〉meldować się (*with* na policji, *w urzędzie*); *measurement*: być 〈zostać〉 zarejestrowanym; *v/t car, measurement etc.* 〈za〉rejestrować; *letter* nad(aw)ać jako polecony; **~ed letter** list *m* polecony

registration [redʒiˈstreiʃn] rejestracja *f*; **~ document** *Brt.* *mot.* dowód *m* rejestracyjny; **~ number** *mot.* numer *m* rejestracyjny

regret [riˈgret] **1.** żal *m*, ubolewanie *n*; *pl* wątpliwości *pl*; **2.** 〈po〉żałować; wyrażać

⟨-razić⟩ żal, przepraszać ⟨-rosić⟩; **I ~ to say** z przykrością muszę stwierdzić

regular ['regjʊlə] **1.** regularny; *customer, job:* stały; *soldier:* zawodowy; *price, time:* normalny, zwykły; **2.** stały bywalec *m*; żołnierz *m* zawodowy

regulat|e ['regjʊlert] ⟨wy⟩regulować; kontrolować, sterować; **~ion** [~'leɪʃn] **1.** przepis *m*; kontrola *f*; **2.** przepisowy

rehears|al [rɪ'hɜːsl] próba *f*; **~e** [~s] ⟨z⟩robić próbę; ⟨prze⟩ćwiczyć

reign [reɪn] **1.** panowanie *n* (*a. fig.*); **2.** ⟨za⟩panować (*a. fig.*)

rein [reɪn] *pl* lejce *pl*

reinforce [riːɪn'fɔːs] wzmacniać ⟨-mocnić⟩; **~ment** wzmocnienie *n*; **~ments** *pl* posiłki *pl*

reject [rɪ'dʒekt] odrzucać ⟨-cić⟩; *applicant* nie przyjmować ⟨-jąć⟩; **~ion** odmowa *f*; odrzucenie *n*

relate [rɪ'leɪt] *v/t* ⟨po⟩łączyć (*s.th. to s.th.* coś z czymś); *v/i* (*concern*) dotyczyć (**to s.th.** czegoś); (*appreciate*) identyfikować się (**to** z); **~d** powiązany; spokrewniony (*a. fig.*)

relation [rɪ'leɪʃn] związek *m*, powiązanie *n* (**to** z); relacja *f*, stosunek *m*; stosunek *m* (**between** między); krewny *m*

(**-na** *f*); **~ship** stosunki *pl* (**between** między, **with** z); związek *m* (**between** między, **with** z); pokrewieństwo *n*

relative ['relətɪv] **1.** krewny *m* (-na *f*); **2.** względny; **~ to** w porównaniu z

relax [rɪ'læks] odprężać ⟨-żyć⟩ (się); rozluźni(a)ć (się)

relay 1. ['riːleɪ] *electr., TV* przekaźnik *m*; *sp.* **~ (race)** sztafeta *f*, bieg *m* sztafetowy; **in ~s** na zmianę; **2.** [rɪ'leɪ] *news* przekaz(yw)ać; *TV* nad(aw)ać, przekaz(yw)ać

release [rɪ'liːs] **1.** zwolnienie *n*, uwolnienie *n*; udostępnienie *n*; (*relief*) ulga *f*; *press:* oświadczenie *n*, komunikat *m*; *video etc.:* nagranie *n*, dzieło *n*; **2.** zwalniać ⟨zwolnić⟩, uwalniać ⟨uwolnić⟩; ⟨o⟩publikować; (*let go*) puszczać ⟨puścić⟩

relevant ['reləvənt] istotny, znaczący (**to** dla); odpowiedni

reliab|ility [rɪlaɪə'bɪlɪtɪ] niezawodność *f*; **~le** [rɪ'laɪəbl] niezawodny; pewny

reliance [rɪ'laɪəns] uzależnienie *n*, zależność *f* (**on** od)

relief [rɪ'liːf] ulga *f*; uwolnienie *n* (**from** od); pomoc *f*; płaskorzeźba *f*, rzeźba *f* (terenu); zmiennik *m*; **~ve** [~v] ulżyć; uwalniać ⟨uwolnić⟩;

position: zwalniać ⟨zwolnić⟩ (*of z*)

religi|on [rɪ'lɪdʒən] religia *f*; **~ous** religijny; pobożny

reluctan|ce [rɪ'lʌktəns] niechęć *f*; **~t** niechętny, pozbawiony entuzjazmu; *be ~t to do s.th.* nie palić się do robienia czegoś

rely [rɪ'laɪ]: **~ on** *or* **upon s.th.** zależeć od czegoś; polegać na czymś

remain [rɪ'meɪn] **1.** pozost(aw)ać; *it ~s to be seen* nie wiadomo; **2.** *pl* pozostałości *pl*, resztki *pl*; szczątki *pl*; **~der**: *the ~der* reszta *f* (*a. math.*), pozostała część *f*

remark [rɪ'mɑːk] **1.** uwaga *f*; **2.** napomykać ⟨-pomknąć⟩; ⟨s⟩komentować (**on, upon s.th.** coś); **~able** zadziwiający, nadzwyczajny

remedy ['remədɪ] **1.** lek *m*, lekarstwo *n* (*a. fig.*), środek (**for** na); **2.** naprawi(a)ć (**s.th.** coś), zaradzić (**s.th.** czemuś)

rememb|er [rɪ'membə] ⟨za⟩pamiętać; przypominać ⟨-mnieć⟩ (**sobie**); **~er me to her** pozdrów ją ode mnie

remind [rɪ'maɪnd] przypominać ⟨-nieć⟩ (**of s.th.** coś, *a. about, of s.th.* o czymś); **~er** przypomnienie *n*; upomnienie *n*

remnant ['remnənt] resztka *f*

remote [rɪ'məʊt] odległy; położony daleko (**from** od);

odosobniony; (*not relevant*) oderwany (**from** od); *possibility etc.*: mało prawdopodobny; **~ control** zdalne sterowanie *n*; pilot *m* F

remov|al [rɪ'muːvl] usunięcie *n*, likwidacja *f*; przeprowadzka *f*; **~e** [~v] zab(ie)rać (**from** z); *clothing* zdejmować ⟨zdjąć⟩; *stain* usuwać ⟨usunąć⟩; **~ed** odmienny; **~er** *stain etc.*: wywabiacz *m*; *nail polish*: zmywacz *m*

rename [riː'neɪm] przemianow(yw)ać

renew [rɪ'njuː] odnawiać ⟨-nowić⟩, wymieni(a)ć; odświeżać ⟨-żyć⟩; *efforts etc.* ponawiać ⟨-nowić⟩; *passport etc.* przedłużać ⟨-żyć⟩; **~al** wznowienie *n*; przedłużenie *n*

renovate ['renəʊveɪt] odnawiać ⟨-nowić⟩

rent [rent] **1.** czynsz *m*; *for ~* do wynajęcia; **2.** wynajmować ⟨-jąć⟩ (od kogoś); **~ out** wynajmować ⟨-jąć⟩ (komuś)

repair [rɪ'peə] **1.** naprawi(a)ć; **2.** naprawa *f*

reparation [repə'reɪʃn] zadośćuczynienie *n*; **~s** *pl* odszkodowanie *n*

repay [riː'peɪ] (*-paid*) *money* zwracać ⟨-rócić⟩; odwdzięczać ⟨-czyć⟩ się, ⟨z⟩rewanżować się (*for* za)

repeat [rɪ'piːt] **1.** powtarzać ⟨-tarzać⟩ (*after* po); **2.** powtórzenie *n* (*a. TV*)

repel [rɪ'pel] ⟨wz⟩budzić odrazę (**s.o.** w kimś); *invaders* odpierać ⟨odeprzeć⟩; *phys.* odpychać ⟨odepchnąć⟩; **~lent 1.** odrażający (**to** dla); **2.** *insect* **~**lent środek *m* odstraszający owady

repetition [repɪ'tɪʃn] powtórzenie *n*

replace [rɪ'pleɪs] zastępować ⟨-tąpić⟩ (**with, by s.th.** czymś); wymieni(a)ć (na nowy); odkładać ⟨odłożyć⟩ (na miejsce); **~ment** zastąpienie *n*; zastępstwo *n*

reply [rɪ'plaɪ] **1.** odpowiadać ⟨-wiedzieć⟩ (**to na**); **2.** odpowiedź *f*; **in ~** (**to**) w odpowiedzi (na)

report [rɪ'pɔːt] **1.** sprawozdanie *n*, raport *m*; *press:* doniesienie *n*; *Brt. school:* świadectwo *n*; **2.** donosić ⟨-nieść⟩, ⟨za⟩meldować; *in press:* ⟨z⟩relacjonować; opis(yw)ać; *to boss etc.:* składać ⟨złożyć⟩ sprawozdanie (**on** na temat); *to police etc.:* zgłaszać ⟨-łosić⟩, **~er** reporter(ka *f*) *m*

represent [reprɪ'zent] reprezentować, przedstawiać, symbolizować; przedstawiać; **~ation** [~'teɪʃn] reprezentacja *f*; przedstawienie *n*, obraz *m*; **~ative** [~'zentətɪv] **1.** reprezentatywny; **2.** przedstawiciel(ka *f*) *m*; *Am. pol.* reprezentant *m*

repression [rɪ'preʃn] represje

pl; *psych.* tłumienie *n* (uczuć, odruchów)

reproduc|e [riːprə'djuːs] *v/t* ⟨z⟩reprodukować, ⟨s⟩kopiować, odtwarzać ⟨-tworzyć⟩; naśladować; *success* powtarzać ⟨-tórzyć⟩; *v/i* rozmnażać ⟨-nożyć⟩ się; **~tion** [~'dʌkʃn] reprodukcja *f*, kopiowanie *n*, odtwarzanie *n*, naśladowanie *n*; rozmnażanie *n*; kopia *f*

reptile ['reptaɪl] gad *m*

republic [rɪ'pʌblɪk] republika *f*; **~an 1.** republikański; **2.** republikanin *m*

repulsive [rɪ'pʌlsɪv] odrażający, wstrętny

reputation [repjʊ'teɪʃn] reputacja *f*, renoma *f*

request [rɪ'kwest] **1.** prośba *f*; życzenie *n*; **on ~** na życzenie; **2.** zwracać ⟨-rócić⟩ się z prośbą, po⟨prosić⟩ (**s.th.** o coś); **~ stop** przystanek *m* na żądanie

require [rɪ'kwaɪə] potrzebować; wymagać; **~ment** wymaganie *n*; warunek *m*; potrzeba *f*

rescue ['reskjuː] **1.** ratunek *m*; akcja *f* ratunkowa; *gol come to the ~* uda(wa)ć się / przychodzić ⟨przyjść⟩ z pomocą; **2.** ⟨u⟩ratować

research [rɪ'sɜːtʃ] **1.** (*a. pl.*) badania *pl*, praca *f* naukowa (**on, into** nad); **2.** badać, prowadzić prace badawcze; **~er** naukowiec *m*

resembl|ance [rɪ'zembləns] podobieństwo *n* (**to** do); **~e** [~bl] być podobnym (**s.th.** do czegoś), przypominać (**s.th.** coś)

reservation [rezə'veɪʃn] zastrzeżenie *n*, wątpliwość *f* (**about** w związku z); *table, plane*: rezerwacja *f; Am.* rezerwat *m* (Indian); **without ~** bez zastrzeżeń, bezwarunkowo

reserve [rɪ'zɜ:v] **1.** *usu. pl* zasób *m; pl* rezerwy *pl* (*a. mil.*); *sp.* zawodnik *m* rezerwowy; rezerwat *m;* (*restraint*) rezerwa *f*, powściągliwość *f;* **in ~** w rezerwie; **2.** ⟨za⟩rezerwować; **~d** powściągliwy; *table, etc.*: zarezerwowany

reservoir ['rezəvwɑ:] zbiornik *m;* zapas *m*

reside [rɪ'zaɪd] zamieszkiwać; znajdować się (**in** w); **~nce** ['rezɪdns] miejsce *n* zamieszkania; rezydencja *f*; zamieszkiwanie *n*, pobyt *m;* **~ permit** zezwolenie *n* na pobyt stały; **~nt 1.** zamieszkały, mieszkający; mieszkający na miejscu, miejscowy; **2.** mieszkaniec *m* (-anka *f*)

resign [rɪ'zaɪn] ⟨z⟩rezygnować; pod(aw)ać się do dymisji, ustępować (-tąpić); **~ o.s. to** ⟨po⟩godzić się z; **~ation** [rezɪɡ'neɪʃn] rezygnacja *f*; ustąpienie *n*; **~ed** pogodzony (**to** z)

resin ['rezɪn] żywica *f*

resist [rɪ'zɪst] stawi(a)ć opór (**s.th.** czemuś); *attack* powstrzym(yw)ać, odpierać; *temptation* nie ulegać ⟨ulec⟩; **~ance** opór *m* (**to** przeciw) (*a. phys.*); *to disease etc.*: odporność *f* (**to** na); **~ant** odporny

resolut|e ['rezəlu:t] zdecydowany, zdeterminowany; **~ion** [~'lu:ʃn] determinacja *f*; (*decision*) postanowienie *n*; *at UN*: rezolucja *f; problem*: rozwiązanie *n*

resolve [rɪ'zɒlv] **1.** postanowienie *n;* **2.** (*decide*) postanawiać ⟨-nowić⟩; *problem* rozwiąz(yw)ać

resonan|ce ['rezənəns] rezonans *m;* **~t** *voice*: donośny; *room*: akustyczny

resort [rɪ'zɔ:t] **1.** miejscowość *f* wypoczynkowa; uciekanie *n* się (**to** do); **as a last ~** w końcu, jako ostatnia deska ratunku; **2.** uciekać ⟨uciec⟩ się (**to** do)

resource [rɪ'sɔ:s] *pl natural*: bogactwa *pl*, zasoby *pl*; (*money*) środki *pl; sg* zaradność *f;* (*source*) źródło *n*, materiał *m* źródłowy; **~ful** pomysłowy, zaradny

respect [rɪ'spekt] **1.** szacunek *m*, poważanie *n* (**for** dla); poszanowanie *n* (**for s.th.** czegoś); *fig.* wzgląd *m;* **treat s.th. with ~** zachowywać ostrożność używając czegoś; **with ~ to** co się tyczy (**s.th.** czegoś); **2.** szanować; wishes spełni(a)ć; **~able** przyzwoity; szacowny; **~ful** pełen szacunku; **~ive** odpowiedni, właściwy; **~ively** odpowiednio

respiration [respəˈreɪʃn] oddychanie n

respond [rɪˈspɒnd] odpowiadać ⟨-wiedzieć⟩ (**to** na, with **s.th.** czymś); reagować (**to** na)

response [rɪˈspɒns] odpowiedź f; reakcja f (**to** na); **in ~ to** w odpowiedzi na

responsibility [rɪspɒnsə'bɪlətɪ] odpowiedzialność f (**for** za); obowiązek m; **~le** [~'spɒnsəbl] odpowiedzialny (**for** za)

rest¹ [rest]: **the ~** reszta f, pozostała część f

rest² [~] **1.** odpoczynek m; oparcie n; spoczynek m (a. tech.); mus. pauza f; **at ~** odprężony; w spoczynku; **put, set s.o.'s mind at ~** uspokoić kogoś; **2.** v/i odpoczywać ⟨-cząć⟩; spoczywać ⟨-cząć⟩; opierać ⟨oprzeć⟩ się (**on** na); choice etc.: należeć (**with** do); v/t body etc. odprężać ⟨-żyć⟩, da(wa)ć odpocząć (**s.th.** czemuś); opierać ⟨oprzeć⟩ (**on** na)

restaurant ['restərɒnt] restauracja f; **~ car** wagon m restauracyjny

restful relaksujący; spokojny, kojący; **~less** niespokojny

restore [rɪˈstɔː] zwracać ⟨-rócić⟩, odd(aw)ać (**to s.o.** komuś); przywracać ⟨-rócić⟩; odnawiać ⟨-nowić⟩, ⟨od⟩restaurować

restrain [rɪˈstreɪn] powstrzym(yw)ać (**from** od); ⟨za⟩hamować, ograniczać ⟨-czyć⟩; **~ o.s.** powstrzymywać się (**from** od); **~t** ograniczenie n; powściągliwość f; umiarkowanie n

restrict [rɪˈstrɪkt] ograniczać ⟨-czyć⟩ (**to** do); **~ed** ograniczony; document: poufny, tajny; area: zamknięty, dostępny dla upoważnionych; **~ion** ograniczenie n (**of / on s.th.** czegoś)

result [rɪˈzʌlt] **1.** wynik m, rezultat m; usu. pl ocena f, stopień m; **2.** być skutkiem (**from s.th.** czegoś); **~ in s.th.** ⟨s⟩powodować coś, ⟨s⟩kończyć się czymś

resume [rɪˈzjuːm] v/t wznawiać ⟨-nowić⟩; seat etc. zajmować ⟨-jąć⟩ powtórnie; v/i trwać dalej; kontynuować

résumé ['rezjuːmeɪ] streszczenie n; Am. życiorys m

retail ['riːteɪl] **1.** detal m, sprzedaż f detaliczna; **2.** v/t sprzedawać w detalu; v/i być w sprzedaży detalicznej (**at** po, w cenie); **~er** [~'teɪlə] detalista m

retain [rɪ'teɪn] zachow(yw)ać; zatrzym(yw)ać

retire [rɪ'taɪə] iść ⟨pójść⟩ na emeryturę; ud(aw)ać się na spoczynek; wycof(yw)ać się; **~d** emerytowany; **~ment** emerytura f

retrieve [rɪ'triːv] odszukać i zabrać; odzysk(iw)ać; *situation* naprawi(a)ć; *hunt.* aportować

retro|active [retrəʊ'æktɪv] działający wstecz; **~active to** z wyrównaniem do; **'~grade** wsteczny; **~spect** ['~spekt]: *in ~spect* z perspektywy czasu; **~'spective 1.** przegląd m (twórczości); **2.** retrospektywny; działający wstecz

return [rɪ'tɜːn] **1.** *v/i* wracać ⟨wrócić⟩ **(to** do); *v/t* odd(aw)ać **(to s.o.** komuś); *book etc.* odkładać ⟨odłożyć⟩; *compliment* odwzajemni(a)ć; *ball* odbi(ja)ć; *jur.* ogłaszać; **2.** powrót m **(to** do); zwrot m; *sp.* return m; *pl* wyniki *pl* wyborów; *econ.* zysk m; **~ (ticket)** bilet m powrotny; **by ~ (of post)** odwrotną pocztą, odwrotnie; **in ~** w zamian **(for** za); **many happy ~s (of the day)** sto lat

reunion [riː'juːnjən] zjazd m; spotkanie n (po latach)

reveal [rɪ'viːl] ujawni(a)ć; odkry(wa)ć; **~ itself** okaz(yw)ać się **(as s.th.** czymś); **~ing** pouczający;

odkrywczy

revenge [rɪ'vendʒ] **1.** zemsta f; **2.** **~ oneself** ⟨ze⟩mścić się **(on** na **for** za)

revers|al [rɪ'vɜːsl] zwrot m (o 180 stopni), odwrócenie n; zamiana f; **~e** [~s] **1.** przeciwieństwo n, coś n całkowicie przeciwnego; porażka f; odwrotna strona f; **~e (gear)** *mot.* (bieg m) wsteczny; **2.** przeciwny, odwrotny; **3.** odwracać ⟨-rócić⟩; zamieni(a)ć; *decision etc.* zmieni(a)ć; *mot.* cofać ⟨-fnąć⟩ f

review [rɪ'vjuː] **1.** recenzja f; przegląd m; analiza f; *mil.* inspekcja f; **2.** ⟨z⟩recenzować; ⟨prze⟩analizować; ⟨z⟩badać; dokon(yw)ać przeglądu (*a. mil.*)

revis|e [rɪ'vaɪz] zmieni(a)ć, ⟨z⟩modyfikować; dokon(yw)ać poprawek **(s.th.** w czymś); powtarzać (wiadomości), uczyć się; **~ion** [~'vɪʒn] korekta f, rewizja f; powtarzanie n wiadomości

reviv|al [rɪ'vaɪvl] ożywienie n; odrodzenie n; wznowienie n; **~e** [~v] *v/t* ożywi(a)ć ⟨o⟩cucić; wznawiać ⟨-nowić⟩; *v/i* odży(wa)ć, odradzać ⟨-rodzić⟩ się

revolt [rɪ'vəʊlt] **1.** bunt m; rewolta f; *v/i* ⟨z⟩buntować się (*a. fig.*); *v/t* wzbudzać odrazę

revolution [revə'luːʃn] rewolucja f; przewrót m; przełom m; *tech.* obrót m; **~ary 1.** rewolucyjny; przełomowy; **2.** rewolucjonista ⟨-tka *f*⟩ *m*

revolve [rɪ'vɒlv] obracać ⟨-rócić⟩ się (**around, round** dookoła); *discussion:* obejmować ⟨objąć⟩ (**around, round**) coś

reward [rɪ'wɔːd] **1.** nagroda *f*; **2.** nagradzać ⟨-dzić⟩; *attention etc.* zasługiwać ⟨-łużyć⟩ na; **~ing** dający satysfakcję, przyjemny

rewind [riː'waɪnd] (**-wound**) *tape* cofać ⟨-fnąć⟩; *film* zwijać ⟨zwinąć⟩

rheumatism ['ruːmətɪzəm] reumatyzm *m*

rhinoceros [raɪ'nɒsərəs] nosorożec *m*

rhyme [raɪm] **1.** rym *m*; rymowanka *f*; wiersz *m*; **without ~ or reason** ni stąd ni zowąd, bez logicznego uzasadnienia; **2.** rymować (się) (**with** z)

rhythm ['rɪðəm] rytm *m*

rib [rɪb] żebro *n*; *pl* żeberka *pl*

ribbon ['rɪbən] wstęga *f*, wstążka *f*; *typewriter:* taśma *f*

rice [raɪs] ryż *m*

rich [rɪtʃ] bogaty (**in** w); *story:* zabawny; *soil:* żyzny; *food:* tłusty, niezdrowy; *colour:* intensywny; **~es** bogactwa *pl*

rid [rɪd] (**rid or ridded**) pozbawi(a)ć (**of** s.th. czegoś); **~ oneself of s.th.** uwalniać ⟨uwolnić⟩ się od czegoś; **be ~ of s.th.** być wolnym od czegoś; **get ~ of s.th.** pozbyć(wa)ć się czegoś

ridden ['rɪdn] *pp of* **ride** 2

riddle ['rɪdl] **1.** zagadka *f* (*a. fig.*); **2.** ⟨po⟩dziurawić; **~d with s.th.** pełen czegoś

ride [raɪd] **1.** przejażdżka *f*, jazda *f*; **2.** (**rode, ridden**) *v/t* jeździć, jechać na (czymś); *v/i* jeździć, jechać na koniu; jeździć, jechać (**in** s.th. czymś); **~ s.th. out** wychodzić ⟨wyjść⟩ cało z czegoś

ridge [rɪdʒ] grzbiet *m*, szczyt *m*; wypukłość *f*; *roof:* kalenica *f*; *meteor.* front *m*

ridiculous [rɪ'dɪkjələs] śmieszny, absurdalny; zabawny

rifle ['raɪfl] strzelba *f*

right [raɪt] **1.** *adj* właściwy, prawidłowy; (*not wrong*) dobry; (*not left*) prawy; **all ~** w porządku, dobrze; **that's all ~** nic nie szkodzi; **that's ~** tak jest; **be ~** mieć rację; **~ angle** kąt prosty; **put ~** naprawić; poprawić; **2.** *adv* prawidłowo; dobrze; *direction:* na prawo, na prawo; **~ away** natychmiast; **~ now** teraz, w tej chwili; **turn ~** skręcać ⟨-cić⟩ w prawo; **3.** *s* prawo *n* (**to** do); dobro *n*; prawa *f* (ręka, strona *itp.*); **the 2** *pol.* prawica *f*; **on the ~** z prawej strony, na prawo; **to the ~** w prawo; **~ful** prawowity, prawnie należny; **~-hand 'side** prawa strona *f*; **~'handed** praworęczny

rigid ['rɪdʒɪd] sztywny, mało elastyczny (a. fig.); surowy

rigo|rous ['rɪgərəs] rygorystyczny; szczegółowy, dokładny; **~u)r** ['rɪgə] usu. pl trud m; law: surowość f

rim [rɪm] krawędź f, brzeg m; wheel: obręcz f; glasses: oprawka f

ring [rɪŋ] **1.** sound: dzwonek m; (impression) brzmienie n; on finger: pierścionek m; wedding: obrączka f; for keys: kółko n; (circle) koło n; people: krąg m; boxing: ring m; circus: arena f; **give s.o. a ~** ⟨za⟩dzwonić do kogoś; **2.** (**rang, rung**) v/t Brt. (phone) ⟨za⟩telefonować (**s.o.** do kogoś); v/i Brt. (phone) ⟨za⟩telefonować; bell: dzwonić; (call) ⟨za⟩dzwonić (**for** po); room: rozbrzmiewać (**with** s.th. czymś); **~ the bell** zadzwonić do drzwi; **~ off** odkładać ⟨odłożyć⟩ słuchawkę; **~ s.o. up** ⟨za⟩dzwonić do kogoś

rink [rɪŋk] ice: lodowisko n; other: tor m

rinse [rɪns] (a. ~ **out**) opłuk⟨iw⟩ać; mouth przepłuk⟨iw⟩ać

riot ['raɪət] **1.** rozruchy pl; colours: bogactwo n; **run ~** wpadać ⟨wpaść⟩ w szał; **2.** wywoł⟨yw⟩ać rozruchy

rip [rɪp] **1.** przedarcie n, rozdarcie n; **2.** rozdzierać ⟨-zedrzeć⟩ (się); ~ **off** zrywać

⟨zerwać⟩; ~ **out** wyr⟨y⟩wać

ripe [raɪp] fruit: dojrzały; '**~n** dojrze⟨wa⟩ć; '**~ness** dojrzałość f

rise [raɪz] **1.** (slope) wzniesienie n; wage, price: podwyżka f; to fame: dojście n (to do); (increase) wzrost m (**of** s.th. czegoś); **2.** (**rose, risen**) unosić ⟨unieść⟩ się; wznosić ⟨-nieść⟩ się; wst⟨aw⟩ać; sun etc.: wst⟨aw⟩ać; river: wzbierać ⟨wezbrać⟩; people: ⟨z⟩buntować się; to fame: dochodzić ⟨dojść⟩ (do czegoś), ~n ['rɪzn] pp of **rise** 2

risk [rɪsk] **1.** ⟨za⟩ryzykować; **2.** ryzyko n; zagrożenie n; **at ~** w niebezpieczeństwie; **put at ~** narażać ⟨-razić⟩ na niebezpieczeństwo; **run the ~** ryzykować (**of** s.th. czymś); '**~y** ryzykowny

rival ['raɪvl] **1.** rywal(ka f) m, przeciwnik m (-niczka f); konkurent(ka f) m; coś n dorównującego, równy m; **2.** dorównywać; '**~ry** rywalizacja f, konkurencja f

river ['rɪvə] rzeka f (a. fig.)

road [rəʊd] between towns: szosa f, droga f (a. fig.); (street) ulica f; **on the ~** w drodze; '**~side** n. pobocze n, skraj m drogi; **2.** przydrożny; '**~way** jezdnia f; '**~works** pl roboty pl drogowe

roar [rɔː] **1.** animal: ⟨za⟩ryczeć; wind, sea: ⟨za⟩huczeć, ⟨za⟩szumieć; ~ (**with laugh-**

ter) ryczeć ze śmiechu; **2.** ryk *m*; **~s of laughter** salwy *pl* śmiechu

roast [rəʊst] **1.** *v/t* meat ⟨u⟩piec; nuts prażyć; coffee palić; *v/i* (feel hot) gotować się; **2.** s pieczeń *f*; **3.** *adj* pieczony

rob [rɒb] ⟨ob⟩rabować (*of* z); *fig.* pozbawi(a)ć (*of s.th.* czegoś), obdzierać (*of s.th.* z); **~ber** rabuś *m*, złodziej *m*; **'~bery** rabunek *m*, kradzież *f*

robe [rəʊb] szata *f*; (dressing gown) szlafrok *m*; bath: płaszcz *m* kąpielowy

rock [rɒk] **1.** skała *f*; (boulder) głaz *m*; Am. kamień *m*; mus. muzyka *f* rockowa; **on the ~s** whisky: z lodem; relationship: skończony; **2.** kołysać (się); building: ⟨za⟩trząść (się); country: wstrząsać ⟨-snąć⟩ (czymś)

rocket ['rɒkɪt] **1.** rakieta *f*; **2.** prices: skakać ⟨skoczyć⟩, strzelać ⟨-lić⟩ w górę

rocky ['rɒkɪ] kamienisty

rod [rɒd] pręt *m*; fishing: wędzisko *n*; divining ~ różdżka *f*

rode [rəʊd] past of ride 2

rodent ['rəʊdənt] gryzoń *m*

roe¹ [rəʊ] (a. roe-deer) sarna *f*

roe² [~] (hard) ~ ikra *f*; soft ~ mlecz *m*

phant: samotnik *m*

role [rəʊl] rola *f* (a. thea.)

roll [rəʊl] **1.** film, toilet paper: rolka *f*; foil: rulon *m*; food: bułka *f*; (list) lista *f*; thunder: huk *m*, toczenie się (grzmotu); drums: warkot *m*; **2.** *v/i* ⟨po⟩toczyć się; (turn over) przewracać ⟨-rócić⟩ się (na bok, plecy itp.); ship: kołysać się; on the floor: tarzać się, kulać się; *v/t* ⟨po⟩toczyć (turn over) przewracać ⟨-rócić⟩ (na bok, plecy itp.); (wrap) zwijać ⟨zwinąć⟩; trousers podwijać ⟨-winąć⟩; cigarette skręcać ⟨-cić⟩; ~ over przewracać ⟨-rócić⟩ (się) (na bok, plecy itp.); ~ up zwijać ⟨zwinąć⟩ (się); sleeve podwijać ⟨-winąć⟩; (arrive) przyby(wa)ć, podchodzić ⟨-dejść⟩; ~ call sprawdzanie n obecności; **~er** walec *m*; pl (curlers) wałki pl; **~er skate** wrotka *f*; **~ing pin** wałek *m* do ciasta

Roman ['rəʊmən] **1.** rzymski; **2.** Rzymianin *m* (-nka *f*); **~ Catholic 1.** rzymsko-katolicki; **2.** katolik *m* (-liczka *f*); **~ numeral** cyfra *f* rzymska

roman|ce [rəʊ'mæns] **1.** romans *m*; (excitement) romantyka *f*; **2.** fantazjować (about na temat); **~tic** romantyczny; idealistyczny, naiwny

Romania [rəʊ'meɪnɪə] Rumunia f; **~n** [~n] **1.** adj rumuński; **2.** s Rumun(ka f) m

roof [ru:f] **1.** dach m; mouth: podniebienie n; **2.** pokry(wa)ć dachem; **~ rack** mot. bagażnik m dachowy

rook [ruk] gawron m; chess: wieża f

room [ru:m, in compound words rum] pomieszczenie n; in house: pokój m; in school: sala f (space) miejsce n (for na); '**~mate** współlokator(ka f) m; '**~y** przestronny

root [ru:t] **1.** korzeń m; gr. rdzeń m; **put down ~s** zapuszczać <-puścić> korzenie, zagrz(ew)ać miejsce; **take ~** zakorzenić (się); <za>korzenić (się); przeszukiwać, przerzucać, przekładać; **~ about, ~ around** grzebać (for w poszukiwaniu); **~ out** wykorzeni(a)ć; wyciągać <-gnąć>; '**~ed** zakorzeniony

rope [rəup] **1.** lina f, sznur m; pl sp. liny pl; **skipping ~** skakanka f; **2.** <z>wiązać liną; **~ off** odgradzać <-rodzić> liną

rosary ['rəuzəri] eccl. różaniec m

rose[1] [rəuz] róża f

rose[2] [~] past of **rise** 2

rosy ['rəuzi] różowy; rumiany

rot [rɒt] **1.** gnicie n; gnić v/i gnić (v ρ). v/t powodować gnicie; rozkładać

rota|ry ['rəutəri] obrotowy;

~te [~'teit] obracać <-rócić> (się); <za>stosować rotacje; **~tion** obrót m; rotacja f

rotten ['rɒtn] zgniły, zepsuty; F fatalny, beznadziejny; F paskudny F

rough [rʌf] **1.** nierówny; skin: szorstki; behaviour: brutalny; life: ciężki; estimate: przybliżony; building: prymitywny; sea: wzburzony; weather: burzliwy; **sleep ~** spać pod gołym niebem; **2.** **~ it** F żyć w prymitywnych warunkach; **~ out** naszkicować

round [raund] **1.** adj okrągły; eyes: szeroko otwarty; **2.** adv dookoła; **~ about** około; **the other way ~** odwrotnie; **3.** prp dookoła; wokół, wkoło; **4.** s runda f; doctor's: obchód m; mus. kanon m; drinks: kolejka f; **5.** v/t okrążać <-żyć>; **~ off** <za>kończyć, dopełni(a)ć; zaokrąglać <-lić>; **~ up** zganiać <zgonić>; '**~about 1.** Brt. mot. rondo n; Brt. karuzela f; **2.** in a **~ way** w pośredni sposób; **~ trip** droga f w obie strony; **~ ticket** Am. bilet m powrotny

route [ru:t] **1.** trasa f; bus: linia f; fig. droga f; **2.** <s>kierować

routine [ru:'ti:n] **1.** stały porządek m, ogranizacja f czasu; (drudgery) nuda f; sp. program m, układ m; F (act) przedstawienie *n*; **2.** rutynowy; typowy

row¹ ['rəʊ] (*line*) rząd *m*; *in a* ~ pod rząd

row² [raʊ] F **1.** kłótnia *f*; spór *m*; hałas *m*; **2.** kłócić się

row³ [rəʊ] **1.** przejażdżka *f* łodzią; **2.** *v/i* wiosłować, płynąć łodzią; *v/t* przewozić 〈-wieźć〉 łodzią; '**~boat** *Am.*, '**~ing boat** łódź *f* wiosłowa

royal ['rɔɪəl] **1.** F członek *m* rodziny królewskiej; **~ty** rodzina *f* królewska; *pl* honorarium *n* autorskie

rub [rʌb] pocierać 〈potrzeć〉 ręką; pocierać 〈potrzeć〉 (*against* o); (*clean etc.*) wycierać 〈wytrzeć〉; *lotion* wcierać 〈wetrzeć〉; ~ *one's hands* zacierać ręce; ~ *down* ścierać 〈zetrzeć〉; *body* wycierać 〈wytrzeć〉 do sucha; ~ *in* wcierać 〈wetrzeć〉; ~ *out* wymaz(yw)ać

rubber ['rʌbə] **1.** guma *f*; *esp. Brt.* (*eraser*) gumka *f* (do mazania); **2.** gumowy

rubbish ['rʌbɪʃ] śmiecie *pl*, odpadki *pl*; *film etc.*: tandeta *f*; F (*nonsense*) bzdura *f*; ~ **bin** *Brt.* pojemnik *m* na śmiecie

ruby ['ruːbɪ] rubin *m*

rucksack ['rʌksæk] plecak *m*

rude [ruːd] niegrzeczny; *joke*: wulgarny; *event etc.*: niespodziewany

rudiment|ary [ruːdɪ'mentərɪ]

tool: prymitywny; *knowledge*: podstawowy; '**~s** ['~mənts] *pl* podstawy *pl*

rug [rʌg] (*carpet*) dywanik *m*; (*blanket*) pled *m*

rugged ['rʌgɪd] *land*: nierówny; *equipment*: solidny

ruin ['ruɪn] **1.** ruina *f*; *pl* ruiny *pl*; **2.** 〈z〉niszczyć

rule [ruːl] **1.** reguła *f*; (*guideline*) zasada *f*; (*regulation*) przepis *m*; (*government*) rządy *pl*; → *ruler*; *as a* ~ z reguły; **2.** *v/t* rządzić; *line* 〈wy〉kreślić; *v/i* rządzić; ~ *out* wykluczać 〈-czyć〉; '**~r** linijka *f*; (*leader*) władca *m*

rumo(u)r ['ruːmə] **1.** plotka *f*; **2.** *it is* ~*ed that* ... ludzie mówią, że ...

run [rʌn] **1.** (*ran*, *run*) *v/i* 〈po〉biec, biegać; (*move*) uciekać 〈uciec〉 (*from* z); *in elections*: kandydować (*for president* na prezydenta, *for parliament* do parlamentu; *train*, *bus*: kursować; *tear*, *river*: płynąć; *tap*: ciec; *border etc.*: przebiegać; *machine*: działać; *text*: brzmieć; *film etc.*: trwać; *butter*: topić się; *fabric*: farbować; *v/t* distance przebiegać 〈-biec〉; *business* 〈po〉prowadzić; *hand etc.* przejeżdżać 〈-je­chać〉; *news item* zamieszczać 〈-mieścić〉; ~ *across* natykać 〈-tknąć〉 się (*s.o.* na kogoś); ~ *down* (*criticise*)

 oczerni(a)ć; *company etc.*:
osłabi(a)ć; *battery*: wyczer-
p(yw)ać się; (*knock down*)
potrącać ⟨-cić⟩; (*find*) znajdować ⟨znaleźć⟩; ~ *in car*
docierać ⟨dotrzeć⟩; ~ *into
trouble* napot(y)kać; (*meet*)
spotkać; (*collide*) zderzać
⟨-rzyć⟩ się; ~ *off* zbiec; ~ *out
money etc.*: ⟨s⟩kończyć się;
passport: ⟨s⟩kończyć się;
~ *out of* już nie mieć; ~ *out on*
opuszczać ⟨-uścić⟩; ~ *over*
(*knock down*) przejeżdżać
⟨-jechać⟩; (*practice*) prze-
ćwiczyć (*a.* **run through**); ~
through list odczyt(yw)ać; ~
up debt nagromadzić; **2.** bieg
m; *ski*: trasa *f*; *in tights*: oczko *n*; *econ. on bank*: run *m*;
on tickets: duży popyt *m*; *in
the long* ~ na dłuższą
metę

rung¹ [rʌŋ] *pp of ring* 2
rung² [~] szczebel *m* (*a. fig.*)
runner ['rʌnə] biegacz(ka *f*)

m; (*messenger*) goniec *m*;
(*smuggler*) przemytnik *m*;
~-up [~ər'ʌp] zdobywca *m*
drugiego miejsca
running ciągły; *water*:
bieżący; *for two days* ~ dwa
dni z rzędu
runway *aer.* pas startowy
rural ['ruərəl] wiejski
rush [rʌʃ] **1.** szczyt *m*; zainteresowanie *n* (*for* czymś); *in
feeling*: napływ *m*, przypływ
m; **2.** *v/i* ⟨po⟩pędzić,
⟨po⟩gnać; ~ *to do s.th.*
spieszyć się by coś zrobić; *v/t*
robić coś pospiesznie; ruszyć na ⟨coś⟩; ponaglać
⟨-lić⟩, poganiać ⟨-gonić⟩; ~
hour godzina *f* szczytu
Russia ['rʌʃə] Rosja *f*; **~n** [~n]
1. rosyjski; **2.** Rosjanin *m*
(-nka *f*)
rust [rʌst] **1.** rdza *f*; **2.**
⟨za⟩rdzewieć
ruthless ['ruːθlɪs] bezlitosny
rye [raɪ] żyto *n*

S

sabotage ['sæbətɑːʒ] **1.** sabo-
taż *m*; **2.** wysadzać ⟨-dzić⟩,
⟨z⟩niszczyć; sabotować
sack [sæk] **1.** worek *m*; **2.** F
zwolnić (z pracy)
sacred ['seɪkrd] święty; *art*:
sakralny
sacrifice ['sækrɪfaɪs] **1.** *to
god*: ofiara *f*; (*something giv-
en up*) poświęcenie *n*; **2.**

składać ⟨złożyć⟩ w ofierze;
(*give up*) poświęcać ⟨-cić⟩
sad [sæd] smutny
saddle ['sædl] **1.** siodło *n*; **2.**
⟨o⟩siodłać
safe [seɪf] **1.** bezpieczny; **2.**
sejf *m*; **'~guard 1.** zabezpieczenie *n*; **2.** ochraniać ⟨-ro-
nić⟩
safety ['seɪftɪ] bezpieczeństwo

n; **~ belt** pas *m* bezpieczeństwa; **~ pin** agrafka *f*

said [sed] *past and pp of* **say** 1

sail [seɪl] **1.** żagiel *m*; *trip*: przejażdżka *f* jachtem; *set* **~** wypłynąć ⟨-łynąć⟩; **2.** pływać, ⟨po⟩płynąć, ⟨po⟩żeglować (*s.th.* (na) czymś); *ship*: płynąć

saint [seɪnt] święty *m* (-ta *f*)

sake [seɪk]: *for the* **~** *of* dla, przez wzgląd na; *for my* **~** dla mnie; *for God's* **~**, *for heaven's* **~** na miłość boską

salad [ˈsæləd] sałatka *f*; *raw*: surówka *f*

salary [ˈsælərɪ] pensja *f*

sale [seɪl] sprzedaż *f*; *pl econ.* (*amount*) sprzedaż *f*; *pl econ.* (*department*) dział *m* sprzedaży; *lower prices*: wyprzedaż *f*; (*up*) *for* **~** na sprzedaż; *on* **~** w sprzedaży; **'~sman** (*pl* **-men**) sprzedawca *m*; handlowiec *m*; **~s manager** kierownik *m* (-niczka *f*) działu sprzedaży; **'~swoman** (*pl* **-women**) sprzedawczyni *f*; handlowiec *m*

saliva [səˈlaɪvə] ślina *f*

salmon [ˈsæmən] łosoś *m*

saloon [səˈluːn] (*a.* **~ car**) *Brt.* limuzyna *f*; *on ship*: salon *m*; *Am.* bar *m*

salt [sɔːlt] **1.** sól *f*; **2.** słony; ⟨po⟩solić; **'~ cellar** solniczka *f*; **'~y** słony

salvation [sælˈveɪʃn] *eccl.* zbawienie *n*

same [seɪm]: *the* **~** taki sam;

the **~ colour** tego samego koloru; *all the* **~** tak czy inaczej; *it is all the* **~ to me** wszystko mi jedno

sample [ˈsɑːmpl] **1.** próbka *f*; **2.** ⟨s⟩⟨po⟩próbować

sanct|ion [ˈsæŋkʃn] **1.** sankcja *f*; (*approval*) aprobata *f*; **2.** dopuszczać ⟨-puścić⟩; ⟨u⟩sankcjonować; **'~ity** świętość *f*

sand [sænd] **1.** piasek *m*; **2.** ⟨wy⟩szlifować (*papierem* ściernym); **~ castle** zamek *m* z piasku

sandal [ˈsændl] sandał *m*

'sand|paper papier *m* ścierny; **'~pit** *Brt.* piaskownica *f*; **'~stone** piaskowiec *m*; **'~storm** burza *f* piaskowa

sandwich [ˈsænwɪdʒ] **1.** kanapka *f*; *cake*: przekładaniec *m*; **2.** **~ together with s.th.** przełożyć czymś; **~ed** (*in*) *between s.th.* wciśnięty pomiędzy coś

sandy [ˈsændɪ] piaszczysty

sane [seɪn] zdrowy na umyśle; rozsądny

sang [sæŋ] *past of* **sing**

sanitary [ˈsænɪtərɪ] czysty, higieniczny; *conditions etc.*: sanitarny; **~ napkin** *Am.*, **~ towel** *Brt.* podpaska *f* (higieniczna)

sanity [ˈsænətɪ] zdrowie *n* psychiczne; zdrowy rozsądek *m*

sank [sæŋk] *past of* **sink** I

Santa Claus [ˈsæntəklɔːz] święty Mikołaj *m*

sapphire ['sæfaɪə] szafir *m*

sarcastic [sɑː'kæstɪk] sarkastyczny

sardine [sɑː'diːn] sardynka *f*

sat [sæt] *past and pp of* **sit**

satellite ['sætəlaɪt] satelita *m*

satir|e ['sætaɪə] satyra *f*; **~ical** [sə'tɪrəkl] satyryczny

satis|faction [sætɪs'fækʃn] satysfakcja *f*; zadowolenie *n*; **~factory** zadowalający; **~fy** ['~faɪ] zadowalać ⟨-wolić⟩; *curiosity* zaspokajać ⟨-koić⟩; *condition* spełni(a)ć

Saturday ['sætədɪ] sobota *f*

sauce [sɔːs] sos *m*; (*cheek*) czelność *f*; **~pan** garnek *m*, rondel *m*; **~r** spod(ecz)ek *m*

sausage ['sɒsɪdʒ] kiełbasa *f*

savage ['sævɪdʒ] **1.** dziki; **2.** barbarzyńca *m*; dzikus *m*

save [seɪv] **1.** ⟨u⟩ratować (*from* od, przed); *money*, *time* oszczędzać ⟨-dzić⟩; (*keep*) przechowywać, odkładać; *computer*: zapis(yw)ać na dysku; **2.** oprócz

saving ['seɪvɪŋ] oszczędność *f* (*in* s.th. czegoś); *pl* oszczędności *pl*

savo(u)r ['seɪvə] **1.** delektować się (s.th. czymś) (*a. fig.*); **2.** smak *m*, aromat *m*; **~y** ['~ərɪ] pikantny; *fig.* chwalebny

saw¹ [sɔː] *past of* **see**

saw² [~] **1.** (*sawed, sawn or sawed*) ⟨prze⟩piłować; **2.** piła *f*; **~dust** trociny *pl*; **~n** *pp of* **saw²** 1

say [seɪ] **1.** (*said*) mówić ⟨powiedzieć⟩; *prayer* odmawiać ⟨-mówić⟩; *that is to ~* to znaczy; **2.** wyrażenie *n* opinii, prawo *n* głosu; **~ing** powiedzenie *n*

scale [skeɪl] skala *f*; *mus.* gama *f*; *fish*: łuska *f*; *of wall* skalować ⟨-lnąć⟩; **~s** *pl* waga *f*

scan [skæn] **1.** przeglądnąć ⟨przejrzeć⟩; ⟨prze⟩badać (wzrokiem); *computer*: skanować; **2.** *med.* badanie *n* skaningowe

scandal ['skændl] skandal *m*; plotki *pl*; **~ous** ['~dələs] skandaliczny

Scandinavian [skændɪ'neɪvjən] **1.** skandynawski; **2.** Skandynaw(ka *f*) *m*

scar [skɑː] blizna *f*

scare [skeə] **1.** histeria *f*; panika *f*; *have a* ~ ⟨wy⟩straszyć się; *give s.o. a* ~ wystraszyć kogoś; **2.** ⟨wy⟩straszyć; ~ *away* odstraszać ⟨-szyć⟩; *be* ~*d of s.th.* bać się czegoś; **~crow** strach *m* na wróble

scarf [skɑːf] (*pl* ~*s*, *scarves* [~vz]) szalik *m*; *head*: chustka *f*; *shoulders*: chusta *f*

scarves [skɑːvz] *pl of* **scarf**

scatter ['skætə] *v/t* rozrzucać ⟨-cić⟩; rozpraszać ⟨-roszyć⟩; *v/i* rozbiegać ⟨-biec⟩ się

scene [siːn] scena *f*; *fig.* miejsce *n*; *behind the* ~*s* za kulisami; **~ry** ['~ərɪ] sceneria *f*, krajobraz *m*; scenografia *f*

scent [sent] woń *f*; perfumy *pl*; trop *m*

sceptic ['skeptɪk] sceptyk *m* (-tyczka *f*); '**~al** remark: sceptyczny; *person*: sceptycznie nastawiony (**about** do)

schedule ['ʃedjuːl, *Am.* 'skedʒuːl] **1.** plan *m*; (*list*) lista *f*; *esp. Am.* train *etc.*: rozkład *m* jazdy; **on ~** według planu; **behind ~** opóźniony; **2.** ⟨za⟩planować (**for** na)

scheme [skiːm] **1.** plan *m*; *evil*: intryga *f*, *large scale*: program *m*, przedsięwzięcie *n*; **2.** knuć

scholar ['skɒlə] uczony *m* (-na *f*); stypendysta *m* (-tka *f*); '**~ship** stypendium *n*; nauka *f*

school [skuːl] **1.** szkoła *f*; *fish*: ławica *f*; **2.** ⟨wy⟩szkolić; '**~age** wiek *m* szkolny; '**~boy** uczeń *m*; '**~ friend** kolega *m* (koleżanka *f*) ze szkoły; '**~girl** uczennica *f*; '**~ing** wykształcenie *n*; '**~teacher** nauczyciel *m* szkolny

scien|ce ['saɪəns] nauka *f*; **~ti-fic** [~'tɪfɪk] naukowy; '**~tist** naukowiec *m*

scissors ['sɪzəz] *pl* (*a.* **a pair of ~**) nożyczki *pl*

scooter ['skuːtə] skuter *m*; *toy*: hulajnoga *f*

scope [skəʊp] zakres *m*; (*opportunity*) miejsce *n* (**for** na); **give s.o. ~ to do s.th.** dawać

komuś wolną rękę do robienia czegoś

scorch [skɔːtʃ] przypalać ⟨-lić⟩; '**~ed** spalony

score [skɔː] **1.** *sp.* wynik *m* (*a. fig.*); *mus.* partytura *f*; *film*: muzyka *f* (do filmu); **2.** *sp.* point zdoby⟨wa⟩ć, **goal** strzelać ⟨-lić⟩; *mark* uzysk(iw)ać

Scot [skɒt] Szkot(ka *f*) *m*

Scotch [skɒtʃ] szkocka whisky *f*

Scots|man ['skɒtsmən] (*pl -men*) Szkot *m*; '**~woman** (*pl -women*) Szkotka *f*

scout [skaʊt] **1.** skaut *m*, harcerz *m*; *mil.* zwiadowca *m*; **2.** przeszuk(iw)ać; ~ (**a**)**round for** poszukiwać

scramble ['skræmbl] *v/i* gramolić się; ⟨po⟩pędzić; walczyć (**for** o); *v/t tech.* ⟨za⟩kodować, ⟨za⟩szyfrować; **~d eggs** *pl* jajecznica *f*

scrap [skræp] **1.** skrawek *m*; *pl* resztki *pl*; (*a.* ~ **metal**) złom *m*; bez ~a ani troszkę; **2.** plan *etc.* odrzucać ⟨-cić⟩

scrape [skreɪp] **1.** *sound*: drapanie *n*, szuranie *n*; (*trouble*) tarapaty *pl*; **2.** *v/t* ⟨o⟩skrobać; (*a.* ~ **away, ~ off**) zeskrob⟨yw⟩ać; **hand** za-drap⟨yw⟩ać (**against, on** o); *v/i* szurać (*save*) oszczędzać

scrap|heap złomowisko *n* (*a. fig.*); ~ **iron** → **scrap 1**

scratch [skrætʃ] **1.** za-drap⟨yw⟩ać; ⟨po⟩drapać

(się); **2.** zadrapanie *n*, draśnięcie *n*; *(mark)* rysa *f*; **from ~** od zera

scream [skri:m] **1.** wrzask *m*; **2.** wrzeszczeć ⟨wrzasnąć⟩

screen [skri:n] **1.** *TV, film etc.*: ekran *m*; *separation*: parawan *m*; **2.** *(hide)* osłaniać ⟨-łonić⟩; *film* wyświetlać ⟨-lić⟩, pokaz(yw)ać; *(examine)* ⟨prze⟩badać

screw [skru:] **1.** wkręt *m*, śruba *f*; **2.** przykręcać ⟨-cić⟩; F *(cheat)* naciągać ⟨-gnąć⟩; **'~driver** śrubokręt *m*

script [skript] tekst *m*, scenariusz *m*; pismo *n*; **~ure** ['~tʃə]: **the** (**Holy**) ℨ(**s**) Pismo *n* Święte

scrup|le ['skru:pl] *(usu. pl.)* skrupuł *m*; **~ulous** ['~pjuləs] skrupulatny, dokładny

scuba ['sku:bə]: **~ diving** nurkowanie *n* z aparatem tlenowym

sculpt|or ['skʌlptə] rzeźbiarz *m* (-arka *f*); **~ure** ['~tʃə] rzeźba *f*

sea [si:] morze *n*; **'~food** owoce *pl* morza; **'~front** nabrzeże *n*; **'~going** morski; **'~gull** mewa *f*

seal¹ [si:l] foka *f*

seal² [~] **1.** pieczęć *f*; *tech.* korek *m*, zamknięcie *n*; **2.** uszczelni(a)ć; *envelope* zaklejać ⟨-leić⟩

seam [si:m] szew *m*; *coal etc.*: złoże *n*

seaman (*pl* **-men**) marynarz *m*, żeglarz *m*

'sea|plane hydroplan *m*; **'~port** miasto *n* portowe

search [sɜːtʃ] **1.** szukać *(for s.th.* czegoś); przeszuk(iw)ać *(for* w celu znalezienia); *person* ⟨z⟩rewidować; **2.** poszukiwanie *n*; rewizja *f*; **in ~ of s.th.** w poszukiwaniu czegoś; **'~ing** *question*: dociekliwy; *look*: badawczy; **'~light** reflektor *m*; **~ warrant** nakaz *m* rewizji

'sea|shore brzeg *m* morski; **'~sick: be ~sick** mieć chorobę morską; **~side** wybrzeże *n; at the ~side* nad morzem; **~side resort** kurort *m* nadmorski

season ['si:zn] **1.** pora *f* roku; *hunting, tourist etc.*: sezon *m*; *Christmas, Easter etc.*: okres; **2.** *food* przyprawi(a)ć; *wood* sezonować; **'~ing** *(a. pl)* przyprawy *pl*; **'~ ticket** *rail. etc.* bilet *m* okresowy; *thea.* abonament *m*

seat [si:t] **1.** miejsce *n* do siedzenia; *in car etc.*: fotel *m*; *parl., thea.* miejsce *n*; *organization*: siedziba *f*; **2.** *building* ⟨po⟩mieścić; **~ oneself** siadać ⟨usiąść⟩; **~ belt** pas *m* bezpieczeństwa

'seaweed wodorost *m*

second ['sekənd] **1.** *adj* drugi; **~ thoughts** wątpliwości *pl*; **2.** *adv* po drugie; jako drugi; **3.** *s* sekunda *f (a. mus)*; *article*: towar *m* wybrakowany; *person*: sekundant *m*; *gear*: drugi bieg; **4.** v/t *proposal* popierać ⟨-przeć⟩; **'~ary** drugorzędny; **~ary education** szkolnictwo *n* ponadpodstawowe; **~ary school** szkoła *f* ś średnia; **~'hand** używany; **'~rate** po drugie; **'~rate** drugorzędny; **~s** dokładka *f*

secre|cy ['si:krəsi] dyskrecja *f*; sekret *m*; **~t** ['~it] **1.** tajny; ukryty; **2.** sekret *m*, tajemnica *f*

secretary ['sekrətri] sekretarz *m* (-arka *f*)

secrete [si'kri:t] (*hide*) ukry(wa)ć; *med.* wydzielać ⟨-lić⟩; **~ive** ['si:krətiv] skryty

sect [sekt] sekta *f*

section ['sekʃn] część *f*; (*department*) oddział *m*; *document:* paragraf *m*; *math.* przekrój *m*

secular ['sekjulə] świecki

secur|e [si'kjuə] **1.** *job:* pewny; (*well protected*) dobrze zabezpieczony; (*fixed*) przymocowany; **feel ~e** czuć się bezpiecznie; **2.** (*obtain*) uzysk(iw)ać; (*make safe*) zabezpieczać ⟨-czyć⟩ (*against I from* przeciwko); (*fasten*) przymocow(yw)ać; **~ity** [~ərəti] bezpieczeństwo *n*

sedative ['sedətiv] środek *m* uspokajający

sediment ['sedimənt] osad *m*

seduce [si'dju:s] uwodzić ⟨uwieść⟩

see [si:] (*saw, seen*) v/i widzieć; *I ~* rozumiem, aha; ~

about s.th. załatwić coś; ~ *through s.o. I s.th.* przejrzeć kogoś / coś; ~ *to s.th.* zająć się czymś; v/t widzieć ⟨zobaczyć⟩; (*view, watch*) oglądać ⟨obejrzeć⟩; *sights* zwiedzać ⟨-dzić⟩; *friend* odwiedzać ⟨-dzić⟩; ~ *a doctor* iść ⟨pójść⟩ do lekarza; ~ *s.o. home* odprowadzać ⟨-dzić⟩ kogoś do domu

seed [si:d] **1.** nasienie *n*; *pl. fig.* ziarno *n*; **2.** *land* obsiewać ⟨-siać⟩; *sp.* rozstawi(a)ć

seek [si:k] (*sought*) poszukiwać; dążyć (*do*)

seem [si:m] wydawać się ⟨być⟩, zdawać się ⟨być⟩; **he ~s (to be) happy** wydaje się być szczęśliwy

seen [si:n] *pp of* **see**

seesaw ['si:sɔ:] huśtawka *f*

segment ['segmənt] część *f*; *math.* odcinek *m*

segregat|e ['segrigeit] oddzielać ⟨-lić⟩; **~ion** [~'geiʃn] segregacja *f*

seiz|e [si:z] chwytać ⟨-wycić⟩, ⟨z⟩łapać (za); *power* przejmować ⟨-jąć⟩; *jur. property* zajmować ⟨-jąć⟩; *jur. person* zatrzym(yw)ać; **~ure** ['~ʒə] *power:* przejęcie *n*; *property:* zajęcie *n*; *med.* atak *m*

seldom ['seldəm] rzadko

select [si'lekt] **1.** wyb(ie)rać; **2.** *group, school:* elitarny; **~ion** (*choosing*) selekcja *f*, wybór *m*; *poems, goods etc.:* wybór *m*

self [self] (*pl* **selves** [~vz])
osobowość *f;* **~adhesive**
samoprzylepny; **~assured**
pewny siebie; **~confidence**
pewność *f* siebie; **~contained** *flat:* samodzielny; *person:* samowystarczalny;
~control samokontrola *f;*
~defence samoobrona *f;*
~'evident oczywisty; **~'interest** własny interes *m;*
'~ish samolubny; **'~less** bezinteresowny; **~possession**
opanowanie *n;* **~reliant**
niezależny; **~respect** poczucie *n* własnej wartości;
~'satisfied zadowolony z
siebie; **~'service** samoobsługowy

sell [sel] (**sold**); *v/t*
sprzed(aw)ać; *v/i* sprzedawać się; kosztować (**at**, **for**)

selves [selvz] *pl of* **self**
semi... [semɪ] pół...

semi ['semɪ] *Brt.* F (*dom*)
bliźniak *m;* **'~circle** półkole
n; półokrąg *m;* **~conductor**
electr. półprzewodnik *m;*
~'final *sp.* półfinał *m*

senat|e ['senət] senat *m;* **~or**
['~ətə] senator *m*

send [send] (**sent**) wys(y)łać;
~ for pos(y)łać po; **~ in**
przes(y)łać; **'~er** nadawca *m*

senior ['siːnjə] **1.** *officer:*
starszy; *post:* wyższy; **~ to**
starszy od; *in organization:*
wyższy rangą od; **2.** student(ka *f*) *m* ostatniego roku; **s.o.'s ~** starszy od kogoś;

~ citizen emeryt(ka *f*) *m*
sensation [sen'seɪʃn] (*ability*)
czucie *n;* (*feeling*) uczucie *n;*
(*excitement*) sensacja *f;* **~al**
sensacyjny; (*very good*) rewelacyjny

sense [sens] **1.** zmysł *m; duty
etc.:* poczucie *n;* (*belief*) uczucie *n;* (*good judgement*)
rozsądek *m;* (*meaning*) znaczenie *n; in a* ~ w pewnym
sensie; **make** ~ mieć sens;
talk ~ mówić do rzeczy; **2.**
wyczu(wa)ć; **'~less** bezsensowny; *bez czucia*

sensib|ility [sensɪ'bɪlətɪ] wrażliwość *f;* **~le** ['sensəbl] rozsądny; (*practical*) praktyczny

sensitive ['sensɪtɪv] wrażliwy
(**to** na)

sensu|al ['sensjʊəl] zmysłowy; **'~ous** oddziałujący na
zmysły

sent [sent] *past and pp of* **send**
sentence ['sentəns] **1.** zdanie
n; jur. wyrok *m;* **2.**
skaz(yw)ać (**to** na)

sentiment ['sentɪmənt] uczucie *n;* (*opinion*) odczucie *n;* **~al**
[~'mentl] sentymentalny;
uczuciowy

separat|e 1. ['sepərət] oddzielać ⟨-lić⟩ (się) (**from** od);
couple: rozchodzić ⟨-zejść⟩
się; **2.** ['seprət] oddzielny,
osobny; **~ion** [~ə'reɪʃn] oddzielenie *n; time:* rozłąka *f;
jur.* separacja *f*

September [sep'tembə] wrzesień *m*

sequence ['si:kwəns] seria *f*; *film etc.*: sekwencja *f*

sergeant ['sɑ:dʒənt] *mil.* sierżant *m*

serial ['sɪərɪəl] **1.** seryjny, kolejny; *computer*: szeregowy; **2.** powieść *f* w odcinkach; *TV* serial *m*

series ['sɪəri:z] (*pl* ~) seria *f*; *TV*: serial *m*

serious ['sɪərɪəs] poważny

sermon ['sɜ:mən] kazanie *n* (*a. fig.* F)

servant ['sɜ:vənt] służący *m* (-ca *f*); *fig.* sługa *m*

serve [sɜ:v] *v/i* służyć; spełniać funkcję (**as, for s.th.** czegoś); *sp.* ⟨za⟩serwować; *v/t* ⟨*supply*⟩ zaopatrywać; *food* pod⟨aw⟩ać; *customers* obsługiwać ⟨-łużyć⟩; *apprenticeship* odb⟨yw⟩ać; *jur.* odsiadywać ⟨-siedzieć⟩; ~ **out, up** *food* pod⟨aw⟩ać

service ['sɜ:vɪs] **1.** służba *f* (*a. mil.*); *train, postal etc.*: usługi *pl*; *in shop etc.*: obsługa *f*; (*job*) usługa *f*; *tech.* serwis *m*; *mot.* przegląd *m*; *sp.* zagrywka *f*; *eccl.* nabożeństwo *n*; **the ~s** *pl* siły *pl* zbrojne; **2.** *tech.* zapewni(a)ć serwis; *mot.* robić przegląd; ~ **charge** dodatek *m* za obsługę; ~ **station** stacja *f* obsługi

session ['seʃn] sesja *f*

set [set] **1.** zestaw *m*; *clothes*: komplet *m*; *math.* zbiór *m*; *TV, radio etc.*: odbiornik *m*; *thea.* scenografia *f*; *sp.* set *m*;

2. ustalony, stały; *work, book*: obowiązkowy; (*ready*) gotowy (**for** na); (*determined*) zdecydowany (**on doing s.th.** zrobić coś); ~ **lunch** *or* **meal** zestaw *m*; **3.** (**set**) *v/t* (*put*) kłaść ⟨położyć⟩; *into surface*: wpuszczać ⟨wpuścić⟩; *with jewels*: wysadzać; *clock, bone* nastawi(a)ć; *hair* układać ⟨ułożyć⟩; *trap* zastawi(a)ć; *time, price etc.* ustalać ⟨-lić⟩; *work* zada⟨wa⟩ć; ~ **an example** da⟨wa⟩ć przykład; ~ **the table** nakry⟨wa⟩ć do stołu; *v/i sun*: zachodzić ⟨zajść⟩; *concrete*: zastygać ⟨-gnąć⟩; ~ **free** uwalniać ⟨uwolnić⟩; ~ **aside** odkładać ⟨odłożyć⟩; ~ **off** *v/i* wyruszać ⟨-szyć⟩; *v/t bomb* ⟨z⟩detonować; ~ **out** wyruszać ⟨-szyć⟩; ~ **to** zabrać się do pracy; ~ **up** *monument* stawiać ⟨postawić⟩, wznosić ⟨-nieść⟩; *apparatus* nastawi(a)ć; *organization* zakładać ⟨założyć⟩; '~**back** niepowodzenie *n*

settee [se'ti:] kanapa *f*

setting ['setɪŋ] *for picnic*: miejsce *n*; *for film*: sceneria *f*; (*environment*) środowisko *n*; *apparatus*: poziom *m*; *gold*: oprawa *f*; *on table*: nakrycie *n*

settle ['setl] *v/t* (*put*) układać ⟨ułożyć⟩; *argument* zakończyć (osiągając porozumienie); *(arrange)* ustalać; *affairs* załatwia(a)ć; *bill* ⟨u-⟩ regulować; *v/i a.* ~ **oneself** siadać ⟨usiąść⟩ wygodnie; układać ⟨ułożyć⟩ się; *dust:* osiadać ⟨osiąść⟩; *jur.* załatwia(a)ć sprawę poza sądem; rozliczać ⟨-czyć⟩ się **(with** z); ~ **down** osiedlać ⟨-lić⟩ się; '~**ment** porozumienie *n (a. jur.)*; *debt:* spłata *f*; *place:* kolonia *f*; *process:* osiedlanie *n*; '~**r** osadnik *m*

'**set-up** F system *m*, układ *m*

seven ['sevn] siedem; ~**teen** [~'ti:n] siedemnaście; ~**th** ['~θ] siódmy; '~**ty** siedemdziesiąt

several ['sevrəl] kilka, kilkanaście

severe [sɪ'vɪə] *damage:* poważny; *critic:* surowy

sew [səʊ] *(sewed, sewn or sewed)* szyć, przyszy(wa)ć

sew|age ['su:ɪdʒ] ścieki *pl*; ~**er** ['su:ə] kanał *m*

sew|ing ['səʊɪŋ] szycie *n*; ~**n** *pp of* **sew**

sex [seks] płeć *f*; seks *m*; *have* ~ mieć stosunek płciowy; ~**ual** ['sekʃʊəl] seksualny, płciowy

shade [ʃeɪd] **1.** cień *m*; *lamp:* abażur *m, glass:* klosz *m; colour:* odcień *m; Am. (blind)* żaluzja *f*; **2.** zacieni(a)ć

shadow ['ʃædəʊ] **1.** cień *m*; *be* pokry(wa)ć cieniem

shady ['ʃeɪdɪ] cienisty; *fig.* podejrzany

shaft [ʃɑ:ft] *axe:* trzonek *m; in machine:* wał *m; in mine:* szyb *m; cart:* dyszel *m; (beam)* promień *m*

shak|e [ʃeɪk] *(shook, shaken)* *v/t* potrząsać ⟨-snąć⟩; strząsać ⟨-snąć⟩ **(from** z); ~**e hands** pod(aw)ać sobie ręce; *v/i* ⟨za⟩trząść się; *voice:* ⟨za⟩drżeć; '~**en 1.** *pp of* **shake**; **2.** *(shocked)* wstrząśnięty; '~**y** roztrzęsiony; *(uncertain)* niepewny

shall [ʃəl, *stressed* ʃæl] *v/aux (past should)* *I* ~ *do it* zrobię to; *we* ~ *see* zobaczymy; *it* ~ *be done* to zostanie zrobione; ~ *I tell him?* mam mu powiedzieć?; ~ *we go now?* pójdziemy już?

shallow ['ʃæləʊ] **1.** płytki *(a. fig.)*; **2.** *pl* mielizna *f*

shame [ʃeɪm] **1.** zawstydzać ⟨-dzić⟩; **2.** wstyd *m; what a* ~ (jaka) szkoda; ~ *on you!* wstydź się!; '~**ful** haniebny; '~**less** bezwstydny

shampoo [ʃæm'pu:] **1.** szampon *m*; **2.** ⟨u⟩myć szamponem

shape [ʃeɪp] **1.** kształt *m; (figure)* postać *f*; **2.** ⟨u⟩kształtować; '~**less** bezkształtny; '~**ly** kształtny

share [ʃeə] **1.** *(use)* dzielić, używać wspólnie **(with** z); *task:* dzielić między siebie; brać udział, włączać się **(in** w); **2.** część *f; econ.* akcja *f*; '~**holder** akcjonariusz *m*

shark [ʃɑːk] (*pl* ~, ~s) rekin *m*

sharp [ʃɑːp] **1.** ostry; *person*: bystry; *change etc.*: nagły; **at three ~** punktualnie o trzeciej; **2.** *mus.* krzyżyk *m*; **F** ~ fis; **'~en** ⟨na⟩ostrzyć; **~ener** ['ʃɑːpnə] temperówka *f*

shatter ['ʃætə] roztrzaskiwać (się); *fig.* rozbi(ja)ć; *hopes* rozwi(ew)ać

shave [ʃeɪv] **1.** (**shaved**, **shaved** *or* **shaven**) ⟨o⟩golić (się); ~ **off** ⟨z⟩golić; **2.** golenie *n*; **have a** ~ ⟨o⟩golić się; '**~n** *pp of* **shave** 1; '**~r** golarka *f*

shaving ['ʃeɪvɪŋ] **1.** do golenia; **2.** **~s** *pl* stróżyny *pl*

shawl [ʃɔːl] szal *m*; *on head*: chustka *f*

she [ʃiː] **1.** *pron* ona; **2.** *s* ona *f*; **3.** *adj zo. in compounds*: samica *f*

shear [ʃɪə] (**sheared**, **shorn** *or* **sheared**) ⟨o⟩strzyc

shed¹ [ʃed] (**shed**) *hair* ⟨s⟩tracić; *clothes* zrzucać ⟨-cić⟩ z siebie; *tears* ⟨u⟩ronić; *blood* przel(ew)ać

shed² [~] *for tools*: szopa *f*; *other*: budynek *m*

sheep [ʃiːp] (*pl* ~) owca *f*; '**~dog** owczarek *m*

sheet [ʃiːt] prześcieradło *n*; *paper, aluminium*: arkusz *m*; *note*: kartka *f*; *glass*: płyta *f*

shelf [ʃelf] (*pl* **shelves** [~vz]) półka *f*

shell [ʃel] **1.** *egg*: skorupka *f*; *nut*: łupina *f*; *snail*: skorupa

f; *building etc.*: szkielet *m*; (*explosive*) pocisk *m*; **2.** *egg* ob(ie)rać; *nuts* łuskać; (*fire on*) ostrzel(iw)ać; '**~fish** (*pl* ~) skorupiak *m*

shelter ['ʃeltə] **1.** schronienie *n*; osłona *f*; *bomb*: schron *m*; *bus*: wiata *f*; **2.** ⟨s⟩chronić (się)

shelves [ʃelvz] *pl of* **shelf**

shepherd ['ʃepəd] pasterz *m*

shield [ʃiːld] **1.** tarcza *f*; *trophy*: odznaka *f*; (*protection*) osłona *f* (**against** przed); **2.** osłaniać ⟨-łonić⟩ (**against** przed)

shift [ʃɪft] **1.** zmiana *f*; **2.** przesuwać ⟨-sunąć⟩ (się); zmieni(a)ć (się); *stain* usuwać ⟨usunąć⟩

shine [ʃaɪn] **1.** połysk *m*; *in eyes*: błysk *m*; **2.** (**shone**) *v/i* ⟨za⟩świecić; ⟨za⟩błyszczeć; *v/t lamp* ⟨s⟩kierować (**on** na); (**shined**) ⟨wy⟩polerować; '**~y** błyszczący

ship [ʃɪp] **1.** statek *m*; **2.** przes(y)łać (statkiem); '**~ment** ładunek *m*; przesyłka *f*; '**~ping** transport *m* (morski); '**~wreck** katastrofa *f* morska; wrak *m*; '**~yard** stocznia *f*

shirt [ʃɜːt] koszula *f*

shiver ['ʃɪvə] **1.** dreszcz *m*; **2.** trząść się

shock [ʃɒk] **1.** szok *m*; *movement*: wstrząs *m*; *electr.* porażenie *n*; **2.** wstrząsać ⟨-snąć⟩; (*offend*) ⟨za⟩szokować

shoe [ʃuː] but *m*; *in s.o.'s* ~**s** na czyimś miejscu; '~**lace**, *Am.* '~**string** sznurowadło *n*

shone [ʃɒn] *past and pp of* **shine** 2

shook [ʃʊk] *past of* **shake**

shoot [ʃuːt] **1.** *Brt.* polowanie *n*; *bot.* pęd *m*; **2.** (**shot**) *v/i* strzelać <-lić> (*at* do); *Brt.* ⟨za⟩polować (na); *v/t* (*kill*) zastrzelić; (*injure*) postrzelić; *film* ⟨na⟩kręcić; ~ **down** *plane* zestrzelić; *person* zastrzelić

shop [ʃɒp] **1.** sklep *m*; (*workshop*) warsztat *m*; **2.** *usu.* **go** ~**ping** robić zakupy; ~ **assistant** sprzedawca *m* (*-wczyni f*); '~**keeper** sklepikarz *m* (*-rka f*); '~**lifter** złodziej *m* sklepowy; '~**ping** zakupy *pl*; ~**ping centre** (*Am.* **center**) centrum *n* handlowe; ~ **window** wystawa f sklepowa

shore [ʃɔː] brzeg *m*; *on* ~ na lądzie

shorn [ʃɔːn] *pp of* **shear**

short [ʃɔːt] **1.** *adj* krótki; (*not tall*) niski; (*rude*) opryskliwy (*with* wobec); *be* ~ *of s.th.* odczuwać brak czegoś; **2.** *adv* nagle; *in* ~ w skrócie; ~**age** [ˈʃɔːdʒ] brak *m*; ~**circuit** *electr.* spięcie *n*; '~**coming** wada *f*; '~**cut** skrót *m*; '~**en** skracać <-rócić>; '~**hand** stenografia *f*; '~**ly** wkrótce; ~**s** *pl* szorty *pl*; '~**sighted** krótkowzroczny; ~ **story** opowiadanie *n*;

'~**term** *loan*: krótkoterminowy; *solution*: tymczasowy; ~**wave** krótkofalowy

shot [ʃɒt] **1.** *past and pp of* **shoot** 2; **2.** strzał *m*; *good, bad etc.*: strzelec *m*; *metal balls*: śrut *m*; *phot.* ujęcie *n*; *med.* F zastrzyk *m*; *sp.* kula *f*; *drink*: kielich *m* F; *have a* ~ ⟨s⟩próbować; '~**gun** strzelba *f* śrutowa, śrutówka *f*; ~ **put** *sp.* pchnięcie *n* kulą

should [ʃʊd] **1.** *past of* **shall**; **2.** *I* ~ powinienem; *he* ~ *do it* powinien to zrobić; *he* ~ *have done it* powinien (był) to zrobić

shoulder [ˈʃəʊldə] ramię *n*

shout [ʃaʊt] **1.** krzyk *m*; **2.** krzyczeć ⟨krzyknąć⟩ (*at* na)

show [ʃəʊ] **1.** (**showed, shown** *or* **showed**) *v/t* pokaz(yw)ać; (*escort*) ⟨po⟩prowadzić; *v/i* być widocznym, ukaz(yw)ać się; ~ **off** popisywać się; ~ **up** F pojawi(a)ć się; **2.** pokaz *m*; (*exhibition*) wystawa *f*; *thea.* show *m*, przedstawienie *n*; *TV* program *m*; ~ **business** przemysł *m* rozrywkowy; '~**down** F decydująca rozgrywka *f*

shower [ˈʃaʊə] **1.** prysznic *m*; *rain*: przelotny deszcz *m*; (*stream*) deszcz *m*, strumień *m*; *have or take a* ~ brać ⟨wziąć⟩ prysznic; **2.** obsyp(yw)ać (*with s.th.* czymś)

show| jumping sp. skoki pl
przez przeszkody; **~n** pp of
show l; **'~room** salon m wy-
stawowy

shrank [ʃræŋk] past of **shrink**

shred [ʃred] **1.** strzęp m; **2.**
⟨po⟩drzeć; **'~der** niszczarka
f

shrink [ʃrɪŋk] (**shrank** or
shrunk, **shrunk**) **1.** ⟨s⟩kurczyć
się; (move) odsuwać ⟨-su-
nąć⟩ się

shrub [ʃrʌb] krzew m; **'~bery**
krzaki pl

shrunk [ʃrʌŋk] past and pp of
shrink'

shuffle ['ʃʌfl] cards ⟨po⟩ta-
sować

shut [ʃʌt] **1.** (shut) zamykać
⟨-mknąć⟩ (się); **~ down** business likwidować; **~ up** F
zamknąć się F; **2.** zamknięty;
'~ter okiennica f; phot. mi-
gawka f

shuttle ['ʃʌtl] **1.** samolot m
wahadłowy; space: wahad-
łowiec m, prom kosmiczny
m; tech. czółenko n; **2.** plane,
bus etc.: wahadłowy

shy [ʃaɪ] nieśmiały

sick [sɪk] chory; **be ~** ⟨z⟩wy-
miotować; **be ~ of s.th.** mieć
dość czegoś; **I feel ~** niedobrze mi

sickle ['sɪkl] sierp m

sick| leave: on ~ leave na
zwolnieniu lekarskim; **'~ly**
chorowity; (unpleasant) obrzydliwy; **'~ness** choroba f;
(nausea) mdłości pl; **~ness**

benefit zasiłek m chorobowy

side [saɪd] **1.** strona f; body,
box: bok m; by road: pobo-
cze n; pl baczki pl; **take s.o.'s
~** brać czyjąś stronę; **2.
with s.o.** trzymać czyjąś
stronę; **3.** boczny; **'~board**
komoda f, kredens m; **'~car**
mot. przyczepa f motocyklo-
wa; **~ dish** przystawka f; **~
effect** skutek m uboczny; **~
kick** pomagier m F;
'~ways 1. adj boczny; **2.** adv
w bok, na bok; z boku

sieve [sɪv] **1.** sito m; **2.** prze-
si(ew)ać; liquid przecedzać
⟨-dzić⟩

sift [sɪft] przesi(ew)ać (a. fig.)

sigh [saɪ] **1.** westchnięcie n; **2.**
wzdychać ⟨westchnąć⟩

sight [saɪt] **1.** wzrok m; something seen: widok m; (look)
spojrzenie n; area: pole n
widzenia; pl atrakcje pl (tu-
rystyczne; gun: celownik m;
at first ~ na pierwszy rzut
oka; **at the ~ of s.th.** na widok czegoś; **catch ~ of** dostrzegać ⟨-rzec⟩; **2.** dostrzegać ⟨-rzec⟩; **'~seeing**
zwiedzanie n; **~seeing tour**
wycieczka f turystyczna

sign [saɪn] **1.** znak m; (gesture) gest m; on door: tabliczka f; at roadside: tablica f; **2.**
podpis(yw)ać; **~ in / out** zameldować / wymeldować się

signal ['sɪgnl] **1.** sygnał m; **2.**
d(aw)ać znak

signature ['sɪgnətʃə] podpis m

signif|icance [sɪg'nɪfɪkəns] znaczenie *n*; **~icant** znaczący; **~y** ['sɪgnɪfaɪ] oznaczać; pokaz(yw)ać

silence ['saɪləns] **1.** cisza *f*; *person's*: milczenie *n*; **2.** uciszać ⟨-szyć⟩ (*a. fig.*); **~r** (*a. mot. Brt.*) tłumik *m*

silent ['saɪlənt] cichy; (*not speaking*) milczący; *I was* **~** milczałem

silicon ['sɪlɪkən] krzem *m*

silk [sɪlk] **1.** jedwab *m*; **2.** jedwabny; **~y** jedwabisty

sill [sɪl] parapet *m*; *mot.* próg *m*

silly ['sɪlɪ] głupi

silver ['sɪlvə] **1.** srebro *n*; *coins*: bilon *m*; *cutlery etc.*: srebra *pl*; **2.** srebrny

similar ['sɪmɪlə] podobny; **~ity** [~'lærətɪ] podobieństwo *n*

simmer ['sɪmə] gotować (się) na wolnym ogniu

simple ['sɪmpl] prosty; (*easy*) łatwy; (*genuine*) uczciwy; (*retarded*) niedorozwinięty

simpli|city [sɪm'plɪsətɪ] prostota *f*; **~fy** ['~faɪ] upraszczać ⟨-rościć⟩

simply ['sɪmplɪ] po prostu; *say, write*: prostym językiem; *live, dress*: skromnie

simulate ['sɪmjʊleɪt] imitować; *illness, conditions* symulować

simultaneous [sɪməl'teɪnjəs] jednoczesny

sin [sɪn] **1.** grzech *m*; **2.** ⟨z⟩grzeszyć

since [sɪns] **1.** *prp* od (*czasu* kiedy / gdy); **2.** *adv* od tego czasu; **3.** *cj* ponieważ, jako że

sincer|e [sɪn'sɪə] szczery; *Yours* **~ely** Z wyrazami szacunku; **~ity** [~'serətɪ] szczerość *f*

sing [sɪŋ] (*sang, sung*) ⟨za⟩śpiewać

singer ['sɪŋə] piosenkarz *m* (-arka *f*); *opera*: śpiewak *m* (-waczka *f*)

single ['sɪŋgl] **1.** pojedynczy; *room*: jednoosobowy; *Brt. ticket*: w jedną stronę; (*not married*) stanu wolnego; **~ parent** osoba *f* samotnie wychowująca dziecko; **2.** *room*: jedynka *f*; *music*: singiel *m*; *Brt. ticket*: bilet *m* w jedną stronę; **3. ~ out** wyb(ie)rać; **~'handed** samodzielnie, w pojedynkę; **~'minded** zdecydowany, uparty; **'~s** (*pl* **~**) *sp.* gra *f* pojedyncza

singular ['sɪŋgjʊlə] **1.** pojedynczy; (*unusual*) niezwykły; **2.** *gr.* liczba *f* pojedyncza

sink [sɪŋk] **1.** (*sank* or *sunk, sunk*) *v/i* (*go down*) opadać ⟨opaść⟩; *ship*: ⟨za⟩tonąć; *voice*: ⟨ś⟩cichnąć; *patient*: ⟨za⟩słabnąć; *v/t* zatapiać ⟨-topić⟩; **2.** *kitchen*: zlew *m*; *bathroom*: umywalka *f*

sinner ['sɪnə] grzesznik *m* (-nica *f*)

sip [sɪp] **1.** łyczek *m*; **2.** (*a. ~ at*) popijać *impf* (*s.th.* coś), wypić *pf* łyk (*s.th.* czegoś)

sir [sɜː] pan m; **Dear** ♀ Szanowny Panie; **yes ~** tak jest

sister ['sɪstə] siostra f; *Brt.* (*senior nurse*) siostra f przełożona; **~-in-law** ['˷ɪnlɔː] szwagierka f; (*brother's wife*) bratowa f

sit [sɪt] (*sat*) v/i *state*: siedzieć; *action*: (*a. ~ down*) usiąść ⟨usiąść⟩; (*pose*) pozować (*for s.o.* komuś); (*belong*) zasiadać (*on* w); v/t (*a. ~ down*) sadzać ⟨posadzić⟩; *examination* przystępować ⟨-tąpić⟩ do; **~ up** siadać ⟨usiąść⟩ prosto; nie kłaść się spać

site [saɪt] miejsce n; *for house*: parcela f

sitting ['sɪtɪŋ] posiedzenie n; **at one ~** na jedno posiedzenie; **~ room** poczekalnia f

situat|ed ['sɪtjʊeɪtɪd] położony, usytuowany; **be ~ed** znajdować się; **~ion** [˷'eɪʃn] sytuacja f; *town, building*: położenie n

six [sɪks] sześć; **~teen** [˷'tiːn] szesnaście; **~th** [˷sθ] szósty; **~ty** sześćdziesiąt

size [saɪz] wielkość f; *clothes etc.*: rozmiar m; **~ up** oceni⟨a⟩ć

skate [skeɪt] **1.** *ice*: łyżwa f; *roller*: wrotka f; **2.** jeździć na łyżwach / wrotkach

skeleton ['skelɪtn] szkielet m

sketch [sketʃ] szkic m; (*outline*) ogólny zarys m; *thea.* skecz m; ⟨na⟩szkicować

ski [skiː] **1.** narta f; **2.** jeździć na nartach

ski|er ['skiːə] narciarz m (-arka f); **~ing** narciarstwo n

skilful ['skɪlfʊl] wprawny

ski lift wyciąg m narciarski

skill [skɪl] sprawność f, umiejętność f, biegłość f; **~ed** wyszkolony; wprawny; **~ed worker** robotnik m wykwalifikowany; **~ful** Am. → **skilful**

skim [skɪm] *cream etc.* zbierać ⟨zebrać⟩; *surface* prześlizgiwać ⟨-gnąć⟩ się po; **~ (through)** *text* przeglądać ⟨przejrzeć⟩ (pobieżnie)

skin [skɪn] **1.** skóra f; *fruit*: skórka f; *on liquid*: kożuch m; **2.** *animal* obdzierać ⟨-obedrzeć⟩ ze skóry; *fruit* ob(ie)rać ze skóry; *knee etc.* zadrap(yw)ać; **~ diving** swobodne nurkowanie n; **~ny** chudy; **~tight** obcisły

skip [skɪp] **1.** podskok m; **2.** v/i podskakiwać ⟨-skoczyć⟩; *over rope*: skakać przez skakankę; v/t F opuszczać ⟨opuścić⟩

skirt [skɜːt] **1.** spódnica f; *on machine*: osłona f; **2.** okrążać ⟨-żyć⟩, otaczać ⟨-czyć⟩

skull [skʌl] czaszka f

sky [skaɪ], *often* **skies** *pl* niebo n; **~jacker** ['˷dʒækə] porywacz m (samolotu)

slack [slæk] **1.** *rope*: luźny;

(careless) niedbały; **2.** nie przykładać się; **3.** *in rope etc.*: zwis *m*, luźna część *f* liny; *econ.* zastój *m*; **~s** *pl* portki *pl*

slam [slæm] **1.** *door etc.* zatrzaskiwać ⟨-snąć⟩; *car* trzaskać ⟨-snąć⟩ *(into* w); **2.** trzaśnięcie *n*

slander ['slɑːndə] **1.** zniesławienie *n*, oszczerstwo *n*; **2.** zniesławi(a)ć

slap [slæp] **1.** uderzenie *n*; *in the face*: policzek *m*, uderzenie *n* (w twarz); *on the back*: klepnięcie *n* (po plecach); *on the bottom*: klaps *m*; **2.** uderzać ⟨-rzyć⟩; *on the back*: klepać ⟨-pnąć⟩; *on the bottom*: d(aw)ać klapsa; **3.** *adv* wprost

slash [slæʃ] **1.** cięcie *n*; *(cut)* rozcięcie *n*; **2.** *v/t* rozcinać ⟨-ciąć⟩; *prices etc.* obniżać ⟨-żyć⟩; *v/i* rzucać się *(at* na)

slaughter ['slɔːtə] **1.** rzeź *f*, masakra *f*; *animals*: ubój *m*; **2.** mordować; *animals* bić

slave [sleɪv] **1.** niewolnik *m* (-nica *f*); **2.** tyrać; **~ry** ['~əri] niewolnictwo *n*

sled [sled] *Am.* → *sledge* 1

sledge [sledʒ] **1.** sanki *pl*; **2.** jechać (jeździć) na sankach; **'~(hammer)** młot *m*

sleek [sliːk] *hair etc.*: gładki, lśniący; *person*: przylizany

sleep [sliːp] **1.** *(slept)* spać; **~ in** *Brt.* odsypiać; **~ on s.th.** przemyśleć coś przez noc; **2.**

sen *m*; **get to ~** zasypiać ⟨-snąć⟩; **go to ~** iść ⟨pójść⟩ spać; *foot etc.*: ⟨ś⟩cierpnąć; **'~er** osoba *f* śpiąca; *rail.* wagon *m* sypialny; *(berth)* miejsce *n* do spania; **light ~er** osoba *f* o lekkim śnie; **'~ing bag** śpiwór *m*; **'~ing car** wagon *m* sypialny; **'~ing pill** tabletka *f* nasenna; **'~less** bezsenny; **~walker** lunatyk *m*; **'~y** śpiący

sleeve [sliːv] rękaw *m*; *for record*: okładka *f*

sleigh [sleɪ] sanie *pl*

slender ['slendə] smukły; *fig.* skromny

slept [slept] *past and pp of* *sleep* 1

slice [slaɪs] **1.** plasterek *m*; **2.** *(a. ~ up)* ⟨po⟩kroić na plasterki

slid [slɪd] *past and pp of* *slide* 1

slide [slaɪd] **1.** *(slid)* ślizgać (się); **~ down** zsuwać ⟨zsunąć⟩ (się); **~ in** wsuwać ⟨wsunąć⟩ (się); **2.** zjeżdżalnia *f*; *on pavement*: ślizgawka *f*; *phot.* przezrocze *n*; *Brt.* wsuwka *f*

slight [slaɪt] **1.** mały; *person*: drobny; **2.** lekceważenie *n*; **3.** ⟨z⟩lekceważyć

slim [slɪm] **1.** smukły; *book*: cienki; *chance*: znikomy; **2.** odchudzać się

sling [slɪŋ] **1.** *med.* temblak *m*; *for cargo*: siatka *f*; *for baby*: nosidełko *n*; **2.** *(slung)* rzucać 〈-cić〉; *przewieszać* 〈-wiesić〉 (*over* przez); *rope* rozwieszać 〈-wiesić〉

slip [slɪp] **1.** v/i pośliznąć się; v/t wsuwać 〈wsunąć〉 (**to** *s.o.* komuś); ~ *away / out* wymykać 〈-mknąć〉 się; ~ *down* ześlizgiwać 〈-gnąć〉 się; ~ *into s.th.* dress etc. narzucać 〈-cić〉 coś na siebie; ~ *on shoes* etc. wsuwać 〈wsunąć〉; **2.** pośliznięcie n się; (*mistake*) pomyłka f; *paper*: kwitek m; *garment*: halka f; '~**per** bambosz m; '~**pery** śliski

slogan ['sləʊgən] slogan m

slope [sləʊp] **1.** pochyłość f; *hill* etc.: zbocze n; (*angle*) nachylenie n; **2.** pochylać 〈-lić〉 się; *surface*: ~ *down* opadać; ~ *up* wznosić się

sloppy ['slɒpɪ] niedbały; (*sentimental*) ckliwy

slot [slɒt] **1.** otwór m; **2.** wsuwać 〈wsunąć〉 (się); ~ *machine* automat m

slow [sləʊ] **1.** wolny, powolny; *be* ~ *watch*: spóźniać się; **2.** (*a.* ~ *down*) zwalniać 〈zwolnić〉; '~**down** spowolnienie n; ~ *motion* zwolnione tempo n

slum [slʌm] slumsy pl

slung [slʌŋ] past and pp of *sling* 2

sly [slaɪ] znaczący; (*cunning*) chytry

smack [smæk] **1.** uderzenie n; *on the bottom*: klaps m; (*sug-* *gestion*) posmak m (*of s.th.* czegoś); **2.** uderzać 〈-rzyć〉; ~ *a child on the bottom* d(aw)ać dziecku klapsa

small [smɔːl] mały; *mistake*, *advertisement*, *print*: drobny; *make* ~ *talk* prowadzić rozmowę towarzyską; ~ **change** bilon m; '~**pox** ['~pɒks] ospa f

smart [smɑːt] **1.** elegancki; *esp. Am.* mądry; **2.** boleśnie przeżywać (*from, under s.th.* coś); *eyes*: piec, szczypać

smash [smæʃ] **1.** v/t rozbi(ja)ć; *window* zbi(ja)ć; *fig.* 〈z〉niszczyć; v/i zbi(ja)ć się; **2.** ~ (*hit*) przebój m sezonu; '~**ing** oczerni(a)ć, *esp. Brt.* F świetny, rewelacyjny

smear [smɪə] **1.** 〈po〉smarować; (*make mark*) pomaz(yw)ać, 〈po〉brudzić; (*slander*) oczerni(a)ć; **2.** smuga f, plama f; (*slander*) oszczerstwo n

smell [smel] **1.** zapach m; *unpleasant*: smród m; *sense*: węch m; **2.** (*smelt or smelled*) v/i pachnieć (*of s.th.* czymś); v/t 〈po〉czuć; (*sniff*) 〈po〉wąchać; *danger*: wyczu(wa)ć; ~ *out* wywęszyć; '~**y** śmierdzący

smelt [smelt] past and pp of *smell* 2

smile [smaɪl] **1.** uśmiech m; **2.** uśmiechać 〈-chnąć〉 się (*at s.o.* do kogoś *a. fortune* etc.: *on s.o.* do kogoś)

smock [smɒk] kitel *m*; (*blouse*) bluzka *f*

smog [smɒg] smog *m*

smok|e [sməuk] **1.** dym *m*; F papieros *m*; **2.** *v/i* palić (papierosy); *chimney*: dymić; *v/t* ⟨s⟩palić; (*preserve*) ⟨u⟩wędzić; '**~er** palacz *m*, palący *m*; *rail.* wagon *m* dla palących; '**~ing** palenie *n*; *no* **~ing** palenie wzbronione; **~y** zadymiony; *fire*: dymiący

smooth [smu:ð] **1.** gładki; *road*: równy; *mixture*: jednolity; *flight*: spokojny; *life*: bezproblemowy; *salesman*: ugrzeczniony, przymilny; **2.** (*a.* **~ out**) wygładzać ⟨-dzić⟩

smuggle ['smʌgl] przemycać ⟨-cić⟩; '**~r** przemytnik *m*

snack [snæk] przekąska *f*

snail [sneɪl] ślimak *m*

snake [sneɪk] wąż *m*

snap [snæp] **1.** zrywać ⟨zerwać⟩ (się) (*esp.* z trzaskiem); (*close*) zatrzaskiwać ⟨-snąć⟩ (się); warknąć (*at* na); *dog*: kłapać ⟨-pnąć⟩ zębami (*at* na); *phot.* F pstryknąć zdjęcie; **~** *one's fingers* strzelać ⟨-lić⟩ palcami; **2.** trzask *m*; *phot.* F fotka *f*; **~** **fastener** zatrzask *m*; '**~py** elegancki; żwawy; '**~shot** zdjęcie *n*

snatch [snætʃ] **1.** wyr(y)wać (*from* z); chwytać ⟨-wycić⟩ (*at* z), (*steal*) ⟨u⟩kraść (*from s.o.* komuś); **2.** urywek *m*

sneak [sni:k] **1.** (*smuggle*) przemycać ⟨-cić⟩; (*tell*) donosić ⟨-nieść⟩ (*on* na); **~** **out** wymykać ⟨-mknąć⟩ się (*of* z); **~** **up** zakradać ⟨-raść⟩ się; **2.** donosiciel *m*

sneeze [sni:z] kichać ⟨-chnąć⟩

sniff [snɪf] *v/i* pociągać ⟨-gnąć⟩ nosem; *v/t* (*smell*) obwąch(iw)ać; **~** **out** wywęszyć

snob [snɒb] snob *m*; '**~bish** snobistyczny

snoop [snu:p] **~** *around* or *about* F węszyć

snooze [snu:z] drzemać

snore [snɔ:] chrapać

snout [snaut] pysk *m*; *pig*: ryj *m*

snow [snəu] **1.** śnieg *m*; **2.** padać; *it's* **~ing** pada śnieg; '**~ball** śnieżka *f*; '**~drift** zaspa *f* (śnieżna); '**~flake** płatek *m* (śniegu); '**~y** śnieżny

so [səu] **1.** tak; *I hope* **~** mam nadzieję, że tak; **~** *am I* ja też; **~** *far* do tej pory; **2.** (*therefore*) (tak) więc; **~** *that* po to by, tak by; **~** (*what?*) no to co?

soak [səuk] (*na*)moczyć (się); **~** *up* wchłaniać ⟨-łonąć⟩

soap [səup] mydło *n*; **~** **opera** saga *f* telewizyjna; '**~y** mydlany; *surface*: namydlony

sob [sɒb] szlochać

sober ['səubə] **1.** trzeźwy; **2.** **~** *up* ⟨wy⟩trzeźwieć so-'called tak zwany

soccer ['sɔkə] piłka f nożna

sociable ['səuʃəbl] towarzyski

social ['səuʃl] społeczny; *life*, *club etc.*: towarzyski; *animal*: stadny, gromadny; ~ **security** *Brt.* system *m* świadczeń socjalnych; '**~ism** socjalizm *m*; '**~ist 1.** socjalista *m*; **2.** socjalistyczny; **~ worker** pracownik *m* socjalny

society [sə'saɪətɪ] społeczeństwo *n*; (*association*) towarzystwo *n*

sock [sɔk] skarpetka *f*

socket ['sɔkɪt] *electr.* gniazdko *n*

soda ['səudə] soda *f*; *drink*: woda *f* sodowa

sofa ['səufə] kanapa *f*

soft [sɔft] miękki; *breeze*: łagodny; *voice*: cichy; *colour*: spokojny; *life*: lekki; ~ **drink** napój *m* bezalkoholowy; '**~en** ['sɔfn] *v/i* ⟨z⟩mięknąć; *v/t* zmiękczać ⟨-czyć⟩; *shock etc.* osłabi(a)ć; '**~ware** *computer*: oprogramowanie *n*

soil [sɔɪl] **1.** gleba *f*; (*territory*) ziemia *f*; **2.** ⟨za⟩brudzić

solar ['səulə] słoneczny; ~ **cell** bateria *f* słoneczna

sold [səuld] *past and pp of* **sell**

soldier ['səuldʒə] żołnierz *m*

sole¹ [səul] jedyny; *right*: wyłączny

sole² [~] **1.** podeszwa *f*; **2.** ⟨pod⟩zelować

solemn ['sɔləm] poważny; *promise etc.*: oficjalny; *procession etc.*: uroczysty

solicitor [sə'lɪsɪtə] adwokat *m*, radca *m* prawny, notariusz *m*

solid ['sɔlɪd] **1.** (*not liquid or gas*) stały; (*not hollow*) lity; (*dense*, *unbroken*) jednolity; *line*, *hour etc.*: nie przerywany; *grip*: mocny; *person*, *building*, *basis etc.*: solidny; *work*, *advice*: konkretny; *evidence*: konkretny; **2.** ciało *n* stałe; *math.* bryła *f*

solid|arity [sɔlɪ'dærətɪ] solidarność *f*; **~ify** [sə'lɪdɪfaɪ] zastygać ⟨-gnąć⟩, ⟨s⟩twardnieć; **~ity** solidność *f*

solit|ary ['sɔlɪtərɪ] samotny; *street*: pusty; '**~ude** ['~tjuːd] samotność *f*

soluble ['sɔljubl] rozpuszczalny; **~tion** [sə'luːʃn] rozwiązanie *n*; (*liquid*) roztwór *m*

solve [sɔlv] rozwiązać; '**~nt 1.** rozpuszczalnik *m*; **2.** *econ.* wypłacalny

some [sʌm, səm] trochę, kilka (kilku *itd.*); *with pl*: niektórzy, niektóre; *unspecified*: pewien, jakiś; *I drank* ~ *milk* wypiłem trochę mleka; *I see* ~ *people* widzę kilku ludzi; ~ *people do it* niektórzy ludzie to robią; '**~body** ktoś; '**~day** kiedyś (w przyszłości); '**~how** jakoś, w jakiś sposób

15 Uni Polish

'~**one** ktoś; '~**place** *Am.* → '~**somewhere**; '~**thing** coś; '~**time** kiedyś; '~**times** czasami; '~**what** nieco; '~**where** gdzieś

son [sʌn] syn *m*

song [sɒŋ] pieśń *f; popular:* piosenka *f; bird:* śpiew *m*

son-in-law (*pl* **sons-in-law**) zięć *m*

soon [su:n] wkrótce, niedługo; (*early*) wcześnie; **as ~ as possible** możliwie najszybciej; ~**er or later** prędzej czy później

soothe [su:ð] uspokajać ⟨-koić⟩

sophisticated [sə'fɪstɪkeɪtɪd] *person:* obyty, nowoczesny; *behaviour:* wyrafinowany, wymyślny; *tech.* skomplikowany

sorcerer ['sɔ:sərə] czarnoksiężnik *m*

sore [sɔ:] **1.** bolący, obolały; **2.** rana *f; ~ throat* zapalenie *n* gardła

sorrow ['sɒrəʊ] smutek *m*

sorry ['sɒrɪ] *state etc.:* kiepski, nędzny; **I'm (so)** ~! bardzo mi przykro!; ~! (*I apologize*) przepraszam!; ~? (*pardon?*) słucham?; **I feel ~ for her** żal mi jej

sort [sɔ:t] **1.** rodzaj *m*, typ *m; ~ of* F w pewnym sensie, coś jakby; ~ *of worried* F trochę zaniepokojony; **a ~ of dress** F coś w rodzaju sukni; *out of* ~**s** F nie w sosie F; **2.**

⟨po⟩sortować; ~ **out** wyb(ie)rać; *fig.* ⟨u⟩porządkować; '~**er** *tech.* sorter *m*

sought [sɔ:t] *past and pp of* **seek**

soul [səʊl] dusza *f*

sound [saʊnd] **1.** mocny; (*healthy*) zdrowy; (*sensible*) wyważony, sensowny; (*correct*) dobry; *econ.* solidny, pewny; ~ *asleep* pogrążony w głębokim śnie; **2.** dźwięk *m* (*a. phys.*); *orchestra etc.:* brzmienie *n;* **3.** *v/i* wyd(aw)ać dźwięk, ⟨za⟩brzmieć; *out:* brzmieć; *you* ~ *unhappy* robisz wrażenie nieszczęśliwego; *v/t* wydoby(wa)ć dźwięk z (czegoś); (*pronounce*) wymawiać ⟨-mówić⟩; *mar.* ⟨z⟩mierzyć (głębokość); *med.* osłuch(iw)ać; ~ **out** wybad(yw)ać; '~**proof** dźwiękoszczelny; '~**track** ścieżka *f* dźwiękowa

soup [su:p] zupa *f*

sour [saʊə] kwaśny; *fig.* skwaszony

source [sɔ:s] źródło *n*

south [saʊθ] **1.** południe *n;* **2.** południowy; **3.** na południe; ~**erly** ['saðəlɪ] południowy; ~**ern** ['saðən] południowy; ~**ward(s)** ['saʊθwəd(z)] na południe

souvenir [su:və'nɪə] pamiątka *f*

sovereign ['sɒvrɪn] suwerenny; ~**ty** ['~rəntɪ] władza *f*

Soviet ['səʊvɪət] *hist.* radziecki; *the ~ Union* Związek *hist.* m Radziecki

sow¹ [saʊ] maciora *f*

sow² [səʊ] (*sowed*, *sown* or *sowed*) ⟨za⟩siać; *field* obsiew(a)ać (*with s.th.* czymś); *~n pp of* **sow¹**

space [speɪs] **1.** miejsce *n*; (*a. outer ~*) przestrzeń *f* kosmiczna, kosmos *m*; *between words:* odstęp *m*; **2.** *usu. ~ out* ⟨po⟩oddzielać od siebie; *'~bar* klawisz *m* odstępu; *'~craft* (*pl -craft*) pojazd *m* kosmiczny; *'~ship* statek *m* kosmiczny

spacious ['speɪʃəs] przestronny

spade [speɪd] łopata *f*; *~(s pl) cards:* pik(i *pl*) *m*

Spain [speɪn] Hiszpania *f*

span [spæn] **1.** (*period*) okres *m*; (*range*) zakres *m*; (*distance*) rozpiętość *f*; **2.** *river etc.:* rozciągać się ⟨po⟩nad (czymś)

Spaniard ['spænjəd] Hiszpan(ka *f*) *m*; *'~sh* hiszpański

spank [spæŋk] (*s.o.*) da(wa)ć klapsa (komuś)

spare [speə] **1.** przeznaczać ⟨-czyć⟩, poświęcać ⟨-cić⟩ (*for* na); oszczędzać ⟨-dzić⟩, ochraniać ⟨-ronić⟩ (*from* przed); (*omit*) przemilczać ⟨-czeć⟩; *to ~* na zbyciu; **2.** zapasowy; (*free*) wolny; *~ (part)* część *f* zamienna; *~ room* pokój *m* gościnny

spark [spɑːk] **1.** iskra *f* (*a. fig.*); **2.** *v/i* iskrzyć; *v/t a. ~ off* wszczynać ⟨-cząć⟩, ⟨za⟩inicjować; *'~ing plug Brt. mot.* świeca *f*; *'~le* **1.** połysk *m*; *fig.* blask *m*; **2.** skrzyć się; *people:* błyszczeć; *'~ler* zimny ogień *m*; *'~ling* błyszczący; *fig.* olśniewający; *~ling wine* wino *n* musujące; *~ plug mot.* świeca *f*

sparrow ['spærəʊ] wróbel *m*

spat [spæt] *past and pp of* **spit¹**

spawn [spɔːn] **1.** ikra *f*; **2.** składać ⟨złożyć⟩ ikrę

speak [spiːk] (*spoke*, *spoken*) *v/i* mówić (*to* do); (*converse*) rozmawiać (*to*, *with* z, *about* o); *v/t word* wypowiadać ⟨-wiedzieć⟩; *truth* mówić ⟨powiedzieć⟩; *~ English* mówić po angielsku; *~ up* mówić głośno; *'~er* mówiący *m* (-ca *f*); *to audience:* mówca *m*; → *loudspeaker*

spear [spɪə] włócznia *f*

special ['speʃl] **1.** specjalny, (*unique*) szczególny; **2.** *TV:* program *m* specjalny; *gastr.* danie *n* firmowe; *'~ist* ['~ʃəlɪst] **1.** specjalista *m* (-tka *f*); **2.** specjalistyczny; *~ity* [~'ælɪtɪ] specjalność *f*; *~ize* ['~ʃəlaɪz] ⟨wy⟩specjalizować się (*in* w); *'~ly* szczególnie; (*exclusively*) specjalnie

species ['spiːʃiːz] (*pl ~*) gatunek *m*

speci|fic [spɪˈsɪfɪk] określony, konkretny; szczególny, charakterystyczny (**to** dla); (*precise*) dokładny; '**.fics** szczegóły *pl*; '**.fy** [ˈspesɪfaɪ] określać <-lić>, <s>precyzować; '**.men** [ˈ.mən] okaz *m*; (*sample*) próbka *f*

spectacle [ˈspektəkl] widowisko *n*; (**a pair of**) '**.s** *pl* okulary *pl*

spectacular [spekˈtækjʊlə] okazały, efektowny; widowiskowy

spectator [spekˈteɪtə] widz *m*

speculate [ˈspekjʊlet] snuć rozważania (**about, on** o, na temat); *econ.* spekulować

sped [sped] *past and pp of* **speed** 2

speech [spiːtʃ] mowa *f*; (*formal talk*) przemówienie *n*; (*language*) język *m*; '**.less** oniemiały

speed [spiːd] **1.** prędkość *f*, szybkość *f*; (*pace*) tempo *n*; *mot.* prędkość *f*; *phot.* czułość *f*; **2.** (**sped**) <po>pędzić, <po>mknąć; **3.** (**speeded**) *mot.* przekraczać <-roczyć> dozwoloną prędkość; **~ up** przyspieszać <-szyć>; '**.boat** łódź *f* motorowa, ślizgacz *m*; '**.ing** przekroczenie *n* dozwolonej prędkości; **~ limit** ograniczenie *n* prędkości; '**.ometer** [spɪˈdɒmɪtə] prędkościomierz *m*; '**.y** prędki

spell [spel] **1.** zaklęcie *n*, urok *m*; *weather*: okres *m*; **under s.o.'s ~** pod czyimś urokiem; **2.** (**spelt** *or* **spelled**) pisać ortograficznie; (*speak letters*) <prze>literować; **~ out** wyjaśni(a)ć; **how do you ~ it?** jak się to pisze?; '**.ing** ortografia *f*

spend [spend] (**spent**) spędzać <-dzić>; *money* wyd(aw)ać

spent [spent] **1.** *past and pp of* **spend**; **2.** zużyty; (*tired*) wyczerpany

sphere [sfɪə] kula *f*; *fig.* sfera *f*

spic|e [spaɪs] **1.** przyprawa *f* (korzenna); *fig.* pikanteria *f*; **2.** przyprawi(a)ć; '**.y** pikantny

spider [ˈspaɪdə] pająk *m*; '**.web** *Am.* pajęczyna *f*

spike [spaɪk] kolec *m*

spill [spɪl] (**spilt** *or* **spilled**) rozl(ew)ać (się)

spilt [spɪlt] *past and pp of* **spill**

spin [spɪn] **1.** (**spun**) obracać <-rócić> (się), wirować; *clothes* odwirow(yw)ać; *thread* prząść; **2.** obrót *m*

spinach [ˈspɪnɪdʒ] szpinak *m*

spinal [ˈspaɪnl] kręgowy; **~ column** *anat.* kręgosłup *m*; **~ cord** rdzeń *m* kręgowy

spine [spaɪn] *anat.* kręgosłup *m*; *book*: grzbiet *m*

spiral [ˈspaɪərəl] **1.** spirala *f*; **2.** spiralny

spire [ˈspaɪə] iglica *f*

spirit ['spɪrɪt] duch *m*; (*soul*) dusza *f*; (*liveliness*) energia *f*; *pl* napoje *pl* alkoholowe; (*mood*) nastrój *m*; '~ual ['~tʃʊəl] **1.** duchowy; **2.** *mus.* spiritual *m*

spit[1] [spɪt] **1.** ślina *f*; **2.** (*spat or Am.* spit) pluć, spluwać ⟨-lunąć⟩

spit[2] [~] rożen *m*

spite [spaɪt] **1.** złość *f*; *in* ~ *of* pomimo; *in* ~ *of oneself* wbrew sobie; **2.** (*s.o.*) robić na złość ⟨komuś⟩; '~ful złośliwy

splash [splæʃ] **1.** plusk *m*; (*drop*) kropla *f*; *colour*: plama *f*; **2.** ⟨o⟩chlapać, ⟨o⟩pryskać

splendid ['splendɪd] wspaniały

split [splɪt] **1.** pęknięcie *m*, podział *m* (*between, into* na, *in* w); *pl sp.* szpagat *m*; **2.** (*split*) *v/i* rozdzielać ⟨-lić⟩ się, rozpadać ⟨-paść⟩ się *wood, dress*: pękać ⟨-knąć⟩; *v/t* rozdzielać ⟨-lić⟩; *lip* rozcinać ⟨-ciąć⟩; ~ (*up*) ⟨po⟩dzielić (się); '~ting *headache*: ostry

spoil [spɔɪl] (**spoiled** *or* **spoilt**) ⟨ze⟩psuć; *child* a. rozpieszczać ⟨-pieścić⟩; ~t *past and pp of* **spoil**

spoke[1] [spəʊk] szprycha *f*

spoke[2] [~] *past*, '~n *pp of* **speak**

'**spokesman** *pl* -**men** rzecznik *m*

sponge [spʌndʒ] gąbka *f*; **2.** wycierać ⟨wytrzeć⟩, ⟨wy⟩czyścić

sponsor ['spɒnsə] **1.** sponsor *m*; **2.** sponsorować *proposal* popierać ⟨-przeć⟩

spontaneous [spɒn'teɪnjəs] spontaniczny

spoon [spuːn] **1.** łyżka *f*; **2.** nakładać ⟨nałożyć⟩ (łyżką); '~ful łyżka *f* (*of s.th.* czegoś)

sport [spɔːt] **1.** sport *m*; (*fun*) zabawa *f*, rozrywka *f*; **2.** nosić dumnie; '~ing sportowy; ~s *adj* sportowy; *behaviour*: honorowy

spot [spɒt] **1.** kropka *f*; *dirty*: plama *f*; *on skin*: krosta *f*, pryszcz *m*; *for picnic*: miejsce *n*; *rain*: kropelka *f*; *on the* ~ na miejscu; *put on the* ~ stawiać ⟨postawić⟩ w kłopotliwej sytuacji; **2.** zauważać ⟨-żyć⟩, dostrzegać ⟨-rzec⟩; '~light *thea.* reflektor *m*

sprang [spræŋ] *past of* **spring** 2

spray [spreɪ] **1.** (*drops*) mgiełka *f*; (*atomizer*) aerozol *m*; **2.** opryskiwać; *with atomizer*: spryskiwać

spread [spred] **1.** (*spread*) *v/t* rozkładać ⟨-złożyć⟩; *butter etc.* rozsmaro(wy)wać (*on* na); *toast etc.* smarować (*with s.th.* czymś); *v/i* rozprzestrzeni(a)ć się; **2.** rozprzestrzenianie *n* się; *food*: pasta *f*; *ideas*: upowszechnienie *n*; *land*: połać *f*;

'**~sheet** *computer*: arkusz *m* kalkulacyjny

spring [sprɪŋ] **1.** (*season*) wiosna *f*; (*coil*) sprężyna *f*; *water*: źródło *n*; **2.** (*sprang or* **sprung, sprung**) skakać ⟨skoczyć⟩; (*fly*) ⟨po⟩lecieć; (*result*) pochodzić, wynikać (*from, out* of z); '**~board** trampolina *f*; *fig.* odskocznia *f* (*for* do)

sprinkle ['sprɪŋkl] *with water*: sprysk(iw)ać; *with powder*: posyp(yw)ać; '**~r** *lawn*: spryskiwacz *m*

sprung [sprʌŋ] *past and pp of* **spring** 2

spun [spʌn] *past and pp of* **spin** 1

spur [spɜː] **1.** ostroga *f*; *fig.* bodziec *m*, impuls *m* (*to* do); **2.** pobudzać ⟨-dzić⟩; (*a. ~ on*) zachęcać ⟨-cić⟩; *horse*: popędzać ⟨-dzić⟩

spy [spaɪ] **1.** szpieg *m*; **2.** szpiegować (~ *on s.o.* kogoś)

squad [skwɒd] *soldiers etc.*: oddział *m*; *police*: wydział *m*; *sp.* drużyna *f*; ~ **car** radiowóz *m* policyjny

squander ['skwɒndə] ⟨roz⟩trwonić

square [skweə] **1.** kwadrat *m*; (*open place*) plac *m*; **2.** (*straighten*) układać ⟨ułożyć⟩; *number* podnosić ⟨-nieść⟩ do kwadratu; *two things*: łączyć (*się*); **3.** *adj* kwadratowy; *with right angles*: prostokątny; *area two*

miles ~ obszar o boku dwu mil; *now we are* ~ F teraz jesteśmy kwita F; **4.** *adv* (*straight*) prosto; (*parallel*) równolegle (*with* do); ~ **root** *math.* pierwiastek *m* kwadratowy

squash [skwɒʃ] **1.** tłok *m*, ścisk *m*; *sp.* squash *m*; → **lemon / orange squash**; **2.** zgniatać ⟨-nieść⟩; (*defeat*) ⟨s⟩tłumić

squeak [skwiːk] ⟨za⟩piszczeć; *door etc.*: ⟨za⟩skrzypieć

squeeze [skwiːz] **1.** *v/t* ściskać ⟨-snąć⟩; *liquid, money etc.* wyciskać ⟨-snąć⟩ (*out* of z); *fruit* wyciskać ⟨-snąć⟩ sok z (*czegoś*); (*fit*) wciskać ⟨-snąć⟩; *v/i* przeciskać ⟨-snąć⟩ się; **2.** tłok *m*, ścisk *m*; *econ.* ograniczenie *n*

squint [skwɪnt] **1.** zez *m*; **2.** ⟨z⟩mrużyć oczy (*at* patrząc na)

squirrel ['skwɪrəl] wiewiórka *f*

stab [stæb] **1.** ukłucie *n*; **2.** pchnąć nożem; (*a. ~ at*) dźgać ⟨-gnąć⟩ (*with s.th.* czymś); ~ *s.o. in the back* F zadać komuś cios w plecy

stabili|ty [stə'bɪlɪtɪ] stabilność *f*; ~**ze** ['steɪbɪlaɪz] ⟨u⟩stabilizować (*się*)

stable¹ ['steɪbl] stabilny; *character*: opanowany

stable² [~] stajnia *f*

stack [stæk] **1.** stos *m*; F

mnóstwo *n*; **2.** (*a.* **~ up**)
układa(a)ć ⟨ułoży(ć)⟩ (w stos);
(*fill*) zastawi(a)ć (**with s.th.**
czymś)

stadium ['steɪdɪəm] (*pl* **~s,
-dia** ['~djə]) *sp.* stadion *m*

staff [stɑːf] personel *m*; *factory*: załoga *f*

stage [steɪdʒ] **1.** etap *m*; *thea.,
pol., econ.* scena *f*; *fig. a.*
teatr *m*; **2.** wystawi(a)ć (na
scenie); ⟨*hold*⟩ ⟨z⟩organizo-
wać; **'~coach** dyliżans *m*

stagger ['stægə] *v/i* zatacza(ć)
się; *v/t* (*shock*) oszałamiać;
~ing ['~ɔrɪŋ] zawrotny

stagnalnt ['stægnənt]
(będący) w zastoju; *water*:
stojący; **~te** [~neɪt] znaleźć
się w zastoju

stain [steɪn] **1.** plama *f* (*a.
fig.*); (*dye*) bejca *f*; **2.**
⟨po⟩plamić (się); **'~less**
nierdzewny; **~ remover** wy-
wabiacz *m* plam

stair [steə] stopień *m*; *pl* schody *pl*; **'~case, '~way** klatka *f*
schodowa

stake [steɪk] **1.** *money, reputation* stawiać ⟨postawić⟩ (**on**
na); **2.** stawka *f*; *pl* pula *f*; **be
at ~** wchodzić w grę

stale [steɪl] *bread*: nieświeży; *bread*:
czerstwy; *person*: przepraco-
wany

stall [stɔːl] **1.** stragan *m*; *information*: stoisko *n*; *in shed*:
stanowisko *n*, boks *m*; *pl
Brt. thea.* parter *m*; **2.** *car*:
zatrzym(yw)ać (się); *per-*

son przetrzym(yw)ać; *event*
opóźni(a)ć

stammer ['stæmə] **1.** *v/i* jąkać
się; (*say something*) mówić
⟨powiedzieć⟩ jąkając się; *v/t
esp.* **~ out** wyjąk(iw)ać; **2.**
jąkanie *n*

stamp [stæmp] **1.** kupon *m*;
postage: znaczek *m* (pocztowy); *rubber*: pieczątka *f*;
(*mark*) piętno *n*; **2.** *v/t envelope etc.* naklejać ⟨-leić⟩
znaczek na (coś); (*mark*)
⟨o⟩znakować; *v/t* nadepty-
wać ⟨-pnąć⟩ (**on** na); **~
one's foot** tupać ⟨-pnąć⟩
nogą

stand [stænd] **1.** (**stood**) *v/i*
stać ⟨stanąć⟩ (*a.* **~ up**)
wst(aw)ać; *law*: obowiązy-
wać; (*run*) kandydować (w
wyborach); *v/t* stawiać
⟨postawić⟩; *test* wytrzy-
m(yw)ać; *I can't ~ it* nie mogę
tego znieść; **~ back** stać
⟨stanąć⟩ z boku; **~ by** stać
bezczynnie; (*be ready*) być w
pogotowiu; **~ by s.o.** po-
zost(aw)ać przy kimś, po-
pierać kogoś; **~ down**
ustępować ⟨-tąpić⟩; **~ for**
abbreviation: oznaczać;
ideas: reprezentować; (*tolerate*) pozwalać ⟨-wolić⟩ (na
coś); **~ in for** zastępować
⟨-stąpić⟩; **~ out** wyróżniać
się; **~ still** stać spokojnie; **~
up for** bronić (czegoś); **~
up to s.th.** wytrzymywać coś; **~
up to s.o.** przeciwstawiać się

komuś; **2.** *vegetable*: stragan m; *information*: stoisko n; *news*: kiosk m; *for spectators*: trybuna f; *furniture*: stojak m; *(position)* stanowisko n

standard ['stændəd] **1.** *(level)* poziom m; *(criterion)* kryterium m; *moral*: zasada f, norma f; *(basis)* wzorzec m, standard m; **2.** standardowy, znormalizowany; *book*: podstawowy; **~ of living** stopa f życiowa; '**~ize** ujednolicać ⟨-cić⟩

standing ['stændɪŋ] **1.** *(permanent)* stały; **2.** pozycja f

stand|point ['stændpɔɪnt] punkt m widzenia; '**~still** martwy punkt m

stank [stæŋk] *past of stink* 2.

staple ['steɪpl] klamra f; *office*: zszywka f; *part*: podstawowy element m; *food*: podstawowy pokarm m; *product*: podstawowy artykuł m; '**~r** zszywacz m

star [stɑː] **1.** gwiazda f; *(asterisk)* gwiazdka f; **2.** oznaczać ⟨-czyć⟩ gwiazdką; *actor*: grać główną rolę *(in* w*)*; **~ring** *s.o.* z kimś w roli głównej

stare [steə] **1.** spojrzenie n; **2.** gapić się *(at* na*)*

start [stɑːt] **1.** początek m; *sp.* start m; *(advantage)* przewaga f; **get off to a bad / good ~** źle / dobrze się zacząć; **2.** *v/i* zaczynać ⟨-cząć⟩ (się);

somewhere: **~ (out)** wyruszać ⟨-szyć⟩; *car etc.*: ruszyć; *v/t career, race etc.* rozpoczynać ⟨-cząć⟩; *panic* wywoł⟨yw⟩ać; *fire* zapalać ⟨-lić⟩; *business* otwierać ⟨-worzyć⟩; *car etc.* uruchamiać ⟨-chomić⟩; **~ to do, ~ doing** zaczynać robić; **to ~ with** po pierwsze, przede wszystkim; '**~er** *food*: przystawka f; *sp.* starter m; *mot.* (a. **~ motor**) rozrusznik m

startl|e ['stɑːtl] przestraszyć; '**~ing** zaskakujący

starv|ation [stɑː'veɪʃn] głód m; *death*: śmierć f głodowa; **~e** [.v] *v/i* głodować; *die*: umierać ⟨umrzeć⟩ z głodu; *v/t* ⟨za⟩głodzić; *(force)* zmuszać ⟨zmusić⟩ *(into* do*)*; **I'm ~ing** umieram z głodu

state [steɪt] **1.** stan m; *(country)* państwo n; **2.** państwowy; **3.** stwierdzać ⟨-dzić⟩ *problem* przedstawia⟨ć⟩; **head of ~** głowa f państwa; **the ~s** F Stany F/pl.; '**~ment** stwierdzenie n; *pol.* oświadczenie n; *bank*: wyciąg m

static ['stætɪk] **1.** nieruchomy; **2.** *radio*: zakłócenia pl

station ['steɪʃn] **1.** *train*: (big), *bus*: dworzec m; *train*: (small), *underground*: stacja f; *police etc.*: posterunek m; *radio*: rozgłośnia f; **2.** ustawi⟨a⟩ć; *mil.* rozmieszczać ⟨-mieścić⟩; '**~ary** nieruchomy; '**~er('s** sklep m papierniczy; '**~ery** materiały *pl* piśmiennicze

statistics [stə'tɪstɪks] *pl* ⟨*sg constr.*⟩ statystyka *f*; ⟨*pl constr.*⟩ dane *pl* statystyczne

statue ['stætʃuː] posąg *m*

status ['steɪtəs] pozycja *f* społeczna; (*prestige*) uznanie *n*; *official*: status *m*; (**marital**) ~ stan *m* cywilny

stay [steɪ] **1.** pobyt *m*; **2.** pozost(aw)ać; (*live*) zatrzym(yw)ać się (**with** u, **at, in** w); ~ **away from** or ~ **out of** trzymać się z dala od; ~ **in** nie wychodzić z domu; ~ **up** nie kłaść się spać

steady ['stedɪ] **1.** stały; *hand*: pewny; *table*: stabilny; *voice*: spokojny; **2.** trzymać prosto; ~ **oneself** odzysk(iw)ać równowagę

steak [steɪk] stek *m*

steal [stiːl] (**stole, stolen**) ⟨u⟩kraść; (*move*) zakradać ⟨-raść⟩ się; ~ **a glance** spojrzeć ukradkiem (**at** na)

steam [stiːm] **1.** para *f*; **2.** *v/i* parować; (*move*) sunąć parując; *v/t* food ⟨u⟩gotować na parze; ~ **up** glass etc.: zaparow(yw)ać się; ~ **engine** maszyna *f* parowa; ~ **er** parowiec *m*; ~**ship** parowiec *m*

steel [stiːl] **1.** stal *f*; **2.** stalowy

steep [stiːp] **1.** stromy; *increase*: znaczny; *fig.* F wygórowany; **2.** food moczyć

steer [stɪə] prowadzić, kierować (czymś); ~**ing wheel**

mot. kierownica *f*

stem [stem] **1.** łodyga *f*; *glass*: nóżka *f*; *pipe*: cybuch *m*; *gr.* rdzeń *m*; **2.** powstrzym(yw)ać; *blood* ⟨za⟩tamować; ~ **from** wynikać z

step¹ [step] **1.** krok *m*; (*stair*) stopień *m*; *pl* drabina *f* składana; **2.** nadepnąć (**on** na); wdepnąć (**in** w); (*walk*) ⟨pójść⟩; ~ **up** zwiększać ⟨-szyć⟩

step² [~] *in compounds*: przyrodni; ~**daughter** pasierbica *f*; ~**father** ojczym *m*; ~**mother** macocha *f*; ~**son** pasierb *m*

stereo ['steriəu] **1.** stereo; **2.** zestaw *m* stereo

steril|e ['steraɪl] sterylny, wyjałowiony; (*infertile*) bezpłodny; ~**ize** ['~ɪlaɪz] ⟨wy⟩sterylizować

stew [stjuː] **1.** food dusić; **2.** gulasz *m*, potrawka *f*

steward ['stjuəd] zarządca *m*; *ship*: steward *m*; ~**ess** stewardessa *f*

stick [stɪk] kij *m*; *thin*: patyk *m*; *walking, dynamite*: laska *f*; **2.** (**stuck**) *v/i* sterczeć (**in** w); (*adhere*) ⟨przy⟩kleić się (**to** do); (*jam*) zacinać się; *v/t* wtykać ⟨wetknąć⟩ (**in** w); *with glue*: przyklejać ⟨-leić⟩ (**on** do, na); (*put*) F wsadzać ⟨-dzić⟩; ~ **out** wystawać; ~ **to** *promise etc.* dotrzym(yw)ać czegoś; *idea, person* trzymać się czegoś / kogoś; ~**er** naklejka *f*; '**~y** lepki; *with glue*: klejący, samoprzylepny; *(hot)* duszny, parny

stiff [stɪf] sztywny; *mixture*: gęsty; *door, lock*: ciężko chodzący; *competition etc.*: ostry; *drink*: mocny; '**~en** *v/t* usztywni(a)ć; *v/i* ⟨ze⟩sztywnieć

still [stɪl] **1.** *adj* spokojny; **2.** *adv* jeszcze; *(nevertheless)* jednak; **3.** *s* fotos *m*

stimul|ant ['stɪmjʊlənt] środek *m* pobudzający; '**~ate** pobudzać; '**~us** ['~əs] *(pl -li)* ['~laɪ] bodziec *m*

sting [stɪŋ] **1.** żądło *n*; **2.** *(stung)* *v/t* kąsać ⟨ukąsić⟩; *v/i* piec

stink [stɪŋk] **1.** smród *m*; **2.** *(stank or stunk, stunk)* śmierdzieć

stir [stɜ:] **1.** *v/t liquid* ⟨za⟩mieszać; *(move)* ruszać ⟨poruszyć⟩; *v/i* ruszać się; **~ up** wzburzać ⟨-rzyć⟩; *feeling* wzbudzać ⟨-dzić⟩; **2.** poruszenie *n*; **~ring** ['~rɪŋ] pobudzający

stitch [stɪtʃ] **1.** *(thread)* szew *m*; *wool*: oczko *n*; *(pattern)* ścieg *m*; *pain*: kolka *f*; **2.** zszywać ⟨zeszyć⟩

stock [stɒk] **1.** zapas *m*; *goods*: zapasy *pl*; *econ. a. pl* akcje *pl*; *trees, houses*: zasoby *pl*; *farm animals*: stado *n*; *rifle*: kolba *f*; *liquid*: wywar *m*; **in ~** na składzie; **out of ~** wyprzedany; **take ~ of** oce-

ni(a)ć; **2.** *expression*: obiegowy; **3.** *goods etc.* mieć na składzie; **~ (up)** *(fill)* wypełni(a)ć; **~ up** ⟨z⟩robić zapasy *(with s.th.* czegoś); '**~bro-ker** makler *m*; **~ed** *lake etc.*: dobrze zarybiony; **~ex-change** giełda *f*; '**~holder** *Am.* akcjonariusz *m*

stocking ['stɒkɪŋ] pończocha *f*

stock market giełda *f*

stole [stəʊl] *past*, '**~n** *pp of* **steal**

stomach ['stʌmək] **1.** brzuch *m*; *organ*: żołądek *m*; **2.** przełykać ⟨-łknąć⟩; '**~ache** ból *m* brzucha

ston|e [stəʊn] **1.** kamień *m*; *commemorative*: głaz *m*; *(pl ~e, ~es) Brt.* jednostka wagi *(6,35 kg)*; *in fruit*: pestka *f*; **2.** kamienny; **3.** *fruit* ⟨wy⟩drylować; *person* ⟨u⟩kamieniować; '**~y** kamienisty; *fig. expression*: kamienny

stood [stʊd] *past and pp of* **stand** 1

stool [stu:l] taboret *m*; *med.* stolec *m*

stop [stɒp] **1.** *v/t car, criminal etc.* zatrzym(yw)ać; *work, conversation etc.* prze-r(yw)ać; *(prevent)* powstrzym(yw)ać; *tooth* ⟨za⟩plombować; *v/i* przest(aw)ać; *storm, road etc.*: ⟨s⟩kończyć się; *watch etc.*: stawać ⟨stanąć⟩; *(cease moving,* *travelling etc.*) zatrzym(yw)ać się; (*cease talking*) przer(y)wać; **~ off** zatrzym(yw)ać się na krótko; *I ~ped to do it* zatrzymałem się by to zrobić; *I ~ped doing it* przestałem to robić; **~ over** ⟨z⟩robić przerwę w podróży; 2. rostój *m*; *bus*: przystanek *m*

storage ['stɔːrɪdʒ] przechowywanie *n*, magazynowanie (*a. computer*)

store [stɔː] 1. (*large shop*) dom *m* handlowy; *esp. Am.* (*shop*) sklep *m*; *computer*: pamięć *f*; (*supply*) zapas *m*; (*building, room*) magazyn *m*; 2. **~** (*away*) ⟨z⟩magazynować

storey ['stɔːrɪ] *Brt.* piętro *n*, kondygnacja *f*

stork [stɔːk] bocian *m*

storm [stɔːm] 1. burza *f*; *take by* **~** brać ⟨wziąć⟩ szturmem; 2. *v/i* wściekać się; *v/t* ⟨za⟩atakować; **~ in** wpadać ⟨wpaść⟩ jak burza; **'~y** burzliwy

story ['stɔːrɪ] opowieść *f*; historia *f*; *written*: opowiadanie *n*; *newspaper*: artykuł *m*; *Am.* → **storey**

stove [stəʊv] piec *m*; *kitchen*: kuchenka *f*

straight [streɪt] 1. *adj* prosty; *answer, talk*: uczciwy, szczery; *whisky*: czysty; 2. *adv* prosto; *drink*: bez rozcieńczenia; **~ ahead**, **~ on** prosto

przed siebie; **~ off** → **~away**
od razu; **'~en** wyprostować (się); **~ out** doprowadzać ⟨-dzić⟩ do porządku; **~'forward** prosty, oczywisty; *person*: bezpośredni

strain [streɪn] 1. *resources* nadwyrężać ⟨-żyć⟩; *patience* wyczerp(yw)ać; *muscle etc.* naciągać ⟨-gnąć⟩; *food* odcedzać ⟨-dzić⟩; 2. obciążenie *n*; (*tension*) stres *m*; *med.* nadwyrężenie *n*, naciągnięcie *n*; **'~er** sitko *n*

strait [streɪt] (*in proper names often*: **~s** *pl*) cieśnina *f*; *pl* kłopoty *pl* (finansowe)

strange [streɪndʒ] (*odd*) dziwny; (*unknown*) obcy; **'~r** obcy *m*

strangle ['stræŋgl] ⟨u⟩dusić

strap [stræp] 1. pasek *m*; *on bus*: uchwyt *m*; 2. przypinać ⟨-piąć⟩ (paskiem)

strateg|ic [strə'tiːdʒɪk] strategiczny; **'~y** ['strætɪdʒɪ] strategia *f*

straw [strɔː] słoma *f*; (*tube*) słomka *f*; **'~berry** truskawka *f*

stray [streɪ] 1. oddalać ⟨-lić⟩ się, ⟨za⟩błądzić; 2. zabłąkany; *dog*: bezdomny

stream [striːm] 1. strumień *m*; *car*: sznur *m*; *insults, questions*: potok *m*; *school*: grupa *f* (*np. wg. zdolności*); 2. *v/i tears etc.*: ciec (strumieniami); *people etc.*: sunąć, posuwać się; *flag*: powiewać (**in** na); *v/t* dzielić na grupy (*np. wg. zdolności*)

street [striːt] ulica *f*; '**.car** *Am.* tramwaj *m*

strength [streŋθ] siła *f*; (*greatness*) potęga *f*; (*toughness*) wytrzymałość *f*; *light etc.*: moc *f*; '**.en** wzmacniać 〈-mocnić〉 (się)

stress [stres] **1.** napięcie *n*, stres *m*; (*emphasis*) nacisk *m*, akcent *m*; **2.** (*emphasize*) podkreślać 〈-lić〉, 〈za〉akcentować

stretch [stretʃ] **1.** *v/i* rozciągać się; *person*: przeciągać 〈-gnąć〉 się; *v/t* rozciągać 〈-gnąć〉; *money etc.*: oszczędnie gospodarować (czymś); **2.** obszar *m*; *time*: okres *m*; *in prison*: wyrok *m*; **3.** *fabric*: elastyczny; '**.er** nosze *pl*

strict [strikt] surowy; (*exact*) ścisły

strike [straik] **1.** strajk *m*; (*attack*) atak *m*; *oil*: odkrycie *n*; **2.** (*struck*) *v/i* strajkować; uderzać 〈-rzyć〉 (**against** w); *illness, troops*: 〈za〉atakować; *clock*: bić, wybijać 〈-bić〉; *v/t* uderzać 〈-rzyć〉; *thought*: przychodzić 〈przyjść〉 do głowy (komuś); (*impress*) robić wrażenie (na kimś); *note* 〈za〉grać; *match* zapalać 〈-lić〉; *gold* natrafi(a)ć na; *pose* przyjmować 〈-jąć〉; **. home** trafi(a)ć w cel; '**.r** straj-

kujący *m*; *football*: napastnik *m*

striking ['straikiŋ] *similarity etc.*: uderzający; (*attractive*) rzucający się w oczy

string [striŋ] **1.** sznurek *m*; *beads*: sznur *m*; *events*: seria *f*; *mus.* struna *f*; *pl* smyczki *pl*; **2.** (**strung**) **. up** wieszać 〈powiesić〉; *bow* naciągać 〈-gnąć〉

strip [strip] **1.** rozbierać 〈-zebrać〉 (się); pozbawi(a)ć (**of s.th.** czegoś); (**down**) 〈z〉demontować; **. off** zdejmować 〈zdjąć〉; *paint* zdrap(yw)ać; **2.** *paper etc.*: pasek *m*; *land etc.*: pas *m*; (*runway*) pas *m* startowy

stripe [straip] pasek *m*; **.d** w paski

stroke [strəʊk] **1.** 〈po〉głaskać; **2.** *brush etc.*: pociągnięcie *n*; *clock*: uderzenie *n*; *swimming*: styl *m*; *med.* udar *m*, wylew *m*

stroll [strəʊl] **1.** przechadzać się; **2.** przechadzka *f*

strong [strɒŋ] silny; (*tough*) mocny, wytrzymały; (*action*) zdecydowany; *drink*: mocny

strove [strəʊv] *past of* **strive**

struck [strʌk] *past and pp of* **strike** 2

structure ['strʌktʃə] **1.** struktura *f*; (*building*) budowla *f*; **2.** 〈u〉kształtować

struggle ['strʌgl] **1.** walczyć (**for** o, **with** z); (*try to get free*) wyrywać się; **2.** walka *f*;

(effort) wysiłek *m*

strung [strʌŋ] *past and pp of*
string 2

stub [stʌb] **1.** resztka *f*; *cigarette:* niedopałek *m*; *cheque,
ticket:* odcinek *m*; **2.** ~ **out**
cigarette ⟨z⟩gasić

stubborn ['stʌbən] uparty;
stain etc.: trudny do usu-
nięcia

stuck [stʌk] *past and pp of*
stick 2

stud [stʌd] nit *m*; *in ear:* kolczyk *m*; *on shoes:* korek *m*;
collar: spinka *f*, ~ **(farm)**
stadnina *f*

student ['stjuːdnt] student *(a
f)m*; *Am.* uczeń *m* (-ennica *f*)

studio ['stjuːdɪəʊ] *painter's:*
pracownia *f*; *photographer's:*
atelier *n*; *TV, film* studio *m*

study ['stʌdɪ] **1.** nauka *f*; *(subject)* przedmiot *m*; *(project)*
analiza *f*; *room:* gabinet *m*;
mus. etiuda *f*; *(drawing)* szkic
m; **2.** studiować; *for test:*
uczyć się

stuff [stʌf] **1.** F rzecz *f*, coś *n*;
clothes, furniture etc.: rzeczy
pl; **2.** wpychać ⟨wepchnąć⟩;
bird wyp⟨ychać⟨wepchnąć⟩;
'~**ed** wyp-
chany; '~**ing** nadzienie *n*; '~**y**
nadęty; *room etc.:* duszny

stumble ['stʌmbl] potykać
⟨-tknąć⟩ się *(on* o); *(discover)* natykać ⟨-tknąć⟩ się
(across, on, upon na)

stung [stʌŋ] *past and pp of*
sting 2

stunk [stʌŋk] *past and pp of*

stink 2

stupid ['stjuːpɪd] głupi; ~**ity**
[~'pɪdətɪ] głupota *f*

stutter ['stʌtə] **1.** *v/i* jąkać się;
v/t mówić ⟨powiedzieć⟩
jąkając się; **2.** jąkanie *n* się

styl|e [staɪl] **1.** styl *m*; **2.**
⟨za⟩projektować; *hair* ukła-
dać ⟨ułożyć⟩; '~**ish** elegancki

subconscious [sʌb'kɒnʃəs]
1. podświadomy; **2.** *the* ~
podświadomość *f*

subject ['sʌbdʒɪkt] temat
m; *school:* przedmiot *m*; *in
experiment:* osobnik *m*; *(citizen)* obywatel *m*; *gr.* podmiot *m*; **2.** [sʌb'dʒekt] narażać *(s.o. to s.th.* kogoś na
coś); **3.** ['sʌbdʒɪkt] narażony
(to na); *be* ~ *to law etc.:* podlegać (czemuś); ~ *to decision
etc.:* według, stosownie do
(czegoś); *~ive* [sʌb'dʒektɪv]
subiektywny

submarine [sʌbmə'riːn] łódź
f podwodna

submerge [səb'mɜːdʒ] zanurzać ⟨-rzyć⟩ (się); ~ *oneself*
poświęcać ⟨-cić⟩ się całkowicie *(in s.th.* czemuś)

submiss|ion [səb'mɪʃn]
uległość *f*; *(proposal etc.)*
zgłoszenie *n*; *~ive* uległy

submit [səb'mɪt] *v/i* ~ *(to)*
godzić się (na coś), ulegać
(czemuś); *v/t* przedkładać
⟨-łożyć⟩

subordinate [sə'bɔːdnət] **1.**
podwładny *m*; **2.** pod-

porządkowany (**to s.th.** czemuś)

subscri|be [səb'skraɪb] **~be to** view etc. identyfikować się z (czymś); **~be to** magazine prenumerować; **~ber** prenumerator m; teleph. abonent m; **~ption** [səb'skrɪpʃn] prenumerata f; society: składka f; charity: datek m

subsequent ['sʌbsɪkwənt] późniejszy; '**~ly** następnie, później

subsid|ize ['sʌbsɪdaɪz] dotować; '**~y** dotacja f

substance ['sʌbstəns] substancja f; (essence) istota f

substantial [səb'stænʃl] znaczny; building: potężny

substitute ['sʌbstɪtjuːt] **1.** zastępować ⟨-tąpić⟩; **2.** substytut m

subtle ['sʌtl] subtelny

subtract [səb'trækt] odejmować ⟨odjąć⟩

suburb ['sʌbɜːb] przedmieście n; **~an** [sə'bɜːbən] podmiejski; **~ia** [~biə] tereny pl podmiejskie, peryferie pl

subway ['sʌbweɪ] przejście n podziemne; Am. metro n

succeed [sək'siːd] v/i dać radę; ⟨po⟩wieść się; in business etc.: ⟨z⟩robić karierę; v/t zastępować ⟨-tąpić⟩; in time: następować ⟨-tąpić⟩ po (czymś)

success [sək'ses] powodzenie n; **~ful** attempt: udany; person: cieszący się powodze-

niem; **~ion** seria f; in **~ion** pod rząd; **~ive** kolejny; **~or** następca m

such [sʌtʃ] taki; **~ a woman** taka kobieta; **~ women** takie kobiety; **~ people** tacy ludzie; **~ a lot of coffee** tyle kawy; **~ a lot of people** tylu ludzi; **~ as?** a mianowicie?; **~ and such** taki (to) a taki

suck [sʌk] ssać; **~ down, in, up** wsysać ⟨wessać⟩

sudden ['sʌdn] nagły; **all of a ~** ni stąd ni z owąd; '**~ly** nagle

sue [sjuː] wnosić ⟨wnieść⟩ sprawę do sądu (**s.o.** przeciwko komuś) (**for s.th.** o coś)

suede [sweɪd] zamsz m

suffer ['sʌfə]; **~ (from)** cierpieć (na)

sufficient [sə'fɪʃnt] wystarczający (**for** do)

suffocate ['sʌfəkeɪt] ⟨u⟩dusić (się)

sugar ['ʃʊgə] **1.** cukier m; **2.** ⟨o⟩słodzić

suggest [sə'dʒest] ⟨za⟩proponować; **~ion** propozycja f; (sign) ślad m; psych. sugestia f; **~ive** niedwuznaczny, prowokujący; charakterystyczny (**of** dla)

suicide ['sʊɪsaɪd] samobójstwo n

suit [suːt] **1.** (outfit) ubranie n, garnitur m; women's, swimming: kostium m; diver's: strój m; cards: kolor m; jur.

rozprawa f; **2.** odpowiadać (komuś); *colour:* pasować (komuś); ~ *yourself* rób jak chcesz; '~**able** odpowiedni; '~**case** walizka f

suite [swi:t] *hotel:* apartament m; *furniture:* komplet m, zestaw m; *mus.* suita f

sulfur ['sʌlfə] Am. → **sulphur**

sulphur ['sʌlfə] siarka f

sum [sʌm] **1.** suma f; *mat.* zadanie n; *in* ~ w sumie; **2.** ~ *up* podsumow(yw)ać

summar|ize ['sʌməraɪz] streszczać ⟨-reścić⟩; '~**y** streszczenie n

summer ['sʌmə] lato n

summit ['sʌmɪt] szczyt m

summon ['sʌmən] wzywać ⟨wezwać⟩; *meeting:* zwoł(yw)ać; ~ *up* zbierać ⟨zebrać⟩; ~**s** ['~z] *sg. jur.* wezwanie n

sun [sʌn] słońce n; '~**bathe** opalać się; '~**beam** promień m słońca; '~**burn** oparzenie n słoneczne

Sunday ['sʌndɪ] niedziela f

sundial zegar m słoneczny

sung [sʌŋ] *pp of* **sing**

sunglasses *pl* okulary f słoneczne

sunk [sʌŋk] *past and pp of* **sink** ; '~**en** *ship:* zatopiony; *cheek etc.:* zapadnięty

sun|ny słoneczny; '~**rise** wschód m słońca; '~**set** zachód m słońca; '~**shade** parasol m; '~**shine** słońce n; '~**stroke** porażenie n

słoneczne; '~**tan** opalenizna f; *get a* ~**tan** opalić się

super ['su:pə] F fantastyczny, fajny F

super... [su:pə] nad..., po- nad...

superb [su:'pз:b] wspaniały

superior [su:'pɪərɪə] **1.** lepszy (*to s.th.* niż coś, od czegoś); (*higher ranking*) wyższy; (*more experienced*) starszy; *smile:* wyniosły, dumny; **2.** zwierzchnik m

super|market ['su:pəmɑːkɪt] (super)market m; ~'**natural** nadprzyrodzony; ~'**power** mocarstwo n; ~'**sonic** ponaddźwiękowy; ~**stition** [~'stɪʃn] przesąd m; ~**stitious** [~'stɪʃəs] przesądny; ~**visor** [~vaɪz] nadzorować; ~**visor** ['~vaɪzə] nadzorca m; (*tutor*) opiekun m

supper ['sʌpə] późny obiad m; *late:* kolacja f

supplement 1. ['sʌplɪmənt] dodatek m (*to* do); *book:* suplement m; **2.** uzupełni(a)ć (*with s.th.* czymś); ~**ary** [~'mentərɪ] dodatkowy; ~**ary benefit** Brt. zasiłek m

suppl|ier [sə'plaɪə] dostawca m; ~**y** [~aɪ] **1.** zaopatrywać ⟨-trzyć⟩ (*with* w); dostarczać ⟨-czyć⟩ (*to* komuś); **2.** dostawa f; (*store*) zapas m; *econ.* podaż f; *usu. pl* zaopatrzenie n

support [sə'pɔ:t] **1.** poparcie n; (*comfort*) pociecha f; *tech.*

podpora *f*; *small*: wspornik *m*; **2.** popierać ⟨-przeć⟩; (*hold*) podpierać ⟨-deprzeć⟩; *family* utrzym(yw)ać; *land* ⟨wy⟩żywić

suppose [sə'pəuz] przypuszczać, sądzić; *I* ~e myślę (że); ~ed [~zd] rzekomy; *I'm* ~ed to do it mam to ⟨z⟩robić; *I'm not* ~ed to do it nie powinienem tego robić

suppress [sə'pres] *rebellion* ⟨s⟩tłumić; *laugh* powstrzym(yw)ać; *information* zatajać ⟨-taić⟩; ~ion *freedom*: ograniczenie *n*

suprem|acy [su'preməsı] przewaga *f*; (*superiority*) wyższość *f*; ~e [~'pri:m] najwyższy

sure [ʃɔ:] pewny (*of s.th.* czegoś); *make* ~ *that* upewnić się że; ~ *enough* faktycznie; ~*!* jasne!, pewnie; *he's* ~ *to win* na pewno wygra; ~*ly* na pewno

surface ['sɜ:fıs] **1.** powierzchnia *f*; *table etc.*: blat *m*; **2.** wynurzać ⟨-rzyć⟩ się; *news etc.*: wychodzić ⟨wyjść⟩ na jaw

surg|eon ['sɜ:dʒən] chirurg *m*; ~*ery* zabieg *m*; operacja *f*; *Brt. place*: gabinet *m*; ~*ical* chirurgiczny

surname ['sɜ:neim] *Brt.* nazwisko *n*

surplus ['sɜ:pləs] **1.** nadwyżka *f*; **2.** dodatkowy, ponadplanowy

surprise [sə'praiz] **1.** zaskoczenie *n*; *pleasant*: niespodzianka *f*; **2.** zaskakiwać ⟨-skoczyć⟩

surrender [sə'rendə] **1.** poddanie się *n* (*to s.th.* czemuś); **2.** *v/i* podd(aw)ać się (*to s.th.* czemuś); *v/t* wyrzekać ⟨-rzec⟩ się (czegoś)

surround [sə'raund] otaczać ⟨-czyć⟩ (*with s.th.* czymś); ~*ing* otaczający; ~*ings pl* otoczenie *n*

survey 1. [sə'vei] przyglądać się (czemuś); *people* ⟨z⟩badać; *land* ⟨z⟩robić pomiary geodezyjne (czegoś); *house* ⟨z⟩robić inspekcję (czegoś); **2.** ['sɜ:vei] *people*: badanie *n*; *land*: pomiar *m*; *house*: inspekcja *f*

surviv|al [sə'vaivl] przetrwanie *n*; ~*e* [~aiv] przeży(wa)ć; ~*or* pozostały *m* przy życiu; *there were no* ~*ors* nikt nie ocalał

suspect 1. [sə'spekt] podejrzewać; **2.** ['sʌspekt] podejrzany *m*; **3.** ['~] podejrzany

suspend [sə'spend] zawieszać ⟨-wiesić⟩; *sp.* ⟨z⟩dyskwalifikować; ~*ed* zawieszony

suspens|e [sə'spens] napięcie *n*; *keep in* ~*e* trzymać w napięciu; ~*ion* zawieszenie *n*; *liquid*: zawiesina *f*; *sp.* dyskwalifikacja *f*; *mot.* zawieszenie *n*

suspici|on [sə'spiʃn] podejrzenie *n*; (*hunch*) przeczucie *n*; **~ous** *glance*: podejrzliwy; *circumstances*: podejrzany; **she became ~ous of me** zaczęła mnie podejrzewać

sustain [sə'steɪn] podtrzym-yw(yw)ać; *sound* przedłużać ‹-żyć›

swallow¹ ['swɒləʊ] jaskółka *f*

swallow² [~] przełykać ‹-łknąć›

swam [swæm] *past of swim* 1

swan [swɒn] łabędź *m*

swap [swɒp] 1. *v/t* zamieni(a)ć *(for* na, *with* z); *views* wymieni(a)ć *(with* z); **we ~ped cars (with each other)** zamieniliśmy się samochodami; 2. zamiana *f*

swear [sweə] *(swore, sworn)* przysięgać ‹-gnąć›; *in court*: składać ‹złożyć› przysięgę; *(curse)* ‹za›kląć, przeklinać; **~word** przekleństwo *n*

sweat [swet] 1. pot *m*; 2. *(sweated or Am. a. sweat)* pocić się; **~er** sweter *m*

Swede [swiːd] Szwed(ka *f*) *m*; **~n** Szwecja *f*; **~ish** szwedzki

sweep [swiːp] 1. *(swept) v/t floor* zamiatać ‹-mieść›; *things* zab(ie)rać; *v/i* ‹po›lecieć, przelatywać ‹-le-cieć›; 2. *move*: ruch *m*; *person*: kominiarz *m*; *land*: połać *f*; **~ing** rozległy; *statement*: (zbyt) ogólny; *generalization*: daleko idący

sweet [swiːt] 1. słodki; 2. *Brt.* cukierek *m*; *Brt. (dessert)* de-

ser *m*; *pl* słodycze *pl*; **~en** słodzić; **~ener** słodzik *m*; **~heart** ukochany *m* (-na *f*)

swell [swel] 1. *(swelled, swollen* or *swelled)* ‹na›-puchnąć; *number*: wzrastać ‹-rosnąć›; *emotion*: nasilać ‹-lić› się; 2. *Am.* F fajny; **~ing** opuchlizna *f*

swept [swept] *past and pp of sweep* 1

swift [swɪft] szybki; *stream*: wartki

swim [swɪm] 1. *(swam, swum) v/i* ‹po›płynąć, pływać; *v/t* przepływać ‹-łynąć› (przez); *go ~ming* iść ‹pójść› popływać; 2. **go for a ~** iść ‹pójść› popływać; **~mer** pływak *m* (-aczka *f*)

swindle ['swɪndl] 1. oszu-k(iw)ać; 2. oszustwo *n*

swine [swaɪn] *(pl ~s)* świnia *f*; *(fig. a. ~s)*

swing [swɪŋ] 1. *(swung)* huśtać (się); ruszać ‹-szyć› (się) (łagodnie po łuku); **the door swung open** drzwi otworzyły się na oścież; **I swung the bag onto my shoulder** zarzuciłem torbę na ramię; **~ round** odwracać ‹-cić› się; *pol. etc.* zmieni(a)ć się; 2. huśtanie *n*; *children's*: huśtawka *f*; *pol. etc.* zwrot *m*; *mus.* swing *m*

Swiss [swɪs] 1. szwajcarski; 2. Szwajcar(ka *f*) *m*; **the ~ pl** Szwajcarzy *pl*

switch [swɪtʃ] 1. *electr.*

przełącznik *m*; *on wall*: kontakt *m*; *Am. rail.* zwrotnica *f*; przejście *n* (**from s.th. to s.th.** z czegoś na coś); **2.** *v/i* przechodzić ⟨przejść⟩ (*from* z, *to* do); (*swap*) zamieni(a)ć się (*with* z); *v/t* (*exchange*) wymieni(a)ć, zamieni(a)ć; **~ off** wyłączyć ⟨-czyć⟩; **~ on** włączyć ⟨-czyć⟩

Switzerland ['switsələnd] Szwajcaria

swollen ['swəulən] *pp of* **swell** 1

sword [sɔːd] miecz *m*

swor|e [swɔː] *past*, **~n** *pp of* **swear**

swum [swʌm] *pp of* **swim** 1

swung [swʌŋ] *past and pp of* **swing** 1

syllable ['siləbl] sylaba *f*

syllabus ['siləbəs] (*pl* **-buses**, **-bi** [**.**baɪ]); program *m* nauczania

symbol ['simbl] symbol *m*; **~ic** [**.**'bɒlɪk] symboliczny; **~ize** [**.**'bəlaɪz] symbolizować

symmetr|ical [sɪ'metrɪkl] symetryczny; **~y** ['sɪmətrɪ]

symetria *f*

sympath|etic [sɪmpə'θetɪk] pozytywnie nastawiony (*to* do); (*understanding*) wyrozumiały (*to* dla); (*concerned*) pełen współczucia (*over* w związku z); *smile*: współczujący; (*nice*) sympatyczny; **~ize** ['**.**θaɪz] współczuć (*with* komuś); (*understand*) identyfikować się (*with* z); **~y** współczucie *n* (*for* dla); *in* **~y** *with s.o.* w solidarności z kimś

symphony ['sɪmfənɪ] symfonia *f*

symptom ['sɪmptəm] objaw *m*

synchronize ['sɪŋkrənaɪz] ⟨z⟩synchronizować

synonym ['sɪnənɪm] synonim *m*

synthetic [sɪn'θetɪk] syntetyczny; *behaviour*: sztuczny

syringe ['sɪrɪndʒ] strzykawka *f*

syrup ['sɪrəp] syrop *m*

system ['sɪstəm] system *m*; *pol.* ustrój *m*; *tabor*: układ *m*; **~atic** [**.**'mætɪk] systematyczny

T

tab [tæb] banderola *f*; nalepka *f*; *pick up the* **~** F ⟨za⟩płacić rachunek

table ['teɪbl] **1.** stół *m*; (*chart*) tabela *f*; *pl multiplication*: tabliczka *f*; **2.** przedkładać

⟨-dłożyć⟩; '**~cloth** obrus *m*; '**~spoon** łyżka *f* stołowa

tablet ['tæblɪt] tabliczka *f*; *med.* tabletka *f*

taboo [tə'buː] **1.** zakazany; *a* **~** *subject* temat *m* tabu; **2.**

zakaz *m*, tabu *n*

tack [tæk] **1.** *thumb:* (duża) pinezka *f*; (*small nail*) gwoździk *m* (tapicerski); (*approach*) podejście *n*; **2.** przybi(ja)ć (gwoździkami), przypinać ⟨-piąć⟩ pluskiewkami; *Brt.* ⟨za⟩fastrygować

tackle ['tækl] **1.** sprzęt *m*; *tech.* wielokrążek *m*; **2.** ⟨za⟩brać się za (coś); *sp.* ⟨za⟩atakować

tact [tækt] takt *m*; '**~ful** taktowny

tactics ['tæktɪks] *mil. pl* taktyka *f*

tag [tæg] **1.** zawieszka *f*; *price:* metka *f*; **2.** ⟨za⟩etykietować

tail [teɪl] **1.** ogon *m*; *pl jacket:* frak *m*; *pl* (*not heads*) orzeł *m*; **2.** F śledzić; '**~light** *mot.* światło *n* tylne

tailor ['teɪlə] krawiec *m*

take [teɪk] **1.** (**took, taken**) *v/t* brać ⟨wziąć⟩; zab(ie)rać (**from z, to** do); (*endure*) znosić ⟨znieść⟩; *stadium etc.* ⟨po⟩mieścić; *courage etc.* wymagać; *decision, risk* podejmować ⟨-djąć⟩; *test etc.* przystępować ⟨-tąpić⟩ do (czegoś); *drugs etc.* zaży(wa)ć; *notes* ⟨z⟩robić; *size of shoes etc.* nosić; *step* ⟨z⟩robić; *oath etc.* składać ⟨złożyć⟩; *temperature* ⟨z⟩mierzyć; *advice* ⟨po⟩słuchać (czegoś); *photograph* ⟨z⟩robić; *math.* odejmować (**from** od); *v/i*

plant: przyjąć się; **~ a look** spojrzeć; **~ a seat** siadać (usiąść); **~ a taxi** (po)jechać taksówką; **~ a walk** iść (pójść) na spacer; **~ offence** obrażać ⟨-razić⟩ się; **~ office** obejmować ⟨objąć⟩ urząd; **~ power** przejmować ⟨-jąć⟩ władzę; **~ after s.o.** być podobnym do kogoś; **~ apart** rozbierać ⟨-zebrać⟩; **~ away** zab(ie)rać; **~ back** odnosić ⟨-nieść⟩ (**to** do); *something said* cofać ⟨-fnąć⟩; **~ down** *message etc.* zapis(yw)ać; *curtains* zdejmować ⟨zdjąć⟩; **~ in** przyjmować ⟨-jąć⟩; (*deceive*) nab(ie)rać; **~ off** *hat etc.* zdejmować ⟨zdjąć⟩; *aer.* ⟨wy⟩startować; **~ a day off** brać ⟨wziąć⟩ dzień wolnego; **~ on** przyjmować ⟨-jąć⟩; **~ out** wyjmować ⟨-jąć⟩; *tooth etc.* usuwać ⟨usunąć⟩; **~ s.o. out** zapraszać ⟨-rosić⟩ (**for** na); **~ over** przejmować ⟨-jąć⟩ kontrolę (nad czymś); **~ to** polubić; **~ up** *as hobby, career:* zajmować ⟨-jąć⟩ się (czymś); *offer, attitude* przyjmować ⟨-jąć⟩; *idea, job* podejmować ⟨-djąć⟩; *time, space* zajmować ⟨-jąć⟩; **2.** *film:* ujęcie *n*; '**~n 1.** *pp of* **take** 1; **2.** *seat:* zajęty; '**~off** *aer.* start *m*

talc [tælk], **talcum powder** ['tælkəm] talk *m*

tale [teɪl] opowiadanie *n*; (*story*) bajka *f*

talent ['tælənt] talent *m*; **~ed** utalentowany

talk [tɔːk] **1.** rozmowa *f*; *(speech)* prelekcja *f*; *(gossip)* plotki *pl*; **2.** mówić **(about, of** o); rozmawiać **(to** z, **about** o); **~ s.o. into doing s.th.** namawiać ⟨-mówić⟩ kogoś do zrobienia czegoś; **~ s.th. over** omawiać ⟨omówić⟩ coś; **~ative** ['-ətiv] gadatliwy

tall [tɔːl] wysoki; **how ~ are you?** ile masz wzrostu?

tame [teɪm] **1.** oswojony; *fig.* potulny, posłuszny; *activity:* nudny; **2.** oswajać ⟨-woić⟩

tampon ['tæmpɒn] tampon *m*

tan [tæn] **1.** opalenizna *f*; **2.** opalać ⟨-lić⟩ się; **3.** jasnobrązowy

tangerine [tændʒə'riːn] mandarynka *f*

tangle ['tæŋgl] **1.** plątanina *f*; *fig.* bałagan *m*; **2.** zapląt(yw)ać (się)

tank [tæŋk] zbiornik *m*; *mil.* czołg *m*

tanker ['tæŋkə] cysterna *f*; *(ship)* tankowiec *m*

tanned [tænd] opalony

tap [tæp] **1.** kran *m*; *tech.* zawór *m*; *on the shoulder:* klepnięcie *n*; *on ~* z beczki; *(available)* do natychmiastowego użycia; **2.** stukać ⟨-knąć⟩ **(s.th.** w coś); *rhythm* wystuk(iw)ać; **be ~ped** *telephone:* być na podsłuchu

tape [teɪp] **1.** taśma *f*; **2.** nagr(yw)ać (na taśmę); *(at-*

tach) przyklejać ⟨-leić⟩ (taśmą)

taper ['teɪpə] zwężać ⟨zwęzić⟩ się; **~ off** ⟨o⟩słabnąć

tape| recorder magnetofon *m*; **~ recording** nagranie *n* na taśmie

tapestry ['tæpɪstrɪ] gobelin *m*

tar [tɑː] smoła *f*

target ['tɑːgɪt] cel *m*; *sp.* tarcza *f*

tariff ['tærɪf] cło *n* przywozowe; *hotel etc.*: cennik *m*

tarnish ['tɑːnɪʃ] *v/t* ⟨z⟩matowić; *reputation* ⟨z⟩psuć; *v/i* ⟨z⟩matowieć, ⟨za⟩śniedzieć

tart [tɑːt] ciasto *n* owocowe

tartan ['tɑːtən] szkocka krata *f*

task [tɑːsk] zadanie *n*; **~ force** oddział *m* specjalny

tassel ['tæsl] frędzel *m*

taste [teɪst] **1.** smak *m*; *good, bad:* gust *m*; **have a ~e of s.th.** ⟨s⟩próbować czegoś; **2.** *v/t* smakować; *v/t* ⟨s⟩próbować; **~eful** gustowny; **~eless** niegustowny; *food:* bez smaku; *remark:* niesmaczny; **~y** smakowity

tattoo [tə'tuː] **1.** tatuaż *m*; *mil.* parada *f*; **2.** ⟨wy⟩tatuować

taught [tɔːt] *past and pp of* **teach**

tax [tæks] **1.** podatek *m*; **2.** ⟨o⟩podatkować

taxi ['tæksɪ] **1.** taksówka *f*; **2.** *aer.* kołować; **~cab** tak-

sówka f; '**~driver** taksówkarz m; **~ rank**, *esp. Am.*
~ stand postój m taksówek
'**tax**|**payer** podatnik m; **~ re-**
turn oświadczenie n podatkowe

tea [ti:] herbata f; → **high tea**;
'**~bag** herbata f ekspresowa;
~ break przerwa f na herbatę

teach [ti:tʃ] (**taught**) ⟨na⟩uczyć; '**~er** nauczyciel(ka) f m

teacloth ścierka f do naczyń

team [ti:m] zespół m; *sp.*
drużyna f

'**teapot** dzbanek m do herbaty

tear¹ [teə] 1. (**tore, torn**)
⟨po⟩drzeć (się); *hole* wydzierać ⟨wydrzeć⟩; 2. rozdarcie n, dziura f; **~ down**
⟨z⟩burzyć

tear² [tɪə] łza f; '**~ful** zapłakany; *voice*: płaczliwy

'**tearoom** herbaciarnia f

tease [ti:z] drażnić

tea| **service, ~ set** serwis m
do herbaty; '**~spoon** łyżeczka f do herbaty

tea towel ścierka f do naczyń

techni|**cal** ['teknɪkl] techniczny; **~cality** [~'kælətɪ] szczegół m techniczny; *jur.* szczegół m formalny; **~cian**
[~'nɪʃn] technik m; **~que**
[~'ni:k] technika f

technology [tek'nɒlədʒɪ]
technologia f

teenage ['ti:neɪdʒ] *person:*
nastoletni; *clothes etc.:* dla

nastolatków; '**~r** nastolatek m

teens [ti:nz] lata pl młodzieńcze (*13-19*)

teeth [ti:θ] pl of **tooth**; **~e** [ti:ð]
ząbkować

teetotal(l)er [ti:'təʊtlə] abstynent(ka f) m

tele|**cast** ['telɪkɑ:st] transmisja f telewizyjna; **~communi-**
cations [~kəmju:nɪ'keɪʃnz]
telekomunikacja f; '**~fax** telefaks m; **~gram** ['~græm]
telegram m

telegraph ['telɪɡrɑːf] 1. telegraf m; 2. ⟨za⟩telegrafować
(**s.o.** do kogoś); **~ic**
[~'ɡræfɪk] telegraficzny

telephone ['telɪfəʊn] 1. telefon m; 2. ⟨za⟩telefonować
(**s.o.** do kogoś); **~ booth, ~**
box budka f telefoniczna; **~**
call rozmowa f telefoniczna; **~**
directory książka f telefoniczna; **~ exchange** centrala f telefoniczna

televise ['telɪvaɪz] nad(aw)ać
w telewizji

television ['telɪvɪʒn] telewizja
f; **on ~** w telewizji; **watch ~**
oglądać telewizję; **~ (set)** telewizor m

tell [tel] (**told**) mówić ⟨powiedzieć⟩ (**of, about** o); *story etc.* opowiadać ⟨wiedzieć⟩; (*order*) kazać pf.
(**s.o. to do s.th.** komuś by coś
zrobił); (*know, guess etc.*) zorientować się; **~ apart**
odróżni(a)ć; **~ s.o. off** udzie-

lać ⟨-lić⟩ komuś nagany; ~ **on s.o.** F ⟨na⟩skarżyć na kogoś; **~er** sekretarz (liczący głosy w wyborach); *esp. Am.* kasjer(ka *f*) *m*; **~tale** wymowny

temper ['tempə] charakter *m*; (*rage*) gniew *m*, wściekłość *f*; (*mood*) nastrój *m*; **keep one's ~** zachow(yw)ać spokój; **lose one's ~** wpadać ⟨wpaść⟩ w złość; **~ament** ['~rəmənt] temperament *m*; **~ature** ['~prətʃə] temperatura *f*

temple ['templ] świątynia *f*; *anat.* skroń *f*

temporary ['tempərɪ] tymczasowy

tempt [tempt] ⟨s⟩kusić; **~ation** [~'teɪʃn] pokusa *f*

ten [ten] dziesięć

tenant ['tenənt] lokator *m*

tend [tend] *v/i* mieć skłonność (**to do s.th.** do robienia czegoś); (*incline*) zbliżać się (**to, towards** do); *v/t* zajmować się (czymś); *land* uprawiać; **~ency** ['~ənsɪ] tendencja *f*

tender¹ ['tendə] czuły; *age:* młody; *meat:* delikatny; *plant:* wrażliwy

tender² ['tendə] *econ.* **1.** oferta *f* przetargowa; **2.** składać ⟨złożyć⟩

tendon ['tendən] ścięgno *n*

tennis ['tenɪs] tenis *m*; **~ court** kort *m*

tens|e [tens] **1.** spięty; *body etc.*: sztywny; *situation etc.*:

napięty; **2.** napinać ⟨-piąć⟩ się; **3.** *gr.* czas *m*; **~ion** ['~nʃn] napięcie *n*

tent [tent] namiot *m*

tentative ['tentətɪv] tymczasowy; *step:* niepewny

tenth [tenθ] dziesiąty

term [tɜːm] **1.** (*word etc.*) termin *m*; (*period*) okres *m*; *school:* semestr *m*; *pol.* kadencja *f*; *pl* warunki *pl*; **~s of** jeśli chodzi o; **in abstract ~s** w sposób abstrakcyjny; **be on good / bad ~s with s.o.** być w dobrych / złych stosunkach z kimś; **2.** naz(y)wać

termin|al ['tɜːmɪnl] **1.** terminal *m*; *bus:* dworzec *m* (autobusowy); **2.** *med. illness:* nieuleczalny; *patient:* nieuleczalnie chory; **~ate** [~eɪt] ⟨za⟩kończyć (się); *v/i bus, train:* zatrzym(yw)ać się na stacji końcowej; *v/t pregnancy* przer(yw)ać; **~ation** [~'neɪʃn] przerwanie *n*; **~us** ['~əs] (*pl* **-ni** ['~naɪ] *or* **-nuses**) stacja *f* końcowa

terrace ['terəs] szereg *m* (domów jednorodzinnych); *street:* ulica *f* o zabudowie szeregowej

terri|ble ['terəbl] okropny; **~fic** [tə'rɪfɪk] (*great*) świetny, rewelacyjny; (*huge etc.*) ogromny; (*powerful*) potężny; **~fy** ['terɪfaɪ] przerażać ⟨-razić⟩

territor|ial [terə'tɔːrɪəl] tery-

torialny; **~y** ['~təri] terytori-
um *n*; (*terrain*) teren *m*, obszar *m*

terror ['terə] przerażenie *n*;
child: diabeł *m*; **~ist** ['~rıst]
terrorysta *m*; **~ize** ['~raız]
terroryzować

test [test] **1.** test *m*; *med.* badanie *n*; **2.** ⟨prze⟩testować;
med. ⟨z⟩badać; *put s.th. to
the* **~** podd(aw)ać próbie

testament ['testəmənt] testament *m*; (*evidence*) świadectwo *n*

testicle ['testıkl] *anat.* jądro *n*

testify ['testıfaı] zezn(aw)ać
(*against s.o.* przeciwko komuś); potwierdzać (*to s.th.*
coś)

testimon|ial [testı'məʊnjəl]
opinia *f*; **~y** ['~mənı] zezna-
nie *n*; (*evidence*) świadectwo
n (*to s.th.* czegoś)

test|tube próbówka *f*; **'~tube
baby** dziecko *n* z probówki

text [tekst] tekst *m*; **'~book**
podręcznik *m*

textile ['tekstaıl] tkanina *f*; *pl*
przemysł *m* tekstylny

texture ['tekstʃə] struktura *f*;
(*feel*) faktura *f*; *mus.* styl *m*

than [ðæn, ðən] niż; *older* **~
her** starszy od niej; *younger
~ me* młodszy ode mnie

thank [θæŋk] **1.** ⟨po⟩dzięko-
wać; (*no.*) **~ you** nie,
dziękuję; **2.** *pl* podziękowania *pl*; **~s!** dzięki!; *~s to* ~
dzięki tobie; **'~ful** wdzięczny

that [ðæt, ðət] **1.** *pron and adj*

(*pl those* [ðəʊz]) ten; *this one
and* ~ *one* ten i tamten; *without pl* to; ~ *was my brother* to był mój brat; **2.** *adv*
tak; *he wasn't quite* ~ *ill* nie
był aż tak chory; **3.** *rel pron*
(*pl that*) który; *the letter* ~
you never opened list,
którego w ogóle nie otwo-
rzyłeś; **4.** *cj* że; *prove* ~ *you
understand* udowodnij że
rozumiesz; ~*'s it* (*exactly*)
tak jest; (*that is the end*) to
wszystko; ~*'s* ~ i na tym koniec; *like* ~ w ten sposób

thaw [θɔ:] **1.** odwilż *f*; **2.**
⟨s⟩topnieć, ⟨roz⟩topić się;
food rozmrażać ⟨-rozić⟩

the [ðə, *before vowels:* ðı,
stressed: ðı:] **1.** *definite article, no equivalent* ~ *speed of
light* prędkość światła; ~
waiter brought ~ *wine* list
kelner przyniósł kartę win;
2. *adv* ~ ... ~ ... im ... tym ...; ~
sooner ~ *better* im prędzej
tym lepiej

theatre, *Am.* **-ter** [ˈθıətə] teatr
m

theft [θeft] kradzież *f*

their [ðeə], **~s** [~z] ich

them [ðem, ðəm] (n)ich,
(n)im, je, nie, nimi

theme [θi:m] temat *m*; *art:*
motyw *m*

themselves [ðəm'selvz] *reflexive:* się, siebie, sobie; *emphasis:* (oni) sami, (one) same

then [ðen] **1.** *adv* wtedy; (*af-*

terwards) potem, później; (*in that case*) w takim razie, wobec tego; **by ~** do tego czasu; **if X ~ Y** jeśli X to Y; **2.** *adj* ówczesny

theology [θɪˈɒlədʒɪ] teologia *f*
theor|etical [θɪəˈretɪkl] teoretyczny; **~y** [ˈ~rɪ] teoria *f*
there [ðeə] tam; **~ is**, *pl* **~ are** jest, są; **~ you are** / **go** co zrobić, no trudno; (*I was right*) nie mówiłem?; (*here you are*) proszę; **~ and back** tam i z powrotem; **~!** no; **~!** no już dobrze; **~abouts** [ˈðeərəbaʊts] coś koło tego; **~fore** [ˈðeəfɔ:] dlatego
thermometer [θəˈmɒmɪtə] termometr *m*
these [ðiːz] *pl of* **this**
thesis [ˈθiːsɪs] (*pl* **-ses** [ˈ~siːz]) teza *f*; (*dissertation*) praca *f*, rozprawa *f*
they [ðeɪ] oni, one
thick [θɪk] gruby; *crowd, hair, liquid, smoke:* gęsty; (*stupid*) tępy; *night etc.:* ciemny; **~en** *v/i* ⟨z⟩gęstnieć; *v/t* ⟨za⟩gęszczać; **~et** [ˈ~ɪt] gaszcz *m*, gęstwina *f*
thief [θiːf] (*pl* **thieves** [θiːvz]) złodziej *m*
thigh [θaɪ] udo *n*
thin [θɪn] **1.** chudy; *cloth etc.:* cienki; *liquid, smoke:* rzadki; **2.** *v/i* przerzedzać ⟨-dzić⟩ się; *v/t* rozrzedzać ⟨-dzić⟩
thing [θɪŋ] rzecz *f*
think [θɪŋk] (**thought**) ⟨po⟩myśleć; **~ of** uważać (*as*

za); (*remember*) przypominać ⟨-mnieć⟩ sobie; (*know*) znać; (*conceive*) wymyślać ⟨-lić⟩; **what do you ~ about** / **of it?** co o tym myślisz?; **~ s.th. over** przemyśleć coś; **~ s.th. up** wymyślać ⟨-lić⟩ coś
third [θɜːd] trzeci
thirst [θɜːst] pragnienie *n*; **~y** spragniony; **I am ~y** chce mi się pić
thirt|een [θɜːˈtiːn] trzynaście; **~y** trzydzieści
this [ðɪs] (*pl* **these** [ðiːz]) ten, ta, to; **~ one and that one** ten i tamten; *without any to:* **~ is my brother** to (jest) mój brat
thorn [θɔːn] cierń *m*; **~y** cierniaty; *fig.* trudny
thorough [ˈθʌrə] dokładny; **~bred** koń *m* pełnej krwi
those [ðəʊz] *pl of* **that 1**
though [ðəʊ] **1.** *cj* chociaż; **as ~** jak gdyby; **2.** *adv* jednak
thought [θɔːt] **1.** *past and pp of* **think**; **2.** myśl *f*; (*consideration*) namysł *m*; (*view*) pogląd *m*; **~ful** zamyślony; (*considerate*) troskliwy; **~less** bezmyślny
thousand [ˈθaʊznd] tysiąc *m*
thread [θred] **1.** nić *f* (*a. fig.*); *tech.* gwint *m*; **2.** nawlekać ⟨-lec⟩
threat [θret] groźba *f*; zagrożenie *n* (*to* dla); **~en** ⟨za⟩grozić; **~ening** groźny
three [θriː] trzy; **~-quarters** trzy czwarte
threshold [ˈθreʃhəʊld] próg *m*

threw [θruː] *past of* **throw** 2

thrifty ['θrɪftɪ] oszczędny

thrill [θrɪl] **1.** podniecać ⟨-cić⟩, ⟨pod⟩ekscytować; **2.** dreszcz *m*; '**~er** dreszczowiec *m*; '**~ing** ekscytujący

thrive [θraɪv] (**thrived** *or* **throve**, **thrived** *or* **thriven**) dobrze się rozwijać, kwitnąć; **~n** ['θrɪvn] *pp of* **thrive**

throat [θrəʊt] gardło *n*

throb [θrɒb] *blood*: pulsować; *heart*: dudnić

throne [θrəʊn] tron *m*

through [θruː] **1.** *prp and adv* przez; *from May ~ October* od maja do października; *let s.o. ~* przepuszczać ⟨-puścić⟩ kogoś; *get ~ teleph.* ⟨po⟩łączyć się (*to z*); *put s.o. ~ teleph.* ⟨po⟩łączyć kogoś (*to z*); **2.** *adj train*: bezpośredni; **~'out 1.** *prp* przez (cały); **2.** *adv* wszędzie, całkowicie

throve [θrəʊv] *past of* **thrive**

throw [θrəʊ] **1.** rzut *m*; **2.** (**threw**, **thrown**) rzucać ⟨-cić⟩; **~ oneself into s.th.** zaangażować się w coś; **~ into prison** wtrącać ⟨-cić⟩ do więzienia; **~ off** odrzucać ⟨-cić⟩; **~ out** wyrzucać ⟨-cić⟩; **~ up** F rzygać V; *dust* wzbi⟨jać⟩; (*build quickly*) sklecać ⟨-cić⟩; '**~away** jednorazowego użytku; *remark etc.*: zrobiony mimochodem; **~n** *pp of* **throw** 2

thru [θruː] *Am. for* **through**

thumb [θʌm] **1.** kciuk *m*; **2.** **~ through** *book etc.* przeglądać ⟨-dnąć⟩; '**~tack** *Am.* pinezka *f*

thunder ['θʌndə] **1.** grzmot *m*; *traffic*: dudnienie *n*; **2.** ⟨za⟩grzmieć; *traffic etc.*: dudnić; '**~storm** burza *f* z piorunami; '**~struck** oszołomiony

Thursday ['θɜːzdɪ] czwartek *m*

thus [ðʌs] *form.* dlatego, z tego względu; tak, w ten sposób

tick [tɪk] **1.** (*mark*) haczyk *m*, ptaszek *m*; (*sound*) tyknięcie *n*; *Brt.* (*moment*) chwilka *f*; **2.** *v/t* odhaczać ⟨-czyć⟩; *v/i* tykać ⟨-knąć⟩; **~ off** odhaczać ⟨-czyć⟩

ticket ['tɪkɪt] bilet *m*; *library etc.*: karta *f*, legitymacja *f*; (*tag*) metka *f*; *speeding etc.*: mandat *m*; *lottery*: los *m*; **~ inspector** bileter *m*; **~ office** kasa *f* (biletowa)

tickle ['tɪkl] ⟨po⟩łaskotać; '**~ish** mający łaskotki; *fig.* wrażliwy; *situation*: delikatny

tide [taɪd] pływ *m*; *high ~* przypływ *m*; *low ~* odpływ *m*

tidy ['taɪdɪ] schludny; **~ up** sprzątać ⟨-tnąć⟩; **~ oneself up** doprowadzać ⟨-dzić⟩ się do porządku

tie [taɪ] **1.** węzeł *m*; *garment*: krawat *m*; (*bond*) więź *f*;

(*draw*) remis *m*; (*match*) mecz *m* eliminacyjny; *Am. rail.* podkład *m*; **2.** (*attach*) przywiąz(yw)ać; *knot, shoelace* zawiąz(yw)ać; (*connect*) ⟨po⟩wiązać; **~ down** ograniczać ⟨-czyć⟩

tiger ['taɪgə] tygrys *m*

tight [taɪt] **1.** *adj clothes*: obcisły; *grip etc.*: mocny; *screw etc.*: dokręcony; *knot*: zaciśnięty, mocny; *string etc.*: naciągnięty; (*packed*) ciasny; **2.** *adv hold*: mocno; *shut*: szczelnie; **'~en** v/t zaciskać ⟨-snąć⟩; *rope* naciągać ⟨-gnąć⟩; v/i *face* ⟨ze⟩sztywnieć; **~ (up)** *screw* dokręcać ⟨-cić⟩; **~-fisted** F skąpy; **'~rope** *circus*: lina *f*; **~s** *pl esp. Brt.* rajstopy *pl*

tile [taɪl] **1.** *floor etc.*: płytka *f*; *wall a.*: kafelek *m*; *roof*: dachówka *f*; **2.** pokry(wa)ć płytkami / kafelkami / dachówkami

till [tɪl] *prp* (aż) do; F → *until*
till² [~] kasa *f*

tilt [tɪlt] przechylać ⟨-lić⟩ (się); *fig.* naginać ⟨-giąć⟩

timber ['tɪmbə] drewno *n*; (*beam*) belka *f*

time [taɪm] **1.** czas *m*; (*period*) okres *m*; (*occasion*) raz *m*; *mus.* rytm *m*; *pl. math.*: razy; **~ is up** czas się skończył; **for the ~ being** na razie; **have a good ~** dobrze się bawić; **what's the ~?, what ~ is it?** która godzina?; **the first ~**

pierwszy raz; **four ~s** cztery razy; **~ after ~, ~ and** (*~)again* wielokrotnie; **all the ~** cały czas; **at a ~** na raz; **at any ~** w każdej chwili; **at all ~s** zawsze; **at the same ~** w tym samym czasie; **in ~** z czasem; *mus.* w tempie; **on ~** punktualnie; **2.** ⟨za⟩planować (*for* na); ⟨z⟩mierzyć; *sp.* mierzyć czas; **'~consuming** czasochłonny; **'~er** *kitchen*: minutnik *m*; *tech.* regulator *m* czasowy; **~ lag** odstęp *m* czasu; **'~less** ponadczasowy; **~ limit** termin *m*; **'~ly** na czas, w samą porę; **~ signal** *radio, TV*: sygnał *m* czasu; **~ switch** *tech.* wyłącznik *m* automatyczny; **'~table** harmonogram *m*; *school*: plan *m* lekcji F, rozkład *m* zajęć; *rail.* rozkład *m* jazdy; *aer.* rozkład *m* lotów; **~ zone** strefa *f* czasowa

tin [tɪn] cyna *f*; *esp Brt. container*: puszka *f*; **~foil** folia *f* aluminiowa; **~ opener** otwieracz *m* do konserw

tint [tɪnt] **1.** odcień *m*, barwa *f*; (*dye*) farba *f* (*do* włosów); **2.** ⟨po⟩farbować

tiny ['taɪnɪ] malutki

tip [tɪp] **1.** koniuszek *m*; *Brt. rubbish*: wysypisko *n*; *Brt.* F (*pigsty*) chlew *m*; *in restaurant etc.*: napiwek *m*; (*advice*) rada *f*; **it's on the ~ of my tongue** mam to na końcu języka; **2.** przechylać ⟨-lić⟩ się (*pour*) wysyp(yw)ać; *liquid* wyl(ew)ać; *Brt. rubbish* wyrzuc‹-cić›; *in restaurant etc.*: d(aw)ać napiwek (**s.o.** komuś); ~ **s.o. off** uprzedzać ‹-dzić› kogoś, ostrzegać ‹-rzec› kogoś; ~**ped** zakończony (**with s.th.** czymś); *cigarette*: z filtrem

tiptoe ['tɪptəʊ] **1.** iść ‹pójść› na palcach; **2. on** ~ na palcach

tire[1] ['taɪə] *Am.* → **tyre**

tire[2] ['~] ‹z›męczyć (się) (**of s.th.** czymś); '~**d** zmęczony; '~**d out** wyczerpany, wykończony; **be** ~**d out of s.th.** mieć dosyć / dość czegoś; '~**less** niestrudzony, niezmordowany; '~**some** (*annoying*) denerwujący; (*boring*) nudny

tiring ['taɪərɪŋ] męczący, nużący

tissue ['tɪʃuː] tkanka *f*; (*handkerchief*) chusteczka *f* higieniczna; *cleaning*: papierowy ręcznik *m*; → ~ **paper** bibułka *f*

title ['taɪtl] tytuł *m*; *jur.* tytuł własności

to [tʊ, tə, tuː] **1.** *prp* do; na; dla; *time*: za; **go** ~ **Spain** jechać do Hiszpanii; **go** ~ **school** iść do szkoły; **with one's back** ~ **the wall** plecami do ściany; **tie s.o.** ~ **a tree** przywiązać kogoś do drzewa; **a letter** ~ **s.o.** list do kogoś; **return** ~ **reality** pow-

rócić do rzeczywistości; **from 7** ~ **11** od siódmej do jedenastej; **from beginning** ~ **end** od początku do końca; **five days** ~ **Christmas** pięć dni do Bożego Narodzenia; **similar** ~ **s.th.** podobny do czegoś; **compare s.th.** ~ **s.th.** porównywać coś do czegoś *or* coś z czymś; **switch over** ~ **computers** przejść (przerzucić się F) na komputery; **a reaction** ~ **s.th.** reakcja na coś; **an answer** ~ **a question** odpowiedź na pytanie; **make sense** ~ **s.o.** mieć sens dla kogoś; **an inspiration** ~ **s.o.** inspiracja dla kogoś; **my surprise** ~ **s.o.** ku mojemu zdziwieniu; **it's five** ~ **six** jest za pięć szósta; ~ **the right** po prawej stronie; **give s.th.** ~ **s.o.** dawać coś komuś; **she seems strange** ~ **me** ona wydaje mi się dziwna; **a secretary** ~ **the manager** sekretarka kierownika; **2.** *in inf* żeby; by; **she went there** ~ **see him** poszła tam, żeby się z nim zobaczyć; **I asked him** ~ **come with me** poprosiłem go, żeby poszedł ze mną; **I want** ~ **tell you something** chcę ci coś powiedzieć; **I am** ~ **do it today** mam to zrobić dzisiaj; **he opened the door** ~ **see Father** kiedy otworzył drzwi, zobaczył Ojca; **I don't know what** ~ **do** nie wiem co robić; **3.** *adv*

toast 460

come ~ odzysk(iw)ać przytomność; ~ *and fro* tam i z powrotem

toast¹ [təʊst] **1.** toast *m*; **2.** ~ *s.o.* wznosić ⟨-nieść⟩ toast za czyjeś zdrowie

toast² [~] **1.** chleb *m* grzankowy; *a piece of* ~ grzanka *f*; **2.** opiekać ⟨opiec⟩; ~ *oneself* wygrzewać się

tobacco [təˈbækəʊ] tytoń *m*

today [təˈdeɪ] dzisiaj, dziś

toe [təʊ] palec *m* u nogi

together [təˈgeðə] razem (*with* z)

toilet [ˈtɔɪlɪt] toaleta *f*; *bowl*: sedes *m*; ~ *paper* papier *m* toaletowy; ~*ries* [ˈ~rɪz] przybory *pl* toaletowe; ~ *roll* rolka *f* papieru toaletowego

token [ˈtəʊkən] żeton *m*; *book etc.*: bon *m*; *love etc.*: symbol *m*, gest *m*

told [təʊld] *past and pp of* **tell**

tolera|ble [ˈtɒlərəbl] znośny; ~*nce* wytrzymałość *f*; ~*nt* tolerancyjny (*of* wobec); ~*te* [ˈ~eɪt] tolerować

toll¹ [təʊl] *bell* bić

toll² [~] straty *pl*; (*fee*) opłata *f*; *the death* ~ liczba *f* ofiar śmiertelnych

tomato [təˈmɑːtəʊ] (*pl* -*toes*) pomidor *m*

tomb [tuːm] grób *m*

tomorrow [təˈmɒrəʊ] jutro; *the day after* ~ pojutrze

ton [tʌn] (*weight*) tona *f* (*Brt.*

1016 kg, *Am. 907 kg*); *metric* ~ → **tonne**

tone [təʊn] ton *m*; *shade*: odcień *m*

tongue [tʌŋ] język *m*; *food*: ozór *m*; *hold one's* ~ trzymać język za zębami, milczeć

tonight [təˈnaɪt] dzisiaj wieczorem

tonne [tʌn] (*weight*) tona *f* (metryczna) (*1000 kg*)

tonsil [ˈtɒnsl] *anat.* migdałek *m*

too [tuː] za; (*as well*) też, także, również

took [tʊk] *past of* **take** 1

tool [tuːl] narzędzie *n*

tooth [tuːθ] (*pl* **teeth** [tiːθ]) ząb *m*; ~*ache* ból *m* zęba; ~*brush* szczoteczka *f* do zębów; ~*less* bezzębny; ~*paste* pasta *f* do zębów

top [tɒp] **1.** *hill etc.*: szczyt *m*; *tree*: wierzchołek *m*; *page etc.*: góra *f*; *street etc.*: (drugi) koniec *m*; *table*: blat *m*; *bottle*: kapsel *m*; *jar*: nakrętka *f*; *carrot etc.*: nać *f*; *clothing*: góra *f* (*toy*) bąk *m*; *on* ~ *of* na; (*in addition to*) oprócz; **2.** *floor etc.*: najwyższy; *end etc.*: najdalszy; *speed etc.*: maksymalny; *person*: czołowy; **3.** *roll etc.* prowadzić w (czymś); *amount* przekraczać ⟨-roczyć⟩; *joke etc.* przebi(ja)ć; ~ *up* uzupełni(a)ć

topic [ˈtɒpɪk] temat *m*; ~*al* aktualny

top-secret ściśle tajny

torch [tɔːtʃ] latarka *f*; *(stick)* pochodnia *f*

tore [tɔː] *past of* **tear**[^1] 1

torn [tɔːn] *pp of* **tear**[^1] 1

tortoise ['tɔːtəs] żółw *m*

torture ['tɔːtʃə] 1. tortury *pl*; *fig.* męczarnia *f*; 2. torturować; *fig.* zamęczać

toss [tɔs] *v/t* rzucać ⟨-cić⟩ *food* ⟨wy⟩mieszać (**with** z) *(wstrząsając w naczyniu)*; *pancakes* podrzucać *(na patelni)*; *head* odrzucać ⟨-cić⟩ *(do tyłu)*; *v/i* rzucać się; ~ *(up)*, ~ *a coin* rzucać ⟨-cić⟩ monetą

total ['təutl] 1. całkowity; 2. ogólna liczba *f*; *in* ~ w sumie; 3. *numbers etc.* dod(aw)ać; *figure*: wynosić ⟨-nieść⟩

touch [tʌtʃ] 1. dotyk *m*; *(act of touching)* dotknięcie *n*; *(improvement)* poprawa *f*; *(style)* styl *m*, podejście *f*; *(small amount)* odrobina *f*; **keep in** ~ być w kontakcie; 2. dotykać ⟨-tknąć⟩ (się); *fig. emotionally*: wzruszać ⟨-szyć⟩; ~ **down** *aer.* ⟨z⟩lądować; ~ **up** poprawi(a)ć, ⟨wy⟩retuszować; ~ *(up)on* **s.th.** nawiąz(yw)ać do czegoś; **'~down** *aer.* lądowanie *n*; **'~ing** wzruszający; **'~y** wrażliwy; *subject*: drażliwy

tough [tʌf] twardy *(a. fig.)*; *(rough)* brutalny; *task*: trudny

tour [tuə] 1. wycieczka *f*;

sight: zwiedzanie *n*; *sp.*, *thea. etc.* trasa *f* objazdowa; 2. objeżdżać ⟨-jechać⟩; *thea. etc.* jeździć ⟨⟨po⟩jechać⟩ w trasę objazdową

tourist ['tuərist] 1. turysta *m* (-tka *f*); 2. turystyczny; ~ **agency**, ~ **bureau**, ~ **office** biuro *n* podróży

tournament ['tuənəmənt] turniej *m*

tow [təu] 1. **give s.o. a** ~ ⟨przy⟩holować kogoś; **in** ~ na holu; F za sobą; 2. ⟨przy⟩holować

toward(s) [tə'wɔːd(z)] *(in the direction of)* w kierunku *(czegoś)*, w stronę *(czegoś)*; *(for a purpose)* na; *(to achieve result)* w celu; **attitude** ~ **s.th.** stosunek do czegoś

towel ['tauəl] ręcznik *m*

tower ['tauə] 1. wieża *f*; 2. górować *(over* nad)

town [taun] miasto *n*; ~ **council** rada *f* miejska; ~ **hall** ratusz *m*

toy [tɔi] 1. zabawka *f*; 2. ~ **with** idea rozważać, zastanawiać się nad *(czymś)*; *object* bawić się *(czymś)*

trace [treis] 1. ślad *m*; 2. znajdować ⟨znaleźć⟩ *(to* w); *development* ⟨prze⟩śledzić; *drawing* ⟨prze⟩kalkować

track [træk] 1. szlak *m*; *planet etc.*, *rail.*: tor *m*; *sp.* bieżnia *f*; *magnetic tape etc.*: ścieżka *f*; *(song)* utwór *m*; *pl* ślady *pl*, trop *m*; 2. ⟨wy⟩tropić; *aer.*

śledzić; ~ **down** ⟨wy⟩tropić; '**~suit** dres m

tractor ['træktə] traktor m

trade [treɪd] **1.** handel m; (*job*) zawód m; **2.** handlować (*in s.th.* czymś); ~ (*off*) wymieni(a)ć (*for* na); '**~mark** znak m handlowy; '**~(s) union** związek m zawodowy

tradition [trə'dɪʃn] tradycja f; **~al** tradycyjny

traffic ['træfɪk] **1.** ruch m; *goods*: transport m; *passengers*: komunikacja f; (*trade*) (nielegalny) handel m; **2.** handlować (*in s.th.* czymś); ~ **circle** *Am.* rondo n; ~ **island** wysepka f; ~ **jam** korek m; ~ **light** światło n uliczne

tragedy ['trædʒədɪ] tragedia f; '**~ic** tragiczny

trail [treɪl] **1.** szlak m; (*marks*) ślad m; **2.** *v/t* śledzić; (*drag*) ciągnąć (*behind one* za sobą); *v/i* ciągnąć się (*behind s.o.* za kimś); ~**er** *mot.* przyczepa f; *Am.* przyczepa f kempingowa; *film, TV:* zapowiedź f, zwiastun m

train [treɪn] **1.** pociąg m; *cars etc.*: karawana f; *events*: ciąg m; *dress*: tren m; **2.** kształcić (się) (**as** na); *dog*: szkolić; ~ trenować (*for* do); ~**ee** [⟨'niː] praktykant m; '**~er** *sp.* trener m; *circus*: treser m; *pl* adidasy *pl* f; '**~ing** szkolenie n; *sp.* trening m

trait [treɪ] cecha f

traitor ['treɪtə] zdrajca m

tram [træm] tramwaj m

tramp [træmp] **1.** włóczęga m; **2.** wlec się

tranquil ['træŋkwɪl] spokojny; ~**(l)izer** *środek m* uspokajający

transatlantic [trænzət'læntɪk] transatlantycki

transfer 1. [træns'fɜː] przekładać ⟨przełożyć⟩, przenosić ⟨-nieść⟩; przewozić ⟨-wieźć⟩; *money* przel(ew)ać; *information, property:* przenosić ⟨-nieść⟩; *employee* przenosić ⟨-nieść⟩ (się); **2.** ['~] przemieszczanie n, przenoszenie n; *bank*: przelew m; *employee, rights*: przeniesienie n; (*decoration*) kalkomania f

transform [træns'fɔːm] zmieni(a)ć (*into* w); ~**ation** [~fə'meɪʃn] zmiana f

transistor [træn'sɪstə] tranzystor m

transit ['trænsɪt] przewóz m; *goods*: transport m; *people*: komunikacja f; ~**ion** [~'zɪʃn] przejście n

translat|e [træns'leɪt] ⟨prze⟩tłumaczyć; ~**ion** tłumaczenie n; ~**or** tłumacz(ka) f m

trans|mission [trænz'mɪʃn] *knowledge, disease*: przekazywanie n; *radio, computer*: transmisja f; *mot.* napęd m; ~**mit** [~'mɪt] przes(y)łać; (*conduct*) przewodzić; *knowledge* przekaz(yw)ać; ~'**mit-**

ter nadajnik *m*

transparent [træns'pærənt] przeźroczysty; *situation etc.*: oczywisty

transplant 1. [træns'plɑːnt] przesadzać ⟨-dzić⟩; *med.* przeszczepi(a)ć; **2.** ['~] przeszczep *m*; **~ation** [~'teɪ∫n] transplantacja *f*

transport 1. [træn'spɔːt] przewozić ⟨-wieźć⟩, ⟨prze-⟩ transportować; **2.** ['~] przewóz *m*, transport *m*; *public* ~ komunikacja *f*; **~ation** [~'teɪ∫n] *esp. Am.* → *transport 2*

trap [træp] **1.** ⟨z⟩łapać w potrzask; *person* nab(ie)rać; *energy* zachow(yw)ać; **2.** potrzask *m*, pułapka *f*

trash [træ∫] F *book, film*: szmira *f*; *painting*: kicz *m*; *(people)* hołota *f*; *Am.* śmieci *pl*

travel ['trævl] **1.** jeździć, ⟨po⟩jechać; *light etc.*: poruszać się; **2.** podróż *f*; ~ *agency* biuro *n* podróży; **~(l)er** podróżnik *m* ⟨-niczka *f*⟩

tray [treɪ] taca *f*

treason ['triːzn] zdrada *f*

treasure ['treʒə] **1.** skarb *m* (*a. fig.*); **2.** cenić; **~r** skarbnik *m*

treat [triːt] **1.** ⟨po⟩traktować (*as, like* jak); *illness, patient* leczyć; *wood* nasycać (*with s.th.* czymś); ~ *s.o. to s.th.* ⟨za⟩fundować komuś coś;

2. przyjemność *f*; *it's my* ~ ja funduję; **~ment** terapia *f*, leczenie *n*; '~**y** układ *m*

treble ['trebl] **1.** trzy razy, trzykrotnie; **2.** potrajać ⟨-roić⟩ (*się*)

tree [triː] drzewo *n*

tremble ['trembl] ⟨za⟩drżeć

tremendous [trɪ'mendəs] ogromny

tremor ['tremə] drżenie *n*; *earth*: wstrząs *m*

trench [trent∫] rów *m*; *mil.* okop *m*

trend [trend] trend *m*, tendencja *f*; '~**y** modny

trespass ['trespəs] *jur.* wkraczać ⟨-roczyć⟩ (*on, upon* na); *no* ~*ing* wstęp wzbroniony

trial ['traɪəl] test *m*, próba *f*; *jur.* proces *m*; *on* ~ przed sądem; *(being tested)* w fazie testowania; ~ *and error* metoda *f* prób i błędów

triangle ['traɪæŋgl] trójkąt *m*; **~ular** [~'æŋgjʊlə] trójkątny

tribe [traɪb] plemię *n*

tribunal [traɪ'bjuːnl] trybunał *m*

trick [trɪk] **1.** sztuczka *f*; *(deception)* podstęp *m*; *cards*: lewa *f*; *play a* ~ *on s.o.* zrobić komuś kawał; *a* ~ *question* pytanie *n* podchwytliwe; **2.** naciągać ⟨-gnąć⟩ (*into* na); '~**ery** oszustwo *n*

trickle ['trɪkl] ciec

trickster 464

trick|ster ['trɪkstə] oszust *m*; '~y trudny

tricycle ['traɪsɪkl] trójkołowiec *m*

trigger ['trɪgə] **1.** *gun*: spust *m*; **2.** (*a.* ~ *off*) wywoł(yw)ać

trim [trɪm] **1.** schludny, zadbany; (*slim*) smukły; **2.** (*decoration*) wykończenie *n*; *in* (*good*) ~ w dobrym stanie; *people*: w formie; **3.** przycinać ⟨-ciąć⟩; *plan* ⟨z⟩redukować; '~ming (*decoration*) wykończenie *n*; *pl* dodatki *pl*; *gastr.* resztki *pl*

trip [trɪp] **1.** wycieczka *f*; *business* ~ wyjazd *m* (służbowy), delegacja *f*; **2.** potykać ⟨-tknąć⟩ się (*over* o); (*walk*) dreptać; ~ *up* potykać ⟨-tknąć⟩ się; *s.o.* (*up*) podstawić komuś nogę

triple ['trɪpl] potrójny; ~ts ['~lts] *pl* trojaczki *pl*

triumph ['traɪəmf] **1.** triumf *m*; **2.** triumfować (*over* nad); ~ant [~'ʌmfənt] zwycięski

trivial ['trɪvɪəl] nieistotny

trolley ['trɒlɪ] wózek *m*; *rail.* drezyna *f*; *Am.* tramwaj *m*

trombone [trɒm'bəʊn] puzon *m*

troop [truːp] **1.** *soldiers etc.*: oddział *m*; *people*: grupa *f*; *animals*: stado *n*; *pl rail.* wojsko *n*; **5,000** ~**s** 5.000 żołnierzy; **2.** ud(aw)ać się grupą

trophy ['trəʊfɪ] trofeum *n*

tropic ['trɒpɪk] *geogr.* zwrotnik *m*; *the* ~**s** tropiki *pl*

trouble ['trʌbl] **1.** kłopot *m*, problem *m*; *pol.* zamieszki *pl*; *tech.* awaria *f*; *med.* dolegliwości *pl*; *in* ~ w kłopotliwej sytuacji; *fig.* w ciąży; **2.** ⟨z⟩martwić; (*hurt*) boleć; '~-free bezproblemowy; *tech.* bezawaryjny; '~maker wichrzyciel *m*, prowodyr *m*; '~some kłopotliwy

trousers ['traʊzəz] *pl* (*a.* **a pair of** ~) spodnie *pl*

trout [traʊt] (*pl* ~*s*) pstrąg *m*

truant ['truːənt] wagarowicz *m*; *play* ~ chodzić, iść ⟨pójść⟩ na wagary

truce [truːs] rozejm *m*

truck [trʌk] *Am.* samochód *m* ciężarowy, ciężarówka *f*; *rail.* wagon *m* towarowy

true [truː] prawdziwy; (*faithful*) wierny (**to s.o.** komuś); *it's* ~ to prawda; *come* ~ *dream etc.*: spełnić się

truly ['truːlɪ] naprawdę; *Yours* ~ *form.* Z poważaniem

trump [trʌmp] atu *n*; ~ (*card*) atut *m*

trumpet ['trʌmpɪt] trąbka *f*

trunk [trʌŋk] *tree*: pień *m*; *person*: tułów *m*; *elephant*: trąba *f*; (*box*) kufer *m*; *Am. mot.* bagażnik *m*; *pl* kąpielówki *pl*; *sp.* spodenki *pl*

trust [trʌst] **1.** zaufanie *n*; *econ.* trust *m*; **2.** ⟨za⟩ufać; powierzyć (*with s.th.* coś); ~

s.o. to do s.th. wierzyć że ktoś coś zrobi; **'~ee** [~'tiː] powiernik *m*; **'~ful**, **~ing** ufny; **'~worthy** godny zaufania

truth [truːθ] *n.* ⟨*s*⟩prawda *f*; *tell me the ~* powiedz mi prawdę; **to tell you the ~** prawdę mówiąc

try [traɪ] **1.** ⟨*s*⟩próbować, starać się, ubiegać się (**for** o); *in court:* sądzić (**for** za); **~ on** przymierzać ⟨-rzyć⟩; **~ out** wypróbow(yw)ać; **2.** próba *f*; **have a ~** ⟨*s*⟩próbować; **'~ing** nieprzyjemny

tube [tjuːb] *metal, glass:* rur(k)a *f*; *rubber:* wężyk *m*; *anat.* przewód *m*; (*container*) tubka *f*; **2** (*London underground*) metro *n*; *tech.* kineskop *m*

tuberculosis [tjuːbɜːkjuˈləʊsɪs] gruźlica *f*

tuck [tʌk] **1.** wkładać ⟨włożyć⟩, wpychać ⟨wepchnąć⟩; **~ away** *money etc.* odkładać ⟨odłożyć⟩; (*hide*) ⟨*s*⟩chować; **~ into** *s.th.* F pogrążać się czymś *f*; **~ s.o. in**, **~ s.o. up** otulać ⟨-lić⟩ kogoś; **2.** zakładka *f*

Tuesday ['tjuːzdɪ] wtorek *m*

tug [tʌg] **1.** pociągnięcie *n*; (*a. ~ boat*) *mar.* holownik *m*; **2.** ⟨po⟩ciągnąć; *mar.* holować

tuition [tjuːˈɪʃn] nauka *f* (*privatna*), lekcje *pl*; (*money*) czesne *n*

tulip ['tjuːlɪp] tulipan *m*

tummy ['tʌmɪ] F brzuszek *m*

tumo(u)r ['tjuːmə] *med.* guz *m*

tuna ['tjuːnə] (*pl ~*, **~s**) tuńczyk *m*

tune [tjuːn] **1.** melodia *f*; *in ~ instrument:* nastrojony; *sing, play:* czysto; *out of ~ instrument:* rozstrojony; *sing, play:* nieczysto; **2.** *mus.* ⟨na⟩stroić; *radio etc.* nastawi(a)ć (**to** na); (*match*) przystosow(yw)ać (**to** do); *tech.* ⟨wy⟩regulować; **~ in** *radio* nastawi(a)ć radio (**to** na); **~ up** *orchestra:* ⟨na⟩stroić się; **'~ful** melodyjny

tunnel ['tʌnl] tunel *m*

turbine ['tɜːbaɪn] turbina *f*

turf [tɜːf] murawa *f*; darń *f*

Turk [tɜːk] Turek *m* (*Turczynka f*); **~ey** Turcja *f*

turkey ['tɜːkɪ] indyk *m*

Turkish ['tɜːkɪʃ] turecki

turmoil ['tɜːmɔɪl] niepokój *m*

turn [tɜːn] **1.** obrót *m*; *car:* skręt *m*; *road:* zakręt *m*; *century:* przełom *m*; **a ~ for the better** zmiana *f* na lepsze; **it's my ~** moja kolej *f*; **by ~s** na przemian; **take ~s doing s.th.** robić coś na zmianę; **2.** *v/t* odwracać ⟨-rócić⟩; *pages* przewracać; *handle, key* kręcić, przekręcać ⟨-cić⟩; *gun* ⟨s⟩kierować (**on** na); *attention* ⟨s⟩kierować; *age* ⟨s⟩kończyć; *ankle* skręcać ⟨-cić⟩; *v/i* odwracać ⟨-rócić⟩ się, zamieni(a)ć się (**into** w); *wheel:* obracać się; *car, road:* skręcać ⟨-cić⟩

(change) przechodzić ⟨przejść⟩ **(from** z, **to** na); *green, sour etc.:* st(aw)ać się; *milk:* ⟨s⟩kwaśnieć; *(shape with lathe)* toczyć; **it has ~ed eight** minęła ósma; **~ against** s.o. zwracać ⟨-rócić⟩ się przeciwko komuś; **~ s.o. away** odrzucać ⟨-cić⟩ kogoś; **~ back** zawracać ⟨-rócić⟩; **~ down** offer odrzucać ⟨-cić⟩; *gas* zmniejszać ⟨-szyć⟩; *radio* ściszać ⟨-szyć⟩; **~ s.o. down** odmawiać ⟨-mówić⟩ komuś; **~ in** F chodzić, iść ⟨pójść⟩ spać; *to police:* wyd(aw)ać; **~ s.th. inside out** odwracać ⟨-rócić⟩ coś na drugą stronę; **~ off** skręcać ⟨-cić⟩, zjeżdżać ⟨zjechać⟩ **(a road** z drogi); *water, gas* zakręcać ⟨-cić⟩; *light, radio etc.* wyłączać ⟨-czyć⟩; **it ~s me off** F to mnie nie podnieca; **~ on** gas, water etc. odkręcać ⟨-cić⟩; *appliance* włączać ⟨-czyć⟩; *light* zapalać ⟨-lić⟩; **~ s.o. on** F podniecać ⟨-cić⟩ kogoś; **~ on** s.o. *(attack)* ruszać ⟨-szyć⟩ na kogoś; **~ out** wychodzić ⟨-yjść⟩ **(right/badly** dobrze/źle **for** s.o. komuś); okaz(yw)ać się **(to be** być, **that** że); *light etc.* wyłączać ⟨-czyć⟩; *(produce)* wypuszczać ⟨-puścić⟩; **~ over** *(think about)* ⟨prze⟩analizować; *(give)*

przekaz(yw)ać **(to** s.o. komuś); *(move)* odwracać ⟨-rócić⟩; **~ to** s.o. zwracać ⟨-rócić⟩ się do kogoś; **~ up** F *(be found)* znaleźć się; *gas etc.* zwiększać ⟨-szyć⟩; *radio etc.* zrobić głośniej; **'~around** *(time)* czas m wykonania; *(change)* zwrot m

'turning przecznica f; **~ point** fig. punkt m zwrotny

'turn|out frekwencja f; *(appearance)* wygląd m; *econ.* produkcja f; **'~over** *econ.* obrót m; *people:* fluktuacja f; **~pike** ['~paɪk] Am. autostrada f (płatna); **'~-up** Brt. mankiet m (spodni)

turpentine ['tɜːpəntaɪn] terpentyna f

turtle ['tɜːtl] żółw m

tutor ['tjuːtə] Brt. univ. opiekun m naukowy; korepetytor m; **~ial** [~'tɔːrɪəl] univ. seminarium n

TV [tiːˈviː] telewizja f; *(set)* telewizor m

twel|fth [twelfθ] dwunasty; **~ve** [twelv] dwanaście

twent|ieth ['twentɪθ] dwudziesty; **~y** ['~ɪ] dwadzieścia

twice [twaɪs] dwukrotnie, dwa razy

twig [twɪg] gałązka f

twilight ['twaɪlaɪt] zmierzch m

twin [twɪn] **1.** podobny; *(dual)* podwójny; **2.** pl bliźnięta pl

twinkle ['twɪŋkl] *star:* migotać, mrugać; *eyes:* skrzyć się

twist [twɪst] **1.** wykręcenie *n*;
in a story: zwrot *m*; **2.**
wykręcać ⟨-cić⟩ (się);
(*sprain*) skręcać ⟨-cić⟩

two [tuː] dwa; *cut in* ~ przecinać ⟨-ciąć⟩ na pół; '~**faced**
dwulicowy; '~**pence** ['tʌp-
əns] dwa pensy *pl*; '~**piece**
dwuczęściowy; '~**stroke** *mot.*
dwusuwowy; '~**way**: ~**way
radio** radiostacja *f* nada-
wczo-odbiorcza; ~**way traffic** ruch *m* dwukierunkowy

tycoon [taɪˈkuːn] magnat *m*

type [taɪp] **1.** typ *m*, rodzaj *m*;
print. druk *m*; *blood* ~ grupa
f krwi; *not my* ~ nie w moim
typie; **2.** pisać na maszynie /
komputerze; '~**script** maszynopis *m*; '~**writer** maszyna *f* do pisania

typhoon [taɪˈfuːn] tajfun *m*

typical ['tɪpɪkl] typowy

typist ['taɪpɪst] maszynistka
f

tyre ['taɪə] *esp. Brt.* opona *f*

U

ugly ['ʌglɪ] brzydki

ulcer ['ʌlsə] wrzód *m*

ultimate ['ʌltɪmət] ostateczny; *power*: najwyższy; '~**ly** w
końcu

ultimatum [ʌltɪˈmeɪtəm] (*pl
-tums, -ta* ⟨-tə⟩) ultimatum *n*

ultra... [ʌltrə] super...;
'~**sound** ultradźwięk *m*;
~**violet** ultrafioletowy

umbrella [ʌmˈbrelə] parasol
m

umpire ['ʌmpaɪə] *sp.* sędzia

umpteen [ʌmpˈtiːn] niezliczo-
na liczba

un... [ʌn] nie...; od...

un\|abashed [ʌnəˈbæʃt] nie
speszony; ~**able**: *be* ~**able
to do s.th.** nie móc ⟨z⟩robić
czegoś; ~**accountable** niewytłumaczalny

unanimous [juːˈnænɪməs]
jednogłośny

un\|approachable nieprzy-
stępny; ~**armed** nieuzbrojony; ~**attached** nie związany (*with z*); ~**attended** bez
opieki

unaware [ʌnəˈweə]: *be* ~ *of
s.th.* nie zdawać sobie sprawy z czegoś; ~**s** ⟨-z⟩: *catch or
take s.o.* ~**s** zaskakiwać
⟨-skoczyć⟩ kogoś

un\|balanced niezrówno-
ważony; ~**bearable** nie do
zniesienia; ~**believable** niewiarygodny; ~**bending**
nieustępliwy, nieugięty;
~**bias(s)ed** bezstronny,
neutralny; ~**born** nienaro-
dzony; ~**button** rozpiąć
⟨-piąć⟩; ~**called-for** nie na
miejscu; ~**certain** niepewny

uncle ['ʌŋkl] wuj *m*

un\|comfortable niewygod-
ny; ~**common** rzadki

~**concerned** [ʌnkən'sɜːnd] niezainteresowany; ~**conditional** bezwarunkowy; ~**conscious** nieprzytomny; ~**cork** odkorkować; ~**cover** odkry(wa)ć; ~**deniable** [ʌndɪ'naɪəbl] niezaprzeczalny

under ['ʌndə] **1.** *prp* pod; *circumstances, conditions, law, construction:* w; *age, amount:* poniżej; ~ *the sea* pod powierzchnią morza; **2.** *adv* pod wodę; pod spód; '~**carriage** *aer.* podwozie *n;* '~**cover** tajny; '~**dog** słabsza strona *f;* ~**done** niedopieczony; ~**estimate** [ʌr'estɪmeɪt] nie doceniać; ~**exposed** [ʌrɪk'spəʊzd] *phot.* niedoświetlony; ~**fed** niedożywiony; ~**go** (*-went, -gone*) przechodzić ⟨przejść⟩, podd(aw)ać się (czemuś); '~**ground 1.** podziemny (*a. fig.*); **2.** *Brt. London:* metro *n;* ~**lie** (*-lay, -lain*) znajdować się u podstaw (czegoś); '~**line** podkreślać ⟨-lić⟩; ~**mine** podkop(yw)ać; *fig.* osłabi(a)ć, zakłócać ⟨-cić⟩; ~**neath** [~'niːθ] **1.** *prp* pod; **2.** *adv* pod spód, pod spodem; '~**pants** *pl* majtki *pl* (męskie); '~**pass** przejście *n* podziemne; ~**privileged** żyjący w niedostatku; '~**shirt** *Am.* podkoszulek *m;* ~**staffed** odczuwający brak pracowni-

ków; ~**stand** (*-stood*) ⟨z⟩rozumieć; ~**standable** ⟨z⟩rozumiały; ~**standing 1.** wyrozumiały; **2.** zrozumienie *n; between nations:* porozumienie *n;* ~**statement** niedomówienie *n;* ~**take** (*-took, -taken*) *job* podejmować ⟨-djąć⟩; ~**taking** przedsięwzięcie *n;* ~**wear** bielizna *f;* '~**world** świat *m* przestępczy

un|deserved niezasłużony; ~**desirable** niepożądany; ~**do** (*-did, -done*) odwiązyw(ać); ~**doubted** niekwestionowany; ~**doubtedly** bez wątpienia; ~**dress** rozbierać ⟨-zebrać⟩ (się); ~**due** nadmierny; ~**earth** odkop(yw)ać; *fig.* odgrzeb(yw)ać; ~**easy** niespokojny

unemploy|ed 1. niezatrudniony; **2.** *the* ~*ed pl* bezrobotni *pl;* ~**ment** bezrobocie *n;* ~**ment benefit** *Brt.* zasiłek *m* dla bezrobotnych

un|ending [ʌn'endɪŋ] niekończący się; ~**equal** nierówny, niesprawiedliwy; ~**erring** [ʌn'ɜːrɪŋ] nieomylny; ~**even** nierówny; ~**eventful** spokojny, monotonny; ~**failing** niezawodny; ~**fair** niesprawiedliwy; ~**faithful** niewierny; ~**familiar** nieznany; nie zaznajomiony (*with z*); ~**fasten** rozpinać ⟨-piąć⟩; ~**favo(u)ra-**

ble niekorzystny; **~'feeling**
niezdury; **~'fold** rozwijać
⟨-winąć⟩; *fig.* st(aw)ać się
jasnym; **~foreseen** nieprzewidziany; **~forgettable** niezapomniany

unfortunate (*unlucky*) pechowy; (*in difficult situation*)
nieszczęśliwy; **~ly** niestety

un|'founded bezpodstawny;
~'friendly nieprzyjazny;
~'happy nieszczęśliwy; niezadowolony (*about* z);
~'harmed bez obrażeń,
cało; **~'healthy** niezdrowy,
szkodliwy dla zdrowia; (*not
well*) chory; *behaviour:* niezdrowy; **~'heard of** nie spo-
tykany; **~'hurt** bez obrażeń

unification [juːnɪfɪˈkeɪʃn]
zjednoczenie *n*

uniform [ˈjuːnɪfɔːm] **1.** jednolity; **2.** strój *m* roboczy; *mil.*
mundur *m*; *school:* mundu-
rek *m*

unify [ˈjuːnɪfaɪ] ⟨z⟩jednoczyć

unimagina|ble niewyo-
brażalny; **~tive** pozbawiony
wyobraźni

uninhabit|able nie nadający
się do zamieszkania; **~ed**
niezamieszkały

un|'inspired bez natchnienia,
~intelligible niezrozumiały;
~intentional niezamierzony

union [ˈjuːnjən] związek *m*;
pol. związek *m* zawodowy;
(*joining*) unia *f*; **'~ist**
związkowiec *m*; **2 Jack** flaga
Zjednoczonego Królestwa

Wielkiej Brytanii i Irlandii
Północnej

unique [juːˈniːk] niepowta-
rzalny, jedyny w swoim rodzaju; ograniczony (*to* do);
(*exceptional*) wyjątkowy,
znakomity

unit [ˈjuːnɪt] całość *f*; (*team*)
zespół *m*; *for measuring:* jednostka *f*; *furniture:* segment
m; *math.* jedność *f*; **~e**
[ˈ~naɪt] ⟨z⟩jednoczyć (się);
~ed zjednoczony; **the 2ed
States of America** Stany
Zjednoczone Ameryki; **~y**
[ˈ~əti] jedność *f*; (*union*) unia
f

univers|al [juːnɪˈvɜːsl] **1.**
powszechny; ogólny; **2.**
pojęcie *n* ogólne; **~e** [ˈ~vɜːs]
wszechświat *m*; (*world*) świat
m; **~ity** [ˈ~vɜːsəti] uniwersy-
tet *m*

un|'just niesprawiedliwy;
~kempt [ʌnˈkempt] zanied-
bany; **~'kind** niedobry,
okrutny; **~'known** nieznany;
~leaded [ʌnˈledɪd] bezołowiowy

unless [ənˈles] (*if not*) jeśli
nie; (*except when*) chyba że

unlike [ʌnˈlaɪk] niepodobny
(do), różny (od); *Bill,* **~ me,
lives here** Bill, w przeci-
wieństwie do mnie, mieszka
tutaj; **~ly** mało prawdopodobny

un|'limited nieograniczony;
~'load rozładow(yw)ać;
wyład(ow)ać (*from* z);

~**lock** otwierać ⟨-worzyć⟩ (kluczem); ~**lucky** pechowy; **be** ~**lucky** mieć pecha, nie mieć szczęścia; ~**manned** [ʌnˈmænd] bezzałogowy; ~**married** stanu wolnego; ~**mistakable** oczywisty, niewątpliwy; ~**moved** niewzruszony; ~**natural** nienaturalny; ~**noticed** nie zauważony; ~**obtrusive** nie rzucający się w oczy; ~**occupied** wolny; *house*: pusty; ~**pack** rozpakow(yw)ać (się); ~**pleasant** nieprzyjemny; ~**plug** wyłączać ⟨-czyć⟩ z sieci; ~**precedented** [~ˈpresidentid] bezprecedensowy; ~**predictable** nie do przewidzenia; *person*: nieobliczalny; ~**questionable** niezaprzeczalny; ~**ravel** [ʌnˈrævl] rozplat(yw)ać (się); *fig.* rozwikł(yw)ać; ~**real** dziwny, nie z tego świata; (*false*) sztuczny; ~**reasonable** nierozsądny; ~**reliable** nieodpowiedzialny; ~**rest** *pol.* niepokój *m*; ~**restrained** niekontrolowany; ~**roll** rozwijać ⟨-winąć⟩ (się); ~**ruly** [ʌnˈruːli] niezdyscyplinowany; *child*: nieposłuszny; ~**safe** zagrożony; (*dangerous*) niebezpieczny; ~**said**: **leave s.th.** ~**said** pomijać ⟨-minąć⟩ coś milczeniem; ~**satisfactory** niezadawalający; ~**savo(u)ry** odrażający;

~**screw** odkręcać ⟨-cić⟩; ~**settled** nieustabilizowany; (*restless*) rozkojarzony; *place*: niezamieszkały; *argument*: nierozstrzygnięty; ~**sightly** nieestetyczny, mało atrakcyjny; ~**skilled** niewykwalifikowany; ~**sociable** nietowarzyski; ~**sophisticated** prosty, niewyrafinowany; ~**sound** błędny, oparty na fałszywych przesłankach; *person*: umysłowo chory; *building*: niepewny; ~**speakable** (*awful*) okropny, straszny; ~**stable** niestabilny; (*not fixed*) luźny; *person*: niezrównoważony; ~**steady** niepewny, niepewnie idący / stojący; *hand etc.*: drżący; ~**stuck**: **come** ~**stuck** odklejać ⟨-leić⟩ się; *plan etc.*: ⟨za⟩kończyć się fiaskiem; ~**suitable** nieodpowiedni (*for* dla); ~**suspecting** niczego nie podejrzewający; ~**tangle** rozplat(yw)ać; ~**tapped** nie wykorzystany; ~**thinkable** nie do pomyślenia; ~**tie** rozwiąz(yw)ać **until** [ənˈtɪl] do; dopóki (nie); ~ **midnight** do północy; **we waited** ~ **they had left** czekaliśmy dopóki oni nie wyszli **un**~**timely** przedwczesny; (*not suitable*) nieodpowiedni; ~**tiring** niestrudzony; ~**told** niesamowity, nieprawdopodobny; ~**touched** nietknięty; ~**troubled** niezmą-

cony, niezakłócony; **~used
1.** [ʌn'juːzd] nieużywany; **2.**
[ʌn'juːst] nieprzyzwyczajony
(*to* do); **~usual** niezwykły; **~varying** niezmienny;
~veil odsłaniać ⟨-łonić⟩;
plans etc. ujawni(a)ć; **~well**
chory, niedysponowany; **~
'willing** niechętny; **be ~wil-
ling to do s.th.** nie wykazy-
wać chęci do zrobienia czegoś; **~wind (-wound)** v/i
odprężyć się; v/t odwijać
⟨-winąć⟩; **~'wrap** rozpa-
kow(yw)ać

up [ʌp] **1.** *adv movement:* w
górę; *position:* w górze; (*on
the wall*) na ścianie; **2.** *prp
with movement:* po; *position:* na; **~ the river** w górę
rzeki; **~ to run, walk etc.:** do;
be ~ to level, standard etc.
osiągać ⟨-gnąć⟩; *something
bad* knuć; **it's ~ to you** to
zależy od ciebie; **be I feel ~ to
doing s.th.** mieć ochotę coś
⟨z⟩robić; **3.** *adj* (*not in
bed*) na nogach; *road:* w na-
prawie; *house:* wybudowa-
ny; *wind:* silny; **~ and about**
w pełni sił (po chorobie); **be
~ three points** *sp.* mieć prze-
wagę trzech punktów;
what's ~? to jest grane? F;
4. ~s and downs *pl* wzloty *pl*
i upadki *pl*

'up|bringing wychowanie *n*;
~'date *information* ⟨z⟩ak-
tualizować; *army* ⟨z⟩moder-
nizować; **~heaval** [ʌp'hiːvl]

zamieszanie *n*; *social:*
przewrót *m*; **~'hill** *adv
move:* w górę; *adj* mozolny,
ciężki; **~'hold (-held)** *law
etc.* przestrzegać; **~holster-
ed** [ʌp'həʊlstəd] tapicero-
wany

upon [ə'pɒn] na; (*after:*) po;
crisis ~ crisis kryzys za kry-
zysem

upper [ʌpə] górny; (*more important, powerful etc.*)
wyższy; **~ case** *letter:* duży;
~ class arystokracja *f*;
'~most *adj* najwyższy; *adv*
najwyżej

'up|right wyprostowany; *ap-
pliance:* stojący, pionowy;
fig. prawy, uczciwy; **~'rising**
powstanie *n*; **~set** [ʌp'set] **1.**
(*-set*) wytrącać ⟨-cić⟩ z
równowagi; *plan etc.* ⟨z⟩de-
zorganizować; (*overturn*)
przewracać ⟨-rócić⟩; **2.** niespokojny, wytrącony z
równowagi; *stomach:* rozstrojony; **'~side:** **~side down**
do góry nogami; **~'stairs 1.**
movement: na górę (schoda-
mi); *position:* na górze; **2.**
(*upper floors*) góra *f*; **'~start**
nowicjusz *m*; **'~stream** w
górę rzeki; **~-to-'date** nowoczesny; *person:* zorIento-
wany; **~ward(s)** ['~wəd(z)] w
górę; **~ward(s) of** ponad

urban ['ɜːbən] miejski

urge [ɜːdʒ] **1.** nalegać, domagać się (*s.o. to do s.th.* by
ktoś coś zrobił); (*advise*) za-

lecać ⟨-cić⟩; *horse etc.* ponaglać ⟨-lić⟩; **~ on** zachęcać ⟨-cić⟩; **2.** żądza *f;* **'~nt** pilny

urin|ate ['juərɪneɪt] odd(aw)ać mocz; **~e** ['~rɪn] mocz *m*

urn [ɜːn] urna *f; tea:* (duży) termos *m*

us [ʌs, əs] nas, nam, nami

usage ['juːsɪdʒ] użycie *n;* (*meaning*) znaczenie *n; energy:* wykorzystanie *n*

use 1. [juːs] wykorzystanie *n; ling.* użycie *n;* **have no ~** nie mieć zastosowania; **be of ~** przyd(aw)ać się; **in ~** w użyciu; **it's no ~** nie ma sensu; **2.** [~z] uży(wa)ć; (*exploit*) wykorzyst(yw)ać; **~ up** zuży(wa)ć

used¹ [juːzd] używany

used² [juːst] **be ~ to** (*doing*) *s.th.* być przyzwyczajonym do (robienia) czegoś; **get ~ to** *s.th.* przyzwyczajać ⟨-czaić⟩ się do czegoś

used³ [juːst]: *I* **~ to live here** kiedyś tu mieszkałem

use|ful ['juːsfʊl] użyteczny; **'~less** bezużyteczny

user ['juːzə] użytkownik *m;* **~'friendly** przyjazny

usual ['juːʒl] zwyczajny; **as ~** jak zwykle; **'~∠ly** [~ʒəlɪ] zwykle

utili|ty [juːˈtɪlətɪ] przydatność *f; public:* usługa *f* komunalna; **~ze** [juːˈtɪlaɪz] wykorzyst(yw)ać

utter ['ʌtə] **1.** *word* wypowiadać ⟨-wiedzieć⟩; *sound* wyd(aw)ać; **2.** całkowity, zupełny; **~ance** ['~rəns] wypowiedź *f;* **'~ly** całkowicie, zupełnie

U-turn ['juːtɜːn] *mot.* zawrócenie *n; fig.* zwrot *m* o 180 stopni

V

vacan|cy ['veɪkənsɪ] wolne stanowisko *n; hotel:* wolne miejsce *n,* wolny pokój *m;* **'~t** wolny; *look, mind etc.:* pusty

vacation [vəˈkeɪʃn] *usu. Brt.* wakacje *pl; jur.* przerwa *f* wakacyjna; *usu. Am.* urlop *m;* **~er** wczasowicz *m*

vacuum ['vækjʊəm] próżnia *f;* **~ cleaner** odkurzacz *m*

vagina [vəˈdʒaɪnə] *anat.* pochwa *f*

vague [veɪɡ] niejasny, niewyraźny

vain [veɪn] *attempt:* bezowocny, daremny; *person:* próżny; **in ~** na próżno

valid ['vælɪd] słuszny; *ticket etc.:* ważny

valley ['vælɪ] dolina *f*

valu|able ['væljʊəbl] **1.** wartościowy; **2.** *pl* kosztowności *pl;* **~ation** [~'eɪʃn] wycena *f; writing etc.:* ocena *f*

value ['væljuː] **1.** wartość f; *it's good* ~ to jest warte swojej ceny; **2.** cenić; (*suggest price*) wyceni(a)ć; '~**added tax** (*abbr. VAT*) VAT, podatek m od wartości dodanej; '~**less** bezwartościowy

valve [vælv] zawór m

van [væn] furgonetka f; *Brt. rail.* wagon m kryty

vandal ['vændl] wandal m

vanilla [və'nɪlə] wanilia f

vanish ['vænɪʃ] znikać ⟨-knąć⟩

vanity ['vænəti] próżność f

vapo(u)r ['veɪpə] (*steam*) para f

vari|able ['veərɪəbl] **1.** zmienny; **2.** zmienna f; '~**ance: be at** ~**ance with s.th.** stać w sprzeczności z czymś; ~**ation** [~'eɪʃn] wariacja f (*a. mus.*); (*change*) odchylenie n

varied ['veərɪd] różnorodny

variety [və'raɪəti] różnorodność f; (*sort*) odmiana f; *theatre etc.*: teatr m rozmaitości, rewia f; **a** ~ **of** ... różnorodne ...

various ['veərɪəs] różny; (*varied*) różnorodny

varnish ['vɑːnɪʃ] **1.** pokost m; **2.** pokostować

vary ['veərɪ] różnić się; zmieni(a)ć się (**with** z)

vase [vɑːz] wazon m

vast [vɑːst] ogromny

vault¹ [~] **1.** skarbiec m; (*tomb*) grobowiec m

vault² [~] **1.** skok m; **2.** (*a.* ~

over) przeskakiwać przez

veal [viːl] cielęcina f

vegeta|ble ['vedʒtəbl] warzywo n; (*plant*) roślina f; ~**rian** [~ɪ'teərɪən] **1.** wegetarianin m (-rianka f); **2.** wegetariański

vehicle ['vɪəkl] pojazd m

veil [veɪl] **1.** welon m; *fig.* zasłona f; **2.** ukry(wa)ć

vein [veɪn] żyła f; *on leaf:* żyłka f

velocity [vɪ'lɒsəti] prędkość f

velvet ['velvɪt] aksamit m

vend|ing machine ['vendɪŋ] automat m; '~**or** [~'dɔː] sprzedawca m (uliczny); *jur.* sprzedający

vent [vent] **1.** wywietrznik m, otwór m wentylacyjny; *give* ~ *to feelings* ⟨za⟩demonstrować; *sound* wyd(aw)ać; **2.** *feelings* d(aw)ać upust (*czemuś* **on** na)

ventilat|e ['ventɪleɪt] ⟨wy⟩wietrzyć; *feelings* ⟨za⟩demonstrować; ~**ion** [~'leɪʃn] wentylacja f; '~**or** [~'leɪtə] wentylator m

venture ['ventʃə] **1.** przedsięwzięcie n; *business:* spekulacja f; **2.** (*take a risk*) odważyć się (**into** na); *opinion* zaryzykować; ~ *out* odważyć się wyjść

verb [vɜːb] *gr.* czasownik m; '~**al** słowny

verdict ['vɜːdɪkt] *jur.* wyrok m; *fig.* werdykt m

verge [vɜːdʒ] **1.** *road:* pobocze n; **on the** ~ **of** blisko, na

verify

granicy; **2.** ~ **on** graniczyć z

verify ['verɪfaɪ] sprawdzać ‹-dzić›

versatile ['vɜːsətaɪl] wszechstronny; *tool etc.*: universalny

vers|e [vɜːs] poezja *f*; (*stanza*) strofa *f*, zwrotka *f*; *Bible*: werset *m*; **~[s]n]** wersja *f*

versus ['vɜːsəs] a; *jur.*, *sp.* przeciw

vertical ['vɜːtɪkl] **1.** pionowy; **2. *the* ~** pion

very ['verɪ] **1.** *adv* bardzo; *before sup*: absolutnie; ***the* ~ *best*** absolutnie najlepszy; ***not* ~** nie zupełnie, nie bardzo; **2.** *adj* sam; ***from the ~ beginning*** od samego początku; ***this* ~ *spot*** właśnie to miejsce

vessel ['vesl] (*ship*) okręt *m*; (*container*) naczynie *n* (*a. anat.*, *bot.*)

vest [vest] *Brt.* podkoszulek *m*; *Am.* kamizelka *f*

veteran ['vetərən] weteran *m*

veterinar|ian [vetərə'neərɪən] *Am.*, **~y surgeon** ['~ɪnərɪ] *Brt.* weterynarz *m*

veto ['viːtəʊ] **1.** (*pl -toes*) weto *n*; **2.** sprzeciwia(ć) się (czemuś, komuś)

via ['vaɪə] przez

viable ['vaɪəbl] *biol.* zdolny do życia; *econ.* opłacalny

vibrate [vaɪ'breɪt] wibrować; **~ion** ['~ʃn] wibracja *f*

vicar ['vɪkə] pastor *m*; **~age** ['~rɪdʒ] plebania *f*

vice¹ [vaɪs] imadło *n*

vice² [~] zło *n*; (*weakness*) słabość *f*

vice- [vaɪs] wice, vice

vice versa [vaɪsɪ'vɜːsə] odwrotnie

vicinity [vɪ'sɪnɪtɪ] pobliże *n*, bliskość *f*

victim ['vɪktɪm] ofiara *f*

victor ['vɪktə] zwycięzca *m*; **~ious** [~'tɔːrɪəs] zwycięski; **~y** ['~tərɪ] zwycięstwo *n*

video ['vɪdɪəʊ] **1.** (*technika f*) video *n*; video(kaseta *f*) *n*; (*machine*) magnetowid *m*; **2.** nagr(yw)ać na video; **'~tape 1.** taśma *f* video; **2.** → **video** 2

view [vjuː] **1.** zapatrywać się na; *house*, *film etc.* oglądać ‹obejrzeć›; **2.** pogląd *m* (**on** na temat); widok *m*; **in ~ of s.th.** biorąc pod uwagę coś; **in my ~** moim zdaniem; **'~er** telewidz *m*; *at exhibition etc.*: oglądający; *for slides*: przeglądarka *f*

vigo|rous ['vɪgərəs] energiczny; **'~(u)r** energia *f*

village ['vɪlɪdʒ] wioska *f*; **'~r** mieszkaniec *m* wsi

villain ['vɪlən] łotr *m*, łajdak *m*; *in books*, *films*: czarny charakter *m*

vine [vaɪn] pnącze *n*; (*grape*) winorośl *f*

vinegar ['vɪnɪgə] ocet *m*

violate ['vaɪəleɪt] *law*, *agreement etc.* naruszać ‹-szyć›; *promise* ‹z›łamać; *peace*

zakłóca|ć ⟨-cić⟩; *tomb* ⟨z⟩bezcześcić; *woman form.* ⟨z⟩gwałcić; **~ion** ⟨~'leɪʃn⟩ *law, agreement etc.*: naruszanie ⟨z⟩ *promise*: ⟨z⟩łamanie *n*; *tomb*: ⟨z⟩bezczeszczenie *n*

violen|ce ['vaɪələns] przemoc *f*; *(force)* gwałtowność *f*; **~t** gwałtowny

violet ['vaɪələt] **1.** fiołek *m*; *colour*: fiolet *m*; **2.** fioletowy

violin [vaɪə'lɪn] skrzypce *pl*

virgin ['vɜːdʒɪn] **1.** dziewica *f*; **2.** dziewiczy

viril|e ['vɪraɪl] męski; **~ity** [~'rɪləti] męskość *f*

virtual ['vɜːtʃuəl] faktyczny; **~ly** faktycznie

virtue ['vɜːtʃuː] cnota *f*; *(advantage)* zaleta *f*; **by ~e of** z uwagi na; **~ous** [~'tʃuəs] cnotliwy

virus ['vaɪərəs] wirus *m*

visa ['viːzə] wiza *f*

vise [vaɪs] *Am.* imadło *n*

visib|ility [vɪzə'bɪlətɪ] widoczność *f*; **~le** widoczny

vision ['vɪʒn] wizja *f*, obraz *m* (*a. TV*); *(sight)* wzrok *m*, zdolność *f* widzenia; *(view)* widok *m*

visit ['vɪzɪt] **1.** odwiedzać ⟨-dzić⟩; **2.** odwiedziny *pl*; *(stay)* pobyt *m*; **pay s.o. a ~** przychodzić ⟨przyjść⟩ do kogoś z wizytą; **~ing hours** *pl* godziny *pl* przyjęć; **~or** gość *m* (**to** w)

visual ['vɪʒuəl] wzrokowy,

wizualny; **~ aids** pomoce *pl* wizualne (do nauczania); **~ize** wyobrazić sobie

vital ['vaɪtl] ważny, istotny; *(energetic)* energiczny, dynamiczny; **~ity** [~'tælətɪ] energia *f*, dynamika *f*

vitamin ['vɪtəmɪn] witamina *f*

vivid ['vɪvɪd] *colour, memories etc.*: żywy

vocabulary [və'kæbjʊlərɪ] słownictwo *n*

vocal ['vəʊkl] wyrażający otwarcie swoje poglądy (**on** na temat); *mus.* wokalny; **~s** *pl* śpiew *m*

vocation [vəʊ'keɪʃn] powołanie *n* (**for** do); **~al** zawodowy

vogue [vəʊg] moda *f*

voice [vɔɪs] **1.** głos *m*; *gr.* strona *f*; **2.** *opinion* wyrażać ⟨-razić⟩

void [vɔɪd] **1.** (*a.* **null and ~**) *jur.* nieważny; **~ of s.th.** pozbawiony czegoś; **2.** pustka *f*, próżnia *f*; *(abyss)* przepaść *f*

volcano [vɒl'keɪnəʊ] (*pl* **-noes, -nos**) wulkan *m*

volley ['vɒlɪ] salwa *f*; *fig. of questions etc.*: grad *m*, deszcz *m*; *sp.* wolej *m*; **~ball** siatkówka *f*

volt [vəʊlt] *electr.* wolt *m*; **~age** napięcie *n*

volume ['vɒljuːm] tom *m*; *phys.* objętość *f*; *trade etc.*: wielkość *f*; *radio etc.*: głośność *f*, natężenie *n* głosu

volunt|ary ['vɒləntərɪ] ochotniczy; **~eer** [~'tɪə] **1.** ochotnik *m* (-niczka *f*); **2.** zgłaszać ⟨-łosić⟩ się na ochotnika (**for** do)

vomit ['vɒmɪt] **1.** ⟨z⟩wymiotować; **2.** wymioty *pl*

vote [vəʊt] **1.** głosowanie *n*; (*choice made*) głos *m*; (*legal right*) prawo *n* głosu; **2.** głosować (**for** na, **against** przeciwko, **on** w sprawie);

'**~r** wyborca *m*

vow [vaʊ] **1.** przysięga *f*; *eccl.* ślub *m*; **2.** przysięgać ⟨-siąc⟩

vowel ['vaʊəl] samogłoska *f*

voyage ['vɔɪdʒ] rejs *m*; *space*: lot *m*

vulgar ['vʌlgə] wulgarny

vulnerable ['vʌlnərəbl] narażony (**to** na), podatny (**to** na)

vulture ['vʌltʃə] sęp *m*

W

wade [weɪd] brodzić

wafer ['weɪfə] wafel *m*; *eccl.* hostia *f*

waffle ['wɒfl] gofr *m*

wag [wæg] *v/t* ⟨po⟩machać; *dog*: merdać; *v/i* kiwać się

wage¹ [weɪdʒ] *usu. pl* zarobek *m*, tygodniówka *f* F

wage² [~] *war* prowadzić

wag(g)on ['wægən] wóz *m*; *Am.* wózek *m*; *Brt. rail.* wagon (towarowy)

waist [weɪst] talia *f*; **~coat** ['weɪskəʊt] *esp. Brt.* kamizelka *f*; '**~line** obwód *m* w pasie

wait [weɪt] **1.** ⟨po⟩czekać (**for** na); **~ at** (*Am.* **on**) **table** obsługiwać; **~ on** s.o. obsługiwać ⟨-łużyć⟩ kogoś; **I can't ~, I can hardly ~** nie mogę się doczekać; **2.** czekanie *n*, oczekiwanie *n*; '**~er** kelner *m*; '**~ing list** lista *f* oczekujących; '**~ing-room** poczekalnia *f*; '**~ress** ['~trɪs]

kelnerka *f*

wake [weɪk] (**woke** *or* **waked**, **woken** *or* **waked**) (*a.* **~ up**) ⟨o⟩budzić (się)

walk [wɔ:k] **1.** *v/i* chodzić, iść ⟨pójść⟩ (pieszo); *v/t road etc.* chodzić po, iść ⟨pójść⟩ po; *dog* wyprowadzać ⟨-dzić⟩ na spacer; *person* ⟨za⟩prowadzić; **~ away from** porzucać ⟨-cić⟩, zostawi(a)ć; **~ away with** (łatwo) zdoby(wa)ć; **~ in** wchodzić ⟨wejść⟩; **~ out** wychodzić ⟨wyjść⟩; (*strike*) ⟨za⟩strajkować; **~ out on** s.o. F opuszczać ⟨opuścić⟩ kogoś; **2.** (*not running*) chód *m*; (*manner*) krok *m*; (*stroll*) spacer *m*; (*path*) ścieżka *f*; (*route*) szlak *m*, trasa *f* spacerowa; '**~er** piechur *m*

'**walking distance**: *it's within ~ distance* można tam dojść pieszo; **~ stick** laska *f* '**walk|out** strajk *m*; '**~over** łatwe zwycięstwo *n*

wall [wɔːl] ściana *f*; *outside*: mur *m*

wallet ['wɒlɪt] portfel *m*

walnut ['wɔːlnʌt] orzech *m* włoski

waltz [wɔːls] **1.** walc *m*; **2.** ⟨za⟩tańczyć walca (**with** z)

wand [wɒnd] różdżka *f* (cza-rodziejska)

wander ['wɒndə] wędrować; (*stray*) błądzić (*a. fig.*)

want [wɒt] *v/i* chcieć; ~ **to do s.th.** chcieć coś ⟨z⟩robić; ~ **s.o. to do s.th.** chcieć żeby ktoś coś ⟨z⟩robił; *v/t* pragnąć (seksualnie); (*need*) potrzebować, poszukiwać; **2.** brak *m* (**of s.th.** czegoś); *pl* żądania *pl*; **for ~ of** z / wobec braku (czegoś); ~**ed** ['~ɪd] poszukiwany

war [wɔː] wojna *f*

ward [wɔːd] **1.** oddział *m*; **2.** ~ **off** nie dopuszczać ⟨-puścić⟩

wardrobe ['wɔːdrəub] szafa *f*; (*clothing*) ubiory *pl*; *thea.* garderoba *f*

ware [weə] *usu.* in compounds; wyroby *pl*, towar *m*; '**~house** magazyn *m*

war|fare ['wɔːfeə] działania *pl* wojenne; '**~head** mil. głowica *f*

warm [wɔːm] **1.** ciepły; **are you ~?** jest ci ciepło?; **2.** *v/t* ogrz(ew)ać; *fig.* nab(ie)rać sympatii (**to** do); ~ **up** *v/t* food podgrz(ew)ać; *person*

rozgrz(ew)ać; *v/i* roz-grz(ew)ać się; ~**th** [~θ] ciepło *n*; ~'**up** rozgrzewka *f*

warn [wɔːn] ostrzegać ⟨-rzec⟩ (**of, against** przed); ~**ing** ostrzeżenie *n*; **2.** ostrzegaw-czy

warrant ['wɒrənt] **1.** nakaz *m*; **2.** usprawiedliwi(a)ć, uza-sadni(a)ć; '**~y** gwarancja *f*

wary ['weərɪ] ostrożny (**of s.th.** wobec czegoś)

was [wɒz, wəz] *1. and 3. sg* past of **be**: **I** ~ (ja) byłem, byłam; **he** ~ (on) był; **she** ~ (ona) była; **it** ~ (ono) było, to było

wash [wɒʃ] **1.** *v/t* ⟨u⟩myć; *clothes* ⟨wy⟩prać; *v/i* ⟨u⟩myć się; *in river, sea etc.*: płynąć, spływać ⟨-łynąć⟩; ~ **away** flood etc.: zmy(wa)ć; ~ **down** food popi(ja)ć (**with s.th.** czymś); ~ **up** *Brt.* zmy(wa)ć; *Am.* in bathroom: ⟨u⟩myć się; *sea etc.*: wyrzu-cać ⟨-cić⟩ (na brzeg); **2.** pra-nie *n*; **have a ~** ⟨u⟩myć się; '**~able** nadający się do pra-nia; '**~basin**, *Am.* '**~bowl** umywalka *f*; '**~cloth** *Am.* ścierka *f* do twarzy; '**~er** F pralka *f*; *person*: praczka *f*; *tech.* uszczelka *f*, podkład-ka *f*; '**~ing** pranie *n*; ~**ing machine** pralka *f*; '**~ing powder** proszek *m* do pra-nia; ~**ing-up** zmywanie *n* (naczyń)

wasp [wɒsp] osa *f*

waste [weɪst] **1.** strata *f*; (*misuse*) marnotrawstwo *n*; (*material*) odpady *pl*; (*land*) nieużytki *pl*; *pl* pustkowie *n*; **2.** ⟨s⟩tracić, ⟨z⟩marnować; ~ *away* usychać ⟨uschnąć⟩; **3.** *material*: odpadowy; *land etc.*: nie używany; '~d niepotrzebny; *person*: zmarnowany; '~ful rozrzutny; ~**paper** makulatura *f*; '~**paper basket** kosz *m* na śmieci

watch [wɒtʃ] **1.** zegarek *m*; (*guards*) warta *f*; **2.** obserwować; (*follow*) śledzić; *TV, match etc.* oglądać ⟨-dnąć⟩; (*look after*) opiekować się (czymś); (*keep an eye on*) uważać na; ~ (*out*) *for s.th.* uważać na coś; ~ *out* F uważaj!; ~ *out!* uważaj!; ~ *over s.o.* opiekować się kimś; '~**dog** pies *m* podwórzowy; *fig.* instancja *f* kontrolna; '~**ful** uważny; '~**man** (*pl* -**men**) dozorca *m*

water ['wɔːtə] **1.** woda *f*; **2.** *v/t plant* podl(ew)ać; *horse etc.* ⟨na⟩poić; *v/i mouth*: ślinić się; *eyes*: łzawić; ~-*down* roz cieńczać ⟨-czyć⟩ (wodą), rozwadniać ⟨-wodnić⟩ (*a. fig.*); ~ **closet** toaleta *f*; '~-**col·o(u)r** akwarela *f*; '~**fall** wo dospad *m*

watering can ['wɔːtərɪŋ] ko newka *f*

water·| [pour] poziom *m* wody; '~**melon** arbuz *m*; '~**proof**, '~**tight** wodoszczelny; *fig.*

sprawdzony; '~**way** droga *f* wodna; '~**works** *sg*, *pl* wo dociągi *pl*

watt [wɒt] *electr.* wat *m*

wave [weɪv] **1.** fala *f*; *hand*: machnięcie *n*; **2.** machać ⟨-chnąć⟩; *flag*: powiewać; *hair, grass*: falować; ~ *s.th. aside* zby(wa)ć coś machnięciem ręki; ~ *s.o. away* od ganiać ⟨-gonić⟩ kogoś; ~ *to / at s.o.* ⟨po⟩machać do ko goś; '~**length** *phys.* długość *f* fali

wavy ['weɪvɪ] falisty

wax [wæks] **1.** wosk *m*; **2.** ⟨po⟩woskować

way [weɪ] **1.** (*manner*, *method*) sposób *m*; *pl* zwyczaje *pl*; (*skill*) talent *m*, dar *m* (*with* do); *route*: droga *f*; *direction*: kierunek *m*; *a long* ~ daleko; *be in the* ~ stać na drodze, przeszkadzać; *by the* ~ przy okazji; *by* ~ *of* jako, tytułem; (*via*) przez; *divide s.th. four* ~*s* dzielić coś na cztery części; *give* ~ ustępować ⟨-tąpić⟩; *mot.* da(wa)ć pierwszeństwo (*to s.th.* cze muś); *go the other* ~ iść ⟨pójść⟩ w drugą stronę; *have one's* (*own*) ~ ⟨z⟩robić po swojemu; *in a* ~ w pewien sposób; *lead the* ~ ⟨po⟩pro wadzić, pokaz(yw)ać drogę; *lose one's* ~ ⟨z⟩gubić się; *make* ~ uda(wa)ć się (*to* do); zwalniać ⟨zwolnić⟩ miejsce (*for* dla); *the other* ~ *round* odwrotnie; **this** ~ tak, w ten sposób; (*in this direction*) tędy; **under** ~ w trakcie (realizacji); ~ in wejście *n*; ~ **of life** sposób *m* życia; ~ **out** wyjście *n*; 2. **the** ~ (*how*) jak; tak

we [wiː, wɪ] my

weak [wiːk] słaby; **'~en** *v/t* osłabi(a)ć; *v/i* ⟨o⟩słabnąć; **'~ness** słabość *f*

wealth [welθ] bogactwo *n*; **'~y** zamożny

weapon ['wepən] broń *f*

wear [weə] 1. (**wore, worn**) *v/t* nosić; *hair, beard* mieć; *v/i* well, badly: nosić się; ~ **away** steps, grass: wycierać ⟨wytrzeć⟩ (się); ~ **down** shoes, teeth: ścierać ⟨zetrzeć⟩ (się); person osłabi(a)ć; ~ **off** pain etc.: mijać ⟨minąć⟩; ~ **out** shoes: zuży(wa)ć (się); person wykańczać ⟨-kończyć⟩; 2. ubranie *n*; (*damage*) zużycie *n*; ~ **and tear** zużycie *n*

weary ['wɪərɪ] wyczerpany (**of** *s.th.* czymś)

weather ['weðə] pogoda *f*; '~-**beaten** ogorzały; *building:* naruszony zębem czasu; ~ **forecast** prognoza *f* pogody

weave [wiːv] (**wove, woven**) ⟨u⟩tkać

web [web] pajęczyna *f*; **~bed** *zo.* płetwiasty

wedding ['wedɪŋ] ślub *m*; (*party*) wesele *n*; ~ **ring** obrączka *f*

wedge [wedʒ] 1. klin *m*; 2. zaklinować

Wednesday ['wenzdɪ] środa *f*

weed [wiːd] 1. chwast *m*; 2. plewić; ~ **out** ⟨wy⟩eliminować

week [wiːk] tydzień *m*; '~**day** dzień *m* powszedni; '~**ly** 1. co tydzień, raz na tydzień; 2. cotygodniowy; 3. tygodnik *m*

weep [wiːp] (**wept**) płakać

weigh [weɪ] ⟨z⟩ważyć; *fig.* ⟨prze⟩analizować

weight [weɪt] 1. ciężar *m*; *metal:* ciężarek *m*; 2. ~ (**down**) obciążać ⟨-żyć⟩; **put on** or **gain** ~ ⟨przy⟩tyć; **lose** ~ ⟨s⟩chudnąć; '~**less** nieważki, pozbawiony ciężaru; '~**lifting** *sp.* podnoszenie *n* ciężarów

weird [wɪəd] dziwaczny

welcome ['welkəm] 1. powitanie *n*; 2. ⟨po⟩witać; (*invite*) mile widzieć; (**you are**) ~ nie ma za co; ~ **to** witamy w; 3. mile widziany, miły

weld [weld] ⟨ze⟩spawać

welfare ['welfeə] dobro *n*; (*state help*) opieka *f* społeczna; ~ **state** państwo *n* opiekuńcze; ~ **work** praca *f* socjalna

well¹ [wel] studnia *f*; *tech.* szyb *m* (*a.* naftowy)

well² [wel] [~] 1. *adv* dobrze; **as** ~ również; **as** ~ **as** jak również; 2. *adj* zdrowy; **be** or **feel** ~ czuć się dobrze; **get**

~ **soon!** szybko wracaj do zdrowia; **3.** *int* no; no więc; **very** ~ **then** w porządku; ~**'balanced** zrównoważony; ~**'being** dobro *n*; ~**'earned** zasłużony

well-'known znany; ~**'mannered** dobrze wychowany; ~**'off** zamożny, bogaty; ~**'read** oczytany; ~**'timed** w samą porę; ~**to-'do** zamożny; ~**'worn** wytarty; *fig.* oklepany

went [went] *past of* **go 2**

wept [wept] *past and pp of* **weep**

were [wɜː] *pl and 2. sg past of* **be**

west [west] **1.** zachód *m*; **2.** zachodni; **3.** na zachód; '~**erly** zachodni; '~**ern 1.** zachodni; **2.** (*film*) western *m*; ~**ward(s)** ['~wəd(z)] na zachód

wet [wet] **1.** mokry; *fish*: świeży; ~ **paint** świeżo malowane; ~ **through** przemoczony; **2.** (*wet or* **wetted**) ⟨z⟩moczyć

whale [weɪl] wieloryb *m*

what [wɒt] **1.** co; jaki; ~ **films do you like?** jakie filmy lubisz?; ~ **about ...?** może ...?; ~ **for?** po co?; **so** ~**?** no to co?; ~ co-kolwiek; **2.** co (do licha)

wheat [wiːt] pszenica *f*

wheel [wiːl] **1.** koło *n*; *mot.* kierownica *f*; *pl* F wóz *m*, cztery kółka *pl* F; **2.** (*push*)

⟨po⟩pchać; (*move*) sunąć łukiem; '~**chair** wózek *m* inwalidzki

when [wen] **1.** kiedy; ~ **did it happen?** kiedy to się stało?; **2.** kiedy, gdy; *he was two* ~ **she died** miał dwa lata kiedy / gdy ona zmarła; ~**'ever** (*any time*) kiedykolwiek; (*every time*) kiedy tylko

where [weə] gdzie; ~ **are you from?** skąd jesteś?; ~ **to?** dokąd?; ~ **are you going?** dokąd idziesz?; ~**'abouts 1.** [weərə'baʊts] gdzież; **2.** ['weərəbaʊts] miejsce *n* pobytu; ~**as** [weər'æz] podczas gdy

wherever [weər'evə] gdzie-kolwiek

whether ['weðə] czy

which [wɪtʃ] **1.** który; ~ **book would you like?** którą książkę chciałbyś?; **2.** co; *she said she was forty, which was a lie* powiedziała, że ma czterdzieści lat, co nie było prawdą; ~**'ever** którykolwiek

while [waɪl] **1.** podczas gdy, w czasie gdy; (*though*) chociaż; **2.** chwila *f*; *for a* ~ przez jakiś czas

whiskers ['wɪskəz] *pl zo.* wąsy *pl*; *man's*: bokobrody *pl*

whisper ['wɪspə] **1.** szeptać ⟨-pnąć⟩; **2.** szept *m*

whistle ['wɪsl] **1.** gwizdać ⟨-dnąć⟩; **2.** gwizd *m*; *policeman's*: gwizdek *m*

white [waɪt] **1.** biały; *go ~* ⟨po⟩siwieć; *(pale)* ⟨po⟩blednąć; **2.** biel *f*; *egg:* białko *n*; *person:* biały *m*; *pl* biali *pl*; **~ coffee** kawa *f* z mlekiem; **~ hot** rozgrzany do białości; '**~n** ⟨wy⟩bielić; '**~wash 1.** wapno *n*; *fig.* mydlenie *n* oczu; **2.** ⟨po⟩bielić; *fig.* maskować, wybielać

who [huː, hʊ] **1.** kto; **~** *did this?* kto to zrobił?; **2.** który; *the only person ~ has class* jedyna osoba, która ma dużą klasę

whoever [huːˈevə] **1.** ktokolwiek; **2.** kto (do licha), któż to

whole [həʊl] **1.** *adj* cały; **2.** *adv* w całości; *a ~ new style* całkiem nowy styl; **3.** *s* całość *f*; *the ~ of Africa* cała Afryka; *on the ~* ogólnie mówiąc; **~foods** *pl* zdrowa żywność *f*; **~'hearted** *support etc.*: pełny; **~sale** hurt *m*; **~sale dealer** → '**~saler** hurtownik *m*; '**~some** zdrowy

wholly [ˈhəʊlɪ] całkowicie

whom [huːm] kto; kogo, komu, kim; *for ~* dla kogo; *to ~* komu; *with ~* z kim; *to ~* któremu, której, którym; *the man ~ I thanked* mężczyzna, któremu dziękowałem

whose [huːz] czyj

why [waɪ] dlaczego; *that's ~* dlatego

wicked [ˈwɪkɪd] paskudny, zły

wide [waɪd] **1.** *adj* szeroki; *eye:* szeroko otwarty; *experience:* duży; **2.** *adv* szeroko; *~ awake* całkowicie rozbudzony; '**~ly** *smile etc.*: szeroko; '**~n** poszerzać ⟨-rzyć⟩; **~'open** szeroko otwarty; '**~spread** rozpowszechniony

widow [ˈwɪdəʊ] wdowa *f*; '**~ed** owdowiały; '**~er** wdowiec *m*

width [wɪdθ] szerokość *f*

wife [waɪf] (*pl* **wives** [**~**vz]) żona *f*

wig [wɪg] peruka *f*

wild [waɪld] **1.** dziki; *(angry)* wściekły; *run ~* zdziczeć; *the ~s* pustkowie *n*; *in the ~* na wolności; '**~cat** żbik *m*; '**~erness** [ˈwɪldənɪs] dzicz *f*; '**~life** przyroda *f*

wilful [ˈwɪlfʊl] *action*: świadomy, celowy; *person*: stanowczy

will [wɪl] **1.** wola *f*; *jur.* testament *m*; **2.** *v/aux (past would)* future tenses: będę, będziesz, będzie itd.; *unemployment ~ continue to rise* bezrobocie będzie nadal rosnąć; *~ you have lunch with us?* czy zjesz z nami obiad?; *~ you help me?* pomożesz mi?; '**~ing:** *we're ~ing to help you* jesteśmy gotowi ci pomóc; '**~ingly** chętnie

willow [ˈwɪləʊ] *bot.* wierzba *f*

willpower siła *f* woli

win [wɪn] **1.** *(won)* wygr(yw)ać; *prize etc.* zdoby(wa)ć; **2.** wygrana *f*, zwycięstwo *n*

wind¹ [wɪnd] wiatr *m*; *(breath)* oddech *m*; F *in stomach*: gazy *pl*; F *(meaningless talk)* bzdury *pl* F

wind² [waɪnd] **(wound)** *road, river*: wić się; *round an object*: owijać ⟨owinąć⟩ **(round** dookoła**)**; *clock* nakręcać ⟨-cić⟩; ~ *up activity* ⟨s⟩kończyć; *business* zamykać ⟨-mknąć⟩; *clock* nakręcać ⟨-cić⟩; *car window* zakręcać ⟨-cić⟩

winding [waɪndɪŋ] kręty

wind instrument [wɪnd] instrument *m* dęty

windmill [wɪnmɪl] wiatrak *m*

window [wɪndəʊ] okno *n*; *bank etc.*: okienko *n*; '**~pane** szyba *f*; '**~shop**: **go ~shopping** oglądać wystawy sklepowe; '**~sill** parapet *m*

wind|**pipe** [wɪndpaɪp] *anat.* tchawica *f*; '**~screen**, *Am.* '**~shield** przednia szyba *f*; **~shield wiper** wycieraczka *f*; '**~y** wietrzny

wine [waɪn] wino *n*

wing [wɪŋ] skrzydło *n*; *Brt. mot.* błotnik *m*

wink [wɪŋk] **1.** mrugnięcie *n*; **2.** mrugać ⟨-gnąć⟩ **(at** na**)**

winn|er [wɪnə] *match, race etc.*: zwycięzca *m*; *prize*: zdobywca *m*; '**~ing** zwycięski; *fig. smile*: ujmujący; '**~ings** *pl* wygrana *f*

winter [wɪntə] zima *f*

wipe [waɪp] wycierać ⟨wytrzeć⟩ **(from** z**)**; **~ away** *or* **~ off** ścierać ⟨zetrzeć⟩; **~ out** F zmiatać ⟨zmieść⟩ z powierzchni ziemi

wire [waɪə] **1.** drut *m*; *electr.* przewód *m*; *Am.* telegram *m*; **2.** ⟨po⟩łączyć; *Am.* ⟨za⟩telegrafować do

wisdom [wɪzdəm] mądrość *f*

wise [waɪz] mądry; '**~crack** F dowcip *m*

wish [wɪʃ] **1.** pragnienie *n*; *last, best etc.*: życzenie *n*; **2.** pragnąć; *I ~ to make a complaint* chciałbym złożyć skargę; **~ s.o. well** / *ill* dobrze / źle komuś życzyć; *I ~ I were younger* szkoda, że nie jestem młodszy; **~ for s.th.** wyrażać ⟨-razić⟩ życzenie otrzymania czegoś; '**~ful**: **~ful thinking** pobożne życzenia *pl*

wit [wɪt] dowcip *m*; *pl* przytomność *f* umysłu

witch [wɪtʃ] czarownica *f*, wiedźma *f*; '**~craft** czary *pl*

with [wɪð] z; *rinse ~ water* przepłukać wodą; *covered ~ dust* pokryty kurzem; *in love ~ s.o.* zakochany w kimś; *are you ~ me?* rozumiesz co ja mówię?; *leave it ~ me* zostaw to u mnie

withdraw [wɪðˈdrɔː] **(-drew, -drawn)** wycof⟨yw⟩ać (się) **(from** z**)**; *(take out)* wyjmować ⟨-jąć⟩ **(from** z**)**; *money*

wypłacać ⟨-cić⟩; (*go*) przechodzić ⟨przejść⟩ (**to** do)

wither ['wɪðə] (*a.* ~ *away*) ⟨o⟩słabnąć; (*dry up*) usychać ⟨uschnąć⟩

withhold [wɪð'həʊld] (*-held*) : ~ **permission** odmawiać ⟨-mówić⟩ udzielenia zgody; ~ **information** nie udostępni(a)ć informacji

with|in [wɪ'ðɪn] wewnątrz, w; ~**in budget** nie przekraczając budżetu; ~**in two miles of the capital** w odległości dwu mil od stolicy; ~**in reach** of s.o. do kogoś; ~**out** [-'ðaʊt] bez

withstand [wɪð'stænd] wytrzym(yw)ać

witness ['wɪtnɪs] **1.** świadek *m*; (*testimony*) świadectwo *n* (**to** s.th. czegoś); **2.** widzieć, być świadkiem (czegoś)

witty ['wɪtɪ] dowcipny

wives [waɪvz] *pl of* **wife**

wizard ['wɪzəd] czarnoksiężnik *m*; *fig.* ekspert *m* (**at** od)

woke [wəʊk] *past*, '~**n** *pp of* **wake**[1]

wolf [wʊlf] **1.** (*pl* **wolves** [~vz]) wilk *m*; **2.** ~ (**down**) pożerać ⟨-żreć⟩

wolves [wʊlvz] *pl of* **wolf** 1

woman ['wʊmən] (*pl* **women** ['wɪmɪn]) kobieta *f*; '~**ly** kobiecy

womb [wu:m] macica *f*

women ['wɪmɪn] *pl of* **woman**

won [wʌn] *past and pp of* **win** 1

wonder ['wʌndə] **1.** zadziwie-

nie *n*; *technological etc.*: cud *m*; **2.** zastanawiać się (**about** nad); (*be surprised*) dziwić się (**at** s.th. czemuś); **I ~ if you can help me?** czy mógłbym prosić o pomoc?; '~**ful** wspaniały

won't [wəʊnt] *abbr. for* **will not**

wood [wʊd] drewno *n*; *often pl* las *m*; '~**ed** ['-ɪd] zalesiony; '~**en** (*a. fig.*) drewniany; '~**pecker** ['-pekə] dzięcioł *m*; '~**work** (*wooden parts*) stolarka *f* (budowlana); (*craft*) stolarstwo (artystyczne); '~**y** *plant*: zdrewniały; *area*: lesisty

wool [wʊl] wełna *f*; '~(**l**)**en** 1. wełniany; **2.** *pl* rzeczy *pl* z wełny; '~(**l**)**y** 1. wełniany, *fig.* mało konkretny; **2.** sweter *m* wełniany

word [wɜ:d] **1.** słowo *n*; (*news*) wiadomość *f* (**of** o); (*order*) rozkaz *m*; *pl song*: tekst *m*, słowa *pl*; **have a ~ with** s.o. zamienić z kimś słowo; **2.** ⟨s⟩formułować, wyrażać ⟨-razić⟩ słowami; '~**ing** tekst *m*; '~ **processing** (komputerowe) redagowanie *n* tekstów

wore [wɔ:] *past of* **wear** 1

work [wɜ:k] **1.** praca *f*; *writer's*: dzieło *n*; ~**s** *sg* zakład *m*, fabryka *f*; ~**s** *pl* roboty *pl*; ~ **of art** dzieło *n* sztuki; **at** ~ w pracy; **out of** ~ bez pracy, bezrobotny; **2.** *v/i* pracować

(on nad); *medicine, machine etc.*: działać; *v/t machine, area* obsługiwać; *person* zmuszać do pracy; ~ **one's way** przedost(aw)ać się; ~ **off** pozby(wa)ć się (czegoś); ~ **out** *v/t solution* znajdować ⟨znaleźć⟩; *(calculate)* obliczać ⟨-czyć⟩; *(understand)* ⟨z⟩rozumieć; *v/i (develop)* rozwijać ⟨-winąć⟩ się; *(exercise)* trenować; ~ **(o.s.) up** ⟨z⟩denerwować się; **~aholic** [~ə'hɒlɪk] pracoholik *m*; **'~er** robotnik *m*

'working hours *pl* czas *m* pracy

'workman *(pl -men)* robotnik *m*; **'~ship** fachowość *f*

'work|shop warsztat *m*; ~ **surface, ~top** blat *m* kuchenny

world [wɜːld] świat *m*; **'~ly** ziemski; *person*: światowy; ~ **power** *pol.* mocarstwo *n*; ~ **war** wojna *f* światowa; **'~wide** ogólnoświatowy

worm [wɜːm] *earth*: dżdżownica *f*; *(insect)* robak *m* F; *(tapeworm etc.)* robak

worn [wɔːn] *pp of* **wear** 1; **~'out** zniszczony; *person*: wyczerpany

worr|ied ['wʌrɪd] zatroskany *(about s.th.* czymś); **'~y** 1. martwić (się); *don't* **~y!** nie martw się; 2. zmartwienie *n*; **'~ying** niepokojący

worse [wɜːs] *comp of* **bad**: gorszy; **~n** ['wɜːsn] pogar-

szać ⟨-gorszyć⟩ (się)

worship ['wɜːʃɪp] 1. uwielbienie *n*; *God*: kult *m*; 2. uwielbiać; *God* czcić

worst [wɜːst] 1. *adj sup of* **bad** najgorszy; 2. *adv sup of* **badly** najgorzej; 3. **the ~** najgorsze; **at (the) ~** w najgorszym wypadku / razie

worth [wɜːθ] 1. wart(y); **~ reading** wart przeczytania; 2. wartość *f*; **'~less** bezwartościowy; **~while** korzystny; **be ~while** opłacać ⟨-cić⟩ się; **~y** ['~ðɪ] wart *(of s.th.* czegoś)

would [wʊd] *past of* **will** 2; ~ **you like ...?** chciałbyś ...?

wound¹ [wuːnd] 1. rana *f*; 2. ⟨z⟩ranić

wound² [waʊnd] *past and pp of* **wind²**

wove [wəʊv] *past*, **'~n** *pp of* **weave**

wrap [ræp] owijać ⟨owinąć⟩ *(round* wokół); *(a. ~ up)* zawijać ⟨-winąć⟩ *(in* w); *goods* ⟨za⟩pakować *(in* w)

wreath [riːθ] wieniec *m*

wreck [rek] 1. wrak *m*; 2. ⟨z⟩niszczyć; **be ~ed** iść ⟨pójść⟩ na dno; **'~age** szczątki *pl* (samolotu itp.)

wrench [rentʃ] 1. szarpać ⟨-pnąć⟩; ~ **off** odrywać ⟨oderwać⟩; ~ **out** wyr(y)wać *med.* skręcać ⟨-cić⟩; 2. szarpnięcie *n*; *tool*: klucz *m* uniwersalny; *med.* skręcenie *n*

wrest|le ['resl] walczyć (**with** z), mocować się (**with** z) (*a. fig.*); '**~ling** zapasy *pl*

wrinkle ['rɪŋkl] **1.** zmarszczka *f*; *in cloth etc.*: fałda *f*; **2.** ⟨z⟩marszczyć (się)

wrist [rɪst] przegub *m*; **~ watch** zegarek *m* na rękę

write [raɪt] (**wrote, written**) ⟨na⟩pisać; **~ down** zapis⟨yw⟩ać; **~ off** pisać (pisma); *debt etc.* anulować; *project* porzucać ⟨-cić⟩; **~ out** report ⟨na⟩pisać; *cheque etc.* wypis⟨yw⟩ać; '**~r** pisarz *m* (-arka *f*)

writing ['raɪtɪŋ] pismo *n*; *pl* utwory *pl*; *in* **~** na piśmie

written ['rɪtn] **1.** *pp* of **write**; **2.**

adj pisemny

wrong [rɒŋ] **1.** *adj* (*not correct*) zły; *information etc.*: fałszywy; *be* **~** *person*: ⟨po⟩mylić się, być w błędzie (*about s.th.* co do czegoś); *you were* **~ to say yes** źle zrobiłeś, że się zgodziłeś; *what's* **~ with you?** co się z tobą dzieje?; *don't get me* **~** nie zrozum mnie źle; *go* **~** *person*: ⟨po⟩mylić się; *plan etc.*: nie ud(aw)ać się; *machine*: ⟨ze⟩psuć się; **2.** *adv* źle; **3.** zło *n*; **4.** ⟨s⟩krzywdzić; '**~ful** *act*: krzywdzący; '**~ly** źle

wrote [rəʊt] *past of* **write**

wrung [rʌŋ] *past and pp of* **wring**

X

X-ray ['eksreɪ] **1.** promień *m* rentgena; *picture*: zdjęcie *n* rentgenowskie; F (*test*) prześwietlenie *n*; **2.** prze-

świetlać ⟨-lić⟩

xylophone ['zaɪləfəʊn] ksylofon *m*; *toy*: cymbałki *pl*

Y

yacht [jɒt] jacht *m*; '**~ing** żeglarstwo *n*

yard¹ [jɑːd] podwórko *n*; (*work area*) zakład *m*

yard² [~] jard *m* (0,914 *m*); '**~stick** miara *f* (*a. fig.*)

yawn [jɔːn] ziewać ⟨-wnąć⟩

year [jɪə] rok *m*; *I've known him for* **~s** znam go od lat;

'**~ly** *adv* (*every year*) co rok; (*once a year*) raz do roku; (*in a year*) rocznie; *adj* (*happening once every year*) coroczny; (*of a year*) roczny

yearn [jɜːn] tęsknić (**for** za)

yellow ['jeləʊ] żółty; **~ pages** *pl teleph.* spis numerów telefonicznych przedsiębiorstw

yes [jes] tak

yesterday ['jestədɪ] wczoraj; *the day before* ~ przedwczoraj

yet [jet] **1.** *adv* jeszcze; *in questions:* już; (*so far*) do tej pory; *I haven't had lunch* ~ nie jadłem jeszcze obiadu; *have you had lunch* ~? jadłeś już obiad?; *not* ~ jeszcze nie; **2.** *cj* jednak

yield [jiːld] **1.** ustępować ⟨-tąpić⟩ (*to s.o.* komuś); ulegać ⟨ulec⟩ (*to s.th.* czemuś); **2.** zysk *m*

yogh(o)urt, yogurt ['jɒgət] jogurt *m*

yolk [jəʊk] żółtko *n*

you [juː]; *ty; pl* wy; *form.* Pan, Pani; *pl* Państwo; *for* ~ dla ciebie / was / pana / pani /

państwa; *see* ~ widzieć ciebie / was / pana / panią / państwa; *with* ~ z tobą / wami / panem / panią / państwem; *about* ~ o tobie / was / panu / pani / państwie

young [jʌŋ] młody; *the* ~ (*animals*) młode *pl*

your [jɔː], ~**s** [~z] twój; *pl* wasz; *form.* Pana, Pani; *pl* Państwa; ~**self** (*pl* -*selves* [~vz]) *reflexive:* się, siebie, sobie; *emphasis:* (ty) sam

youth [juːθ] młodość *f*; (*young man*) młodzieniec *m*; (*young people*) młodzież *f*; ~**ful** młodzieńczy; ~ **hostel** schronisko *n* młodzieżowe

Yugoslav ['juːgəslɑːv] Jugosłowianin *m* (-anka *f*); ~**ia** [~'slɑːvɪə] Jugosławia *f*

Z

zero ['zɪərəʊ] (*pl.* -**os**, -**oes**) zero *n*

zigzag ['zɪgzæg] zygzak *m*

zinc [zɪŋk] cynk *m*

zip [zɪp] **1.** zamek *m* błyskawiczny; **2.** (*a.* ~ *up*) zapinać ⟨-piąć⟩ na zamek; ~ **code** *Am.* kod *m* pocztowy; ~ **fastener**, ' ~**per** zamek *m* błyskawiczny

zodiac ['zəʊdɪæk]: *the* 2 zodiak *m*

zone [zəʊn] strefa *f*

zoo [zuː] zoo *n*

zoolog|ical [zəʊə'lɒdʒɪkl] zoologiczny; ~**ical garden** ogród *m* zoologiczny; ~**y** [zəʊ'ɒlədʒɪ] zoologia *f*

zoom [zuːm] **1.** ⟨po⟩mknąć, ⟨po⟩pędzić; *prices:* skakać ⟨skoczyć⟩; ~ *in phot.* ⟨z⟩robić zbliżenie; **2.** → ~ *lens phot.* obiektyw *m* ze zmienną ogniskową

Czasowniki nieregularne
List of Irregular Verbs

Bezokolicznik – Czas przeszły – Imiesłów czasu przeszłego
Infinitive – Past Tense – Past Participle

alight – alighted, alit – alighted, alit

arise – arose – arisen

awake – awoke, awaked – awoken, awaked

be – was (were) – been

bear – bore borne; – born

beat – beat – beaten, beat

become – became – become

beget – begot – begotten

begin – began – begun

bend – bent – bent

bet – bet, betted – bet, betted

bid – bade, bid – bidden, bid

bind – bound – bound

bite – bit – bitten

bleed – bled – bled

bless – blessed, blest – blessed, blest

blow – blew – blown

break – broke – broken

breed – bred – bred

bring – brought – brought

broadcast – broadcast(ed) – broadcast(ed)

build – built – built

burn – burnt, burned – burnt, burned

burst – burst – burst

buy – bought – bought

can – could

cast – cast – cast

catch – caught – caught

choose – chose – chosen

cling – clung – clung

come – came – come

cost – cost – cost

creep – crept – crept

cut – cut – cut

deal – dealt – dealt

dig – dug – dug

do – did – done

draw – drew – drawn

dream – dreamed, dreamt – dreamed, dreamt

drink – drank – drunk

drive – drove – driven

dwell – dwelt, dwelled – dwelt, dwelled

eat – ate – eaten

fall – fell – fallen

feed – fed – fed

feel – felt – felt

fight – fought – fought

find – found – found

flee – fled – fled

fling – flung – flung

fly – flew – flown

forbid – forbad(e) – forbid(den)

forecast – forecast(ed) – forecast(ed)

forget – forgot – forgotten

forsake – forsook – forsaken

freeze – froze – frozen

get – got – got, Am. a. gotten

gild – gilded – gilded, gilt
give – gave – given
go – went – gone
grind – ground – ground
grow – grew – grown
hang – hung – hung
have – had – had
hear – heard – heard
hew – hewed – hewed, hewn
hide – hid – hidden, hid
hit – hit – hit
hold – held – held
hurt – hurt – hurt
keep – kept – kept
kneel – knelt, kneeled – knelt, kneeled
knit – knitted, knit – knitted, knit
know – knew – known
lay – laid – laid
lead – led – led
lean – leant, leaned – leant, leaned
leap – leapt, leaped – leapt, leaped
learn – learned, learnt – learned, learnt
leave – left – left
lend – lent – lent
let – let – let
lie – lay – lain
light – lighted, lit – lighted, lit
lose – lost – lost
make – made – made
may – might
mean – meant – meant
meet – met – met
mow – mowed – mowed, mown
pay – paid – paid

prove – proved – proved, Am. a. proven
put – put – put
quit – quit(ted) – quit(ted)
read – read – read
rid – rid, a. ridded – rid, a. ridded
ride – rode – ridden
ring – rang - rung
rise – rose – risen
run – ran – run
saw – sawed – sawn, sawed
say – said – said
see – saw – seen
seek – sought – sought
sell – sold – sold
send – sent – sent
set – set – set
sew – sewed – sewn, sewed
shake – shook – shaken
shall – should
shave – shaved – shaved, shaven
shear – sheared – sheared, shorn
shed – shed – shed
shine – shone – shone
shit – shit(ted), shat – shit(ted), shat
shoot – shot – shot
show – showed – shown, showed
shrink – shrank, shrunk, – shrunk
shut – shut – shut
sing – sang – sung
sink – sank, sunk – sunk
sit – sat – sat
sleep – slept – slept
slide – slid – slid

sling – slung – slung
slit – slit – slit
smell – smelt, smelled – smelt, smelled
sow – sowed – sown, sowed
speak – spoke – spoken
speed – sped, speeded – sped, speeded
spell – spelt, spelled – spelt, spelled
spend – spent – spent
spill – spilt, spilled – spilt, spilled
spin – spun – spun
spit - spat, *Am. a.* spit – spat, *Am. a.* spit
split – split – split
spoil – spoiled, spoilt – spoiled, spoilt
spread – spread – spread
spring – sprang, *Am. a.* sprung – sprung
stand – stood – stood
steal – stole – stolen
stick – stuck – stuck
sting – stung – stung
stink – stank, stunk – stunk
stride - strode – stridden
strike – struck – struck
string – strung – strung

strive – strove – striven
swear – swore – sworn
sweat – sweated, *Am. a.* sweat – sweated, *Am. a.* sweat
sweep – swept – swept
swell – swelled – swollen, swelled
swim – swam – swum
swing – swung – swung
take – took – taken
teach – taught – taught
tear – tore – torn
tell – told – told
think – thought – thought
thrive – thrived, throve – thrived, thriven
throw – threw – thrown
thrust – thrust – thrust
tread – trod – trodden
wake – woke, waked - woken, waked
wear – wore – worn
weave – wove – woven
weep – wept – wept
wet – wet, wetted – wet, wetted
win – won – won
wind – wound – wound
wring – wrung – wrung
write – wrote – written

Liczebniki – Numerals

Liczebniki główne – Cardinal Numbers

0 zero *nought, zero*
1 jeden, jedna, jedno *one*
2 dwa, dwie *two*
3 trzy *three*
4 cztery *four*
5 pięć *five*
6 sześć *six*
7 siedem *seven*
8 osiem *eight*
9 dziewięć *nine*
10 dziesięć *ten*
11 jedenaście *eleven*
12 dwanaście *twelve*
13 trzynaście *thirteen*
14 czternaście *fourteen*
15 piętnaście *fifteen*
16 szesnaście *sixteen*
17 siedemnaście *seventeen*
18 osiemnaście *eighteen*
19 dziewiętnaście *nineteen*
20 dwadzieścia *twenty*
21 dwadzieścia jeden *twenty--one*
22 dwadzieścia dwa *twenty--two*
23 dwadzieścia trzy *twenty--three*

30 trzydzieści *thirty*
40 czterdzieści *forty*
50 pięćdziesiąt *fifty*
60 sześćdziesiąt *sixty*
70 siedemdziesiąt *seventy*
80 osiemdziesiąt *eighty*
90 dziewięćdziesiąt *ninety*
100 sto *a* or *one hundred*
101 sto jeden *a hundred and one*
200 dwieście *two hundred*
572 pięćset siedemdziesiąt dwa *five hundred and seventy-two*
1000 tysiąc *a* or *one thousand*
1998 tysiąc dziewięćset dziewięćdziesiąt osiem *nineteen (hundred and) ninetyeight*
500 000 pięćset tysięcy *five hundred thousand*
1 000 000 milion *a* or *one million*
2 000 000 dwa miliony *two million*
1 000 000 000 miliard *a* or *one billion*

Liczebniki porządkowe – Ordinal Numbers

1. pierwszy *first*
2. drugi *second*
3. trzeci *third*
4. czwarty *fourth*
5. piąty *fifth*
6. szósty *sixth*
7. siódmy *seventh*
8. ósmy *eighth*
9. dziewiąty *ninth*
10. dziesiąty *tenth*
11. jedenasty *eleventh*
12. dwunasty *twelfth*
13. trzynasty *thirteenth*
14. czternasty *fourteenth*
15. piętnasty *fifteenth*
16. szesnasty *sixteenth*
17. siedemnasty *seventeenth*
18. osiemnasty *eighteenth*
19. dziewiętnasty *nineteenth*
20. dwudziesty *twentieth*
21. dwudziesty pierwszy *twenty-first*
22. dwudziesty drugi *twenty-second*
23. dwudziesty trzeci *twenty-third*
30. trzydziesty *thirtieth*
40. czterdziesty *fortieth*

50. pięćdziesiąty *fiftieth*
60. sześćdziesiąty *sixtieth*
70. siedemdziesiąty *seventieth*
80. osiemdziesiąty *eighteeth*
90. dziewięćdziesiąty *ninetieth*
100. setny (*one*) *hundredth*
101. sto pierwszy (*one*) *hundred and first*
200. dwusetny *two hundredth*
572. pięćset siedemdziesiąty drugi *five hundred and seventy-second*
1000. tysięczny (*one*) *thousandth*
1998. tysiąc dziewięćset dziewięćdziesiąty ósmy *nineteen hundred and ninety-eighth*
500 000. pięćsettysięczny *five hundred thousandth*
1 000 000. milionowy (*one*) *millionth*
2 000 000. dwumilionowy *two millionth*

Brytyjskie i amerykańskie jednostki miary

1. Miary długości

1 inch = 2,54 cm
1 foot = 30,48 cm
1 yard = 91,439 cm
1 mile = 1,609 km

2. Miary powierzchni

1 square inch = 6,452 cm²
1 square foot = 929,029 cm²
1 square yard = 8361,26 cm²
1 acre = 40,47 a
1 square mile = 258,998 ha

3. Miary objętości

1 cubic inch = 16,387 cm³
1 cubic foot = 0,028 m³
1 cubic yard = 0,765 m³
1 register ton = 2,832 m³

4. Miary pojemności

1 British *lub* imperial pint
= 0,568 l, *am.* 0,473 l

1 British *lub* imperial quart
= 1,136 l, *am.* 0,946 l
1 British *lub* imperial gallon
= 4,546 l, *am.* 3,785 l
1 British *lub* imperial barrel
= 163,656 l, *am.* 119,228 l

5. Wagi handlowe

1 grain = 0,065 g
1 ounce = 28,35 g
1 pound = 453,592 g
1 quarter = 12,701 kg
1 hundredweight =
112 pounds = 50,802 kg
(= *am.* 100 pounds
= 45,359 kg)
1 ton = 1016,05 kg, *am.*
907,185 kg
1 stone = 14 pounds
= 6,35 kg

Waluta angielska

£ 1 = 100 pence

Monety

1 p (a penny)
2 p (two pence)
5 p (five pence)
10 p (ten pence)
20 p (twenty pence)
50 p (fifty pence)
£ 1 (one *lub* a pound)

Banknoty

£ 5 (five pounds)
£ 10 (ten pounds)
£ 20 (twenty pounds)
£ 50 (fifty pounds)

Waluta amerykańska

1 $ = 100 cents

Monety

1 ¢ (one *lub* a cent, a penny)
5 ¢ (five cents, a nickel)
10 ¢ (ten cents, a dime)
25 ¢ (twenty-five cents, a quarter)
50 ¢ (fifty cents, a half-dollar)

Banknoty

$ 1 (one *lub* a dollar, F a buck)
$ 5 (five dollars)
$ 10 (ten dollars)
$ 20 (twenty dollars)
$ 50 (fifty dollars)
$ 100 (one *lub* a hundred dollars)